FORGED IN GOLD

The Golden One Trilogy: Book One

NOELLE EDWARDS

For my late grandfather, Ken.
Thank you for showing me the power of storytelling. It changed my life.

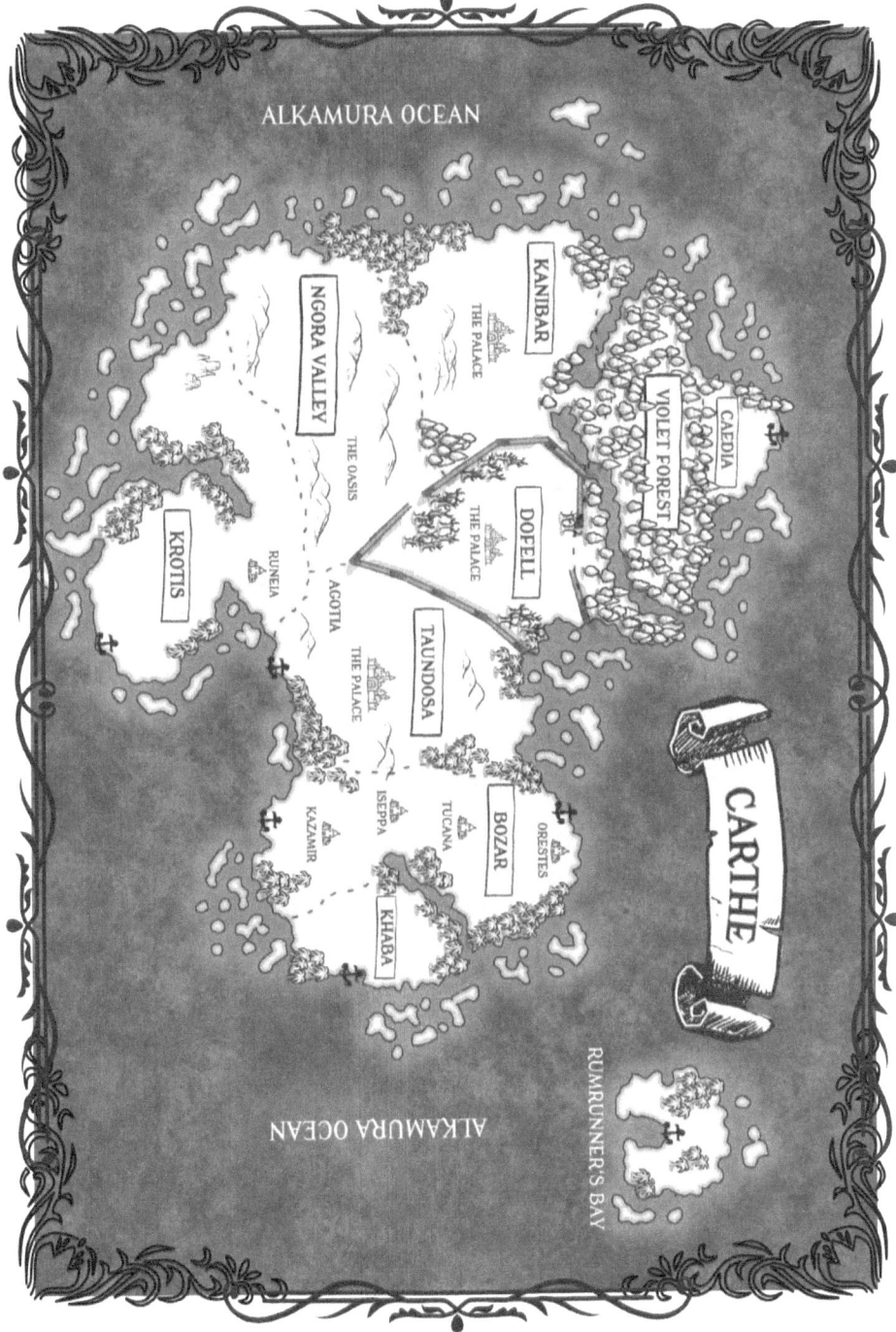

ALKAMURA OCEAN

KANIBAR

NGORA VALLEY

THE PALACE

VIOLET FOREST

CAEDIA

KROTIS

THE OASIS

DOFELL

THE PALACE

RUNEIA

AGOTIA

TAUNDOSA

THE PALACE

KAZAMIR

ISEPPA

TUCANA

BOZAR

ORESTES

KHABA

CARTHE

ALKAMURA OCEAN

RUMRUNNER'S BAY

Forged

in

Gold

Prologue

1965 Post Creation

dmund Brentwood did not care for propriety.

On a warm summer day bathed in sunlight, the last thing the King of Akkinor wanted to do was mull over paperwork in his cramped, windowless study. Rather, he wanted to spend the day doing the only thing proven, time and time again, to fill his heart with unparalleled joy: run about the palace gardens with his seven-year-old daughter.

She was perched on his shoulders, her arms outstretched and a ferocious roar gurgling in her throat, as she imagined she were a dragon taking flight. Edmund bounded across the lawn while she bobbled on his shoulders, trying his utmost to act like the creature she loved so much.

It was perhaps the most inappropriate thing he might've done as a man of his status, and he loved every second of it.

When Edmund grew breathless, he set his daughter, Crown Princess Aurelia, on the grass beneath an enormous weeping willow. It ached his soul to pull her from the branches when she began to climb, but her mother only allowed him to remove Aurelia from her lessons because Edmund had promised to resume her studies himself. He was ever the dutiful husband, despite his heart demanding that he allow his firstborn to find simple joys in the world while she still had the chance.

"Come here, little darling." He patted his leg as he sat with his back to the trunk of the willow tree. Aurelia, with her pale pink frock already covered in dirt, sighed and climbed onto his lap. He wrapped his arms around her and rested his chin atop her head. "Master Barrien says you have an examination tomorrow on your history lessons. Tell me—what do you recall about the Creation?"

He knew she was scowling—how she despised her studies! "'Humanity was born with the spilling of celestial blood,'" she said reluctantly.

"Is that all? Pfft!" Edmund ruffled her hair. "Anyone with their wits about them can recite the first line of the Creation Story. The future Queen of Akkinor must prove that she is both a diligent student and an educated leader—not merely that she is capable of reading from a book."

Aurelia huffed like a woman five-times her age. "Ten—no, *twelve*—gods created the realm in the image of their home in the heavens. At first, they sent some of their creatures from the heavens to live in the new realm, but they got bored, so they decided to make humans like us. Then there was...there was a big rainstorm that filled the realm with the gods' golden blood. When the Great Storm ended, the First Mortals were left behind."

"Very good. Where did the First Mortals live?"

"Here in Akkinor and in Carthe to the east. Master Barrien says it took many years for the First Mortals to migrate to other places, like Quapebet and Espos, and they only did so because the Elementals gave them the power to do it."

"Who are the Elementals?"

Aurelia's sigh was riddled with exasperation. "Everyone knows who they are, Papa." She sighed again, likely sensing the sternness etched onto his face, and tried again: "The Elementals were humans born from the gods' flesh and blood. They were supposed to introduce magic to humanity and show the First Mortals how to live in harmony. They created mages by having children or choosing worthy mortals, but some mortals weren't happy when they weren't chosen. Humans are greedy and selfish, so they turned on mages and hurt them. That's what Master Barrien thinks."

Edmund hooted with laughter. "And what do *you* think?"

She pondered for a moment as her frizzy, coppery curls tickled his nostrils. "I think mortals were scared of magic, so they tried to get rid of it. That's why they hurt magical creatures, too."

"Why do you suppose the gods failed to intervene?"

"Because they were scared, too."

A sincere smile formed on his lips. "That's a wise conclusion to come by. Many believe the gods were fearful of interfering in human life during other instances, too. Can you think of a time like that?"

"Hmm." She brought a tiny hand to her face and inquisitively tapped her chin. "No, Papa. I'm sorry."

He lifted her from his lap, turned her to face him, and sat her on the grass between his knees. When she refused to meet his gaze, he gently took her chin between his fingers and lifted her head. Her eyes—a more vibrant blue than his own—were bright with embarrassment.

"Don't ever be ashamed of not knowing something, Aurelia. One may never learn if one is too afraid to ask." He released her chin and clasped her hands in either of his. "Many centuries ago, a chieftain called Robert Cherrane conquered all of Akkinor. The kingdoms as we know them now were independent of one another until King Robert unified the continent. Only Omara was spared. It was—and still is—protected by the Monastery of Dhylo. The rest of the continent wasn't so lucky. They prayed to the gods for assistance so they could maintain their unique ways of life, but the Twelve failed to answer. Some believe the gods remained silent because King Robert's conquest was destined to happen. Others believe the gods were afraid of participating in such violence and horror."

A crease formed between her eyes as she contemplated. "Did the people feel the same way during Oleander's Rebellion?"

Edmund paused for a moment as he smiled at her insight. He'd worried that she hadn't been paying attention during her history lessons, but she'd proven him wrong yet again. That was one of the many wonderful things about his only daughter: she never failed to prove anyone wrong when they doubted her.

"It's certainly possible," he replied. "The two wars were quite different from one another, though. It's said that the gods *did* intervene during the rebellion—just in a different way. Has Barrien told you about the Ones Forged in Gold?" Aurelia shook her head. Edmund leaned forwards and released her fingers long enough to brush a spiraled curl from her eyes. "The Creation story refers to them as saviors born from the flesh and blood of the gods. A bit like the Elementals, I suppose, but their purpose wasn't dependent on magic. The stories claim that the gods, every so often, delivered a person Forged in Gold to the earthly realm to eventually serve as humanity's salvation—as a bringer of peace during a tumultuous time. Many Akkinorians believe Oleander Brentwood was Forged in Gold, though it's never been proven. Those Forged in Gold *must* weep golden tears as the gods did before them."

Edmund's distant ancestor, Oleander the Great, rose to power as a young man originally meant to inherit an Akkinorian dukedom. His plans for the future changed when Akkinor's queen at the time, Alora Cherrane, inflicted chaos across the realm. The queen, alongside every person of prominence within the monarchy, drove the continent into poverty, debt, and famine. To prevent foreigners from settling in Akkinor (Akkinorians hardly had enough resources for themselves, let alone for those seeking refuge), the country sealed its borders to the world and fell from glory within itself. The decrease in trade with Akkinor severely impacted the economies of other civilizations—so much so that Akkinor was threatened with war by both their enemies and their former friends.

After a bloody five-year war, the rebellion ended with the overthrowing of the Cherrane family and the crowning of Oleander Brentwood. Only after Queen Alora's defeat did Omara, the last independent kingdom on the continent of Akkinor, agree to join the nation as its sixth and final territory. After that, those who praised Oleander's name were completely and utterly convinced that the gods had chosen the new king to restore harmony to the realm.

Alas, that much had never been proven. Not a soul had witnessed the only inarguable event confirming Oleander's identity as Forged in Gold: golden tears falling from his eyes.

"In summation," Edmund finished, "Robert Cherrane nearly destroyed the continent because he wished to seize as much power as he could. Oleander Brentwood led Akkinor to greatness because he wished to save it from injustice and dishonor. Many believe that humanity is incapable of acting with such selflessness on our own—that's why they think Oleander the Great was divinely chosen to serve as Akkinor's hero."

Aurelia blinked her wide, round eyes up at her father. "Do *you* think we are too selfish to do those things on our own?"

Overcome by her incredible wisdom and insight for the second time that day, Edmund merely stared at her, dumbfounded. Sometimes when she spoke, she sounded so much like a grown woman that he forgot she was practically still in leading strings.

"No, sweetness. No, I don't." He pulled her into his arms and held her close. He was almost tempted to rock her as if she were still a newborn babe, but he knew she wouldn't like that. She liked to be treated like an adult, even if those days were years ahead of her. "Chosen by the gods or not, those Forged in Gold are human. That much has always been true. Their purpose in the realm may have been predetermined by the gods, but the things they achieved were direct results of their own actions. That, my dearest daughter, is the majesty of free will—free will, honor, and the need to do what's right for the betterment of all."

Aurelia, suddenly acting like a girl her age, wrapped her arms around Edmund's neck and rested her cheek on his shoulder. A warm, delighted smile graced his lips when he felt her heart beating against his. He hadn't felt such a wonderful sensation since she learned to walk—since she learned what it was to rely on herself.

"Papa?"

"Yes?"

"I hope I can be selfless like Oleander the Great when I'm queen."

He chuckled. "You already are. One day, you shall have the opportunity to show the realm exactly who you are. Your golden heart will shine for all to see. Perhaps you may even shock us all by weeping tears of gold!"

Aurelia's small body rumbled with laughter. "Don't be silly."

Had she been looking at him, she would've seen the sincerity in his eyes. She was only a young thing, still with many decades of life to live, but her character shone like the ever-risen sun. If the time came in the near future for One Forged in Gold to save the realm from its downfall, Edmund had no doubt that Aurelia Brentwood, future Queen of Akkinor, would be the gods' first choice.

BOOK ONE: SORROWS

1983 Post Creation

Laurenia Falwell had seen the inside of a potato sack over a dozen times before. As a child, she'd often fallen victim to her brother's schemes: he'd pull a canvas sack over her head, tie her hands behind her back, and laugh until he wept while she ran about the cottage in circles like a headless chicken. It was all good fun, of course, and she'd gotten her revenge more than once.

This time was different.

One moment, she'd been snoring beside her husband, Cullen, while their two young children slept down the hall. The next, she was being ushered awake by an all-too-familiar phenomenon: the rough, spud-laden interior of a canvas potato sack—still stinking of earth and roots—being tugged over her head while scratchy rope bound her hands behind her back. She heard voices she didn't recognize, along with her husband's muffled protests, and found herself unable to speak with a wad of cloth tucked in her mouth.

She was forced to walk by what she thought was a group of three or four men. They spoke in hushed, raspy tones as they escorted Laurenia and Cullen out of their home and onto the cold, damp streets of Whiteholm, where sharp fragments of ice and powdery snow seeped into the cracks between her toes. Had she been granted her sight, her vision would've been clouded by the misty haze of her own breath intermingling with the frosty Sadian air.

She would've been frightened if the men were common criminals, but they weren't. She knew by the smell of cleanliness and colognes, by the familiar feel of luxury textiles when their clothing touched her skin: these weren't thieves, rapists, or radicals seeking to sacrifice the Falwells, but important highborn individuals desperately in need of clandestine services.

Soon enough, her captors swapped the freezing midnight air for the cozy warmth of a hearth. She didn't know where they were just yet, but the lingering scent of hoppy ale, sweat, and yeast suggested it was a tavern. A surprisingly gentle grip on her elbow guided her shoeless feet across dense, creaking floorboards. She obeyed and lowered her rear until it came in contact with the firm surface of a wooden chair. Not a minute after she was seated, the potato sack was violently removed from her head and the cloth was torn from her mouth. Laurenia found herself face-to-face with a group of seven highborn men while Cullen, also with his hands bound behind his back, sat in a chair directly to her left. His eyebrows were furrowed with confusion and his cheeks were flushed from the cold, but his demeanor was calm and relenting.

"Mister and Madam Falwell." The tallest of the men, wearing a full suit of bronze armor and a helmet concealing his face, was the first to speak. "Forgive us for the method in which we brought you here. Trust me when I say it was the best way."

Cullen pursed his lips. "You look like respectable gentlemen. We could've discussed this—whatever it is—over tea and biscuits at the cottage. Was kidnapping us truly a necessity?"

"Yes." The next man to speak was more of a boy, Laurenia thought, based on his lanky build and the high pitch of his voice. "It's our understanding that you, Mister and Madam Falwell, are currently accepting new assignments. We'd like to hire you."

"You could've asked, you know."

The boy's face and hair were covered by a thick wool scarf, but his cool blue eyes were piercing. He narrowed his gaze at Cullen with such ferocity that Laurenia surged backwards in hopes of inching as far away from him as possible. Rather than retaliating, the boy simply turned to glance at a redheaded man to his left. The man, too, had his face covered by a scarf.

"Show them," the boy commanded.

Obeying, the redheaded man fetched a thick knapsack from the corner of the room (a tavern, and one Laurenia recognized) and dropped it on the floor at Cullen's feet. He opened the bag enough to show the Falwells its contents: enough gold, silver, and bronze coins to make them richer than half of Sadia's noblemen.

"There's more, but you won't receive the second half until the job is done," the boy informed them. "The job *must* be completed exactly ten days before the Changling. You won't be the only souls attempting to eliminate this target, either. Your payment is relative to your attempt and your ability to keep your word—*not* on whether you succeed. You'd be fools to decline."

Cullen continued staring at the coin until his gaze found Laurenia. For a moment, the two had a silent conversation with their eyes. They needed the coin desperately—both to afford repairs to their home and to purchase new clothing for their fast-growing children—and the amount before them was more than enough to cure their woes.

Even so, the promise of coin wasn't nearly enough to ensure their commitment. Laurenia and Cullen Falwell, a pair of veteran and esteemed assassins, didn't accept assignments at the jingling of coins. It was a dark and dangerous thing to claim a life on another's behalf, and while many assassins wouldn't have thought twice about the proposition, the Falwells were different. To them, the cause was as valuable as the reward.

"You shall have to offer us more than coin," Laurenia murmured. All eyes snapped in her direction when she spoke for the first time. She could see in their disparaging gazes that they hadn't wished to negotiate with *her*, but with Cullen; at the least, the men had researched the assassins enough to understand that one didn't proceed without the other. "Who is the target? Where might we find them? How would you like it to happen?"

"You'll find the target in the Folly," the boy replied. "I don't care how you do it, so long as it's done. It'll be easier than you think. Your path will be cleared beforehand. Before we continue, though, I must inform you of several conditions. You will not speak of this to another living soul. When the job is done, you will not discuss it even to each other. We'll pretend this conversation never happened. Is that understood?"

Cullen frowned. "You still haven't given us a name."

The ensuing silence was deafening. Laurenia could hear every tiny, insignificant noise now that the men had lost their voices: the crackling of the fire in the hearth behind her, the hooting of the owls outside, the gurgling of her captors' stomachs. She understood exactly what their silence meant: the target, whoever they were, was one of prominence.

As she gazed at the faces in the tavern, Laurenia identified two beyond a reasonable doubt. The first—a middle-aged, waxen man with a shaggy beard and one blind eye—was the owner of the tavern. He'd served the Falwells a few times before. The second, a dark-skinned man with a bald head and a gray beard, was the Earl of Whiteholm. He hadn't made any effort to conceal himself, likely because he hadn't expected the Falwells to recognize him.

She didn't recognize the redheaded man who'd delivered the coin until he removed his scarf to dab at the beads of sweat dripping over his cheeks.

The mole above his left nostril gave him away. She'd done business with him before at the Bank of Akkinor. He was Tyren Silio, an apprentice at the bank, and the second son of a Sadian duke.

There were at least two highborn men among them. That meant one thing: the Falwells would soon find themselves taking the greatest risk of their lives.

Laurenia's voice was nothing short of a whisper. "Who is it?"

The boy's knifelike gaze found hers. "Her Majesty the Queen."

Cullen made a noise that sounded more like a gurgle than a chuckle. "You're mad. The lot of you. Stark-raving mad."

"Cullen," Laurenia murmured, warning him.

He ignored her and turned his turquoise gaze to the men. "There's a difference between murdering a stranger and murdering one's leader. No amount of riches could sway us into claiming the queen's life. It's a death sentence."

"Not for two assassins of your expertise." The armor-clad man crossed his bulky arms over his chest. "As mentioned, your path will be clear. That's why it's so important for you to complete the job on the provided date."

"No." Cullen shook his head. "I apologize for the trouble, but we must refuse. The coin isn't worth the risk."

Laurenia's heart hammered as she awaited their captors' responses. None came. She glanced at the boy and gulped when she saw the way he was seething at them. Until then, she'd regarded him as a child. Now, the malicious glint in his eyes made him look as seasoned as a man four times his age. It was the same glint she saw in the gazes of the hardened men who'd trained her in the art of death: the tiny, unmistakable spark of a person who equated a human life to that of a rodent.

"You were recommended by reliable individuals," the boy said after a moment of silence. "I can't take no for an answer, Mister and Madam Falwell. If coin isn't incentive enough, I'd be most inclined to fetch your children from their beds. Perhaps you'll be swayed upon seeing little Alis's hands scalding in a pot of boiling water or young Soren's severed fingers garnishing the pig's trough."

Laurenia's muscles seemed to calcify beneath her flesh. Cullen gritted his teeth and struggled against the rope binding his hands. In that moment, she was grateful for the rope; if Cullen hadn't been bound, he'd lunge at them—using his bare hands as weapons—and the owner of the tavern would spend the rest of the night mopping Cullen's blood from the floor.

Cullen's face radiated pure, unbridled rage. "How dare you—"

"I've said all I needed to," the boy continued. "Accept the assignment or spend the rest of your lives tending to your impotent children. Take your pick."

Laurenia met Cullen's gaze once more. There was no point in discussing it—the decision had already been made for them.

Not an hour later when husband and wife returned to their cottage, they carried their sleeping children into their bedchamber and held them close. Their silent conversation continued as they stared at one another in the darkness, both desperately searching for an escape—an escape that wouldn't leave their children to suffer for their own cowardice.

When daybreak arrived, the light from the rising sun reflected on the knapsack of coin resting in the corner of the Falwells' bedchamber, and Laurenia knew their fates had been sealed.

I

Linden Elliot had mastered the art of silence.

He could glide across the marble floors of the palace without making a sound, climb a tree without disturbing the birds in their nests, and melt into the shadows so skillfully that people wondered if he was human or a creature of old. He was, of course, *human*, but the Hand of the Queen would never fail to be a subject of great intrigue and debate for those who made his acquaintance.

Aurelia Brentwood, Queen of Akkinor, liked those things about him. She liked how he could sneak up on her like a ghost, giving her a brief jolt of fright and a long fit of laughter. He was a skilled and valiant soldier, but that'd never been enough to hire someone so close to the monarch. Linden stood at her side because of his undying loyalty, his fierce compassion, and the way he could make her belly laugh unlike anyone else in the world.

There *were* things about Linden, though, that the queen could've done without. He always knew where to find her when she disappeared for a brief escape. There weren't many places for the queen to hide in a palace full of people, and Linden knew all of them. Hiding from him was like hiding from the gods—it couldn't be done.

Early one morning, she heard him coming as soon as the gates to the gardens screeched open. She kept as still as possible in hopes that it would take him some time to find her. She was wrong, of course. She didn't look up from the book in her lap until she heard his amused chuckling from down below.

"Lord Reilly has arrived for you, my queen."

Aurelia sighed and thanked him, but she was unable to keep the displeasure from her voice. After marking her page, she closed the book on her lap and nestled it in the narrow crevice between the tree trunk and a thick, curved branch, where three of her favorite novels were waiting to be read again. She swung her legs over the side of the large branch she'd been sitting on and hopped to the ground. When she straightened, she saw amusement flickering in his eyes.

"What?" she demanded.

"Nothing, nothing." He offered her his arm to take, trying—and failing—to conceal his smirk. "Might I suggest a change of clothing? You have a bit of mud on your gown."

She stifled a laugh and glanced down at her muddy hem. Perhaps Lord Reilly might've been offput by her improper appearance, but every other soul in the palace was accustomed to it. It was no secret to them that the gardens were the queen's favorite place on the property. If she'd had her way, she would've moved her study and her bedchambers to the gardens. Nobody could blame her; the gardens at the Palace of Akkinor were, inarguably, the most exquisite place in the nation's capital.

She must have walked along the cobblestone path over a million times in her life. On either side of it, short hedges organized like a maze seemed to carry on for miles. Statues and birdbaths sat scattered between the patterns in the hedges. Halfway through, the path forked to the left and right. Following the walkway to the left would lead to the greenhouse, where lavender wisteria flowers grew along the sides of the glass building and crawled upwards onto the roof. The path to the right led to a building called *the Little House* where Madame Vittoria Bettley, the palace stewardess, resided with her family.

The halfway point of the gardens was marked by monumental, intricate marble water fountains that housed the clearest, bluest water in the Folly. There were always frogs snoozing on lily-pads, bright blue songbirds resting on the marble, and citrine lotus flowers growing along the edges. Sometimes, if the gods were kind, a flower nicknamed the *Widow's Bell* would grow from the sparse patches of grass between the fountain and the cobblestone ground. The petals were a deep, striking magenta with curved stems, thus creating the illusion of blossoms that appeared to be weeping.

Just beyond the fountains was Aurelia's favorite part of the gardens: the lawn. The vast field was home to more species of trees, flowers, and bushes than Aurelia could keep track of. The trees—oak, crabapple, dogwood, cherry—were all quite massive and perfect for climbing. The beds and fields of flowers created an incredible contrast of colors that attracted swarms of insects during the warmer seasons. When the magenta cyclamens bloomed between the droopy violet petals of the irises and the startling red of the geraniums, the sheer beauty of the flowerbeds was cause enough for anyone to stop for a brief moment of serenity.

A flash of brown—the only bland color in the gardens—caught Aurelia's attention as she and Linden approached the rear doors of the palace. Buck, a stable hand, was impressively lugging a weighty canvas sack of apples plucked from trees on the lawn. He paused to rest his arms and seemed to sense Aurelia watching him, as he raised a hand in her direction in a nonchalant, halfhearted hello. She returned his smile, but not his greeting; she couldn't give the soldiers at the doors reason to believe something unseemly lingered between the two. Their suspicions would've been correct, of course, but a queen couldn't allow potentially ruinous rumors to run ramped in her subjects' imaginations. After all, a woman without her maidenhood was a woman destined for life as a spinster—queen or peasant.

Aurelia tore her gaze away from Buck to greet the soldiers as they opened the doors. She released a contented, blissful exhale at the sudden balminess in the corridor after braving the chill of the autumn air. Winter was nearly upon them, and it wouldn't be long before the gardens she loved so dearly were covered in a blanket of snow and frost.

Linden brought her to the monarch's suite on the second floor of the eastern corridor. "Here you are. I'll have someone escort you to the morning room while I chat with Lord Reilly. I'd like to inspect his pockets for myself. They always seem fuller whenever he visits. I suppose I shouldn't have left him alone, now that I think of it."

After exchanging a fit of laughter, he bowed to her as two soldiers took their positions outside of her door. When she entered, her three lady's maids curtsied and ushered her over to the changing screen with a clean dress. Linden must have given them notice to have something prepared. She never anticipated how filthy she could become after time outdoors, but Linden always did. After all, he'd been helping to clean the mud from her shoes since the day she learned to walk.

When she was dressed, she plopped down at her vanity and remained perfectly still while her maids prepared her for the audience. They combed her tangled curls, nonchalantly plucked tiny twigs from the snarls in her hair, and slipped comely white shoes onto her feet. After adding the finishing touches—a glittering diamond diadem and a bit of coral rouge on her cheeks—the girls wished her luck and sent her off.

The soldiers outside of her door escorted her downstairs to the morning room while she admired the humble splendor of her home. She smiled at the servants as they hung new drapes on the windows, fixed the peeling gold-and-white wallpaper, and scrubbed stubborn spots from the floors. She always wanted the palace staff to know how much she appreciated them, and even something as minute as a smile was enough to make them blush with joy.

When the soldiers opened the door to the morning room, the two men inside immediately rose to their feet. Linden clasped his hands behind his back and remained silent after bowing to her. The man who'd been sitting in the armchair across from him, three-and-twenty-year-old Lord Bradley Reilly, seemed so taken by her that he almost forgot to bow. She could tell he'd been riding all day: his uniform was crumpled, his hair somewhat tousled, and his cheeks pink from the cool autumn breeze. He was a tall man, very lanky, with short brown hair and chestnut eyes. His pale skin was peppered with freckles, including a sizable pink spot on his left cheek. He once claimed that a priest in Laynoa referred to the spot as *a kiss from the gods*, but Aurelia didn't believe that for a second.

"Your Grace." Lord Reilly accepted her outstretched hand and kissed her knuckles. "As always, it's a pleasure to see you."

"Likewise, my lord." She sat on the couch closest to Linden and crossed her ankles. Neither of the men followed suit until she was seated. "Welcome back to the Folly. I trust your journey was pleasant?"

"Very pleasant. The trek from Laynoa to the Folly is a long one, yes, but it's worthwhile. Unfortunately, my visit must be brief. Forgive me for being blunt, Your Grace, but have you given any thought to what we discussed?"

It took her longer than usual to respond, as his thick Laynoan accent made itself painfully known. She often struggled to understand most native Laynoans (save Linden, who'd lost the accent after so many years in the Folly), particularly when they spoke quickly like Lord Reilly tended to. A Laynoan's tone was ceaselessly dry, rough, and emotionless. There was little distinction between their tones, and their voices were somewhat low. While a Follian would've pronounced *must* or *discussed* with an *uh* sound, a Laynoan pronounced them with an *oo* sound. More than one battle had been fought throughout history simply due to one misunderstanding another's native accent—usually a Laynoan's.

"I have," she told him. His eyes lit up with excitement. She almost felt sorry when she realized how quickly it would turn into defeat. "I'm afraid you must forgive me, too. I'd like a bit more time to decide."

His eyebrows furrowed. "My queen, it has been—"

"—five years, yes. As you may know, governing a country is quite taxing work. I hardly have time to say my prayers before I sleep at night. Your proposal is most flattering, but I must ask for more time before I can give you a proper answer. I'm terribly sorry, Lord Reilly. I hate to see the disappointment in your eyes. Please believe me when I tell you that an answer will come in due time."

He nodded. "Of course, Your Grace, but—"

Linden cleared his throat. "Forgive the interruption, but the Assembly has requested a brief audience in ten minutes, my queen. You know how they hate to be kept waiting."

"Yes, of course." She knew there was no meeting with her advisors, but she was grateful for his interception. She rose from her seat as Lord Reilly did the same. "I wish you safe travels. Your people must be missing you."

His smile trembled with force. "I should hope so. Thank you for your time, Your Grace."

"Your satchel will be packed shortly," Linden added. His face, usually welcoming and charismatic, was stained by a mask of apathy. Normally, he'd never be caught lacking the propriety expected of the queen's best man, but his aversion to Lord Reilly was impossible to conceal. "Her Grace has asked our staff to supply you with anything you should need for your travels. I hope it's satisfactory."

"It will be." The young lord took the queen's hand again and kissed it tenderly. "Until we meet again."

She smiled and tipped her head in response. She waited for the door to close behind him before tiredly slumping on the couch. Linden sat beside her, gazing at her with amusement in his eyes, as she massaged her temples and exhaled.

"I should've told him." She shook her head in shame. "I should've given him an answer."

"Do you know your answer?"

"Not quite, but—"

"*Not quite* is good enough. You're not a noble lady, Aurelia. You're not a peasant girl waiting for the highest bidder. You're the *queen*. Marriage isn't something to be approached without due consideration. Until you've made your decision, you can't act with such haste. Lord Reilly will come to understand."

"Maybe." She eyed him humorously and smiled. "An Assembly meeting? That was clever thinking. Once again, you've saved me."

"Will he ever stop pining for you?" he teased. When she snorted, he allowed himself a booming laugh. "A silly question. The love of his life could knock on his door, and still, he'd turn her away. Nothing is good enough for a Reilly. He'd rather die hoping for the queen than live with the woman of his dreams. It's a bit sad, actually."

"I suppose." She leaned her head back and stared at the fresco painting on the ceiling. "My parents suggested the union with Lord Reilly five years ago. I was hardly twenty then. When they died not long after...I thought the arrangement had unraveled. The king and queen were dead, the entire country was ravaged with grief, and I was forced into a role I wasn't yet prepared for. Somehow, the line of suitors at my door grew longer. Are they really so desperate to marry the queen that they'd sacrifice something better without question?"

"It's a shame. Lord Reilly could've been married with children by now if he'd ceased his attempts to court you. He wanted to marry the Crown Princess, and now he wants to marry the queen. There's a difference."

Aurelia reached for the small, cylindrical locket hanging from her neck. She curled her fingers around the golden tube as she often did when she was deep in thought. Linden's dark umber eyes watched her while she toyed with it; he knew she was troubled simply by observing the way she clutched it.

"It'll be all right, you know," he avowed.

She snapped out of her daze to look at him. The sunlight pouring into the parlor made his armor glow like a candle. The contrast of the shimmering bronze against his dark skin drew attention to his features: his wide, pearly-white smile, the sleekness of his bald head, and the few, coarse whiskers around his nose that he'd missed while shaving.

"I know." She sighed and rested her head on his shoulder. "May I tell you something?"

"Always."

"Sometimes I wonder if it'd be easier to be nobody."

"I do, too."

"For yourself or for me?"

He wavered for a moment. "Either one." He shifted enough to press a kiss to the top of her head. "Let's not dally on this any longer. It's a painfully sore subject, and there are other things for us to attend to today."

The pair stood from the couch and exited the parlor arm-in-arm. Linden left her in the hall to attend to business in his study, so Aurelia searched for other ways to occupy herself in his absence. As she roamed, she couldn't help but think back to her audience with Lord Reilly. Linden was right: the decision to marry—and the decision regarding *who* to marry—wasn't one to be made with haste. What neither opted to mention, though, was how five years' worth of unanswered proposals was exactly the opposite of haste.

She'd given an incredible amount of thought to marrying Lord Reilly, but she still hadn't decided if the benefits outweighed the downsides. For one, he was the lord of an Akkinorian kingdom. Normally, the law would prevent him from abandoning his title to live and reign in another kingdom. He'd made it clear that Laynoa would be fine without him, as his younger brother was well-prepared to take his place as lord.

By all accounts, Bradley Reilly wasn't supposed to be Laynoa's leader. Grandson of the late Clyde Reilly II—a man who'd sired more children than five generations of Brentwoods combined—he'd only come into power after the deaths of three uncles, his father, and his elder brother. Every sister, daughter, and niece was overlooked by the men of the family until Aurelia, wanting to respect Akkinor's laws of succession (which stated that all heirs, regardless of sex, were eligible to hold power), decreed that Bradley's three elder sisters were next in line to rule Laynoa after their eldest brother perished. All three women died within weeks of one another under mysterious circumstances, thus allowing Bradley to seize power.

Aurelia and those closest to the monarchy had their suspicions regarding Bradley's ascent, but no accusations could be made without risking an uprising. It was considered a tremendous act of dishonor to accuse a nobleman of such treachery, and without proof, Aurelia could do nothing but hope and pray that Bradley Reilly was a kinder soul than his predecessors had been. Hope allowed him to keep his title, but it wasn't enough to offer him a place at the queen's side.

Either way, she didn't particularly *like* Laynoa. The northeastern kingdom valued hardships and heritage as a means of earning good favor with the gods. Their values (while innocent and noble enough to the untrained eye) were rooted in male dominance. While it was traditional for boys to be named after heroes of old, it was traditional for girls to be named after gemstones, both as an ode to Laynoa's mining culture and as a means of solidifying male superiority. All men were regarded as heroes, and all women as prizes to be won. Aurelia wasn't exactly fond of the idea of marrying a man who'd been raised to believe such things.

"Your Grace! Your Grace!"

Aurelia turned, eyebrows raised, when she heard a high-pitched voice hollering from behind her. All thoughts of Bradley Reilly disappeared as a young maid slowed to a stop before the queen and fumbled into a curtsy.

"I was instructed to bring these samples to your attention at once, Your Grace. Madame Bettley would like you to select linens for the Changling. Would you prefer white or beige?"

Aurelia glanced between the two folded sets of sheets in the maid's arms. "I think white will do nicely. Oh, and tell Madame Bettley to ensure that Lady Tarre is given a suite closest to the west wing. She tends to call on her staff at the latest hours of the night—we mustn't allow her to disturb the entire palace when she finds herself craving a cup of warm milk and honey. It will be best for everyone if she resides closest to the servant's quarters."

The maid suppressed a giggle. "Yes, Your Grace. Thank you, Your Grace."

When the young girl scampered off, Aurelia exhaled tiredly and continued on her way. Sometimes she desired the simplicity of common life—it made for quite the impersonal existence when one was perpetually called *Your Grace*. People seldom called her by her first name now that she was queen, but her reign had already broken more rules than one, and she wouldn't break another by telling the servants to call her *Aurelia*.

Now that autumn was nearing its end, the palace was chaotic as the staff prepared for the Changling Celebration. The extravaganza had been implemented centuries prior as a means of marking the end of a new season and the beginning of another. It was quite a grand event: nobility from across Akkinor visited the Folly for five days of tournaments, balls, and performances. It wasn't limited to Akkinor's nobility, either. Even lowborn individuals were allowed to participate, though most couldn't afford to do so for the entirety of the five-day commemoration.

Though the festivities weren't set to begin for another two weeks, there was much to be done. The guests' suites needed dusting, polishing, sweeping, and restocking of things like firewood, soaps, and linens. Some guests required hot water bottles in their beds or rooms with the best lighting for reading and corresponding. The kitchen staff had to prepare menus for all five days of the celebration—breakfast, luncheon, dinner, dessert, teatime, liquor. Even the gardeners, stonemasons, and woodworkers worked tirelessly to prepare the grounds for visitors.

Aurelia, despite being hostess and mistress of the estate, didn't have much to do in preparation for the Changling. Madame Bettley tended to oversee most matters pertaining to grand events. Still, Aurelia was expected to voice her opinions. She had to approve the menus, the porcelain, the linens, the performers. It was her responsibility to choose which knights would be participating in the jousts, to finalize the schedule of events, and to ensure that the needs of her guests were met.

While promenading across the palace, Aurelia stopped briefly in the doorway of the throne room. Cicely Poole, her lady-in-waiting and dear friend, was perched on Aurelia's throne and, on Aurelia's behalf, greeting the commoners who'd arrived with gifts for the queen. Normally Aurelia did so, but Cicely insisted upon taking the job for herself after a former incident saw a peddler throw himself onto Aurelia's lap and press a sloppy, wet kiss to her lips before her guards could stop him.

Aurelia's heart warmed as she watched her friend accept a basket of quail eggs from a shaky elderly woman. Cicely—whose mother previously served as a lady's maid for Aurelia's mother, thus allowing the two girls to grow up alongside one another—was perhaps the most exceptional example of a lowborn transformed into a highborn. She had no title or status, and yet, she held herself with all the poise, elegance, and propriety of someone born into power. Other than Linden, Cicely was the only person in the palace whom Aurelia trusted fully to assume her duties.

Moments later as she prowled the halls in search of entertainment, she heard her name echoing in the corridor. As always, she failed to hear Linden's approaching footsteps until he was directly in front of her. She didn't scold herself too harshly for falling victim to his spiderlike movements that day, though. Between the yelling of the servants, the clatter of tools, and the heavy footsteps pounding across the halls, she could hardly hear her own breath.

She smiled brightly at him. "I'm glad you've found me. Would you care for a turnabout the gardens? I won't have nary a second of peace before I'm bombarded by floral arrangements and porcelain patterns, so we must move quickly!"

"Not exactly your definition of a leisurely afternoon," he joked, laughing. "A promenade shall have to wait, though. I've just come from examining the country's financial records from the last five years. Would you care to know what I found?"

She rolled her eyes. "No, I should think not. What a terribly boring subject." When he stared blankly at her, she made an impatient gesture with her hands. "Out with it, then!"

"Your sarcasm is less than appreciated, Your Grace," he said playfully. She chuckled. "It would appear that the financial plan we developed at the beginning of your reign has proved as fruitful as we'd hoped. Akkinor has surpassed every other civilization in wealth and prosperity. Congratulations, dear friend. Your country is now the most affluent in the realm."

Her heart skipped a beat. "H-How?"

"You don't mean to tell me that you doubted yourself, do you?"

She hadn't meant to reveal the truth of her skepticism when she averted her gaze and bowed her head. As his demeanor softened, he set a comforting hand on her shoulder and murmured, "Every monarch questions themselves at some point. That's nothing to be ashamed of. You should welcome this as fuel for your confidence. That plan of yours was an excellent development, Aurelia. Whatever path you choose in the future shall certainly yield the same remarkable results."

Tears swam in her blue eyes. "Are we truly the most prosperous country in the world? Have we finally done it?"

"And then some. The gods haven't forgotten us."

The Brentwood name—and its legacy—carried more weight than the entire mass of Akkinor combined. Aurelia was a direct descendent of the man who'd saved the country from the dark ages, and every monarch since Oleander the Great had done their utmost to bring honor to his name. Even so, it took centuries for the country to recover from the harrowing effects of rebellion, war, famine, and persecution. When one kingdom began to flourish, another seemed to crumble. When one noble proved good and honorable, another revealed his or herself as corrupt and deceptive. The obstacles in the monarchy's path towards greatness seemed abundant and unavoidable.

Aurelia's father, King Edmund II, had reigned during the beginning of Akkinor's betterment. Though he and Queen Cressida were lost at sea before he had the opportunity to implement his plans, Aurelia tried her best to see them in practice. He'd developed a new system for producing and distributing goods throughout the country, and Aurelia made it better by commissioning the clearing of land for farms, purchasing livestock for farmers to raise, and theorizing about possible alternatives for supplies provided by the environment.

Aurelia had produced her own plans for Akkinor's financial betterment, too. Early into her reign, she decreed that exports from across Akkinor wouldn't be transported to each kingdom on demand, but brought to the Folly first to be sorted, packaged, and distributed. It was difficult for the average Follian citizen to find work—particularly during the colder seasons—and her new plan offered jobs to thousands. The nobility hadn't been pleased with her decree, but her subjects certainly were.

The results proved effective almost immediately. Within two seasons of the plans being approved by the Assembly, Aurelia's board of advisors, the welfare of the entire country shifted. Civilians who'd been unemployed now worked sorting and distributing goods, on farms, or as construction workers. The increase in livestock meant more food, dairy products, wool, pelts, and fertilized land. People taught themselves how to utilize the natural gifts of their environments, too: the Sadians, for example, lived in the northernmost kingdom where the two long seasons were limited to a harsh winter and a cool spring. The kingdom had been paying for shipments of medicinal remedies for decades until Aurelia's plan inspired them to look elsewhere. Now, rather than paying hundreds in silver, the Sadians combined their native buzz button plant—a natural numbing agent—with fresh snow to create a topical therapy for treating burns and other superficial wounds.

It brought her tremendous pride to know that she'd contributed to her country's prosperity. Had her plan failed, the commoners might've attempted to overthrow her. They hadn't been pleased with a female monarch to begin with, and her failure would've supported their belief that she, as a woman, was incapable of ruling. She would've become one of the many forgotten names scattered throughout the Brentwood family tree. In a thousand years, nobody would remember Aurelia Emmeline Brentwood, First of Her Name, the seventeenth Brentwood monarch to rule Akkinor.

Now they would. Now there was no doubt that her country would never forget her name. She never wanted fame, of course, but she knew better than most that there was a fine line between eternal glory and a dark, ignominious smudge on the Brentwood family's legacy.

***

If there were anything Bradley Reilly despised more than halfhearted rejections, it was the boisterous, somewhat childish ambience of the Folly. Akkinor's capital—overrun by hooting children chasing chickens into establishments while the latter attempted to escape slaughter—was perhaps the young lord's least favorite place in the country. The thought of trading the stillness of Laynoa for a life among rambunctious, aptly named Follians made his skin crawl with displeasure, and yet, he was no less determined to make the Folly his home.

He sat by his lonesome in an empty tavern, skinny fingers wrapped around a mug of steaming black tea, with the hood of his cloak pulled over his head to conceal his face. Across the way, the barkeep eyed him while cleaning mugs and chalices with a cloth. Both were impatiently awaiting the arrival of someone new, but with the grating sounds of peasant life rattling their eardrums from outside, they couldn't hear so much as the shuffling of boots against cobblestone or the jingling of a knight's armor.

Bradley spotted a handful of Reilly soldiers posted outside of a window to his left. Like Bradley himself, they wore long, thick brown cloaks— purchased not an hour prior from a civilian's tailor shop—to conceal all evidence of their profession and their familial loyalty. After all, they were meant to be riding back home to Laynoa at that time, not lingering in a filthy, yeasty-smelling tavern in the heart of the Folly.

As his patience grew thinner, he glanced down at his reflection in the tea. His cheeks warmed as a melodic, yet insincere female voice echoed in his head: *I'm afraid you must forgive me, too. I'd like a bit more time to decide.*

A snort vibrated his nose. Five years was more than enough time to answer a proposal, he thought. Despite his frustrations, he wouldn't cease his efforts until a proper answer was provided. Enough persistence would surely wear her down, but how much more persistent could he be after five years of failed attempts?

Bradley had the opportunity to become the most powerful person in the country—the first Reilly King of Akkinor. Queen Aurelia wouldn't last long when she was finally wedded, and Bradley would be viewed as the man who rescued Akkinor from yet another incompetent queen. His name would be known on all corners of the world, and it'd never be forgotten.

A chilly gust of wind smacked him in the back. He grimaced when a shrill, youthful howl of laughter pierced his ears. The barkeep nodded his head in greeting to whomever had entered the tavern, and by the time the door closed—silencing the pesky Follian voices—a hooded man wearing Akkinorian bronze armor had slid into the seat across from Bradley's with his head bowed. The Lord of Laynoa couldn't see his companion's face (nor did he know the man's name), but he didn't need to see it to know that this was the person he'd been waiting for.

"My lord." The knight's gravelly voice was briefly interrupted when the barkeep shattered a glass. "Thank you for meeting with me. I'd hoped to catch you before your return to Laynoa."

"Your message was persistent," Bradley replied. "What's so important that it couldn't be discussed in writing?"

The soldier cleared his throat. "The reason for your visit to the Folly is no secret. I take it your immediate return to Laynoa means you were denied once again?" At Bradley's grimace and brooding silence, the man exhaled. "We thought as much. I'll be frank with you, Lord Reilly. Her Grace's position has always been fragile. She's a glass simply awaiting the day when she is shattered beyond repair. That day is fast-approaching. There are plans...plans I can't utter aloud until I have your full cooperation."

Bradley sucked in a breath through his teeth. "Do you mean—?"

"Indeed. My master requests your assistance in executing his plans. Your manpower and your peoples' familiarity with certain architectural obstacles would be most useful. My master will offer you extensive compensation, of course, upon your agreement."

He chewed on the insides of his cheeks. "If this is what I believe it to be, I won't be granted the only thing I desire. Your master plans on seizing the throne—as do I."

"Take no offense, my lord, but Akkinor would find itself embroiled in yet another rebellion if a Reilly called himself king."

Bradley's face burned as both the soldier and the barkeep stifled laughter. He knew how society considered both himself and the Reilly name: weak, spineless, incapable, feeble—but only one individual, so it seemed, found value in those qualities.

"All right." Bradley ignored his humiliation and eyed the stranger. "What would I receive?"

"Enough coin to make you richer than the Brentwoods. A permanent position on my master's court. Any bride, estate, or property of your choosing. Is that satisfactory?"

Bradley chewed on his cheek again, contemplating. He'd spent years of his life envisioning a grand future: his marriage to the most powerful woman in Akkinor and, eventually, his ascent to the forefront of the monarchy after appealing to society's preference for a male leader. The queen would be disposed of—imprisoned, exiled, or killed, but only after birthing Bradley's sons—thus allowing Bradley to become Akkinor's hero while serving as the first king of a new dynasty. Now he was envisioning an entirely new path: offer his resources to whomever was brave enough to usurp and murder the queen, receive any number of riches and luxuries he desired, and uphold a coveted position of prominence on the monarch's court.

Marrying the queen and forcing her abdication would make him a king; a merciless, dishonorable, and selfish king, but a king, nonetheless. Not a soul in Akkinor would dare laugh in his face or undermine his power ever again. Contributing to her assassination and usurpation—while preventing him from seizing the throne—would provide him with all the benefits of kingship without the title or miseries associated with it. He'd be revered and praised for his involvement in removing Queen Aurelia from power without his name eternally connected to her assassination. Nobody would laugh at him or undermine him in that scenario, either, but only because he'd earned their respect rather than demanded it.

Inhaling precariously, Bradley reached out to shake the soldier's hand. "Tell your master I accept."

The soldier's smile shone beneath the shadow of his cloak. "A bottle of your finest wine, sir," he called to the barkeep. He removed his hood to reveal dark eyes and a bald head. "We have quite a bit to discuss, my lord."

II

Having never ventured beyond Akkinor's borders, Aurelia knew the greatest wonders of the realm had yet to be seen with her own eyes. From the vibrant rainforests of Quapebet to the black sand beaches of Glacier Bay, she'd only ever heard or read stories about them. Even if the days came when she *did* set her gaze upon such wonder, she knew—without a fraction of a doubt—that no place in the realm would ever bring her as much joy as her country's capital.

A place of simplicity and order, the Folly was home to three groups of people: the royal family and their closest allies, like the Lord Hand and the Assembly; soldiers, bankers, and others who directly served the monarchy; and, of course, a substantial population of working-class civilians. Aurelia's native kingdom was one characterized by hard work and duty, by soldiers training to defend the country from those who would harm it, and by common people working tirelessly to maintain a state of stability. It was often said that the Folly bred the best leaders and the best soldiers in Akkinor, as it was a Follian value to defend the country and serve as its primary lifeline.

There was nothing particularly unique about the Folly. With both rural and urban areas, it could be either sleepy and peaceful or chaotic and meddlesome. It was the most temperamental of the six Akkinorian kingdoms: sometimes it was lush and blooming with springtime flowers, or so boiling with summer heat that one couldn't walk the streets without shoes for fear of scalding their feet. It was especially lovely in the autumn when every cobblestone and every roof was blanketed in colorful leaves. Other times, it was nearly impossible to leave one's house, as torrential rainfall flooded from the massive hills to the streets at sea level and froze like ponds. It wasn't a terrible nuisance, though: children and adults alike tended to skate or sled their way throughout the kingdom rather than sheltering in their homes until the ice melted.

Aurelia knew everything about the Folly—even things the villagers were often unaware of. She knew where the yellow daffodils grew in the spring, where the schools of catfish frequented within the River Gilsad, where herds of deer tended to roam in search of meals. She knew which farmlands would flood during severe rainfalls, which species of birds would fly south to Quapebet following the first frost, and which colors would appear when the hyacinths bloomed throughout the villages.

It hadn't been commonplace for the monarch to stroll about the kingdom until Aurelia was crowned. She was aware that some of her people found her behavior quite strange, but others took pride in how often she immersed herself in the lives of civilians. After all, most highborn preferred to be doted on by servants in the comfort of their extravagant estates rather than trekking through bustling working class villages.

Some of the older folk recognized her, but many citizens did not. She never strolled about the Folly in her best gowns, most expensive shoes, or flashiest tiaras. To the untrained eye, in her modest cream frock with her wild curls straining within a knot on the back of her head, she looked like the average civilian. She was glad for that—if the people knew who she was, they wouldn't allow her to have nearly as much fun as she desired.

Three days after her meeting with Lord Reilly, Aurelia found herself in the village of Mistcairn, the closest civilian settlement to the Palace of Akkinor. Linden was at her side, as always, scouring their surroundings in search of potential threats. After so many years of visiting the village, Aurelia had long since stopped worrying about danger. The humble commoners of the Folly's villages were, without a doubt, as harmless as butterflies. The small yet lively village was busy but never overwhelming, always smelling of yeast and magnolias, and as willing to befriend a stranger as a hound was to chase a chicken.

She never grew weary of studying the palace from the streets of Mistcairn. The interior of the estate was grand, of course, but it was nothing compared to the view from beyond. The stone walls surrounding the property did little to conceal the structure—they weren't very tall nor much of an obstacle—and the Akkinorian bronze gates, though more practical than sightly, were almost constantly open to patrons who came from near and far for a tour of the palace's public corridors.

She'd left the palace with the intention of approving the decorations on the bailey for the upcoming Changling. Though breezy, it wasn't cool enough to warrant a cloak for such a brief excursion, so she'd left wearing nothing but her short-sleeved frock. She'd been halfway through her rounds, marveling at the village in the distance, when Linden arrived with her cloak in hand. He'd anticipated where the day would take her as soon as she set her sights on Mistcairn—well before she herself had any intention of leaving the palace grounds.

"Oh, Linden, look at them!" Aurelia sunk to the ground before a large terracotta potter overflowing with hyacinths. "I don't remember the last time they bloomed like this! What would you call this color? Apricot?"

"Salmon?"

She wrinkled her nose, making him laugh, and decided *apricot* was a more suitable name. Careful not to disrupt the entire arrangement, she gently uprooted four flowers from the pot. When she had a bouquet of hyacinths in hand, she buried her nose in the petals and inhaled the sweet scent she loved so much. Hyacinths—her favorite—struggled to grow properly in the palace gardens, but somehow, they never ceased to bloom across the villages. The racemes of star-shaped blossoms were the only ones of their kind to grow in the Folly, and both their size and vibrancy made them the most exquisite decoration in the kingdom.

"These will do nicely in my study," she decided. "Do you suppose I should fetch a bouquet of violet ones for Madame Bettley? Violet is her favorite color. She deserves a token of my appreciation—what better way to do that than with a gift from the natural world?" She paused to take a dagger from Linden's girdle, then carefully severed the bulbs from the bottoms of the stems. He chuckled a bit as she buried the bulbs in the dirt, staining her hands and wrists with damp brown flecks, and covered them with soil to ensure their rebirth. "The pink and blue hyacinths are in abundance this season, but it appears most of the violet ones have already died. Nevertheless, I won't cease my search until I find them!"

"Ever the stubborn ass, Your Grace."

Aurelia grinned at him. Had anyone else referred to the Queen of Akkinor as a *stubborn ass*, they'd be thrown in the dungeons without a moment's hesitation. But Linden was more than Hand of the Queen—he was her best friend. There was nothing in the world that he could say that would offend her in the slightest, and better yet, she could speak to him with the same lighthearted and teasing tone without worrying that he'd lose respect for his queen.

As they strolled in search of violet hyacinths, they came across a group of children playing a game of knucklebones beside a rickety well. Aurelia paused briefly to peer inside the well and frowned at the bone-dry stones scattered over the bottom. It'd been dry for so long that someone had already removed the bucket. Aurelia turned to Linden, intending to ask him to remind her about the problem when they returned home, but he was already scribbling a note in the handheld leather journal he always kept on his being.

That was one of the many things she adored most about him: he could read her mind before she'd even conjured her thoughts.

The duo approached the children (who didn't so much as look up at their intruders) and watched in silence as the six youngsters hollered over a handful of sheep's talus bones. The sight reminded Aurelia strongly of her childhood—of hiding from her tutors with Linden ever at her side, munching on stolen sweets and bickering over knucklebones like they had absolutely nothing better to do.

"How close you were," Aurelia mused. One of the children, who'd dropped the bones rather than catching them on the back of her hand, huffed in frustration as another child took her turn. "You mustn't be disheartened," she advised, sinking to the ground. "This is a game of chance. Do you know what that means?"

The girl, no older than six, shook her head. "No, missus."

"It means there's little skill involved. Most people who excel at this are simply lucky. The game isn't a reflection of your talent, little one." She tapped the girl's nose, making her giggle, and raised her eyebrows at the group. "Might I have a turn?"

Behind her, Linden masked his sardonic laughter with a cough. Aurelia ignored him and took the five talus bones from one of the boys. She shook them about in her hand, teasing the children as they anticipated her toss, then threw them high into the air. She quickly flipped her hand over and managed to catch all five bones on the back of her hand. While the children gasped, she balanced the bones before jerking her hand into the air again. On her second toss, she managed to catch four bones in her palm while the other clattered to the ground.

She couldn't help herself when she muttered, "Bollocks."

"Rotten luck." One of the boys swiped the bones and gazed at his friends. "I'm in the lead. Have I won? Can I have the bread?"

Aurelia frowned. "Whatever do you mean?"

"This is for the winner." Another boy swiveled to the side and reached for a lump wrapped in filthy white cloth. When he unwrapped it, Aurelia's stomach churned at the sight of a hard, burnt loaf of bread. "Pa said to feed it to the birds. I didn't want to because I was hungry. Then we made a game out of it!"

A little girl made a face. "But it's *black!* You can't eat that!"

"No, you can't." Aurelia was silent for a moment, eyebrows furrowed and stomach churning with guilt, as the children bickered over whether the burnt bread was edible. Finally, she removed the bracelet from her left wrist and reclaimed Linden's dagger. She ignored her friend's protests as she used the tip of the blade to pry the gemstones from her bangle. By then, the children had ceased arguing out of sheer curiosity. "I'd like you to listen to me closely," she continued as the first ruby fell from the bracelet. "Each of you must take this home to your mamas and papas. If they bring the stone to the bank, you shall never have to eat burnt bread again."

After three rubies and three diamonds were pried from the bracelet, she handed one stone to each of the children and sent them on their way. The older few understood what the stones were, as they hollered breathless thanks while they ran down the street to their homes. The younger children simply clutched the stones to their chests for fear of losing them, though they hadn't fathomed the true value of what they'd been given.

"That was extremely generous," Linden said as Aurelia rose to her feet. She slipped the bracelet—with just three stones left—back onto her wrist and brushed off her dirty skirt. "We shall have to bring that to the jeweler at once. He can repair it for you."

She waved her hand dismissively. "I like it this way. It shall forever remind me of a good deed and a *very* entertaining game."

He chortled at her. "I believe you owe me thanks. It was *I* who taught you how to play. I've always regretted it, in fact. Luck has never worked in my favor since I introduced you to that wicked game. How old were you when you first defeated me? Six?"

"Five."

"Ahh." He nodded his head towards something across the way. "I think I see violet hyacinths up ahead. Perhaps after we've fashioned a bouquet for Madame Bettley, you and I might play a round or two of knucklebones in the gardens. I've a strong feeling that I shall emerge victorious today."

Aurelia firmly grasped his hand and shook. "I wouldn't trust that gut of yours. I shall always reign supreme when the two of us compete. You have only yourself to blame—it was you who taught me the true meaning of competition!"

Linden was grinning. "Gods help us all."

***

Aurelia, as still and mute as a statue, sat with her back straight and her hands folded on the desk before her as she listened to the frenzied ramblings of Lord Henry Rudal, a member of her Assembly of advisors. Lord Rudal was a wonderful asset in every way that mattered, but more often than not, Aurelia found herself irritated by his chaotic speech as he struggled to make sense of his own thoughts.

When he finally finished speaking, she rose from her seat and approached a slim table lined up against a wall in her study. Neither spoke as she lifted the violet hyacinths she and Linden had plucked earlier in the day. After bringing the flowers to her nose and inhaling their scent, she reached for the culinary knife on the table and began trimming the stems.

"Your Grace?" Lord Rudal's hands danced anxiously along the brim of his hat until the fabric was wrinkled and bent. "Have you any opinion on the matter, or shall I bring it to the Lord Hand?"

She smiled and placed a trimmed flower into an empty glass vase. "I've yet to be informed on what exactly the trio was doing in Seaport this afternoon, my lord."

"I believe they were hoping to commandeer a ship, Your Grace."

"The word *commandeer* has many meanings. Did they arrive in Seaport with the express intention of thieving one of our ships, or did they hope to buy passage on one of our vessels?"

"Only one of our ships sails to the north, Your Grace. If they were hoping to buy passage, the vessel would take them as far as the Syren Isles. We don't have any commissioned ships that sail to Glacier Bay. If they sought direct passage to their homeland, they would've stolen a ship."

She paused to consider the copious amount of information she'd received. While she and Linden frolicked through the Folly that morning, Lord Rudal apprehended three Isalder men who'd been spotted roaming the streets of Seaport. Residents of the coastal town reported seeing the trio pulling a dinghy to shore *without* an Isalder ship in sight. Isalders seldom traveled south—particularly a trio of men rather than several dozen—so nobody was convinced that they'd come with pure intentions.

Lord Rudal's feelings on the matter were made clear by the beads of sweat peppering his forehead, the anxious darting back-and-forth of his eyes, and his intense, white-knuckled grip on his hat. It wasn't in her nature to feed the worries and fears of others, so she maintained her composure by offering him smile after smile, calm word after calm word. She hoped he couldn't see through her mask of indifference. As far as he knew, she wasn't concerned by the news.

That, of course, wasn't exactly true.

"And you've put them into custody?" she asked, shifting the hyacinths from one place to another. He nodded. "That's very well. We can't send them back until we know exactly what they hoped for upon their arrival. Send word to Glacier Bay at dawn—perhaps the Isalders are missing our little trio." Now satisfied with the arrangement, she turned to meet his eyes. "Who knows about this?"

"Just you and I, Your Grace."

"I should like to keep it that way," she told him. The mousy-looking man nodded vigorously. "I shall inform the Lord Hand upon his return from the city. He'll conduct the interrogation. Until then, I'd like you to keep an eye on the prisoners. It'd be a terrible shame if they managed to dig their way out of the dungeons before we've decided how to proceed."

He cracked a smile. "Understood."

When Lord Rudal was dismissed, Aurelia returned to the arrangement of hyacinths and pulled the purple ribbon from her hair. As her curls sprung free, she tied the ribbon in a bow around the neck of the vase. She opened the door to her study and called for a maid, who scurried inside as the queen was scribbling a note on a piece of parchment. Aurelia instructed the maid to deliver the vase and the note to Madame Bettley as a token of her gratitude.

Following the maid's departure, Aurelia returned to her desk and kneaded her knuckles into her temples. She'd felt a fierce pressure behind her eyes from the moment Lord Rudal came to her about the predicament. It wasn't a migraine like the kind her mother was prone to, but a physical warning of sorts. Normally it was just an ache, but every now and then, it became so excruciating that she couldn't see or hear anything around her.

The first time she'd experienced such a feeling had been before her coronation. A grim-faced Linden had found her in the gardens one sunny afternoon, and before she could clearly see his face, she'd known something was wrong. It was the sharp pain behind her eyes, the turning of her stomach, the black spots clouding her vision—as if her body already knew something awful had happened. Not five minutes later, Linden told her that her parents had been lost at sea, and her people were expecting her—not as Crown Princess, but as the new Queen of Akkinor.

Now as she considered what Lord Rudal told her about the Isalders, the inexplainable aches returned. She didn't want to believe that something nefarious was occurring, but she trusted her body. She had no choice but to assume that his fears weren't misplaced.

She knew extraordinarily little about the Isalders of Glacier Bay. They were one of four powerhouses of the realm along with the Akkinorians, the Carthinians, and the Quenosi. While the latter three traveled the world (alongside the pirates of Espos, whose numbers were smaller and whose behaviors were much less civilized), the Isalders only ever left their continent to wreak havoc or gather supplies. They were overly concerned with preserving the purity of the Isalder race, and, as such, didn't wish for their people to intermingle with foreigners in any capacity.

Aurelia herself had only interacted with Isalders once in her lifetime at her parents' twentieth anniversary celebration. Her father had invited the

Isalder king to the bash as a token of good faith, and King Viggo Styrmodr responded by sending his younger brother in his place: not to break bread with Akkinorians, but to propose a union between Aurelia and the Crown Prince of Glacier Bay. Though the Isalders didn't normally condone foreign relationships, the king saw an opportunity to ally his nation with the strongest in the realm by promising his then-seven-year-old son to the fourteen-year-old daughter of King Edmund II. The Isalders hadn't considered that Edmund would name his daughter as his heir. Isalder culture was exceptionally oppressive of women—even compared to Akkinor—and believed that Akkinor, too, would've chosen a male heir in place of a firstborn daughter.

Edmund, with all the poise he could muster, had politely informed the prince that Aurelia couldn't be betrothed to a Crown Prince while she herself was a Crown Princess. Rather than accepting defeat, the Isalder royal proposed an arrangement between Aurelia's younger brother, Prince Archie (who was eleven at the time), and his nephew's twin sister. Edmund had declined.

Aurelia hadn't seen or spoken to an Isalder since that day, but she'd once observed an Isalder ship sailing away after pillaging a coastal town in northern Sadia. Linden had written to King Viggo the next day, and the latter hadn't responded. Even Aurelia didn't know for certain if King Viggo had ordered his men to pillage Sadia or if rogue Isalders had simply ventured off on their own. Either way, it was a rare occurrence, and Aurelia hadn't wished to incite hostility between Akkinor and Glacier Bay unless her reasons were foolproof—even if the most prominent voices in Akkinor demanded that she respond.

The Isalders, like the Esposi pirates and the radical bandits who roamed the forests of Akkinor, were small foes. Aurelia, despite the wishes of her people, decided not to retaliate against the meager acts of indecency committed by her challengers. War was costly in more ways than one, and only a monarch understood exactly what was at stake when war loomed on the horizon.

She wouldn't act on the news for now. It wasn't worth giving her people reason to fear their neighbors to the north, and it wasn't worth risking ill-will with the Isalders until she had cause, beyond a reasonable doubt, to accuse them of something.

She set the document aside and moved on to the next, but even as she tried to forget about it, the dull ache behind her eyes didn't fade. It wouldn't—not until whatever she was forewarned about made itself known.

III

I don't know how I might further express my gratitude." Burly, gentle Silas Crowland peered down at Aurelia with a fatherly sort of affection. "I'm afraid I've earned myself a reputation as something of a nuisance, Your Grace."

Aurelia laughed. "Impossible!"

The Lord of Myra cracked a smile as the pair strode. "I do hope I haven't disturbed you. Your engagement diary must be quite full."

She didn't wish to tell him that, prior to receiving his plea for an audience the night before, the sole item on her agenda for the day was sparring with Linden in the gardens. It was better, she thought, that her subjects believed she was up to her ears in royal duties rather than taking advantage of an inactive day.

She'd been close to sleep the night prior when Linden entered her bedchamber with a message from Lord Crowland. The latter, having an unexpected opening in his schedule for the following day, requested an urgent audience with the queen. His wife was confined to her bedchamber after delivering a stillborn child. Unwilling to leave her, Lord Crowland requested that Aurelia travel to Wentworth Castle—capital of Myra and home of the Crowland family—to meet with him.

It wasn't habitual for nobles to host the monarch at their estates, as private audiences between monarch and noble were normally held at the palace. Aurelia made an exception for Lord Crowland. He was her closest ally among the five reigning nobles of Akkinor. That, and excluding the Folly, Myra was perhaps the most beloved Akkinorian kingdom in the queen's heart.

Of course, having visited each kingdom extensively throughout her lifetime, Aurelia found something to admire about them all. She particularly loved the rolling hills and wildflower-laden valleys of Omara;

the snowcapped mountains and frozen lakes of Sadia; the rocky shorelines and massive cliffs of the Holosi coast; and the glittering quarries of Laynoa where, long ago, one may have found dragon hatchlings learning to fly.

Myra was different, and not because the first Brentwoods in Akkinor had called the kingdom home before they were royals. There was something prepossessing about the southwestern kingdom of Akkinor—something that made Aurelia feel as though she was closest to the heavens whenever she breathed Myran air.

The Templar's Road, a series of paths that connected each kingdom to the others, offered views of nothing but vineyards, orange trees, and olive trees the instant one crossed the border into Myra. The smells of wine, fruit, and goods from the kingdom's infamous bakeries were nearly impossible to ignore. For as far as the eye could see, there was nothing but greenery, cobalt skies, and vibrant colors bleeding together as the fields of wildflowers in the distance seemed to unite under the beaming Myran sun.

It was the wealthiest Akkinorian kingdom, second only to the Folly, and while the latter earned its riches in duty, the former harvested it from gifts from the natural world. With plantations, seasonal farmland, and an overabundance of livestock, Myra's luxurious food and drink solidified their importance to the country. What produce they couldn't grow came from Omaran farms and was used to prepare specialty dishes. Sauces, soups, jams, wines, cheeses, and baked goods were exported not only across Akkinor, but also to Quapebet.

Aurelia enjoyed her rare visits to Myra nearly as much as she enjoyed her audiences with Lord Crowland. The middle-aged nobleman radiated a sense of compassion native only to the fathers of beloved daughters. The sound of his voice—the smooth, posh intonation common to Myrans, Follians, and Omarans—was nothing short of comforting, even when he didn't intend to be. He habitually greeted her with a basket of fresh oranges from the courtyard at Wentworth during her visits, and Aurelia was so touched by his kind gesture that she hadn't the heart to inform him of her dislike for oranges even ten years after receiving her first basket.

When they reached his study, Lord Crowland offered his chair and his desk to Aurelia while two of the queen's knights stood guard on the other side of the door. He collected a pipe from a wooden box on the desk, lit the contents with the flame of a candle, and sunk into a chair across from Aurelia while exhaling plumes of smoke.

"Now that it's just the two of us," Aurelia mused, "what would you like to discuss?"

Lord Crowland released a melancholy exhale. "It's my children, Your Grace. If you recall, my eldest—Silas, my namesake—was knighted by your father seven years ago, and young Alder wishes to revoke his noble status to become a High Priest at the monastery." He set the pipe aside and rubbed the heels of his palms along his thighs. A nerve-induced crimson rash crept up to his neck from his chest. "Neither of my sons may inherit my title. We'd hoped for another son throughout my lady wife's most recent pregnancy, and for a moment, our prayers were answered. Alas, our boy was dead before he was born."

A shiver traced Aurelia's spine. The only thing worse than a miscarriage, she thought, was carrying a babe to term only for the child to be still at birth. She'd been ten years old when her mother delivered a stillborn child—a son they called Rien, after Cressida's favorite brother—and the harrowing shrieks that'd ripped from her mother's throat would scar Aurelia's memory forever. She hoped the Crowlands' four children had been far away while their mother's wails shook the castle.

"And what of your girls?" she inquired.

"Liliana is all but ten. Dahlia has just turned sixteen. She's of marrying age, though I don't wish to force marriage upon her if she's not ready. Unfortunately, Your Grace, I fear it must be done."

Aurelia sighed. She should've expected this conversation.

Lord Crowland's predicament was clear: while both of his sons were unable to inherit his title due to the constraints of knighthood or priesthood, and while both of his daughters were unmarried, he had no heir. The queen was expected—not forced—to marry before taking the throne. A noblewoman, on the other hand, couldn't inherit *until* she was married. If Lord Crowland died before either of his daughters were married, both Aurelia and the Crowlands risked the highborn families of Myra battling one another for the kingdom.

"This is a problem I've fought tirelessly to solve," Aurelia muttered. "The Assembly has yet to agree on my proposal to change the law. They believe the country will protest if women are given the opportunity to govern territory without husbands at their sides. I've considered drafting an executive order, but as you know—"

"—we nobles don't take well to executive orders." He offered her a wry smile. "I'm beginning to feel my age, Your Grace, but I can't allow myself to rest until my line has been secured."

Aurelia raised an eyebrow. "What is it you want, my lord?"

Wincing, he took another drag from his pipe before setting it aside again. "My Dahlia is quite...well...*nervous*. She's aware of what her future may hold, and she is fearful of marrying beneath her status." His eyes locked on hers. "May I speak freely?"

"Please."

Lord Crowland swallowed. "I believe my daughter's fears for her future aren't so different from your own."

Aurelia understood exactly what he meant. The fear he spoke of was partly to blame for Aurelia's hesitance to accept Bradley Reilly's proposals—along with several other highborn suitors, too. It'd taken centuries for Akkinor to accept women in power, and even now, most men seized any and every opportunity to use a woman for her status. Just as Aurelia feared for her suitors' true intentions, Dahlia Crowland worried that no man worthy of becoming her husband would truly respect her. Any and all potential husbands for the future Lady of Myra would propose marriage not because they liked or even respected her, but because they hoped to manipulate her into surrendering control of Myra.

"Any suitors of equal status to hers are highly unlikely to accept her hand," Aurelia told him. "She can't marry a man due to inherit lordship of another kingdom, but..."

The queen's gaze turned to her immediate left, where a painting hung on the wall between two tall bookshelves. The portrait depicted General Rowan Blackwolf, a man who'd made it possible for Oleander Brentwood to win the rebellion against the Cherrane family with his clever strategies and insatiable valor. Aurelia knew about Blackwolf not because of her lessons, but because of her brother. Archie was particularly fascinated by Oleander's greatest war general. She didn't know why Archie idolized Blackwolf so—only that he did. In fact, Archie had been trying to seize the portrait for as long as Aurelia could remember. She'd tried purchasing it from Lord Crowland several years earlier as a name day gift for Archie, but he'd declined to keep the portrait in its ancestral home.

Lord Crowland seemed to remember this when he followed her gaze. "Has His Royal Highness expressed interest in marriage?"

"No. That would be far too easy." She sighed in defeat. "He's stubborn as a mule, my brother. If we're able to convince both he and Dahlia of the benefits of their union, however..." Her eyes lit up with excitement. "When he marries, Archie will officially inherit the dukedom of Eldford here in Myra. There's no law that prevents one spouse from ruling a kingdom while the other rules a dukedom or earldom. As a prince, he has nothing more to gain from marrying a noblewoman. Dahlia wouldn't have to fear for her reign by marrying above her status rather than below it."

He raised an eyebrow. "Would His Royal Highness be willing to marry beneath him?"

"Heavens if I know." She chewed on her lower lip as she stared at the portrait. She didn't want to admit that Archie wouldn't be pleased if he were a mere duke while his wife was a noble lady. "Perhaps if they shared both duties equally—"

"That depends on what the pair of them decide. Unless, of course, Your Grace commands it."

"I won't command your daughter to share her power simply because my brother was born a prince," she asserted. "He'll do his duty to our country as every second son has done before him. My father's younger brother was born a prince, too, and now he's happily married to a countess. He may have exchanged his royal status for that of an earl, but alas—there were no princesses to marry other than his sisters!"

The two laughed. "If only cross-cultural relations were commonplace," Lord Crowland said lightheartedly.

Aurelia knew the lord's comment was meant to be humorous, but even hours later as she rode back to the Folly, she couldn't stop thinking about it. What *if* the various cultures of the realm decided to intermingle in such a capacity? There were, naturally, dozens of Akkinorian commoners and outlaws who traveled the world and formed relations with other cultures— commoners and outlaws, but never royals or nobles.

Highborn rules existed for a reason, and Aurelia wouldn't claim responsibility for altering the status quo. If her great-great-great grandchild wished to risk their reign by wedding a savage from Carthe, so be it. Akkinor's current monarch, on the other hand, was risking her reign enough as it was just by being a woman.

***

"Was it a pleasant trip?"

Aurelia shrugged as she massaged a thick pearly cream onto her hands. "Pleasant as ever. Lord Crowland is a kind and generous host, and while I'm certain that our conversation would've reached the same conclusion via written correspondences, I'm grateful for his companionship." She eyed Estylle's reflection in her vanity mirror before turning in her chair and clutching the backrest with dewy hands. "The conversation left me curious, though. How long might I have before the people insist I marry?"

Estylle sighed as she tidied Aurelia's bedchamber. "I fear you won't see your thirtieth name day. Certainly the Assembly has mentioned this to you."

She nodded, grimacing. "Linden, too, though he continues to remind me that selecting a husband isn't a task to be taken lightly."

"No, it's not. Your mother—" Estylle stopped herself as she scrubbed wax from a candelabra. Her sandy brown skin was already rosy with embarrassment. "Forgive me. I don't wish to overstep."

Aurelia waved her hand dismissively. Her former governess (now head housemaid at the palace) had grown increasingly mindful of the things she said to Aurelia since the latter's coronation. Before Aurelia was queen, though, there was nothing that couldn't be shared between child and governess. She admired Estylle's respect, but she longed for the days when Estylle—and so many others—treated her like a friend, not a queen.

"Women are told from the moment we're born that our only duty to the realm is furthering family lines—our father's, our husband's—and so rarely are we allowed to consider our own legacies. It doesn't matter how we as mothers, daughters, or queens are remembered, so long as our children bear the surnames of the great men who came before them. I'd like to change that manner of thinking." A trembling breath escaped her lips. "The moment I marry, everything changes. I'll be deemed an unfit ruler while I carry my children because a woman in a delicate state is apparently too weak to govern a nation. I'll be scorned for excusing myself to feed my child from my body. The instant I provide an heir, I'll be seen as a mother—nothing more. It won't matter how many nurses, governesses, and tutors are hired to care for my children. A mother who allows her children to be raised by others is a dreadful one, and a queen who chooses to raise her own children is a selfish one. Either way, the people will turn to my husband as their leader, and I'll face one of two scenarios: I'll be forced to raise arms against my husband and my country to keep my throne, or I'll be forced to surrender my throne to prevent bloodshed and civil war. Linden thinks my woes are misplaced, but I'll continue to disagree until I meet an Akkinorian man unwilling to usurp his wife for the chance to rule."

Estylle's mahogany eyes were solemn. "You risk becoming a villain to your people simply by marrying and producing heirs. It's something that all highborn people must do at some point in their lifetimes, and yet, you may be scorned simply for wearing a crown."

"I've known this for my entire life. It's terrifying if not perfectly maddening." She eyed the governess, debating her next words. "Archie agrees with them, you know." Estylle raised a thick brown eyebrow as she plumped the pillows on Aurelia's bed. "He thinks I should be married by now. I was hoping to wait until after he leaves the palace to do so. That time may be fast approaching."

Estylle stilled. "How do you mean?"

"I came to an agreement with Lord Crowland today. We believe that a union between Archie and Dahlia will greatly benefit both families. His Lordship wishes to formalize a betrothal as quickly as possible. He fears for his health, and without an heir, Myra may be at war with itself. There are far too many noble families in Myra who believe they have a claim to the kingdom with the Crowlands gone. It'd be disastrous for the country if he were to perish before securing his line."

"Oh, dear." Taking a long, deep breath, Estylle abandoned her task and sat on the edge of the bed to face Aurelia. "In theory, it's a wonderful plan. In practice, I don't think Archie will take well to an arranged marriage. Perhaps he would've obliged if your parents still lived, but with his sister at the helm..." She trailed off and chewed on her lower lip. "What will happen to the Crowlands if he refuses?"

"I shall have to discuss that with Linden and His Lordship. The fate of Myra may very well rest entirely on Lord Crowland's two daughters." She raised a skeptical eyebrow. "You truly believe he'll refuse?"

Of course she does, she thought. *She raised him.*

"I can't say for certain." Estylle reached over to set a hand on Aurelia's. "When you speak to him at dinner tonight, be mindful of your temper. Asking him to do what's best for the country is a much better alternative to commanding him."

"I shall do my best by him."

"I know you will." She placed her cool palms on either side of Aurelia's face and smiled. "So much like your mother."

Aurelia beamed.

IV

*taring into your gaze is like losing oneself among the midnight stars. It is so much like your mother's, and yet so different. Tell me, Your Grace—is red hair prominent in your family? What a sensation it would be to see the late queen's hair on my children!*

Aurelia scoffed as she read. "Ridiculous."

I greatly look forward to seeing you at the upcoming Changling. It will be a wonderful opportunity to get to know you. I'd like to request a seat in the royal viewing box so we may watch the tourneys together. If not, I shall know exactly how to find you. You stand out like a beacon, my queen. A beacon of grace, beauty, and poise. I shall count the days until we meet.

She couldn't bring herself to finish reading. She'd gone to her study that evening expecting a vast pile of paperwork, and instead found about a dozen letters stacked on a bronze platter. Every single letter was written by an Akkinorian nobleman attempting to win her hand in marriage. The content ranged from empty promises to love poems to pleas soaked in desperation; none of which had ever been enough to impress her.

This particular letter had been sent by a middle-aged Holosi duke who, as a young man, had attempted to court Aurelia's mother. She'd never met him before, but he sent a letter to her desk once every season in hopes of wooing her. He may very well have been the lone suitor who didn't wish to marry the queen for the prospect of incredible power, but rather because he'd been smitten with her mother, and Aurelia was the closest thing to Cressida Brentwood left in the realm.

He spoke of midnight eyes that shone like stars, and Aurelia's gaze was nothing like the one he described. Her eyes were pale blue and clear like the cloudless sky, not dark and mysterious like her mother's. He spoke of her red hair, too, but Aurelia didn't have Cressida's rich auburn locks. It would've been one thing if the duke *assumed* she resembled her mother, but he'd done more than that: he'd created a visual of her in his head (a visual strikingly similar to her late mother), ignorant of how odd it was to praise a woman's looks without ever setting eyes on her.

"Apologies, my lord." She crumpled the letter and tossed it into the wastebasket. "Perhaps you'll have better luck next season."

The next letter was signed by Bradley Reilly. She didn't make it beyond the first sentence before discarding it. The thought of seeing him again—so soon after his last visit—made her stomach churn with dread. He'd spend the entire five-day Changling Celebration attempting to win Aurelia's heart, and he wouldn't be alone in his endeavor, either. The male nobles seemed to view each Changling as nothing but opportunities for courting their queen. The event's true purpose had been lost to them from the moment Aurelia came of age, and it would continue to evade them until a King Consort stood at her side.

Lord Reilly wasn't even the worst of them. The older ones were just as relentless as the younger ones, but they weren't nearly as polite. Aurelia may have outranked them, but their seniority and ancestral authority gave them enough leeway to test her patience. Linden repeatedly told her the same thing during each attempted courtship: *They're treating you exactly how they'd treat a king—only in this case, they're offering* themselves *rather than their daughters.* That made it easier to swallow, but not by much.

During the Changlings when Aurelia had no choice but to entertain them, they'd purchase seats in the royal viewing box at Robert's Arena (the Follian site for tournaments and sporting events), claim the seats nearest to her, and spend the duration of the event attempting to charm her. She tried her hardest to remain patient and polite, but it wasn't a simple feat. Between clouds of breath stinking like rotten mung beans and wrinkled hands desperately searching for an excuse to touch her, she was almost persuaded to do away with the Changlings for good.

When the dinner bell chimed, Aurelia left her study and made her way to the dining hall. Upon her arrival, she saw her four dinner guests positioned around the table. Each of them rose and either bowed or curtsied to her. As always, Aurelia sat at the head of the table with Archie on her left and Linden on her right. Cicely claimed the seat to Linden's other side while Ser Frederick Baylor, an Assembly advisor, fumbled with a servant from his spot beside Archie after accidentally spilling wine on his lap. Upon Aurelia's arrival, he told the servant to forget about the stain and leave him be.

"Good evening," she said cheerfully. Nobody so much as flinched until she was seated. As soon as she was comfortable, her guests reclaimed their seats, and footmen arrived to deliver the first course. She took a sip of burgundy wine from her chalice and raised an eyebrow at Archie. "I've hardly seen you today, brother. Your lurking is usually quite conspicuous. How are you?"

He shrugged, cheek squished against his palm, as he impolitely leaned his elbow on the table and trained his eyes on his soup. "Just fine. Practiced my playing for a bit. Went for a ride. It wasn't nearly as enthralling as *your* day must've been."

She ignored the twinge of bitterness in his voice. "It sounds to me like you had a marvelous day." She cleared her throat and minded Estylle's voice in her head. "I was hoping you'd accompany me to Wentworth tomorrow. Lord Crowland—"

"I'm not interested in his daughter, Li."

It didn't shock her that Archie predicted exactly what she was going to say. She'd been pressuring him to find a wife since he came of age at sixteen, not a season after her coronation. She'd even approved of a list of potential brides created by their father before his death, and Dahlia Crowland had been at the top of that list.

Her eyes narrowed. "You can't live like a bachelor forever. You understand the terms of your inheritance as well as I do. Father was clear in his instructions: you can't inherit Eldford until you're married."

Archie scoffed. "If that's your only persuasion tactic, you shall have to think of something better. You speak of my inheritance like it's something to be proud of. It's not." He took a long gulp from his chalice before setting it down with a bang. "Becoming Duke of Eldford means trading my royal status for something lesser. No prince with his wits about him would consider *that* a proper inheritance."

"Regardless of what your future holds, you'll never be stripped of your royal title. You know that."

"It's not the same."

She shook her head at him as she sipped a spoonful of creamy mushroom soup. "To be frank, I expected a stronger sense of duty from you. The Brentwood name was born in Eldford. We wouldn't be kings and queens today without our ancestry there. It's a tremendous honor to rule such an influential dukedom. You should be counting your blessings, but instead, you're fighting your inheritance with everything you have. I don't understand it."

"How could you? Your status has only grown in recent years, whereas mine has been destined to shrink," he retorted. "Say what you will, sister, but I won't marry beneath me simply to inherit something not worth inheriting."

"You shall never find a woman of your status in this country. That's what it means to have royal blood. We will both marry nobles, brother, and that is final."

His eyes were glazed with frost. "*You* have yet to marry, too. You're five-and-twenty."

"I'm also the queen," she snapped. Cicely and Lord Baylor jumped when her attempt to gently set her spoon on the table failed, causing the metal to shriek and the table to rumble. "You wish for me to act the villain? All right. You will accompany me to Myra tomorrow, you will *consider* Lord Crowland's eldest daughter as a potential wife, and we will continue the search if she is not fit. If you can't decide on a wife, I shall decide for you. Am I understood?"

The siblings seemed to stare at each other for hours. Their gazes were as dangerous as it was to stare at the sun for a moment too long. If they were still children, they would've stared at one under until they were physically torn apart.

Having exhausted his efforts, Archie retired his spoon and dabbed at his mouth with a napkin. His blue eyes were sharp against the blonde of his outgrown hair and the reddish-brown of his trimmed beard. The scowl on his face looked like it'd been there for years. As far as his sister knew, it had.

"I'd like to be excused, if Her Grace would be so kind."

Wordlessly, Aurelia gave a slight nod. His chair screeched when he stood and presented her with a mocking bow. She watched, fuming, as he stormed out of the dining hall without another word. She couldn't take her eyes off the doors even as a servant arrived to clear his place setting. Her guests hadn't uttered a word, and they wouldn't as long as she remained silent. After another battle with her brother, though, silence was the last thing she wanted.

She asked her guests about their days, their work, their worries. She tried to pay close attention when Lord Baylor discussed the overspending of the Spirre family, the nobles of Sadia, but her attention was frayed by thoughts of her brother.

Archie had seen her as his worst enemy since the deaths of their parents. He disrespected her both publicly and privately because he knew she adored him too much to punish him. He ignored her requests, rolled his eyes when she spoke, and abashed anything she said that he didn't entirely agree with. Everyone knew why he'd become so frosty towards her, though nobody dared say it aloud: he was jealous. Before their parents, kings had hidden their firstborn children away, disposed of them, or faked health concerns if the infants were daughters. Her own great-grandfather sent his firstborn daughter to be raised by servants in Sadia so his second son, Edmund I, could inherit the crown. When a girl happened to be born first, she never saw the throne—not until Aurelia, whose parents valued her birthright more than others' opinions.

While training to inherit the throne, Aurelia's father gave her two firm instructions. The first was, naturally, to marry well and produce heirs— but only with a man she loved and trusted. *I'd sooner wish for the Brentwood line to end with you than watch from the heavens while you suffer at an incompetent man's hand,* he'd said. The second was to find her brother a wife before he turned two-and-twenty. Though all Akkinorians came of age at sixteen (and were therefore eligible to receive their inheritance), Edmund had been clear that the circumstances for Archie were different. Archie's poor sense of duty was evident even at an immature age, and Edmund hoped that a strong wife would offer Archie enough direction and stability to be successful in his eventual role as Duke of Eldford. So long as Archie refused to marry, though, he'd remain under Aurelia's roof, just awaiting the day when he was offered something more.

When she snapped out of her daze, she realized her dinner guests were still discussing Sadia. The northwestern kingdom had been a constant topic of conversation as of late, and it was perhaps the only situation more worrisome to Aurelia than her brother's stubbornness. Lady Daena Spirre (the lone child of the late Lord Daene Spirre, who'd usurped Aurelia's maternal grandfather for control of Sadia), along with her cousin-husband and their family, had been taking advantage of their return to power since long before Aurelia's birth. They were mindful of their behavior while Aurelia's father sat on the throne, as they didn't wish to inspire further ill-will with Edmund after usurping his wife's family. Now that Edmund was gone, they'd begun to reveal their true colors. They didn't seem as intimidated by Aurelia as they'd been by her father.

Akkinor as a country may have surpassed every civilization in the realm in wealth and prosperity, but a closer look at financial records proved that Sadia hadn't contributed much to Akkinor's successes. The Spirres spent most of their family fortune on material luxuries—the finest gowns, jewels, architecture, and the like—before Aurelia took the throne, and now that their funds were dwindling, they'd begun using coin intended for the whole of Sadia to accommodate their avaricious lifestyle.

A sizable portion of Sadian coin, according to Lord Baylor, had been recently withdrawn from the Bank of Akkinor by the Spirres. Lady Spirre claimed it was used to improve the conditions of the schoolhouses, most of which hadn't been built to withstand the sharp winds and harsh snowfalls common to Sadia. Instead, she'd spent the coin on extravagancies for she and her family. While hundreds of Sadian children turned blue with cold during their lessons, the Spirres were expanding their collection of jewels or decorating every inch of Arrenwood Castle with one-of-a-kind antiques that, individually, costed more than Aurelia's collection of tiaras.

Aurelia had but two options: restrict the Spirres' spending by whatever means necessary (like threatening their rule in Sadia), or turn a blind eye to their antics in hopes of maintaining peace. She hoped the predicament wouldn't take her to Lady Spirre's doorstep. Nobody, not even desperate Bradley Reilly, made her skin crawl like Daena Spirre could. The noblewoman had the petrifying yet fascinating ability to make even the fiercest of people feel no greater than ants. When her gaze—one green eye and one brown—landed on someone, that individual, even for a fraction of a second, became half the person they'd been before.

"The Spirres have never turned down anything that glitters," Aurelia stated. "Send troops to Sadia at dawn, Lord Baylor. I'd like a full report on the peoples' livelihoods. If the Spirres prove to be negligent beyond a reasonable doubt, I'll pay for fresh supplies for the civilians using Lady Spirre's collection of gems and furs."

Lord Baylor smiled at her. "Yes, my queen."

Whenever Aurelia questioned herself, wondering if Archie really was better suited for the throne, she looked to the faces at her dinner table. She saw the sheen of surprise in Lord Baylor's eyes, as he hadn't expected her to be so outright. He was impressed with her. Then she glanced at Linden and Cicely, who were both beaming with such pride that Aurelia couldn't stop herself from blushing.

As long as her friends could smile and laugh at the queen's dinner table, she'd succeeded. She never wanted to see the day when they were too frightened to look her in the eye or too timid to share their honest thoughts on her reign. That would be the day when they became too afraid to smile in her presence.

When dinner and dessert came to an end, Aurelia politely declined Lord Baylor's offer to join him for an evening drink, as she had a lengthy list of engagements to attend to before the night ended. Normally the pair did so once a week: he'd host her at his private apartments for brandy or wine, and the two would discuss everything from displeasure with his fellow advisors to Aurelia's list of suitors to the new species of wildflower planted in the gardens. It wasn't an audience she was expected to endure, but an hour or two she chose to spend unwinding with someone she trusted.

She'd known Frederick Baylor since she was seven years old. At the time, he was married with two children, a former royal banker, and recently appointed as the newest member of her father's Assembly. His daughter had been one of Aurelia's playmates until she died of scarlet fever on her eleventh name day. Lord Baylor's wife, in her grief, claimed her life as a result. He had no choice but to send their surviving child, a six-year-old boy, to be raised by an aunt in Holos. He hadn't paid much attention to little Aurelia until the day he buried both his wife and daughter. The ten-year-old princess had offered him her handkerchief when she saw him crying, and ever since, he'd treated her like family.

As she mulled over paperwork in her study, she wished she hadn't left so much to do, as the only thing she desired was to feel the familiar burn of brandy on her tongue while Lord Baylor joked about the many letters she'd received from potential suitors. He'd say something clever about an elderly earl's wandering eye or a desperate duke's strange habit of clicking his tongue after every sentence, and she'd laugh until her cheeks ached and tears bubbled on her lashes.

She realized she'd been staring off into nothingness—imagining she were fogging her brain with liquor rather than answering tedious correspondences—when her eyes burned. She blinked, rubbed her tired eyes with her knuckles, and stood from the desk to fetch herself a cup of water from the jug across the room. While she coated her parched throat, she admired the vase of hyacinths in front of her, then turned her gaze to the portrait hanging on the wall behind it. She hadn't noticed how close she was to the portrait until she felt Oleander the Great's sapphire gaze staring into her soul.

When she was a girl, she used to wonder if the portrait was a good likeness. She'd spend hours staring at Oleander's head of long bronze hair and his thick beard to match; his midnight blue eyes that somehow glowed like real jewels; the jagged scars that disfigured his face with horrible white lines; and the charismatic, tender smile that played on his lips, as if the painter were the love of his life. Ten-year-old Aurelia had decided that Oleander's gaze wasn't as soft as it'd been painted. A usurper like Oleander Brentwood wouldn't have been so kind and temperate.

Now that she was older, her mind wandered to other things. She wondered about how the kingdoms of Akkinor had responded to Oleander's defeat of the Cherrane family. Every question that ran through her mind was political, and despite her position as queen, she yearned for the days when her sole concern was whether the painter had accurately captured the color of Oleander's eyes.

A sharp rap vibrated the door. Aurelia tore her eyes away from the portrait and gave permission for the knocker to enter. Both Linden and Cicely slipped into the study and sat themselves in the chairs across from her desk. By the look of Cicely's tousled hair and swollen lips, Aurelia knew immediately why they were still awake at that hour. They didn't seem intent on hiding it—they never did.

As a knight and a lady-in-waiting, Linden and Cicely, respectively, had sworn oaths to spend their lives unmarried and childless. There was no such oath, however, that forbade them from enjoying each other's company—so long as no surprises came as a result of it. Aurelia used to pity them for being unable to experience the joys of passion and romance, but every ounce of sympathy disappeared when she saw their flushed faces and sly smiles. They may not have been able to immortalize their love in marriage, but they'd always have a partner who loved them. It would've made more sense, she thought, for her friends to pity *her*, as she was the only member of their trio without a partner.

"Corresponding with the Spirres again?" Cicely asked. Aurelia nodded. "I thought so. You always look terribly peevish when working with Sadia." She gestured to the half-written letter on the desk and smirked a bit. "Forgot the blotter, did you?"

Aurelia peered down at the parchment and cursed. She'd been so distracted by her thoughts that she'd forgotten all about her correspondence. She'd put too much pressure on the quill, so there was now a thick splotch of black ink smudged across the parchment.

"That's very well." She balled the parchment and tossed the crumpled letter into a wastebasket. "The first half was just gibberish anyhow."

Linden sighed. "Your humbleness is never anything but admirable, but I do wish you wouldn't be so gracious."

"How do you mean?"

"The Spirres don't deserve your kindness. You claim this is a conversation between the two of you—I'd say it's more of a chastising. The Spirres are your nobles, your subordinates. They carry themselves as if they're your equals. Their greed and disobedience have been entertained for long enough. You mustn't continue to show them leniency."

Aurelia frowned. "Cicely? What do you think?"

Her friend shifted uncomfortably and tucked a lock of hickory hair behind her ear. "I agree with Linden. The Spirres were egotistical enough to overthrow Brennen Normindi while his daughter was married to the king. Your parents were merciful to allow them to proceed without royal intervention. Now they think themselves mighty enough to challenge yet *another* Normindi! This behavior must come to an end."

The queen sighed. "The Spirres have only worsened since they conquered Sadia. The kingdom isn't the extravagant place it once was when my mother's family governed the territory. If they continue on like this, Sadia will be penniless within the year. I suppose the time has come for me to give them an ultimatum. I'll request an audience with Lady Spirre so I might deliver this news in person. If she can't agree to my terms, she'll be forced to surrender control of the kingdom. That's what must be done to ensure the welfare of the Sadians."

"A wise decision," Linden said with a smile. "They won't be happy that you've reduced their spending, but they won't risk losing control of Sadia. The noble title means far too much to them. They wouldn't dare sacrifice Sadia in exchange for their family's former role as Duchy of Northacre."

"I should've come to this conclusion sooner." Aurelia inwardly cursed herself as she massaged her throbbing temples. "My father would've intervened years ago. Of course, the Spirres wouldn't have dared to act as they have if my father were still alive. They're disobedient because they don't consider me a threat."

"It's pitiful," Cicely agreed. "Worry not, my friend. You shall prove to them that you're as formidable as King Edmund was. Rest his soul."

"You've been the queen for less than five years," Linden reminded her. "Your training was interrupted by tragedy. Don't torture yourself over this, Aurelia. It takes a tremendous amount of time and effort for a monarch to find their footing. If I know anything, it's that you're more capable than any who came before you. The entire world could be yours if you desired it."

"Even the Carthinian heathens?" she joked. Her friends laughed. "You know, I've often wondered why my predecessors failed to acquire territories in Carthe. I suppose it's a rather elementary reason: the continent is crawling with uncivilized savages."

Cicely shrugged. "So the stories say. None of us have ever visited the continent. Your parents traveled there often, but they always returned with the same report. The western continent—"

"—is a dangerous and unpredictable place," Linden finished. "Even so, their visits to Carthe were limited to Caedia. We can't know for sure if the rest of the continent is as brutish as the stories claim."

Aurelia snorted in a vastly unladylike manner. "The tales alone are enough. Consider the kingdom of Dofell: their Almighty is Myenar. Mythology points to Myenar as the most pernicious of the Twelve. I trust I don't have to remind you of the stories."

Her friends grimaced in understanding. Myenar was one of the Twelve gods responsible for the Creation of the realm. Every civilization in the world believed in the same twelve deities, but their individual religions were quite different. No two civilizations worshipped the gods in the same way. The primal deity (known across the realm as the Almighty) of Akkinor was Buen, god of prosperity. In Taundosa, it was Gianla, the sun goddess. To the north, the Isalders of Glacier Bay mainly worshipped Hzarl, god of the hunt. Every civilization had one primal deity whom they viewed as the all-powerful among the gods. There were still temples in Akkinor dedicated to Gianla and Hzarl and the other deities, but Buen was the only god whose name was spoken in the prayers of every civilian at the end of each day.

Of the Twelve, Myenar, god of judgement, had perhaps the poorest reputation. Legends told of Myenar judging individuals before they had the opportunity to perform sinful acts. In rare cases, his premature judgement prevented individuals from doing so: a divine curse was placed upon their soul to hinder their autonomy. In other cases—like an individual who merely *considered* performing a sinful act, but who bore no intention of carrying it out—was cursed unfairly, thus ensuring an inadequate quality of life and preventing them from earning a place in the heavens.

"I rather think," Cicely drawled, "that we must thank the Almighty thrice this evening for allowing us to live in Akkinor instead of Dofell." The trio laughed. "Anyway," she added, rising from her seat, "it's time for me to retire for the evening. Good luck with your correspondences, Aurelia. Remember this: you have something the Spirres and the Carthinians do not."

The queen raised an eyebrow. "Which is?"

Her old friend smiled. "The heart of the hero. That alone shall lead you to greatness."

V

hen the oil lamp beside her burned out, Aurelia let her eyes fall shut with an open book lying on her stomach. Then a thunderous bang and an earth-shattering jolt echoed throughout the palace, and suddenly she was more awake than she'd ever been. She sat up in her massive bed, eyes wide and heart racing, as the door to her suite flew open without so much as a knock.

It was Linden. "Aurelia," he gasped, locking the door behind him. He rushed over to her and pulled her out of bed by the wrists. Only a fool would've missed the thick smear of blood across his cheek. "We have to leave. The palace has been breached. It-It appears to be an uprising."

"An *uprising*—"

"They're coming for you." He dragged her into the closet and tore through her belongings. "I-I don't know who's responsible for this, but it's been meticulously planned. I spotted a handful of assassins on my way to you." The blood drained from her face. "We know what to do, but we must make haste. The soldiers outside won't hold them forever. T-There are too many of them."

Her stomach twisted into panicked knots. "Linden—"

"Everything will be fine." He held up a bundle of clothing. "Change into these. Riding clothes. I already have our bags packed."

She tried to focus on her breathing as she changed out of her nightdress, but her hands were trembling too much. When she was as decent as she could be, she threw a cloak around her shoulders and pulled the hood over her head to conceal her telltale, curly locks: a unique shade of light copper woven with strands of golden blonde.

Linden slung two hefty bags over either shoulder while she secured the cloak. "Are you ready?"

"I have to be." She lifted a hand to his bloodied cheek and observed. "It's not yours."

He grimaced. "No, it's not. Come."

He kept her close to him as he opened the door. She could finally hear the signs of conflict: the guttural screams of innocent lives being snatched; the clanging of swords as their blades met; and the pounding of heavy boots against tile, immediately followed by shattering glass and deafening crashes as the intruders destroyed everything in their wake.

Linden grabbed a nearby soldier (who, along with a dozen others, had been guarding Aurelia's bedchamber) by the wrist and tugged him along as they set out for the opposite side of the palace. Doing so meant passing the foyer, where everyone—friend and foe alike—would see them.

Linden took a long, deep breath and dashed forwards with Aurelia and the soldier hot on his heels. Bile rose up in her throat when she saw the scene around them. Blood was splattered on the beautiful wallpaper, shoeprints smudged the blood on the tiles, and precious pieces of artwork were either torn apart or smashed to pieces. Her heart constricted at the sight of a servant lying dead on the floor with an arrow through his neck. She'd seen him hours earlier when he was polishing the floors. He'd smiled at her.

Suddenly, a strike from behind had the soldier hollering in pain. Before the assailant could deliver the killing blow, Linden sent a dagger sailing into his forehead. Aurelia didn't have time to wince before Linden pulled her away again, leaving the poor soldier behind. He took her into a musty-smelling room once used to host guests. While he pushed a heavy dresser in front of the door and sealed the windows to the best of his ability, Aurelia dove into the closet and searched for a hidden door. She pulled the latch and exhaled in relief when the door lifted from the floorboards.

"I've found the door. B-But the assailant, he-he looked like—"

"Like an Isalder." His eyes shone with understanding. "Mercenaries."

There was no questioning that the assailant was an Isalder—they had the most conspicuous features in the realm. Most had pale skin, hair so fair that it appeared white, light eyes, and clothing made of thick textiles and furs. In a fight, Isalders were ruthless and brutal. Their weapons weren't terribly impressive, but they didn't need the finest materials to bash a man's skull and turn his brain to mush with one whack of a wooden club. They were fierce and merciless, so they were often sought out by those seeking to inflict maximum damage.

She remembered the trio of Isalders who'd been apprehended in Seaport a week earlier, locked in the dungeons by Lord Rudal, and her stomach sank to her knees. The ache she'd felt behind her eyes when he told her the news was, indeed, a warning—one she'd chosen to ignore for the sake of keeping the peace.

Assailants pounded on the door, so Aurelia knew somebody must have seen them slip into the room. She glanced at Linden frantically, and it would've been impossible to miss the doubt flickering over his face.

"Go," he instructed. "I'll be just behind you."

She hesitated. "What about Archie? Cicely? Lord Baylor? Perhaps we have time to—"

"There's no time. The soldiers are responsible for guiding them to safety. The only thing we must concern ourselves with is safely delivering you to your destination." He sucked in a long, deep breath and clenched his jaw. She could see in his eyes that he, too, was much more concerned for their loved ones than he let on. "I shall meet you at the end of the tunnel. I have to stop at the dungeons first anyway, and it's safer for me to go on without you. There's something we need down there."

She knew: magic. "Be safe, Linden. Please." She took the locket from her neck and set it on his palm. "Good luck."

"The same to you." He put the locket around his neck and inhaled. "I'll get you out of this city safely, Aurelia. You have my word."

She tried to smile, but it was unconvincing. "I'll see you soon."

Banging on the door intensified the need to quicken her pace. She carefully climbed into the hatch and down the ladder, salvaging her last few seconds of light, before Linden closed the door and sealed her in. It wouldn't be long now before he was ambushed, and even a knight as exceptional as Linden wouldn't emerge unscathed.

She observed nothing but empty darkness from all angles. There were no candles, no torches, no tiny slivers of moonlight peeking out from any cracks above. She was glad for the darkness—she would've frozen and yelped if she saw the roaches and spiders undoubtedly climbing the stone walls only inches from her face. For one so fond of the outdoors, she despised insects.

Other than the soles of her shoes clanging on the metal prongs and the dripping of water against stone, the only sound she heard was the dull roar of combat. The vertical tunnel was built between walls and extended from the highest point of the palace to the lowest: even if Aurelia's only surroundings were damp stone walls and roaches, she was much closer to the conflict than she appeared. If she smashed through the tunnel walls, she'd likely find herself in a parlor or hallway.

When she reached the bottom of the ladder, she firmly planted her feet on the ground and reached for the closest stable structure. It wasn't long before she felt the damp, firm wall of the tunnel. She kept a hand on the wall as she walked straight ahead, turning only with the curve of the tunnel.

Finally, she saw a tiny spark of light in the distance. She increased her pace until she was practically splashing in puddles and scraping her fingers on the rock wall. She slowed down upon reaching a thick, sturdy wooden door. Light was peeking out from the empty keyhole. She bent down to peer through it in hopes of seeing Linden on the other side. Instead, a pit formed in her stomach upon observing the Folly. Houses and wagons were ablaze, horses ran wild through the street, and bodies lay strewn about like ragdolls. Civilians were running in search of shelter, screaming for their loved ones, begging for mercy. A man to the left was writhing around in pain, pleading with anyone who would listen, crying out for the arm that was no longer attached to his body.

She looked away and pressed her back against the door. Her breathing labored as she struggled to comprehend the state of her kingdom. Whoever executed the rebellion was bold to call for the queen's head, but even bolder to wreak havoc on the capital and its inhabitants. No Follian still with their head would allow such horror to be forgiven or forgotten.

"Aurelia?"

The voice startled her. She nearly stumbled to the ground as she struggled to open the door. Just a crack was enough to see the anxiety in Linden's eyes. When he, too, relaxed at the sight of her, he opened the door wider and ushered her out.

As she followed him through the wreckage, she couldn't help but notice the way the firelight stressed his time away from her. His face was bleeding from a cut on his temple, and he was clutching his fighting arm against his abdomen. The knight's cape that trailed behind him was torn— so much so that nobody could distinguish him from other soldiers.

He dragged her behind an abandoned home where a soldier was waiting with three horses and three emergency packs. He quickly removed the locket from his neck and pulled it over Aurelia's head. She made sure the necklace was secure, gave it a brief touch for reassurance, and pulled the hood of her cloak over her head again. Somehow, the return of her most sacred possession didn't bring her the comfort she'd hoped for.

Aurelia mounted her horse as the soldier tied her supplies to the saddle. Linden did the same, biting through the pain in his arm as he did so. As she waited, the sound of clanging swords intensified. Somebody screamed nearby, so piercing that it echoed through the trees of the forest to their right. Linden told the soldier to keep watch while he finished tying Aurelia's supplies for himself.

"Listen to me," he said. Both winced at the sound of a garbled scream. It was so close that they both knew the soldier wouldn't be returning. He hurriedly finished tying the pack and looked up at her with fear in his dark eyes. "We know where we must go if we hope to stand a chance. Whatever happens, we must make it to our destination tonight—even if we must crawl there on our hands and knees. Your parents trained us for this moment, Aurelia. Everything we've feared has finally come to pass."

Bile rose up in her throat. "If we're too late—"

"It's never too late." He mounted his horse and curled the reins around his wrist. "If we're followed, I—"

His hurried speech was interrupted by the whizzing sound of something slicing through the air. Both gasped when a spear—Isalder-made, judging by its gargantuan size—pierced the ground only a foot from where Linden's horse was standing. The stallion reared and whinnied in terror, thus tossing Linden from his back and sending the Lord Hand rolling across the dirt. Aurelia cried out for him upon hearing the clanging of his armor coming in contact with the ground. Within a millisecond of hearing her voice, Linden was on his feet again, sword in hand and body posed for combat.

Aurelia's heart hammered at the sound of deep, gruff grunts from the other side of the dwelling. Though she couldn't understand a lick of it, she recognized the Isalder tongue well enough.

"Go." He shifted his grip on his weapon as if weighing it, then bounced on the balls of his feet in anticipation. "Don't stop until you arrive. I'll be just behind you."

"Linden—"

She was interrupted when an arrow flew passed her head, narrowly missing her. She wasn't given the chance to react before barbaric war cries rattled her eardrums. In the blink of an eye, the two were caught in an ambush by a handful of Isalder mercenaries.

Linden killed the first to approach with a sword through the neck. The second recognized Linden's skill without hesitation. While Linden prepared to strike, the second Isalder swung his club, and a sickening crack echoed throughout the Folly when the wood came in contact with Linden's armor. Aurelia cried out as he hollered in pain and fell to one knee, temporarily disabled by the vibration of his bones rattling against metal.

With Linden immobilized, only one threat to the mercenaries' success remained: the queen herself. They stepped closer to her, moving slowly as if to intimidate her, all while bearing their weapons for her to see. She urged her horse backwards a few paces, increasing the gap between them, and prayed to every god in the realm that Linden would find his footing again.

He did. While the mercenaries were distracted by Aurelia, Linden rose to his feet and approached one from behind. The Isalder's throat was cut, and as a result, his comrades returned their attention to Linden, now seeking vengeance for the murders of their two friends. Linden wiped the sweat and blood from his face, adjusted his grip on his sword, and met Aurelia's gaze with a sense of desperation and urgency she'd never seen before. She knew exactly what that meant: he was telling her to go, to leave him there, to save herself if nothing else.

Aurelia increased her horse's pace and set out for the forest. She didn't want to leave him, but she had no choice. He was right: if she didn't make it out of the Folly, she wouldn't live to see another day.

She didn't dare look back. She could still hear the sounds of war coming from the Folly, even as it became no larger than a candle's flame, and tried to keep as far from the road as possible to avoid being spotted by anyone venturing towards the capital. When she found herself drifting towards the path—where she could hear the laughter of battle-crazed men and the trotting of horses—she brought her steed to a stop and waited until the noises passed. She didn't move again until it was silent. Even in the darkness, she knew the people who invaded the Folly were the same type of people who could hunt human beings with their eyes closed. She'd leave nothing to chance.

Finally, she heard the calming melody of rushing water and smelled the horrible stink of days-old fish. She'd safely arrived at Seaport, the coastal town west of the Folly, which served as Akkinor's primary harbor. Most people who worked in Seaport preferred to live in the Folly, as the town was far too small and busy for a peaceful existence. The people who *did* live there, though, liked the village for its lack of nobility. It was inadequate for a noble family, let alone a castle. They were close enough to the Folly that the monarchy could keep an eye on them, but far enough to have a bit more freedom than the other kingdoms.

Aurelia tied up the horse and grabbed her supplies from his back. She was grateful for the darkness now. Most Seaport residents abided by a strict daily schedule, so the streets were empty. Only a few lanterns lit the pathways while most homes were as dark as the sky. She cautiously padded through the neighborhoods in search of one particular home: a white cottage with blue doors and blue hydrangeas tied to the messenger box. When she found it, she knocked three times before pulling her cloak down to cover her face.

The door creaked open to reveal an elderly man on the other side. "May I help you?" He froze. "Your Grace. Come inside."

She rushed into the home without a word. While the man locked the doors and closed the shutters, she turned to the only other face in the room: an old woman stamping out the fire in the hearth and blowing out the candles illuminating their quaint home.

"You're in luck, Your Grace." The woman rushed to the kitchen and snatched a loaf of bread from the dining table. "My husband is leaving for Carthe at dawn."

"C-Carthe?" Her stomach twisted into flustered, mortified knots as she widened her eyes. "I'm meant to leave Akkinor for a continent overrun by hedonistic savages?"

The couple exchanged looks. "Aye, Your Grace," the woman said tentatively. "Where else would you go?"

"I wouldn't know where to begin."

"We may be able to help with that." The man sat on the couch across from her while his wife encouraged her to eat and drink. She eyed him carefully as he unlocked a wooden box he'd taken from a nearby bookshelf. He set the box's contents—a single letter stamped with the seal of the Brentwood family—on the table between them. "From your parents."

The woman sighed. "There was so much they wanted to tell you. It was too dangerous. They didn't want you to know unless it was absolutely necessary. That's why they left this letter for you—to tell you themselves when the time was right. Open it when you're safely aboard the ship. We must get you onboard before your enemies raid the village."

Shivers crawled up Aurelia's spine. "But the Lord Hand—"

"If he's not with you, the situation is worse than we feared. Your father and Ser Elliot were clear with us, Your Grace. Waiting for him isn't worth the risk."

It took every ounce of self-control in her body to keep from vomiting. Aurelia never truly imagined herself being forced to flee the country, but if she had, she would've imagined Linden at her side. She would've waited for him in that little cottage until her usurpers broke the door down—but if she did, she'd be signing her own death warrant.

She hadn't had the stomach to eat when the old woman brought out a tray of bread and jam, so the couple wrapped it up for her and put it in her pack. She tried to decline when they offered more food, but they gave it away anyhow. When it was time to go, the old man put on his hat and coat while his wife kissed him goodbye.

"Be safe, Your Grace." The old woman smiled and clasped Aurelia's hands. "I wish you the best of luck."

The queen offered her a weak smile. "Thank you, madam."

When the old man opened the door, she ducked out and let him guide her towards the docks. The village was still quiet, so she knew the riots were far away. That would buy them some time. He led her to a dingy floating in the docks and helped her climb inside while he untied it. When the boat was free from the dock, he pulled the rope inside and started to row.

She peered over her shoulder at a merchant's vessel anchored in the distance. Ships like it frequently traveled to and from the continent of Carthe to the west, and sailors often resided in small coastal villages like Seaport. Aurelia wondered if the old man had been a sailor all his life or if he'd changed professions after meeting her parents. After all, the elderly couple hadn't begun growing blue hydrangeas in their garden until they met the Brentwoods.

Upon arriving at the ship, they climbed onboard without making a sound. "Nobody's here," he confirmed, opening the hatch that would take them below deck. "You should be safe, Your Grace."

She smiled faintly and followed him below deck to a cluttered storage room—the orlop—which was filled with more barrels of whiskey and ale than she could fathom. He pushed aside a toilsome metal gate that led to an opening behind a tall stacks of barrels. There was nothing but a few feet of cobweb-laden space, a musty blanket, a bucket, and a damp box of matches.

"This is the best I can do." He averted his eyes and flushed. "I'll bring food and water as often as I can."

"Thank you for your kindness. This is a debt I'll never be able to repay."

He shook his head. "This is our way of repaying *our* debt to your parents. You owe us nothing." He bowed and turned to leave. He paused in the doorway as Aurelia sat down on the floor behind the barrels. She could hardly see him in the darkness, but something told her he was smiling. "Long live the queen."

***

Laurenia sat at the dining table beside her husband, caked in thick layers of soot and the blood of innocent souls, as moonlight peeked through a nearby window and gleamed on the pile of coin spread over the table. She tore her eyes from their spoils to study Cullen's face—the ash melted into the deep lines on his forehead, the still-oozing cut over his eyebrow, and the haunted, tortured look in his turquoise eyes. The look mirrored exactly what she felt in her heart: guilt, disgrace, and enough terror to make two veteran assassins shake in their boots.

Your path will be cleared beforehand. The blue-eyed boy's assurance echoed in her head. The Falwells assumed he'd meant that the dozens of soldiers guarding the palace would be incapacitated; they never would've imagined what he truly had planned. Instead of finding a few pesky obstacles removed from their path, the Falwells arrived in the Folly to find it ablaze and riddled with civilian corpses. The queen's soldiers weren't the only threat to the highborn who'd hired the Falwells—apparently, they needed every Follian removed from the equation.

Laurenia, a native Follian before her permanent move to Sadia, hadn't recognized her own village when she and Cullen trekked through the carnage to reach the palace. She never would've known that she was walking through Mistcairn, the place she'd called home for the first seventeen years of her life, while it was gray and flaming and inhabited only by screaming souls desperately seeking salvation.

"It's done." Cullen's voice pierced the silence in the cottage like a blade. His normally melodic tone was rough and gravelly. "They were true to their word, at least."

Laurenia didn't reply. The coin spread over the table was double the amount they'd been given upon accepting the assignment. When they returned to the cottage that night after attempting—and failing—to assassinate the queen, they found a second bag of coin sitting on their doorstep.

Laurenia cleared her throat. "Do you think she's—?"

"Dead? No." Cullen inhaled and rubbed the heels of his palms along his thighs. "We would've heard by now. If she hasn't yet escaped the Folly, she's hiding somewhere nearby. How many others do you suppose they hired?"

"Assassins?" Laurenia chewed on her lip, contemplating. "I don't know. I saw two others, but there must've been more."

"I'd assume so." He shook his head, chuckling a bit, and rolled a gold coin between his fingers. "There were at least four assassins and several dozen mercenaries hunting her. If none of us managed to kill her tonight, nobody ever will. It's a lost cause."

"Maybe. I'm just glad..." She trailed off, but she didn't need to finish for Cullen to know what she meant to say: *I'm just glad that we fled before we found her.* They hadn't had any intention of assassinating Queen Aurelia when they accepted the assignment, as they only wished to protect their children. That, however, would've meant very little if they'd found themselves face-to-face with their target. Fortunately, the Falwells were able to slip away while the attack was at its peak. They'd done what they promised by trying (however halfheartedly), and they'd managed to avoid having their names forever tied to the murder of Akkinor's queen.

Even if they *had* finished the job, it would've been worth the infamy and the shame. Everything would've been worth it if it meant keeping Soren's fingers from the pig's trough and Alis's hands from a pot of scalding water. There was nothing a parent wouldn't do for their children—even murdering the crown.

VI

A urelia lost track of how long she'd been at sea. It had to have been at least three days, as they'd stopped briefly after her second night aboard to gather supplies at Marooner's Chain. The cluster of isles—an independent civilization until its conquering in the days of old—was a port for restocking supplies close to the mainland. It was a short trip, so the ship was only docked for a few hours, but she'd recognize the stench anywhere: filth, rotting flesh, and stale liquor. She'd stopped counting the days and nights after that.

The old man had been true to his word when he said he'd look after her on their travels. He came down every day, only once, to deliver food and water. She decided to dump her waste bucket through a porthole and into the ocean, saving herself from embarrassment and her savior from unnecessary tasks.

With so little to do, her mind kept wandering to what she'd run from. She could still see Linden as he sent her off and prepared to face an army alone: bouncing on the balls of his feet, smearing blood across his face as he wiped sweat from his brow, and staring at his own face in the mirrorlike metal of his sword.

She thought about Archie. Archie, Cicely, Estylle, Lord Baylor, Lord Rudal, Buck, Madame Bettley. She remembered seeing the bodies strewn about the halls, the blood caked on the walls like paint, the shoes left behind by those who'd attempted to flee. She wondered who'd survived and who was already dead. Those closest to her—those with even a lick of influence within the monarchy—would've been led to safety by the soldiers, but the rest of the palace's residents wouldn't have been so fortunate.

The most obvious means of infiltrating the palace—the front or rear doors—wouldn't have been the attackers' point of entry for exactly that reason: it was too obvious. If Aurelia had sought to invade her own home, she would've taken the cleverer route: the servants' entrance. Only two soldiers guarded the door at all times of the day. The entrance led directly into the kitchens, which offered direct routes to almost every corridor on the ground floor. If there'd been anyone lingering in the kitchens after dark, it would've been Shela, the six-and-seventy-year-old cook who'd prepared the royal family's meals since Aurelia's father was an infant. Ma Shela, as she was affectionately known to all, tended to stay up until the middle of the night preparing Aurelia's favorite breakfast dish (a complicated pastry for which Shela was known). The old woman wouldn't have put up a fight, but the attackers would've killed her anyhow.

It didn't matter that the vast majority of the palace's residents were servants or that more than half of the palace staff had children who lived with them in the estate. The servants weren't soldiers or fighters, but innocent men, women, and children who desired nothing more than to build the most wonderful lives they could with what they had. They'd been hired to service the Brentwoods because it was their best chance, and now that chance had been stripped from them as quickly as it'd been given.

As she leaned her head back against the damp wood behind her, Aurelia closed her eyes and thought back to the attack. She couldn't understand how the usurpers were able to infiltrate the palace without forewarning her men until it was too late. It occurred to her then that perhaps her soldiers hadn't been bested or overwhelmed by the intruders. Perhaps those tasked with protecting the queen had betrayed her for the promise of coin or glory. Perhaps they'd allowed enemies to enter the property and lay siege to the palace. Perhaps they'd even told the intruders—mercenaries, assassins, and Akkinorian soldiers alike—exactly where to go and what to do when they made it beyond the gates.

Soldiers weren't enough to accomplish what the invaders hoped for, either. Whoever orchestrated the uprising would've required assistance from others, too: handmaidens, footmen, messengers, and even Aurelia's advisors knew things most people didn't, like where to find her if she weren't in her bedchamber or her study, what time she normally retired for the evening and when she woke each morning, and how many guards were stationed outside of her bedchamber. She trusted the majority of those closest to her, but no monarch with their wits about them could trust everyone in their inner circle.

Of her eight advisors, she trusted three with her life: Henry Rudal, Frederick Baylor, and Alwen Gideon. She desperately wanted to trust Zinnia Summerhill, the newest member of the Assembly, as Zinnia was the only advisor whom Aurelia herself had appointed. The others served on her father's Assembly, so after one former advisor died, Aurelia sought to replace him with a woman. She'd hoped for a strong bond with Zinnia until she learned of an ongoing affair between the advisor and Archie. Zinnia hadn't given Aurelia reason to distrust her yet, but Aurelia was made uneasy by her apparent preference for Archie.

The remaining four sat on the Assembly for one reason and one reason only: they'd been loyal, honorable advisors to both Edmund I and Edmund II. Aurelia hoped their loyalty to the Brentwood family would apply to her reign, too, but she'd never been convinced. Stephen Wallace and Braddock Median were Sadians, and as such, were heavily dependent on Sadia's primary value: stability over pleasure. They believed arranged marriages were necessary for familial lines and power, so the idea of marrying for love or even friendship was a foolish one. The only thing they cared about was pushing a King Consort unto their queen. She'd never know how they truly felt about her until she was married.

Leith Rowe and Calder Byrd, on the other hand, were Holosi. The people of Holos valued community, so the noblemen were mainly concerned with Aurelia's relationships with her subordinates. They'd been urging her to mend her poor relationships with Sadia and Laynoa (by allowing the Spirres to continue their greedy endeavors and by marrying Lord Reilly, respectively) rather than paying heed to more important matters across the country. In their eyes, pleasing her nobles was the most crucial aspect of Aurelia's reign. Every wonderful thing she'd done for her country was overlooked while tensions with her nobles prevailed. She could've saved every impoverished soul in Akkinor, and still, Rowe and Byrd would've told her to ignore the poor in favor of the wealthy.

She couldn't decide if her advisors' qualities and values made them her friends or her enemies. Wallace and Median may have wanted her to marry as quickly as possible, but were they impatient and traditional enough to use her negligence as justification for a rebellion? Rowe and Byrd may have wished for Aurelia to please her nobles by whatever means necessary, but was their desperation for unity and cordiality reason enough to betray her?

No, she decided. Her advisors may have thought extraordinarily little of her, but she didn't think little of them. She wouldn't allow herself to become as cynical as others were. She believed in their loyalty and honor as every Akkinorian monarch should; only time would tell if her faith was misplaced.

The damp floorboards of the orlop creaked, startling her. The noise was quickly followed by the old man's kind voice: "Only me, Your Grace."

She exhaled. While she stood, the man rearranged the barrels and crates to find her in the tiny space. Had he been anyone else, she might've been embarrassed. She was a queen, and there she was, hiding out in a crawlspace of filth like a common criminal being smuggled across the sea.

"Here you go." He handed her a canteen, a loaf of bread, and a few pieces of dried beef wrapped in white cloth. She didn't hesitate to chug the contents of the canteen as soon as she had it in her clutches. She coughed and sputtered when the burning sensation of foul mead ravaged her throat. "Begging forgiveness, Your Grace. I thought you'd like something with a kick."

She *was* desperate for liquor. While the mead was meager at best, it was the closest she'd get to a glass of wine or brandy. She thanked him, but before the old sailor could return to his crew, he sat himself on the floor across from her.

"A raven found us from Seaport this afternoon," he shared. Immediately, she abandoned the food and straightened up to give him her undivided attention. "My wife reported a raid of the village. Every residential, public, and private building in Seaport was searched. They found nothing. Your enemies don't think you escaped from Seaport. They've turned their attention to the border of Quapebet at Vilgh-Ahzor."

A sigh of relief escaped her lips. "That's certainly consoling. Has she...Has she heard much else? From the Lord Hand, perhaps?"

"I'm afraid not, Your Grace."

"Oh. That is...That is very well. It's better to hear nothing at all than to hear bad news."

"A wise conclusion," he said with a smile. "If you don't mind my saying so, I'm pleased to have had the chance to know you now. You were so young when we met for the first time. It's a tremendous honor to know you as a queen and as the continuation of your dear papa's incredible legacy. I can hear his voice echoing yours."

Despite herself, Aurelia blushed. "You flatter me, sir. There's no greater honor than to be compared to my father." She hesitated for a moment, debating between safety and curiosity. "Would it be all right if you told me how you came into my parents' service?"

That made him sigh. "We met your parents many years ago. You were young then—no older than six, I'd wager. They were visiting Seaport during a time of dire financial troubles. The town magistrate was collecting debts by seizing our property. If we couldn't pay, we couldn't properly care for our children, either. The debt collectors were taking babes from their mothers' breasts by the dozens to be brought to orphanages."

"I beg your pardon?"

The old sailor grimaced. "Aye. Your parents happened to be riding by our neighborhood when the magistrate arrived to take our children. Your mother climbed out of a moving carriage to intervene. She and His Grace were kind enough to pay the debts of everyone in the village. They forced the magistrate to return every child who'd been taken. Our children would've been separated and delivered to orphanages if your parents hadn't intercepted. When they saved our family, we offered them our services in return. It was your mother's idea to use our home as a safe house in the event that you were ever forced into hiding."

Aurelia hadn't heard the full story until that moment. For as long as she could remember, her parents and Linden told her that even a monarch's safety was never truly assured. *There might come a day,* her father had said, *when you will find yourself forced to escape the Folly—and perhaps the country— to save your own life.* She never believed him until he and Linden showed her the secret tunnel. Even then, she didn't understand the severity of it until she was brought to a small cottage in Seaport with a blue door and hydrangeas on the messenger box. She met the elderly couple for the first time when she was twelve years old, when they promised to do their utmost to ensure her safety.

"Thank you," she murmured. "For offering."

"It's been the honor of our lives to repay your parents." He brought himself to his feet and smiled at her. "Get some rest, Your Grace. The journey has just begun."

***

There wasn't much to do in the orlop for entertainment. So many days and nights of hiding out in a cramped space forced Aurelia to become creative. She'd torn several spouts from the barrels of ale to use as makeshift knucklebones. The game proved entertaining for a while until she heard the sailors bellowing from above deck about broken barrels, and she knew it wouldn't be long before they decided to examine their cargo with a closer eye.

She had company, at least. About five days into the voyage, she noticed a pod of orca whales swimming alongside the ship—seemingly following the vessel across the entire length of the Crystal Sea. She spent hours watching them battle the current in flashes of ebony and ivory, cut through the waves as they crested atop one another, and disappear into the depths of the azure water only to reappear moments later. She imagined they were there for her, having sensed her loneliness, but she wasn't delusional enough to believe it.

When the whales disappeared from view, she turned her gaze away from the porthole and to her knapsack. Her parents' letter was buried somewhere deep within the canvas bag as it awaited her eyes. The moment she thought of it, the beating of her heart grew restless and unsteady, and her stomach churned like she'd swallowed a jug of sour milk. The pain behind her eyes became something fiercer and sharper, as if someone had stuck a white-hot branding iron through her eyeballs and into her skull. Normally the pain went away with a decent distraction, but she couldn't continue to avoid it. She needed whatever information the letter contained, even if it physically pained her to open it.

Her parents' instructions for times of peril began with the palace tunnels and ended with the little cottage in Seaport. She understood why they hadn't disclosed any further details when they first told her about the plan: they knew exactly what she'd say if she knew where they were sending her, and it wouldn't have been anything particularly proper for the future queen to utter aloud.

Carthe. The idea was baffling, as the continent across the sea was irrefutably forbidden to her. Her parents would visit often for trading purposes, but she was never allowed to accompany them. *Carthe is a dangerous and lawless place, my love,* her mother would say. *It matters not who you are, so long as you have silver in your pocket.*

Every Akkinorian knew the nature of Carthe. Of the seven territories, every last one of them had tales of horror and indecency tied to their names. Some were better than the others, of course, but that did little to convince Akkinorians that the continent was anything more than a melting pot of barbarians and heathens.

In the kingdom of Kanibar, the monarchy used branding irons to identify certain types of people. Thieves and rapists strolled the streets with a *T* or an *R*, respectively, burned into the flesh of their wrists. Traitors, on the other hand, were marked with an *X*. Even orphaned children, the poor things, were branded with an *O*. And in every Carthinian kingdom excluding Krotis, a popular punishment for criminals was the removal of one's tongue. Even a starving child convicted of stealing a loaf of bread was forced to spend the rest of their life as a mute. Another popular punishment in Carthe was crucifixion: while most perished after being staked to cross-shaped planks of wood, some survived and lived for years without full or proper use of their hands and feet.

Such horrid punishments and traditions didn't exist in Akkinor. Criminals were often flogged for severe crimes, but more commonly, they were merely arrested or executed. Akkinorian culture didn't believe in torture or lifelong physical punishments.

Carthe was more than its seven kingdoms, too. Each kingdom was relatively small, particularly when compared to Akkinorian territories, and a substantial portion of the continent consisted of unoccupied terrains where anyone (or anything) could do as they pleased without repercussions. There were no laws in those parts of Carthe, no governments to keep the people in check, and nobody in the kingdoms who cared enough to do something about the horrors that occurred there.

Aurelia flinched when she heard footsteps above her head. She didn't move a muscle until a familiar face appeared on the other side of the barrels.

"Good afternoon, my queen." The old man bowed. "We're arriving in Carthe. My crew is staying the night at an inn and setting sail for Akkinor tomorrow evening. I'll come back for you tonight when they've left."

She frowned. "Will they think it suspicious for you to be going all the way back to the ship once they've gone?"

"That's one of the great things about Caedia. The water is deep enough for the ship at the docks. There's no need for me to take a dinghy out to fetch you. It'll be a quick trip, and most of them will be too drunk to notice I've left the tavern." He bowed again while she chuckled at his lighthearted quip. "I'll be back for you soon. I'd suggest reading that letter before your feet touch land. I'll melt the wax in the fireplace tonight. We don't need anybody finding the seal of Akkinor on you."

"That's a fair point. Thank you."

When he left, she knew she was running out of time to read the letter before she stepped foot on foreign soil. She'd have to be careful now, as Carthinians weren't known for their love of Akkinor. Shielding her identity as queen was one thing, but shielding her identity as an Akkinorian was even more imperative if she wanted to survive.

She sucked in a long, deep breath before rummaging through her pack for the letter. It stung her to break the seal, knowing that the last person to touch the letter was long dead. She could see herself as a young girl, browsing through her father's study as he sealed an envelope. She'd watch his long, slender fingers pour the hot red wax over the envelope and stamp it with her family's sigil: a falcon with a scythe in either talon.

"Why a falcon, Father?" she'd asked him. "Why scythes?"

"Oleander the Great used a scythe when he overthrew Queen Alora," he'd replied. "In those days, the Brentwood family raised falcons like soldiers. They were our second-in-command. Our spies, our messengers, our eyes above."

"Why do we no longer train falcons?"

"Falcons are small, sweetness, and we are not small people."

She hadn't understood what he meant, not then, but she knew it was just a matter of time before her family's secrets became her own. Now, so many years later, she wished her parents had shared their secrets before they were taken away so suddenly. If not, her heart wouldn't be pounding as much as it was, and her hands wouldn't be shaking uncontrollably at the sight of a mere letter.

With a heavy heart, she opened the envelope and removed the letter. Her eyes burned when she set her gaze on her father's handwriting. She could practically see him before her, eyes furrowed in concentration, as he focused on every curve, every line, every space. She used to tease him for paying so much attention to his handwriting. *A king shouldn't have to worry about what people think of his hand*, she'd proclaimed. He'd merely chuckled at her and replied, *A king must write as mindfully as he swings his sword. So must a queen. Soldiers won't follow a commander whose hands tremble when she writes, for they shall also tremble when she is facing the enemy.*

She'd soaked in every word of it. She wanted to be brave and strong, a true leader like her father, but now, she didn't feel very brave. Her father's handwriting was enough to make tears spill from her eyes and smudge the decade-old ink. She brushed her tears away and took a deep breath before focusing her eyes on the letter.

My dearest Aurelia,

If you're reading this, I am long gone, and something terrible has happened to threaten your reign. The safe house will protect you only for a short while; with that, it's in your best interest to find safe passage to Carthe. These foreign lands aren't like ours, and you'll find that your name and title mean nothing to them. Many diverse souls live on the continent: people who will try to kill you, people who will take you for ransom, people who will protect you, and people who will want to follow you. The name you must remember on your quest is Arian Cristos. Find him, and he will guide you home again.

I wish I could tell you this in person, and I pray your mother still lives so you may hear it from her lips: Aurelia, my sweet child, your mother and I have lied to you from the moment we first held you in our arms. For many years, we struggled for a child. When we were certain the world was pitted against us, we visited an old friend in Carthe, where we met a beautiful newborn baby girl. We took you home with us and claimed you as our own. When your mother held you in her arms, you became Princess Aurelia Emmeline Brentwood, First of Her Name, rightful heir to the Akkinorian throne. Despite your blood, you're no less our child than Archie. You will be the most wonderful queen, and we've never doubted that you will continue to make us proud regardless of what obstacles you face.

You may have been raised in Akkinor, but you have Carthe in your veins. You know what that means. On this journey, don't forget that you are a Brentwood, but don't forget where you come from, either.

With love from a thousand lifetimes,
Father.

***

Aurelia didn't know how long she spent rubbing her own saliva onto her hands, desperately attempting to clean her skin of the ink stains that'd melted into her fingertips after her tears turned her father's letter into dribbling black smears. She rubbed until her skin was red and raw, until every last speck of black ink disappeared.

She knew she had a vivid imagination, but never before had she maintained the capacity to envision her new reality. She never had to imagine herself as queen; after all, she'd been raised to inherit the throne if nothing else. She may not have inherited the title until her father died, but a part of her had always been queen. It was her birthright, her destiny—or so she thought.

She remembered being a young girl, not yet a woman, having overheard the palace guards snickering at Edmund's decision to name Aurelia as his heir. She'd sobbed in her father's arms after hearing the soldiers' desire to see her then-eight-year-old brother on the throne rather than herself.

Edmund had tried his utmost to console her. "You mustn't pay them any heed. In due time, you'll come to understand that their apprehensions are just that—apprehensions. They won't know what you're capable of until your time comes. That doesn't mean you're any less suited for the throne than your brother. You, Aurelia Brentwood, are the firstborn child of the king. There's nothing anyone can say that will change what your blood demands."

The eleven-year-old princess hadn't been convinced. "But I'm a *girl!* They will never like me so long as I'm a girl."

"Hmph! They'll learn to love you for who you are. It matters not the sex of the monarch, Aurelia. What matters is a monarch's spirit, their heart, their blood—and you, my darling girl, have excelled in all three. You have the spirit of a true leader, the heart of a hero, and the blood of the greatest kings and queens of the realm. You are a piece of my heart, my soul, my flesh; that much will never change."

She'd believed every word. She believed everything her father had told her. He was the most honorable person she'd ever known, and a man like Edmund Brentwood didn't lie to those he loved. If he believed that she was as worthy of ruling as her brother, then she had to believe it, too.

Now she wasn't so sure. Now she found herself questioning everything she thought she knew about her life, her legacy, her reign. She wasn't

Edmund Brentwood's flesh and blood. She wasn't the firstborn child of the king. She didn't have the blood of Akkinor's greatest rulers running through her veins. Her blood was a mystery, and so was she.

The throne wasn't hers by birthright. It was hers because Edmund had deemed it so—not because she had any real claim to it whatsoever. She was a queen, an orphan, a deserter, an imposter. Now that she knew the truth, she couldn't help but wonder if the loss of her crown had been fated.

Perhaps the Brentwood line *would* end with her, just as the Cherrane line had ended with a queen—but could the dynasty end with an individual who wasn't a trueborn Brentwood?

No, she thought. The Brentwood line wouldn't end with Aurelia, First of Her Name, adopted daughter of Edmund II. It *couldn't* end with her. The blood running through her veins may not have been the blood of Oleander the Great, but the heart in her chest beat to the same rhythm as every Brentwood who'd come before her, and so long as that remained true, Akkinor belonged to her.

That was, of course, if she could silence her inner demons long enough to fight for what had been gifted to her by her parents—by her parents, by the gods, and by the country that burned like an eternal flame in her heart.

VII

I couldn't possibly—"

"I insist," the old man interrupted. Aurelia bit the insides of her cheeks as she curled her fingers around his leather coin pouch. "You'll need it on your expedition. It's been an honor to serve you, my queen. I wish you the best of luck."

She smiled. "Thank you. I hope to see you again, sir. Preferably on the other side of the world."

"As do I, Your Grace."

He tipped his head to her and slipped into the tavern before he could be missed by his fellow sailors. She exhaled and tucked the pouch into her bag for safe keeping.

Her ally was true to his word when they docked on the northern coast of Carthe at a port province called Caedia. He'd successfully smuggled her out of the ship and onto dry land where a horse, Scotch, was waiting for her. He gave her directions, the coin in his pocket, and a loaf of bread to start her on her quest. The only thing he couldn't give her, though, was the answer to her most pressing question: *Where do I go from here?*

The only thing she knew was that she had to find a man named Arian Cristos, wherever and whoever he was, on the massive continent. She understood why her father hadn't disclosed Arian's precise location: if the letter happened to fall into the wrong hands, her enemies would know exactly where she was going. It was a risk they couldn't take—even if it meant creating yet another burden for her to bear.

"Come, Scotch," she murmured, taking hold of the horse's reins. "Shall we look for a place to spend the night?"

He only stared straight ahead as they wandered. She sighed. It'd be an awfully long journey with nobody to talk to, but that was the only way she could ensure her survival. If anyone knew who she was, she'd be in grave danger. If people from Akkinor decided to search for her in Carthe...not only would *her* life be in danger, but she'd be putting any potential allies in the line of fire, too.

After walking the dirt path for a bit, she came across an adobe building that looked promising. Tavern by day, inn by night, according to the sign posted by the door. She knew it'd be wise to leave Caedia as soon as possible, but she was desperate for a hot meal, a cozy bed, and a bath. She removed her belongings from Scotch's saddle and tied him up in the stables with the other horses. She entered the tavern, immediately wrinkled her nose at the smell of stale mead and body odor, and approached the counter. The innkeeper—a somewhat emaciated middle-aged woman whose gray hair grew in tufts on her bald head—was counting coins.

"Lookin' for room or drink, girl?" Like most northern Carthinians, the innkeeper spoke the common tongue, which was also the native language of Akkinor. In other places, though, Aurelia was prepared to find people who spoke the native tongues of Carthe—languages in which Aurelia wasn't fluent, but that she could decipher in bits and pieces.

She swallowed. "Both, if you'd be so kind. Possibly a meal, too, if that isn't too much to ask."

The woman snorted. "You Akkinorians and your damn words." Aurelia's eyes widened. Had she already given herself away? She kept mum as the woman set a pint of ale and a key on the counter. "Here. Somebody will be out with a bit of scran in a minute or so."

"Thank you."

She wrinkled her nose. "You look and smell like you ain't seen daylight in weeks. I'll donate some soap. Everythin' else is ten silver."

Donate. What a thing, Aurelia thought, to be a queen one day and a beggar the next.

She fished around in her bag before setting the coin on the counter. The innkeeper snatched it, then exchanged the coin for a bar of soap. Aurelia felt her cheeks darken when she slipped the soap into her bag. She'd gotten so used to her own scent that she hadn't realized how pungent it was.

She scanned the tavern for a place to sit. Sailors, travelers, and merchants sat at the long wooden tables, roaring with laughter, drinking, and talking so loudly that she could hear every conversation taking place. Barmaids walked around carrying trays of food and ale, though the men appeared more interested in the women themselves than the refreshments. None of them seemed to care much about Aurelia when she took a seat by the fireplace in the back. Perhaps, she thought, it was more common for a woman to travel alone in Carthe than it was in Akkinor.

A barmaid arrived with a tray of hot food. Aurelia's mouth watered as she thanked the woman for the meal. She was eternally grateful for the old man's hospitality while aboard the ship, but surviving on scraps of sailor's meals had been close to misery. She was ecstatic to see a bowl of stew, two generous slices of bread, and a bowl of candied nuts—a Carthinian token of gratitude for her business.

Aurelia couldn't help but wince when she sipped the ale. She'd expected better, seeing as though Caedia was home to Carthe's primary trading port. Merchants from around the world sold and traded goods there. She shouldn't have been surprised to taste something so foul, though. After all, the taverns weren't concerned with returning customers. They only existed for travelers who needed a hot meal and a warm bed before returning to the road or the sea.

"The days were old, the nights were cold!" She glanced up as a group of warbling men stood from their tables with their cups raised in the air. "The fires burned bright like the sun, and soon the war was done! The bells rang through the night..."

She closed her eyes and listened. These were Akkinorian men likely preparing to sail home. The song dated back to the old days: a bard had written it about the end of the war when Oleander the Great seized Akkinor. It was a celebration, an omen of good fortune, and a few simple chords that reminded the people of their history.

While the singing drowned out her thoughts, she quickly finished her meal and found her way to the bathhouse. It was empty, so she scurried into the lady's section and undressed before somebody could join her. She'd never taken a bath in a public place before—even her own lady's maids had left her to bathe on her own, which was uncommon for a highborn. She slipped into the lukewarm water, clutching the bar of soap to her chest, and wrinkled her nose as soon as her legs disappeared below the surface. There was no way for her to know how clean the bathwater was, but after over a week hidden away on a ship, she was willing to sacrifice the idea of sterility for a decent washing.

She lifted a lock of her wet, stringy hair. It was a warm-toned blonde, almost like honey, with coppery undertones that made it appear goldish or bronze, depending on the lighting. People used to say that her hair was a perfect mix of her parents: her mother's hair was auburn while her father's was blonde. She couldn't help but wonder where the color of her hair really came from—where *everything* about her really came from.

As she thought about it, though, she realized it didn't matter who her birth parents were. Edmund and Cressida Brentwood had raised her, loved her, protected her. Nothing would change the relationship between them, even if they weren't connected by blood. Her parents were gone now, though, and she was more alone than she'd ever been. If her birth parents were still out there, maybe their blood bond would be enough for them to love and protect her as the Brentwoods had. Maybe *that* was why Edmund and Cressida sent her to Carthe: to find her family.

Arian Cristos. As she climbed out of the bath and dressed herself in clean clothing, she eyed the letter in her pack. Her parents left her with no destination other than the name of one man. She'd never heard of him, but her parents wouldn't have told her to find him if they doubted his ability to assist her. Maybe *he* was the family she was searching for. As hard as it would be, she was going to find him. She just needed a place to start.

When she left the bathhouse, she returned to the tavern before looking for her room. The innkeeper was still counting coins at the counter when she approached. The woman only raised a bushy gray eyebrow rather than speaking.

Aurelia cleared her throat. "I'm looking for someone. I was hoping you may be able to give me directions."

The innkeeper sighed. "Got a name?"

"Cristos."

"Don't know. Surnames endin' wit *tos* are common on the other side of the valley. Lots of 'em in Taundosa. Maybe you'll have luck there."

She furrowed her eyebrows. "The valley?"

"So clearly a stranger," the innkeeper drawled, chuckling. Aurelia's face burned. "The Ngora Valley is the desert dividing Carthe in two. In the north, you have Caedia, Dofell, Kanibar, and the Violet Forest. In the south, you have Taundosa, Bozar, Krotis, and Khaba."

Taundosa, commonly referred to as *the City of Gold* (which Aurelia thought was strange, as it was a kingdom, not a city), was the wealthiest civilization in Carthe. Queen Reyna of Taundosa was even younger than Aurelia when she took the throne. Aurelia hadn't heard much about her, but she knew Taundosa was a force to be reckoned with. In Carthe, they had the largest army, the vastest territory, and the most prominent influence. The only country in the world with more supremacy was Akkinor. The two civilizations kept their distance from one another to avoid conflict, but it was said to be the most glorious kingdom in the realm, and the only one made almost entirely out of gold.

"What's the best way to reach the other side of the Ngora Valley?" Aurelia asked. When the innkeeper scoffed and rolled her beady hazel eyes, Aurelia frowned. "Madam?"

"You travelin' alone, girl?"

She shifted her weight. "Yes."

"That won't help you." The woman locked the coin in a safe behind the counter and scratched at her balding head. "Maybe you can get through the forest. Cuttin' through Dofell is your only way to the desert—ain't no access from Kanibar. Won't be easy, though. They ain't fond of you Akkinorians." Aurelia gulped. "You get invited in, great. If not, you best travel with a group. They let groups pass through. But the valley is what you should worry about. Near impossible to get through it by yourself."

"How far is Taundosa from the Ngora Valley?"

"Right on the other side. The district of Agotia is closest to the border of the valley. The capital's a stone's throw from Agotia. They will let you pass, but gettin' to the other side of the palace is difficult without reason. Lookin' for one man ain't reason enough."

She wasn't worried about that. When she was close, she knew what had to be done to receive an audience with Arian Cristos. For now, it was just a matter of finding him.

"Thank you, madam," Aurelia murmured. "I sincerely appreciate your help and your hospitality today. You've been so kind."

"Sure. Good luck."

She felt the innkeeper eyeing her as she took the narrow, spiral staircase to the second floor of the tavern. She matched the room to the number on her key and unlocked it with caution. After glancing around to ensure her privacy, she locked the door and collapsed on the squeaky bed.

The room was nothing like her suite in the Folly. It was austere and plain with nothing but a bed, a table and two chairs, a chamber pot, a fireplace, and a drying rack for clothing. She'd rinsed her dirty clothes in the bathhouse, so she was now able to leave them out to dry. After doing so, she tied her wet locks in a braid and sprawled out on the bed to rest her aching feet.

She could still hear the sailors laughing and singing in the tavern. Outside, animals howled, and travelers spoke more languages than she could keep track of. If the innkeeper was right, Aurelia would have no choice but to make friends with the travelers. She'd never make it to Arian Cristos on her own. Everyone had warned her to keep a safe distance from the people of Carthe, so either way, she was risking death. If she continued on her own, she'd never survive to see Akkinor again. If she trusted the wrong people, she'd only see her homeland again from the heavens.

Sighing, Aurelia swung her legs out of bed and fumbled through her pack for the letter from her parents. The sight of her father's handwriting made her stomach churn with anguish. The old man from Seaport had taken the seal and burned it aboard the ship, knowing that even a glimpse of Akkinor's seal could reveal her identity to passersby, but the letter itself would reveal nothing unless it fell into the wrong hands. That's what convinced her to bring the letter to the fireplace and toss it into the flames without a second thought. She remembered everything her father had written, so there was no point in possessing such a liability.

While she watched the parchment shrivel and burn, her fingers instinctively curled around her locket. She hadn't opened it in ten years, but she didn't need to open it to appreciate it. The necklace had a way of making her feel safe in the world. Even here, across the sea in foreign lands, a wave of comfort washed over her as soon as her skin touched the gold.

She'd given the locket to Linden when they parted ways on the day of the attack for a reason, and it hadn't been for good luck on his mission. The man he'd gone to visit in the dungeons—a sorcerer, a type of mage who utilized only dark magic—was the only person they knew who could remove the protection spell on the necklace, thus giving Aurelia the opportunity to open it if the situation called for it.

Only a mage could remove the spell, and the prisoner was the only known mage in the Folly. Akkinor, like Quapebet, Glacier Bay, and even Espos, hadn't welcomed mages since before the magical persecution in the old days. Only Carthe still crawled with mages and magical creatures. Aurelia often wondered why her parents had gifted her with something that could only be unlocked by magic—magic that didn't exist on their side of the world.

Her parents claimed the locket had been hers since birth. When she was young, it was kept in the palace vault for increased security. When she was old enough to value the locket, not a day passed when it wasn't hanging from her neck. It was the one thing she'd possessed since the day she was born. A powerful heirloom, meant only for her, that she cherished more than her own existence. She couldn't help but wonder if her parents were telling the truth when they said the locket had been hers since birth. If that was true, the locket didn't come from Akkinor or from the Brentwood family. It came from Carthe.

Her head was spinning with everything that'd happened since the uprising. Not only was she concerned with finding a way home, but she also had questions that needed answering. She wanted to know who she was and where she came from. Above all, she wanted to know how to reclaim her throne from the people who'd wreaked havoc upon her home.

One way or another, the Queen of Akkinor was going home. The throne may not have been hers by blood, but it was hers by birthright. She was the firstborn child of a king. She'd brought prosperity to Akkinor in her few years as queen, and her people had loved her for it. She knew they were waiting for her return, but a few loyal families wouldn't be enough to stop the people who'd forced her from her home. She needed allies in Carthe. If she could bring them home with her, the usurpers wouldn't stand a chance.

Aurelia moved away from the fireplace and approached the dirty mirror hanging on the wall. She saw no difference between the Queen of Akkinor and the woman staring back at her, but starting then, they were no longer the same person. They couldn't be.

***

As water seeped into his nostrils and clogged his airway, Linden Elliot was reminded of a harrowing yet welcomed childhood memory. For a moment, he was a twelve-year-old boy diving for lost treasures in the River Gilsad, unaware of the limitations to breathing underwater. He'd been moments away from losing consciousness when his dearest friend pulled him to shore—battling against the fierce current and her own lack of physical strength—and calmly urged him to cough the remaining water from his lungs. It was his gods-given duty to protect her from the moment she was born, but that day, the seven-year-old Crown Princess of Akkinor had saved *him*.

Upon wheezing for air, reality returned to him. He wasn't a young boy who could be rescued by his best friend, but the Lord Hand of a usurped queen with a jug of filthy sewage water being poured over his face and a cloth pressed to his mouth and nose.

His throat gasped instinctively, but he managed to control his other bodily responses. He wouldn't thrash or kick or beg for mercy from his torturers—that's exactly what they wanted. They were wearing him down not because they wanted his knowledge (even lackies like these were smart enough to recognize his undying loyalty to his queen), but because they sought to punish him simply because they could.

When the cloth was torn from his face, Linden felt a sharp boot slam into his sternum. The force was enough to catapult him (and the chair he was tied to) backwards onto the stone floor. His restraints came loose upon impact, allowing him to roll from the chair and onto the floor. Two laughing voices—one breathy and one guttural—mocked him as he felt around in the darkness for something to use as leverage for standing. He imagined his cell in the palace dungeons was illuminated by torches, but he couldn't be certain. His eyes were still swollen shut from being beaten within an inch of his life when the usurpers apprehended him following

Aurelia's escape. He hadn't been able to see more than a sliver of his surroundings for days.

His tormentors muttered something, but Linden couldn't distinguish their words over the roaring of blood pounding like drums in his ears. One of the men dragged him—naked except for a scrap of cloth to conceal his manhood—back to the chair, retied his restraints, and brandished a set of gleaming bronze knuckles.

"Let's try another question, eh?" the man quipped. "Where did she go?" Linden only bowed his head, silent. An *oomph* sound escaped him as the man struck him in the mouth. "Try again."

Linden spit a mouthful of blood—and a tooth—onto the floor. "I don't know."

"*Lies!*"

A blow to the cheek angered a preexisting cut. His head turned with the force of the strike, but he didn't so much as grunt or grimace in response. He wouldn't give them the satisfaction of knowing they'd hurt him, even if he'd felt his cheekbone fracture when the bronze knuckles connected with his face.

Having exceeded their patience with him, the two men left him—but only after clobbering him with wooden paddles so fiercely that he lost feeling in his legs. They loosened his restraints enough to taunt him with the prospect of freedom, but not enough for him to escape.

As he sat shivering and alone in a damp, rat-infested cell, he listened to the men's voices grow distant as they left the dungeon. He didn't recognize their voices, but their dry, emotionless drawls were unmistakably Laynoan. It wasn't much of a surprise that whoever usurped his friend had enlisted the help of Laynoan torturers—they were, without a doubt, the most notorious interrogators in Akkinor. Their brutish ways were no secret to the masses.

He peeled his eyes open as much as he could and turned to the small, narrow window to his left. An iridescent white shimmer dominated his vision: moonlight. He wondered what the stars looked like that night, and he wondered if Aurelia—wherever she was—could see the same ones.

VIII

Aurelia pulled Scotch forwards until they were safely beneath the leaking roof of the stables, then tied his reins to a post as he shook rainwater from his mane. Her cloak hadn't done much to protect her from the heavy rainfall—she was soaked through and through, freezing, and numb to her bones. The innkeeper had warned her of the weather when she left that morning, but she wasn't afraid of a bit of water. She hadn't realized why there were so few people on the roads until the rain came down in buckets. Apparently, the weather in Carthe was much more violent and unpredictable than it was in Akkinor.

She'd been spitting out mouthfuls of rainwater for hours before her fingers turned blue. Luckily, she spotted a tavern on the edge of Caedia where she could wait out the storm. She hoped to cross the border from Caedia to the Violet Forest that day, but now her travels were delayed. She had no choice but to wait for the rain to stop if she wanted to avoid sickness.

After taking a seat inside the tavern, a barmaid offered her a bowl of ale, soup and bread. She wrinkled her nose immediately once the steaming bowl of soup was set before her. It was mostly broth and potatoes with a few pieces of an unidentified meat floating on the surface.

"It's hum," a voice said. Aurelia glanced up at the young woman sitting at the other end of the table. It took her a moment to understand the stranger's accent, but when she did, she realized the woman had said *ham*. As she nodded in understanding, the stranger took her belongings and moved to sit across from Aurelia. "Kaia Bolas. I stay here every now and then. Haven't seen you before. What brings you here?"

"I'm just avoiding the storm."

"You should hang your cloak by the fire to dry."

Aurelia blinked at her. "I hadn't thought of that. Thank you."

"Sure. What's your name?"

"Lily. Lily, erm, Linden."

She surprised herself with her answer. She hadn't thought of an alias until then. *Lily* was her childhood nickname, and she hadn't heard it since she was a young girl. Even more surprising was where the nickname had come from: Linden's father, Robert. The former Hand of the King once proclaimed that Aurelia needed a truncated name (after all, her father was tenderly known as Ed, her mother as Cressy, and her brother as Archie) but he didn't like *Ellie* or *Ella* as suggested by Linden. He decided to call her *Lily* instead, though the nickname was short-lived.

For a fraction of a second, Aurelia thought about her brother. The only true nickname she'd ever had in her life was coined by him. Archie couldn't pronounce her name as a young boy, so for the first six years of his life, he referred to her as *Li*. The affectionate moniker was used less and less as they grew older, but every now and then, Archie surprised her with it. It was the last shred of evidence proving that, once upon a time, Archie had adored his sister as much as she adored him.

Kaia laughed at her. "I'm sure it is." Aurelia kept quiet as she hung her cloak and returned to her seat. "I'm not going to ask why you're lying about who you are. That's your business. I know an Akkinorian when I see one, though. You must be running from something—or someone. If not, you wouldn't be here."

Aurelia's eyes stung as they enlarged. "How did you—?"

"It's fairly obvious. You have that look in your eyes. Like a lost animal. Akkinorians are more poised than the rest of us, too. Your people hold yourselves very highly, as if everyone else in the world is beneath you."

She scowled. "That's awfully presumptuous."

"Like I said, I know an Akkinorian when I see one. Especially a noble."

"I'm not—"

"I don't care who you are. Or who you *were*," Kaia clarified. Aurelia's heart was pounding, but something in the stranger's inviting eyes felt reassuring. Kaia didn't seem like a threat—not yet. "None of my business. I just wanted to know if I was right about you. What brings you to Carthe, Lily of Akkinor?"

"I don't think it wise for me to share that information."

"I won't tell. I don't know anyone from Akkinor."

"People are searching for me. I'm doing you a favor by withholding my story from you." She hesitated as she remembered what the innkeeper said about traveling to Taundosa. "I have to cross the Ngora Valley. I'm going south."

"Good luck," Kaia quipped. Aurelia frowned at the sudden lack of sincerity in Kaia's tone. "Some advice? Try to relax. You look far too anxious and out of place. Maybe change your clothing, too. You dress like an Akkinorian."

Aurelia laughed breezily. "Thank you for the suggestions."

"My pleasure."

Kaia Bolas would've stuck out like a sore thumb in Akkinor. Her pale brown skin differed greatly from Akkinorians of mixed backgrounds, as it was cool toned, fawny, and peppered with moles and freckles. She was taller than Aurelia by several inches and noticeably slim compared to the queen, who had slender limbs, wide hips, and relatively broad shoulders. Kaia's long hickory locks, pulled back in a ponytail, were pin-straight with creases from where she'd previously tied it. Her face was slim like her body—almost gaunt—with a broad nose, full rosy lips, and pale green eyes like a cat's. Patches of thread in assorted colors along her brown trousers suggested they'd been repaired more than once. She wore muddy shoes that might've been white when purchased, and a bland ivory shirt with loose sleeves and a low neckline. Everything she wore was too big for her, like it'd been stolen from somebody taller and heavier. There was some sort of a mark peeking out from beneath her shirt—a scar on her wrist— but it was hard for Aurelia to see in the dim lighting.

"I'm on my way home to Kanibar," Kaia continued. "Where are you going? You must have a specific destination in mind." When Aurelia didn't reply, Kaia's eyes found her locket. "You're going to Taundosa."

Aurelia shifted uncomfortably. "How could you possibly know that?"

"Lucky guess. Taundosa is a marvelous kingdom. I've yet to visit myself, but everyone hears the stories. It's a place of tremendous wealth. I should hope that you know someone who lives there. If not, you can expect a bit of resistance. People don't simply pass through Taundosa. If you enter the kingdom, you must have a reason."

"I do." She stirred her spoon through the now-cold soup. "I'm looking for someone. I don't anticipate much of a struggle, but it'd certainly help if he knew to expect me."

"It would." Kaia finished her ale and stood from the table, then peered to her left at the window. The shutters were cracked open for a bit of fresh air, so they could see that the rain had lightened to a drizzle. "It looks like the rain has calmed down. I'd better get going. If you'd like, I can take you as far as the Ngora Valley. No offense, but you look like you could use all the help you can get. I don't mind acting as your travel guide for the next few weeks."

Aurelia's eyes widened with astonishment. "The next few *weeks?* How long does it take to cross the Violet Forest?"

"That depends entirely on luck." Kaia threw her pack over her shoulder and shrugged. "I've crossed in nine days. I've also crossed in four weeks. Sometimes the journey is simple, and sometimes it's dangerous. We simply can't know what to expect." She raised her eyebrows. "Are you coming or not?"

"I appreciate the offer, but it's far too dangerous. I can't put your life at risk."

Kaia snorted. "You gave me a false name, and you won't tell me why you're here. If somebody comes looking for you, I technically don't know who you are. I couldn't betray you if I wanted to—and I wouldn't, by the way. I like you, Lily of Akkinor. You can trust me."

Aurelia looked into Kaia's jade eyes, contemplating. Everyone had told her to be mindful of who she trusted on this journey. Even her parents had warned her about trusting strangers in Carthe, but they'd also told her that along with the people who would betray her, there would be people who might help her. She'd have to take a chance on someone eventually.

"You're putting yourself in danger by offering to help me," Aurelia disclosed. "I need you to understand that."

Kaia shrugged as a defiant smile formed on her lips. "I can hold my own. I've always been drawn to a bit of danger, anyway."

Aurelia stared at her. "Are you certain?"

"Quite." Kaia smiled and nodded her head towards the window. "Come. We should get moving before we're no longer the only people on the road. You don't seem keen on finishing that soup, anyway."

"No." Aurelia wrinkled her nose as she stood from the table and gathered her belongings. "Thank you, Kaia."

Her new ally beamed. "My pleasure. If I were a stranger in *your* country, I'd hope that someone would show me the same kindness." The pair left the tavern together and approached the stables to untie their horses. "How long have you been here?"

"One night."

"You have so much to learn," Kaia said with a chuckle. Aurelia ignored the burning embarrassment bubbling up in her chest. While she tied her pack to Scotch's saddle, Kaia approached another horse and guffawed. "Men. Such imbeciles. What kind of fool leaves their weapon in the stables?"

"What?" Aurelia observed, mouth agape, as Kaia removed a sword and its sheath from a horse's saddle. "What are you doing? Stealing another traveler's property?"

"For you," Kaia mused. Aurelia's eyes enlarged when the sheath was set in her hands. "You need some sort of weapon to protect yourself. This man shouldn't have been so careless with his belongings. Just take it."

Aurelia didn't approve of stealing. She was raised on high standards of honor, and theft was considered to be one of the worst dishonors one could commit. Though she knew she had no choice but to accept the weapon, Kaia's actions confirmed Aurelia's opinions of Carthinians: they were as lawless and immoral as the stories claimed. When Aurelia caught sight of the bow and sheath strapped to Kaia's back, she couldn't help but wonder which poor soul the Kanish girl had stolen them from.

The pair led their horses from the stables and climbed on their backs. Straight ahead, Aurelia spotted signs offering directions. They were approaching the edge of Caedia, so it'd only be a mile or so before they reached the Violet Forest. The directions told her that the major kingdoms, as well as the Ngora Valley, were south of their location. While Aurelia was studying the directions, Kaia was leading her horse to the left. She seemingly had no intention of following the road.

"Why are you taking to the woods?" Aurelia asked, following. "Is it not in our best interest to follow the path?"

"No. People like you who have no idea what you're doing or where you're going tend to follow the roads. Enemies will be looking for new and oblivious travelers. If we stay hidden, we're safer from the people of the forest."

Aurelia gulped. "People of the forest?"

Kaia's eyes twinkled with amusement. "You don't know much about Carthe, do you?" The monarch didn't answer. "I'm sure it's not much different from Akkinor. There will always be cruel people who prey on easy targets. Thieves, rapists, kidnappers, murderers. The tribes are what you really have to worry about, though."

"The tribes?"

"The Violet Forest and the Ngora Valley are like the provinces. Ungoverned. No monarchs, no nobles, no soldiers. Anyone can do as we please. The nomadic tribes of Carthe live in the forest because their way of life isn't tolerated elsewhere. Some want peace with the continent, but others are barbarians. They follow their own rules."

"What are they like?"

"You'll know when you see them. Their weapons are poorly made or stolen. They never wear armor. Too sure of themselves and too willing to accept death rather than defeat."

"I'm assuming they aren't fond of negotiation."

Kaia winced. "I've never known someone to survive an interaction with tribesmen. Some may ignore us if they see us. Others...I suppose it depends on the tribe. They may want to take us as slaves. They may rob us, rape us, and leave us to die. Or..."

She didn't need to finish. Aurelia could fill in the blanks for herself: *Or they'll rob us, rape us, and cook our flesh on spits like pigs.* The thought made her shudder.

As promised, Kaia took on the role of traveling guide as they rode through the forest. While Aurelia didn't think much about the things they saw, Kaia treated every overturned stone and every bird in the sky like the most valuable thing in the world. She identified animal tracks, which berries and plants were safe for consumption, and which were poisonous. She'd even stopped them by a small crevice at the bottom of a hill that'd collected fresh rainwater during the storm. They refilled their canteens, plucked berries from the bushes, and caught a fish in a nearby stream to eat for dinner.

Even with its many dangers, Aurelia couldn't deny that the forest was beautiful. It seemed to carry on forever in every direction. Most of the trees were extremely tall, blooming with bright green leaves just sparse enough for the sky to be visible beyond the canopy. Their path was accompanied by thick bushes, hills, valleys, streams, woodland creatures, and vibrant flowers that seemed to sing with the wind. Everything was wet from the rain, but the water droplets only emphasized the luminous colors.

It felt too serene to be home to Carthe's most dangerous people, but as Aurelia had come to understand in her five-and-twenty years, looks were as deceiving as words.

When the sky darkened, Kaia found the perfect place to camp for the night: a narrow spot between a handful of enormous trees where they'd be concealed from all sides. Aurelia wasn't particularly eager to sleep in the middle of a forest, but it was the only option they had.

Aurelia took it upon herself to build a fire with twigs and leaves, though she wasn't making excellent progress. While Kaia crafted a spit, Aurelia sparked a conversation by asking about how Kaia had become so proficient at surviving in the wilderness.

"My parents died when I was thirteen. My older brother used to be a soldier, but he retired to raise us and work closer to home. He sells goods in Kanibar with a friend of his. Our younger siblings make jewelry and such. We weren't making as much as we needed in Kanibar, so I started selling the jewelry in Caedia. Sailors are always hunting for things to take home for their ladies. My brother has to stay home in Kanibar with the children, so I have no choice but to do this alone."

"That's awfully noble of you."

"Necessary, not noble, but I appreciate your kindness." Kaia finished working on the spit and admired the fire. "Look at that! You've made your first fire."

Aurelia grinned. "How do you know this is my first?"

"Noble ladies in Akkinor don't tend to their own fires," she commented, stifling a laugh. She softened a bit when Aurelia flinched. "I meant what I said. I don't care about who you are or why you're hiding. Your reasons are your own, though I can't imagine what would make you so nervous."

"I think it's better if I keep that to myself."

"Isn't it awfully lonely?"

"Isn't *what* lonely?"

Kaia's eyes reflected the sorrow in Aurelia's heart. "You're alone on another continent. You're the only person who knows who you are. You can't trust anybody. You can't tell anyone what you're running from or how to help you. You haven't told me anything about your life, but you already know so much about mine. Isn't it lonely, having nobody to confide in?"

Aurelia looked up at the trees. Dusk was settling in, so the stars were barely twinkling through the thick foliage above them. She wondered if they were the same stars she'd see in Akkinor, late at night when the entirety of the Folly was asleep, when she and Linden would sneak out to the observatory to admire the midnight sky. Certainly not, she decided. The stars seemed to talk to her in Akkinor. The stars in Carthe were silent.

"*Lonely* isn't the word I'd use," Aurelia drawled. "Frustrating, yes. I'd love to confide in someone, but other things are more important than talking. I can't put my entire purpose on this continent at risk because of loneliness or frustration."

"I understand." Flames danced in Kaia's eyes as she stared at the fire. "If you grow tired of hiding, I'll be here. I don't think you're a threat, Lily. I think you're someone who needs help but is too afraid to ask. Whatever or whomever you are running from, I know it wasn't your fault. I can feel it. That's worth more to me than leaving an innocent person to a terrible fate."

Warmth flooded through the queen's veins. "Thank you, Kaia."

"I'm always happy to make a new friend." She removed the fish from the spit and raised an eyebrow. "Can we eat, or is there more for us to discuss?"

"Oh, I don't think I can—"

"You have to eat," Kaia insisted. "I know it's not what you must be used to, but this is all we can afford. Honestly, you're *terrible* at blending in. I'm beginning to regret my offer."

Aurelia laughed, and so did Kaia. They shared their dinner over a crackling fire and the howling of hounds somewhere in the distance. If she'd been alone, her surroundings would've frightened her—but she wasn't alone anymore, and because of that, she was no longer afraid.

She should've been.

***

"Ahem."

Oona ignored the impatient voice behind her as she separated her coins by size and color. She exhaled dryly at the sound of the man's shoe pattering against the floor. Her initial response of, "Just a minute!" clearly hadn't been enough.

When she turned to address him, she scowled at the sour, twisted expression on his lips. He'd been staring at the back of her head, at the uneven tufts of gray hair sprouting over her smooth, bald scalp. His reaction to imperfection was enough to identify him as Akkinorian. He ogled the middle-aged innkeeper with judgement in his eyes, as if she'd *chosen* to surrender her once voluminous mahogany curls to look like a featherless duckling.

Oona raised an eyebrow. "Lookin' for room or drink?"

"Neither." The golden-haired, flat-faced man surveyed the tavern with a quick glance. "I'm searching for someone. She may have passed through your establishment in recent days." He reached into the pocket of his trousers and produced a folded piece of parchment. "Take a look. Have you seen anyone of her likeness?"

The innkeeper frowned and unfolded the parchment. A charcoal drawing of a young woman—with scribbled notes referencing red hair and blue eyes—stared back at her. The drawing was detailed enough for Oona to identify the woman's features. She *had* seen the person in question just days prior. The woman was searching for a man well-known to native Carthinians, but Oona hadn't bothered pointing her in the right direction. No foreign commoner could survive the journey to Taundosa on their own, and even if they did, someone like Arian Cristos was much too powerful a man to concern himself with a desperate peasant.

Recognition must have flashed in her eyes, as the man perked up and leaned closer. "You've seen her, haven't you?"

"Maybe. Can't be sure."

A low rumbling sound vibrated his chest. "Either you've seen her, or you haven't. I don't suppose there are many red-haired, fair-skinned women roaming Caedia by their lonesome. She'd be difficult to miss."

Oona's hazel eyes narrowed. "You'd be wastin' time lookin' for a redheaded girl. It ain't red. It's...sunnier."

"Sunnier?"

"She means *blonder*." A tall woman with dark features manifested at the man's side. She'd been standing in the corner of the tavern—lurking, as if in anticipation—with her arms folded over her chest as she listened to her male companion from afar. The woman raised an eyebrow at Oona. "Right?"

Oona nodded. "Right."

"So you *have* seen her," the man concluded. Oona stared at him, silent. "Which direction did she take when she left here? Was she alone?"

"Don't remember where she went. Had a horse wit her."

"Can you remember anything else?"

"Nope."

The man sighed. "All right. I suppose what you've given us is good enough."

Oona brushed off her irritation. "What do you want wit her?"

"That's none of your concern," the woman snapped. "Thank you for your cooperation."

She took her companion's elbow and guided him away. Oona watched them exit the tavern as a chill traced her spine. Guilt twisted her insides into knots—why, she didn't know. Perhaps it was the sheer enormity of the pair's swords or the intensity glowing in their eyes. The poor woman who'd stayed at Oona's inn wasn't the first foreigner to seek refuge in Carthe, and her presence suggested only one possible scenario: she was being hunted.

Only then did Oona realize that she'd told the hunters exactly what they were looking for. She'd given them crucial information, and she couldn't help but wonder if the woman's blood would be on her hands, too, if the hunters managed to find her.

What wracked her brain even more, though, was this: what on earth had the kind, soft-spoken woman with golden hair done to deserve being treated like a pig for slaughter?

Oona decided it didn't matter what the woman had done or who she was—she'd never see her again. The woman would become just another passing face whose soul, desperately seeking a safe haven in an unfamiliar world, was lost to Carthe forever.

IX

H ere's dinner." Aurelia tossed a dead rabbit onto the ground by Kaia's feet. Kaia stared at the rabbit, glanced up at Aurelia, then turned back to the rabbit with her lips pursed. Clearly, she hadn't expected Aurelia to succeed after sending her off with her bow and sheath of arrows. Not only had Aurelia secured their next meal, but she'd also proven the depth of her skill: it was a clean shot, right through the eye, giving the pair enough meat for the next few days.

"Huh." Kaia's eyes twinkled. "I underestimated you."

Aurelia could only smile for fear of revealing more than she already had. Kaia had been right to assume that noble ladies weren't soldiers in Akkinor. Most had never even touched a sword, but some noble women were the ladies of their kingdoms, and by default, the commanders of their armies. Aurelia was included in that group. She was the Commander of the Royal Army, and she'd been trained to use every weapon in Akkinor's armory. Until now, she never had to strap a sword to her waist or sling a sheath of arrows over her shoulder—Akkinor hadn't seen battle in decades.

She'd never hunted anything before, but it proved easier than she'd expected. She'd merely done what she loved most: climbed a durable tree as high up as she could go, camouflaged by thick clusters of leaves, and perched on a branch until a poor critter came into view. After that, it'd only been a matter of utilizing her training to ensure the animal was slaughtered quickly and efficiently.

The two had been traveling through the Violet Forest for over a week. Besides a few fellow travelers, they hadn't come across anyone on their expedition. Only two men had made snide comments towards them, but they hadn't been threatening.

"How long before we reach the valley?" Aurelia asked.

"Maybe a week. Maybe two. I told you—it's hard to say." She skinned the rabbit with the skill and ease of someone who'd been doing it their entire life. "We passed a landmark two days ago. The waterfall with the pretty blue azaleas. We're halfway through the forest now, but we traveled northeast to avoid the path. We'll be closer to Kanibar than Dofell if we keep to this route."

Aurelia didn't speak for a moment. "When do our paths sever?"

"I can take you to the border. Kanibar is west of Dofell and north of the Ngora Valley, so it's not far from my original path. Maybe a day or two out of the way."

"I don't want you to prolong your journey for me."

"I'm not. I like traveling with a friend."

Aurelia smiled. "All right."

She'd grown fond of her new friend. She didn't like to think about the day when they were meant to separate. Kaia had a family and a home in Kanibar, and Aurelia couldn't ask her to follow her into the unknown. Regardless of what the future held, Aurelia wouldn't complete her quest with Kaia Bolas at her side.

In a week, Kaia managed to change Aurelia's opinions of native Carthinians. She didn't seem like the immoral brutes from the stories. Every questionable deed attributed to her name had been necessary for her survival—and for the survival of her three siblings. It was admirable if not somewhat familiar.

"You remind me of someone, you know," Aurelia told her. "A friend from home. His father worked closely with mine, so we grew up together. I miss him terribly."

"Is he still there? In Akkinor?"

She winced. "I hope so."

"What does that mean?"

"He was locked in combat when I saw him for the last time." As she stared at the rabbit cooking on the spit, she envisioned Linden's blood-spattered face as they hid behind a flaming house in the Folly. She remembered the fear in his deep brown eyes—she'd never seen true terror in his gaze until that night. "He was helping me escape. I don't know what happened to him."

Kaia paused. "I'm sure he's just fine."

Aurelia didn't believe her. She knew what she left behind when she escaped the Folly. She remembered the chaos, the wreckage, the bloodshed. If the usurpers succeeded, the heir to the throne and the Hand of the Queen would've been their first targets. There was no doubt in her mind that Linden and Archie were either dead or locked away in the dungeons.

If her forces *had* managed to stop the usurpers, there was still no way for her to know what'd happened to Linden. When they'd seen each other for the last time, he was standing in the middle of a war-torn city with no reinforcements in sight. Maybe he managed to survive the battle, or maybe he was gone as soon as she turned her back on him.

A sudden thought popped into Aurelia's head. "If your village was raided, and going back for your loved ones meant giving your life, would you do it?"

Kaia blinked at her. "Wherever did you think of such a question?"

"Call it nothing more than mere curiosity."

"All right." She leaned in closer to the fire, the flames reflecting in her pale eyes like a mirror, and appeared torn between answers. "I don't know. I suppose I'd try to go back for them. I doubt they'd be incredibly happy if I got myself killed in the process, though. My loved ones would rather see me survive than have me die while attempting to retrieve them." She tore her eyes from the fire and glanced at Aurelia. "You must've asked because it happened to you. Who did you leave behind?"

The queen's gaze grew cold and withdrawn. "Everyone."

***

Bloody handprints streaked across golden wallpaper and mahogany panels. Pools of thick crimson so massive they threatened to flood every inch of the marble floors and beige carpets. Dying men convulsing and thrashing on the floor as they desperately awaited a rescue that would never come. Maids, fresh out of training, pinned to the walls with arrows and spears before they'd lived two decades of life. Horses galloping through the streets ablaze like hellfire, trampling the corpses of adults and children alike until the bodies were buried beneath layers of mud and ash.

Aurelia saw nothing else when she closed her eyes. A blissful sleep had been impossible to come by since the uprising. Every evening when the moon took the sun's place in the midnight sky, she closed her eyes in vain, knowing her dreams would be haunted by memories of her home being burned to the ground while the people she cared about were violently murdered. All because of her.

Unable to return to sleep and terrified of what she might find if she did, Aurelia tossed and turned as best she could while cramped in her tiny campsite. Kaia snored softly beside her and didn't seem affected by Aurelia's restlessness. For a moment, Aurelia debated waking Kaia so her ally might distract her from her waking nightmare. She eventually thought better of it; the only time she could truly be herself was at nighttime, when nobody was awake to watch her shoulders shake with silent sobs as she recalled the past.

She'd done something to the person—or people—responsible for the uprising. It wasn't enough to see her shackled to the dungeons with only rats for company. They wanted her dead. They wanted everyone who served her and everything that mattered to her to fall to ruin. Dozens upon dozens of people had lost their lives, homes, careers, property. Now she'd carry that burden with her for the rest of her life, knowing that everything the Folly had suffered since the uprising was ultimately her fault.

Linden would've told her to stop being ridiculous. Like her father, he was a firm believer in one rule: she wasn't to blame for any incident that she herself didn't execute. She hadn't given the order to murder every man, woman, and child in the Folly. She hadn't given the order to torch every home, every barn, every tree and every stone. She hadn't given the order to lay waste to an entire city as a demonstration of unbridled power.

Perhaps it wasn't her fault at all. Perhaps it was simply meant to feel like it was.

***

"Oh, this is *nice*." Kaia dunked her hands into the rushing stream and splashed her face with cool water. Her voice was a dull murmur when she attempted to speak over the roaring waterfall a stone's throw from where the pair had stopped. "If we had waterfalls and rivers like this in Kanibar, I'd never leave!"

Aurelia waded out of the water, dripping from head to toe, and sat beside Kaia on a bed of orange ranunculus flowers. "I don't know much about Kanibar. What's it like?"

"Which part?" She brought a damp hand to the back of her neck. "The western half of the kingdom borders the ocean. It's inaccessible by ship because of the Cliffs of Morinna, which are hundreds of feet above sea level. The winds are strong there, but beyond the cliffs is the only place in the realm where one can find mermaids."

"Mermaids?" Aurelia couldn't conceal her awe if she tried. She'd never met someone who'd seen mermaids in the flesh. As far as she'd known, mermaids had disappeared alongside the dragons, phoenixes, and other magical species. "Are you jesting?"

"Not at all. I've seen my fair share of them. They normally reside in the western half of the Alkamura—it's safer there. When they were being hunted, they were forced to find homes in the only body of water humans couldn't reach."

"How tragic."

"Indeed." Intent on changing the topic of conversation to something cheerier, Kaia added, "My village is located inland on the eastern side of the kingdom. That's where you'll find the Kanish countryside. It's rather lovely, I think. If we were neighbors with Taundosa or Bozar instead of Dofell, I'd wager that Kanibar would be the most sought-after place of residence in Carthe."

Aurelia frowned. "What's so wrong with Dofell? Other than its Almighty, of course."

"It was once called the Great City. All native Carthinians believed it to be the center of the world. Then it fell. Simple as that." Kaia's eyes were glazed with sorrow as she watched a leaf coast through the air and flutter to the surface of the stream. For a moment, the only sound for miles was the whistling of sharp winds tearing leaves from their branches. "The kingdom has reached a state of poverty unknown to the rest of the realm. Every inch of the border is encased in ghastly stone walls to discourage people from settling there. The soldiers have strict orders—nobody can enter the kingdom without the intention of leaving. They can't afford to shelter and feed those searching for a new beginning."

Aurelia's stomach churned. That was almost exactly what'd happened in Akkinor during the last years of the Cherrane Dynasty. Akkinor was saved from ruin by Oleander the Great, but no one had even attempted to save Dofell.

"Western Kanibar offers a mesmerizing view of the sea," Kaia continued, "and eastern Kanibar offers a harrowing view of stone walls and murdered vegetation. At least one good thing has come from our neighbors' failure—our rulers will never let us fall from grace as the Dofelli have."

Aurelia smiled sadly. "No ruler should've allowed such a thing to begin with. Kings and queens, lords and ladies...We all have a duty to our people and our kingdoms. How could anyone care so little for their peoples' welfare?"

"I agree." She cocked her head to the side, fingertips still grazing the surface of the stream, and studied Aurelia with unblinking eyes. "You said *we*. You counted yourself as a highborn. I *knew* I was right about you."

Desperate to change the subject from her lapse in judgement, Aurelia urged, "Tell me more about Kanibar."

"As you wish, Lily of Akkinor." Kaia's laughter was lighthearted, as if Aurelia hadn't just given herself away. "There's no kingdom like it. Not in Carthe, anyway. I suppose we have the monarchy to thank for that. The royal family has always valued privacy and serenity. Every vast city from the days of old has been broken down into smaller settlements and villages. We don't care for the noise and chaos of urban life. You won't find another kingdom so quaint and peaceful."

When Kaia spoke of her home, Aurelia could visualize it in her head with as much detail and clarity as a native Kanish. She saw the dirt roads built into mossy hills, the spacious valleys where villagers settled in cottages adorned with climbing ivy, and the blooming fields of tulips and snapdragons. She could almost feel the breeze blowing her hair from her shoulders as curious gulls and pelicans soared overhead.

When Kaia removed her top to wash it in the stream, Aurelia caught sight of the mark on her wrist. Her lessons came flooding back to her when she saw the O-shaped brand burned into Kaia's flesh.

Not wanting to reveal her highborn education, she asked Kaia what the branding meant. Kaia smiled and glanced down at her wrist like it was something to be proud of rather than something to despise.

"The O stands for *orphan*," she explained. "In Kanibar, if a child is orphaned, they may bear this symbol as a means of announcing their status to others. Most people—usually the older folk—will offer the child something to eat, a piece of clothing, blankets, or even medicine. The Kanish look after our orphans. It's the only way to ensure the survival of the next generation."

"Isn't it terribly painful?"

"Not as painful as losing one's parents," she replied. Aurelia firmly bit the insides of her cheeks. She knew that better than anyone—except Kaia, of course. "It's something we must endure if we wish for assistance. A few moments of physical pain is nothing compared to years of starvation."

Aurelia was frowning. "Must it be a brand? It's just as effective for a child to slather some paint on a piece of wood. That's harmless compared to a permanent marking."

Kaia's smile turned solemn. "If it were that effortless, then just about anyone could masquerade as an orphan, couldn't they?"

The thought made Aurelia shiver. She struggled to imagine Kaia as a young girl, freshly orphaned, squirming in pain while a stranger with a hot branding iron stamped a letter onto her skin. Aurelia herself hadn't had to worry about starving or freezing to death after her parents were lost at sea, but Kaia—like so many orphans in the world—knew what it was to fear for her life at an early age.

As she thought about it, she realized how awful it was of her to consider the tradition barbaric and sinful. She'd often turned her nose down on the Kanish for forcibly branding their people for life like they were cattle. Kaia offered a new perspective: of the many Kanish who were branded, one particular group—orphans—had *chosen* to bear the permanent marking and undergo the pain associated with it.

"I believe," Kaia declared, "you now owe me a tale of your own. What's *your* home like?"

Aurelia hesitated. Even if she chose to describe the most remote village in the Folly, she risked Kaia putting the pieces together and learning the truth. But her home wasn't limited to the kingdom in which she resided. All of Akkinor was her home, and she was free to choose anywhere in the country to share with Kaia.

"There's a dukedom in the kingdom of Myra called Eldford," she said. "My family has lived there for generations. I suppose Myra is similar to Kanibar, in a way. We have many cities, but Eldford is far less urban. The settlements were built on valleys and fields, and the bordering hills make it difficult to reach the villages if one isn't adept at hiking. Most people who live in Eldford tend to make a living by working in the vineyards."

"You must have the best wine in Akkinor."

"That is, of course, why most Akkinorians view Myrans as lazy drunkards."

Kaia laughed. "What else?"

For the next several hours, the pair seemed to forget that they had a destination and a long journey ahead of them. They sat by the stream, laughing and yelling over the deafening rushing of the waterfall, and traded stories about their homes until there was nothing left to share.

For the first time since arriving in Carthe, Aurelia remembered Akkinor as it was. She forgot about the bloodstains on the walls, the flaming horses, the trampled children in the streets. She stopped thinking about stepping over the bodies of her lady's maids, stopped recalling the feel of Linden's blood on her fingertips, stopped hearing the sounds of royal knights choking on their own blood.

For a moment, she was happy. Content. Peaceful.

Then she remembered.

X

ays after their excursion at the waterfall, Aurelia and Kaia stopped at a secluded spot in the forest to eat a meager lunch of rabbit and sugared nuts. It was cool that day—the coolest she'd felt since arriving in Carthe—and Aurelia relished the feel of the breeze lifting her hair from her shoulders rather than the humidity gluing her curls to the back of her neck. Even Kaia, who was quite adapted to the heat, seemed to be enjoying the brief change in weather.

A rustling from behind made Aurelia freeze. She exchanged looks with Kaia (who had a piece of rabbit meat stuck to her lip) and said nothing as her ally brought her finger to her lips. As slowly and quietly as a cougar hunting its prey, she stood from the ground and hefted Aurelia's sword. Aurelia, too, grabbed Kaia's bow and sheath as she rose to her feet. As she nocked an arrow, Kaia held the sword high and cautiously crept around a corner. The rustling and the footsteps grew louder as Kaia raised her sword just in time for two people to appear in front of them.

"Watch it!" A man held up his hands and took a few steps back. The woman with him staggered backwards, too, and nearly slammed into a tree. "We're sorry. We didn't know anyone was here. We'll just be going."

Kaia lowered her weapon and exhaled. Aurelia kept an arrow nocked as the couple eyed them while they walked. When the pair passed the campsite, they stopped and looked over their shoulders.

"Might we use your spit?" the man inquired. "We found a bird's nest and a handful of eggs. You don't seem to need yours anymore. It'd be immensely helpful if—"

"Yes, yes," Kaia said. "Take it. We're through."

"Thank you. Bless you."

Kaia and Aurelia stood back while the man carefully tended to the remainder of their fire. The woman produced a few bird's eggs from her pack and gave them to him. While they prepared their meal, Aurelia and Kaia collected their belongings. They'd been hoping to sleep there, but they couldn't risk staying now that two people knew where they were.

Aurelia studied the couple as she packed her things. The man wore typical peasant's clothing: brown breeches, riding boots, and an olive-green shawl covering the upper half of his body. His greasy, golden blonde hair (rivaling Aurelia's in length) was tied back with a piece of string. His eyes, solid blue like sapphire, were hidden beneath pale lashes. A massive iron sword peaked out from beneath his shawl.

The woman hadn't uttered a word since their initial meeting. Her light, fawny skin was mostly concealed by a thick charcoal-gray shawl, which matched her pants and riding boots. Her long carob hair flowed like a river down her back, straight as a pin and shinier than her chestnut eyes. Her features were defined like Kaia's, but her eyes were large and circular rather than sharp and feline.

Their physical traits weren't cause for concern—it was their body language that made Aurelia's heart pound. The woman's darted around wildly, like she was waiting for something. The man kept looking up from the spit while the eggs cooked, eyes shifting back and forth between Kaia and Aurelia. It was clear that Kaia was in charge, but he seemed particularly drawn to Aurelia. She noticed bulging in his boots, too—concealed weapons. As she analyzed the woman, she saw something catching the light against her clavicle—goldish, shiny, bulky. Akkinorian bronze. It was a rare material used primarily for battle armor, as it was the strongest metal in the world and the only thing that could bend a blade like clay. Aurelia would know it anywhere.

Kaia slung her pack over her shoulder and turned to the strangers. "Put the fire out and dispose of the spit when you're finished unless you want to attract the tribes. We should be going now."

"You're from Akkinor," Aurelia observed, ignoring her friend. The two strangers exchanged surprised looks. She raised her eyebrows at their prolonged silence. "Aren't you?"

The man stood and approached her with his hand extended. "Indeed." She shook it gingerly, taking note of the awkward placement of his thumbs, and narrowed her eyes. "Oren Lowstone of Myra. My lovely companion here is Alda Port of Holos."

"Lily Linden and Kaia Bolas of Kanibar," Aurelia stated. She may not have looked much like a native Kanish, but she had to trust that her Akkinorian kin struggled to differentiate the Carthinian cultures. "Charmed to make your acquaintance."

His eyes narrowed for a moment, but it was so quick that she thought she imagined it. "Likewise. We appreciate your generosity. I'm well-aware of the tension between our two continents. It's humbling to learn that some are not as cruel towards Akkinorians."

"Certainly." Kaia stepped between them with her arms crossed over her chest. "We'll be going now that we have our things together. You'd be wise to do the same."

"Of course. Good luck on your travels." His eyes passed over Aurelia. "Forward, ever forward."

Her breath caught in her throat, but she couldn't so much as blink in response. She and Kaia simply watched and waited, curious, as the two went on their way. Aurelia refused to move a muscle until Oren Lowstone and Alda Port were out of sight.

Forward, ever forward. Every Akkinorian knew those words. They were first uttered by Oleander the Great during the battle of Folly Hill. He was losing badly, his army was reduced to a mere four-hundred soldiers, and his enemies were growing stronger by the day. If he could successfully capture the landmark of Folly Hill, Akkinor would fall into his grasp. One of his soldiers, frightened as they waited for enemy troops to arrive on the battlefield, asked, "Where shall we go from here, my liege? Shall we turn back?" Oleander had smiled at him and replied, "Forward, good man, ever forward."

When travelers crossed paths on the Templar's Road, they'd stop to exchange news and wish each other safe travels with those parting words. If a civilian's business was struggling, someone might speak those words to them to keep their spirits high. Aurelia remembered hearing her father say it to her mother when she was in labor with Archie. It was an expression of perseverance, strength, and good fortune.

Everyone in the world knew about King Oleander's famous words. Foreign visitors in Akkinor would often say their rendition to Aurelia as a token of peace, but it was never quite right. *Forward march!* the southerners of Quapebet would say. *And still we move forward!* was a favorite of the Isalders to the north. The Carthinians came closest: *Forward, ever forth!* but still not quite right.

Only trueborn Akkinorians referenced the entire saying—all five of Oleander's words, not three for shorthand. That was one of the nation's great tricks. Few foreigners knew the precise saying, so Akkinorians could find one another while out in strange lands by relying on just those five words. It was a sign of kinship and of trust, and it was something never to be broken by anyone but a traitor.

Oren Lowstone knew exactly who Aurelia was, and now she knew he was a traitor. While she watched her tongue to avoid revealing herself, his omission of the full phrase was intentional. He knew she'd recognize that he wasn't a friend by failing to utilize the complete phrase. He wanted her to know that she'd lose her life that day, that he'd return to claim her head after the amusement of watching her squirm. Killing her as she sat in the clearing was far too simple and dull for people like Oren and Alda; they sought the thrill of the chase, the satisfaction of releasing prey into the wild only to hunt it down and slaughter it for sport.

Aurelia dashed over to Scotch and untied his reins. "What are you doing?" Kaia asked. "They're gone. We don't have to rush."

"We have to go." Aurelia didn't bother tying her pack to the saddle. She kept it slung over her shoulder as she climbed on Scotch's back. "We can't stay here, Kaia. Not now that two Akkinorians know we're out here."

She sighed. "Lily—"

With one sharp look from Aurelia, she fell silent and followed suit. When both were safely on their horses, Aurelia held out the bow and arrow for Kaia to take. She expected her friend to accept the weapons and exchange them for Aurelia's sword, but the Carthinian only smiled at her and said, "You hold onto that. You're better with a bow. I'm better with a sword."

They started moving again, traveling deeper into the trees, as she glanced over her shoulder in search of the two Akkinorians. Even Kaia had grown nervous. She was normally quite talkative, but now, she was mute.

After a few moments, Kaia cleared her throat. "What was that about?"

"I beg your pardon?"

"The Akkinorians. What's the problem? There are lots of Akkinorians in Carthe. What are you so worried about?"

Aurelia bit the insides of her cheeks until she tasted blood. "I know my people. You have to take my word for this."

No reply. Then Kaia yanked her horse's reins and increased his pace until they were in front of Aurelia and Scotch. She pulled her horse to a stop, trotting in place so she blocked Scotch's path. Aurelia sighed at her as Scotch slowed in front of the new obstacle.

"Kaia—"

"I asked *you* to join me," her friend snapped. "I pushed you into this. I told you to trust me so we can both make it to our destinations in one piece. I know what I said to you. I don't care about who you are or why you're running from Akkinor, but if my life is in danger, I need to know why."

Aurelia stared into her eyes and struggled to think of a suitable lie, but as her mind fabricated a story to appease Kaia, a pit formed in her stomach.

She didn't like lying to Kaia. She didn't like the person she'd been forced to become in Carthe. Kaia was her friend—one of the few friends the queen ever had—and she was knowingly putting her life in danger to help Aurelia. The least she could do was explain herself.

When she opened her mouth to reply, she was silenced by a whizzing sound that grazed her ear. In the blink of an eye, the tip of an arrow was poking out from Kaia's shoulder blade. It wasn't enough to knock her from her horse, but she cried out and teetered anyhow. Aurelia immediately reached for her bow and nocked an arrow. Kaia flattened herself against her horse and guided him behind a tree as Aurelia searched for the source of the arrow. Anger flowed through her veins when she saw a glittering Akkinorian bronze breastplate from across the clearing. Oren Lowstone and Alda Port were sitting on their horses, perched on a hill, with their shawls discarded and their weapons drawn. When Aurelia saw the black strip of fabric tied to their left arms, she realized they were assassins.

"Kaia! Go!"

Her friend was already turning gray. Kaia used her good arm to jerk the reins and send her horse galloping through the forest. Another arrow flew towards them and missed Aurelia by inches. She shot an arrow towards the assassins, just missing Alda's horse, and quickly followed Kaia through the foliage.

The clearest path for them to take was narrow, so it was almost impossible for their horses to fit beside one another. Kaia was gritting her teeth in pain as they rode, still with the arrow in her shoulder, but she seemed less frightened and more enraged by the situation. Aurelia's blood boiled when she heard the assassins whooping and calling after them. They weren't far behind, and Aurelia and Kaia were running out of places to go.

When they came to a fork, Kaia looked at Aurelia with wide eyes. She was glistening with sweat now, covered in her own blood, but her mind was as sharp as ever. Aurelia only nodded as the two led their horses in opposite directions. She wasn't surprised when she heard the assassins following her path rather than Kaia's. They had no need for a random Carthinian girl. They'd come only for Aurelia.

She couldn't see them behind her, so she dismounted Scotch and pulled him behind a tree. After quickly tying him to the trunk, she nocked an arrow and leaned her back against the bark. Her heart was pounding violently in her chest, both out of fear for her own life and worry for Kaia, but she'd been trained by some of the greatest soldiers in Akkinor, and she wouldn't let this moment reflect poorly on their lessons. The Queen of

Akkinor and the Commander of the Royal Army wouldn't be taken down by two lowly assassins.

In front of her, she saw a stream at the bottom of a hill. She heard movement behind her and studied the reflection in the water. It was angled enough to see the top of the hill behind her, so, as she hoped, it wasn't long before she saw something bronze shimmering against the water. With a deep breath, she turned around and sent an arrow towards the hill. It lanced Oren in the thigh, making him holler as he fell from his horse.

Alda was quick to respond. She threw a dagger towards Aurelia, piercing the tree she was hiding behind, and quickly took her horse down the hill. Aurelia barely had time to duck before a sword slashed the tree trunk where her head had been moments before. In the time it took Alda to turn her horse around, Aurelia had nocked another arrow and sent it flying. The arrow pierced Alda's horse in the gut, causing him to throw the rider to the ground and gallop away.

Oren was still struggling to stand at the top of the hill, and Alda was gasping for breath a few feet from Aurelia. The queen didn't waste any time. She climbed on Scotch's back and galloped towards Kaia, leaving the assassins behind to watch her go. Alda threw another dagger, but her aim was sloppy, and the weapon landed several feet from where Aurelia was riding. After a few moments, she looked over her shoulder and was pleased to see nothing in her wake.

She found Kaia waiting for her by a stream. She hadn't removed the arrow yet, and her skin was still sticky and shiny with blood. Luckily, she was sitting upright and appeared more annoyed than hurt.

Kaia sighed in relief when Aurelia joined her. "Okay. I understand. It was a good idea to leave."

Aurelia shook her head. "I'm so sorry, Kaia."

"It's only an arrow and it's only my shoulder." She forced a weak smile. "I'll be fine. There's a tavern nearby where we can rest for a night or two. We can make it there before it gets too dark." She raised her eyebrows and winced as she turned to look at her wound. "Do you think it wise to walk into a tavern with an arrow through my shoulder?"

"I can take it out."

She laughed nervously. "Lily—"

"Trust me." Aurelia rode up next to her so she could get a better look at the arrow. It'd gone straight through her flesh. Other than a bit of pain and time to heal, there was nothing more to worry about. Even so, Kaia didn't seem fond of the idea of Aurelia removing the arrow. "You *do* trust me, don't you?"

Kaia stared at her. "I do. I don't know why, but I do."

"Good. It's mutual."

Aurelia hoped their shared trust in one another—and their friendship as it was—wouldn't lead to Kaia taking another arrow. If it did, she'd have to add Kaia's name to the lengthy list of souls whose lives had been taken to see Aurelia removed from the world.

XI

When they fell asleep the night of the attack, Kaia was herself. When they woke the next morning, she was a stranger.

She hadn't seemed too bothered by the arrow. Removing it was painful, but that was the worst of it. The most they could do was smear a bit of healing salve over the wound to prevent infection and wrap it in bandages. She'd complained about the discomfort when they fell asleep nestled in a cluster of bushes, but that was expected. She was still smiling, making jokes, and teasing Aurelia like she normally did. She was even excited to show her siblings her battle wound, as they were always eager to hear stories of her travels.

At dawn, Aurelia noticed a severe shift as soon as Kaia opened her eyes. Kaia's fawny skin had turned gray, her hair and clothing were damp with sweat, and her arm seemed limp rather than sore. She refused to eat and could barely finish a full sentence, though she insisted she was stable enough to keep moving. Aurelia didn't argue even when Kaia struggled to mount her horse. She was practically falling asleep as they rode, barely able to hold herself upright, and she held her shoulder like it was a worthless piece of flesh attached to her body.

Aurelia spent the next two days insisting they rest or search for a medic, but Kaia wouldn't have it. She was insistent on reaching the border of the Violet Forest as quickly as possible. Aurelia heard a traveler in passing on their way back from Dofell who'd said they'd been traveling for a week. The edge of the forest wasn't nearby. That's what motivated Aurelia to force Kaia into resting, as she knew that her friend would never make it to Dofell unless she cared for herself.

"Eat." Aurelia set a pouch of berries in Kaia's hand as her friend sat with her back to the trunk of a tree. She was in a daze, barely present, but

Aurelia wouldn't let her disappear more than she already had. "You must eat something, Kaia. You'll starve."

"I had some bread."

"That was yesterday. Eat."

Kaia didn't move. "I'm not hungry."

Aurelia said nothing for a moment. "We should change your bandages while we're resting, then." She crouched down next to Kaia's injured shoulder and waited for her friend to respond. When no reply came, she exhaled and carefully peeled away Kaia's shirt. Blood had soaked through the bandages, so she cut them away to reveal the wound. Immediately, her breath caught in her throat and her heart plummeted to her knees. "Oh..."

No response from Kaia. Aurelia was glad for that; she didn't know what she'd say if Kaia asked about the injury. The puncture wounds had turned a sickly shade of green, like mucus, and began to ooze when the bandages were removed. The sensitive skin surrounding the puncture marks was bright red, inflamed beyond repair, and the veins of her arm had started to blacken. It looked like spiderwebs were crawling along her skin, surrounding a crusting red mark with green gunk bubbling from her flesh.

"Is it bad?" Kaia croaked.

Aurelia cleared her throat. "It's fine. A bit more salve should do the trick. Stay still while I apply the bandages."

Aurelia hated lying to her friend, but she couldn't tell Kaia about the severity of the injury. She was simply glad that Kaia hadn't seen it for herself. Anyone could recognize the effects of phoenix blood. The incredibly rare poison had been used extensively in the old days before the entire realm prohibited the slaughter of phoenixes. Soldiers would coat their blades in poison to inflict an excruciatingly slow, painful death on their enemies. It was extremely uncommon to find phoenix blood in Aurelia's time, but some people (mainly assassins) still sold or purchased it at illegal markets.

Preventing death after being poisoned with phoenix blood was nearly impossible. As soon as the poison entered the bloodstream, a person was destined for death. It could only be stopped if one were able to remove all traces of the poison from the victim's blood, which was incredibly difficult, even for the most talented of medics. Death could take hours or days, depending on the person.

Aurelia wasn't worried about time. She was worried because she knew that her only friend on this side of the world was going to die, and it was entirely her fault.

Kaia didn't need to know. She wouldn't find the strength to make the most of her last moments if she knew her time was running out. This knowledge was a burden for Aurelia to bear on her own.

Kaia fell asleep before Aurelia could finish tying her bandages. Not knowing what more to do with herself, Aurelia leaned back, still kneeling on the dirt, and wiped her gunky hands on her clothing while monitoring the sound of Kaia's labored breathing. Suddenly, a burst of rage erupted like a ball of fire in her chest, and she couldn't stop herself from throwing everything in her reach.

She was angry at the assassins, angry at the person or people who'd sent them, and angry at herself for putting Kaia in such a position to begin with. She suspected that hundreds of innocent souls had perished the day of the uprising, and now—even across the sea in foreign lands—another innocent was close to death. The innocents in the Folly had been strangers, but Kaia was a friend, and that made the guilt and the pain all the worse.

Closing her eyes, Aurelia took a long, deep breath and forced herself to stand. She collected everything she'd thrown, one by one, until her satchel was full again. She couldn't let Kaia see the evidence of her despair.

When Kaia woke, she didn't seem to know what Aurelia had done moments earlier. She simply smiled at her friend, accepted assistance when it was time to move, and clutched her bandaged wound as if ensuring it was still there.

"Can you ride?" Aurelia asked. Kaia nodded. "All right. Let's try."

She carefully helped her friend stand and mount her horse. Kaia was practically falling asleep against her horse, so it was up to Aurelia to collect their belongings and erase all traces of their presence at the campsite. When she, too, was safely perched on Scotch's back, the two started towards Dofell. Aurelia made sure to stay close to Kaia's side, but her watchful eye wasn't enough. They were riding for only a few moments when Kaia's condition worsened. She made a small, weak noise in the back of her throat while her eyelids began to flutter.

"Kaia—?"

No response. Just then, the Kanish native began coughing and leaning to the side. Aurelia let out a strangled cry as she reached out to grab Kaia's shirt, but her efforts were in vain. She was already jumping down from Scotch's back when Kaia fell from her horse, directly impacting her good shoulder, right onto a cluster of ivory azaleas. While Aurelia rushed to her aid, Kaia lay there limply, still blinking furiously and moaning in pain.

"Everything is fine." Aurelia leaned Kaia against a thick tree trunk and rummaged through her bag for a canteen of water. "Drink this. You're probably dehydrated and malnourished. You need to eat and drink."

Her friend shook her head. "I want to see it."

"See what?"

"T-The wound."

Aurelia hesitated. "Kaia—"

"Please."

The desperation in her voice forced Aurelia to comply. She gently peeled away Kaia's shirt and unraveled the bandages. Kaia took one long breath before glancing down at her shoulder and gasping. Aurelia winced. Kaia knew what phoenix blood's poison did to a person. She knew she'd been infected. The thing Aurelia tried shielding her from had been exposed, and now both of them knew that Kaia wouldn't live to see Kanibar again.

"I-It's poison, Lily."

"I'm sure it's nothing more than a minor infection."

Kaia's pale eyes welled with tears. "No, it's not."

Aurelia didn't reply. She rebandaged the wound and told Kaia to get some rest. She didn't know what else to say. The most she could do was keep Kaia comfortable, but it was hard to focus on anything but the idea of losing a friend. Kaia lay her head in Aurelia's lap while the queen gently stroked her hair, humming the old Akkinorian lullabies once used to soothe her when she was distressed as a young girl.

When Kaia woke up coughing, white foam dripped from the sides of her lips as red liquid bubbled in her nostrils. It wasn't long before blood was dripping from her nose and mixing with the foam around her mouth. Aurelia quickly wiped it away before Kaia could notice. That's when she saw how bloodshot her friend's striking green eyes had become, and how the onyx veins on her arm had already managed to spread towards her chest and neck.

"I-I'm sorry," Kaia wheezed. "I'm...I'm slowing us down."

"It isn't your fault. It's mine."

She shook her head. "Y-You told me we had to-to go." She coughed again, foaming blood dribbling down her chin, as her chest rattled with each breath. "I didn't listen. You were right, Lily. I-I should have listened to you."

"You wouldn't be in this position if not for me."

"I made that choice."

Aurelia hesitated and gnawed on her lips. "Why? Why did you wish to accompany me so desperately?"

Her smile was weak, but it was still there. "I-I was going to leave you at the-at the crossroad, but I couldn't do it. I-I looked over at you, and-and I saw this look on your face that..."

She paused to release a dry cough from her chapped lips. Aurelia hurried to unscrew her flask, then dribbled a bit of water onto her friend's lips.

"Th-Thanks," she croaked. Aurelia offered her a weak, faltering smile. "I-I looked at you, and I felt like...like a child again. Like waking up to my mama singing while she-while she cooked, a-and my papa feeding the birds in the y-yard." Aurelia hushed her, hearing the strain in her voice, but Kaia wouldn't listen. Her eyes were wide, very wide, and she wasn't blinking. "Suddenly I had my...my spirit for adventure back, Lily. The spirit I ha-had before my parents died. To do something brave an-and daring. It was right there, in your eyes."

Aurelia could do nothing but stare at her until burning tears forced her to blink. She looked away, sniffling, as Kaia released a rattling cough and a deep, aching moan. Aurelia couldn't bring herself to reply. Until recently, it'd been Kaia who saved them from an awkward silence when Aurelia couldn't answer. Now, for the last time, she'd be saving them yet again.

"Lily?" She looked up at Aurelia with dull, glistening eyes. They were no longer wide with angst, but drooping and fluttering with weakness. Her lips were stained crimson, and her skin was so ashen that she appeared drained of blood. Around them, the white azaleas were splattered with red after Kaia's coughing fits. "C-Can you...can you tell me the truth about who...about who you are?"

The queen stilled, lips parting, as her friend stared at her, expectant and pleading. She knew there was nobody around to overhear them, just as she knew that if there were any time to tell Kaia the truth, it was now. But she liked who she was when she was with Kaia. She liked the person she was becoming when everyone around her wasn't bowing or curtsying or calling her by a title rather than her own name. That's how she wanted Kaia to remember her. Still, after everything she'd endured, Kaia deserved honesty.

"All right." Aurelia sniffled and gently combed her fingers through Kaia's damp hair. "I, too, am an orphan. My parents were lost at sea about five years ago. You may know of them—Edmund and Cressida Brentwood, King and Queen of Akkinor."

Kaia's eyes widened. She finally showed an emotion: amazement. "So, you're—?"

"Aurelia Brentwood, First of Her Name, Queen of Akkinor." Aurelia offered her a middling smile. "It's a pleasure to formally make your acquaintance, Kaia of Kanibar."

She was the liveliest she'd been in days. "My word. I-It's nice to meet you, Your Grace. B-But why are you here? In Car-Carthe?"

"I don't know, exactly," she admitted. "I was forced to escape Akkinor when the palace was attacked. The Lord Hand—the friend I told you about—thought it was an uprising. Usurpers came to seize my throne. My parents left a letter for me in the event of something like that. They told me to escape to Carthe and find the one person capable of assisting me."

"A-And you came here all...all alone?"

Aurelia nodded.

"If I could stand, I would-I would curtsy."

That made Aurelia laugh. "No need. Friends should not have to curtsy." When she saw how shallow Kaia's breathing had become, she kept talking. "After I find what I need in Carthe, I'll locate your siblings and tell them what you did for me. They'll know that you died a hero."

Kaia's eyelids fluttered. "Thank you."

After a few moments, Kaia's hand in hers became limp and fell to the ground. Her eyelids stopped moving, her chest stopped rising and falling, and the sound of her labored breaths disappeared. Aurelia bit back tears as she gently rested Kaia's head on the ground. She knelt beside Kaia's body and stared at her friend's face. The fight was finally over, and Kaia had returned to the heavens with her parents. She was gone.

She didn't let herself cry. Kaia would've hated that. Instead, she simply kissed Kaia's forehead and murmured a goodbye. *Forward, good man, ever forward.* Kaia didn't know what it meant, but it would've brought her comfort if she did. Few Akkinorians spoke those words as a goodbye for foreigners. It was a tremendous honor, and that day, it'd been bestowed personally by the queen.

As she stared at Kaia's lifeless face, something fell from above and landed on Kaia's chest. Aurelia looked up and smiled when she realized they were beneath a magnolia tree. Pink blossoms were blowing with the breeze, covering the friends in a lovely blanket of petals, and nestling on the ground between the azaleas. Aurelia wiped her running nose with her sleeve and backed away from Kaia's body. She simply watched, both awestruck and grief stricken, as the petals surrounded Kaia's remains and laid her to rest in the most serene way Aurelia could've imagined.

Only a few minutes after leading Scotch away from the clearing, Aurelia was stopped by a sharp, severe pain in her chest. She brought a hand to her breast, attempting to steady her racing heart, but instead felt another sharp pain jabbing her in the ribs. It was a feeling she knew all too well, and it was one she'd hoped never to feel again. Grief was a tricky opponent to play against one's emotions—it was strong enough to render a person as lifeless as the one they mourned for.

Overcome with weakness, Aurelia reached out for the nearest stable structure—a boulder—and lowered herself onto the rounded surface. Within a moment of sitting, she found herself struggling for breath as harsh, merciless sobs wracked her entire being. She hunched forwards, head between her knees, and dry-heaved over the ground until the few contents of her stomach made a reappearance. Even after her stomach had been emptied, she continued to weep for her fallen friend, knowing she'd never find another like Kaia.

XII

While attempting to fashion a spit over a dwindling fire, Aurelia caught her hand on a sharp twig. She gasped, cursed, and immediately pressed her bleeding palm against her dirt-stained trousers. It was one of many injuries she'd sustained in the past three days since Kaia's death. Without her friend to assist her, her survival skills were being harshly tested.

After wrapping her hand in a piece of cloth she'd ripped from her shirt, she fetched her last piece of game—a squirrel—from her satchel and tied the skinned animal to the spit. Her hand burned both from the cut and the heat of the fire, but she swallowed the pain for the sake of her empty stomach. The discomfort, however, wasn't worth it in the end, as the tiny squirrel did little to soothe her hunger.

She glanced at her bandaged hand, then at the bloody tear on the left sleeve of her shirt. Like a fool, she'd fallen asleep the night before while her game was still cooking on the spit. The smell attracted a fox, and when she woke to the sound of the animal pawing at the spit, she'd startled both of them so greatly that the fox swiped at her with his claws. She'd managed to protect her face with her arm before the fox scurried off into the trees. She attempted chasing it, hoping for a better meal than a meager squirrel, but the creature was much faster than she.

A combination of frustration, rage, and self-pity caused her to lash out. She'd kept her temper under control prior to Kaia's death—and, miraculously, throughout her entire journey—but now that she was alone again without Kaia or even the old man from Seaport, anger was beginning to consume her. Losing the fox had awakened that temper of hers again, and the disappointment that followed hurt more than the gash on her arm.

She'd hollered, kicked at the tree trunks, thrown rocks, cursed the gods. Scotch attempted to comfort her by nuzzling her neck, and she'd responded by aggressively pushing him away. She hadn't known that horses whimpered until then. She was filled with guilt when she saw the way he shied away from her, but even that wasn't enough to calm her anger.

She'd always had a short temper. Nobody knew where it came from. Cressida was the gentlest person she'd ever met, and Edmund had such control over himself that it was almost unfathomable. Her mother never raised her voice, and her father only did so when it was warranted. Aurelia, on the other hand, tended to fall victim to fits of anger and frustration quite often.

She remembered being nine years old, having spent five hours locked in a room with her tutor, wanting nothing more than to abandon her studies and enjoy the first warm day of the summer. When her tutor forbade her from leaving the classroom, she'd shouted at him, carved profane words into her desk, and thrown her books onto the floor. She'd learned her lesson after a lengthy conversation with her father, and ever since, she'd been mindful of her temper.

Mindful of it, but not submissive to it.

The last time she'd experienced an angry fit like that had been two years earlier. She became aware of something that not even her father had known about: highborn families were using buildings across the country— abandoned castles, temples, and even taverns—for clandestine purposes like private brothels, trading posts, and banks. It wasn't illegal to do so, only frowned upon, but the highborn were risking ill favor with the monarchy by hiding their activities.

Since her reign began, she'd considered converting the structures into public buildings for civilian use. She thought it would benefit the common people to have additional schoolhouses, infirmaries, and the like. When she learned of the nobles' activities, she politely requested that they cease everything for the good of the masses. They'd declined, and she was forced to command them to do so.

It was the disrespect of her nobles that sparked her temper. Some of them had undermined and belittled her without directly insulting her authority, thus allowing them to keep their heads. She was always torn between keeping them happy and doing what was right for her people— even if the latter asserted her nobles' belief that she, as a woman, was an unfit ruler. The frustration of it had sent her into a blind rage, and without Linden to steady her, she might've done more than allowing her nobles to leave with a mere slap on the wrist.

They hadn't been happy with her decision, but they had no choice but to accept her plans. Some of them, like Lord Crowland, respected her more for refusing to let such influential people interfere with her plans. Others, like Lady Spirre, came as close to insulting Aurelia as she could without meeting the hangman at the gallows.

When thoughts of the fox and her wretched temper disappeared, Aurelia pondered once more about her father's letter. In moments such as this when her only company was her own thoughts, she almost always found herself thinking back to the letter. She still wasn't certain that she believed the message it contained. Knowing that she hadn't come from Edmund and Cressida Brentwood weighed down on her each and every day. They may have raised her and loved her as their own, but she wasn't theirs by blood.

Her birth parents were Carthinian—that much was clear—but from where? Did they come from the serene countryside of Kanibar, or from the impoverished streets of Dofell? Was she born in the modest world of Krotis, or in the booming cities of Bozar? Had she taken her first breath in the City of Gold, or in a lonely province like Khaba or Caedia?

She'd been chosen as Edmund's heir, but for all she knew, she'd been born to be nothing but another passing face in the poor villages of Carthe. Whoever she'd been before she was the daughter of Edmund and Cressida Brentwood, she certainly hadn't been meant to rule Akkinor.

With a sullen, defeated sigh, she began to pray for both her survival and her own worth. It wasn't enough to simply endure—she had to earn the gift her parents had given her, and she had to prove to herself that being chosen to rule was as valuable as being born to rule.

***

"Do you remember your sixteenth name day?"

A hoarse, raspy female voice croaked in response. "Yes."

"I believe you're the only servant in history to have received such a grand celebration for your coming of age." Linden smacked his dry lips together. Talking so much parched his already bone-dry throat, but he knew it was the only thing keeping her from slipping away. "The king and queen thought it odd—as did my father—but Aurelia wouldn't have it. She was insistent that we celebrate you for who you are: someone with the heart and soul of a queen. Of course, the only people in attendance were servants, but the entire royal family came, too. Even the king's sisters. I still don't know how Aurelia managed that. She must've enticed them under some sort of ruse." He shook his head and chuckled. "Rotten little cheat, isn't she?"

A breathy exhale escaped her throat. "In the most-the most marvelous way."

"Indeed." Sitting with his back against the bars of his cell, Linden turned to press his face against the iron rods as he tried to glance at the hallway to his left. He saw nothing but the dark dreariness of the dungeon and the faint twinkle of a torch at the other end of the hallway. "Where do you suppose she is right now?"

No reply. He turned again, now with the front of his body melting into the bars, and ignored the brief jolt of pain coursing through his abdomen from the pressure of open wounds against iron.

"Cee? Are you awake? Cicely?"

Silence. Mustering what little strength he had, Linden rose to his feet and practically squeezed his head through the bars. He still couldn't see her clearly, what with her cell being directly adjacent to his, but he could see one of her arms limply dangling between the bars of her cell.

He called out for her again, and with each lack of a response, he increased his volume until he found himself yelling. The sudden commotion summoned the Laynoan soldier at the end of the hall who'd been tasked with guarding the dungeons. The first thing the soldier did was approach Linden and push him backwards using the sharp tip of an iron fire poker. While Linden fell backwards, blood spouting from a fresh cut on his chest, the soldier moved on to the cell to Linden's right. He muttered something Linden couldn't hear, then hollered for soldiers stationed at other posts throughout the dungeon.

"What is it?" Linden scrambled to his feet and clutched the bars again. "What's happened?"

The soldier manifested in front of his cell in the blink of an eye. When Linden spotted the fire poker aimed in his direction, he staggered backwards to avoid another injury.

"She's dead." The soldier's voice was dry and emotionless, as if something as silly as sympathy was far beneath him. "They'll be around to collect the body before the stink sets in."

The soldier hesitated outside of the cell for just a moment longer, seemingly anticipating that Linden would throw himself at the bars in a halfhearted attempt at vengeance. When Linden merely lowered himself onto the cold stone floor, silent, the soldier lowered the poker and walked off without another word.

Linden parted his lips to speak one last time. "Cee?"

At her silence, his body tensed as if he were swallowing himself whole, forcing him to curl up in a ball like his limbs had calcified. He knew he'd be punished for his sobs, so he covered his mouth with both hands while ceaseless tears flooded his cheeks.

Cicely would've told him not to cry. She would've reminded him that he needed every drop of water in his body to survive. He could almost hear her voice in his head: *Don't waste your tears on me, my love. They are too precious to be spent on the dead.*

She'd known from the moment she was locked in the dungeon that she was going to die, but Linden hadn't believed it. The woman he loved—soft spoken, compassionate, and as innocent as a newborn babe—had taken an arrow to the gut while shielding a maid's young son with her own body. Rather than killing her when she was found after the siege (alive but wounded), the usurpers locked her in the dungeon to die slowly and painfully: a death befitting of someone eternally loyal to the new king's nemesis.

She'd managed to survive for a few weeks with the arrow still lodged in her abdomen. Linden had seen people survive much worse injuries in his lifetime—he was confident she'd make it through. His confidence, however, was nothing but a veil preventing him from accepting the inevitability of her demise. She'd known full well that she was going to die in that cell, and Linden had refused to say goodbye for fear of proving her right.

Nobody came to collect her body. Nobody came until the decaying smell of her remains was pungent enough to waft upstairs whenever the doors to the dungeon were opened. By the time they arrived to carry her away, she was exactly where she'd been at the moment of her death: slumped against the door of her cell, one arm dangling between the bars as if reaching for the man she loved, and her would-be response to Linden's inquiry still pursed on her lips.

***

Aurelia's slow, paced breaths vibrated the bowstring kissing her lips. She narrowed her eyes, focusing, as her fingers on the arrow began to ache. With one quick movement, the arrow was released, and she allowed herself a satisfied smile when it found a home between the eyes of a runty brown rabbit. She hopped down from her hiding spot in the thick branches of a towering tree, clicked her tongue for Scotch to follow, and maneuvered through the uneven forest floor to collect her next meal as she slung her bow over her shoulder.

When she was a few feet from the rabbit, she found herself unable to budge. Frowning, she stared down at her feet as she willed her legs to move. She was stuck in place as if trapped in quicksand, and she quickly understood why after the rabbit rose into the air and flew through the trees as if caught in a cyclone.

"Hello?" She looked around, heart hammering, as Scotch kneaded her shoulder with his nose. She tried lifting her feet again as she scanned her surroundings. "Is someone there? Hello?"

With one more yank, her left foot rose from the ground. She was so startled by her sudden freedom that she stumbled, though she was able to keep herself from falling by grasping Scotch's reins. She blew escaping wisps of hair from her face and took a few cautious steps forwards. Though she couldn't see where the rabbit went, she followed its path through the trees and eventually heard something that sounded like humming.

Just a few feet away, she saw a clearing in the woods where a small, cloaked figure sat on a fallen tree trunk. The individual seemed to be preparing for dinner: they were spreading a large green leaf over the tree trunk and positioning hand-carved cutlery on either side of the makeshift plate. While the figure organized their place setting, the rabbit was being skinned with a hunting knife—on its own.

The figure shifted, causing the hood of the cloak to slip, and Aurelia's pounding heart steadied when she realized the individual was a child. The young girl was no older than twelve or thirteen at most. Even from a distance, Aurelia recognized the girl's features as Dofelli, thanks to Kaia's many lessons on Carthinian culture. The girl was tall and slim without a lick of muscle or fat on her body. She had a long, freckled face with sallow skin, narrow golden eyes, and matted black hair. Her hands—like her cheek and her neck—were caked in dried blood.

Aurelia took a few slow steps forwards. "Hello, there." The girl jumped, alarmed, and dove behind the log to shield herself. "It's all right. I'm not here to hurt you. I'm just wondering if you happen to know where my rabbit went. I seem to have lost it."

The girl's cheeks turned crimson. "Forgiveness. Very hungry."

Judging by her thick accent and improper vocabulary, Aurelia assumed the girl didn't speak the common tongue. She may have understood it—many Carthinians did, according to Kaia—but she didn't speak it well.

When Aurelia stepped closer, she realized the girl wasn't alone. A wicker basket beside the log wasn't filled with food or supplies, but rather serving as a bassinet for a small, sleeping babe wrapped in blankets.

"Oh, dear." Aurelia tore her eyes away from the baby and frowned at the girl. "Are you here alone? Where are your parents?"

The girl blinked at her, then lifted her index finger to her neck and pretended to slit her own throat. The poor children, like Aurelia herself, were orphans.

"May I sit?" she asked. The girl merely stared at her as she lowered herself onto the ground beside the smoldering fire. "My name is Lily. I'm all alone, too. My parents are gone. As you can imagine, I'm as hungry as you are. Might we share the rabbit?"

The girl wavered, visibly nervous, before nodding once. She cautiously climbed over the log and resumed her earlier position. Her eyes didn't leave Aurelia's face. Aurelia, on the other hand, turned her attention to the snoozing babe. He was a bit younger than a year old, but he was severely underweight for a babe of his height.

She snapped her gaze to the right when the hunting knife clattered to the ground. She watched in awe as the skinned rabbit slowly moved through the air before positioning itself over the fire. The animal turned as if on a spit, cooking over the flames, but there was no such mechanism to be found.

Aurelia had seen magic before, but never so directly. She'd never stood in the presence of a mage who used their power without a second thought. Nearly everything she knew about magic came from her studies, from books and stories and ancient documents. Until now, she hadn't known how magnificent it truly was.

"Your magic is wonderful," she murmured. "What's your name?"

The girl shifted uncomfortably. "Liat."

"It's lovely to meet you, Liat. Is this your brother?"

She nodded. "Jaco."

Aurelia peered into the basket and smiled. "Hello, Jaco."

It was clear to her that Liat was still uneasy, and she didn't blame the girl for being afraid of her. For all she knew, Aurelia was pretending to show her kindness only to thieve her supplies and leave her for dead. What the poor little thing didn't realize was that Aurelia was afraid of *her*. Magic in any form was deadlier than a blade or an arrow. If she so desired, Liat could simply command her hunting knife to find a home in Aurelia's heart, and the Queen of Akkinor would be killed by a twelve-year-old girl.

When Jaco began to cry, Liat immediately sprang into action. She reached for a smooth leaf while a leather canteen rose from her little backpack. As she folded the leaf and touched the tip to Jaco's mouth, the canteen unscrewed, and the mouth of the bottle positioned itself at the other end of the leaf. The canteen tipped slightly, causing a trickle of white liquid to seep down the leaf and into Jaco's mouth.

Aurelia assumed it was goat's milk, a popular alternative to breastmilk in both Akkinor and Carthe. She didn't know how Liat had managed to acquire a canteen of goat's milk, but she'd have to do so again quickly, as Jaco finished the last of it within minutes. He didn't have teeth yet, and unless Liat managed to find a food mushy enough for him to eat, he'd starve to death.

For a second, Aurelia toyed with the idea of bringing them along on her journey. She wouldn't take them all the way to Taundosa, but she could find someone along the way who'd be willing to take them in. It was unlikely—not impossible—that someone would take the children simply to help them, but more likely that someone would offer them shelter and food in exchange for service of some kind. That, she thought, was a better fate than leaving them to suffer in the wilderness.

She decided almost instantly that it was a poor idea. The pain and guilt of Kaia's death was still fresh in her heart, even eight days later, and she had no intention of risking an additional two innocent lives. Her desire for company and her urge to protect the children weren't reasons enough to put the two in harm's way.

If Kaia were still alive, perhaps things would be different. Perhaps Kaia would take the children back to Kanibar with her after she and Aurelia parted ways. Kaia knew more about the forest and the continent than Aurelia did, and someone with such little experience couldn't possibly claim responsibility for the lives of two young children. Aurelia could hardly ensure her own survival, let alone that of Liat and baby Jaco.

"Pretty."

Aurelia snapped out of her daze. "I beg your pardon?"

"Pretty." Now that Jaco was fed and sleeping once again, Liat scooted away from him and sat on her knees beside Aurelia. She was pointing at Aurelia's locket. "Pretty."

"Why, thank you. It was a gift from my parents. I—"

She stopped when she felt the locket vibrating against her skin. Puzzled, she looked at Liat and gasped when she saw the way the child was staring intently at the necklace. She knew what was happening: Liat was attempting to open the locket with magic.

"I'm afraid it's empty," Aurelia lied. Liat relaxed, exhaled, and ceased using her magic. A sigh of relief escaped Aurelia's lips when the locket stilled. "You have very powerful magic. It's a wonderful gift so long as you use it for good. Are you good, Liat?"

"Very good!"

"You must be, because most little girls wouldn't care for their brother so diligently. He's fortunate to have you."

Liat beamed. She scooted over to the basket again, gripping the sides, and peered down at her sleeping brother with nothing but adoration in her bright eyes. She was dirty, bloody, and thinner than a twig, and yet, the only thing she seemed to care about was Jaco.

Kaia once told Aurelia a story about her neighbors in Kanibar. When the three siblings were orphaned, the eldest—thirteen years old—understood how difficult it would be to keep the other two alive. It became even harder when the youngest, just a year old, contracted typhus. The eldest let the babe die rather than working for the coin needed for medicine. When the babe passed, the eldest sibling sold the middle child, a five-year-old girl, to a couple in Dofell who needed an extra set of hands on their farm. He never saw her again.

Aurelia couldn't imagine doing such a thing. From the moment her brother was born, she knew it was her duty as his elder sister to protect him. When he did something naughty, she confessed to their governess on his behalf and earned herself five whacks on the hand with a stick. When the loudness of the Changling Celebration scared him out of his wits, she guarded his hiding spot and ushered people away until he was ready to emerge. Before she knew what it was to be a princess or a queen, she knew what it was to be a sister—it was the only role she'd understood perfectly since she was three years old.

She cursed herself for listening to the instructions given to her by her parents and Linden—instructions which stated that under no circumstance was she meant to worry for anyone but herself during times of peril. Taking Archie along with her had never been part of the plan. She'd been given an order by the King and Queen of Akkinor to protect only herself, and yet, every fiber of her being was screaming at her for failing to go back for her brother.

In moments like this one, Aurelia hated being queen. She despised the fact that she was the most important person in Akkinor—as such, she could risk her life for nobody but herself. She couldn't do everything in her power to protect her brother like Liat was doing for Jaco. Her crown was both gift and curse, and while she roamed the Carthinian wilderness by her lonesome, unaware of her brother's fate, her crown felt useless.

While Aurelia joined Liat for a meal consisting of rabbit meat and sugared nuts, a gigantic brown bird with crimson-tipped wings flew overhead. Liat gasped and jumped to her feet, awestruck. The bird circled over the clearing thrice before resting in the branches. For the first time, Liat acted like a girl her age when she ran around in circles with her arms outstretched like a bird taking flight.

Aurelia chuckled. "You'd make a dear little bird, Liat."

She beamed, then paused and raised an eyebrow. "You fly?"

Aurelia knew what she meant. The little girl wanted to know if Aurelia ever pretended to be a bird, too. Humans could swim like fish and walk on their hands and knees like monkeys, but they couldn't fly. Pretending was the closest they ever came.

The Queen of Akkinor, on the other hand, was different.

A dizzy spell washed over her as she wrapped her fingers around the locket. "Yes." Her voice sounded distant and hazy, as if it were not her own. "I know what it is to fly."

For all she knew, she was the only person alive who did.

XIII

Aurelia ran her fingers along the cool, damp fabric of the shirt she'd been wearing for the last few days. It still wasn't dry, so she changed into a new outfit she'd stolen from the bathhouse of an inn with Kaia. It was more Carthinian for certain, but she didn't like wearing something that identified her as a native. Though her goal was to keep her identity hidden, she liked having a piece of Akkinor with her—even something as simple as the stitching of trousers or the comfortable soles of riding boots.

The tavern was quiet (most travelers didn't like stopping in the middle of the Violet Forest), and the only visitors present, like Aurelia, had come solely for the bathhouse. Kaia had warned her not to stop—travelers would steal Scotch if they saw him in the stables. People would wait for her to leave if they saw her enter the tavern, especially if they noticed the coin pouch hanging from her belt. Nowhere was safe in the Violet Forest, but after ten days alone out there, she desperately needed a change of scenery.

When she paid the clerk for the soap she'd purchased, she asked, "How much farther to Dofell?"

"Few miles. Maybe you could make it there by tomorrow or the day after." He counted the coin and poured it into a linen bag. "Can I get you something for your travels?"

"Bread would be fantastic. Maybe a pouch of candied nuts, too, if you wouldn't mind."

The old man blushed when he saw her smiling at him. "Of course. Three silver, please."

She exchanged the coin for food. "Thank you. I greatly appreciate your hospitality. You've been far too kind."

He blushed again. "Good luck out there, lass."

She thanked him with a slight nod of her head. He counted the coins and quickly realized she'd given him an extra two pieces of silver. When he smiled at her, she saw a mouth full of yellow or missing teeth. She knew it was unwise to give away unnecessary coin, but she wouldn't be herself if she turned a blind eye to someone in need. People didn't smile much in Carthe, she noticed, and she didn't like that one bit.

Outside, Aurelia found her horse in the stables. "Good morning, Scotch. I'm sorry we couldn't rest more than we did. It's time to leave again."

He didn't respond. She knew he'd never talk back to her, but she needed *someone* to talk to. Her short interaction with little Liat and baby Jaco had given her a taste of what it was like to be human again, and ever since, the deafening silence of solitude had only worsened.

She didn't know what happened to the children after she left them in the clearing, and she didn't *want* to know. The terrible possibilities were endless. She felt horrible for leaving them alone, but they were better off without her. Everyone was.

She chatted to Scotch as she tied her pack to his saddle, climbed on his back, and led him towards the dirt road. She decided it was safe to take the main road to Dofell, as she was close enough now to take such a risk, so she kept her eyes peeled and her ears on high alert.

As they rode, Scotch started to snort. She put a hand on his mane to sooth him, but he soon began trotting in place and shaking his head like an insect was nibbling at his face. She tried to find the source of the problem, but he was moving too quickly and too aggressively for her to get a good look. When he started walking backwards, she tightened her grip on the reins and murmured comforting words.

"It's all right, Scotch. It's just the two of us here. Nothing to worry about."

He didn't settle. She carefully dismounted and tried to approach him from the front, but she didn't get the chance. As soon as her feet were on the ground, something from behind whacked her in the back and sent her plummeting. Scotch was spooked by the sudden interruption and galloped off into the woods, leaving Aurelia alone in the dirt. As she brought herself to her feet, a formidable force shoved her backwards until she came in contact with the thick bark of a nearby tree. Her head was spinning, and as she slowly regained her stability, she saw two men pinning her against the tree with hunger in their eyes.

"Release me at once!" she shouted. "You have no—"

"Shut up!" One of the men revealed yellowed teeth and near-black gums when he snarled at her and wrapped his hand around her throat. She couldn't bring herself to speak even when the other man bound her hands above her head with rope. "Pretty girls should know better than to go walking through these woods alone."

She struggled, trying to kick him or bite him or *something*, but it was impossible. The second man, sallow and stout with eyes like slate, looped her arms through a branch above her head. The branch was so high that her heels just barely grazed the grass. While she strained and hollered, one of the men ran his hands along her sides as the other untied his pants.

Her eyes widened. "No. No—"

"*Quiet!*" The gray-eyed man untied the front of her pants and punched her in the gut when she tried to kick him. He wrapped his hand around her throat while she gasped for air. "Save yer screams, girl. There will be plenty of time for that soon enough."

She spat at him. He only grinned as a thick, bubbling wad of saliva dripped down his cheek. He made no effort to wipe it away.

When she felt his breath on her neck, she lifted her knee into his groin with all the strength she could muster. He cursed and stumbled backwards, nearly falling to his knees, as the yellow-eyed man yanked her hair back and held a knife to her throat. He pressed his face against her shoulder and inhaled, making bile rise up in her throat, while his free hand grazed the side of her leg. She struggled still, even as the other man came towards her again, and prayed for a miracle while begging for her release.

The man with the yellow teeth didn't seem bothered by her resistance. In fact, it seemed to fuel him. While his partner held her back by her hair, the knife still pressed against her throat, he grabbed the front of her shirt and tore it open. She yelped as her underthings were exposed, her new shirt torn in half, and her pants now riding low on her hips. She closed her eyes and told herself to be strong, but she knew in her heart that she would not.

Then she heard something.

She barely had time to react as an arrow pierced the bark of the tree, just above the man's head as he held her from behind. While he ducked, the other man simply released her and turned with his hand on his sword. A man appeared from within the foliage, a bow in his hand and an enormous sword sheathed at his side. She recognized the bow and the sheath slung over his shoulder: both were hers.

He nocked another arrow. "I'd suggest you do as the lady requested, gentlemen. You won't receive another warning."

"Get out of here, boy," the gray-eyed man snarled. "Find yer own or mind yer business."

The man cocked his head to the side. "I believe the lady asked you—several times, actually—to release her. There are plenty of whores for filth like you in the brothels." As he strode towards them, both of Aurelia's captors pointed their weapons at him. He set the bow down and raised his hands in defense. "I want no trouble. I cannot, however, allow you to treat a lady with such foulness."

"We only gonna tell ye one more time." The man with the yellow teeth pointed the tip of his skinny sword at the stranger's chest. "Get outta here or die wit her. Take yer pick."

Aurelia's heart hammered. She stared at the stranger, hoping he was as gallant as he seemed, but she couldn't make sense of what he was thinking. She wouldn't have been surprised if he valued his life more than hers and left her at the rapists' mercy.

Finally, he exhaled. "Very well. I do wish you'd done as the lady asked. I'd hate to get blood on my clothing."

In the blink of an eye, his sword was drawn and the man with the yellow teeth was choking on his own blood. Aurelia barely had time to react before the gray-eyed man behind her charged the stranger. When he raised his sword, she managed to kick him in the back of the legs. He fell to his knees, giving the stranger the opportunity to cut his throat without making a sound. In less than a minute, both of her captors were lying in puddles of their own blood.

"That was invigorating," the stranger declared, running a hand through his hair. He gazed down at his clothing and beamed. "And not a drop of blood on my new trousers!" When she cleared her throat, he looked up and chuckled a bit. "Oh, yes. Apologies."

She stared into his eyes as he untied her wrists. "Thank you. I owe you my life. How can I repay you?"

"I don't believe in debts." As soon as her hands were free and her feet touched the ground again, she quickly redressed herself, though she was forced to wear her shirt backwards because of the massive rip across the front. The stranger, like a proper gentleman, averted his gaze from her exposed body. "It was the right thing to do. I found your horse wandering, and I couldn't believe someone would leave behind such an impressive bow and a full sheath of arrows. I've tied him up with my horse. I do hope everything belongs to you. If not, now you have a horse and a bow."

She chuckled. "It all belongs to me." While he sheathed his sword, she extended her hand for him to shake. "Lily Linden. It's a pleasure to meet you."

"Jack Sherbourne." As they shook hands, she noticed the strange placement of his thumb—tucked under her hand rather than over it so their thumbs were interlinked. He seemed to notice the way *her* thumb was placed, too. Something flashed in his eyes as they neglected to release one another. "I haven't seen another Akkinorian so far into Carthe in years," he drawled.

"You're the first I've come across," she replied, telling him a fraction of the truth. When they retracted their hands, neither broke eye contact. "I arrived about four weeks ago. Maybe less, maybe more. I don't know. Yourself?"

"It's been over five years for me."

She couldn't hide her surprise. *"Five years?"*

Amusement danced in his eyes. "Little was left for me in Akkinor. It was never much of a challenge. Carthe has been an experience, to say the least. And you? What's a lovely Akkinorian woman doing in Carthe by herself?"

She studied him, starting with the silly smile on his face that looked both innocent and wicked at the same time. It was wicked, she decided, after seeing the way it matched his gaze. His big blue eyes were much darker than hers with patches of gray and green that reminded her of seafoam. It was like waves were cresting over the surface of the ocean, right there in his cunning eyes. He was tanned from the sun—extremely tanned, judging by the pale lines on his wrist where he wore leather bracelets. His thick black hair was wavy and unruly with wisps falling over his forehead and into his eyes. His nose was rather large, but then again, so was everything about him. He towered over her like a subspecies of giant, and now that he was closer to her, she wondered why her would-be rapists hadn't bolted at the mere sight of him.

"Your use of the word *woman* is disheartening," she accused, walking uphill towards the horses. He wasn't far behind. "It's not normal for *any* Akkinorian to be wandering through Carthe, and yet, here we are. You believe it perfectly suitable for yourself to be here, but not for a woman. Why is that?"

"I meant no offense. I was only speaking due to recent occurrences. You must be careful here. Carthe has plenty of terrible people and not enough laws to keep them contained. They're looking for people like you."

"I've noticed." She rubbed Scotch's nose as she slung her bow and sheath over her shoulders. "If you must know, I'm in Carthe because I wish to find someone. I've learned that he's most likely residing in Taundosa. That's where I'm going."

"What a coincidence! I'm on my way to Taundosa, too. Shall we accompany one another?"

"I appreciate the offer and your help today, but I'd much rather continue on my own," Aurelia muttered as she climbed on Scotch's back. She was now looking down at Jack rather than up, but only by a few inches. "Thank you again. Good luck on your travels."

"It's nearly impossible to cross the Ngora Valley on one's own," he said pointedly as she turned Scotch away from him. "You'll have better luck with an ally!"

"I'm better off alone than with someone who eats for three," she grumbled under her breath.

"I heard that."

Aurelia rolled her eyes. She led Scotch away from the clearing and released a long, tired exhale. Her body was still sore from where the men had beaten her, and she knew she'd be smelling the foulness of their breath for the next fortnight. Besides the assassins from her homeland and Kaia's murder, she'd been somewhat lucky on her journey. No Carthinian had tried to attack her until that day. A part of her hadn't realized how dangerous they actually were. Maybe *that's* why she was attacked—because she wasn't as cautious as she should've been.

Her ears pricked when she heard something from behind. She barely had time to look over her shoulder before Jack appeared beside her. Again, he towered over her, just as his sleek black horse towered over Scotch. The size of his stallion made Scotch look like a mule.

"What are you doing?" she demanded.

"I'm following you," he declared. She started to protest, but he talked over her. "I'll ride with you until we reach the road. If I haven't convinced you to let me join you, then I'm certain we'll see one another at the border of the valley. We can go our separate ways and hope that life leads us back to one another." She snorted. The sound made him grin. "Why are you so convinced you must travel this great distance on your own?"

"You have your reasons for leaving Akkinor and I have mine. I can't afford the liability of a two-hundred-pound veteran Akkinorian swordsman at my side." When his lips parted and his eyebrows lifted, she exhaled. "I know a soldier when I see one, and you're far too skilled with a sword to be just anyone."

He chuckled. "Clever. Even alone, we're in danger here. But if we're together, we have a better chance at surviving to see another day. It's fascinating when you think about it. There are only a handful of Akkinorians on this continent, yet two of us managed to find each other today. Two of us, both fearful of our own kin, aiming for the same destination. It's marvelously poetic."

She hesitated. "I thought Akkinor was boring you. Now you say you're fearful of our people. Telling me that you're being hunted isn't a very wise persuasion tactic, you know."

"*Hunted* is a strong word, and one that came from your lips, not mine," he said with a laugh. Her cheeks grew hot with embarrassment. "Both are partly true. I may have left Akkinor eventually, but the target on my back was particularly convincing at the time."

Aurelia stared at him. He seemed normal enough, and if he wanted to hurt her, he would've done so by now. He could've stolen her supplies when he found Scotch and left her for dead. Instead, he saved her life, killed two men in the process, and was now practically begging to join her. She didn't know why. Maybe he felt safer with somebody at his side, or maybe he needed some sort of pawn. She wondered if he could've been an assassin, too, but she pushed the thought from her brain. An assassin would've waited for the two men to have their way with her before killing whatever was left of her in the name of her usurper.

Jack Sherbourne wasn't there to hurt her. He was there because something had forced him to escape their country, and he'd decided to start his life anew in Carthe. Aurelia might've ended up in the same position if she failed to find Arian Cristos.

Still, she had to ask: "How do I know you aren't an assassin from Akkinor? Or someone who would kidnap me and sell me for profit?"

"I'm Omaran."

Those two words were enough to make her understand. He must've known it, too, just as he must've known that he should've begun with that when he decided to pursue her.

Omara was the newest kingdom to join the nation of Akkinor, and it was also the most different from the others. The scenic landscape was as pristine as it was centuries ago, as it was never ravaged by war and reduced to ruins. Omarans weren't fighters—the nobles only rallied their soldiers and their bannermen when the situation was dire. In fact, they didn't engage in any type of violent behavior without a dignified cause.

It was no wonder he'd risked his life to save her—such kindness was etched into the bones and souls of the Omaran people.

His blue eyes shimmered. "Have I passed your tests, Lily of Akkinor? Am I permitted to travel with you?"

"I promised myself I'd do this alone. I already lost one friend since I arrived here." She glanced down at her hands on the reins as a sudden thickness coated her throat. Despite her tireless efforts to scrub it away, Kaia's blood still lingered beneath her fingernails. "I'd hate to put your life in danger, too."

"Our lives are constantly in danger here. It makes no difference if we're alone or together. What matters is surviving, which we have a better chance of doing if we're together." He looked over at her, amused. "You don't have to trust me, you know. I don't exactly trust you, either, but we've already worked so well together—it'd be a shame to separate us so soon."

She paused. She thought about Kaia, whose short life had been taken from her because she decided to help a stranger. The same was possible for Jack, but Kaia was a Carthinian native, and Jack wasn't. He could've been promised wealth, women, or anything else his heart desired by Akkinorians. They'd trade anything for Aurelia. She didn't doubt that he'd betray her for those assurances. Even so, he was right: she'd never make it across the Ngora Valley by herself. She'd barely made it through the Violet Forest by herself. If she was going to find Arian Cristos, she needed an ally.

She sighed. "Fine. You may accompany me for now, but I reserve the right to continue in solitude if I'm even the *least* bit displeased with you. I don't anticipate that you and I will last long together, Mister Sherbourne. You'd be wise to remember that."

"Understood." His smile brightened as he stared straight ahead at the road. She thought of something that made her chuckle, which captured his attention. He glanced over at her and raised an eyebrow. "What on earth is so funny?"

"I don't understand. I've met two people so far who've begged to accompany me in spite of the threat of impending assassination."

Jack turned away from her again, smiling. "I suppose the thrill of it entices me."

XIV

*I*n light of gold the story was told
a tale of glory and creatures of old.
Fires of man and god burned bright
on land and sea to the sailor's delight.
To children and babes on their mother's breast
to the Great King and his royal guest."

A low, aggravated growl emerged from deep within Aurelia's throat. She resisted the urge to look over her shoulder at her unwanted accomplice, knowing her attention would only fuel him further. So long as she proceeded to ignore him, she hoped he'd become less tempted to rattle her at every opportunity.

Jack Sherbourne had been following Aurelia for exactly one day. She was less grateful for the company and more frustrated by his apparent lack of incentive. There she was, a monarch searching for a way home to her country and her people, traveling with a man whose primary concern was reciting an archaic Akkinorian poem as if he were performing it for the queen herself (which, of course, he was).

He knew he was irking her, just as he knew that it was in his best interest to remain several paces behind her if he didn't wish for a scolding so ear-splitting it frightened the birds from the trees. He was observant—she'd give him that much—but he was a nuisance if nothing else, too.

"*In light of gold the story was—*"

"For heavens' sake!" Yanking Scotch's reins, Aurelia maneuvered so they were positioned sideways, thus blocking Jack's path. He quickly slowed his horse, Sterling, to a stop and scowled at her. "Must you continue repeating that horrid poem?"

"It isn't horrid. It's historical."

"It was written by the son of a Holosi soldier who fought in Oleander's Rebellion for *two days* before he was injured. There's nothing historical about it, Jack. It's just a silly piece of literature."

He wrinkled his nose, though the fullness of his cheeks and the wobbling corners of his lips suggested he was refraining from laughter. "Not fond of poetry, are you, Lily dear?"

A shiver raced up and down her spine. "Don't call me that." Now he *did* laugh, and the sound made her even more irritated than she'd been before. Remembering her power, Aurelia sat up straighter on the saddle and urged Scotch forwards again. "You'll do well to remember that I'm not in any danger at present, and therefore, I'm not in need of your protection. If you continue to behave like a child, I shall be on my merry way, and we may meet again in the desert. Gods willing, of course."

"Of course." He rode up beside her, ignoring her scoffs and protests, and offered her a cheeky grin. "They won't allow you into Dofell on your own, you know. They have a certain suspicion of lone travelers. If you wish to cross the gates into the valley, you must have someone with you. Everyone knows that. Everyone except for you, apparently."

Aurelia gritted her teeth and swallowed the less-than-respectable retaliation she had planned for him. Even if she didn't fully trust him, she knew he was right. Kaia had told her something similar about Dofell. Whether she liked it or not, she needed Jack to reach and cross the kingdom. That, or she'd be forced to join other travelers under some sort of ruse. She wasn't fond of that idea.

"Fine." She tightened her grip on the reins. "Get behind me. I can't bear to hear your incredibly obnoxious breathing from such a close proximity."

"Gee, thanks."

Ignoring him, she urged Scotch forwards to increase his pace while Jack fell behind. *He follows commands, at least,* she thought. She was eternally grateful for the Omaran soldier trapped somewhere inside Jack Sherbourne. Without his former profession to balance him, she would've smothered him in his sleep with his own blanket.

Aurelia's opportunity to enjoy the serenity of the forest was quickly interrupted by Jack's voice: "How do you do? I'm well, thank you."

"Jack!"

"What?" he said innocently. When she cast a glance over her shoulder, she huffed immediately at the silly, ridiculous grin on his face. "Since *you* refuse to speak to me, I've turned to the trees. I need company of some sort if I'm to survive this journey."

Exhausted, Aurelia ignored him and continued to ride, lacking the energy she required to argue with him again. Soon enough, as they brushed low branches from their faces and navigated their horses through uneven ground, she found herself smiling while listening to the one-sided conversation Jack was having with the trees. She realized she hadn't smiled—a real, joyous smile—since before Kaia died.

It felt wonderful.

The closest she'd come to such a smile had been during her brief encounter with little Liat and baby Jaco. She'd thought of them often since meeting Jack. A guilt-ridden part of her wondered if the children would've had a better chance of surviving if she'd taken them with her—after all, she'd met Jack only days after leaving the children, and a man like him would've known exactly where to take them. Another part of her, though, believed Liat could keep both herself and her brother alive. Liat bore powerful magic for one so young, and the odds of her survival were greater because of it.

Thoughts of the children compelled her to speak again. "May I ask you something, Jack?"

"Oh, please do!"

She bit her cheeks to keep from chuckling. "Have you encountered much magic in the time you've been in Carthe?" When he didn't reply, she added, "I only ask—"

"—because our country is void of magic, and you wish to know more about it." He was riding beside her now so she could see him (and smell him, gods help her) with perfect ease. "Mages and magical creatures may be free here in Carthe, but their numbers have dwindled more and more with each passing day. It used to be that one couldn't avoid spotting a magical creature in these woods. Today, individuals are considered fortunate to have seen one."

"You count yourself as a fortunate one, then?"

"I've seen my fair share. Mutated dragons, as you know, are commonly used here in Carthe as domesticated servants. They're difficult to miss. I saw a basilisk once when crossing the valley, but they're not the terrifying beasts they once were. Evolution has changed them. The average size of the basilisk has decreased significantly—no larger than a common rattlesnake. They no longer bear the ability to inflict death for humans by making eye contact with their victims, either. I suppose we've become immune to it."

Aurelia frowned. "I can't decide if that's tragic or favorable."

"For us, it's favorable. For the basilisk, it's an utter tragedy." He tossed a sidelong glance at her and smiled. "Do you know what I'd like to see most before I die?"

"I haven't a clue."

"I'd like to visit the Syren Isles. Many Carthinian sailors who travel there claim to have seen sirens off the coasts of the islands. I'm desperate to know if the sailors were lucky or mad."

"Haven't you heard the tales?"

He shook his head. "I haven't. Tell me, won't you?"

For the next several minutes, Aurelia told Jack the story exactly as it'd been told to her by her father. Edmund had loved a good story, and this one—even if it hadn't been proven beyond a reasonable doubt—was a favorite of his.

It was said that, during and after the persecution, the Isalders sought to save one species and one species only: sirens. The subspecies of mermaid, known for casting spells on sailors via song and luring them to their deaths, lived exclusively in the north of the realm. Many ancient intellectuals believed that sirens lived in underwater cave systems beneath the archipelago south of Glacier Bay. Hence, the chain of islands was called *the Syren Isles.*

To protect Glacier Bay from enemies—pirates, rogue Carthinians, and even some Akkinorians—the Isalders made a deal with the sirens: they would be protected from harm so long as they used their power not on the Isalders, but on other civilizations.

Nobody knew for certain if the sirens still existed. The Isalder king who'd ruled during the persecution claimed his men had murdered the sirens to prevent other world leaders from hunting them in Isalder territory. No one suspected that the sirens survived the persecution until many years later. Even in Aurelia's lifetime, it was still a great debate across the realm—the Isalders, however, refused to contribute to the speculation.

When the sun began to set, Aurelia realized that she and Jack must've been conversing for hours. She'd hardly noticed how much time had passed until the sky darkened. Since her initial inquiry, there hadn't been a moment of silence, awkwardness, or aggravation between the two. It almost felt like she'd been conversing with an old friend.

She was glad to have someone to talk to, someone to answer her questions, someone to laugh with—it was the only thing that made her feel less alone than she was.

***

Unable to sleep, Aurelia pushed herself up on her elbows and looked to her left. Jack was sleeping on the ground a safe distance away from her. She refused to let him sleep within several yards of her; she'd spent one night with her newest ally, and she was still unsure if he could be trusted. The last thing she wanted was to be betrayed by him while she was unable to defend herself.

Even so, he was grateful for his knowledge and companionship. She finally had someone to talk to other than Scotch—and an Akkinorian, no less. That, and Jack was perhaps as skilled at surviving in the Carthinian wilderness as Kaia had been. If Aurelia didn't know any better, she might've assumed that he, too, was a native Carthinian.

For the most part, Kaia had been insistent that the pair of them sleep in shifts. When one was sleeping, the other was keeping an eye out for potential threats. Jack had chuckled (almost patronizingly) and brushed her off when Aurelia questioned who would take the first shift as watchman. He had his own methods of keeping watch, methods so clever that Aurelia couldn't help but wonder where he'd learned them. He'd reached for whatever was nearby—empty bottles stolen from taverns, rope from his pack, twigs, stones—and fastened them together to create what she *thought* was a trap.

"It's not a trap," he'd corrected. "It's a warning bell."

As he must have done a thousand times before, Jack established a perimeter around their campsite and spread his contraptions around the grass in a circular formation. As he did so, he explained that no intruder (animal and human alike) could enter the circle without stepping on the contraptions, nor could the contraptions be avoided when concealed by leaves and darkness. When an intruder stepped on any part of the contraption, a chain reaction of thunderous noises followed, thus alerting them of any approaching threats.

Aurelia hadn't been convinced. "This doesn't seem practical. It's possible that this creation of yours could fail, and we'll both be dead before we have the chance to defend ourselves."

"I've survived on this continent for five years by trusting this method, and still you doubt me?" he'd asked. She'd rolled her eyes at him as he clutched his heart with both hands. "You wound me."

"This isn't a joke, Jack. You're leaving our lives in the hands of twigs and bottles."

He'd sighed, now somber as he sensed her genuine fear. "I learned this from a native Carthinian of eight-and-fifty years. Back then, I had no choice but to trust the word of a man who knew every survival tactic ever attempted on this soil. Now I'm asking you to trust the word of a man whose life has been saved by this trick more times than I care to admit. Can you do that for me, love?"

Gnawing on her lower lip as she contemplated, Aurelia offered him a reluctant nod. "I will trust you," she decided, "and you will cease calling me *love* this instant."

A silly grin formed on his lips. "As you wish."

Now, one day later as she lay awake at the center of a booby trap, she wondered if she had the cleverness to continue on her own. Between Kaia's death and meeting Jack, Aurelia had slept with one eye open each and every night. She'd been so exhausted from being half-conscious at all times that she'd often fallen asleep on Scotch's back. She'd had no choice but to pray that she roused herself in time to flee if she were attacked. She never would've thought to use empty liquor bottles and twigs as makeshift warning bells.

She still couldn't make up her mind about Jack Sherbourne, and she still didn't feel comfortable endangering yet another ally. She hadn't decided whether she'd allow Jack to join her for the remainder of her quest. On one hand, she needed his knowledge and expertise not only to reach Dofell, but to cross the Ngora Valley into Taundosa. On the other, she had more than enough coin to purchase a traveling guide whose job it was to take people from the gates of Dofell to the gates of Taundosa.

She could slip away while Jack slept and carry on without him. The opportunity was right there, waiting for her to take it.

She realized then—when the only sound for miles was Jack's snoring—that she didn't want to carry on without him. It wasn't because of his company or his experiences, either. It was because Jack Sherbourne was the closest thing she had to home, and without him, she feared Akkinor would slip from her grasp.

She wondered what was happening at home at that moment. Had the usurpers been identified and apprehended, or had they managed to seize control of Akkinor? If the usurpers *had* been defeated, did that mean that Aurelia's closest allies—Linden, Archie, her advisors—were searching tirelessly for her? And if the usurpers were still there, sitting on her throne and wearing her crown, what did that mean for the state of her country? Her people?

The more she thought about it, the more she realized that it was foolish of her to believe her usurpers had been defeated. Rather than assassins tracking her throughout Carthe, it would've been Linden and more than half of the Royal Army. Linden didn't need to wonder to know where she'd gone—he only needed to visit the little house in Seaport with the blue door and hydrangeas on the messenger box. The elderly couple would've told him exactly what happened after Aurelia arrived at their home, and after that, all of Akkinor would be scouring Carthe for their queen.

That left one of two conclusions: either Linden was dead, leaving nobody to know where Aurelia might've fled to during the uprising, or the usurpers still controlled Akkinor, making it impossible for anyone with loyalties to her to go on searching.

She wouldn't find these answers while in Carthe—news from Akkinor meant extraordinarily little to the natives, and it was doubtful that word from Akkinor had spread to Carthe in the time since the uprising. If it had, Jack might've realized that he wasn't traveling alongside a peasant girl called Lily Linden, but rather Aurelia Brentwood, Queen of Akkinor.

Aurelia would never know what was happening in Akkinor until she found Arian Cristos. Until then, she couldn't distract herself with theories and possibilities. Nothing she'd conjure in her head would come close to satisfying her desperate craving for the truth. For now, the only thing she could worry about was what was directly in front of her: a massive, charming Omaran swordsman with a fascination for magic and talking to inanimate objects.

XV

urelia blew a sweaty lock of hair from her face as she filled a canteen in a stream. A gust of wind forced her to inhale the scent of her own body odor. She wrinkled her nose and held her breath as she waited for the smell to pass. She'd almost gotten used to it by that point—*almost*.

She gathered the freshly filled canteens from the ground and returned to the campsite. Jack was thoroughly concentrated as he struggled to use giant leaves as shade from the boiling Carthinian sun. Aurelia glanced down at her red, blistered skin as it burned beneath the warm golden light. Kaia had never been worried about sun poisoning, as she was practically immune to the harsh weather of her homelands, but Aurelia's fair skin seemed perpetually angry at her. Jack's blisters matched her own. Clothing just wasn't enough to protect their sensitive Akkinorian skin from the boiling sun.

"Thank you, lovely," he mused when she returned with the canteens. She ignored his comment as he hefted a rabbit from the ground. "This little creature came for a visit while you were gone. Now we have dinner."

"Wonderful." She crafted a spit for the fire while he finished building the shelter. "How much longer? I thought we would've reached Dofell by now."

"Tomorrow." He pointed east through a clearing. "There's a river up ahead. Travelers stop there regularly, but it's dangerous. Natives are constantly waiting for victims and opportunities by the river. If not, that's where we'd be. Dofell is on the other side of the river. It's getting dark now, though. I don't recommend crossing the river when darkness isn't our friend."

She understood that well enough. The sun was starting to set, so they had a few moments to cook their dinner before it was time to stamp the fire out. Jack and Kaia both told her that natives tended to lurk closer to the border of Dofell, so anything could be used as a signal: smoke, fire, horses, loud talkers. If the river was as popular as Jack claimed, it wasn't safe for them to cross until morning.

"I've got this." Jack took his hunting knife in one hand and the rabbit in the other. "You can go clean up while this is cooking. I've seen you gag at your own scent three times today."

Her face flushed. "This isn't exactly normal for me. This isn't normal for anyone in Akkinor. I'd be charmed to know how *you* became so accustomed to life in the wilderness." He snorted into a laugh. "You read my mind, though. I won't take long."

"No, please. Take as long as you need."

She gave him a nasty look, making him chuckle. While he prepared dinner, she practically ran back to the stream and stripped off her clothing. That was something she liked about Jack—even if he *could* see her at the bottom of the hill, he wouldn't have looked. She could bathe peacefully without having to worry about someone watching her from behind a tree.

She still had a sliver of soap from the last bathhouse she'd visited, but it'd gone faster than she'd hoped. She had no choice but to wash most of her body, hair, and clothing in nothing but stream water. When she was as clean as possible, she dressed in her spare outfit and squeezed water from her sopping hair. She was pulling her locks into a braid when someone approached from behind and covered her mouth with a thick, clammy hand. A shriek rose up her throat, but it disappeared when she saw Jack from the corner of her eye. He was slowly walking them backwards, still covering her mouth with his hand, and redirecting her towards the campsite.

When he released her, she stared at him with wide eyes. For a moment, she thought he was betraying her. Then she saw him raise a finger to his lips, telling her to stay silent. He turned and pointed towards something in the distance. When she followed his gaze, she saw a mountainous plume of smoke rising into the sky.

They tied their belongings to the horses' saddles, strapped their weapons to their bodies, and destroyed any trace of their presence there. Jack tied the skinned rabbit to Sterling's saddle and broke the spit into pieces. When Aurelia put her foot in one of Scotch's stirrups, preparing to mount, Jack shook his head and gestured to the reins. With a frown, she stepped down and grabbed Scotch's reins to walk him through the forest rather than ride him.

"Jack—"

"It's the Bobolon tribe. They're bonded with the tribes in the Ngora Valley, so they tend to lurk in this area. They're known for sending smoke signals when they spot prey."

She didn't understand. "So why are we leaving?"

He stared at her. "We're the prey, Lily. The Bobolons are cannibals."

"Jack—"

"Just keep moving. We have to get as far from here as possible. The signal summoned the tribesmen back to base camp so they can form a hunting party. Try to be as quiet as you can. We may not be able to see them, but we'll certainly hear them."

Aurelia didn't say a word. She bit the insides of her cheeks so hard that she tasted blood filling her mouth. When she looked up, the sight of an amber glow kissing the midnight blue sky told her that the sun was only a few moments away from setting. It was dangerous enough to travel through the forest at nighttime, but with a tribe of cannibals on their trail...she hoped Jack was as decent at surviving as he claimed to be. Hearing about the tribes was one thing, but interacting with them was something she never wanted to experience.

Jack brought them to a halt when voices echoed through the foliage. They hid behind a few thick trees and peered through the bushes to get a better look. A small group of travelers sat around a fire in a clearing. A man was cutting away at a fox trap while his companions tended to the fire and built a spit.

A rustling sound made Aurelia's ears perk. It was quiet—so faint that she wondered if she'd imagined it—but she trusted her gut and followed the sound with her eyes. When she looked up at the trees towering over them, she froze as her heart pounded rapidly in her chest. A young man was perched in the branches, partially concealed by the trees, with a bow in hand and an arrow ready to fly. He wore nothing but a pair of filthy, too-small trousers, torn and frayed at the knees, and a leather holster for carrying weapons strapped to his back. Every inch of him was painted with mud and adorned with twigs and leaves for camouflage. Had it not been for the whites of his eyes gleaming through the darkness, she wouldn't have seen him.

"Jack." She set a trembling hand on his arm. He paid her no attention as he scoped an escape route. "J-Jack."

He finally met her eyes. When he saw that she was looking above him, he followed her gaze and inhaled sharply. The travelers at the campsite were laughing loudly, completely oblivious to what was happening behind them.

That's when Jack grabbed Aurelia's waist, pulled her close to his chest, and removed his sword from its sheath. He lifted his sword and slashed through the air in time to deflect an arrow shot by the cannibal in the trees. He shouted commands at her while the tribesman made an earsplitting, high-pitched noise deep in his throat. Aurelia and Jack barely had time to mount their horses before the rest of the tribe responded to the signal. They were all around, invisible in the trees and in the darkness, and they'd be upon the pair in moments.

Aurelia held her breath as Scotch galloped through the forest behind Jack and Sterling. The travelers gasped in alarm when the pair cut through the campsite and knocked two of them to the ground. They didn't stop to look over their shoulders as they attempted to gain as much distance as possible. The sound of screaming and whooping echoed through the forest. When Aurelia finally mustered the courage to look back, she saw the campers' fire had been completely stamped out. An ear-piercing shriek echoed throughout the trees, closely followed by a battle cry that made her stomach churn.

"Jack," she called, "w-we have to go back for them! We have—"

"Don't look! We have to keep moving! Don't look at them, Lily!"

She didn't have to look. She could still hear their screams. Jack and Aurelia had escaped the tribe, but the campers weren't so lucky. Even if they'd been warned, they wouldn't have had time to escape. That was the only thing that brought Aurelia peace. If she and Jack had tried to help, the tribe would've claimed six bodies rather than four.

When they were a safe distance away, Jack slowed Sterling's pace, and Aurelia mimicked him. They rode side-by-side, breathless and trembling, as both struggled to relax after nearly looking death in the face. If the campers hadn't been ruthlessly butchered, Aurelia might've laughed at their grand escape. Instead, all she could do was think about what the tribe had done to them.

She mirrored him when he dismounted Sterling, opting to walk the rest of the way, and found it nearly impossible to place one foot in front of the other, what with the formidable trembling of her knees hindering her movements. Without Scotch to steady her, the combination of terror and guilt bubbling up in her gut would've sent her plummeting to the ground.

"Jack—"

"There was nothing we could do." He was still shaking, his skin was a sickly shade of green, and his knuckles white as he gripped Sterling's reins. "It was us or them."

"W-We have to go back. Maybe someone...maybe someone survived."

"The Bobolons don't leave survivors." A raspy, haunted tone usurped his voice, which was usually charismatic and smooth. "Their brutality is something I've witnessed more times than I can count. Being a traveler in Carthe requires extreme selfishness, unfortunately."

"We can't just go on our way like nothing happened. We-We have to at least *ensure* that everyone was killed. What if the tribe *did* leave survivors? What if someone is wounded and awaiting rescue? What if—"

"*Lily.*" A sudden ferocity filled his voice as he dropped Sterling's reins and held out his arm to halt the horses. As she watched him, her eyes wide with alarm and her chest rising and falling with every shaking breath, he placed his massive hands on either side of her face and looked deeply into her eyes. "Take a breath. You'll harm yourself if you fall into a panic."

"I-I can't calm down, Jack! I can't move on without knowing if-if…"

"They're gone, lovely." His fingers, so long they disappeared into her hair, tensed against her scalp as he rubbed his thumbs along her cheeks. "If we go back, we'll find nothing but the remains of their camp and however many tribesmen are still lingering there. It's a trick of theirs—they stay behind waiting for travelers seeking to steal whatever supplies the campers left behind."

Aurelia's chin trembled. "The campers—"

"—were innocent, just as we are." Now that her breathing had stabilized, he removed his hands from her face and pulled her into a soothing embrace. Desperate for comfort, she wrapped her arms around his middle and pressed her cheek against his warm chest. "The Bobolons care not for who they target. Princess or rapist, nobleman or thief, native or foreigner. They take what they can get and leave nothing behind."

Her eyelids fluttered shut. "How many times have you seen something like that?"

"You've been here four weeks. You lost one friend in that time. I've been walking these woods for five years, and you're not the first friend I've made."

She said nothing. They were still getting to know one another, but she knew less than she wanted to about Jack. Five years was a long time for an Akkinorian to be in Carthe. He had his reasons, she knew that, but he'd experienced more than she could imagine in that time. She wondered if she'd ever hear about the things that happened to him—or maybe his past was as much of a secret as hers.

***

145

Jack didn't seem happy when they reached the river. It was long and wide, stretching as far as Aurelia could see in either direction, and the current was too strong for them to cross in the dark. Luckily, there were no other travelers nearby. That didn't stop Jack from keeping an eye out while he led them towards a colossal cluster of boulders to their right. Once again, he proved his familiarity with the land when he showed her a cave hidden within the boulders. They quietly tied Scotch and Sterling to a grove of trees behind the rocks, then ducked inside with their supplies and tried to feel their way through the darkness.

Aurelia ran her hands along the cold, damp rock walls of the cave. It reminded her of the tunnels within the Palace of Akkinor. She hadn't thought about the night she escaped in some time. For the last few weeks, the only thing on her mind was finding Arian Cristos and returning home, but now, the small reminder of that night made bile rise up in her throat. She could still hear her people begging for mercy, smell the sickening aroma of burning flesh, and feel the terror in Linden's body as he led her to safety. Those things would stay with her until the end of her days—she was sure of it.

Jack left for a few moments and returned with an armful of twigs and logs for a fire. As soon as the fire blazed, the cave was cast in a warm orange glow, and Aurelia could see clearly again. Bugs crawled along the ground, water leaked from the walls and the ceiling, and there was barely room enough for both of them to lay comfortably. While Jack tended to the fire, Aurelia spread out their blankets and tried to organize a makeshift campsite.

Neither of them spoke as they burrowed beneath their blankets. They'd wordlessly agreed not to eat the rabbit, as the events of the evening had caused both of them to lose their appetites. Aurelia only had one blanket, so she was forced to lay on the ground while using her shawl as a pillow. Their backs were facing one another, but they were so close that she could feel every breath he took. He normally fell asleep quickly while she struggled to drift off, though that night was different. She wondered if he was thinking about the people he'd lost in Carthe; she certainly was.

"Jack?"

"Hmm?"

"What happened to the friends you made here?"

He took a deep breath. "I met Varn in Caedia. He was as Carthinian as they come: a native of Kanibar whose family line traced back to the old days. We met at a tavern in Kanibar a few weeks after I arrived in Carthe. I wanted to see the continent, so he offered to take me along to Bozar. His bride fashioned beautiful Kanish quilts—he hoped to sell them in Bozar.

We came across a group of five men when we were crossing the valley. Like Varn, as Carthinian as they come. Driven by coin rather than comradery, though. They recognized me as an Akkinorian and spit at me. Called me wealthy scum. That's how some Carthinians view us, you know."

"I can imagine."

He grimaced. "They accused me of abandoning my good fortune to invade their poor lands. People like them think everyone in Akkinor lives like royalty—they couldn't understand why I'd turn my back on such privilege to inhabit a land where I wasn't welcome. Varn defended me. He wasn't one to let others slander a good man's name. They told him he was no true Carthinian and killed him for it, right in front of me. I hadn't lifted my sword to a Carthinian until that day. All five of them fell at my hand."

Aurelia swallowed. "At least you know he was your friend. I don't know how many people would do that for me."

"I could say the same. That's a downside of Akkinor—you don't always know who you can trust."

She nodded in understanding. "Was there anybody else?" When he didn't answer, she added, "You don't have to tell me—"

"It's all right. I just haven't had anyone to talk to about my adventures in a long time." Jack rolled onto his back, setting his hands on his chest, and stared at the ceiling of the cave. "Louisia. I called her Lou. We met at a tavern in Krotis about two years ago. She was like me—walking the ends of the earth and back again in search of her purpose. We were here in the Violet Forest on our last day together. I'd just started the fire and was setting up camp when she left to hunt. I heard her return, and when I looked up, there was a spear in her stomach." Aurelia winced and closed her eyes in despair. "A tribe found us. The way she looked...They must have raped her and sent her back as a warning. It was a game they played. Send her running, then spear her before she could scream for me. She died right there in my arms. I took her horse—Sterling, actually—and left everything behind. That's when I started stealing to survive. I had nothing after that. Only a few coins in my pocket and whatever was attached to Sterling's saddle."

Aurelia was quiet for a moment. She knew there was more to the story by the tone in his voice. It wasn't hard to deduce that Louisia had been more to him than just a traveling companion. He spoke of her like Linden often spoke of Cicely: with fondness and longing.

"You loved her, didn't you?"

"I don't know," he admitted after a moment of silence. "I've never loved anyone like that before." He turned his head to the side, finally meeting her gaze. She could hardly see him in the darkness, but the glow from the fire reflected in his oceanic eyes. They were misty with emotion. "And you? Have you ever loved like that?"

"I'm yet to have the pleasure."

"I find that hard to believe."

She raised her eyebrows, amused. "Oh? How so?"

Even in the darkness, she saw his face redden. "A beautiful young Akkinorian woman who's never known romance. Most people are married with children at your age. If I'd stayed in Akkinor, I probably would've been, too."

"Life doesn't always work that way." She leaned up, using her elbows to support her upper body, and smirked down at him. "I said I've never known love. I said nothing about never knowing romance."

"Forgive me. My mistake." His teasing tone made her chuckle. He yawned and rolled onto his side, facing away from her. "I firmly believe someone will catch your eye when you return home. Akkinor is in no short supply of bachelors."

She lay down again and folded her hands under her cheek. "Neither is Carthe."

No reply. As the fire dimmed, she watched him and waited for some sort of a response. When nothing came, she closed her eyes and listened to the rushing water of the river outside. She shivered against the cool ground beneath her and drew her legs to her chest. As her body adjusted to the temperature and as her eyelids finally began to fall, she felt something brushing against her skin. Warmth settled in, spreading from her toes to her fingers, as something thick and rough tickled her exposed arms. It didn't take long for her to realize that Jack had covered her with his blanket.

Aurelia smiled. As she slowly drifted off to sleep, she listened to the melodic rush of the river and the rhythmic hum of Jack's heavy breathing—a perfect lullaby if there ever was one.

XVI

"Welcome to Dofell." Jack smiled. "Don't worry—it isn't as intimidating on the other side."

Aurelia gulped, doubtful. The walls surrounding the kingdom of Dofell were enormous—she couldn't see so much as a tree or the towers of a castle from where they stood. A set of thick, tall wrought iron gates stood between the two halves of the wall. Four soldiers guarded the gates, all heavily armed, and there were six more on the watchtowers atop the wall.

When they approached the gate, an emotionless guard demanded, "State your identities and your objective in the Great City."

"Jack Sherbourne," he told the guards, "and my wife, Lily. We intend to cross the Ngora Valley at dusk in hopes of reaching Taundosa. We seek only safe passage through the Great City."

The soldier nodded. "Very well." He gestured to the other guards to open the gates. "Should you decide to stay rather than continue on your journey, you will be forcibly removed. Am I clear?"

"Certainly, sir," Jack said patiently. "Thank you. We appreciate your hospitality."

The guard said nothing. When Jack gave her a reassuring look, Aurelia swallowed and followed him through the gates. She would've snapped at him for calling her his wife, had he not fashioned each of them a wedding band made of twine. When they left the cave that morning, he'd insisted that families were only people allowed beyond the gates of Dofell. Lone travelers were too suspicious and untrustworthy. While they were in Dofell, Jack and Aurelia had no choice but to masquerade as a couple unless they wanted to be forcibly removed from the kingdom.

The first thing she noticed was the filth. Everything was muddy, as if it'd rained nonstop for the past two seasons, leaving any crops or plants to drown rather than to thrive in the soil. Most of the houses were void of shutters on the windows, chimneys on the roofs, and locks on the doors. The shelters were barely standing with leaking roofs and tilted walls from apparent landslides. Farm animals roamed the streets, free of their pens, while children in ratty clothing chased after them on shoeless feet.

The forest had been nothing but foliage, bushes, streams, hills, valleys, and wildlife. Dofell was a flat terrain with hills of human and animal waste rather than earth and grass. The water in the wells wasn't clean, and it ran through the lowest points of the streets, collecting in puddles. Even the paths and streets were buried under inches of dirt, mud, and garbage. The walls outside of the city were surrounded by nature, but inside there was nothing. A few trees might've been planted as decoration years ago, but they'd all withered into nothing more than sticks. The air felt thicker in Dofell, and the stench of numerous foul odors—human filth, rotting meat, and sour milk—made Aurelia's stomach churn.

In the distance was the first remarkable sight in Dofell: the palace. It was a few miles away, standing taller than every other structure in the city and glittering against the sunlight. It was white and made entirely of marble with several expansive balconies, towers, and terraces. A flag hung from the tallest tower, blowing violently in the warm breeze, with tall golden gates surrounding the estate. The palace was beautiful, yes, but it was nearly impossible to appreciate while standing in the heart of such poverty.

"It's..." She tried to finish, but words escaped her.

Jack sighed. "Dofell isn't the grand place it once was. A former king spent most of the kingdom's money on the new palace, and four generations since then have lived through its construction. The current king is the first to live in the completed structure. As you can imagine, almost two-hundred years of poverty has taken its toll on the people. They make their money by selling whatever they have left to the taverns, inns, and brothels on either side of the valley."

Jack stopped them outside of a quiet tavern in the middle of the kingdom. He didn't seem particularly worried about theft when they left the horses in the stables. She could tell that this particular tavern used to be an inn, but the lack of overnight guests must have forced the owner to convert the inn into nothing more than a tavern. The room keys still hung behind the counter, collecting dust from years of neglect, and the staircase was blocked off with rope.

They didn't hesitate to order hot meals. There were only two other customers in the tavern, so they sat down in the nearest empty seats and waited for the barmaid to arrive. The clerk visited them first with two pints of ale, and the barmaid wasn't far behind with their meals. Aurelia had expected worse than what was provided, even if the food resembled slop more than she would've preferred. The singular slice of pork on her plate was thin, gray, and tasteless with a small dollop of brown gravy, and served with underboiled, skinless potatoes and a piece of stale bread.

As they practically swallowed their food without chewing, a group of men waltzed into the tavern. They were filthy and wearing identical clothing, so Aurelia knew they must've just finished work for the day. By the look of their blackened faces and garments, they were miners, as Dofell's primary (and only withstanding) commodity was iron. They walked in laughing, hooting, and yelling over one another like children. As soon as they were seated, the clerk visited them with a tray of empty cups and two jugs of ale. The men didn't hesitate to serve themselves, spilling ale over the wooden table and even drinking it straight from the jugs.

As she turned away from them, a glimmer of rage formed in Aurelia's heart when she caught sight of a runty creature chained up by the hearth. The dragon—mutated and domesticated over many centuries—was no bigger than a young cattle dog. Its scales, an iridescent combination of lime green and saffron yellow, were dull and muted beneath a thick layer of dirt and ash. The creature still had wings (unlike many of its kind, whose wings had been clipped ages before), but Aurelia doubted that it could fly more than a few feet above the ground. It certainly couldn't go anywhere while shackled to the wall with a ring of heavy iron around its neck. The dragon was sleeping like a hound with its head nestled on its scaly feet, but the clerk would undoubtedly wake the poor creature as soon as the fire began to dwindle.

As she stared at it, the locket resting between her breasts began to burn, and a shiver traced every vertebra of her spine from the base of her tailbone to the nape of her neck.

Her attention was redirected once more when the bard in the corner of the room, who'd been silently mulling over a pint of ale, suddenly stood and began to play his dusty guitar. It wasn't long before the workers began singing along to the tune. They were standing and swaying, spilling ale all over the floor, as they sang completely out of tune.

"He almost makes me miss the bards in Akkinor." Jack nodded his head towards the musician. He swallowed a gulp of ale as a man threw a piece of bronze at the bard. "If he wanted to play because he enjoyed it, he would've done so before there was a crowd to please. At least Akkinorian bards aren't so desperate for money. They play for nobody but themselves and the gods."

The bard began playing a new song—one Aurelia recognized all too well. "Funny you should say that. This is an Akkinorian lullaby. One of my favorites." She closed her eyes as she listened, trying to focus on the tune rather than the singing of the already-drunken patrons. When she opened her eyes, she saw Jack staring at her, puzzled. "What? Why are you looking at me like that?"

"This is the ballad of the highborn children. How do you know it?"

"My mother was stewardess to Lady Spirre of Sadia." She cursed herself for how quickly and easily the lie slipped from her tongue. "I was raised with the Spirre children. Not exactly a privileged childhood, but close enough." She hesitated when a realization struck her. "You must've been a nobleman, Mister Sherbourne. How do *you* know the ballad?"

He winced. "I was an Omaran soldier, remember? Because there were so few of us, we worked closely with the Ashford family. I was exposed to many highborn privileges."

Neither of them spoke again. She wanted to trust his word, but how could she? If it were this easy for her to lie to him, it'd be just as easy for *him* to lie to *her*.

Before she could get lost in her thoughts, he reached out towards her face and brushed his thumb over the corner of her mouth. She jumped, startled, as a hearty chuckle escaped his lips. Her face burned when she saw a drop of brown gravy on the pad of his thumb. His eyes didn't leave hers as he licked it from his skin. Her face must've turned ten shades redder (from both embarrassment and the slightest bit of arousal), as he lowered his gaze to his meal, hiding a smile, like nothing had happened.

"Can I ask you something?" he inquired. She nodded, grateful for the distraction from what he'd just done, and nonchalantly dabbed at her mouth with her napkin. He didn't notice. "You mentioned a friend in Carthe who was killed for helping you. May I ask what happened?"

Aurelia shifted. "Assassins. They recognized me as an Akkinorian when they found our campsite. I knew who they were, so I told Kaia that we needed to get as far from our camp as possible. It was too late. She was shot with a poison arrow. Phoenix blood."

He winced. "Akkinorian assassins?"

She nodded.

"How can you be sure?"

"Akkinorian bronze armor. One of them said something to me, too. *Forward, ever forward.*"

He snorted. "A purposeful mistake, I'd imagine."

"I thought so. I should think they're still here, searching for me."

"Who sent them?"

She shrugged. "One was from Holos, the other from Myra. I've wronged nobody in either kingdom, but I suppose that doesn't matter. Assassins can be hired from any kingdom when deployed by the capital." As realization sank in, she experienced a whirlwind of emotions: fury, betrayal, and utter stupidity. "They were sent from the Folly."

He raised an eyebrow in amusement. "What did you do to piss off Queen Aurelia?"

"Nothing." She flinched at the sound of her name on his lips. He had absolutely no idea that Queen Aurelia and the girl across from him were one in the same. "She had nothing to do with it. But..."

She trailed off as her thoughts overwhelmed her. The person responsible for the uprising had known how to sneak an army into the Folly undetected, and they'd needed royal authority to deploy assassins. Other than Aurelia herself, the Lord Hand, and the entire Assembly after a unanimous vote, there was only one other person who—with Aurelia out of the way—possessed that kind of power.

The only son of the last Akkinorian king.

The only heir to the throne.

Archie.

It all came together, filling her veins with fire and her heart with ice. If she were removed from the equation, he could take the throne for himself. Nobody would suspect that he'd participated in the attack or in Aurelia's disappearance. They'd simply be grateful to have a Brentwood on the throne—especially one who'd rescued them from an army of foreign attackers.

He couldn't have done it alone, either. One man (royal blood or not) couldn't sneak an army of mercenaries into the capital without help. Even a prince couldn't withdraw the amount of coin needed to fund a mercenary army and hire assassins. Perhaps a handful of his allies had been threatened into compliance, but Aurelia wasn't foolish enough to believe that everyone who'd helped her brother had needed coercing. There were plenty of Akkinorian souls who'd been praying for the late king's son to take the throne since the day Archie was born.

Aurelia never paid those people any heed. They weren't a threat to her while they were alone. Archie, on the other hand, had apparently been keeping tabs on those who didn't kiss Aurelia's shoes or obey her every whim. He'd been steps ahead of her, like a ruthless game of chess, the entire time.

If she was right, she wouldn't be returning to Akkinor to face one enemy, but an army of them.

The stool beneath her screeched against the floor when she stood. "I need a bath," she announced. Jack furrowed his eyebrows at her as she tossed a few pieces of coin onto the table. "You can have my ale. That should be enough to cover my share."

"Lily—"

"I'll see you later. I smell like Scotch."

He cracked a smile, but the worry in his eyes didn't fade. She said nothing more as she purchased a bar of soap from the clerk and made her way to the bathhouse. Nobody was there, but she couldn't bring herself to bathe yet. She simply sat on the ground, staring at the murky water, and pictured her brother's face in her head. An unsettling feeling coursed through her as she realized something: when she pictured her brother, he was never smiling. He'd always looked at her with a scowl on his lips, as if any love he might've had for her sunk to the bottom of the ocean with their parents.

When her eyes burned, she realized she was crying. She'd always chosen to see the best in people, but she didn't know if she'd been hopeful or blind when it came to Archie. If her judgement hadn't been so clouded by love, maybe she'd still be in Akkinor.

The worst part was that she could still remember a time when Archie loved her. Even if he hadn't loved her as a brother should, he gave her enough reasons to believe he did.

She recalled the extravagant ball thrown at the palace to commemorate her sixteenth name day. Now that she was no longer considered a child, every available suitor in the country had attempted to win her heart. She'd been surrounded by men between the ages of sixteen and fifty from the moment she entered the ballroom. She'd been overwhelmed and intimidated by the attention, and of all the friendly faces at the party, only one came to her rescue: Archie.

Her thirteen-year-old brother had cut through the crowd of suitors and asked her to dance. Archie hadn't taken enough dance lessons to be as proficient as his sister, so he soon found himself stepping on her toes. He'd flushed and fumbled over an apology, but Aurelia merely laughed and brought him into a tight embrace.

"Thank you, brother," she'd whispered.

Archie hesitated before returning her embrace. "'The greatest honor in one's life is to protect one's family,'" he'd said, quoting Oleander Brentwood. "You deserve better than the men who want you only for your crown, Li."

She'd tightened her grip on him and rested her cheek on his shoulder. "I love you, Archie."

Her brother didn't return her affection, but instead pulled away from her and spun her under his arm. Surprised at the sudden movement, Aurelia stumbled, and the siblings' laughter echoed through the ballroom, louder even than the blaring music of the orchestra.

As the memory faded, so did every other recollection of a time when Archie genuinely cared for her. When the opportunity came for him to choose between the crown and his only sibling, he'd chosen the crown, and because of that, the two Brentwood siblings were now at war with one another.

She lifted her locket to her lips and closed her eyes. She thought about her parents and the gift they'd given her. When she asked about the locket as a child, they told her it was a family heirloom that'd once come from a land across the sea. *The entire city is made of gold,* her mother had told her. *One can see it glittering from miles away.*

The memory furthered her belief that Taundosa was her place of birth. She wondered if Archie knew—then she thought about where Linden had gone when they separated during the attack. While she was finding her way through the tunnels, he was fighting his way to the dungeons to visit a sorcerer. Linden wouldn't have left such a valuable person alive in the middle of an uprising. She had to believe that the sorcerer—the only person other than her parents who would've even *suspected* her illegitimacy—was gone. If not, she risked Archie learning the truth about something that could've ruined her.

Even if Archie *was* aware, he didn't know how much power she really had. He wouldn't know unless they met again on opposite sides of the battlefield. Still, his greed and pride were much too strong for any one man. He wouldn't surrender unless he was dead.

Aurelia had spent the last several weeks worrying about what had happened to her brother when she left him behind. Now, until she returned to Akkinor, she'd be worrying about how his grand plan would end. One of them wouldn't survive to see the sun rise over the hills of the Folly again. She hoped it wasn't her, but she also didn't want it to be him.

Of all the people in the world, her greatest enemy was her baby brother. She knew what that meant, just as she knew that when the time came, only she could pass the sentence.

***

Estylle lost track of how long she'd been staring at the door, fist raised as if to knock, while swallowing the bile that'd risen up in her throat. It must have been longer than she thought, as a nearby soldier stomped over and rapped his fists on the door. Her cheeks burned when he glared at her before returning to his post across the hall. Not a moment later, she heard a voice on the other side of the door beckoning her, and her chance to turn back faded into oblivion.

Until recently, she'd never been nauseous with anxiety when visiting the monarch's study. In her twenties, the man sitting behind the desk wasn't merely her king, but her friend. Decades later when Edmund's daughter sat behind the desk, Estylle visited the study to converse and giggle with the queen she'd raised from infancy. To her, Edmund and Aurelia Brentwood weren't monarchs, but the closest thing to family she had left.

Now, the person sitting behind the desk was no more a grown man than Estylle was a housecat. Naivety and ignorance shimmered like a veil over his face, highlighting the boyishness he'd fought tirelessly to wipe from existence. He was as unfamiliar with a comb as he'd been as a young boy, causing the crown on his head to be partially concealed by outgrown locks of unkempt blonde hair. The crown and the many medals pinned to his shirt—his father's medals—offered the illusion of power and authority.

"My king." She curtsied. "You wished to see me?"

"Yes." Archie casually leaned back in his chair with his hands folded over his stomach. He didn't offer her a seat. "It was brought to my attention that you may have some knowledge of my sister's whereabouts. I thought I'd give you the chance to explain yourself before my advisors urge me to make rash decisions."

Her heart rattled with fear. "I-I haven't the slightest idea, Your Grace. I am not—nor have I ever been—in a position that would permit me to know such valuable information."

"I thought so. My sister wouldn't have told the *governess* of her plans to abandon her country." His icy eyes narrowed. As he gazed at her, she realized she hadn't heard him utter Aurelia's name since before the invasion. He'd only referred to her as *my sister* in recent weeks. "I can't help but wonder where these rumors originated from, though. Have you any idea?"

"None, Your Grace."

"Hmm." His eyes narrowed even further until they nearly disappeared behind his golden lashes. "I shall have my advisors thoroughly interrogated, then. That is, of course, unless the former Lord Hand relents and tells me what I wish to know."

Estylle swallowed. "Whatever Your Grace believes is right."

He exhaled and tapped his fingers on his thigh. "Where do you think she might've gone to?"

"Vilgh-Azhor, perhaps. She may have fled into Quapebet."

"Unlikely. Quapebet is a place for exile, not refuge."

The Quenosi would beg to differ, she thought.

"Wherever she is, she'll get what's coming for her," Archie continued. Estylle flinched. "There's a debt to be paid by those who abandon their people in times of need. She won't emerge from this unscathed, I assure you."

Estylle surprised herself with her courage when she asked, "What does Your Grace have in mind for her?"

He gawked at her for a moment, shocked by her inquiry, before he cleared his throat and straightened in his chair. "That's yet to be determined. My instinct is to have her executed on various counts of treason. My advisors have other plans in mind. They think she's too beloved by the civilians—our subjects would rebel if I have her killed. They suggested marrying her to Bradley Reilly and shipping her off to Laynoa. She'd be locked away, of course. Lord Reilly is insistent that if I choose to keep her alive, I mustn't harm her. He needs her strong and healthy if she's to carry his heirs." He raised an eyebrow. "What do you think of that?"

Estylle's blood turned to ice in her veins, paralyzing her. She pictured Aurelia's face in her head—not the face of a queen, but of a little girl looking to her governess for guidance, love, and protection. She couldn't imagine the girl she loved so dearly being hunted around the world only to be murdered or locked away in a tower as a childbearing tool for a foul nobleman. It was as inhumane as it was beyond belief.

Estylle had sworn an oath before the gods to adore and defend the Brentwood children with her life—*both* of them. She never imagined having to choose between them, but she should have.

The entire country should have.

Knowing he was awaiting her response, she sucked in a breath. "Either option will certainly prove to be a wise decision by Your Grace."

He offered her a smug smile and leaned back in his chair, satisfied. "You've always been so good to me, Estylle. I hope to never see the day when that changes."

She shivered at the cool and somewhat threatening tone in his voice. Her silence was apparently response enough, as he waved his hand to signal her departure. She held her breath as she turned on her heel and exited the study, and she didn't allow herself to breathe again until the door was closed between them.

At first, Estylle wanted to believe that Archie hadn't been involved in the attempt on Aurelia's life. He'd played the role of a loyal, concerned brother (and reluctant heir) in the days following the tragedy, but his loyalty and concern morphed into something darker when Aurelia failed to return home after several weeks. After that, he'd traded hope in her return for confidence in her betrayal. He wasn't worried about finding her and bringing her home safely, but about finding the best way to punish her for abandoning her country.

That left one of two possibilities: either Archie had adopted an extremist's perspective of the law regarding treason, thus making him blind to honor and family loyalty, or it'd been his plan all along to see Aurelia thrown to the wolves.

Estylle didn't know which was worse.

She'd changed his diapers from the day he was born to the day he learned to use the chamber pot. She'd stayed awake with him for hours upon hours when terrors plagued his dreams. She'd sung to him and rubbed his back when he was ill, slept beside him under his bed when he insisted on hiding from monsters that didn't exist, and helped him regain control of his words when the adolescent prince allowed his nerves to transform his speech into garbled stutters. She'd given him her blood, sweat, and tears for more than two decades, and despite all of it, he was prepared to send her to the gallows beside his sister if she breathed even one wrong word.

Archie Brentwood, her beautiful, blue-eyed little boy, held her life in his hands like she were a snowball—like he could close his fist and crush her into dust without a moment's hesitation.

The boy she once knew was gone, and in his place was the very same monster Estylle, once upon a time, had protected him from.

XVII

urelia had felt Jack's eyes on her from the moment they left the tavern. They were riding their horses across the filthy streets of Dofell, as they had no choice but to reach the border before nightfall. There was no time to spare, though Jack didn't seem concerned about it. He was more worried about pressing Aurelia for information. Eventually, she shot him a sharp glare and set her lips in a thin line, hoping he'd understand her peeved expression.

"What?" His long, dark eyelashes fell gently over his bright eyes. "Why are you looking at me like that?"

"You know why."

"We may not know one another well, but I can see that something is troubling you. You've hardly uttered a word since dinner. What's on your mind?"

She glowered at him. "I've already told you—"

"—you don't want to tell me anything that could get me into trouble." He offered her a silly, lopsided grin. "I'm not afraid, Lily. I'd simply like a bit of reassurance from you. If you continue to keep everything to yourself, I may have to trade you in for the bard. At least he'll speak to me on this expedition. I hope."

That made her smile, but it soon faded. "I think I know who sent the assassins. It had to have been my brother."

Jack furrowed his eyebrows. "Why did you flee, anyway? Who are you running from? Your brother?"

"I didn't think so. Not at first," she admitted. She begged forgiveness from the gods as she prepared to utter yet another lie. "I-I made a mistake. It was an unfortunate business deal with the Reilly family of Laynoa. There was a bounty on my head, so I had no choice but to escape. My brother...my brother thinks I've wronged him in more ways than one. He has powerful friends. Rich friends. The Reilly family may want me to collect a debt, but my brother wants me gone. All he had to do was ask for a favor."

"Your own brother." A disgusted scoff rose up in his throat. "Why would he do that? Why does he want you dead?"

A sharp pang pierced her heart. "I took something from him without knowing it. Do you have siblings, Jack?"

"I do."

"Think of it as your parents' inheritance. What would your siblings say if your parents left their entire inheritance to you? While your siblings received nothing, you received every piece of your parents' legacy. How would your siblings take to that?"

He grimaced. "Not well."

"Not well. You had absolutely no opinion on the matter, but your siblings would've despised you, nonetheless. That's how my brother feels. He was jealous of something that neither of us could control. I should've predicted this, but I didn't want to consider that he was involved until it was directly in front of me."

"I'm sorry, Lily. I don't blame you for being so upset. Hopefully this Taundosan fellow can help you bring an end to his schemes."

Her smile wavered with uncertainty. "Hopefully."

A shiver ran down her spine when a gust of wind blew through the air. It was cool, and paired with the dark blue of the sky, she knew nighttime would soon be upon them. She hadn't been fond of the idea of traveling through the Ngora Valley at nighttime, but Jack assured her that it was their best option. Walking the desert beneath the blazing Carthinian sun was a challenge. At least after nightfall when the sun rested for the day, they could travel without their skin turning to blisters.

They came across a small-scale marketplace on the other side of the palace. Few people were walking around and shopping, but merchants were still trying to make sales. Only a handful were selling things like jewelry, ornaments, artwork, or hand-crafted household necessities. Most were selling things that pertained to the travelers of the Ngora Valley, not the residents of Dofell. She saw several shops and stands selling travel-sized packs of food, hunting knives, sun shields, and water canteens. Jack stopped to purchase an insect net for Sterling's face while a merchant convinced Aurelia to buy a *fjardel*: a thick, yet lightweight piece of cloth worn to protect one's face from the sun and sand. In the common tongue, the word translated to *sandsilk*.

"Oh, darling girl!" A man's eager voice rang out. Aurelia barely had time to react before a merchant was standing before her, tightly grasping her hands in his. He stared intently at her chest—or, more specifically, at her locket. "I have been searching for a necklace to complete my set. Would you care to see it? Maybe it would interest you. If not, I'd be glad to offer ten gold for your necklace!"

Jack appeared at her side. *"Ten gold?"* His eyes nearly bugged out of his head. "Lily—"

"I'm not interested. This is a family heirloom," she told the merchant. His face fell. "Thank you for your offer, though. You have some beautiful pieces in your collection."

He nodded and stepped away. She felt Jack gawking at her as they climbed on their horses and continued towards the gates. He didn't say a word to her until they were a safe distance from the marketplace. When the merchants were far behind, he rode up beside her and gave her a look that made her want to strike him.

"Lily—"

"Jack," she snapped, "mind your business."

"Ten gold," he repeated. She shook her head in exasperation. "Of course, I doubt the poor man even *has* ten gold—he'd probably have to pay in installments—but for him to offer such richness at all is outstanding. That kind of coin could feed an entire family for a *year*."

"Not in exchange for my necklace. This is the one thing I would barter my own life for. End of discussion."

He held his hands up in defense. "All right. I was just trying to make a point. We're going to the City of Gold, after all. It isn't exactly cheap living." He raised an eyebrow at her. "You said you're going to Taundosa in search of someone. Who? Why?"

"His name is Cristos. He was good friends with the people who helped me escape Akkinor, but I know extraordinarily little about him. An innkeeper in Caedia told me that surnames ending in *tos* are common on the other side of the Ngora Valley—mainly in Taundosa. I don't know for certain if he actually lives there."

"So why are you going?"

She shrugged. "I have to try."

"What will you do if you can't find him?"

"Live out the rest of my days in Carthe, I suppose." The thought filled her mouth with a bitter, metallic taste. She didn't want to die on this continent, even if it happened blissfully in her sleep at the ripe age of ninety. "You don't happen to know anything about him, do you?"

"I'm afraid not. Any person capable of achieving what you desire hasn't concerned themselves with worthless nomads like me. Not yet, anyway."

She wasn't as disappointed as she should've been—she'd expected that response. "You're not worthless."

"Anyone in Carthe without a title or land attached to their name is worthless. Nobody of prominence concerns themselves with us." Even while attempting to convince her of his insignificance, he smiled and beamed like she was the only person ever to disagree with the statement. "Thank you, though."

She returned his smile. "What about you, Jack Sherbourne? What awaits you in Taundosa? A pretty maiden and her warm bed, perhaps?"

"Good gods. *No.*" His flushed cheeks made her laugh. "Nothing, really. I'm on my way to Khaba. Taundosa is just a stop on my journey. Khaba has always interested me, you know. It's a peculiar place, to be sure, but..."

While they rode, they talked about Carthe, its territories, and the many things they had to adapt to as foreigners. In Akkinor, a monarch governed the six kingdoms. Aurelia was Lady of the Folly, what with it being the nation's capital, while lords and ladies oversaw the other five kingdoms. The smaller territories in each kingdom were governed by bannermen—low-ranking highborn families. Before Oleander overthrew the Cherrane family, he'd been Duke of Eldford in the kingdom of Myra. As Eldford was the Brentwood family's ancestral home, Aurelia's title officially included *Duchess of Eldford*. It wouldn't be removed from her list of titles until Archie married and moved into the estate to become duke.

None of that applied in Carthe. The five major kingdoms—Dofell, Kanibar, Krotis, Taundosa, and Bozar—were all governed differently. A monarch ruled some, and others were ruled by several lords and ladies working collectively to function on a feudal system. Dofell, for example, had been ruled by numerous lords and ladies for centuries before an uprising turned it into a monarchy.

Jack jerked his thumb over his shoulder at the palace behind them. "King Elrin of the Phyre family, Third of His Name. His great-great-grandfather began construction on the palace after he'd fought the lords and ladies for sole control of the Great City. Because his wealth was lost to the war, he relied on money from the city to pay for the palace. The current king is still paying off his great-grandfather's debts. That's why Dofell is so...well, you know."

"I see." Aurelia wrinkled her nose. "What kind of leader does such a thing to their people? It's repulsive."

He exhaled. "I don't understand it, either. After King Edmund and Queen Cressida died, I heard that many people in Akkinor expected the worst from Queen Aurelia. Young nobles are reckless and irresponsible. The power goes to their heads, as seen with King Elrin's ancestor. He was used as an example against Queen Aurelia. I left Akkinor before she was crowned—before she had a chance to prove the speculators right or wrong."

Aurelia knew how her people had responded to a young female heir to the throne. She'd heard whispers from the common people who claimed she'd played a hand in her parents' deaths because she was too eager for power. The rumors never failed to make her laugh. Her parents were her world, for one. For another, no twenty-year-old girl wanted the weight of a nation on her shoulders.

She cleared her throat. "Have you heard anything about her? Has word traveled to Carthe?"

"A bit here and there."

"What do you think of her?"

Jack shifted. "I think the people can't help but serve her." She furrowed her eyebrows, frowning, and watched him inquisitively in hopes of elaboration. "They want desperately to despise a woman on the throne, but they can't. There's something about her that makes her intoxicating. Akkinor can't help but adore her."

"But what do *you* think?"

"Me?" Jack pondered for a moment. "I don't know. I never gave her a chance." He paused, still contemplating. "I remember hearing about her coronation day. They say every bell in Akkinor rang for the new queen. I knew then that the country believed in her. If they hated the idea of a female ruler so much...nobody was forcing them to ring the bells, you know?"

She hadn't thought of it like that. One of her older maids, who'd been serving the Brentwood family since Aurelia's grandfather sat on the throne, once told her that only the bells in the Folly rang for every new monarch. It was rare for every kingdom to collectively support each monarch who took the throne, so the bells seldom chimed outside of the capital. There was always a problem: Sadia didn't like the new king's bride or Myra thought he was too young or Holos didn't like his new policies. If Jack was right about the day she was crowned, then her people believed in her more than she realized.

"I've heard stories about her, too," he continued. "Sailors like talking about their queen. Most are lonely men who will take anything they can get when it comes to a pretty woman. They're constantly yammering on about her, even if most of it is crafted in their imaginations. I once heard a man say her bed was never cold, though her own vanity prevented her from marrying. She was too beautiful for any one man, and she knew it. I know she must be beautiful, but I can't imagine the daughter of Edmund Brentwood acting like such an ass."

She laughed. "You said it yourself—it was probably another tall tale."

For the most part, she thought. Her parents hadn't stifled her when she was younger; they let her be herself, even when it got her into trouble, and tried their best to keep the chiding to a minimum. It was their belief that if she were confident in herself as a normal girl, she could be confident in herself as queen. Her father didn't know about her more *unrefined* activities, but her mother did. She couldn't hide anything from her mother.

"Mhm. Maybe." He glanced over at her and donned a wicked smile. "She's the queen of the most powerful nation in the world. If she doesn't want people to know something, they won't."

A warm blush colored her cheeks. "Your sailor friends are playing you for a fool, Jack."

He laughed. "Maybe so. My point is that I don't know much about her. She was just the Crown Princess when I left Akkinor. She's been *your* queen for some time. What do you think about her?"

Her stomach churned. What *did* she think? It didn't feel right to talk about herself like that. Then again, Aurelia knew she had her faults. She knew she wasn't the greatest ruler in history. If there was ever a time to be honest with herself, it was now, with someone who would listen and respond without predisposition.

"She seems to be doing well. Poverty has been diminished. The numbers are the lowest in one-hundred years. But the nobles have always been uncontrollable. You must know that. Until she can properly control the nobility, her hands are tied. They've been in power since before the Brentwood family ruled Akkinor. There's only so much she can do."

"Pity. The nobles have never been easy to work with, but at least she's made a difference to the people. She's proven them wrong so far, right?"

She forced a smile. "So far."

"When you're safely in Akkinor again, you shall have to write to me. I'd like to hear about what you think of her after begging her for a pardon." Aurelia couldn't help but laugh. Jack lifted an arm, still clutching Sterling's reins, and pointed to something ahead. "You're one step closer to Akkinor and our queen, Lily. We're here."

Our queen. Hearing those words from his lips caused a shiver to trace her spine.

The gates were a terrifying sight to behold. They were enormous, made of the same iron as the gates on the other side of the kingdom, and so thick that Aurelia couldn't see through to the other side. Soldiers were standing guard as if waiting for the precise time to open them. She wondered if their irritating choice of architecture had been purposeful. Maybe the people who built the gates thought it best that travelers didn't see what was waiting for them. The thought made her shudder.

Jack nodded his head to several groups of people surrounding the gates. "We won't be alone on this journey. I would've been surprised if we were the only people here tonight. Normally, the other travelers want no trouble—just to cross the desert in one piece. Most groups will be escorted by expert guides who want even less trouble with us than the travelers. Causing problems isn't good for business."

"Shouldn't *we* have an expert guide?"

A cocky grin lit up his face. "*I'm* our expert guide."

Aurelia rolled her eyes at him. He erupted into a hearty, booming fit of laughter. She knew better than to argue with him—he was right, of course. Jack had crossed the Ngora Valley more times than he should have. He knew as much as the guides, but on this particular mission, he happened to come free of charge.

"We need to gain distance from the wall," he continued. "That's where the desert tribes lurk. Following the wall keeps travelers close to civilization and offers a quicker route to Taundosa—it's the perfect hunting ground. Victims have a low probability of fleeing while they're surrounded by tribesmen on three sides and an unbreachable wall on the other. Our route will be long, but our odds of survival will be high."

Aurelia gulped. She didn't want to admit that she was grateful for him, but right now, she couldn't imagine what she'd do without him.

Die, probably.

When a bell in the distance chimed six times, the soldiers posted at the gates shifted. The groups of travelers quickly scrambled to their feet after double-checking their supplies. The guides, who identified themselves with blue-and-yellow *fjardels,* were coercing donkeys tasked with pulling wagons of supplies. Aurelia held her breath in anticipation as the guards opened the gates to reveal her first glimpse of the infamous Ngora Valley.

"Six chimes." Jack's eyes were bright and dancing with excitement. "If you want to change your mind, now's the time."

She shook her head. "No. I'm ready."

"Good. I hope you're better suited for the desert than you look."

She glowered at him. While Sterling and Scotch took them through the gates, she secured the *fjardel* around her face and took a long, deep breath. Beneath the moonlight, the cacti and sand dunes didn't look so threatening. She could practically see the City of Gold on the horizon line.

Then a wolf howled in the distance, closely followed by the sound of war cries, and the air became thick with dust as the horses galloped into the abyss of sand and darkness.

XVIII

O h, Jack, *must* you—"

"Shh."

Aurelia gave him a nasty look. She watched with her arms crossed over her chest as he squinted at something in the distance. The string of her bow grazed his lips as he held a nocked arrow between his fingers. After a few seconds of silence, he released the bowstring, and the arrow flew across the desert in the blink of an eye. A painful howl echoed around them as Jack triumphantly set the bow aside to collect the bounty, and soon returned holding a lifeless lump of white fur.

She shook her head at him. "You shouldn't have done that."

"What should I have done?" He knelt down in the sand, sweat shimmering on his brow, and began skinning the dead animal with his hunting knife. "We need to eat. If you'd rather survive on sugared nuts and forest berries, be my guest. I've no problem feasting on my own."

"That's not what I meant." She tended to the fire and built a spit while he worked on the carcass. "There are other animals in the desert for us to hunt. You could've been killed for that."

He grinned. "I certainly am lucky, aren't I?"

She rolled her eyes at him. When he finished skinning the animal, it was virtually impossible to identify the species. The only way for someone to recognize it was by the pelt resting on the sand. It was a stunning creature, but its glittering ivory coat and black-tipped ears made it difficult for the animal to go unnoticed in the desert. The Ngoran Fox was protected by most Carthinians because it was endangered after centuries of being hunted for its pelts and meat. Slaughtering one came with the penalty of death. As long as nobody was around to see what he'd done,

Jack didn't care about breaking the law. He only cared about filling his belly—even if it meant killing one of the rarest creatures in Carthe.

Aurelia didn't like that, but she had no choice unless she wanted to starve. The food they'd collected before entering the valley hadn't been enough. Supplies were already running low after three days of crossing the desert. Luckily, Jack told her about a lone tavern in the middle of the desert built for travelers. There, they could replenish their supplies before their inventory ran out. Jack claimed there was a small oasis closer to the border of Taundosa, too, where they could refill their water supply.

She worried about the horses. Some of the other travelers took camels instead of horses, as the former were better suited for the desert, but the pair refused to leave Sterling and Scotch in Dofell. It wouldn't matter if Aurelia and Jack had enough supplies to make it through the valley—it mattered if the *horses* had enough supplies. Unfortunately, horses weren't particularly fond of fox meat and sugared nuts.

While they dined beneath the moonlight and the humid desert air, Jack asked, "What do you know about this Cristos fellow?"

"Not much."

"Hmm. Your source was right, though. Surnames ending in *tos* are common in Taundosa. If I were looking for someone named Cristos, I'd start there." He chewed a bite of fox meat and gazed at her. He almost looked sheepish. "Is it some sort of arranged marriage?"

"Heavens, no!" She laughed awkwardly. "Arranged marriages may be common in Akkinor, but I'd never use another's power for my own personal gain. That's not how we function in my family." She'd become defensive—why, she didn't know. "I don't know how he'll help me if he agrees to it. I was only told in a letter that a man named Cristos can help me return to Akkinor. That's all."

"May I read the letter?" He laughed when he saw the grimace on her lips. "I suppose I should've expected that. You're cleverer than you let on. You know..." She raised an eyebrow when he trailed off, and that sheepish smile of his—ineffective when paired with the wickedness in his eyes—returned. "I should've left you in the forest that day. I regret nothing, of course, but my actions are still surprising—even to myself. The thrill of the adventure entices me. As do you."

She blushed. "It seems like you should be crediting the danger, not the adventure. Maybe it was the prospect of reward that enticed you, Mister Sherbourne. Maybe if you came with me, you'd be presented with an opportunity you couldn't refuse."

Something dark and haunting passed over his face. He was offended by her words, but the emotion was gone as quickly as it came. Still, even when the look disappeared, his eyes lacked the playful ambience that normally illuminated his oceanic irises.

She hadn't intended to offend him by suggesting that he'd betray her. On the contrary—she simply wanted to observe his reaction to her statement. Had he been anything other than offended, she might've revisited her former suspicions of him, but he *had* seemed hurt by her words. That secured her belief that he could be trusted. He'd been given more than enough opportunities to do her harm or to alert assassins of her whereabouts. His actions had earned her trust, but only proof from the heart could calm her fears for good.

"If I wanted to betray you, I would've done so before we began trekking through the desert," he said. "It's nearly impossible to travel the desert on one's own. I'd be a fool to betray you now. I'd be a bigger fool if I betrayed you after surviving this place together. I may not be in Akkinor anymore, but I still have my honor. Not even Carthe can take that away from us."

She smiled a bit. She liked that her country had such a formidable reputation for being honorable. There'd always be individuals who lacked this common Akkinorian trait, but most of her people shared the same morals. She was glad to know Jack hadn't lost the trait after so many years in Carthe.

"I feel a strange pull towards you," he continued. "Almost like we've met before. Maybe that's what entices me."

Her lips quirked. "I think we'd both know if we had."

"Maybe."

"Do you think we would've been friends in Akkinor, had we known one another?"

"I like to think so." His playful demeanor returned as his eyes danced with imagination. "There's something about you. I can't quite put my finger on it. But if we *had* known one another in Akkinor, I would've done exactly what I did here in Carthe."

Aurelia raised an eyebrow. "Pray tell."

"I would've followed you."

Her cheeks warmed. "Followed me where, exactly?"

"Does it matter?"

No, it didn't. Not to her. She thought about her parents' letter and how her father had warned her about the types of people she'd meet in Carthe: *people who will try to kill you, people who will take you for ransom, people who will protect you, and people who will want to follow you.* Jack knew so little about her, and yet, he still wanted to follow her, even if it led him straight into the enemy's arms. She wanted to believe that he was a thrill-seeker who would've followed anyone on an adventure, but when she looked into his eyes, she knew there was another reason—a reason even Jack himself didn't understand.

Something about her was familiar to him. Captivating, tempting, *enticing*. He didn't know what it was, but she could see the answer on the tip of his tongue. If he ever learned the truth about her, he'd finally know why he'd fought so hard to be her companion. She doubted he'd be surprised. It was all right there in front of him, just waiting for him to put the pieces together.

Jack, to her understanding, was no nearer to learning the truth than he was on the day they met. To him, she was Lily Linden, a young woman trying to escape an angry little brother and a debt to the noblemen of her country. To him, Queen Aurelia was across the sea on her golden throne, toying with men's hearts because she was too vain to marry. The two women couldn't have been more different to Jack, and Aurelia didn't know if he'd be elated or furious to learn the truth. A part of her wished he'd never find out.

***

"This one would do nicely." Tyren Silio, Hand of the King, paused to adjust the emerald ascot tucked into his too-tight collar. The blotchy red skin on his neck strained and stretched in protest. "She's strong and healthy, according to the examiner, and young enough to service you for many years."

Daena Spirre pressed her lips in a thin line. "She's awfully thin."

Without a word, Tyren nodded and guided the noblewoman to the next. "This one is a bit plumper—she's recently given birth, so I've been told—but she's strong. The king had her tongue removed not a fortnight ago. She won't give you much trouble."

"Was she known to bleat in the night?"

Tyren chuckled. "And then some."

The Lady of Sadia waved her hand dismissively. "Show me another."

He took a few steps forwards before stopping once more. "I wouldn't waste my time on this one, my lady. She's a bit slow in the head. Can't tell the difference between a food trough and a water trough."

Daena narrowed her eyes—one brown and one hazel—and crouched to the ground before the contender. The girl, no older than twenty at most, mirrored the positions of the dozen others in the room as she knelt on the tiled floor with her head bowed and her wrists tied behind her back. She was rather plump for one so short with a mousy face and dull, frizzy brown hair cropped to her ears. A small whimper escaped her lips when

Daena took her chin, forcing the girl to look the noblewoman in the eye. The girl, like Daena herself, had eyes of two different colors: one brown and one blue.

Daena smiled. "I shall take this one."

Tyren blinked at her, surprised, but didn't question her decision. "As you wish." He pulled the girl to her feet and untied her wrists as she wobbled whilst finding her footing—only to tie her hands over her stomach rather than behind her back. "Tell us your name, girl."

Her chin trembled. "A-Aysia."

"Aysia," Daena repeated. "You're Sadian-born?"

"Y-Yes, milady."

"You'll do well with my family in Arrenwood, then." Daena scanned the girl's body in search of any potential deformities, then smiled when none could be found. "What was your position here in the palace?"

Aysia swallowed. "I was a lady's maid for the queen."

"Former queen," Tyren corrected.

"I've no need for another lady's maid," Daena replied, ignoring the Lord Hand. Aysia bowed her head again as her face turned crimson. "My son's intended will be residing at the castle with us until both come of age to marry. You will tend to her." As the girl nodded, Daena turned her gaze to Tyren. "Would it be terrible of me to ask you to summon the king? I'd like to say my goodbyes before we leave for Sadia."

He bowed. "At once."

Tyren exited the room, leaving the remaining eleven women and girls behind. They were former servants to the now disgraced Queen Aurelia, who'd all been imprisoned after surviving the siege on the palace.

Daena escorted her new servant towards the foyer. "There's something else," she murmured when the two were alone. Aysia only stared at her, wide-eyed, as her shoeless feet skidded against the floor. "I've considered an alternate path for my son's intended—the daughter of my husband's brother. I hope to see Spirre blood ruling Akkinor one day, dear Aysia. If my niece can win His Grace's heart, the next king will be both Brentwood and Spirre. You've worked in the palace long enough to know what the king prefers in a woman. I'd like you to train my niece for a place at his side. Help her become exactly the woman he'd like to take for a bride. If he grows smitten with her, you'll be generously rewarded."

A small gasp escaped Aysia's throat. "My lady—"

"Can you manage that, or would you prefer to return to the dungeon?"

"I-I can!" She tried to curtsy, but it was clumsy and lacking poise because of her bound hands. "I'll do my best by you, my lady."

"I thought as much. If you succeed, you'll have done a great service to all. The king may very well have a wife and an heir by this time next year. Those who continue to support his sister, wherever she may be, will have no choice but to declare loyalty to the king while she remains unmarried and childless. He will have an heir, and she will have no means of securing the Brentwood line. Akkinor won't forget your service if you manage to secure a wife for our king—and, subsequently, an heir."

The weight of the task seemed to settle on Aysia's shoulders, as the emaciated young woman whimpered and hunched like a wagon of bricks had fallen on her back.

Spotting Tyren and the king approaching from the other end of the corridor, Daena nodded her head towards a nearby Spirre soldier. When he approached, she set a hand on Aysia's shoulder. "Escort the young lady to the carriage. I'll be there shortly."

The soldier nodded his head, bowed, and took a trembling Aysia by the wrists. As they left for the bailey, Daena met both the king and the Lord Hand halfway across the foyer. As customary for the new king, she curtsied before taking his outstretched hand and pressing a kiss to his knuckles.

"Your Grace." She rose from her curtsy and smiled. "I'd like to thank you for donating one of your girls. Young Elria will be pleased with her. In fact, I'd like to bring Elria for a visit to the palace in the near future. She's rather infatuated with Your Grace—how overjoyed she is to see the rightful King of Akkinor on the throne!"

King Archie's face was blank and expressionless, but his eyes shone with smugness. "I should hope so. I hope the girl is satisfactory."

"She will be. It's been a trying thing to find help suitable enough for a highborn girl in Sadia. Elria is the first Spirre daughter born since I myself arrived on the earthly realm. The gods seem to have a fondness for bestowing daughters when they aren't wanted."

"I'd say so." The king, taller than Daena by only a few inches, peered down his nose at her with his hands clasped behind his back. "I shall be most displeased if my future bride produces a firstborn daughter. I'd have no choice but to send the child away."

Daena chuckled. "Your parents were seen as the jesters of the realm when they failed to dispose of your sister!"

Daena didn't see the king move, but the next thing she knew, one of his hands was tightly wrapped around her throat while his hot breath warmed her face from only an inch away. She felt her body tilted backwards, her feet scraping the floor, as his hand on her neck lifted her body with surprising strength. A choked sound escaped her lips as her eyes bugged out of her skull, and the only thing she could see was the king's blazing blue eyes piercing hers.

"Say what you will about my sister," he seethed, "but if you wish to keep your head, you will never disrespect my parents in my presence again. Am I understood?"

Daena must've nodded, as the king released her without another word. As she stumbled and gasped for air, he merely muttered something to Tyren before clasping his hands behind his back again and walking off in the direction he'd come from. Daena rubbed her tender throat, startled and humiliated, as Tyren barked at the nearby servants—who'd been watching the interaction as if it were a theater performance—to get back to work.

Tyren brushed dust from the shoulder of his suitcoat. "You shall have to forgive His Grace. He's just received word that his sister escaped a pair of assassins in Carthe. He's rather sore about it." As if she hadn't been choked into seeing spots only a moment earlier, he smiled cheerfully and offered his arm for her to take. "May I escort you to the carriage?"

***

While Jack snoozed beside her, Aurelia gazed around their campsite to observe where the midnight sky met the sand dunes in the distance. Jack claimed that his makeshift warning bells weren't as effective in the desert; it was one of many reasons why he refused to cross the Ngora Valley on his own. The pair would have to sleep in shifts for the remainder of their time in the desert—if they didn't, one or both would have to sleep with one eye open.

Jack was less worried about the threat of animals and other travelers than he was about the desert folk. Like the Violet Forest, the valley was crawling with tribal people who'd adapted to living in the desert. Some were harmless, some were cannibals, and some were skilled thieves who stole most of their supplies from innocent travelers. Jack explained that most tended to stay close to the borders of the valley's surrounding kingdoms where they were sure to find victims. Even so, he seemed concerned, and he'd advised Aurelia to sleep with her knife in hand.

Aurelia didn't mind having to sleep in shifts. She'd done it before with Kaia, so her body was somewhat accustomed to being conscious for more than a day. Being liable for her own safety—and Jack's—gave her a sense of purpose and responsibility she hadn't felt in weeks. She'd spent so long relying on Jack and Kaia that she'd forgotten what it was to rely on herself.

As she listened to Jack's chest rumble with each snore, she thought about the friend she'd lost. The few weeks she'd spent with Kaia felt like another lifetime. Her memories of Kaia had already begun to fade—exactly as her memories of her parents started to fade after their deaths—and when she found herself unable to conjure the sound of Kaia's laughter, her eyes stung like someone had poured acid over her face.

Maybe, she wondered, Kaia wouldn't have been so adamant about assisting her if she'd known who Aurelia was upon their first meeting. Maybe Jack, too, would've been less enticed and more frightened by the idea of following her if he knew the truth. She'd warned them as much as she could without revealing herself, but it wasn't enough.

She glanced over at Jack as a jolt of adrenaline coursed through her veins. For a moment, she debated waking him and telling him everything. He was an Akkinorian, after all, and an Omaran at that—perhaps he could've helped her further if he knew who she was.

She was shaking him awake before she realized what she was doing. Until his eyes opened, she had every intention of introducing herself not as Lily Linden, but as Aurelia Brentwood, Queen of Akkinor. When he blinked and met her gaze, though, every bit of courage in her heart fizzled away. She *couldn't* tell him. She couldn't put the burden of knowledge on his shoulders, and she couldn't ask him to keep such a powerful secret.

"Lily? Is everything all right?"

Aurelia swallowed the lump in her throat. "Fine. I was just-um-well, my mind was wandering, and I was desperately bored, so I thought I'd wake you."

"How considerate of you," he joked. She cracked a smile as he rolled onto his back and stretched. "What's on your mind?"

"I don't know. Too many things, all at once. Could you...Could you tell me something, Jack? Something to distract me?"

"Like what?"

She smirked a bit. "I'd like to hear about that lady of yours. Louisia, wasn't it?"

"Yes. Lou." He tucked his hands under his head and stared at the dim stars above them. "She was born in Khaba. Her mother was a concubine, her father an Esposi pirate. He was killed not six weeks after her conception, and her mother died in childbirth. She was raised by her mother's friends at the brothel. Left when she turned fourteen. She would've been indentured as a concubine if she'd stayed a day longer."

"How did you meet?"

"I mistook her for a barmaid, and she hit me over the head with a metal pitcher," he recalled, laughing. "We shared a drink after making amends and found ourselves walking together for some time before we decided to make the arrangement permanent. We were both desperate for intimacy at the time, too. Better to lay with someone you admire than with someone who only wants you for your silver." He turned his head to raise an eyebrow at her. "And you? What was your last partner like, Lily dear? Was he a brawny lumberjack trapped in a loveless marriage, or a skinny shepherd aiming to propose marriage after the first kiss?"

"You presume an unmarried peasant girl such as me would engage in a thoughtless, passionate affair with the highest-bidding farmhand?"

Even in the darkness, she saw his face redden. "I didn't mean—"

"I'm only teasing you," she said with a laugh. He grunted. "He wasn't a farmhand, nor a lumberjack or a shepherd. He was the son of the groom at our local stables. Everyone called him Buck, though I haven't the slightest idea as to why, and I never learned his true name."

He was curious now. "What happened to him?"

"He moved away," she lied. "I never saw him again."

She didn't know what had happened to Buck. His father, Gus, had worked in the palace stables since before Aurelia's father was crowned king. She grew up seeing Buck each and every time she took her horse from the stables, as he worked there with his father. When they were older, she visited him more frequently, but there was never any longing or love between them—only lust.

She'd visited him for the last time just a few weeks before the uprising. She'd gone for a walk late at night, hoping to clear her head after receiving an infuriating letter from Lady Spirre, and soon found herself at the stables. Only Buck was there. Linden, ever the loyal friend, guarded the stables from afar while Buck romanced their queen atop bales of hay. When they finished, he'd bowed to her and said, "Always an honor, Your Grace." They'd laughed so hard that Linden, mistaking their laughter for sounds of terror, rushed into the stables to rescue her before Aurelia had finished buttoning the front of her gown.

Something deep in her soul told her that Buck was dead. Buck, Gus, and the many others who worked in the stables. Aurelia had shared a cordial relationship with her staff, and her fondness for the stable hands was no secret. She often spent her leisurely time helping them care for her mare, Delilah. Once, she'd even broken protocol by inviting them to the palace for dinner simply to express her gratitude. They were good and honorable workers who'd become more like friends than staff—the least she could do was invite them into her home for a meal befitting of royalty.

Archie would've gone after anyone in the Folly whom he knew Aurelia favored. He'd order his men to torture them for information regarding her whereabouts: Linden, Cicely, Estylle, Ma Shela, her lady's maids, her secret lovers. Everyone she'd ever cared for was likely a victim of Archie's greed. She wondered if those lives would've been spared if she hadn't followed her parents' instructions to run away to Carthe.

"Jack?" she whispered.

"Hmm?"

"Would you mind terribly if I slept?"

A pause. "Not at all."

She considered lying down on her blanket a ways away from him, but the rhythmic rising and falling of his chest called to her like a beckoning from the gods, and she soon found herself curled up against his side with her cheek on his chest and her arm splayed over his stomach. He sucked in a sharp breath, surprised, and rested his arm over her back as he gently pulled her closer to his side.

The weight of his arm on her body and the feel of his veins bulging against her skin reminded her of Buck. The two didn't often lay in each other's arms after their endeavors, but every once in a while, they'd find themselves lying there beside one another, too absorbed in the effects of intimacy and desire to move. Even so, she'd never known what it was to lay in a man's arms for nothing more than comfort. It was her body that Buck and her other lovers had sought to please, not her soul.

Jack was different. She could feel it in the way he held her, hear it in the pattern of his breathing as his cheek touched the top of her head. Despite the refreshing change of pace, she wondered what it would feel like to have him tangled in her limbs, naked and hot with desire. She wondered if he'd know his way around her body instinctively, or—like the others—if it'd take him a time or two to grow familiar with the curves of her muscles, the dipping of her hips, the swelling of her chest. She wondered if he'd be gentle and sensual like a devoted husband drowning in love for his wife, or rough and demanding like a young bachelor desperate to leave his mark on a woman's willing body.

She prayed he couldn't feel her body temperature increase while her brain ran ramped with imaginings, dreams, desires. She didn't wish for him to know—or even *speculate*—that she thought such things about him. It wasn't just that she knew he'd mock her for it, as he liked getting a rise out of her in any way he could. It was because she could feel the way he craved her, too—feel it filling the hollows of her body when he rubbed her back in comforting circles, feel it inching down her throat when the heavy mass of his leg pressed against hers. He imagined her the same way she imagined him, and the moment he sensed the way she starved for him, there'd be nothing left for them to do but sink into one another until everything else faded into oblivion.

Her country, her throne, her secrets and unanswered questions...everything would be locked away in some inaccessible corner of her mind, swallowed whole and hidden by a veil of indifference, the moment Jack obstructed her senses with those dangerously capable hands warming her skin and that beckoning, wicked mouth taunting hers.

Aurelia was a pyre, a bland and dry stack of wood with nothing to do but prevail until her moment of promise arrived. Jack was a spark of life, a burning ember just awaiting the cue to turn a lonely pyre into a blazing inferno.

Aurelia knew better than most that an inferno couldn't be stopped once it'd begun. Human autonomy or not, the instant she and Jack made their imaginations a reality, she'd be at his mercy. No woman with half a brain could lay with a man like Jack and want anything except to be engulfed by him.

As the sound of his heartbeat lulled her to sleep, she felt the tiniest bit of moisture on her forehead. A small, unintended sound of contentment escaped her when his lips lingered on her skin for just a moment too long. She yearned for the warmth of his mouth when he pulled away, but fear—not of rejection, but of loss—prevented her from seeking more than a mere kiss on the forehead.

At least one man had almost undoubtedly lost his life for being the recipient of Aurelia's tenderness and affection. Her fondness for Buck (among others) may not have been common knowledge, but it wouldn't have been difficult for Archie to ascertain after a few clever interrogations. Even if Archie wasn't in Carthe to observe her growing affection for Jack, his assassins were, and what better way to break her spirit and hinder her motivation than to claim the life of the man she so adored?

The recessive part of her wanted nothing more than to deny the way her body and soul yearned for Jack, but the dominant part of her—the part that'd never forget what fate befell those who showed any degree of fondness for the Queen of Akkinor—sought to bury that yearning with everything she had.

XIX

Days later, there was still nothing to be seen for miles other than sand, sparse plants, and the occasional animal roaming the terrain. Aurelia and Jack hadn't spotted another person since they left Dofell. Jack wanted to stay a safe distance behind the other travelers in the event of some sort of attack, so the groups were far ahead of them. As they continued to move forward, though, Aurelia spotted figures in the distance huddled around a fire.

"Jack—?"

"I don't know." The lines on his forehead deepened with worry. "Let's ask, shall we?"

When they rode up to the travelers, all eyes turned to the pair. She followed Jack's lead when he dismounted Sterling and led him forward by the reins. While keeping Scotch close, she studied the travelers' makeshift campsite. The group was sitting together around the fire, dining on some sort of meat, with their supplies not far behind.

"Hello." Jack stopped a few paces from the group with his hand on the hilt of his sword. "What's going on here?"

"We're stopping for the night," the guide replied. "There's a sandstorm coming tomorrow. We have to seek shelter in the tavern for the day and the night. We've stopped here to warn travelers of the storm. If you get caught in that, you won't see Taundosa."

"Thank you for the warning, but why stop now? Why not keep moving forwards to the tavern?"

"There's been an increase in travelers passing through the valley. Not enough room in the tavern to host so many travelers each day and night. Every visitor is allowed one night's stay—no more than that. We need to make our one night count if we want to avoid the sandstorm."

"You're welcome to join us," a woman said. "It seems the other groups have already moved on."

Her distinct features—a long, broad nose, feline eyes, and fawny skin—reminded Aurelia of Kaia, so she assumed the woman was a northern Carthinian. "The tavern is a few miles from here. We'll be leaving before the sun rises."

Jack smiled and thanked her. He and Aurelia sat in the sand with the travelers and shared the water in their last full canteen. She was aware of the travelers watching them closely, but she pretended not to feel their eyes. The last thing she needed was for one of them to find her suspicious—*especially* if she and Jack weren't the only Akkinorians present.

"What are you two going east for?" the guide asked. "Riches? Work? A place to start a family?"

Jack held up his left hand. "These were a sham." Aurelia exhaled when she saw the twine wedding band on his finger. They'd both forgotten to remove the rings after leaving Dofell. "Just a precaution. We're not married. Lily's searching for a friend in Taundosa, and I'm simply her traveling companion."

"How sweet!" A young woman with white hair practically swooned. If Aurelia had to guess, she would've believed the woman to be a native Isalder of Glacier Bay. "We are looking for a new home. The north hasn't been kind to us." She elbowed the man sitting to her left. "I told you we should've made passage for Akkinor. There's nothing left for us in Carthe."

A short, stubby man next to Jack scoffed at the woman and pointed a clean animal bone at her. "Akkinor is no better than Carthe. I've heard the king is corrupt. Taking money from the people to fund his adventures. You're better off here than under the command of a thief like that."

Aurelia's blood boiled, but she forced herself to maintain her composure. This wasn't the time nor place for her temper to make a reappearance.

Another man, dark-skinned and rather short, shook his head. "No, no, you've got it all wrong. Edmund hasn't been king in years. There was the shipwreck, remember? His girl took the throne after he and the queen drowned on their way home from Carthe." The pendant around his neck told her he was formerly an Esposi pirate, as most pirates wore necklaces identical to his. The symbol stamped onto a pirate's pendant identified their allegiance to their ship and its captain. "I don't know what was so fascinating to them about this place, anyway. Cost them their lives, in the end."

"Drowned." The husband of the white-haired woman snorted. His gravelly, guttural accent—paired with his pale blond hair and gray eyes—confirmed his identity as an Isalder. "It was foul play, undoubtedly. The King and Queen of Akkinor don't simply *drown* on a routine trip to Carthe." Both Jack and Aurelia shifted uncomfortably while the man gave his wife a pointed look. "*That* is why we didn't go to Akkinor, my dove. Even the king wasn't safe there."

Aurelia's gut twisted. Of course, upon learning that her parents were lost at sea, she considered that something nefarious had been at play. Until survivors of the shipwreck washed up on the coast of Quapebet, all of Akkinor wondered if their king and queen had been murdered somehow. Though their deaths had been officially labeled as accidental, there were still those who believed there was more to the story Aurelia didn't have the strength to face those rumors. It was enough that her parents were dead—she didn't need to spend the rest of her life wondering about their last moments.

The stubby man beside Jack took a swig of wine from his canteen. "I saw her once, y'know. The queen. Back when I was a rower aboard the *Tigress*. We transported silver ore to Seaport from an independent merchant in Caedia. She was there, watching while we unloaded. Very pretty. Had this long brown hair that got in the way of everything. She could barely see with the wind blowing it in her eyes."

Jack was frowning. "From what I've heard, the Queen of Akkinor has blonde hair, not brown."

"Lies. I've seen her."

"I don't know, mate," the Esposi muttered. "I've heard it's blonde, too."

"This is irrelevant." The Kanish-looking woman popped a handful of sugared nuts into her mouth. "We ought to feel bad for her. The poor thing lost both of her parents in an instant."

The stubby man was unfazed. "She gained a crown, didn't she?"

"That doesn't compare," the Isalder woman argued. "It's a terrible thing for any child to lose their parents—royal blood or not."

"They don't call her the *Queen of Sorrows* for nothing," her husband added.

Aurelia stilled. *Queen of Sorrows?*

Jack raised an eyebrow, frowning again. "I've never heard such an absurd moniker used to describe Akkinor's leader. Wherever did it come from?"

"Don't be daft," the Carthinian woman snapped. "That girl is younger than any of us in this circle, and yet, her life has been one of great tragedy. Her parents are lost at sea, and she's immediately expected to take her father's place as monarch. Half of her people would rather see her dead than bow to her simply because of her sex. If she hasn't married already, she'll be pressured to do so, and those in power will secretly prefer her husband—whomever he may be—to her. They'll argue that she's unfit to rule while she bears children, yet they'll expect her to have as many as she can. After all, it's her duty to ensure the line of succession." The woman sighed as if the situation was personal to her. "She's as sorrowful as they come. I give it ten years before the poor thing is overthrown or murdered."

Aurelia didn't bat an eye. "I give it five."

When she spoke for the first time, all seven people seated around the fire turned to stare at her. The stubby man snorted in agreement, the Carthinian woman sighed again, and the others changed the topic to discuss something cheerier. Even Jack only exhaled as if he, too, agreed with her.

Hearing them talk about her like that made Aurelia feel odd—as if she really *was* Lily Linden, and Queen Aurelia was someone else entirely. In that moment, Aurelia Brentwood felt like a distant friend, like someone she'd known once upon a time when everything was right in the world. It was difficult to remember that the person in question was herself.

Queen of Sorrows. Perhaps, she thought, it was a nickname coined by native Carthinians to describe Akkinor's queen. Given what little information they had on the Queen of Akkinor, it wasn't so difficult to believe. Only terrible, despondent news from Akkinor reached the average Carthinian individual, and with that came the opportunity to invent even more terrible and despondent stories.

The Carthinian woman was right about it all. Aurelia had earned the pity of thousands because of her parents' tragic deaths, but that was only the beginning. It wasn't enough that Akkinor was the most stable and prosperous country in the realm; so long as she was a woman ruling a country dominated by men, she'd never be a ruler as admired and beloved as her father.

When she'd asked Edmund why their people despised a female monarch so fiercely, he'd blamed the ill-fated rule of Queen Alora. When she'd asked her mother the same thing, Cressida had a different answer:

"Women have something that men do not: the ability to create life. Whether you are Queen, Queen Consort, or lacking a title, that remains the same. Only you can provide heirs for the Brentwood name. Do you remember how ill I felt when Archie was in my belly?"

Of course she did. She'd only been three, and still, she'd been mortified. Cressida was confined to bedrest for half a season, and in the last two weeks before Archie's birth, she'd been perfectly miserable. Cressida's screams during her labors had shaken the palace and haunted little Aurelia's dreams.

"You will experience the same feelings when you are with child," Cressida continued. "Because of that, many of your subjects will argue that you are unfit to rule. I pray your childbearing years will be over by the time you take the throne, but we can't be certain of anything. What you must remember is this: our country believes that women are weaker than men because we have a power they do not. Men can't harness what the gods granted us, so instead of worshipping and protecting us, they aim to control us. It's silly, really, but it's the way of the world. You must show them that you are anything but weak if you wish to keep your crown."

When she was older, Aurelia understood exactly what her mother meant. If she wanted to keep her throne, she had to prove to her people that she could be both mother and queen—that she could balance the two roles without neglecting her country as Queen Alora had.

That was one of many items on her engagement diary for the near future. Maybe if she returned to Akkinor and defeated her brother, it'd be enough to show her people that she deserved to sit on the throne. If not, she'd have to find another way to prove herself before she faced yet another uprising—and as far as she knew, the odds of her reclaiming her throne for a second time were poorer than they ought to be.

Queen of Sorrows. Perhaps it *was* a fitting moniker after all.

***

Still trapped in her thoughts and fighting the urge to pity her own life, Aurelia said goodnight to Jack and the travelers while they continued chatting around the fire. They were all drinking wine from the stubby man's flask, chuckling and conversing, as the sky grew darker and the moon brighter above their heads.

She couldn't sleep, not with their voices cutting through the silence of the desert like knives, so she hoped and prayed that her woes would serve as a lullaby. Even letting her despair lull her to sleep was impossible, what with Jack's energetic voice practically rattling her eardrums. The blithering idiot wouldn't sleep until their comrades were sleeping, too. He liked to talk, she'd noticed, to anyone—or anything—who'd listen. He'd be wide awake until the only person left for him to converse with was himself.

"She sleeping?" The stubby man's voice interrupted a brief period of silence. When Aurelia felt Jack's leg twitch against hers, she knew they were talking about her. "Pretty lady. You're a lucky man."

Jack tittered. "No, no. It isn't like that."

"Should be."

"How did you two meet?" It was the Isalder woman's voice that rang out next, as sharp as the northern winds of Glacier Bay. "Have you been together long?"

"Somewhat," Jack replied. "I saved her from a pair of forest maggots. She saved me from being alone. It's been quite the partnership."

Aurelia could practically hear the woman swooning. "How romantic! I hope you aren't separating when you reach Taundosa. I'd hate to see the two of you part from one another."

"We haven't spoken of it. I agreed to follow her into Taundosa, but neither of us knows where life will take us after that. I suppose we'll have to wait and see."

Aurelia held her breath. She could feel him looking at her.

"Well, if you want my opinion, *I* think the two of you make a beautiful couple," the Isalder woman said. Aurelia could practically see the white-haired woman leaning closer to Jack, eyeing him, when she added, "You really haven't so much as kissed her?"

He coughed. "No."

"What a shame. At least you managed to fool the guards at the gates, though. It's odd, isn't it? I shall never understand why Dofell demands we travelers take such absurd measures simply to cross the kingdom."

"Couples, families—they're all looking for new beginnings, and they won't find that in Dofell. They don't *want* that in Dofell." Aurelia recognized the guide's voice when he spoke next. He'd been kind and soft-spoken earlier, but now his tone oozed with bitterness. "Lone travelers know what awaits them when they cross those gates. We have no soldiers beyond the walls protecting us from the outside world. You saw what strides our people make to earn a living. The man who offered ten gold for the girl's locket? He used to be earl of the very same lands we were standing on until his family's debts caught up to him. Lost his home, his title. He lives as a commoner now, forced to sell whatever hadn't been taken from him to keep his family from starving."

Aurelia's chest constricted as she withheld a gasp. He was talking about her. She hadn't even known the guide was nearby when the Dofelli merchant stopped her to inquire after her locket. She could almost see the guide's dark umber eyes burning the words into Jack's gaze—Jack, a supplement for Aurelia while she pretended to snooze.

"Highborn fall from grace, too, you know," he continued. "Happens all the time. Anyway, my point is that lone travelers tend to be like vermin: they infest you. They disappear for a time, long enough for you to think they've gone, and return when you're at your lowest. They know where you live, where you work, what you sell—then they take it from you, and they go on their way to get richer somewhere else. Half the population is too weak to stand a fighting chance against people like that. The other half never had anything of value to begin with." Something resembling a scoff escaped him. "The king can't afford to get involved. I'd wager the rotten fool eats nothing but potatoes for dinner more often than not, too, like the rest of us. Until he and his idiot advisors find a way to pay what they owe to the continent, they're as useless as planting anything other than potatoes in that gods-forsaken soil."

He laughed, and soon the others did, too—all except Jack and the Isalder couple, though the latter quickly feigned chuckles of understanding.

Aurelia shuddered. A place where next to nothing grew in the ground, where one man's selfishness had damned an entire population. She wondered if Myenar had placed a curse on the kingdom—or the Phyre family, at least—for the late king's failures. After all, debt alone didn't lead to the land decaying or the awful, constant dreariness encapsulating the entire kingdom. Their Almighty had cursed them to live in barren lands, leaving them very little to offer as a means of making money.

She hadn't had a very high opinion of Dofell before arriving in Carthe, and her thoughts hadn't changed upon seeing it for herself. She hadn't known how truly horrible it was, even while trekking through mountains of filth and waste, until now.

Later in the night when the fire turned to nothing but ash and soot, Aurelia rolled over to face her fellow travelers and sighed when she saw that each of them was asleep. She sat up on her blanket, still unable to sleep, and stared at the dunes in the direction they'd come from. For a moment, she imagined the dunes were the rolling, grassy hills of the Folly—then an awful howl echoed in the distance, and she reminded herself that she was a long ways from home. She'd never hear something like *that* in the Folly.

She looked back at the travelers. Two were Isalders, if not free citizens of the Syren Isles; one was a former Esposi pirate; the traveling guide was a native of Dofell; and the other two were natives of Carthe, though she couldn't be sure about which kingdoms they called home. Four distinct cultures sat huddled in a group together, relying on one another for one night and one night only—and while Aurelia never imagined she'd find herself surrounded by such an eclectic group, a part of her found it incredible that all eight of them had managed to put their differences aside to see each other to safety.

Carthe is a dangerous place overrun by dangerous people. That's what Aurelia had been told all her life. She never thought to expect any degree of kindness, hospitality, or mercy from Carthinians until she experienced the continent for herself. The lore surrounding Carthe—which made most Akkinorians terrified of the western world—was proving to be more like mythology than fact.

She'd have to do something about that when she reclaimed her throne. Kaia Bolas deserved that much, as did every innocent Carthinian who'd been branded as heathen or savage by the realm's most influential nation.

"Lily?"

To her left, Jack rubbed his tired eyes and pushed himself upwards to a sitting position. Only then did she realize that she'd been anxiously tapping her fingernails against the soles of her shoes. It wasn't a particularly loud noise, but loud enough to wake a man who slept with one eye perpetually open.

When she didn't respond to him, he sat beside her with his legs bent and his arms draped over his knees. He looked especially handsome that night with his hair tousled and his eyes glistening with sleepiness, and when he ran his tongue over his cracked lips, she resisted the urge to throw herself onto his lap and press her mouth to his.

It was getting more difficult by the day to remember that acting on her ever-growing fondness for Jack meant putting him at an even greater risk of being targeted by Archie's assassins—that finally giving in to the way she craved him meant providing them with one more person to use as leverage against her.

Jack, too, was staring at the dunes in the distance. He was silent for several moments until he turned to her with a raised eyebrow and frustration etched into the lines of his face.

"The queen. Her hair is blonde, isn't it?"

Aurelia chuckled. "I suppose it could be."

She nonchalantly glanced down at the frizzy, frayed ends of her braided hair. The color had changed more times than she could count throughout her lifetime. Before she turned three, it was so blonde that it could've been mistaken for Isalder white. Her curls darkened to a pale, orangey-red in the years that followed, and between the ages of eleven and fifteen, it was as auburn as her mother's. After that, her hair settled on a permanent hue: blonde etched with wisps of coppery red, giving the illusion of locks that seemed to radiate a golden glow.

Jack nodded his head towards the stubby man sleeping beside them. "The fool must've mistaken a noblewoman for her. I don't suppose the queen inspects cargo at Seaport, anyway."

"I wouldn't think so."

"Who do you think it was? The brown-haired woman?"

Aurelia's heart raced. "I wouldn't know where to begin."

Another lie. It made her chest ache to lie to Jack, but she wouldn't dare tell him the truth—that the brown-haired woman in question was Cicely Poole, close friend and lady-in-waiting to the queen, who often visited Seaport with the queen's men to deliver gifts to sailors and their families. After so many years at the queen's side, Cicely appeared and acted like nobility. Aurelia didn't blame the stubby man for mistaking her friend for her.

"I wonder what she's doing at this very moment," Jack added.

"Who?"

"The queen, of course."

Aurelia's throat felt thick. She'd had quite enough of talking about "the queen" for one day. At the very least, the inquiries made by Jack and the other travelers were proof that news of the uprising hadn't yet reached Carthe.

"I don't know," she murmured. "Why do you ask?"

"Curiosity. It's nice to think of her like she's as normal as you and I."

Fearing her voice would betray her, Aurelia swallowed the lump in her throat and clamped her jaw shut. Instead of replying, she exhaled and rested her head on Jack's shoulder. He froze, surprised by her sudden movement, but didn't jerk away. Instead, he rested his head on hers and mirrored her exhale. Neither uttered a word until Aurelia mustered the courage to speak again:

"Jack?"

"Hmm?"

"I'm sure she likes to think of herself as normal, too."

He paused. "Thinking like that must make them more tolerable. Her sorrows."

Her eyelids fluttered shut. "As tolerable as sorrows can be."

XX

As Aurelia, Jack, and the group crossed the barren desert, the Queen of Akkinor wrapped her fingers around her locket and weighed it in her hand. For some reason, the necklace seemed to grow heavier as they drew nearer to Taundosa. If she couldn't find Arian Cristos in the City of Gold, the locket hanging from her neck would be all she'd ever have left of her home.

Home. Whenever she'd leave the palace, she dreamt of returning. She craved the familiarity, the comfort, and the safety of the Folly. Each time she left, she thought about the things she was excited to see when she returned. Cicely would wait for her carriage on the front steps of the palace, wanting to be the first person to welcome Aurelia home. She loved walking the halls after time away and catching up with her staff about changes in their lives that she may have missed, like the birth of a cook's first child or the marriage of a footman to a lady's maid.

She even looked forward to the sound of the pianoforte, which Archie tended to play for hours on end. She'd understood that he never intended to welcome her home with a song, but she liked to think he did. It was easier to greet him when she chose to believe that he was happy to have her home again.

She never dreaded coming home to her brother. Sometimes she even missed him. She always thought of him when they were apart, despite how unfazed he was by her existence, and she was always disappointed when she returned home to him—mainly because *he* was disappointed to see *her*.

Archie hadn't always despised her. They were close as children and even as teenagers, though his resentment grew as they did. It wasn't until her coronation when he became something different. Until their parents died, Aurelia and Archie Brentwood were siblings. After the shipwreck, they were nothing but two people who lived under the same roof and dined at the same table.

"Lily?"

For a moment when she glanced up and to her left, she saw her brother. Scrawny and pale with icy blue eyes, overgrown blonde hair that no governess or stylist could ever tame, and freckles spotted over his nose and arms. A permanent scowl was etched on his lips, the glare in his eyes as sharp as ever. Then Archie faded away and morphed into someone taller, someone stronger and kinder. Jack Sherbourne now sat on Sterling's back with his swirling blue eyes and unruly black curls. The malicious glint in Archie's eyes turned into a playful, charismatic shimmer in Jack's bright orbs.

She snapped out of her daze when he held out a canteen. "Oh. Thank you."

"We should be there shortly. Taundosa is about another week's journey from the tavern. It won't be long before we find this mystery man of yours. You shall be reunited with your family before you know it."

She smiled woefully. "No, I won't."

He furrowed his eyebrows in confusion but didn't press her for details. She gave the canteen back and kept her eyes forward as they crossed a tall dune. The wind was picking up now (making it obvious that a sandstorm was coming), but luckily, they'd arrived at their destination. A long, wide two-story structure became visible when they reached the top of the dune. It looked sturdy enough and offered plenty of protection from the elements—helpful for surviving a sandstorm—but she didn't understand how it existed.

"How on earth is it still here?" The smell of yeast and spices made her stomach growl. "I wouldn't think to build a tavern in the middle of a desert."

"It's the only way to keep people like us from starving to death. This building has been in Carthe for as long as I have, at least. No sandstorm or poor weather has managed to tear it down. Rumor has it that the mages of Carthe have it protected with some sort of spell. And surprisingly, the food and ale are spectacular. Merchants deliver supplies each week from both sides of Carthe."

She didn't need to trust his word. The scent alone was enough to tell her that the food was divine—at the least, it'd be better than what they'd been surviving on. She could hardly contain her excitement when they left the horses in the stables, which were built as sturdily as the tavern itself. The pair gathered their belongings and followed the group inside. When the door closed behind them, leaving the sun, sand, and heat on the other side, she removed her *fjardel* from her head and neck with unparalleled joy.

The clerk at the counter handed them each a pint of ale. "Oh," Aurelia murmured, startled by the hasty service. "Thank you."

He grunted in response and jabbed his thumb over his shoulder. "Bath's that way. Room's upstairs to the left. Food will be out soon." He dropped a singular key on the counter. "Don't break anything."

"We won't." Jack furrowed his eyebrows as he reached for the key. "Is this all you have? We'd prefer separate rooms."

"You get one room."

Aurelia frowned. "But—"

"Look," the clerk interrupted, irritated, "there's too many of you and not enough rooms. You can stay here, or you can brave the storm. Don't much matter to me." He folded his arms over his chest and stuck his nose up at Jack. "What's the problem? Don't trust yourself in bed with a fair maiden? Take the floor, lad."

Jack's eyes flashed. "Will do. Thank you for your hospitality." When they turned and walked up the stairs to their room, he released a frustrated exhale. "Bloody scoundrel."

Aurelia cracked a smile. When they found the room matching the number on the key, Jack unlocked it and opened the door for her. Like most of the inns she'd visited before, there wasn't much to see: a large bed beside a nightstand that bore nothing but an oil lamp, a window that appeared impossible to open, a chamber pot, and a basin for washing. It was dimly lit by candles and the lamp, smelled faintly of ale and smoke, and barely had enough floor space to comfortably host someone as gargantuan as Jack.

"Don't worry. I'll take the floor," he assured her, winking. "You're an awfully aggressive sleeper."

She snorted. "You're worse than I am. Your snoring could wake the dead."

"I beg your pardon?"

"I believe you heard me."

"I heard you. Half of Carthe probably heard you. Your voice carries like dragon fire."

She allowed herself a small, snarky smile. He was preparing a makeshift bed on the floor using his own two blankets, but she felt guilty for taking the bed to herself. She gave him two of the four pillows on the bed, which he seemed to appreciate, and removed her extra set of clothing from her pack. She wouldn't miss an opportunity to bathe and wash her clothes. As soon as there was a hot meal in her stomach, she'd be first in line for the bathhouse.

They rushed down to the tavern when everything had been settled in the room. Every traveler who'd left Dofell with them was there, eating and drinking and talking amongst themselves. Almost as soon as they sat down at an empty table, the clerk arrived with meals. Aurelia's mouth watered at the sight of bread, meat pie, vegetables, and a hearty portion of Carthinian sugared nuts. She ate it so quickly that her bowl was empty before Jack's. The way he stared at her—a combination of amusement, surprise, and admiration—made a fiery blush rise up on her cheeks.

While she finished her ale, he cleaned his bowl and immediately reached into his pocket. Her eyes widened when he produced a bar of soap similar to the one in her own pocket. They'd been thinking the same thing, which meant sharing the bathhouse rather than bathing separately (even a screen dividing the male and female baths did little to appeal to one's preference for privacy).

He raised an eyebrow when she held out her soap. They stared at one another for a moment, realizing they had the same intention, as a silent game ensued between them. Aurelia couldn't help but wiggle her eyebrows at him, which seemed to both excite and challenge him.

A smirk danced on her lips. "How would you feel about a race?"

His response was a grin. Then, just like that, he was gone. She barely had time to scramble to her feet before he rushed across the tavern towards the door leading to the bathhouse. Unfortunately for Jack, the inn hadn't been constructed for persons of his build. He was more of an obstacle than anything, while Aurelia was quick and light on her feet. She slipped right by him when he struggled to fit through the crowded doorway. As her laughter rang through the bathhouse, he quickly caught up to her and grabbed her by the waist. She let out a squeal as he lifted her from the ground, holding her directly over the male bathtub. Luckily, it was empty.

"Jack!" She clawed at his arms and kicked his legs. "Put me down, you filthy bastard!"

"Put you down? If you insist." When his grip on her waist faltered, threatening to send her plummeting into the water, she yelped and swatted at him. "All right, all right. I'll let you go—but only if you admit that I let you win."

She gaped. "That's outrageous!"

"Lily, dear—"

"Okay! Okay." She gave in when she felt herself slipping. She clutched his forearms and reluctantly stopped kicking him. "You let me win. Put me down before your bathwater turns red."

"Scary," he teased, setting her down. She ran a hand through her tousled hair before folding her arms over her chest. He offered her a sheepish, cheeky smile. "I saw an opportunity and I took it. Forgive me?"

She jabbed her finger into his hard, muscular chest. "Keep an eye out, Jack Sherbourne."

Her breath caught in her throat when his hand, rough and calloused, captured her chin and tilted her head backwards, forcing her to meet his gaze. She swallowed at his uncharacteristic dominance as he lowered his face close to hers, just barely grazing her lips with his. Her eyelids fluttered shut as she waited for a real kiss, but they quickly opened again when the warmth of his mouth disappeared. He must've felt the violent shiver that wracked her body, as his lips curled into a grin to reveal a full set of sparkling teeth.

Unwilling to let *him* taunt *her,* she wrenched herself from his grip, turned on her heel, and untied the front of her shirt. She shrugged the loosened garment from her shoulders to reveal her near-naked back. As she did so, she sauntered over to the other side of the bathhouse, where a thick screen divided the male bath from the female bath. She tossed a glance over her shoulder before slipping behind the curtain. When her eyes found his peeking out from above the curtain, she saw a new emotion glittering in his eyes: lust.

"I won't let you get away with that again," she warned.

"I should hope not." His voice was overcome and a bit isolated, like his head was lost among the clouds. "Go on, then. You smell like Scotch."

She rolled her eyes at him and finished undressing. When the garments were peeled from her body, she sniffed and immediately wrinkled her nose. She *did* smell like Scotch. The soap and water wouldn't be enough to remove the smell entirely, but she spent the next few minutes trying, nonetheless. She scrubbed until her skin was burning, red, and flaking. It felt wonderful to wash her hair after so long, as her curls had become matted and brown from sleeping on the sand. A foul taste filled her mouth when she washed her clothing and saw the cloud of murky brown water that appeared before her.

"I do miss this about Akkinor," Jack called out from the other side. "I never had to worry about being filthy at home. Here... Nobody wants to come close to a man who smells more like his horse than his horse does."

She snorted. "You've never had to worry about that. No matter which establishments we've visited, women have ogled you until the moment we left. Your stench doesn't seem to bother them."

"I could say the same about you." His voice was persistent, as if he were trying to convince her of something. "You tend not to notice them, but I certainly do. Men can't help but feel drawn to you. They're always staring, whispering, imagining. But you don't notice them, do you?"

She wasn't thinking about that. She was thinking about what he said: *Men can't help but feel drawn to you.* It was almost exactly what he'd said to her when they were discussing his opinions on Akkinor's queen: *I think the people can't help but serve her.*

"I don't pay much attention to the fantasies of men," she admitted, wringing her wet clothing. "I have more important priorities to concern myself with."

A pause. "Is that so?"

"Indeed it is."

No reply. She exhaled and dressed in her clean, dry clothing before gathering her belongings and peeking her head out from behind the curtain. She joined him when she saw that he was dressed. He was putting a knife back into his pocket and dabbing at his neck with a piece of cloth. He'd cut himself shaving, probably due to the absence of a mirror in the bathhouse, but she was glad he'd erased the scruff on his face. She thought he was much more handsome when he was clean-shaven. The thick hair of his beard tended to conceal the curve of his jaw, the sharpness of his cheekbones, and the dimple on his chin.

"What a miracle!" She grinned when she joined him. "You smell like a king, Jack."

"And you like a queen, Lily dear." She winced, but he didn't seem to notice. "I'd no longer mistake you for a stable girl, had we just met."

She made a face. "Is your mission in this world to torture me?"

"How ever did you know?"

They snorted into laughs. Together, they left the bathhouse and trekked upstairs to their room to retire for the night. It wasn't particularly late, but they were both exhausted from a long day. The sandstorm had forced them to travel beneath the unforgiving sun and the torrid desert heat, so they were tired in more ways than one.

In their room, Jack lowered himself onto the floor while Aurelia crawled beneath the bed sheets. It felt incredible to sleep on a mattress with a pillow under her head and a plush comforter over her legs. It was the first bed she'd seen in weeks. She buried her toes in the sheets and snuggled her face against the thick, supple pillows. She would've fallen asleep right then and there, had Jack not spoken:

"Goodnight, lovely. Sleep well."

"And you, Jack."

She was lying on her side, staring at the wall, as the oil lamp beside her began to burn out. The sight reminded her of the night of the uprising.

She'd fallen asleep to the sight of an oil lamp burning into nothingness, and not a moment later, Linden arrived. The memory made her shiver and turn to her other side, where she was facing Jack. She stared at his back as he struggled to sleep on the hard wooden floor, despite the pillows and blankets cushioning him. She waited for a snore, a deep breath, an unconscious twitching of his legs. Apparently, that night, they were both wide-awake.

What irked her more than the thought of him sleeping on the cold, hard floor was the thought of him sleeping so very far from her. They'd always kept to themselves while they slept, but they'd been close enough for her to feel his body heat, too. It didn't feel right to spend even one night apart from such warmth. They were in the hottest place in the realm, and yet, Aurelia was combatting violent shivers and chattering teeth like they were stuck in the frigid north—all because of him.

It wouldn't do. Not now, and not ever again, if she could help it.

"Jack?"

"Yes?"

"There's room here for two, you know."

He peeled his upper body from the floor, using his elbow as leverage, and grinned at her. "I have to refuse. I'd hate to be a bother."

She scoffed. "Since when do *you* care about being a bother?"

"Since you nearly elbowed me in the face the last time I slept within a foot of you. You're quite the acrobat when you sleep."

Her cheeks warmed. "If I promise not to bloody your nose, will you cease your incessant chatter and join me? You can't possibly be comfortable down there."

"It's a bit rough on the old back, but I must admit—I'm enjoying the view from down here. It's rather entertaining to watch you shiver while in such a warm place. Are you cold, Lily dear?"

Her entire body burned with embarrassment. He knew as well as she did that she wasn't shivering because she was cold, but because her body had no other response to being separated from his.

"I'm just fine. You, on the other hand, have ten seconds to join me before I reconsider my offer."

"As you wish." He wouldn't admit it, but he was clearly glad to be sleeping in a bed rather than on the floor. She practically hugged the other end of the mattress while he climbed under the covers beside her, leaving a safe distance between them. "Thank you."

She made a soft, quiet noise in response. She didn't trust herself to speak. Maybe she'd say goodnight and fall asleep before he could reply, or maybe the warmth of his presence would become too tempting for her to bear. She couldn't be sure. The only thing she was thinking about was the way he slept facing her back, as if he were waiting for her to turn around and look into his soul.

That's exactly what she did.

When she rolled onto her other side, he opened his eyes and gazed into hers. She could feel his warm breath on her face and the heat of his body spreading throughout the bed. The dim lamplight cast a faint orange glow on his chiseled face. Even laying down, she had to tilt her head upwards to look into his eyes. She lifted her hand and splayed it over the side of his face, smiling when she saw how tiny her hand was against his cheek. He covered her hand with his and tilted his head so he could press his lips to her palm, all without breaking eye contact. His hand dropped from hers and settled on her hip, bunching fistfuls of her muslin trousers and forcing them to strain against her legs.

He broke eye contact, but he was still staring at her—more specifically, at her mouth. A quiet, fleeting noise escaped her throat when his hand on her hip pulled her closer to him. He propped himself up on his elbow, now gazing down at her, as he tucked his arm behind her head and tipped his head downwards. Butterflies erupted in her stomach when his nose brushed against hers. Her eyelids fluttered as he grazed her lips with his, the hand on her hip so hot it threatened to sear her. She sneaked her arms around his middle and hooked one of her legs over his. When he knew for sure that her thoughts mirrored his own, he lowered his head and kissed her like he was starving for her, like she was the cure to his every plague and every woe.

He pulled away enough to brush pesky hairs from her face. "I've been wanting to do that since the moment we met."

Her heart leapt to her throat. "Really?"

"Well, sort of. It was when you accused me of eating for three that I knew I had to have you."

She tightened her leg on his, teasing him, and smiled as he grunted. "I'd say the same, but you were an awful nuisance those first few days."

Pulling at the strings of her shirt to reveal her chest, he kneaded his hand against her breast and grinned at the way her back arched in response. She tried to meet his mouth with hers when he leaned closer to her face, but instead of kissing her, he blew hot breaths of air against her neck before dipping his tongue into her ear. She shuddered in spite of herself, knowing her reaction to his taunting would bring him nothing but the utmost pleasure.

"A nuisance." He didn't meet her eyes as he peppered kisses along her neck and chest. "Women have called me many things before, but never a *nuisance.*"

Another shudder ravaged her. "You...You..."

He lifted his lips from her neck long enough to pierce her gaze. "What was that?"

"You...*prick.*" Her words were garbled, nearly unrecognizable, but she didn't care—she'd never known anything greater than the feel of his lips on her skin.

Laughing, he shrugged out of his shirt and trousers while she wiggled out of her loosened pants. He lifted her shirt over her head, practically growling with desire, and immediately began caressing the curves of her body and kissing every inch of her from her neck to her belly to her thighs. Their legs were tangled together by then, both entirely naked, as he cupped her face in his hands and sneaked his hips between her legs. She ran her hands up to his back and sides until they settled on his abdomen. She memorized every curve of every muscle on his body until she was sure she could find her way around him in her sleep.

"I've dreamt of this every night." Jack kissed her again, slowly and tenderly, as her body arched to join his. "Dreamt of *you.*"

She swallowed the thickness in her throat as she traced his cheekbones with her fingertips. "Am I how you imagined I'd be?"

His nose brushed against hers. "What you are is beyond my imagination." The silly side of him returned for just a moment as that wicked grin she adored so much illuminated his face. "Did you imagine me like this, Lily dear? Naked and burning beside you?"

"Once or twice."

He guffawed, but it soon faded when the tenderness returned to his face. "At least we can finally allow our imaginations to rest."

He kissed her again, and when she felt his tongue inching down her throat, she brought her hands to his head and tugged at his hair, forcing him closer to her. A low, sultry moan rattled her eardrums—a moan so passionate and filled with lust that it must have come from Jack, but when he grinned against her mouth, breaking the kiss for a moment, Aurelia knew that it had been she herself who'd channeled the primal noise. She'd never heard such a sound from her own lips before. It was terrifying, maddening, tempting—everything deemed improper for a woman of her status.

Her body trembled at the feel of his blazing palm against her inner thigh, and she couldn't stop herself from shrieking with delight when he covered her breasts with his hands. Everything he did to her was teasing, but it wasn't intentional anymore; she knew by listening to the pattern of his breathing and by the flicking of his tongue. He simply aimed to memorize every curve, scar, blemish, and bruise on her body. It was like they were locked in a trance, timeless and immortal, with nothing to do other than claim the other with everything they had.

Patches of her skin felt warm and sharp from where his mouth had been, and she knew she'd be bruised when they woke up the next day. She could already feel the tender spots on his body where *his* bruises would form, too. The bruises would taunt her mercilessly come dawn, and she'd welcome it like an old friend.

When Jack gasped her name, she was unable to think about anything but the disappointment that followed when it wasn't the name she wanted to hear. *Aurelia!* She wanted to scream at him, to shout the truth right in his face. *My name is Aurelia!*

Only she couldn't tell him that. Not now, when his lips were stuck to hers like glue and while his hands traced the curvature of her spine as if she were a part of him. But she knew then that she wanted him to know the truth. She could only hope that he'd continue to look at her and hold her as he did when her secret was revealed. When she felt the way he yearned for her, she knew he would.

XXI

urelia brought her fingers to her lips and winced. They were swollen and tender, sore to the touch, and her bottom lip was peppered with tiny red marks from where Jack had nibbled the sensitive skin. She could barely press her lips to the mouthpiece of her canteen without flinching in pain. She debated spreading a bit of healing salve over her mouth to numb the discomfort, but that would only make it easier for Jack to mock her.

"Oh, dear." He glanced at her with amusement twinkling in his eyes. "Are your lips ailing you today?"

She scowled. "Shut your mouth."

"I'm sorry." He didn't look very apologetic. He was perched on Sterling's saddle without a care in the world, and judging by the way he smirked, he seemed to be enjoying the suffering he'd caused. "It's quite funny. I won't laugh anymore, though. You have my word."

A jolt of pain coursed through her when Scotch took her over a small dune, causing the saddle to slam against her sore groin. Jack snorted at first, but the look on her face must've been more amusing than she thought, because he soon burst out laughing. She squirmed uncomfortably and shot him the dirtiest look she could muster. It seemed to work, as the silly grin disappeared from his lips while his face went slack. Despite the discomfort she felt, she allowed herself a smile. At least she was menacing enough to stop *him* in his tracks.

"How much farther?" she whined.

"Not far. A few miles, maybe. Don't worry. You can stretch your legs and relax for as long as you wish. Maybe we can stretch other things, too." When he saw the look on her face, he hooted with laughter. "I'm only teasing you. I'm sorry, lovely. I seem to have gotten carried away."

"As usual. Good heavens, Jack. What were you thinking?"

"You didn't complain then."

"I am now, you big idiot."

His smile was both sheepish and suggestive. "I really am sorry, you know. Deeply sorry."

"No, you're not."

Jack threw his head back and laughed. "No, I'm not."

Aurelia glowered. They'd been traveling the desert for over a week at that point, but they were still a long ways away from Taundosa. They'd been allowed to stay at the tavern for an entire day while the sandstorm raged. With nothing else to do, the pair spent the entire day in bed together. Not much changed when they left the tavern, either. They quickly found that enjoying each other's bodies was as easy to do on a blanket in the sand as it was to do in a warm bed.

She was grateful for Jack—not because of his loyalty or his lovemaking, but because it was *him* rather than another handsome stranger. He wasn't frightened by the post-intimacy awkwardness like many of Aurelia's former lovers had been. His charismatic, teasing nature (aggravating on the average day) was the one thing keeping her from blushing and going mute each and every time he glanced in her direction.

But the closer she got to Jack, the more she worried for him. It was one thing to save a strange girl from rapists and offer to guide her to her destination, but it was something else to find oneself pitted against elite assassins. Before their first night together, he might've left her to save himself if assassins caught them. She wasn't so sure of that now. A man who looked at her the way Jack did wouldn't listen if she instructed him to flee, and if he died because of her, she'd never forgive herself.

According to Jack, they were getting close to the oasis, which was both a survival necessity and a landmark—but only for those who already knew where to find it. Jack claimed he'd been taken to the oasis by a guide during his first trip across the desert. If he hadn't, he and Aurelia would've walked right past the oasis without realizing it, as a protective enchantment concealed it from the naked, untrained eye.

When they arrived, they could stop to rest, replenish their water supply, and gather whatever natural resources the area provided. The oasis meant that Taundosa was another week away, depending on how quickly they traveled, and the pair didn't have enough supplies to last an additional seven days in the desert. Aurelia hoped that Jack was better at surviving than he appeared. If not, the only way she'd see Taundosa was if Arian Cristos went looking for her himself.

Though there was no competition with the other travelers headed for Taundosa, Aurelia was relieved that she and Jack had fallen behind. Other than the people they'd shared a night with, the groups were composed of strangers, and seeing them all clustered together in the tavern made her especially uneasy. She didn't want to be among them when the food and water ran out after the oasis. Fortunately, they were long gone—all thanks to Jack and Aurelia's decision to remain in bed for hours after the sandstorm while the others immediately departed.

"Lily, darling." When she glanced over at Jack, she saw him staring at something above: a flock of birds. "Look."

She followed the birds as they flew east. Her heart nearly stopped when she saw a patch of green in the distance. As they rode closer, the oasis became clearer and larger. She released a sigh of relief at the sight of vibrant plants, clear fresh water, and a plethora of berry bushes that seemed to summon her. In the blink of an eye, they were galloping across the sand so quickly that even the *fjardel* couldn't protect her face from the harsh granules of sand burning her skin.

When they were close enough, the pair decided to dismount their horses and walk the rest of the way. Aurelia's legs were still shaking, but now with excitement rather than pain from riding. The smell of sour berries, crisp water, fresh air...it was a combination of aromas she'd missed while trapped in the desert.

She clutched his forearm and squeezed. "Oh, Jack. It's *beautiful.*"

He smiled as he gazed down at her. "I'd certainly say so."

When they finally reached the oasis, both practically drooling, they tied the horses to the palm trees and collapsed on the sand. Aurelia reached her hands into the pool, relishing the feeling, and splashed warm water on her face. She and Jack both lifted handfuls of water to their mouths and swallowed as it dribbled over their chins and onto their shirts. She tried to clean herself as best she could without getting undressed, as even a few patches of clean skin was better than nothing. When they were both clean and hydrated, Aurelia filled the canteens and buckets while Jack gave the horses a chance to drink.

She gathered as many berries as she could and packed them into an empty leather pouch. Jack did the same but spared a handful to enjoy right then and there. The two sat down in the sand by the pool and gorged themselves on berries, fresh water, and the bread they'd managed to save from the tavern.

"I hope we have enough." She frowned as she examined their inventory. "If we aren't dead by the time we arrive in Taundosa, we'll be very ill."

"We'll be fine. I've survived the Ngora Valley on much less than we have now. As long as the horses are hydrated, we'll see Taundosa. I promise."

He lifted a canteen to his lips and tilted his head back. Aurelia snickered when he stopped and turned the canteen upside down. It was already empty. He gave her a look and refilled it in the pool while she fed apples to Scotch and Sterling. While she was doing so, her ears pricked at the sound of footsteps across from them. Both Aurelia and Jack slowed their movements and nonchalantly reached for their weapons. Jack sighed when two travelers emerged from the other side of the oasis, flinging themselves to the ground and practically drowning in the pool. Three horses stood behind them, and one of the stallions carried a fly-laden corpse on its back—a corpse wearing a blue-and-yellow *fjardel*. Aurelia wrinkled her nose in disgust when the scent of decaying flesh finally reached her nostrils.

"That's terribly unfortunate." Jack lowered his voice as he eyed them. "Looks like the guide's been dead for a few days now. The travelers should be thanking their lucky stars he managed to see them here before he died. They might not have known the oasis existed without him."

Before Aurelia could reply, Scotch began snorting and shaking his head. Jack stood to console him, believing Scotch was annoyed by pesky insects or sand in his eyes, but Aurelia knew her horse well enough by then. She recognized the sounds he made, the anxiety in his movements, the detection in his body language. She looked more closely across the pool at the two travelers (who were mostly camouflaged by the oasis) and studied them as best she could without giving herself away. When one of them moved, their cloak shifted, and she saw the familiar shine of Akkinorian bronze beneath their clothing.

Her breath caught in her throat. "We have to go."

"What? Why? We've—"

"*Now*, Jack."

He stared at her. The fear in her eyes must have been enough to convince him, as he quickly gathered their supplies without another word. She, too, didn't waste a moment. The day Kaia died had started just like this one, and she refused to lead Jack to the same fate.

Before they could climb on their horses, a whizzing sound sliced through the air. An arrow pierced the tree behind her—so close that it could be nothing if not a warning shot. Wild-eyed, she and Jack peered to the side at the two travelers. Anger, hatred, and vengeance curdled in her stomach when she saw Oren Lowstone and Alda Port standing before them, armed to the teeth and ready to earn the vast compensation they'd receive in Akkinor.

It was no wonder the guide—an expert at traveling across the Ngora Valley—had died before making it to the oasis. Assassins didn't care for witnesses, nor did they like asking for assistance. The only reason they'd hired him was to use his body (a body whose soul, like Jack's, was already familiar with the magical landmark) to access the oasis.

"You're right," Jack decided. "We should go."

While Alda nocked another arrow, they climbed on their horses and left the oasis without looking back. Oren was already on his horse, following them, as one of Alda's arrows pierced the sand in front of Aurelia. She refused to look back, even when she heard them behind her, and tried her best to nock an arrow while remaining safely on Scotch's back.

"Lily," Jack called, "we've nowhere to go! We're in the middle of the gods-forsaken desert!"

She knew what that meant: the only way they'd see Taundosa was if they fought their way out.

"Gods forgive me," she murmured.

She gritted her teeth and turned her body as best she could, bow in hand and arrow ready to fly. Oren was getting closer to them, but Alda was lagging behind as she sent arrow after arrow flying towards them. Just as one of her arrows hit the sand where Jack had been riding, Aurelia brought the bowstring close to her lips and whispered a silent prayer. When she released the bowstring, her arrow sliced the side of Alda's neck. Aurelia shot another arrow, this time at Alda's horse, causing the massive beast to fall to its side with Alda still on its back. Alda managed to release one final arrow as her legs and torso were crushed beneath the weight of her horse. As her garbled screams echoed throughout the desert, her arrow hit the sand just ahead of Scotch.

Spooked, Scotch threw Aurelia from his back and galloped off into the distance. She emitted a guttural *oomph* when she collided with the sand. Pain spread throughout the side of her body as she brought herself to a sitting position. Alda was dead, if not close to dead, but Oren was still approaching them with his sword raised and hunger in his darkened eyes.

Jack looped Sterling around and came back for Aurelia without a second thought. He leaned to the side, nearly falling from the saddle, and held out his arm for her to take. As soon as her fingers were wrapped around his bicep, he yanked her from the sand and pulled her onto the saddle. She wrapped her arms around his waist and held on for dear life as he rode, desperately trying to lose Oren and catch up with Scotch.

"Jack," she wheezed, "you need to go. He's here for me. I-I'll catch up with you."

His muscles tensed. "I'm not leaving you."

"I'm not asking you to leave me. I'm asking you to save yourself. I refuse to let another person die because of me. Please, Jack."

When he refused to respond, she reached over him and grabbed Sterling's reins. With one hard yank, the stallion skidded to a stop and whinnied. Aurelia ignored Jack's protests and hopped down from the saddle. She could see his face now, and it was clear by the angry flushing of his cheeks and the taut clenching of his jaw that he wasn't pleased with what she'd asked of him. The bow and arrows wouldn't do her much good when Oren finally caught up with her, so she drew her sword instead and waited for him to arrive. Jack simply stared at her, even as Oren came closer, and silently struggled to decide.

Aurelia smiled at him. "Forward, good man—"

"—ever forward." Jack returned her smile, but it was painful rather than hopeful. "I shall see you soon."

With that, he jerked Sterling's reins and galloped away. She wanted to watch him go, to see for herself that he was safe, but there was no time for that. Oren Lowstone was approaching.

He looked the same as he had on the day he'd wounded Kaia—the only difference was the vengeance in his eyes. Now, it was no longer assassin versus target, but two people seeking revenge for their fallen friends.

Oren slowed in front of her and bowed mockingly on his horse. "Your Grace. Oren Lowstone of Myra, a dedicated citizen of Akkinor and an honored assassin of the crown. A pleasure to meet you—again."

"You're no citizen of mine."

"The crown is no longer yours," he retorted. Aurelia's blood boiled. "You're no longer the Queen of Akkinor. You're a traitor and a shameful smudge on your family tree. You sacrificed your throne, your rights, and your freedom when you failed to return to your people in their time of greatest need. For that, you will die."

She narrowed her eyes. "I won't die today, Mister Lowstone. I'm sorry to disappoint."

He adjusted his grip on his sword. "Let's see what the Commander of the Royal Army is capable of, shall we?"

The assassin had enough decency to offer her a fair fight. His horse stayed put after he dismounted so both he and Aurelia were on their feet. They circled one another with their swords raised, sizing each other up, but neither was intimidated. Oren may have been an assassin, but Aurelia had trained alongside Akkinor's most esteemed soldiers. Assassins were sloppy people who wanted nothing more than gold in their pockets. Aurelia had something stronger to fight for.

Oren was the first to move. When he swung his blade, she swerved out of the way and left him slicing through nothing but air. She took the opportunity to strike, but he was faster than she expected and managed to block her swing. The sound of steel kissing steel echoed throughout the desert as their swords found each other over and over again. She swung again, and he was forced to bend backwards to avoid decapitation. He grabbed the hilt of his sword in both hands and brought it downwards. She blocked it with her own sword, but his was much heavier than hers. She gritted her teeth as he pushed the weapons downwards, inching closer and closer to her collarbone.

When she saw the greed and triumph in his eyes, she lifted her knee to his groin and left him howling. She stumbled backwards and regained her composure as he hunched over in pain, but that wasn't enough to stop him. He reached into his armor and produced a concealed blade before throwing it in her direction. A brief, sharp pain spread throughout her arm as the blade fell onto the sand. He'd managed to cut her, tearing through her shirt and reopening the scabbed wound she'd earned after battling a fox several weeks earlier.

Just then, Aurelia heard the unmistakable thud of hoofprints in the sand. When she glanced over her shoulder, careful not to let her guard down, she gasped at the sight of Jack, Sterling, and Scotch galloping towards her. She wanted to be angry at him for refusing to obey her wishes, but at the same time, she was eternally grateful for his courage and loyalty. She needed it now more than ever.

"How invigorating," Oren taunted, grinning. "Now I shall have two bodies to claim today!"

Aurelia gritted her teeth. "You won't touch him."

When he charged her, the two clashed with their swords while Jack and the horses inched closer. After she sliced Oren's side and sent him stumbling, the assassin grabbed a handful of sand and threw it at her face, temporarily blinding her. She managed to stagger out of the way when he struck the spot where she'd been standing seconds before. She could hear the whipping sound of a rope against air—the same rope Jack had often used when crafting his warning bell contraptions in the Violet Forest.

Gritting her teeth, Aurelia snatched Oren's bloody dagger from the sand and threw it. Just as she'd hoped, it sailed passed him and fell to the sand by his horse's hooves. He taunted her again, commenting on the weakness of her aim and of her entire being, as they circled one another.

She didn't stop moving until he retrieved the dagger, now with his back facing Jack—exactly where she wanted him.

"You're as foolish as the king claimed," Oren growled. "A silly, incompetent little girl who has no business wearing a crown."

For the first time, her infamous temper didn't rise. She felt it burning in her chest, but she didn't let it see the light of day. Perhaps she would've, had she been alone; but she wasn't, and so long as that remained true, her temper was a foe as easily defeated as Oren Lowstone.

On Jack's signal—a chaotic waving of his arm—Aurelia dove to the side and landed several feet to Oren's left. He began to laugh, unaware of how close Jack was, and raised his sword in preparation to defeat her for good. As he lifted his blade above his head, Jack and Sterling rode up beside Aurelia with Scotch directly across from them on Oren's other side. One end of Jack's rope was in his hand, and the other end was tied to Scotch's saddle.

Oren turned in time for the rope to collide with his throat. The force of the impact sent him sailing backwards, where he landed on his back with a thud. He was gurgling, gasping, and wheezing for air. The rope hadn't simply knocked him to the ground—it'd crushed his windpipe. That, paired with the way his back slammed against the ground, restricted his ability to breathe.

Aurelia climbed to her feet and looked to the side. Jack and the two horses were a ways away as they slowed down in preparation to turn back. Even with the throbbing pain coursing through her body, she knew her time alone with Oren was limited. She'd have to act fast before Jack was within earshot.

She approached a gurgling Oren as he clutched his throat. Only then did she notice that his legs weren't moving despite his upper body squirming in pain. The force of his collision with the ground must have inflicted some sort of fracture to his spine. If she was right, then he was either paralyzed or close to it.

"You deserve no mercy from me." Her chest heaved as she towered over him. "Despite this, I swore an oath to show mercy to my subjects— all of you."

His gasps for air weren't enough to fill his lungs, let alone to give them the strength needed to talk. He didn't need to reply for her to discern exactly what he was thinking, though: *long live the king.*

Without a second thought, she pushed the tip of her blade through his throat, and the light faded from his eyes before she could remove the blade from his flesh. His blood, so dark it was nearly black, seeped from his body and stained the sand. Normally she would've uttered a prayer for his soul, but her friend's murderer deserved no kindness. Instead, she simply left him where he was and staggered towards Jack.

Her shoulder and hip were still aching from her fall, and the cut on her arm was deeper than she first realized. Blood was dripping down her arm and staining her shirt. At least, she thought, Oren's weapons hadn't been laced with phoenix blood like Alda's arrowheads (neither his sword nor his dagger shimmered with the telltale silvery sheen associated with the poison). If they had been, she would've let him kill her.

When he was close enough, Jack slowed the horses and jumped onto the sand before Sterling came to a complete stop. He was in front of her within seconds, wrapping his arms around her and pressing her head against his chest, muttering something about how deeply sorry he was for leaving her—even if they'd only been apart for a few moments.

"You never listen." She blinked at him when she felt his arms trembling. There was an emotion in his eyes she'd never seen before: fear. "I told you I'd catch up."

Jack smiled and took her face in his hands. "I couldn't let you win. Not this time." He tipped his head downwards to kiss her. When they parted, his smile morphed into a smirk, and she was instantly reminded of the valiant, lighthearted swordsman who'd saved her in the Violet Forest. "A simple thank-you would suffice, you know."

A small, tired smile formed on her lips. "Thank you, Jack."

He tilted his forehead against hers and buried his fingers in her hair. "The pleasure was mine, Lily dear."

XXII

For heaven's sake, Jack! Stop it!"

"No. You need to drink, Lily. I won't hear another word of your fussing about it."

Aurelia glared at him. She reluctantly accepted the canteen, peeled her head from his chest to sit up, and took the final sip of their water supply. There was still water in the bucket they used for the horses, but they hoped it wouldn't come to that. At the least, they had enough food to last them the duration of the journey—if the heat and dehydration didn't kill them first.

It'd be a terrible way to die.

By that point, Aurelia had cut off the sleeves of her shirt and the legs of her pants to combat the heat, so most of her body was sunburnt. Patches of skin had bubbled over scars from previous burn blisters. Only her face and neck had been protected from the harsh sun, thanks to the *fjardel* she'd purchased in Dofell.

Aurelia licked her dry, cracked lips and wondered if any amount of water would ever return them to normal. Now that the sun had set, she'd removed her *fjardel*, but her hair was still matted to her skin with sweat. Jack's black curls were flat and straight against his forehead and neck, glued to his skin as beads of sweat rolled down his face. Neither looked nor felt their best, but they were hopeful that Taundosa was just around the corner. As soon as they were in the City of Gold, the Ngora Valley would be a distant memory.

She lifted her head from his chest again and reached up to brush a damp piece of hair from his forehead. As she admired him, she saw something she hadn't noticed before—a crescent-shaped scar above the slanted tail of his left eyebrow. It was an old scar, white and raised, that he must've earned many years prior.

"What happened here?" she murmured, brushing her fingertip over the scar.

He grimaced. "I was playing with friends in the ruins of the old Cromwell estate in Myra. I must've been eight or so at the time. Fell from the scaffolding and almost cracked my skull." His chest rumbled with laughter. "I bled until my skin was translucent, but it's still one of the happiest days I can remember from my childhood."

She paused for a moment. "Do you ever miss Akkinor?"

"Sometimes." She could feel his hand moving on her stomach, so she knew he was making gestures while he spoke. He never realized what he was doing. "I miss feeling safe there. I suppose there were the radicals on the Templar's Road, but other than that...how many rapists prowled about in Akkinor? How many murderers? Thieves? Predators?"

"Not many."

"Not many. It used to be that people could leave their doors unlocked. Women could walk the streets alone at nighttime without being afraid of nasty men. Parents let their children play outside without supervision. Is it still like that?"

"It was. I've been gone for some time, though. I don't know what it's like now."

"How much can change in less than a year?"

More than you think, she thought. She hoped she was wrong. She hoped the country was exactly like she remembered it—exactly like *Jack* remembered it—when she finally returned.

She wondered what was happening in Akkinor at that moment. When they reached civilization, surely someone would've received word of Queen Aurelia's overthrowing, as it was highly unlikely that word hadn't spread to Carthe's leaders. Hopefully, when she found Arian Cristos, she'd learn about everything Archie had done since the uprising and everything her people had endured since her departure. She was itching for the truth, but she knew it was better to be ignorant while Jack was at her side. He was a clever man—it wouldn't take him long to put the pieces together once he learned of Queen Aurelia's disappearance.

Jack brushed his fingers against her arm. "Does it hurt much?"

"No." She looked at the makeshift bandage around her arm. It was stained with blood, but it hadn't bothered her much in the days that'd passed since Oren managed to slash her. "I'm afraid it'll leave a nasty scar, though. My time in Carthe has left me with one too many. I wish there were a way to remove them from my body forever. I'd rather not have a permanent reminder of the terrible things that happened here."

"They're not reminders of terrible things. They're reminders of how strong you are," he insisted. "If you really want to be rid of them so badly, we can ask around in Taundosa. The City of Gold is partly renowned for its incredible mages. We may have to sell everything we have to pay for one, but they can do it."

She furrowed her eyebrows. "Mages." As thought after thought filled her brain, she sat up in the sand and looked down at him. "This Mister Cristos could be a mage, couldn't he?"

"I don't know."

"There's a mage—a sorcerer, really, he isn't very pleasant—in my, uh, village. He owed two debts to my parents. He repaid them once when I was younger. I claimed the second in their place when I fled Akkinor. My parents told me to keep near to him, should anything happen, despite his dark nature. I was told to find him in the event of an emergency to claim the second favor. I needed him to escape. Now, you're telling me that Taundosa is renowned for its mages."

He stared at her like she'd gone mad. "I'm not exactly following."

Aurelia sighed. "For as long as I've been alive, I've kept a secret. Because of this, my parents told me that there was only one person in Akkinor who could help me, should I ever need it."

"The sorcerer."

"Yes. Do you remember when you asked me about how Mister Cristos might help me return home?"

He cracked a smile. "I asked if it was an arranged marriage."

"I sincerely hope it's not," she stated, making a sour face. "I'd decline, obviously, but that's beside the point. I don't know how Mister Cristos is going to help me, Jack. I have no idea why he's the answer I've been searching for, but they made it perfectly plain that I was to find the sorcerer if I was ever in trouble. What if it were impossible for me to find him? What if I was forced to leave Akkinor without finding the sorcerer first?"

Realization flashed across his eyes. "If you couldn't find the sorcerer in Akkinor, they may have sent you to the only other mage whom they trusted." She nodded. "That would solve the problem of the mage you required, but the person who will help you return to Akkinor can't simply be a mage. There must be something else about him."

"I don't know what it could be."

"Your parents never mentioned him? Not once?"

She shook her head.

"I wouldn't know where to begin." He scrubbed a tired hand down his face. "I suppose we'll find out shortly. Taundosa is just a few days away. We'll be standing before Mister Cristos in the blink of an eye."

Aurelia forced a smile. "I certainly hope so."

"I pray he's as rich as most in Taundosa." He yawned. "Maybe he can buy you an army to overthrow the Reilly family. That would send quite the message, wouldn't it?"

She winced at his mention of her lie. "Money doesn't solve every problem in the world, Jack."

"No," he said with a wicked smile, "but it solves most."

***

As the Lord of Myra gazed at the dozens of filthy men lugging limestone bricks and iron rods across a construction site, his eyes focused on their feet: more specifically, on the grapes being squished beneath heavy boots as laborers navigated the remnants of curly vines scattered in the dirt. What had once been the largest and most extravagant vineyard in Myra was now a flattened valley marred by ugly tools and empty liquor bottles.

"...this, my lord?"

Silas Crowland turned when he realized he was being spoken to. A dozen Myran nobles sat around an ovular table in the symposium of Sherwood Manor—the capital of Clyren, a Myran dukedom, and home of the Sherwood family. Nobles from across Myra had answered Silas's summons for a meeting in Clyren that day, but many were missing, as they were too fearful of retaliation from the monarchy to risk the audience.

Silas cleared his throat. "You were saying?"

"We are discussing the estimates provided by our Coinmasters," Duke Sherwood explained. "What with the cost of the king's menagerie and the absence of revenue from Sherwood Vineyards, we will lose up to seven-and-twenty percent of our annual income. Myra can survive on such numbers without severe ramifications for four years, if we're lucky. We can combat our losses by cutting costs elsewhere, but it'd be a risky endeavor."

Duke Summerhill massaged his temples. "That's excluding the commission costs of the menagerie. Because the structure will exist on Myran soil, the king has insisted that all coin be taken from Myra's funds at the Bank of Akkinor. He's already spent a quarter of it on materials and laborers."

"And another quarter on the animals," added the Earl of Murdock.

Silas exhaled and looked over his shoulder at the window. Soon enough, soldiers loyal to Emperor Kaplo of Quapebet would ride into Myra with a caravan of exotic animals—tigers, panthers, snakes, monkeys, and the like—to fill the menagerie. The king, under the ruse of expanding Akkinor's cultural identity, ordered the demolition of Sherwood Vineyards because he believed it was the prime location for the menagerie he desired.

Duke Summerhill removed his spectacles and tossed them onto the table. "I've already decreased my staff's pay by five percent. I was forced to release two hundred soldiers without pay. My lady wife has begun selling her jewelry for fear of our children's inheritances being snatched. How much longer must this last?"

All eyes turned to the Lord of Myra. For the first time in his life, Silas didn't know what to say. Only so much could be said without implicating himself as a traitor to the crown. He couldn't deny the king his desires without risking poor reception, which would undoubtedly lead to his execution. If Silas Crowland were executed, leaving no heirs while his daughters were unmarried, the nobles of Myra would have no choice but to battle one another for the kingdom. Other nobles from across Akkinor would flock to support whomever they preferred as Silas's replacement, and soon enough, the conflict would evolve into a full-fledged civil war. Silas's daughters would be killed to prevent them from attempting to seize power while they were still unmarried, and his sons would be killed simply for being men. Regardless of their inability to inherit lordship, they were still threats to anyone who wished to rule Myra.

If there were any reason good enough to hold his tongue, it was to spare his wife from burying her husband and four children all at once. His beloved was too pure a soul to endure such torture.

"I never imagined I'd say this," said Duke Caplight, "but we need *her*."

There could only be one *her* in question: Aurelia Brentwood, rightful Queen of Akkinor. Her brother, King Archibald, claimed she'd fled Akkinor during an invasion by rogue Isalders. Rather than staying behind to fight for her people and her country, she escaped, seemingly without any intention of returning. Archie, her only heir, somehow managed to survive the invasion only to emerge as a king and a hero, come dawn. Silas, like so many others, was highly suspicious of that story. He had a great fondness and affection for the queen, and he knew her character as well as he knew his own. Someone like Aurelia Brentwood—a person whose very being radiated selflessness, valor, and compassion—never would've abandoned her people unless she had a plan for their salvation.

The nobles of Akkinor may have disapproved of a woman on the throne, but now that she was gone, they'd finally recognized her value.

"We have nobody but ourselves to blame for this," Silas muttered. His bannermen stared at him, not understanding, as he shook his head in shame. "Each of us in this room pledged fealty to Queen Aurelia, and yet, we broke that oath almost as quickly as we promised it. It was our duty to protect her reign and honor her name, and we've failed her. Perhaps if we hadn't been so occupied with finding her a husband, we may have realized her worth before it was too late."

Earl Northwood clenched his jaw. "We are not responsible for this. Whatever happened—whatever *truly* happened—we had no part in it."

"Maybe not," Duke Caplight said, "but the intruders were bold enough to attack for a reason. They sensed our reluctance in supporting her reign. They knew many of us wouldn't protest if she were removed from power. Our lack of support in her rule may not have caused this madness, but it certainly didn't prevent it."

Duke Woodgard, the eldest of the noblemen, looked weary and close to tears. "If the late king were alive to see what we've allowed to happen..."

"We as a kingdom failed to honor and defend her name for five years," Silas said, squaring his shoulders. "When she returns—and she will—we mustn't allow ourselves to fall into our old ways. She'll return to save us from our downfall, and it's our duty to do the same for her."

The Earl of Murdock sucked in a breath through his teeth. "If our suspicions regarding her departure are proven correct, my lord, that will be much easier said than done. Our support alone isn't enough to assure her victory, and if she fails, each of us in this room will find ourselves all too familiar with the royal executioner."

Silas narrowed his eyes. "That, my friend, is a risk I'm willing to take. I'd rather sign my own death warrant than watch in vain as that poor girl is led to a terrible fate. Wouldn't you?"

None of the noblemen responded, but they didn't have to—Silas knew they agreed with him. They were simply too afraid of potential eavesdroppers to utter it aloud.

Silas Crowland had lived nearly six decades of life by then. He'd seen many terrible things—things that would haunt him until the day the gods called him home—but until recently, he'd never experienced true horror for himself. The things that'd happened in his country since the invasion were, without a doubt, acts of evil hitherto unheard of on Akkinorian soil.

The new king had recently hosted an audience at the palace for all reigning nobles of the Akkinorian kingdoms. Lord Ashford of Omara made the unfortunate mistake of asking what might be done to Queen

Aurelia if she were found and returned to Akkinor. The king's reply had terrified Silas so greatly that he hadn't returned home to Wentworth Castle after the audience. Instead, he visited his two sisters to make amends for every silly, petty, childish squabble they'd ever endured. He hugged each of them for the first time in decades, promising both sisters—and himself—that he'd never forget the love between siblings again. When he returned home, he gave all four of his children a firm talking to and made them promise to never raise a hand against the others.

If Lord Reilly of Laynoa wished for the queen's hand in marriage, she'd be imprisoned and kept alive only until she provided him with a suitable number of heirs. When she was no longer needed, she'd be delivered to Oleander's Valley in the Folly, where an amateur executioner (she was unworthy of an experienced killer, the king claimed) would strike her neck with an axe—not a sword as customary—until her head was severed from her body. The king would leave her body by the chopping block to be abused, mutilated, and torn apart by spectators until she was unrecognizable. The people would take chunks of her hair and maybe a tooth or two as souvenirs. Men would battle each other for the opportunity to defile her corpse, and women would strip her of every jewel and every scrap of clothing on her body. Whatever remained of her, the king had said, would be buried in an unmarked grave on the outskirts of the Folly where it might never be found, only to be covered in lime to assure a quick decomposition.

Silas was prepared to do everything in his power to prevent that, and he was prepared to command his bannermen to do the same. He'd be risking countless lives and legacies by doing so, particularly if the masses were convinced by the king's story regarding his ascension to the throne, but it'd be worth it in the end. He trusted Aurelia Brentwood to see her people to salvation, and he wouldn't stray from his loyalty to her—even if such loyalty saw his corpse, headless and forgotten, buried beside hers.

XXIII

urelia must have spent hours staring at the stars while Jack snored beside her. His bulky arm was still draped over her chest, but she didn't dare move him—he wasn't all that pleasant when he was prematurely woken.

Normally Jack would've been the one to insist upon traveling at nighttime when the sun was set and the air was cool, but the pair and their horses were far too exhausted to make it another mile without stopping.

Heartache and just a touch of guilt had compelled them to stop when they did, too. Earlier in the day, they'd come across a sight so grotesque that both of them vomited what little they had in their stomachs: six crucified corpses, rotting and stinking, left to fester within several yards of one another while still nailed to wooden stakes. They'd been stripped naked, their jaws dislocated, and their tongues ripped from their mouths.

The worst part was that Aurelia and Jack recognized the six bodies—after all, the pair had spent a night with them beneath the desert stars not long before reaching the tavern.

Aurelia wondered what might've happened if she and Jack had stayed with the group instead of moving on alone. Maybe an extra two swords would've saved them. She shouldn't have felt guilty, but she did—especially when she saw the Isalder woman's rounded, bulging belly, which she hadn't noticed before. Perhaps a few of them, like the narcissistic stubby man and the bitter Dofelli guide, had been crossing the valley simply for work, but the others had been searching for new beginnings in southern Carthe. Their dreams for a brighter future had been crushed before they'd even made it to the gates of Taundosa.

Jack hadn't been *entirely* shocked by the scene. One desert tribe in particular, he claimed, had an affinity for crucifying their victims and leaving the latter to rot—a decision intended to taunt other travelers if nothing else. He'd never seen such horror up close before, though, and Aurelia hoped neither of them would ever see anything like it again.

She shook the memories from her mind when Jack choked on a snore, dragging his arm from Aurelia's chest and rolling onto his side. His snoring ceased completely by then, so she knew he was either awake or enduring a light sleep. Ravaged by boredom, anxiety, and fear, Aurelia pushed herself onto her side and set a hand on his shoulder.

"Jack." She shook him a bit. "Are you awake?"

"I am now." His voice, deep and husky from sleep, didn't sound as aggravated as she'd expected. He rolled over to face her and smiled through half-open eyes. "Couldn't sleep?"

"No." She sat up fully and brought her knees to her chest. "I was thinking about home again. Compared to this place, to the things we've seen here...Thinking about Akkinor is the only thing keeping me from losing faith in humanity. In the gods."

No reply. It took him a moment to wake up completely, but when he did, he gave her his undivided attention. He sat with his legs on either side of her hips, facing her, and comfortingly ran his palms along her arms. She didn't have the heart to tell him that the callouses on his hands were making the sunburns on her skin sting like his palms were hot coals.

"Tell me a story, Jack. Tell me a story from home."

"What kind of story?"

"Anything. Whatever you wish."

"All right." Now with his hands in hers, his eyes shifted to something behind her as his gaze grew nostalgic and far away. "I had quite an eventful childhood, you know. My mother taught us how to dig for blue slinkers in the flowerbeds across the villages—those strange little insects that birds like to eat. The blue slinkers were rare, so we'd make a game out of it. Whoever found a blue slinker would get an extra bite of dessert that night."

Aurelia smiled. "It sounds like your family was close."

"Somewhat. I was closest to my mother. She liked for her children to make the most out of life—every day was a new adventure. My father wasn't so lenient, though. He believed that we had a responsibility to work and provide for our village. He wanted his sons to become strong and affluent, and his daughters to become graceful and poised. He was never the easiest man to impress."

"What was he like?"

A strange, twisted look formed on Jack's face. "He was...he was quite stern. A disciplinarian. He never took to my sense of humor, and his wasn't particularly good. He valued duty above pleasure. He was unfathomably unaware of who his children were at heart, too. To him, we were heirs and responsibilities. I do believe he loved us very much, but he had a terribly indifferent way of expressing it. My mother was his polar opposite, though I suppose that's why they got on so well. She radiated such kindness and warmth. We used to say she was a beacon—people were drawn to her. She loved being a mother, but she loved my father even more. She contradicted him when it came to marriage, though. She wanted her children to marry for love."

"Is that why you never married?"

"Maybe. I couldn't say." He snapped his eyes over to hers and smiled. "And you, Lily dear? What were your parents like?"

Aurelia laughed uncomfortably. "Well..."

"Come on now." He gave her sides a gentle, playful squeeze. "I've told you all about mine. It's only fair that you tell me a story of your own."

"All right, all right," she relented, making him grin. "My parents...I don't know where to start. They were both so lovely. I suppose there was something off-putting about my father at first, but those closest to him knew the kind of man he was. He had a wonderful sense of humor. That biting wit of his was unparalleled—I've never met another soul so capable of drawing a laugh out of even the most neurotic of people. He did have a terribly gruff side to him, though. He could be stern and firm when the situation called for it. I know many people were frightened of him when he was angry, but I never saw that side of him."

"Papa's little princess, eh?"

Aurelia made a sour face. Luckily, the darkness of the night provided a veil decent enough to keep Jack from noticing.

"Yes. He was so warm and gentle with me. He taught me how to manage our property, our finances, our responsibilities. He was the most exceptional teacher I've ever known. That much never changed when my brother came along. Not once did he ever disregard me in favor of a son."

As Jack rubbed her legs comfortingly, she found herself picturing Edmund's face in her head. Those piercing, icy blue eyes of his—a mirror image of Archie's—seemed cold and stern to anyone who didn't know him well. To Aurelia, his gaze was perpetually twinkling with amusement and bursting with life. His hair, long and sunny in his youth, had shortened and turned gray by the time he passed. Aurelia wondered if he would've chosen to wear his hair long again if he'd lived. She'd often wondered if his face would look different with long hair falling over his wrinkled forehead.

Whenever she imagined Edmund, Cressida followed. It was impossible to think of one without the other. She remembered her mother's eyes as being less vibrant and intense than her father's: they were a magnificent dark blue that seemed to pair perfectly with the deep, fiery red of her hair. Unlike Edmund, anyone's first impression of Queen Cressida was that she was sent directly from the heavens. It was something in the way she seemed to smile through her eyes. She had a way of bringing comfort, understanding, and tenderness to anyone with nothing more than a glance.

Thoughts of her parents only aggravated her solemnness. She climbed to the space between Jack's legs and sat with her back against his chest. As he wrapped his warm arms around her middle, she leaned her head back and rested it on his shoulder. For a moment, neither said anything as they gazed up at the stars.

"Tell me another story," she whispered.

He pressed his lips to her cheek. "All right."

He told her about a time during his adolescent years, and when that story ended, Aurelia reciprocated in kind by telling him a tale of her own. It was a memory from the day she and Cicely were stopped by an elderly blind woman on the streets of Mistcairn, who'd offered them each five pieces of bronze in exchange for assisting her while she churned butter. Jack may not have found anything strange about that—peasant children were always being offered odd jobs by their neighbors. *He would've laughed if he knew the truth*, she thought. He would've understood why the memory was so fond if he realized the Crown Princess of Akkinor had skipped her politics lessons in favor of churning butter with a lonely old blind woman.

Aurelia lost track of how long they stayed awake talking, dreaming, and reminiscing. By the time their conversation came to a brief pause, the sun was beginning to rise over the massive dunes in the distance. For a moment, Aurelia could've sworn she saw a twinkle of gold reflecting against the sunlight.

Taundosa was near.

***

Aurelia leaned her head against Scotch's body as her eyelids fluttered shut. When she felt herself stumbling, her feet skidding against the boiling sand, she opened her eyes and straightened up. She looked to her right at Jack, who was loosely holding Sterling's reins while practically sleepwalking. Neither of them had to think about walking anymore—it was as if their legs couldn't be stopped by anything other than a stone wall.

"Jack." He snapped his eyes open and pretended like he was on high alert. The redness in his eyes was impossible to miss. "What's left of the water?"

He peeked into the bucket attached to Sterling's saddle. "Maybe a mouthful."

She sighed and leaned against Scotch again. In a desperate effort to reach Taundosa as quickly as possible, they'd been riding all night and all day. Almost a week had passed since their encounter with the assassins at the oasis. If Jack's memory served, they'd arrive in Taundosa in less than a day. They'd been so tired when they first left their campsite that they'd slept while riding their horses. Unfortunately, that resulted in Aurelia falling from Scotch's back and Jack causing Sterling a world of discomfort. Ever since, they'd decided to walk the horses to keep themselves awake. It was growing more and more difficult by the minute.

"I'm worried about Scotch." Her horse looked as terrible as she felt: ribs straining against his chestnut hair, head and neck bowed with fatigue, and his eyes droopy. "We won't make it much further unless we rest."

"There's nowhere to stop." His voice, usually smooth and melodic, was rough and hoarse from dehydration. "If we stop, we die. We can't afford to take a break." She couldn't argue with that. "We're nearly there. Maybe if you're lucky, I'll let you beat me to the gates."

She snorted. "Even the desert can't tarnish your imagination."

That made him laugh, but it stopped sooner than expected. "Lily, dear!" The abrupt, thrilling change in his voice persuaded her to glance up at him. "Look."

She followed his gaze to the path ahead, and almost immediately, a gasp rose up in her throat. Peeking out from behind a gargantuan sand dune were the greatest set of gates she'd ever seen. They practically disappeared into the clouds. Between each set of gates was a tall, rectangular marble pillar, each with some sort of golden plaque nailed to the center. Rather than bars of metal designed to keep people out, the gates were a piece of architecture that should've been worshipped. They were made entirely of gold with long, cylindrical bars connected to ornate golden sculptures. As they inched closer, the sculptures became clearer: gods, mythical creatures, animals, symbols, *people*. Everything was woven along the bars like a painting or tapestry, molded together so marvelously that even one missing piece would destroy the entire scene.

"Oh." Words didn't seem applicable. "Jack…"

She couldn't finish. She was too enchanted, too captivated. Every story she'd heard about Taundosa was true, and she hadn't even entered the kingdom yet.

Eight soldiers guarded the main gates, each of whom wore the colors and emblems of different noble families. Three stood on the outside, three on the inside, while two manned either watchtower. The main gates themselves were simple—nothing but golden bars—but there was a large circular plaque that separated in two halves when the gates were opened. It was stamped with the emblem of the Caltheos family, the monarchy of Taundosa. The other plaques on the stone pillars were stamped with the emblems of the reigning noble families, all of which had been in power for over seven hundred years. No noble family in Akkinor had been in charge for that long—not even the oldest of them.

"State your identities and your purpose in the City of Gold," one of the guards demanded.

Jack's voice was clear and strong. "Jack Sherbourne and my partner, Lily Linden. We're passing through the City of Gold on our way to Khaba. We humbly request a night's rest before we take to the road again."

The soldier nodded. As his comrades opened the gates, he turned to Jack. "You'll find that there are ample places to stay for the night. You are now entering the district of Agotia. The capital is on the other side. There are directories in Agotia to assist you further. Welcome to Taundosa, Mister Sherbourne and Miss Linden. Her Grace is pleased to host you."

"Thank you, sir," Jack said kindly. Now that the gates were opened, the exhaustion on his face was evident again. "Your hospitality is most gracious."

Aurelia's heart skipped a beat when the guards stepped aside to allow the pair into the kingdom. She held her breath as they took a few steps into the place she'd been dreaming about for weeks. Reality wasn't so different from her dreams.

Now, the only thing left for her to do was find Arian Cristos—wherever and whomever he was.

XXIV

Compared to Dofell, Taundosa was the most incredible place in the world. There were no filthy, starving, homeless civilians skulking in the shadows. Children played in the streets, women hung wet clothing on drying lines, and men drove wagons of supplies to their shops. The shutters and doors of every home were open. The smell of freshly baked bread and sugary blue wine wafted through the air. The people walked arm-in-arm down the streets, sipped wine as they strolled, and hollered at one another from the rooftops.

"This is wonderful," she breathed, eyes wide. "I-It's just like—"

"Like home," Jack finished. A glimmer of nostalgia passed over his face, but it was gone as quickly as it came. "I know a place where we can stop to rest. It's just up ahead."

Taundosa *did* remind her of Akkinor, but there were things about it that were entirely unique. Everywhere she turned, she saw palm trees, tropical flowers, animals, plants, and insects. Bright blue butterflies flew in flocks, something she'd never seen before, and yellow-spotted lizards scurried between her feet whilst chasing mice and massive insects. As they walked the cobblestone streets, Jack told her about the other species of larger animals that called Taundosa their home. In the south, he said, herds of enormous brown elephants tended to roam the valleys and plateaus alongside gazelle, jackals, and numerous species of deadly snakes.

It was as if flakes of gold were imbedded in every last structure. Every building—homes, shops, taverns, inns, infirmaries—was made of adobe, but the material sparkled like it was gold. Each of the doors and windows were made of wood, but stained with gold-infused paint. In Akkinor, most businesses identified themselves with signs crafted with wood and cheap paint or ink. Here in Taundosa, all public buildings were adorned with engraved golden plaques.

Perhaps, Aurelia thought, Akkinor could adopt a thing or two from the districts of Taundosa—but only if her country was willing to trade bronze for gold.

After a few minutes of walking, Aurelia identified an apothecary shop, a woman's hospital (with three mages serving as medics, according to the inscription on the plaque), a bakery, a mercer, multiple craftsmen's shops, and a blacksmith's forgery. Merchants were stationed at little markets outside of their homes, where they sold all kinds of goods and produce from across Taundosa.

"This is a shortcut." Jack nodded towards a narrow alleyway between two towering adobe buildings. "If memory serves, we'll emerge in eastern Agotia. Careful now—this is private property. I've had a shoe thrown at my head three times before by old women who think I've come to steal their knickers."

The alley was too narrow for she and Jack to walk their horses through side-by-side, so she and Scotch trailed behind. Even Sterling seemed to know where he was going. Of course, the alley didn't do much to represent the splendor and beauty of Taundosa. The ground beneath their feet was a mixture of dirt and sand as opposed to the cobblestone of the streets, and the buildings that towered over either side of them completely concealed the sunlight. The buildings must have been residential, given the clothing lines strung up between them. When Aurelia looked up and to her left, she saw a young girl sitting in the tallest window with a book on her lap. Below the girl, an elderly man was peering out from another window, carefully eyeing Aurelia and Jack.

"Jack," she murmured, "how do Taundosans take to foreigners?"

He glanced over his shoulder at her. "Non-Carthinians, you mean?" She nodded. "I suppose I don't really know. Most people in southern Carthe take one look at me and assume I'm a crossbreed. I'd pass as a full-blooded Bozari if I were smaller and a bit darker. I personally haven't been the victim of any intolerance, but when I've seen other outsiders in the kingdom...the natives keep their distance. They don't want any trouble."

When they emerged on the other side of the alley, Aurelia wasn't surprised to find that eastern Agotia wasn't so different from the western half of the district. Here, though, there was a palpable increase in soldiers wearing specialized, one-of-a-kind armor. They were known as the Goldmen, and they'd served as the Taundosan monarchy's elite force of royal knights for centuries. Because eastern Agotia was so close to the capital—the Palace of Taundosa—there were more soldiers on patrol. They didn't seem particularly concerned with anything around them, though. In fact, the Goldmen appeared as leisurely and carefree as the commoners.

Jack stopped them by an extravagant golden water fountain. He bent down by the edge of the structure before turning to Aurelia with one beautiful, vibrant flower in hand. The five petals, rounded at the tips, were a radiant lime-green in the center but gradually turned blue towards the tips.

"For you, Lily dear," he said with a smile. "They call it *plumeria*. It only grows here in Taundosa. The plumeria flower can live for up to six weeks after it's been plucked. Now you shall have a lovely hair accessory to adorn throughout our time in Taundosa."

"Thank you." She took the flower, rolled the stem between her fingers, and inhaled the sweet scent that somehow reminded her of the hyacinths in the Folly. When she tucked it behind her ear, she raised a playful eyebrow at him. "Well? How do I look?"

His oceanic eyes sparkled. "Like a goddess."

"You mustn't fuel my hubris, Jack. Not here. Not now."

He held out his arms and grinned from ear to ear. "Look where we are. If you were looking for somewhere to be humbled, you've come to the wrong place."

***

Jack stopped them at an inn about halfway through the district. They tied up the horses in the stables, where Scotch and Sterling immediately began to snooze after nearly drowning themselves in water from a trough. The inn beside the stables was as lovely as the other buildings in Agotia, but it appeared more expensive than any establishment Aurelia had visited in Carthe thus far. What cost her seven pieces of bronze in Dofell ended up costing three pieces of gold in Taundosa. Her pockets felt bare after handing the coin to the innkeeper.

After purchasing a room for the night, a pitcher of water, a loaf of bread, and two bars of soap, Aurelia and Jack found their way to their bedchamber and collapsed on the bed. She was suddenly aware of the intense throbbing in her feet, the aching of her hips, and the sharp pain in her head. When she cast a sidelong look over Jack, she saw him massaging his temples with a bitter look on his face.

"I hadn't realized how sore I am until now," he shared, as if reading her thoughts. "I almost forgot about how taxing the valley is on one's body."

"You might've thought to mention that before."

"What difference would that have made? There are no masseuses in the desert."

"No, but there are better shoes."

He laughed. She desperately wanted to sleep, but the growling of her stomach made it difficult to keep her eyes shut. They finished the entire loaf of bread and pitcher of water in one sitting but decided to bathe before ordering dinner. Jack thought it best for them to take it slowly—apparently, it wasn't uncommon for people to vomit after their first meal following a trek through the desert.

In the bathhouse, Aurelia scowled at the state of her body. She looked thinner. Her face was gaunt, but she couldn't decide if it was due to malnutrition or exhaustion. Her face was ashen, her lips cracked and pale, and her eye sockets sunken. Her skin was either white as a pearl or red as a tomato. Most of her blisters had turned into scars, but some patches of sunburnt skin were still purple. The warm bathwater felt like glass against her burns. It wasn't very pleasant against the wound on her arm, either. She stopped thinking about the pain when she saw how murky the bath water had become. Dirt, sand, and grime from over two weeks without a bath had certainly left its mark.

When she was clean as a whistle, she dressed in the only clothing she had left that wasn't torn, bloody, or filthy. Jack was waiting for her by the exit, damp but pristine, and holding a wad of filthy clothing just as she was. On their way to the tavern, they threw the clothing in the wastebasket without a second thought.

A barmaid brought them a pitcher of water and two pints of ale when they were seated in the tavern. It wasn't long before she returned with two bowls of steaming stew, a loaf of bread, a bowl of sugared nuts, and a plate of assorted cheeses. Aurelia didn't know where to start. As she lifted her spoon to the bowl of stew, she saw Jack handing two pieces of silver to the barmaid. He shrugged when she raised her eyebrows at him.

"Gratuity is customary in Taundosa." He winced when he peered inside his coin pouch. "I really do hope this Cristos fellow is rich."

While she scoffed, the man at the end of their table perked up. "Cristos?" he repeated. Aurelia and Jack stared at him. *"Arian* Cristos?"

"You know him?" Jack asked.

The man's dark eyes twinkled with amusement. "Everyone in Agotia knows Arian Cristos! He's been our lord for the last six-and-twenty years."

Aurelia's eyes widened. "Arian Cristos is Lord of Agotia?"

"Not only that! He's Hand to Her Majesty the Queen."

Jack choked on a sip of ale. *"What?"* He turned to Aurelia, wild-eyed and startled beyond measure, as foamy liquid dribbled down his chin. "The man you're looking for is Hand to Queen Reyna?"

"Apparently so." She turned so she was fully facing the Taundosan man. "What more do you know about him?"

"Lots of things. Doesn't come cheap, though," he said, eyeing the pouch hanging from her girdle. She rolled her eyes and tossed him a piece of silver. He caught it easily and grinned. "Thank you, miss. Anyway, if you're looking for Lord Cristos, you better hope he's expecting you. He's the most powerful person in Taundosa, second only to Her Majesty. Comes from a lengthy line of mages, too. Authority, wealth, magic...everyone wants to make an impression on Arian Cristos. You aren't the first lost souls to go searching for him."

Aurelia lit up. "He's a mage?"

"Oh, yes. The Cristos family is one of the oldest in Taundosa. Some say they come from the Elementals."

Jack snorted. "That's rubbish."

"It's true," the man snapped. "As the story goes, anyway."

Aurelia was silent. *The Elementals. Impossible,* she thought. But then again, it didn't seem as impossible as she imagined. The Elementals were the first mages in the world. Everyone knew about them—even those whose ancestors called mages *heretics* and burned them alive. The Elementals were, without a fraction of a doubt, as prominent across the realm as the gods themselves.

Some would argue that all mages were descended from the Elementals. She didn't know what was real and what was legend, but none of that mattered. The one important thing she gathered was that Arian Cristos was a formidable man—exactly the kind of person she needed.

"Thank you very much," Aurelia said to the stranger. "You've been so helpful."

He grinned. "Sure thing."

She turned back to Jack and lowered her voice. "We should leave for the palace in the morning. He's likely residing there rather than here in Agotia. A monarch's Lord Hand would—"

"Slow down." He didn't look nearly as enthused as she was. "Think about this for a moment. Lord of Agotia, Hand of the Queen, descendent of the Elementals...is this really the man you've been looking for?"

She shrugged. "I know as much about him as you do. I have to trust that I was sent here for a reason."

"A man with that kind of power won't concern himself with a stranger."

"He will."

He was growing frustrated with her. "How do you know that?"

"I feel it," she insisted, instinctively reaching for her locket. "I didn't come all this way to be turned away. I didn't lose Kaia and nearly get both of us killed for nothing. One way or another, he'll see us. I know it."

He didn't look convinced. "Okay. I trust you."

"You do?"

"Of course I do." He took her hand from the table and kissed it. "I adore you, Lily, in more ways than one. There's no adoration without trust, is there?"

"No." She hesitated for a moment. "I adore you, too."

Jack grinned and lifted his cup. "I'll drink to that."

XXV

I have a bad feeling about this." Jack gazed around cautiously as they rode through Agotia. The Palace of Taundosa was visible now beyond the border that divided Agotia and Taundosa's capital. "This is the queen's palace, Lily. It isn't a lord's castle. Do you know how they'll take to two strangers demanding entry? Not well."

"We can barely see the palace, and already you have cold feet?"

"My entire body will be cold if they refuse us entry," he retorted. "You're not so skilled at taking no for an answer. Soldiers don't take kindly to that kind of attitude. We'll both be cold and long dead by the time Arian Cristos hears news of us—*if* he hears news of us."

She glared at him. "Your pessimism is dejecting."

"So is your obliviousness."

"I'm not oblivious. I'm hopeful."

He clenched his jaw. "*Hope* isn't enough for us to enter the queen's palace. You must know that."

Of course she did. Even if it was hard to remember in Carthe, she was a queen, too. If two exhausted, armed, ratty-looking civilians requested entry into the Palace of Akkinor, Aurelia's soldiers would've turned them away without a second thought. If the strangers were as persistent as Aurelia planned to be, the soldiers would've disposed of them as they deemed fit. Nobody dared to enter the monarch's residence without invitation, cause, or escort. Aurelia had all three—the problem was that she was the only person who knew it.

"If you're so worried about this, maybe you should wait at the inn," she suggested. "I'm going one way or another. If you're uneasy, I won't ask you to accompany me."

Hurt and disappointment flashed across his face. "You don't wish for me to come?"

"That isn't what I said."

"It sounded like that's what you meant."

"I didn't intend for it to sound that way." When she heard the bitterness in her voice, she exhaled and ran a hand through her curls. "I'm sorry. You must understand, Jack—Arian Cristos is the last hope I have. If I want to go home, I need to try, even if I fail. I want you to try with me. I can't imagine coming so far together only for it to end because of this, but I won't ask you to put yourself in harm's way again. If you're uneasy, I won't ask you to proceed, and I will understand."

He hesitated. "If you want me to stay, I shall stay." He reached over and set his hand on hers. "I spend my life traveling this continent. There's nothing for me to do but walk the land. I was an arrow that flew without destination until I met you. You've given me a purpose again, Lily. I wouldn't walk away from you."

Warmth spread throughout her entire body. "Have I told you recently how much I adore you?"

"I believe you showed me last night."

She pushed him away. "You're a scoundrel."

"And *you* are the loveliest creature since Xienia."

Aurelia blushed furiously. Xienia was the goddess of beauty. Jack certainly knew how to charm a woman, and the way he looked at her made her positive that no other woman would ever be as lucky as she was.

And yet, she was risking him for something as unpredictable as hope. A pit filled her stomach as she gazed up at the palace. She couldn't see much of it yet, but even a glimpse was enough. It was made entirely of gold with enormous towers, wide balconies, and intricate golden sculptures. Everything about it sparkled and shined against the sun. It was smaller than the Palace of Akkinor, but its beauty rivaled even that of Xienia. The palace itself wasn't nearly as intimidating as the thought of the truth being revealed, though. When Aurelia set her gaze on Arian Cristos for the first time, every secret she'd hidden from Jack would be brought to light. Would he still look at her that way when she was his queen rather than his partner?

She didn't see it that way. She liked who she was when she was with Jack. She liked that she could be herself in every way. No formalities, no pristine behavior, no expectations. They were simply two people who cared for one another—two strangers who'd met by chance and formed a bond that she valued more than she thought possible. As soon as they stepped foot in the palace, though, they would be seen as nomad and queen. She only hoped that Jack saw them for what they were at heart like she did.

When she looked at him, her fears seemed to melt into nothingness. She studied the curve of his jaw, the shape of his lips, the swirling blue of his eyes, the fall of his dark curls against his tanned skin. She admired the hefty, brawny hands that caressed her body with the gentleness of a butterfly and the strong arms that held her each night when nightmares had her thrashing in her sleep. But the thing she admired most about him was the heart in his chest that seemed to beat only for her. In the brief time they'd known one another, he'd shown her the kindness, selflessness, and protection she thought was missing from the world. She knew exactly the kind of man he was. If anyone in the world could forgive her for keeping such a secret, it'd be Jack.

They stopped briefly to leave the horses at nearby stables. They were arriving at the palace now, and Aurelia thought it best to walk the rest of the way. As they were tying the reins to posts, she caught sight of a Taundosan man doing the same thing across the way. He was observing them like they'd just announced plans to lay siege to the kingdom.

"Jack," she whispered. He raised an eyebrow. "That man is watching us. Rather closely."

He followed her gaze and sighed. "He knows we aren't Carthinian. He's likely wondering what we're doing so far into the continent."

"How could he possibly know that?"

"On this continent, we're Akkinorians versus Carthinians. We're not Akkinorians versus Taundosans or Bozari or Kanish. In Akkinor, on the other hand, we're Myrans versus Omarans, Sadians versus Holosi, and so on. The number of foreigners who trek across this continent under false identities is astronomical. It's impossible to take one's word that they're a native of one particular kingdom. The Carthinians have gotten into the habit of identifying themselves as just that—Carthinians." Jack finished tying Sterling's reins and offered his arm for her to take. "Shall we?"

Smiling, Aurelia wordlessly accepted his arm and let him guide her towards the palace grounds. She absorbed everything she could about Taundosa and its people while they trekked: the adolescent boys abandoning their streetside game—without a moment's hesitation—to assist an elderly man who'd dropped an armful of books; a trio of expectant mothers fanning their faces, whispering, and giggling from their rocking chairs while their husbands massaged their swollen feet; a group of men, having formed an assembly line that spanned from one side of the street to the other, delivering supplies to repairmen working on a rooftop; and the children, varying in age from three to thirteen, working together to bring trays of food and drink to the laboring adults.

Aurelia spent the majority of her life entertaining a somewhat vainglorious perspective of her country. Even before Akkinor surpassed all other civilizations as the realm's most prosperous, she believed her country was the best of them. She frowned upon other countries and kingdoms because she didn't understand them, because they were different from hers; now that she'd learned so much about the culture and character of Carthe, her opinions were changing before her eyes.

These people weren't savage barbarians looking for any excuse to attack and defile foreign visitors. They weren't heathens who'd chosen to ignore divine guidance for immoral lifestyles. They were just....people. Normal, average people who wanted nothing more than to survive and to exist in peace, just as the gods intended. The only thing that truly made Akkinorians and Carthinians different from one another was this: the former was created to dominate the east, and the latter created for the west.

A nervous lump formed in Aurelia's throat when she and Jack arrived at the palace grounds. There were a dozen guards posted at the gates, and another dozen guarded the front doors of the palace. Eight more manned the four watchtowers atop the gates. Before Aurelia and Jack could get close to the gates, a soldier stepped forwards with his hand raised to stop them. His other hand sat comfortably on the hilt of his sword.

"That's far enough," the soldier declared. "Civilian entrance is prohibited without an invitation. Turn around and be on your way."

Aurelia kept her head high. "I'm looking for Lord Arian Cristos. I was told that he serves as Hand to Her Majesty the Queen."

"That's right."

"I've come for an audience with Lord Cristos, should the gods be kind."

"What's your business with His Lordship?"

"I'm a friend from Akkinor."

He scoffed at her. "The Lord Hand is far too busy to entertain a peasant girl from Akkinor." Anger bubbled up inside of her, but for the sake of entry, she kept it contained. "Leave now or you will be removed from the premises."

Jack set his hand on her elbow. "I think we have our answer."

She tugged her arm away. "I'd suggest reconsidering my request," she told the soldier. She'd made it to the gates—she didn't plan on leaving so soon. "His Lordship would be terribly upset if he learned of my dismissal today."

"Careful, girl." The soldier narrowed his eyes at her and adjusted his grip on his sword. "I won't tell you again. If you leave and return with an invitation, I will open the gates. If you can't acquire an invitation, you will be executed upon your return. Do I make myself clear?"

She stared at him with a look in her eyes that made him recoil. "Let's make a deal, shall we?" She removed the locket from her neck and held it out for him. "Bring this to Lord Cristos. If you return without him, I shall take my leave without protest. You have my word." He said nothing as she set the locket in his palm. Before releasing it, she grasped his hand tightly and leaned forwards. "I won't leave this spot until my possession is returned to me. I assure you, if you can't give me your word and remain true to it, there will be consequences."

His eyes flashed. "A man's word can always be trusted in Taundosa."

"As it can in Akkinor. Thank you for your cooperation."

He didn't seem fond of her tone. Without another word, he turned on his heel and walked towards the gates. The other soldiers opened them for him, and the soldiers posted at the front doors allowed him inside without question. When he disappeared, Aurelia released the breath she'd been holding and stepped back to join Jack.

His mouth was agape with bewilderment. "What on earth was that?"

"What?"

"*That!*" He gestured towards the gates, wild-eyed. "A man once offered you enough gold to make us rich. You refused because your necklace is a precious family heirloom worth more to you than your life. Now you've given it to a soldier who threatened you. What if he doesn't bring it back?"

"He will. He gave me his word."

"And you trust him?"

"I have to. We're out of options."

He shook his head at her. "Why would you risk your most prized possession for the chance to meet Arian Cristos? Why would a trinket mean anything to him?"

She didn't answer him. She didn't know what the right answer was. All she knew was that her locket had been in her possession since she was born, and given the revelations about her birth and the distinct gold of the locket, she had to assume it came from Taundosa. It'd been with her when she was born on the continent, and Arian Cristos was the one person in the world who could give her the answers she needed. She had no choice but to hope that the locket meant something to *him*, too.

They'd been waiting for so long that they decided to sit on the ground rather than stand and lurk like outsiders. They were sitting in the grass, picking wildflowers from the ground, when the palace doors opened again. As the couple scrambled to their feet, the soldiers perfected their posture and wiped the emotions from their faces. Aurelia's heart pounded rapidly when a man appeared in the doorway, radiating a type of power that made even the queen break a sweat.

He wasn't what she imagined. He wore a clean, loose-fitting blue tunic and matching trousers that concealed most of his thin, short body. He had brown skin, shoulder-length graying hair, and a neatly trimmed gray beard that was both thick and clean-cut. His bushy gray eyebrows, when furrowed, nearly concealed his deep-set eyes from view. There were age lines on his forehead and around his eyes, but the smile lines around his mouth were even more defined. He held himself high with pristine posture and the unrelenting vigor of a nobleman.

When his eyes found Aurelia, everything about him seemed to change. In the blink of an eye, he was no longer the most powerful nobleman in Taundosa, but a small, withered middle-aged man who looked like he was staring into a phantom's gaze.

He took a few slow, hesitant steps forwards without taking his eyes from hers. He was studying everything about her, just as she was doing to him. She minded every move he made as he walked down the stairs and inched towards her, eyes wide and unbelieving. The soldier was trailing behind him as the guards opened the gates for their lord. When the gates were opened and nothing was obstructing her view of him, she saw her locket dangling from his hand. It was held tightly in his fist—tighter than necessary. He was as worried about losing it as she was. It *had* meant something to him after all.

When he was standing directly in front of her, neither of them uttered a word. He simply stared at her with a dumbfounded look in his deep brown eyes. When she regarded him more closely, she saw his hands were trembling and his lip was quivering. He didn't look like the kind of man who could've conquered the entirety of Carthe if he felt so inclined. He looked...frail. Small.

Finally, he spoke: "Where did you get this?"

"I don't know," she said honestly. When he held out his hand, she did the same, and he dropped the locket into her palm. She didn't hesitate to put it around her neck again. "It was given to me on the day I was born. I was hoping you may be able to help me put the pieces together." No response. "I assume your soldier informed you of where I come from. Now, I'm assuming you know who I am and why I've come."

He said nothing. The soldier took a few steps forwards and glared at her. "What would you like me to do with her, my lord? Shall I send her away?"

"Certainly not." Arian Cristos finally sounded like a nobleman when he spoke again. He peered at the soldier sternly, if not disapprovingly. "Please learn of Queen Reyna's whereabouts. I must inform her of our guests' arrival if they're to stay in the palace."

The soldier furrowed his eyebrows. "My lord? Do you know this woman?"

"Mind your tone, soldier. You know her as well as I do." The lord stepped back and straightened up. Aurelia's heart pounded violently when he clasped his hands behind his back and bowed to her. "Welcome to Taundosa, Your Grace."

An enormous grin spread over her face, so wide that her cheeks ached. "Thank you, my lord. The City of Gold is as lovely as I imagined it."

He smiled. "Show some respect, gentleman," he called to the guards. Each soldier gawked at him, confused. "You stand in the presence of Her Majesty, Aurelia Brentwood, First of Her Name, Queen of Akkinor." His eyes sparkled as he gazed at her. "I've been waiting a very long time to meet you, Your Grace."

Intermission

There'd been something unusual yet intriguing about her from the moment they met. Jack could've sworn he'd seen her before, but he knew he'd remember if he had. A man didn't forget a woman like her if he could help it. Even so, that was exactly the reason he'd decided to follow her into the unknown. She was familiar to him, and he was hellbent on uncovering the reason why.

At least, that's how it started. By the time they traded the unpredictable Violet Forest for the barren Ngora Valley, he found himself riding alongside her for a different reason.

He'd fallen in love with her.

Before meeting her, Jack thought he knew exactly what love was: eternal loyalty born from the utmost respect and affection. It took time, patience, and selflessness to acquire, and it didn't simply fall onto one's lap. It was something he had to earn, had to fight for, until he risked losing everything. Only then would he finally be worthy of the love he sought.

That, of course, had been his father's perspective. Jack should've known better than to believe such things.

Upon meeting the blue-eyed, golden-haired woman who'd found her way into his heart, Jack felt like a fool for adopting his father's interpretation of love. It wasn't something one needed to earn to experience, but something one had to accept for what it was before it was lost forever.

It was something in the way she looked at him—as if she were a lion preying on a gazelle when he irritated her, and as if he were a god promising her eternal salvation while she lay in his arms. It was the way her laughter melted into the sounds of birdsong and rushing streams, like she was one with everything the gods had created to supply the realm with beauty and serenity. It was the way her eyes reflected every emotion she felt, forcing him to adopt those same emotions to prevent her from experiencing them by herself. It was how she hummed in her sleep in a way that sounded like singing, how she greeted each new sight and every unfamiliar experience like she'd never known anything greater, and how she blatantly refused to admit that she needed him on her journey— because she didn't. Her aptitude illuminated her being like the setting sun against the horizon, and the only thing keeping the ferocity in her soul from breaking free was the humble heart beating in her chest.

The heart that'd begun to beat to the same rhythm as his.

He tried to deny his feelings. It wasn't in his nature to love the women he lusted for. It'd been impossible from the start to ignore the way he craved her, but when the craving transformed into longing, he tried to convince himself that he was imagining it. Perhaps it was the heatstroke and the dehydration. Both were known to inflict oddities on the human brain, and loving a mysterious woman—practically still a stranger—was about the craziest thing he could think of.

In spite of his better judgement, her name had been carved into his heart, and his soul had begun to sing for her.

What had once been a mission to place her in his memories had quickly become a desire to be wherever she was. He didn't know where life would take him next when she found what she was looking for in the City of Gold. Maybe she *wouldn't* find it, and she'd give up on the idea of returning to Akkinor so she could begin anew in Carthe.

A part of him hoped she wouldn't find what she was searching for. The wiser part of him, though, recognized that a woman like Lily Linden wouldn't stop until she had what she desired. He could see it in her eyes: her spirit was too strong. That alone would carry her home.

He didn't want to part with her, nor did he want to return to the place he'd run from five years earlier. If he followed her, she'd finally know why he ran and why he never returned. She'd learn that he'd been lying to her since the day they met, and she'd look at him like a stranger. He'd have no choice but to accept her decision if she left him. A woman like her deserved better than a liar like him.

There was one thing, however, that Jack hadn't considered until he found himself standing outside the Palace of Taundosa with the woman he loved at his side: she may have been lying to him, too.

And she was.

It crashed over him like a tidal wave swallowing a village. In an instant, he understood exactly why she was so familiar to him: he knew her. He'd never met her personally, of course, but he'd seen her back home in Akkinor when they were children. Perhaps if he'd stayed in Akkinor long enough to catch a glimpse of her as an adult, he might've known who she was upon their first real meeting in the Violet Forest.

He'd seen her, but she'd never seen him—and yet, somehow, he hadn't put the pieces together until the truth was directly in front of him. He'd been so infatuated with her that he believed every word she'd said to him. He believed she truly was Lily Linden, daughter of a noble lady's stewardess, seeking assistance in Carthe after an unfortunate arrangement with dangerous highborn individuals.

He never stopped to consider that she might've been Aurelia Brentwood, Queen of Akkinor—the one individual who, if Jack ever returned to his homeland, would be responsible for deciding his fate.

Even with the truth turning his brain to mush, Jack maintained his own charade. Now more than ever, he couldn't tell her who he was. She wouldn't look at him the same way if she knew, nor would she ever love him as he loved her. It was a risk he couldn't take.

Jack Sherbourne would've gone to the ends of the earth and back again for Lily Linden, but she wasn't Lily Linden, and he wasn't Jack Sherbourne.

They were, for lack of a better phrase, strangers united by tragedy— tragedy and, of course, sorrows.

BOOK TWO: ASHES

Someone was coming.

He didn't know who, and he didn't know when, but Arian Cristos was certain of it: someone was coming.

The day his instincts proved accurate wasn't a special one, but it was different. The sun was hotter, the air was drier, the sky was brighter—almost as if some sort of spell had been cast over the glittering kingdom of Taundosa, alerting every living creature of the arrival of something destined for the City of Gold.

Every part of his daily routine was marked by goosebumps and risen hairs on the back of his neck. He washed, dressed, ate, promenaded, read—and with every step, he felt himself growing closer and closer to whichever force of nature was due to arrive at the palace gates.

It was late morning when he found himself in his study. He ignored the mountain of documents awaiting his signature and instead began to pace. He couldn't understand how he, a veteran mage of exceptional skill, couldn't identify what was coming. Was it friend or foe? Mage or mortal? Stranger or familiar? Or, even worse—was this feeling of his nothing but rubbish and hogwash?

Arian stopped pacing, craned his neck backwards, and focused his dark eyes on the ceiling. The sundial above his head—a particular type of time-telling device unique to Taundosa—was moving slowly, very slowly, from one end of the study to the other along a thin golden line marked by the hour. A sculpture of a dragon, wings outstretched as if taking flight, was connected by its talons to a large sun. The iron sculptures traveled along the golden line as the hours changed, and due to the magical properties of the sundial, didn't need to be exposed to the outdoors to correctly display the time.

The sundial had been a source of comfort for Arian for almost thirty years. He remembered the first day he sat in the study as Lord Hand to Reyna Caltheos, Queen of Taundosa. Back then, he'd felt the same anxiety he felt now bubbling up in his chest. He'd just buried both of his parents, let his youngest sister disappear into the continent, and accepted a position as the kingdom's second-most powerful individual. It was just a matter of time before his nerves consumed him.

He would've lost himself to that anxiety had it not been for his beloved sister, Katryna. She'd found him there, short of breath and gray in the face, pacing across the room with such force that his knees had gone numb. She'd taken him by the wrists, looked into his eyes, and turned her gaze to the ceiling.

"Look up. You must find your peace again, Arian. Look up."

He'd tilted his head backwards and watched the sundial as it moved in miniscule increments across the ceiling. He focused his eyes on the dragon and his mind on the feeling of Katryna's gentle fingertips applying pressure to the pulses of his wrists. When his trembles faded away, he glanced down at his sister again and exhaled.

"It's all right." She removed her necklace—a cylindrical golden locket hanging from a matching gold chain—and set it on his palm before smiling and curling her fingers around his. "Let this be a comfort for you, brother. You are my eternal solace; today, may this be yours."

He'd squeezed her fingers and returned her smile. "Thank you, Kitty."

"It's you and I. Always."

Katryna Cristos hadn't lived much longer after that, but her memory would exist for eternity. Whenever he found himself falling victim to his nerves, he looked at that glorious, silly little sundial and imagined his sister was there with him. Imagining was the only way he could survive a world without her.

Now he stood alone in the study, staring at the sundial, and rotated his body enough to see it from all angles. He felt his eyes well with tears as he watched the dragon, which appeared to wield the sun in its talons like a child might hold a toy.

Only a dragon, he thought, bore the power to wield the sun.

A vigorous knock at the door startled him. He regained his composure, squared his shoulders, and blinked the emotion from his eyes. Upon opening the door, he was greeted by a breathless knight of Taundosa who appeared both frustrated and intrigued at the same time.

"Forgive the interruption, my lord," the Goldman wheezed. "There's a peddler woman at the front gates. She insists upon an audience with you, but she hasn't a formal invitation to the palace."

Arian sighed. This wasn't the first peasant to seek an audience with him, and she certainly wouldn't be the last.

"Send her off. Without an invitation—"

"I informed her of that, my lord, but she's rather persistent. She claims to be a friend from Akkinor. I was instructed to give this to Your Lordship as some sort of incentive for meeting with her."

When the knight unclasped his hand, Arian nearly lost his footing. He stared at the knight's palm for a moment, awestruck, before lifting the object with trembling fingers. It was a locket, but not just any locket—it was the same necklace worn by Katryna for her entire life. It was one-of-a-kind, and the last time he'd seen it, it was boarding a ship destined for Akkinor.

Arian didn't realize that he'd started walking until the knight hurried to match his pace. He knew the knight was speaking to him, but he heard nothing but garbled words and noises. It wasn't a long walk from his study to the front doors of the palace, but that day, it felt like he'd crossed the entirety of the Ngora Valley.

He knew exactly where that locket came from, and better yet, he knew exactly *who* it'd come from: the very same *who* he'd spent the last several weeks waiting for.

He saw her immediately when the guards opened the doors for him. He descended the front steps slowly and cautiously, one by one, as she waited patiently on the other side of the gates.

In that moment, he didn't notice the numerous Goldmen nor the elephantine male companion waiting behind her. He didn't notice the curious faces watching from the streets, nor the eavesdropping servants observing from the windows and balconies of the palace. In that moment, he saw nothing but the golden-haired woman with his sister's face staring into his eyes.

This was no peddler woman. This was no *woman* at all—this was a queen, and Arian was certain that he was the only person present who knew it.

Aurelia Brentwood, Queen of Akkinor, had returned to the City of Gold.

XXVI

The Queen of Akkinor often prided herself on her ability to recognize a face. She could her gaze on someone and recall the exact moment she saw them for the first time—even if they were a stranger she'd seen in passing while roaming the streets of the Folly.

As she followed Arian Cristos through the glittering golden halls of the queen's palace, Aurelia felt a sense of frustration coursing through her veins. She was certain she recognized him, but she couldn't place him in her memories. It was almost as if she'd seen him in a dream, long ago when everything was simpler, like an omen or prophecy written by the gods.

She listened intently while he spoke, observed his body language, analyzed his facial expressions. She stared at the dark curls streaked with gray as they bounced on his head, the scars on his hands, the star-shaped birthmark on the left side of his neck—and yet, even with so many distinguishing aspects of his being, she couldn't determine where or when she'd seen him before.

For a moment, she considered a somewhat obvious explanation: she'd spent so many weeks wondering about him that she'd simply imagined his familiarity. Then the left sleeve of his tunic lifted towards his elbow as he raised his arm, and when she saw the golden bangle on his wrist adorned with diamonds and amethysts, the realization struck her: Arian Cristos was familiar not because she'd seen him before, but because every aspect of his demeanor—from the way he strolled to his speech patterns to the way he smiled—reminded her hauntingly of her father. Now more than ever, she needed to know why Edmund had instructed her to find Arian in her hour of greatest need.

Aurelia snapped out of her daze when Arian halted in front of an open door. "I must ask you to wait here for a few moments. It's imperative that

I find Her Majesty and inform her of your arrival. She'll be most eager to meet you."

She smiled at him. "Take all the time you need."

When he left, deafening silence struck Aurelia like a club to the back, highlighting the sheer enormity of Arian's presence. Only then did she finally turn to glance at Jack, who hadn't said a word since Arian announced the arrival of Akkinor's queen. Now that Arian had left the pair to themselves, she had no choice but to face the crushing weight of a horrible, gut-churning revelation: her entire relationship with Jack had been built on lies. She'd always known it, of course, but now that Jack did, too, she was forced to admit that she'd been playing him like a fiddle from the moment he saved her in the Violet Forest.

He was standing beside a plush cream-colored couch, looking ghoulish with his ashen skin and wide, startled eyes. She wanted to take his hands and kiss him in celebration of her success, but she stopped herself when she caught a glimpse of his face. Jack's mouth was contorted in a bitter sort of way, twisted and curled as if caught between a sneer and a scowl, and the expression resulted in his nose wrinkling in disgust.

She'd glanced at him fleetingly after Arian identified her, and she wished she hadn't. The guilt that followed nearly swallowed her whole. His skin was tinged with green, his knuckles whiter than a sheet, and his eyes void of the charm she'd grown to love. He'd been so shocked that he hadn't even *looked* at her. In fact, he hadn't lifted his eyes from the ground until the moment they stepped foot into the palace—and even then, it seemed like the last thing he wanted to lay eyes on was Aurelia.

She didn't blame him. She'd deceived him, and regardless of the reason for it, her lack of transparency translated into an act of disloyalty. She would've reacted similarly, had their roles been reversed, but her temperament wouldn't have allowed her to remain as composed as Jack. She had his Omaran blood to thank for that.

Aurelia had been terrified of his reaction to learning the truth from the very beginning. When he was nothing more than an insufferable swordsman who'd insisted upon accompanying her to Taundosa, she wasn't inclined to trust a rogue Akkinorian in Carthe. She assumed he would've sold her out to anyone hoping to deliver her head to her usurper. As she found herself trusting him and falling victim to his insatiable charm, though, her terror was rooted in her betrayal. With every stride their relationship took, the agony of secrecy only worsened. Now, the time for hiding had finally come to an end.

"Jack—"

"Yes, Your Grace?"

She frowned at the bitterness in his voice. "Please don't make this more difficult than it already is."

"Queen Aurelia." He shook his head and scoffed. The anger in his eyes made him look like a different person—a person who, unlike the Jack she adored, was riddled with hostility. "All this time..."

"I wanted to tell you," she insisted. "It was for my protection, Jack, and yours. You know what might've happened if anyone discovered the truth. It wasn't worth the risk while we were traveling. I never intended to hurt you or lie to you. I did what was necessary to ensure our survival."

He clenched his teeth so tightly that the taut muscles of his jaw wobbled. "You're not just another Akkinorian. You're the queen. *My* queen. And I had absolutely no clue. Have you any idea how humiliating that is?"

"I'm sorry, Jack." She took a few steps towards him and held out her hands, hoping to find strength and comfort in his touch, but he didn't move a muscle. She sighed and dropped her arms to her sides. "What would you have done if you knew?"

"Exactly what I've already done."

"So why does this change anything?"

"Because, Lily—" He stopped short when he realized his mistake. When she winced, he exhaled irritably and ran a hand through his curls. "Because it was all a lie. Everything we've done together...I thought I was doing it all with someone who was like me. A civilian who wouldn't be missed in Akkinor, searching Carthe for answers and purpose. I confided in that person. I gave advice to that person. I *lay* with that person, for heaven's sake. If I knew..."

She surged backwards, hurt. "You would've treated me differently?"

"Of course I would've! You're the *Queen of Akkinor!*"

"There's no difference between the woman you know and the woman I am. I've always been true to myself—*especially* with you."

No reply. She saw the wheels turning behind his eyes, and it wasn't difficult to infer what was running through his brain. Though he was several years older than her, they'd still grown up in Akkinor at around the same time. Perhaps Jack had visited the Folly in the past—maybe even on a day when Aurelia was strolling through the villages in disguise. Or maybe, given his position as a soldier for the noble family of Omara, he'd accompanied the Ashfords to the palace for a tournament, where he saw the princess sitting in the viewing box with her parents.

As she watched him ponder, she recognized the expression on his face as one of realization. He finally understood that nearly everything Lily Linden had told him about her life was true—mainly the bit about her brother and the inheritance he believed she'd stolen from him. Jack may have been upset at her deception, but at the very least, he now knew two things for certain: the exact reason Aurelia had left Akkinor for Carthe, and that she'd trusted him with as much as she could regarding her predicament without revealing her identity.

A glimmer of pity sparkled in Jack's eyes. "Prince Archie. He planned the uprising against you?"

"I believe so."

"Why?"

"Why do you think? He wanted the crown, and our parents chose me to wear it. The uprising was a perfect opportunity for him to take it because nobody would suspect him of foul play. He's my only heir, after all. In their eyes, he was there to save them when I wasn't. They're probably eating out of his hand by now—if he hasn't led them to ruin, that is."

"Royal life isn't so glamorous, is it?"

She smiled pitifully. "No, it's not."

He studied her. "I want so badly to be angry with you. I wish I could yell and fight and leave you here, but I can't. We've been together all this time, and all along you've been someone else. I understand why you did it, though, as much as I wish I didn't."

"I'm so sorry, Jack," she said earnestly. He finally accepted her hands when she reached for his. As always, the feel of his skin against hers—warm, calloused, and strong—brought her peace. "You haven't any idea how guilty I've felt. With you, with Kaia. I never expected to meet people in Carthe whom I trust with my life. I was lucky enough to find two of you. Every day, I've thought about telling you the truth so I can finally sleep in your arms without feeling ashamed." She traced his forearms with her fingertips as if to claim him with ancient runes and long-forgotten spells. The gesture must've brought him as much comfort as it did her, because the tension in his muscles melted away with every move she made. "It was better this way. It was better for you to know me as someone who doesn't exist."

When his eyes locked on hers, she knew they were thinking the same thing: Lily Linden *did* exist. She may have been a woman created on a whim, but she'd lived a life in Carthe. Lily Linden had been free, but Aurelia Brentwood was not. She'd been unfamiliar and frightened of that freedom at first, but now, she was unsure if she was prepared to lay Lily to rest and be chained, once again, to the chaos and turmoil eternally bonded to the throne.

They didn't get the chance to discuss it further. Not a moment later, Arian returned to the parlor with a living work of art on his arm: Reyna Caltheos, Queen of Taundosa.

Aurelia often imagined the Golden Queen as she was at the time of her coronation, several years before Aurelia's birth: a fourteen-year-old girl with dark hair, brown eyes, and brown skin so warm it appeared golden. In the flesh, Reyna wasn't at all like Aurelia pictured her. The only thing Aurelia managed to assume correctly was Reyna's complexion: a stunning, dewy shade of almond brown accentuated by mauve powder on her sharp cheekbones and deep plum lipstick on her mouth. Her sleek, glossy hair fell like a sheet of obsidian over her back, so long that the ends licked her hips. Dark powder was smudged over her eyelids and beneath her lower lashes to draw attention to her eyes. Her nose was thin but long and hooked at the tip (characteristic of native Taundosans). Her eyebrows, plucked thinly with sharp arches, were painted with enough black powder to conceal balding spots. It was clear she'd used the same cosmetic on the roots of her hair to conceal the gray, as her scalp was dusted with flaking black powder and tinged charcoal.

However, her loveliest and most striking quality was her gaze. While the majority of her features were visibly Taundosan, her eyes were, without a doubt, Bozari: enormously round and bluer than pure azurite. They were so bold and bright that they appeared to be glowing, as if there were a tiny source of light desperately trying to break free from its prison behind Reyna's eyes. If not for Reyna's gaze serving as a reminder, Aurelia would've forgotten that the Queen of Taundosa was born to a Bozari mother.

"Your Majesty." Aurelia smiled. "I'm charmed to make your acquaintance. Taundosa is as lovely as claimed by the stories that have reached Akkinor."

The queen beamed. "Thank you. I've heard many stories about the Queen of Akkinor, too. I'm pleased to formally meet you. Should you require anything at all, you need only ask. We queens must stand together and support one another, after all." She winked. "I'd imagine you feel the same way."

"I do. Your kindness is admirable, Your Majesty. When I've safely returned to Akkinor, you will forever have a place at my hearth. I would be honored to host the queen of such a handsome and prosperous country."

Queen Reyna smiled. Then she saw Jack, who'd been awkwardly standing several paces behind Aurelia. When he saw the queen's eyes on him, he cleared his throat and bowed to her while Aurelia introduced him.

His past as an Omaran soldier was more evident, she noticed, now that such dominant individuals surrounded him.

"On behalf of the monarchy, welcome to Taundosa," Reyna mused as she glanced between her guests. "Your chambers are being prepared as we speak. The palace is your home for as long as you need, Your Grace. I will leave you to attend to business with Lord Cristos, but if you require anything at all, please don't hesitate to find me."

Aurelia thanked her with a weak, wobbling smile. The expression—paired with the faint stinging of her eyes and the sudden dryness of her throat—warned her of impending tears before they could flood down her cheeks. She hadn't known what to expect when she learned that Arian served the Queen of Taundosa. She was delighted (and a bit shocked) at Reyna's hospitality and willingness to host Aurelia as if the two were old friends.

Jack cleared his throat when Reyna disappeared. He looked weary, as if the reveal of Aurelia's true identity had caused him to age twenty years. "I think I should retire to my chambers. This is a conversation for the two of you to have privately. I-I've a bit of thinking to do in the meantime."

Her heart hammered. "Of course. I shall see you later on."

The last thing she wanted was for him to leave her alone with Arian Cristos. She trusted Arian as her parents did, but she knew their upcoming conversation would be difficult if not painful, and having Jack at her side would bring her calmness and comfort. She felt stronger when Jack was near, despite the little voice in the back of her head reminding her that she didn't need him to be strong. His presence was a matter of preference, not necessity—but if it'd been the other way around, she knew he would've stayed regardless of his displeasure with her. That was just the kind of man he was.

When Jack left, Arian raised an eyebrow at her. "He didn't know who you were until today, did he?"

She shook her head.

"All for the best, undoubtedly," he replied. She couldn't so much as shrug. When he offered her his arm, she took it and allowed him to escort her into the hallway. "He reminds me of someone. I can't quite place it. What kingdom does he hail from?"

"Omara."

His eyes flashed. "There it is. Only an Omaran can hold his head high in the midst of inner turmoil. They're a special kind of people, aren't they?"

Aurelia didn't answer. She was too distracted by their surroundings, which she hadn't noticed during her initial walkthrough of the palace with her thoughts running ramped through her brain. The exterior of the palace was breathtaking, but the interior was unlike anything she'd ever seen. If the entire kingdom itself wasn't deserving of the moniker *the City of Gold*, then the palace certainly was. For a fraction of a second, a pang of jealousy pierced her soul, and she wondered if she'd ever look at the Palace of Akkinor the same as she once did now that she'd seen Taundosa with her own eyes.

Though only the foyer and the main corridor were visible to her, she knew the remainder of the palace wouldn't stray far from the entrance's beauty. The floor was composed of a shiny polished wood, a light maple or oak, though they strolled along a taupe carpet embedded with gold thread. Enormous ivory pillars bordered the carpet from the front doors to the end of the corridor with tall arches between them. Several gold-and-crystal chandeliers hung low to the ground in the center of the corridor. Golden artifacts, statues, and other decorations were nestled in the niches built within the white walls and gold trim. Even the murals and mosaics on the ceiling—which all seemed to depict the early days of Taundosa's existence—were made with gold paint or tiny pieces of solid gold.

He soon stopped in front of a door with a plaque on the wall identifying it as the personal study of Arian Cristos, Hand of the Queen. He opened the door for her and allowed her inside before he followed. It was simple inside, with a desk and chair, two armchairs on the opposite side, a small sofa, a tea table, and bookshelves lining the walls. She started to sit in one of the armchairs, but he insisted that she take the spacious leather chair at the desk. He seemed to know that she'd never been on the receiving side of a nobleman's desk before.

"Now," he said, smiling, "where shall we begin?"

XXVII

My lord—" Aurelia began.

"Arian, please." He quieted for a moment as he studied her, causing a blush to warm her cheeks. "Forgive me, Your Grace. I've always wondered what you looked like as an adult. You're exactly as I envisioned you, and somehow, you look like Cressida."

She smiled, but it faded quickly when memory served. "I don't know how that's possible." When she saw the look in his eye, she knew she'd been right about where to find her answers. "You don't know how it's possible, either. Do you?"

"Not quite. I wondered if they'd ever tell you the truth. When did you find out?"

"When I escaped Akkinor. My parents left a letter for me, but I'm afraid I've burned it. They told me the truth about my birth and that the one person who can help me is you. I've never heard your name before, and yet, here we sit."

"Here we sit," he repeated. "I've waited for this moment for many years. I wondered if it would ever come."

Her eyes snapped downwards to his lap, where the golden bangle on his wrist shimmered against the candlelight. As far as she knew, only four bangles identical to his had been created by a former Brentwood family jeweler. Her paternal grandmother, Queen Consort Charlotte, gifted the bangles to her four children. Aurelia's aunts and uncle still wore their bracelets every day. Edmund's was likely at the bottom of the Crystal Sea, having drowned in the shipwreck that claimed his life.

"Your bracelet," she murmured. "Where did you get it?"

His eyes twinkled. "Where do you think?"

"My grandmother. She had four bracelets made for each of her children. Amethysts to symbolize the Brentwood family, and diamonds to symbolize the Steel family of Holos—hers."

Arian lifted his arm to admire the bangle. "You're almost entirely correct. Your grandmother, rest her soul, had five bracelets created. One was intended for me." He removed the bracelet and handed it to her. "Take a look at the inscription."

Perplexed, Aurelia accepted the bracelet and studied the engraving. Her father's bangle had been inscribed with a message from his mother, too: *For the boy who made me a mother.* Arian's wasn't so different: *For the boy who made me a better mother.*

"I don't understand." She looked up at him as she clutched the bracelet between her hands. "You wear a bracelet made by my grandmother for her children. You remind me of my father—so much so that it frightens me, in truth. You knew who I was simply by identifying my necklace. My parents mentioned you by name as the only person whom I can trust during times of peril. All of this, and yet, I don't understand. Why you?"

Arian cleared his throat and scratched at the back of his head. He didn't answer her immediately, but rather turned his gaze upwards to stare at the ceiling. She couldn't decide if he seemed more nervous or relieved; then his gaze found hers again, and what he said next was unlike anything she'd expected to hear.

"Five-and-twenty years ago, you were born at Ardiham Castle in Agotia. Your mother's name was Katryna Cristos. She was my younger sister."

A dizzy spell washed over her. *"W-What?"*

While his mouth was twisted in pain, his eyes shone with relief. "Your father, Eric, had left Taundosa by that point. Katryna died in childbirth. I was meant to raise her daughter as my own, as the future heir of Agotia, but I wasn't prepared for it. I worried about the quality of life I'd give you. Fate came into play not two days after you were born. My best friends, Edmund and Cressida Brentwood, arrived in Taundosa to visit me. Your parents had been struggling to conceive at the time. They took one look at you and knew you were meant for them. I, too, knew they were the parents you deserved. They'd give you a beautiful life—much better than what I was capable of offering you. When they left Taundosa after their visit, they returned to Akkinor with a daughter and an heir to the throne."

Her head spun. "Y-You're...my uncle?"

"I am." He smiled so brightly that it breathed life into his grief-stricken face. "It's wonderful to see you again, Aurelia."

There were only a handful of instances in her lifetime in which the Queen of Akkinor failed to summon words. There were so many questions she wanted to ask and so many comments she wanted to make—and yet, every last syllable turned to mush before she could formulate a sentence.

She'd spent the last several weeks wondering where she came from. It kept her awake at night, nibbling away at her from the inside out, threatening to wear her down until nothing remained of her identity except for a haunting little sliver. Now that she finally knew where she'd come from, she could almost feel those missing pieces tethering themselves to her soul, filling her heart with warmth and her gut with bubbling, gurgling amazement.

Arian gestured towards his neck as a distant look washed over his face. "That locket is the only piece of your birth family that left Carthe with you. When the soldier brought it to me today...I knew. Without a second thought, I knew."

"It's been my most valued possession." She blinked in surprise at the sound of her own voice: hoarse, low, and lacking emotion for fear of displaying weakness. "I've protected it with my life. My mother used to say that it came from a place that could be seen glittering from miles away. I assumed it came from Taundosa, but I never imagined that *I* came from Taundosa, too."

"Our family has ruled Agotia for centuries. Katryna was meant to be Lady of Agotia, but our parents' deaths changed that. If everything happened as it should have, you would be heir to Agotia."

The thought made her shiver. On one hand, if her parents never adopted her from Taundosa, she would've been raised to become a noblewoman. On the other, as the adopted daughter of Edmund Brentwood, she was raised to become Queen of Akkinor. Either way, her life had been blessed since before she was born. She couldn't imagine how one person could be so fortunate without realizing it.

"You're Lord of Agotia and Hand of the Queen," she summarized. "I don't recall my parents doing business with Taundosa. How were you acquainted?"

Something flashed in his eyes that made her feel guilty for asking the question. He looked...*distraught*. She knew the reason without having to think about it: if what he told her was true, then her parents were his best friends, and they hadn't mentioned his name even once before.

"Your grandfather, Dyron Cristos, was associated with Edmund the Elder," he explained. She bit the insides of her cheeks, surprised. Nobody in Akkinor had called her grandfather *Edmund the Elder* since she was a little girl.

"The story of how that came to be is long, so I shall save it for another day. My father took me with him when he worked in Akkinor. At first, I was meant to study diplomatic relationships to better myself for lordship. I was just a boy then. So was your father—Ed and I were raised together as brothers. When our fathers realized the value of our bond, they considered solidifying my presence in Akkinor. I was meant to be Ed's Lord Hand while Katryna was meant to be the future Lady of Agotia. When my father died, I returned home to put him to rest. My mother passed three days later—of a broken heart, so it seemed. I made the difficult decision to remain in Agotia with my sisters and become lord. Katryna never wanted to rule Agotia, and as our father's eldest child, I knew it was my duty to take that burden from her. Ed had no choice but to choose Robert Elliot as my replacement. Because of my experience, Her Majesty asked me to be her Lord Hand after the death of her first. Katryna was supposed to become Lady of Agotia once again when my position with the queen was determined. She never made it there."

Aurelia assumed her parents had met Arian on one of their many trips to Carthe when they were trading or organizing business deals in Caedia. She'd never heard of Dyron or Arian Cristos working in the palace with her father and grandfather. As far as she knew, her father's Lord Hand was always meant to be Robert Elliot, Linden's father. Edmund hadn't mentioned a word of a childhood friend who lived in Carthe. It was like all traces of the Cristos men in Akkinor had been erased from existence.

She swallowed the lump in her throat. "You have another sister?"

He smiled, but it was riddled with more pain than joy. "Yes. Anysa. She was an accident, as horrible as it is to utter aloud. My mother became pregnant with her when my father returned to Agotia for a short visit. My father and I barely knew Anysa when she was growing up. She wasn't particularly fond of either of us. After our parents died, she fled Taundosa with the boy she loved and was never seen again. She was thirteen."

"*Thirteen?*"

"She was so much like Katryna, yet so different. They were both adventure-seekers. Your mother was aware of her boundaries, but Anysa didn't understand the world as well." He shook his head and exhaled. "I searched the continent for her for many years. When Katryna died, I wanted Anysa to know. I thought it'd be enough to bring her home. I still haven't found her."

He held out his hand with his palm facing the ceiling. A gasp escaped Aurelia's throat when a ball of light appeared hovering over his palm: pure, iridescent white with a deep blue center that seemed to pulsate.

The stories were true—Arian Cristos was a mage.

Aurelia could barely summon her voice. "What-What *is* that?"

"Anysa. Her soul. Mages of the same bloodline can channel each other's souls. Each morning when the sun rises, I search the magical realm for my sister. Her heart hasn't stopped beating. Wherever she is in this world, she's alive. That's enough for me." When the sphere disappeared, another took its place. This one had a lighter blue center, but it wasn't pulsating like the first. The white light surrounding the blue core was dull and muted rather than bright and glowing. "Do you know who this belongs to?"

She didn't waste a breath. "My mother."

"Yes." His face crumpled for a fraction of a second, but it was smooth again when she blinked. As he stared at the ball of light, Aurelia knew he must have done it more often than he cared to admit. "Her heart no longer beats, but so long as there's light, there's a soul. *That* is how I know she made it safely to the afterlife. Her soul still exists in the universe—even if it's not here with us."

The light disappeared, and Arian closed and opened his hand again. Aurelia could feel the heat from the light when another enormous ball of magic appeared above his hand. It was white, like the two before it, but the core was different. The blue shade was brighter than the other colors while streams of purple, gold, and red flowed through the core, too.

"This is yours," he said, answering her internal question. "Have you heard the saying that blood is thicker than water?"

"Yes."

"Any decent mage will tell you that this is untrue. A gaze into one's soul is all the proof one shall require. See the blue? That's your blood tie to the Cristos family. That's Katryna. The dull red color is in honor of your birth father—the second half of your biological whole. The purple and gold are the colors of royalty. The colors of the Brentwood family. In your soul, at the very core of your existence, you aren't simply the daughter of Katryna Cristos and Eric Haze. You're the daughter of Katryna, Eric, Edmund, and Cressida. The gods knew it before you did."

Her breath caught in her throat. While she watched the colors swirl, she could practically hear her parents' voices echoing in her head. Before learning the truth, she worried about losing the relationship she had with her parents. She wondered if she was less of their daughter than she'd been led to believe. After seeing them within her own soul, she knew nothing could change the bond that tied them together—not even her true heritage.

Arian was right. She'd been meant for Edmund and Cressida Brentwood since before she was born.

***

Aurelia had risked her life to find Arian Cristos for two reasons: to learn the truth of her birth, and to seek assistance in returning to Akkinor. Now that she'd gotten her answers, it was time to tell him exactly what'd happened to bring her to his doorstep.

A part of her felt terrible for being the person to tell him about Archie's betrayal. While she didn't wish for Arian to choose sides between the Brentwood children, she had no choice but to tell him everything. Both knew that Edmund and Cressida hadn't raised their son to be so heartless and greedy—maybe if they had, the truth would've been easier to swallow.

"Unbelievable." Arian shook his head when Aurelia finished telling her story. "The things he's done are unspeakable. I pray he doesn't know the truth of your heritage."

She winced. "I should think not. If he does, there would've been no need for the attempt on my life. My people would've turned against me as soon as he spread the word. It would've saved him quite a bit of money and resources. He doesn't know a thing."

He never would. Aurelia knew her secret was one that could never be shared with the world. Her country had no laws against adopted children inheriting their parents' title, wealth, assets, and legacies—mainly because it was unheard of for a highborn to raise a child who wasn't their own. It was a regular practice among the lowborn, but until it became commonplace for Akkinor's leaders, it wasn't important enough to warrant regulation. No law stated that the adopted child of a king or queen was forbidden from taking the throne. It wasn't a matter of legality, but of preference. Nobody wanted a Carthinian on the throne of Akkinor, even if she'd lived in the country for her entire life. If the people of Akkinor learned the truth, Aurelia's return would be pointless.

"I always worried the truth would be revealed," Arian said lowly. "Your parents were remarkable when it came to protecting you, though. On their last visit to Taundosa, they left me with a letter to be opened in the event of their deaths. They worried about the people learning the truth after they were gone and using it against you. When news of their deaths reached Taundosa..." His face crumpled for a moment, but he regained his composure in the time it took her to blink. "I wanted to sail to Akkinor immediately, but your father was clear in his letter. He asked me to remain in Carthe in the event that you should need my assistance. I promised them that I'd protect you—even if it meant missing the memorials of my two greatest friends." A short, humorless laugh escaped him. "Even then, they seemed to know that they'd arrive in the heavens together—or, at the very least, that one wouldn't survive long after the other was gone. It's exactly as your mother once said to me: her life began when she married Ed, and her life would end when his did. I don't suppose she realized how right she was."

A mournful, longing feeling coursed through Aurelia's veins. She'd always attributed those words to her father. *Before I met your mother*, he'd said, *it always felt like I was trapped in quicksand—like the entire world was moving around me, and I was stuck in place. That feeling didn't change after we met. The only difference was that I had someone stuck beside me now, someone with whom I could watch the realm move forward without feeling like I was alone in it. The day she returns to the heavens is the day I'm forced to stand alone again—the day my life ends.*

Apparently, the two were more alike than either of them had realized. She smiled sadly. "You must miss them as much as I do."

"Every moment," he said with a solemn sigh. "Did you know that we wrote to each other every day? Of course, the letters were never delivered on time, but we wrote to each other every day anyhow. I still have every letter your parents wrote to me. Sometimes I read the letters when I miss them. Some of your father's papers still smell like him. Sage and—"

"—peppermint," she finished. Her chest tightened; she hadn't thought about that in a long time. "He was always burning sage in his study. I don't recall ever seeing his desk without a tin of peppermint hand salve, either. He had terrible callouses on his palms. They drove him mad."

Arian laughed. "I remember."

Her eyes burned, but she refused to let herself cry. "I wish he were here. He always had the answer to every question, the last piece to every puzzle. He was a firm believer in his children coming to our own conclusions, though. When I asked him for help, he'd stare at me and smile until it dawned on me. That's how he taught us to trust in ourselves."

Aurelia could've asked him the simplest question in the world, and her father wouldn't have responded unless absolutely necessary. He'd watch her, jolly blue eyes twinkling, as the wheels turned in her brain. When she finally figured it out, he'd take her chin in his hand and beam at her. *Never before has there been a person so perfectly suited for a crown*, he'd say. His methods made her confident in her ability to make decisions, and even more confident in her ability to make the *right* decisions.

"Let's try it your father's way, shall we?" Arian suggested. She raised an eyebrow. "You sought me out because you need a means of returning to Akkinor and reclaiming your throne. How can we do that?"

"I-I don't know," she admitted. "I was hoping you would tell me."

"Pfft! What would your father say to that?"

"'A true ruler relies not on the ideas of others, but on the ideas that will benefit others,'" she quoted. When she saw his eyes brighten, she knew they'd been thinking the same thing. "I know noble families in Akkinor are still loyal to me. Most aren't so foolish to believe that Archie's ascent to the throne was honest. Unfortunately, there's no way to contact them without risking interception. I have no way across the sea, no secure means of battling Archie's forces, and no way of discerning how many people will pledge fealty to me."

"You have me. The Army of Agotia will stand behind you. So will half of the Goldmen—the half I insure. We can discuss it with Her Majesty, if need be, but I'm certain she'll agree to some sort of arrangement between the two of you. If that happens, you'll have the entire force of the Goldmen, the Agotian Army, and Taundosa's navy to escort you across the sea. But you're forgetting one very important thing, Aurelia."

She clutched her locket. "What is it?"

He laughed. "You forget who you are. You've changed Akkinor for the better in a brief period of time. Now, Akkinor is being ruled by a king who's still a boy. Boys like to fight. They like to win things. When Archie's no longer concerned with you, he'll grow bored of Akkinor and look elsewhere for a bit of challenging excitement. Akkinor and the kingdoms of Carthe aren't allies, but we're neutral. If Archie threatens that neutrality, there will be chaos across Carthe. No king, queen, lord, or lady wants to battle Akkinor. Most Carthinians already know your character, and soon they'll know his. My people would rather fight for you for a chance at keeping the peace than ignore you and risk war with Akkinor."

"Are you telling me to extend an olive branch to the kingdoms of Carthe?"

"Not quite. I'm suggesting that you extend an olive branch to several *rulers* of Carthe. There are a few nobles who promised to fight for Taundosa if need be. I'd start with them, but if they lend you a sword, you must remember that you may need to lend them a sword in the future."

"Alliances go both ways," she affirmed. "I'm prepared to serve my allies in Carthe if needed, so long as they do the same for me."

He smiled. "Where would you like to start?"

"With your queen. Akkinor and Taundosa recognize each other, yes, but there's no formal alliance between us. There's no formal alliance between *any* two kingdoms on different continents. Even Akkinor's relationship with Quapebet is limited. I should think Queen Reyna would like to better Taundosa's reputation by forming an alliance with Akkinor. If she consents, the lords and ladies you mentioned may do the same."

"I will organize an audience with Her Majesty as soon as possible," he assured her. "She'll be absent from dinner tonight, but there will be time for a meeting later on."

"Wonderful. I have another situation to handle before that, anyway."

He raised an eyebrow. "Mister Sherbourne?"

She nodded.

"I wish you the best of luck." When she stood from the desk, he followed suit. He led her to the door and opened it for her, smiling. "Forward, my queen, ever forward."

XXVIII

After leaving Arian's study, Aurelia was escorted upstairs by a servant who seemed awfully afraid of standing before Akkinor's queen. She tried to make polite conversation, but the poor girl only squeaked in response. Aurelia sighed as they walked in silence. She was already starting to miss the simplicity of being Lily Linden. Nobody had ever been afraid of *her*.

The servant showed Aurelia to her own bedchamber rather than Jack's. As much as she yearned for a bath and a plush bed, she wouldn't let herself rest before talking to him. She still didn't feel right about their earlier conversation. Instead of settling in, she crossed the hall to Jack's room and knocked twice on the door. He opened it a moment later, wearing clean clothing with his damp hair combed back, and appeared somewhat surprised to see her.

She frowned. "Did you expect me to return to Akkinor after an hour of knowing Arian Cristos?"

"No, but I assumed the two of you would be conversing for quite a while." He opened the door wider and stepped aside for her. A soft, slow exhale of relief escaped her lips. At the least, he wasn't so upset that he wished to remain parted from her. "He seems like a kind man, but I must admit, I remain suspicious."

She raised an eyebrow and mimicked him as he sat on the edge of his bed. "Oh? How so?"

"He's an unmarried nobleman of middle age with no heirs. Are you absolutely certain you haven't come all this way to unite Akkinor and Taundosa in marriage?"

"Good gods! *No.*" A deep crimson blush rose up on her cheeks. "May I tell you a secret?"

"Of course."

"I'm the trueborn daughter of Arian's younger sister, Katryna. My parents adopted me as their own after Katryna died in childbirth. They were good friends with Arian, so I've been told."

While intrigued, Jack didn't necessarily appear shocked. "Huh. I suppose that makes a great deal of sense given where we are and why we've come." The corner of his mouth twitched. "But discussing Arian Cristos, while enticing enough, isn't the reason you're here, I presume."

"No, it's not. I thought we'd pick up where we left off earlier—but with less shouting."

His lips quirked into a funny-looking smile, but it was gone when she blinked. "I haven't much more to say on the matter. We've said all we needed to. I'm not angry with you. I'm just...processing."

She exhaled. "I really am sorry, Jack."

"Lily—" He stopped short when he used the wrong name. "That'll never become easier, will it?" She stared down at her hands in her lap, silent. "I told you, lovely. I've forgiven you. I just...I just don't want anything to change between us."

She frowned. "Why would anything change?"

"Because you are my queen, and I am your subject."

"I don't care."

"You should. I'm nothing, and you are everything."

Aurelia gave him a look. "You're not nothing. *You* are everything. Wherever we end up...I adore you, Jack. I'll always adore you."

He cupped her face in his large, warm hand. "On the day we met, I knew you were a woman I'd remember for the rest of my life. I didn't know how long we'd be together. I didn't know what would come of our relationship. I didn't know the first thing about you. Even so, I knew I'd always remember you. I'd be on my deathbed, reminiscing on one-hundred years of life, and I'd remember Lily of Akkinor."

"And now? Will you always remember Aurelia of Akkinor?"

He leaned forwards and touched his forehead to hers. "I'll never forget you. It's like you said—you were still yourself as Lily Linden. You're still the same woman I met in the forest. I never should've doubted you. It was foolish of me to think a title means so much. I'm sorry."

She set her hands on his chest. "All is forgiven."

With that, Jack sealed the gap between them and pressed his lips to hers. A sigh of relief escaped her at the familiar feeling, which seemed to please him. He took her face in his hands, hot fingers brushing her neck as they buried in her hair, and deepened the kiss like it was the last one they'd ever share. Aurelia swung her legs over his lap and straddled him with her arms around his neck. When he let himself fall backwards against the bed, they threaded their hands together on either side of his head while losing themselves in the feeling of their bodies being welded together.

When the grandfather clock chimed an hour later, Jack's once-pristine bedchamber looked like it'd been ravaged by a tempest: clothing was strewn around, either piled on the floor or hanging from decorations; the comforter and pillows were tossed aside, leaving nothing but a sheet on the bed; the candles had burnt out, decorations were knocked from the nightstands, and the bed itself had shifted several inches forward. Aurelia was lying on top of Jack with a sheet covering the lower half of her body, her head resting on his chest as she traced the curves of his biceps with her fingers. His hands worked up and down her bare back, following the path of her spine. Sweaty pieces of hair stuck to her face and Jack's clammy chest. She could hear his heart beating beneath her ear—a slow, rhythmic hum that reminded her of a lullaby.

"Do I have to call you *Your Grace* from now on?" he murmured.

"Yes."

His body rumbled with laughter. "Twenty years from now, I'll still call you *Lily*."

"Twenty years from now?" She lifted her head from his chest to meet his eyes. "Is this your playful little way of telling me that you'll be returning to Akkinor?"

When his face went slack, she realized she'd misinterpreted. "Oh. Well..." He trailed off as his hands on her back fell to his sides. At his sudden change in demeanor, she shifted so she was sitting beside him rather than on top of him. "I don't know. I told you I'd follow you, but...may I be plain with you?"

"Always."

"Until today, I didn't think you'd return to Akkinor," he admitted. "I wasn't so convinced that Mister Cristos would give you what you were looking for. As far as I was concerned, you were a common girl from Akkinor escaping debt. A stranger in Carthe—especially a man like Arian Cristos—would have no reason to assist you. Lily Linden was one of many Akkinorians who came to Carthe in search of something that could never be found. I-I thought you and I would live out our days in Carthe. I thought you'd become just like me. Now that I know who you are and why you *must* return...I left Akkinor for a reason. I swore I'd never return."

She furrowed her eyebrows. "You told me you left Akkinor because there was nothing left for you. You have me now. Isn't that enough?"

"It isn't that simple."

"Pray tell."

"My family..." He sat up against the headboard, frustrated. "I'm not so sure I'd be welcomed home with open arms. Even if I stayed in the Folly with you...Is that what you want? For me to live in the capital with you? We haven't known each other for exceptionally long, Lil—uh, Aurelia. How will it look when the Queen of Akkinor returns to the Folly with a peasant on her arm?"

Her frown deepened. "You're confusing me."

"Our worlds are different," he pressed. "You belong in Akkinor. I don't know where I belong. I'd hate to cause problems for you or get in your way or—"

"You've done nothing but care for me since the day we met," she said sharply. He winced at the tone of her voice: the tone of a queen, and one he'd never heard from her lips before. "I don't want to *remember* you, Jack. I want to be with you." He didn't answer. Instead, he swung his legs out of bed and removed the sheet from his body. Her lips set in a thin line when he began to dress himself again. "This isn't about me, though. There's another reason for your hesitation. What is it?"

He scrubbed a hand down his face. His shirt was still in his grasp, so he set it aside so he could kneel in front of her and take her hands. "What will happen if I go with you? Will the most powerful woman in the country marry a commoner who deserted his homeland for a worthless, nomadic lifestyle? Or will I be one of many suitors who spends his life pining for a woman who can never be his?"

She removed her hands from his and scowled. "I don't care for what others have to say about my personal choices. Not a soul in Akkinor has the authority to tell me who I can and can't marry. If the most powerful monarch in the world isn't free to make her own decisions, is she really the most powerful monarch in the world?"

His response was pure, deafening silence. Scoffing, she climbed out of bed and redressed as he watched her without a word. If they were still trekking through the Violet Forest or the Ngora Valley, her instinctive response would've been to snap at him and throw horrible, misplaced accusations in his direction. *You're not acting like the man I know,* she might've said. *I don't know who you are anymore.*

But she wouldn't say any of that now. She *couldn't*. She was a queen again, not a desperate peasant girl with nothing but a golden locket and a few pieces of silver to her name. Now more than ever, she had a reputation to uphold, and she couldn't allow her temper to get the best of her. Jack didn't deserve her cruelty, either—even if she didn't deserve the heavy stream of tears he'd inflicted upon her as she flew out of his chambers and slammed the door.

What a shame, she thought as she flopped onto the bed, *to ruin such lovely satin sheets with senseless tears.*

It was a combination of recent events that fractured the dam, but her conversation with Jack that flooded it. It was grief for Katryna Cristos, her poor mother, who hadn't been given the chance to live a proper life before the gods took her away. It was sympathy for Edmund and Cressida, her wonderful parents, who hadn't truly anticipated what fate would befall their firstborn child when they adopted her from the western continent. It was sympathy for Arian, too, who'd lost everyone he'd ever loved only to have his memory wiped from every hall, every stone, and every blade of grass on Akkinorian soil. There was even a bit of self-despair to blame: she'd spent her entire life believing she knew exactly who she was, only to learn that she was someone else entirely.

She'd hoped that having Jack at her side would make the grief, the sympathy, and the despair more bearable. Now she was beginning to wonder if she'd been foolish to rely on him for solace. He was supposed to be her light in the darkness, her voice of reason—and now, much to her disappointment, he was becoming yet another source of her anguish.

Jack Sherbourne wasn't necessary for her return to Akkinor. If she left him in Carthe, nothing would change. She'd return to her country, defeat her enemies, and reclaim the throne as Akkinor's rightful queen. If the gods were kind, her life would continue as it had before the uprising. But for the rest of her existence, she'd look back on her time in Carthe and remember Jack. She knew not a day would pass when she didn't think about him: the way he protected her, respected her, adored her, fascinated her.

She didn't want to finish her quest without him. She didn't want to fight on the battlefield without Jack at her side. She didn't want to present herself to her people without the man who'd saved her life in more ways than one. It didn't seem right. A life without him didn't seem right.

She knew she loved him. She might've known for some time by then. She'd never been in love before, but she knew what it was like. Edmund and Cressida had shown her for twenty years. She loved him, and she was fairly certain that he loved her, too. If it were entirely up to Aurelia, she'd marry him as soon as they were safely in Akkinor again.

It wasn't entirely up to her, though. The decision was his to make as much as hers. Unless he changed his mind, she'd spend the rest of her life knowing she'd finally found the love she'd always wanted, only to have it disappear almost as quickly as it'd arrived.

XXIX

Good morning, Your Grace." The maid on the other side of Aurelia's door smiled cordially as she balanced a hefty white garment box in her hands. "This is a gift from Queen Reyna. Shall I bring it inside for you?"

"Oh, please do." Aurelia stepped aside for the maid, who placed the box on the vanity. "Thank you. Please extend my gratitude to Her Majesty."

The maid nodded. "Of course. If you require my services no further, I'd be most inclined to begin my daily duties."

Aurelia thanked her and turned her attention to the gift. While she removed the ribbon and the lid, the maid busied herself by making the bed. Aurelia smiled when she produced a lovely periwinkle gown from the garment box. It was the most glorious piece of clothing she'd seen since arriving in Carthe: the silk fabric appeared metallic against the light, creating an optical illusion of a shade that seemed to shift between blue and violet, and it was breathable enough for the long, billowing sleeves to be practical in the Taundosan heat. Unlike Akkinor, it wasn't commonplace in Taundosa for gowns to be accompanied by corsets or hoopskirts (nor did Taundosan woman wear underdresses or stockings due to the heat), so while it'd be strange to feel the fabric clinging to her like the gown was made of liquid, it'd be a welcomed oddity.

She returned the gown to the garment box and headed to the washroom for a bath, which a previous maid had drawn not long before. As she walked, already untying her dressing robe, she felt the maid's eyes on the back of her head. The feeling brought her immense discomfort, but she reminded herself of the Taundosan natives' utter unfamiliarity with Akkinorians. The maid, like so many others, was simply trying to understand the foreign queen's character.

Curiosity, as Edmund used to say, was often misinterpreted as malice.

Aurelia dropped her dressing robe and carefully stepped into the steaming copper tub. The sight of oils, salts, and blossoms floating in the soapy water made her moan with delight. While every bit of tension in her body faded, she lifted rose petals from the silky water and rolled them between her fingers. Only then did she notice that her palms were crimson and irritated, like they'd been scorched beneath the desert sun. She felt a slight sting when her palms came in contact with the steaming water, but she didn't think much of it—she assumed the bathwater was still a bit too hot and had merely aggravated her sensitive skin.

She slid her rear along the bottom of the tub, sucked in a deep breath, and let the full length of her body slip beneath the surface. She liked the pressure of being encased in water; it was like a warm, weighty hug across her entire being. For a few seconds, she could feel the comfort of an embrace while being completely and utterly alone.

As the last breath of air in her lungs bubbled to the surface, she lifted herself out of the water, but she wasn't given the chance to inhale before an aggressive force shoved her head underwater again. Her heart leapt to her throat as she thrashed and grappled with the force—a hand—while water laden with rosehip oil and rosemary sprigs crept into her airway like ruthless little termites.

The fingers covering her face loosened their grip enough for Aurelia to free herself. She gasped for air, unhinged her jaw, and clamped her teeth down on the weblike flesh between the assailant's thumb and index finger. The attacker released a shrill, feminine howl as Aurelia spit a mouthful of flesh and blood into her bathwater. Though her vision was blurry from lack of oxygen, she spotted the assailant—the maid—stumbling backwards against the wall and clutching her bloody hand to her chest.

The shock of what Aurelia had done paralyzed the maid long enough for Aurelia to pull herself out of the tub. She slipped as soon as her damp, slimy feet came in contact with the tiled floor. She was hunched over, naked and dripping, and trying to run for her bedroom as her feet refused to find traction on the tiles. She was a step away from the carpeted floor, gripping the doorframe of the washroom for support, when she heard the maid growl from behind. She didn't make it another two steps before the maid grabbed her by a chunk of sopping hair and yanked her to the ground.

When she hit the floor, every breath in her lungs was seized as if clenched within a fist, and the sole utterance from her lips was a horrible, humiliating gurgle. The maid hovered over her and wiped dripping blood from three parallel scratches on her cheek—scratches Aurelia had inflicted while the maid was holding her head underwater. Aurelia barely registered the missing chunk of flesh on the maid's hand as the latter, now wielding a dagger she'd taken from the garter beneath her skirt, straddled the queen and pressed the sharp blade against her throat. The only thing Aurelia could do as she struggled to breathe was grunt and peer directly into the maid's emotionless walnut eyes.

"Don't you know?" the maid seethed. "No place is safe from the King of Akkinor, *Your Grace.*"

Aurelia's eyes fell shut as her gut twisted into knots. She hadn't thought about the possibility of Archie's assassins following her into Taundosa, never mind into the palace. It was dangerous and risky to send assassins into another monarch's home, but then again, Archie never cared much for consequences.

"You serve a usurper." Aurelia managed to find her voice, but it sounded more like wheezing than speech. "If you release me, I will spare your life. I can't say the same for my brother if you return to him without my head."

"From where I stand, it should be *you* begging for your life."

When the blade pressed deeper into Aurelia's skin, drawing blood, the queen lifted her knee and jabbed the maid in the stomach. While the woman howled, she retracted the knife enough for Aurelia to spring up from the floor. She barely had time to reach for her sword on the vanity before the maid charged her again. It was much too difficult to combat a knife-wielding assassin with a sword rather than a weapon of equal size. Before she knew it, Aurelia was dropping her weapon and using her hands to stop the maid's wrists before the knife could come in contact with her face.

Their gazes met as they struggled. The maid sneered at her with eyes as hard as stone. For a second, time seemed to still, and Aurelia recognized the maid's distinctive features—the almond shape of her eyes, her broad nose, and her high cheekbones—as Kanish. She would've been beautiful, Aurelia thought, without the bloody scratches marring her face.

Aurelia kicked her in the leg, causing the maid to stumble backwards, and reached for her sword again. The two women of equal strength, agility, and experience sparred back and forth until the maid shoved Aurelia into the vanity and forced her to drop the sword. Aurelia used one hand to keep the knife as far from her throat as possible while the other reached for something beside her. The maid inched closer and closer until her nose was practically touching Aurelia's forehead. Aurelia could smell the metallic remnants of her own blood on the blade as it wavered in front of her.

"The great Queen Aurelia, finally bested," the maid declared, "and by my own hand! My name will be known across all corners of the world."

"Nobody will know your name," Aurelia hissed. "They will only know mine."

Something flashed across the woman's eyes—a glimmer of victory, thinking she'd won. Then her eyes widened, and a deep, guttural sound emerged from her throat. Her knife clattered to the floor as she staggered backwards. She peered down at her body and slowly removed an arrow from her side. She stared at it, blood dripping onto the carpet, before falling backwards and collapsing to the floor in a heap. She gasped, trembled, and shuddered for a few seconds before she froze completely, her eyes still open and wide with the awareness of her impending demise.

Aurelia blew a strand of hair from her face and glanced at the side of the vanity, where her bow and sheath of arrows were resting. Once again, she owed her life to Linden. When she spotted them during the struggle, she'd thought to use the arrow as her final effort after remembering one of her many sparring lessons with Linden. When she'd had the upper hand, he'd reached for a sizable rock and brought it close to her head. If it'd been a real fight, he would've defeated her by crushing her skull. *In my experience, it matters not the strength of either foe,* he'd told her. *A quick thinker will always emerge victorious. Anything can be used to defend oneself, so long as one is as observant as one is determined.*

A knock at the door tore her from her thoughts. Before answering it, she wrapped her naked body in the nearest garment she could find—her old cloak—and fetched a cloth from the vanity to hold against the wound on her neck. When she opened the door, she saw another maid holding a garment box nearly identical to the first.

"Good morning, Your Grace," the maid said cheerfully. "This is a gift from Her Majesty. A token of her hospitality." Her eyes widened when she saw the bloody cloth. "You're bleeding, Your Grace. Shall I summon a medic?"

"Please." She looked over her shoulder at the body. The maid gasped in alarm when she saw the corpse. "And Lord Cristos, if you wouldn't mind. I'm afraid Taundosa isn't as safe as we thought."

***

"That was quite clever of you," Arian told Aurelia as soldiers removed the maid's body from her chambers. He was marveling at the bloody arrow. "What made you think to do that?"

Aurelia sighed. "An old friend."

He eyed her curiously but didn't press for details. "Fortunately for you, I pride myself as a mage more than I do as a man." He slowly waved his hand over her throat, and a warm, tingly feeling spread over her skin. A strange taste filled her mouth: a combination of burnt nutmeg and citrus fruit. The taste of magic, according to historical texts she'd read during her lessons. When he dropped his hand, both the blood and the cut were gone. "There we are. Good as new."

"Thank you." She admired the reflection of her unscathed neck in a handheld mirror, then turned to face him fully as he sat beside her on the edge of her bed. "The Cristos family is descended from a long line of mages, yes? I've heard rumors that we're descended from an Elemental."

He chuckled. "An old wives' tale. Our earliest descendent was gifted with their power by an Elemental, yes, but not born from their flesh and blood. You're correct, though. The Cristos family has been blessed with magic since the first of us walked the earth."

"Does that include me?"

"It did," he said, making her frown. "If a mage hasn't been trained by their coming of age, their powers disappear and return to the universe. Think of it like recycling magic—because your powers weren't touched, the realm gifted them to another." He smiled encouragingly when he saw the disappointment in her eyes. "Mages aren't common in Akkinor, but they're unheard of within highborn bloodlines. Your parents and I thought it safest for you to remain oblivious about your nature, even if it meant sacrificing your magic. Nobody could know."

She sighed. "I understand."

His smile became pitiful. "In this particular situation, though, I do wish you had the advantage of magic. Look here." He rose from the bed and pointed to the garment box on the vanity—the garment box delivered as a ruse by the assassin. As he pointed, the periwinkle gown lifted from the box at his command. "Mages have heightened senses. I smelled something odd the moment I entered your bedchamber. Peridot."

Peridot. Not the green gemstone, but rather the poisonous powder of the same name. Native only to Laynoa, it was the byproduct of mining Akkinorian bronze. When bronze ore was collected, an olive-tinted powder was left behind that could only be acquired if one scraped it from the cavern walls. It was a difficult task, as the dampness of the mines transformed the powder into useless sludge if it wasn't harvested quickly enough, but the benefits of peridot were worth the struggle: when mixed with willow bark and clove oil, it became a lethal poison that could kill an individual within minutes. In the old days, people would store the powder in rings to discreetly taint a target's food or drink.

"The mortal nose can't detect peridot," Arian continued. "It's a strange smell—like a combination of soil and spice, I suppose. This assassin was certainly clever. It seems like her original plan was to poison the gown. The silk has been dusted with peridot. If you'd worn the gown, it would've been just a few moments before the poison took effect."

When Aurelia glanced at her hands in her lap, she remembered the way her palms had looked prior to the attack: red, irritated, and slightly bubbled as if burnt by the sun.

"I touched it," she whispered. "The gown. I took it from the box."

Arian reached for her hands and inspected them. They were still a bit red, but no longer irritated or raw. "The bathwater likely rinsed the poison before it could reach your bloodstream. It takes time for poison to work when absorbed through one's skin. You'd probably be dead if you ingested the peridot somehow—or if it'd touched an open wound, for that matter."

It would've been more effective for the maid to taint Aurelia's drink, but she'd chosen a more entertaining route: rather than watching Aurelia die within minutes of ingesting the poison, she'd opted to watch Aurelia meet an excruciating death while the poison slowly seeped into her bloodstream through contact with her flesh. Oren Lowstone and Alda Port had chosen to elongate their attempt on Aurelia's life, too—all because it was more enjoyable to watch her squirm and suffer than it was to offer her a clean, painless death.

Aurelia retracted her hands and balled them into fists. "She was certainly motivated, wasn't she?"

"I'd say so." He grimaced as he eyed the crimson stain on the rug to his left. "If you weren't such a fighter, you may have died today. That's the advantage you have over your brother and his assassins. They view you as a damsel rather than as a leader or warrior."

She cracked a weak, wry smile. "What a world it would be if all women were given the recognition we deserve."

"You'll receive that recognition soon enough. I'm certain of it."

He patted her knee affectionately, then stood from the bed and crouched beside the bloodstained rug. The lines on his forehead deepened in concentration as he held his hand out with his palm facing it. She watched him intently as his eyes fluttered shut and his breathing shallowed. A gasp escaped her lips when a sudden breeze—lacking a source—slithered across the bedchamber. She shivered and wrapped her dressing robe tighter around her body when the cool air made her sopping locks feel like icicles against her back. The invisible breeze seemed to caress Arian as every drop of blood disappeared from the rug within seconds.

"My word," Aurelia breathed. "How did you do that?"

Straightening up and smiling at his handiwork, he replied, "Restoring something to its original state is an area of magic taught to most young mages during our training years. A tree bearing dead leaves, for example, can be reborn with a mage's assistance. A shattered mirror can be repaired as if it were never broken at all."

"How fascinating! Mages have elemental specialties, too, don't you?"

"Indeed. I was born with an aptitude for water magic—a useless proficiency given my place of birth," he joked. She chuckled; there certainly weren't many opportunities in the desert of Taundosa for a water mage to flaunt their power. "That's why I trained so diligently in other fields—I had to seek power elsewhere. Most mages nowadays don't bother expanding their magical capacity if they excel at their elemental specialty. What they were born with is good enough."

The corners of her lips sagged downwards as a thought popped into her head. "You spent your prime years in Akkinor. How were you able to train so proficiently when you were forced to conceal your power?"

His smile was nothing short of melancholy. "There are some things your father never had the chance to tell you, my dear, in life or in writing."

"How do you mean?"

"The monastery," he replied, blinking at her. He was eyeing her as if awaiting an *ah-ha!* moment that would never come. Her lack of a reaction was confirmation that whatever Arian knew, Edmund hadn't managed to communicate to Aurelia before his death. "It's a safe haven for mages. Many of your priests are mages, in fact. A mage may seek refuge at the monastery—either to live amongst their kin or to educate themselves in magical fields—and the High Priests are sworn to keep their nature secret. The number of mages at the monastery has dwindled over the decades, though. Civilians simply can't afford residence."

Aurelia stared at him, bewildered, and searched his gaze for any sign that he was mistaken. She knew better than to believe that, though. A man like Arian Cristos didn't make mistakes. That left one plausible explanation: dozens (if not hundreds) of her subjects knew that magic existed in Akkinor, and better yet, they knew exactly where to find it. But the queen—the one person in Akkinor expected to know everything that occurred on her soil—hadn't known a thing about it.

"That can't be right," she insisted. "If that were true, I would've known. Someone would've told me. Linden, my advisors..."

"They don't know. They shouldn't, anyway. Mages with connections to the monastery will spread word to their kin, but there are no mages among the Akkinorian highborn. Only the monarch and the priests are aware of the arrangement. The Assembly hasn't a clue."

Now she was scowling. "That's preposterous. My father would've told me."

"I believe you're right, but I'm afraid he never got the chance."

Guilt simmered in her chest, but it was gone as quickly as it'd come. She knew there were things her parents never had the chance to tell her, just as Arian said, but understanding didn't lessen her frustration. Her father, like so many others across the realm, assumed he'd have another few decades of life to live. He hadn't gotten the chance to tell her in person, but he hadn't thought to leave it for her in writing, either. This, she thought, was one of many things Edmund might've mentioned in his final letter—the letter that'd guided her to Arian Cristos.

"Anyway," Arian resumed, sensing her swelling aggravation, "I spent quite a bit of time at the monastery while I was in Akkinor. A High Priestess by the name of Orlanna taught me to excel in most magical fields. Your father studied there, too. His lessons didn't involve anything relating to magic, of course, other than its history. He studied everything all Akkinorian rulers are expected to know—yourself included. First and foremost, the monastery is an educational institution for highborn. It just so happens to be a place of refuge and training for mages, too."

Aurelia bit the insides of her cheeks, silent. She couldn't help but wonder if Arian would've been permitted to study magic at the monastery if Edmund hadn't been educated there, too. After all, Arian was expected to accompany Edmund everywhere back then. One couldn't exist without the other. If Edmund hadn't been educated at the monastery, Arian likely never would've had the opportunity to become as proficient a mage as he was.

Desperate to change the subject, she cleared her throat. "And my mother? What was her specialty?"

Arian's bright eyes seemed to dance with a light that hadn't been there before—a glowing, flickering light in shades of amber and carmine. "Fire."

A grin blossomed on Aurelia's face, so wide that her cheeks ached and trembled as she withheld a tremendous burst of laughter.

She should've known.

***

Not long after their conversation, Arian left Aurelia to herself (and under the watchful eye of the trusty soldier he tasked with ensuring her safety) to discuss the assassination attempt with Reyna. Aurelia worried that Reyna would ask her to leave the palace immediately. Regardless of the assassin's intended target, her presence in the palace was a threat to

Reyna, her children, and her associates. It would be safer to remove Aurelia from the premises, even if the possibility of another attack was slim to nothing.

Arian hadn't seemed overly concerned. He assured her that he and Reyna only intended to discuss an increase in security measures. It'd been their staff who'd hired the maid anyway—the attack may not have happened if the palace employees had been stricter with who they allowed within the walls.

With the soldier trailing a few feet behind her, Aurelia took a walk throughout the palace to stretch her legs and clear her head. She overheard three footmen whispering to each other about the attack while pretending to dust the golden statues on display in the halls.

"I saw the body," shared the youngest of the trio. "She was Kanish. No doubt about it."

The tallest of them, distracted, buffed his own hand rather than the statue before him. "How did the Scorpion of Akkinor manage to hire a Kanish woman as an assassin?"

Aurelia shivered. In Akkinor—and apparently in Carthe, too—scorpions had been associated with traitors since the old days. It didn't surprise her that such symbolism had been turned into a nickname for her brother, nor that the moniker had been coined so quickly. The rest of the world may not have known about Archie's treason, but Reyna's staff had likely been eavesdropping since the moment Aurelia arrived at the palace. All they needed was to overhear one conversation about the uprising, and gossip would spread throughout the palace like dragon fire.

"It's not so hard." The last and eldest of the footmen, a middle-aged man with one missing ear, shrugged at his companions. "Nothing appeals to this continent more than coin, and he's got plenty of it. All he had to do was order his men to find nine willing killers on our soil—one for each Carthinian territory. They've probably been prowling their assigned territory for weeks now, just waiting to hear word of the queen's arrival in one place or another so they could finally act."

"Since when has murder become such a coveted profession?" the young one asked. "If it's that easy to find and hire assassins from across the sea, then there must be more of them than we thought."

The tall footman grimaced. "The price of death has surpassed the price of life, my friends."

As she left the trio behind, Aurelia couldn't stop the man's words from echoing in her head.

The price of death has surpassed the price of—

"Lil—Aurelia!"

She was shaken from her thoughts by the sound of her name. As she reached the second floor and turned towards her bedchamber (still with the soldier trailing her), she looked over her shoulder and saw Jack rushing towards her, panicked, from the bottom of the staircase. She sighed in relief when she saw his face. She was desperate for a nap now that she'd exerted herself with a promenade, but she wasn't ready to return to the scene of the attack by herself. They hadn't spoken since the evening before, but she was willing to face whatever tension remained if it meant feeling safe in his arms.

When he finally reached her, his momentum made it difficult for him to slow down, so she reached out to steady him as he skidded to a stop. He didn't seem fazed—he simply took her face in his hands and tilted her head at all angles, inspecting the spot on her neck that'd been cut by the assassin. When he realized she was unharmed, he exhaled and took her in his arms. She chuckled, returned his embrace, and waved her hand to dismiss the soldier.

"I was just told of the attack," he muttered, cradling her head. "I've been searching everywhere for you. What happened?"

"It was an assassin disguised as a maid. We had a bit of a battle, but it's all right—she's dead. Arian's currently discussing an improvement in security measures with Reyna."

He pressed his lips together. "I should've been there." She sighed and shook her head as he followed her into her bedchamber. "I should've been with you. I'm so sorry, Aurelia."

"You have nothing to apologize for. There was no way for us to know that assassins infiltrated the palace. The only person to blame is my imbecile of a brother," she replied. That made him laugh. She placed her hands on either side of his face and smiled when his curls tickled her fingers. "I'm sorry for how our conversation ended last night. I overstepped. I shouldn't have pushed you as I did."

He covered her hands with his. "I'm sorry, too. I shouldn't have said those things to you. It-It's a difficult conversation to have, and I'm not quite ready for it. Allow me some time to settle into this new revelation, yeah?"

She leaned up on her toes and brushed her nose against his. "Yeah."

Jack grinned. When he leaned down to kiss her, it wasn't long before he was wrapping his arms around her waist and lifting her feet from the ground. She smiled against his lips as he carried her over to the bed and set her down, running his hands along her sides. She locked her legs around his waist to hold him closer, then switched their positions before he could blink. He looked startled when he realized that she was now straddling him, hands burrowing beneath his loose-fitting white shirt, with the drooping neckline of her dress revealing more of her upper body than intended.

Instead of kissing her again, Jack gazed at her, somewhat astonished, with his hands on her hips. "You're not the most ladylike queen in the world, are you?" They simply stared at one another until Aurelia broke eye contact by laughing. "No, really. It was never even a possibility in my mind that you could be the queen."

"What *did* you think of me?" She perched beside him with her legs crossed as he sat up against the headboard. Seeing as though the moment had been spoiled, she fixed her dress and wiped traces of Jack's saliva from her mouth.

He shrugged. "I thought you were the daughter of Lady Spirre's stewardess. A girl trying to escape debt with the Reilly family and her wretched brother. I thought you were exactly who you told me you were."

Aurelia's heart felt heavy. "I'm so sorry, Jack. It was never my intention to deceive you. Nobody could know until it was absolutely necessary, until we were under Arian's protection. I didn't want you to carry the weight of my secret. Had you known..."

He brushed a curl from her face and smiled. "I meant what I told you before. I don't know much about Queen Aurelia, but I do know *you*. Akkinor is extremely fortunate to have someone like you on the throne. Archie wants it because he believes it to be his birthright, but you want it because you know you can make a difference for our country. I didn't believe in Queen Aurelia when I fled Akkinor...though I certainly believe in her now. I believe in *you*."

Her lower lip trembled. "Does that mean—?"

"I'm returning home with you?" he finished. She could only stare at him. A sheepish smile formed on his lips. "Yes, my love. Yes."

The relief flooding through her veins was akin to what she felt when Jack rescued her in the Violet Forest. She was so close to Akkinor that she could practically taste it, but Jack had been a piece of the puzzle that hadn't fit quite right. Now, she was only a few moves away from returning home. As long as Jack was by her side, she didn't doubt that the next pieces would fall into place on their own.

XXX

urelia's eyes narrowed to slits as her gaze trailed Ser Normyn Barvel, General of the Goldmen, from across the palace foyer. She'd found him barking orders at soldiers when she arrived in the entryway moments before to meet Arian. The general—the third-most powerful person in Taundosa after Reyna and Arian—had hesitated to make her acquaintance when she introduced herself. She'd hoped to build some sort of relationship with him, and he hadn't seemed even remotely interested in her presence. It was clear that he, like so many Carthinians, had been conditioned to despise any and all Akkinorians.

Ser Barvel was an older, taller, and less welcoming version of Arian. The combination of his distinctive features—medium brown skin the color of walnut, round russet eyes, and shoulder-length, gray hair that had once been black—made Aurelia certain that he was Taundosan. He was taller than Arian by several inches but significantly shorter than Jack (as was everyone), and for a man in his early sixties, he was surprisingly buff. His right eyelid was swollen and droopy, a sign of a previous infection, and the flesh along his left forearm was somewhat glossy and wrinkled, having never properly healed after what appeared to be a nasty burn. He wasn't the most pleasing man in the realm to look at, but his appearance resembled his temperament so vividly that it was almost frightening.

She spotted Arian crossing the foyer from the direction of his study. He nodded his head in greeting to the general, who reciprocated in kind, before halting beside Aurelia with his hands clasped behind his back.

"Forgive my tardiness, my dear," he said. She waved her hand dismissively but didn't tear her eyes from the general's icy demeanor. Arian followed her gaze and sighed. "You needn't worry about him. He may not be the personable sort, but his heart is true."

The queen exhaled. "When I first arrived, everyone observed me like a mythical creature brought to life. Nobody knew what to make of me. Now, your staff can barely look at me without scowling or whispering to one another. I've made them afraid. I'd rather not prolong my stay when I seem to have such a negative effect on your people."

"They're not afraid of *you*." He patted her hand as they crossed the corridor. "They're afraid of what your presence in Taundosa may bring."

She furrowed her eyebrows. "What's that, exactly?"

"The world is changing, Aurelia. Things have been the same for centuries. Generation after generation has experienced the same lifestyle, the same culture, the same comforts. Now, the Queen of Akkinor is here to form an alliance with the Queen of Taundosa. When's the last time an alliance was formed in the world?"

"When Oleander the Great still walked the earth."

"In other words," Arian mused, "it's been many centuries. You're the first foreign monarch to personally request an alliance in Carthe. The first eastern monarch to request an alliance in the west. Things are changing, and the people are finally starting to realize it. They're not afraid of you, nor do they wish to do you harm. You must simply give them the opportunity to adjust."

She wanted to believe her uncle, but the whispers, stares, and frowns were eating away at her. Four days had passed since her arrival in Taundosa and three since the attack by Archie's assassin. The palace staff had become increasingly cold towards her, and she was beginning to wonder if the deal she'd made with Reyna would have to be broken for the good of all. If Reyna's employees were too frightened by Aurelia's presence, the Queen of Taundosa would have no choice but to send Aurelia home as soon as possible—*before* either of them had the chance to pledge fealty to one another.

Upon reaching the rear of the palace, Arian brought them to a halt in front of two tall, sparkling frosted-glass doors. The soldiers standing guard tipped their heads to Arian before opening the doors. Aurelia smiled when she saw what lay beyond: the gardens. She'd been searching for an excuse to explore them from the moment she caught a glimpse of them through Jack's bedchamber window.

"Welcome to the gardens," Arian proclaimed as they strolled along the stone pathway. "This is my favorite place in Taundosa. It was Cressida's favorite spot, too. She could hardly bring herself to leave when she visited. She loved nature, your mother."

"I remember." She reached her hand out and brushed her fingers along the hedges lining the pathway. Tall palm trees were planted between the hedges and the enormous gates that surrounded the gardens, and the branches hung overhead like a roof of vines and leaves. As a balmy breeze lifted her curls from her shoulders, shivers caressed her spine. "Was Katryna fond of nature?"

"Quite. Our mother used to chide her because she liked to swing from trees like a monkey."

Aurelia erupted in a grin. "Now I know where I inherited that from."

Delight flashed across his eyes. "You're more like her than you know. You have her spirit, her cleverness, her eyes. So much of Katryna lives on through you, but sometimes, you remind me of your father, too. You're responsible like him. Level-headed, logical, practical. The voice of reason. Sometimes when you speak, you sound exactly like him."

She wasn't sure how to feel about that. If what her uncle told her was true, then her birth father abandoned a pregnant Katryna and disappeared before Aurelia was born. He might've loved Katryna, but he hadn't given himself the chance to love Aurelia. She didn't know if it was a good thing that she sounded or acted like him. In fact, she didn't know much about him at all.

"Did you know him well?" she asked. When Arian grimaced, she hurriedly continued, "I only ask because—"

"Because he's your father, and you want to know what he was like," he finished. She released a soft exhale in response. "It's all right. In fact, I knew him well. Your mother was about Archie's age when they met. Eric had been hired as a replacement for her personal guard. We became good friends in the time he spent with us in Agotia." He chuckled a bit as he recalled a memory. "Oh, Katryna was infuriated when he first arrived! She wanted nothing to do with him."

"Why?"

"He was Darryn's replacement." He said it simply, as if he expected her to know who he was talking about. He seemed to realize his mistake when he added, "Darryn Atwood had been Katryna's protector and trainer since she was an infant. He was the father to her that ours couldn't be while we were in Akkinor, but they were the best of friends, too. Her Majesty asked him to lead a troop tasked with disarming a threat in the north, and he was one of hundreds who perished out there. Katryna never fully recovered from his loss. They'd adored one another in a way I'll never understand. Her life was never the same without him—it was like the light faded from her eyes."

A fleeting, instinctive smile formed on her lips before she could stop it. The way Arian described Katryna's relationship with Darryn reminded her of the way Aurelia often described her own relationship with Linden.

"What changed? With my parents?"

Arian sighed. "They fell in love."

She paused, debating whether or not to press for more details, until a realization struck her: "Where was he from? I don't suppose I inherited my hair and my fair complexion from a southern Carthinian."

A cross between a chuckle and a snort escaped him. "No, no. He was Akkinorian, in fact."

"What?"

He grimaced. It was clear that he hadn't wanted to disclose that to her—after all, it meant her birth father could've been one of her subjects, and she'd had absolutely no idea.

"He hailed from northern Holos. Just on the Laynoan border, I believe," he continued. "He didn't speak about Akkinor very often. In fact, he claimed to be the son of outlaws from Castoffs Cove—the pirate island south of Glacier Bay. He told me he moved to Taundosa to start anew. I didn't know the truth of his heritage until my sister told me after he was gone. For whatever reason, he hadn't wished for anyone to know where he came from. The only person he trusted with that knowledge was Katryna."

"Do you suppose he returned to Akkinor when he left?"

"I should think so. Emely—my stewardess in Agotia—believes he left a family behind in Holos and returned to them after Katryna fell pregnant." He shook his head and scoffed. "He left his honor behind when he fled Akkinor. Apparently, his love for my sister wasn't enough to restore it. Katryna was never cross with him for leaving her, though. That's why I think Emely's theories are accurate. Katryna would've sent him home if she knew he'd left a family behind. I know she would've."

Aurelia forced a smile. "She made a great sacrifice for him, then."

"Indeed." He turned to her and lifted a curl from her shoulder. "Eric traveled with a small portrait of his late sister. She was three when she died of typhus. Her hair was the *exact* color of yours. Kitty and I used to tease him relentlessly about his complexion, too—he'd be redder than a cardinal after only a few moments outdoors. He was always a sore sport about it."

"What was he like?"

Arian scratched and pulled at his bushy beard. "He was...different. He had a kind and loyal heart, but he was easily enraged. There was an awful lot of anger hidden within him. I suppose that's why he and Katryna connected so well. She was infamous for her cheek, my sister, but never her temper. She had a way of showing everyone how to find their serenity and peace of mind. He became a better man in the time he spent with her."

She smiled. "I seem to have inherited that from him, too."

272

That made him laugh. "Oh, yes. Your father wrote to me often about that temper of yours." She blushed. "It's not the terrible quality you think it to be, though. Nothing is."

"How do you mean?"

"Katryna used to say that it's better for one to be angry than to be numb. She was a firm believer in the power of one's emotions to change the world. Do you suppose Oleander the Great would've succeeded if he were numb to Alora's actions rather than angered by them?"

"No. His fury at the things she inflicted on the Akkinorian people is what instigated the rebellion."

"Exactly. A person who understands their emotions—and who allows those emotions, however positive or negative, to be seen by those who trust them—is a person whose victory is almost always guaranteed." Arian smiled and gestured to a marble bench beneath a tall tree with pink blossoms. "Shall we sit?"

As they did so, Aurelia squinted through the bright sunlight, watching birds fly from their hiding spots in the trees. Everything around her was so vibrant that her eyes began to ache. The gardens of Taundosa, so full of life and majesty, made the gardens of Akkinor look like peasantry. Aurelia wasn't surprised that her mother had fallen in love with the gardens of Taundosa. If Aurelia knew her mother, she knew Cressida would've slept there if she could. Aurelia didn't have a drop of Cressida's blood in her veins, but somehow, she'd managed to adopt that much from her mother.

"Uncle?" When the wind blew a lock of hair into her eyes, she tucked it behind her ear and exhaled. "I'm facing a predicament only you can solve for me."

"What is it?"

A sharp pang pierced her heart. "It's silly, really. I-I can't seem to remember what Mother and Father's voices sound like. I haven't for quite some time. Is that terrible of me?"

"Not at all. Time can have that effect, especially for someone so young as yourself." He set his hands on his knees and gazed out at the gardens as a humble smile formed on his lips. "Your mother had the voice of a goddess. Your father used to say that the birds sang when she spoke. She could begin a sentence with the gentleness of a mother and end it with the authority of a monarch."

Aurelia closed her eyes, imagining her mother's beautiful face in her head, and struggled to keep tears from leaking down her cheeks.

"And your father." Arian laughed a bit. "My friend. He was gruff, wasn't he? Even as a boy. He had an authoritarian voice, though he always sounded like he was holding back a chuckle. I never knew if he was prepared to scold someone or laugh at them. Even when he was being serious, I thought he'd erupt in a fit of laughter."

With her eyes still closed, Aurelia pictured her parents in front of her. They were sitting on a rose-colored futon in one of the palace's many sitting rooms, silently and adoringly listening to Aurelia as she played a song on the pianoforte. Cressida clasped her hands to her mouth in awe as tears sparkled in her eyes. Edmund closed his eyes and listened to the tune, beaming with pride, while quietly humming along and tapping his fingers against his thighs.

The memory wasn't complete without Archie, who stood leaning against a pillar in the corner of the room with his arms folded over his chest. His outgrown blonde hair fell over his forehead, his bright blue eyes were narrowed, and the scowl etched on his face was so hateful and twisted that it was almost unnatural.

In her vision, her brother was a child. Maybe she'd been wrong about when his resentment first began. Maybe he'd been waiting to rid her from the world since they were too young to fathom what that meant.

"What do you think they would do?" When she opened her eyes, she saw Arian staring at her, confused. "My parents. What would they do if they were alive to see what I've endured?"

Arian grimaced. "If someone threatened their daughter, they'd go to the ends of the earth and back again to keep you safe."

"Even if my assailant was their trueborn son?"

"You're as much their child as Archie." If not for the compassion in his eyes and the ghost of a smile on his lips, she might've mistaken his firmness for a scolding. "Don't forget that, Aurelia. You saw your own soul reflected back at you. How can you ever doubt that you aren't their trueborn child?"

Aurelia's cheeks warmed with embarrassment. She knew that blood changed nothing about her relationship with her parents and her role in Akkinor, but she still wasn't entirely comfortable with the truth. If Edmund and Cressida were alive to see what Archie had done to her...he was their son by blood. If her parents ever found themselves torn between children, would they choose the firstborn daughter they took in, or the trueborn son they created?

Edmund and Cressida Brentwood weren't the type of people to choose between their children, but then again, the emergency escape plan they crafted for her didn't include Archie. They never intended for brother and sister to escape Akkinor together. Was it possible they'd known what Archie was? If not, Aurelia didn't want to think about why her parents would save one child and not the other. Letting her mind wander there would make her question everything she thought she knew about them.

"Oh!" Aurelia gasped in alarm, shaken from her thoughts, when something cool and slimy wrapped around her ankle. She released a yelp of fear at the sight of a long, lavender-scaled snake at her feet. "Mother of—"

Arian made a *tsk* noise with his tongue when she tried shaking it off. "Fear not, my dear!" He bent down and collected the snake, which immediately wrapped itself around his arm. "This is a Bozari python. He's quite harmless, I assure you. Haven't you heard of them?" She shook her head, still uneasy, as the snake's forked tongue lapped at the air. "It's a magical species. They managed to survive the persecution because mortals were unaware of their existence. Many still are."

She swallowed. "It doesn't look magical to me."

"Pfft!" His face was illuminated with a childlike excitement. "When the female Bozari python lays her eggs, only one will hatch as a newborn. The others—normally between three and five—contain a stone called *elvemar*. When an elvemar stone is placed in the mouth of any living creature that's been mortally wounded, that creature is instantly healed."

"My word," she breathed. The python, now disinterested in the pair, slithered down Arian's leg and disappeared into the bushes. "I've never heard of this. Why has such power remained secret?"

"If mortals knew about it, elvemar might be used to revive the most wicked of people. Nowadays, the Bozari python can only be found on the southern half of Carthe. Many rulers have considered sharing the python with the rest of the world, but that shall never come to pass. After all, our little friend gives us something nobody else has—appreciation. Would you appreciate him as much if his kind were everywhere, like rabbits?"

"Rabbits aren't magical."

"Aren't they?"

When she looked up at him, she expected to see him grinning with a teasing look in his eyes. Instead, his face was slack, and his eyes were inquisitive rather than playful. He was completely genuine. Aurelia didn't know how to respond to someone with such an imagination; she only wished she could see the world as he did.

"The magic of the world is protected for a reason." His eyes sparkled as his gaze turned to her locket. "You know that as well as I do."

A shiver traced her spine as she smiled and nodded. She *did* know. And for a moment, she could've sworn she felt her locket trembling against her chest as if it, too, was responding to her uncle.

XXXI

"We have one final stop on our journey today," Arian stated. "Though your powers have disappeared into the universe, I'd like for you to see what our people are capable of. I'm truly sorry that you were unable to utilize your power. It was a necessary sacrifice, I'm afraid, and one I urged your parents to make. Had anyone learned that you were a mage, the truth of your parentage would've been revealed rather quickly."

Aurelia understood that much, though she couldn't help but grieve for the gift she'd lost. She'd spent most of her young life reading or hearing stories about mages and their great adventures, and she might've had a place among them if the world had been a kinder place.

The magical persecution, to her understanding, had been rather ironic. Mortals hunted and slaughtered both mages and magical creatures because of one thing: fear. Fear of what they couldn't control, and fear of being destroyed rather than being the destroyers. Mages had every opportunity to massacre mortals and become an untouchable force in the realm, but they refused. They didn't want magic to become a thing to be feared, but a gift for all to enjoy. The one-sided war saw the instigators and eventual victors doing exactly what they feared would be done to them—*without* the use of magic.

Arian escorted her through numerous long, winding hallways until they reached a door leading to the courtyard: a massive, rectangular-shaped bit of outdoor space in the heart of the palace. Unlike the gardens, the courtyard wasn't a place of serenity and relaxation, but something of a training field for Taundosan mages.

There were about two dozen individuals in the courtyard, and every last one of them was different from the others. The mages, both men and women, varied in age, size, strength, and speed. There were people old enough to be Aurelia's grandparents training alongside people young enough to be her children. The one thing that bound them together, it seemed, was magic.

"Had you been raised in Taundosa," Arian mused as they watched from the sidelines, "you'd have a place among them. The people you see here are members of my coven. We train together, and during times of war, we answer the call to arms together. There are other covens across Carthe, but none so close as ours."

"Why is that?"

"We spend all of our time here—training, learning, growing. It's the safest place for us to be what we were born to be. If the existence of covens was common knowledge around the world, those who disapprove of magic would hunt us down and destroy us. We're untouchable within the palace walls, though. Here, it doesn't matter who you are or where you come from. Mage or mortal, Taundosan or Akkinorian...Here, we are a family. We protect one another, and we guide each other to greatness."

She wondered (hoped, really) if there were any such covens living in secret in Akkinor. Most mages were too fearful to reveal their power because of Akkinor's participation in the persecution. Even so, she wondered if there were enough of them in her country to form an organization as grand as this.

Arian, pulled aside by a woman seeking his help, left Aurelia to wander on her own. She took a turn around the courtyard, observing in silence, while bursts of light and beams of magic illuminated the field. She was particularly stunned by one man—about seventy years old—who rose a boulder into the air with nothing but his mind. As he stood facing the rock with his arms outstretched, it cracked into hundreds of miniscule fragments. When he turned his arms so his palms were facing the sky, the rock fragments flew through the air towards a straw, human-shaped dummy across the training field. Some of the fragments merely lodged themselves in the straw, but the others struck the dummy with such force that it fell backwards onto the grass.

Then the old man clenched his hands into fists, and the rock fragments rose into the air once more. Aurelia watched, mouth agape, as the fragments joined together to reform the large rock from the beginning of the demonstration. Slowly and cautiously, the mage lowered the boulder to its original place, then wiped his hands on his trousers and smiled triumphantly.

He caught her staring at him and widened his smile. "I haven't managed that since I was forty years old."

"That was wonderful," she said honestly. "How is it possible?"

He twirled the curved ends of his bushy gray mustache. "Mages have specialties, you see. Most of us have the same general powers, then something else that makes us unique. If something's broken, I can fix it. I found that power when I was a boy—only six, if you can believe it! I broke my leg after a fall from a tree. Mended my own bone right then and there."

"My word! How remarkable." A realization struck her. "Have you been unable to use this power until now?"

"Not entirely." He sighed in defeat. "I did it to myself. Started using it for money. People hired me to fix things—wagons, houses, all of it. I spent so long repairing manmade things that I nearly lost my ability to repair elements of the natural world. Some call it a mage's downfall. Our power comes from nature, and when we lose sight of that, we lose the true depth of our abilities."

She offered him a hopeful smile. "It seems to me like you've regained your power, sir. Rather brilliantly."

His ears reddened with humble pride. "Why, thank you, miss! Only took me thirty years!"

She laughed. The old man excused himself to continue his training, and only then did she realize he'd called her *miss*. She didn't know if it was a slip of the tongue or if he was unaware of her identity, but either way, she liked it. She'd never enjoyed being alienated by her titles. For a brief moment, she felt normal—human, even.

Some of the mages, like the old man, were training on their own. Others were training in pairs. She stopped to observe one pair, a young woman and an adolescent boy, as they tested each other's abilities. The boy was hurling balls of fire at the woman, and the latter was deflecting them using shimmering, iridescent shields that glowed upon contact with the flames.

The boy seemed to realize that his offensive strategy wasn't working. He inhaled sharply and shrugged his shoulders, causing his arms to ignite with flames from his fingertips to his shoulders. Streams of fire shot themselves at the woman, as if his arms were dragons. Her protective shields weren't strong enough nor produced quickly enough to defend herself. Instead, the shields formed one enormous sphere that encapsulated her entire body. The flames disappeared immediately upon contact with the shield.

"You're a rotten cheat, Alryn," the woman snapped. The shield had disappeared by then, and the boy's arms were now back to normal. "We agreed on first pitch."

"It was far too easy," he argued.

"You might've offered me a warning before escalating to third!" Just then, she spotted Aurelia watching them, and her entire body stiffened. "Excuse our quarreling. Alryn here is still learning the rules."

Aurelia waved her hand dismissively. "You've both kept me quite entertained. Answer this for me—what's pitch?"

The two exchanged amused looks. "Strength stages of magic," the woman replied. "First pitch refers to our lowest and weakest form. There are four pitches, with the fourth being the full extent of our power."

Her lips parted, awestruck. "You mean to tell me that what I just witnessed was only third pitch? There's *more?*"

"There's more, but it's an exhausting task to perform fourth." Alryn yawned, suddenly weary, and rolled out his shoulders. "In fact, I'm fatigued as it is. Shall we reconvene tomorrow, Lyra?"

The woman sighed. "All right. Go on and have something to eat." Alryn yawned again before scurrying off into the palace. Lyra smiled at Aurelia as she approached the queen. "He's a good lad, but he hasn't quite gotten used to the way things are done here. He hadn't trained with other mages until last season."

"I see. Tell me—what does fourth pitch look like for each of you?"

"For me, I can extend a protective shield to anyone in my vicinity. For Alryn, he can ignite his entire body with flames. He hasn't mustered the courage to attempt it on his own yet." She tucked a lock of dark hair behind her ear. "Have you come to join the coven?"

Aurelia blinked. "I-uh-not exactly, no."

"Pity. You strike me as a valiant fighter."

"I'm handy with a bow and a sword, but I'm afraid I haven't any magic."

Something flashed in Lyra's brown eyes. "You're her. The queen. I heard you were in Taundosa, but I hadn't expected to find you here, of all places."

"Lord Cristos thought it prudent for me to be properly educated on magic. As you know, we don't have any covens like this one in my country. Akkinorian mages masquerade as mortals. They've been doing so since the persecution."

Lyra frowned. "You're the queen. Don't you have the power to change that?"

Aurelia surged backwards, offended, as she struggled to keep her temper under control. But as she thought about her words, she realized there hadn't been an accusatory note in Lyra's voice. And she was right— *didn't* Aurelia have that kind of power?

Aurelia relaxed and released a long, pitiful exhale. "I'm here partly because my people don't approve of a woman on the throne. Every move

I've ever made has been scrutinized, however noble or beneficial to the masses. Some have enough humility to admit that I've done right by them, but others search for endless reasons to see me stripped of my crown. I fear my decision to urge mages out of hiding would upset the masses and put those mages in danger. People would turn on one another—and on me. Again."

Lyra thought about that for a moment. "If you want my opinion, Your Grace, I think it's worth trying."

"That's easy for you to say. *You* aren't the face of Akkinor."

"No," she agreed, laughing, "and I thank the Almighty kindly for that. I'd much rather be a simple mage than an omnipotent ruler." She curtsied and smiled. "A pleasure, Your Grace."

When Lyra walked off, Arian took her place. "I hope she wasn't too formidable. Our Lyra isn't the most subtle of people."

Aurelia chuckled, but it sounded more forced than she'd intended. "Do you think it wise for me to reconsider the role of magic in Akkinor? To urge mages out of hiding?"

His eyes grew distant. "Your father asked me the same thing many years ago. He believed that having a mage as his Hand would inspire the Akkinorian people to welcome magic into the country again. I suppose that idea perished when I returned to Taundosa, though I believe he would've done it, had I stayed."

"That's not an answer."

"No, I suppose not." He was smiling now. "That choice must be yours, my dear. What do *you* think?"

She gazed around at the training field, marveling at the explosions of magic that warmed her face, and mirrored his smile with her own. She didn't have to speak for him to know what she thought. It was right there in her eyes, nestled just beside flashes of magical light and the glittering reflection of dancing flames.

***

Aurelia stared at the ceiling, arms folded over her chest, as the reverberation of Jack's snoring nearly drowned out her thoughts. She hadn't stopped wondering about the presence of magic in Akkinor since her visit to the training field earlier that day. Lyra's words—and Arian's— had been echoing in her head for hours.

She'd always been fascinated by the idea of magic. Every last one of her childhood lessons regarding the old days included tales of magical heroics. She remembered learning about the adventures of Alder the Gallant, the fourth King of Akkinor and the great-grandson of Robert Cherrane I. A half-blooded mage on his mother's side, Alder rose to fame by using his power to create two bodies of freshwater—Holyvern Lake in Laynoa and the Stogus River in Myra—after a prolonged period of drought left more than half of Akkinor's population without drinking water. Records from witnesses offered varying interpretations of exactly how Alder managed it, but they all seemed to agree on one thing: what they observed made them feel as close to the gods as humanly possible.

Akkinor would be an unstoppable force in the realm if it welcomed mages as it had before the persecution. Rarely was there a problem magic couldn't solve. Civilians often perished in substantial numbers due to infected wounds or undiagnosed illnesses; a mage could identify the problem and cure the patient simply by touching them. The many hundreds of people living in northern Sadia and Laynoa, too, feared freezing to death during the harshest point of the bitter winters; mages could keep them warm and alive with fires that burned forever, if need be.

There were more reasons to reintegrate magic than there were to keep mages hidden from society. Aurelia knew the people would be uneasy at first, but they'd grow to accept and cherish it when they realized how beneficial magic was to their everyday lives. If she really *did* wish to bring magic back to Akkinor, though, her greatest adversary would be—yet again—the nobility.

Desperate for guidance and a second opinion, she rolled onto her side and poked Jack's bicep. "Jack. Wake up." He groaned and rolled over, now with his back facing her. She scowled and shook his arm. *"Jack."*

"Good heavens, woman!" He sprung up to a sitting position, eyes wide and bleary, and gazed down at her like she'd stabbed him in the back with a branding iron. "What is it?"

She glowered. "I can't sleep. I-I need your opinion on something."

He collapsed onto his pillow and rubbed his eyes. "It's the middle of the night. What could possibly be so important?"

She gnawed on her lower lip. "If you were a highborn in Akkinor—say, the Lord of Omara—would you be pleased or furious if mages emerged from the shadows to bring magic back to the country?"

He winced and turned onto his side again. "I haven't the slightest idea. I'm certainly no lord, Aurelia. I couldn't say. Besides—what does it matter what the nobles think? You're the queen."

"Well, yes, but—"

"Aurelia," he said tiredly, "your faith in yourself grows lesser with each day that passes. From what I've heard about your reign, you were never one to let the opinions of others interfere with what you thought was best for your country. Your time in Carthe has stripped you of your confidence."

She blinked at him, hurt. "That's an ugly thing to say."

"I promised to be honest with you. This is as honest as it gets." He yawned. "I'm going to sleep now. Goodnight."

She glared at him, still upset, as he began snoring again in a matter of seconds. Unsatisfied with his response—mainly because she knew he was right—she climbed out of bed, snatched a candle from the bedside table, and quietly padded out of their shared bedchamber. She didn't know where she was going; so long as she had a quiet place to think, she was content.

After roaming the palace for a time, alone except for the soldiers guarding the entrances and exits, she paused by the door of Arian's study. Light was flickering from beneath the door. She knocked, hoping he was awake, and sighed in relief when she heard his tired voice on the other side. When she entered the study, she found him hunched over his desk, mulling over paperwork.

"Aurelia." His eyebrows lifted in surprise. "Why, it's the middle of the night! What's troubling you?"

"I might ask you the same thing." She sunk into the chair across from his. "What are you doing?"

If she blinked, she would've missed the flash of guilt that passed over his face. "I was woken by a guard not long ago. A letter arrived for me." He winced. "A letter from Akkinor."

She nearly fell out of her seat. "What?"

He rubbed the sleep from his eyes and sighed. "I took the luxury of writing to an old friend of mine in Laynoa. He's married to the sister of a Laynoan Coinmaster. I wrote to him hoping he'd provide an update on the current conditions in Akkinor. He reported that his brother-in-law withdrew a substantial amount from the Bank of Akkinor by order of Lord Reilly. He believes the coin was used as payment for Isalder mercenaries who've been spotted taking shelter in Laynoan hostels."

Aurelia sighed. She'd expected that. Lord Bradley Reilly had been attempting to court her for over five years, and despite the queen's obvious indifference, he'd been insufferable. She knew it was just a matter of time before his desperation morphed into rage.

"It seems Lord Reilly has finally exceeded his patience with me," she mumbled. "Laynoa will most certainly support my brother. Lord Reilly won't be charmed by my attempts at negotiation. I daresay the Spirres will raise arms against us, too. They aren't exactly pleased with the restrictions I've placed on their spending habits."

"My thoughts exactly. As of now, I'm confident that both Laynoa and Sadia will stand behind your brother. The Royal Army will be divided, I think, but I'm uncertain about the other kingdoms. Lord Crowland—"

"—has always been a friend." A sudden thought struck her. "I have other friends in Akkinor, too. *Family.*"

"Your aunts and uncles." His eyes brightened as he rose from his seat. Now that she'd excited him, all traces of grogginess disappeared from his being. "The Spirres seized Sadia from your grandfather. Lord Brennen may be dead, but his heir isn't. All five of your mother's siblings still live. They may not wish to choose sides between their niece and nephew, but if Andren Normindi is promised Lordship of Sadia upon your victory, surely that would be incentive enough to inspire his support."

Aurelia grinned from ear to ear. "If I restore my mother's family to power in Sadia, I'll remind them of Archie's misguided loyalties to the Spirre family and his lack of care for his own blood. That's more than reason enough for the Normindies to support me—and for those who wish to see a Normindi ruling Sadia again to support me, too."

"Precisely. And if I remember correctly, you have other friends in Akkinor. Friends with powerful connections. Need I continue?"

A gasp of both shock and delight escaped her lips. *"Linden."*

When the sparkle in Arian's eyes matched his smile, she knew she'd mirrored his thoughts. She was embarrassed for failing to think of it first. Linden was her closest friend in the world, and she'd nearly forgotten that he, too, came from a family with highborn connections. His parents may have been long dead, but his younger sister, Gemma, was very much alive.

Their mother, Sapphira, died in childbirth with Gemma. Overwhelmed with his duties as Lord Hand (and with raising Linden to inherit the title), Robert sent Gemma to the Monastery of Dhylo when she was four years old. She was raised and educated by her tutors at the holy educational institution, but she was never given the opportunity to utilize the skills she learned there. Her marriage to Lucan Stone, Laynoan Duke of Lockshaven, was arranged when she was eight years old and finalized nine years later.

Aurelia didn't know Gemma well anymore, but she was fond of her best friend's sister. They used to spend hours chasing Linden around the palace grounds when Gemma was permitted to visit her family in the Folly. The trio shared many great childhood memories together, and more than that, Gemma looked up to Aurelia as something of an elder sister. It was Aurelia who'd explained the marital act to teenage Gemma prior to her marriage, and it was Aurelia who'd sent the greatest physicians in Akkinor to Gemma's doorstep during her labors with her sons.

"The Reilly family can't remain in power after the battle is won," Aurelia said thoughtfully. "I won't have a traitor's blood ruling one of my kingdoms. If I must appoint a new noble family of Laynoa, it might as well be the family of a friend. The only problem I can sense is the duke. If I grant control of Laynoa to Gemma, he may contest her rule."

"He can't. Robert, Sapphira, and Gemma Elliot were all born in Laynoa. So long as a native highborn of the kingdom serves as its leader, such a decree can't be contested. Besides—he'd be a fool to deny becoming Lord Consort of Laynoa in favor of living as Duke of Lockshaven."

Aurelia cracked a smile, but she wasn't so convinced. "Perhaps if I allow Duke Stone to maintain Lockshaven, he'll be swayed. Their eldest son will inherit Lordship of Laynoa upon Gemma's death. Their second son will inherit Lockshaven. Gemma may be granted more power than her husband, but he'll still maintain his current status. Only a blithering idiot would contest something like that." Arian laughed. "Restoring the Normindies to power—and granting the Stones with greater noble power—will assure their support. Their bannermen will follow their lead, too. I maintain hope for Myra, but Omara..."

Arian waved his hand dismissively. "Fear not for Omara. The bond between Brentwood and Ashford, however strained, prevails. I have faith."

"I suppose we should send word to Akkinor, then." She glanced up at him with worry in her pale eyes. "May the Almighty ensure that our letters aren't intercepted by Archie's men."

Arian forced a smile, attempting to assure her that interception wasn't a major concern, but it was less than convincing. Both knew that if the letters fell into the wrong hands, the consequences would be dire, and all hopes of victory would be crushed like ants under boots.

"Now that we've discussed my reason for being awake at this ungodly hour," he teased, "what are *you* doing roaming the halls?"

Aurelia winced. "I was thinking about my conversation with Lyra today. Then Jack said something to me, and I don't know what to make of it." When he raised his eyebrows, she briefly recapped her conversation with Jack. "Do you think I've lost faith in myself, too?"

He stared at her like he wasn't sure how to respond. "I think you've experienced more trials than people twice your age. Carthe is a magical continent, yes, but it's also a place that challenges even the greatest among us. It doesn't surprise me that your confidence is dwindling after everything you've experienced here. That, however, doesn't mean you're less capable than you were before."

"I don't—"

"Aurelia," he continued, leaning his elbows on his desk, "three years ago, you ordered the demolition of numerous buildings across Akkinor. Those buildings were being used by your nobles for various purposes— secret brothels, banks, and the like. You had them destroyed so schoolhouses and infirmaries could be built in their place. Five thousand impoverished children were given the same education as highborn children because of that order. How did the nobles take to that?"

She smiled a bit. He'd certainly been following her reign, even from across the sea. "Not well."

"Did you allow their disapproval to stop you?"

"No."

"Why not?"

"Because it was for the good of the people."

He leaned back in his chair, smiling. "You're still the same queen who ignored the complaints of greedy nobles for the welfare of the masses. Your time in Carthe has changed you, yes, but that woman still exists within you. Don't allow her fire to dwindle simply because you're afraid. We're all afraid, Aurelia. Don't forget that."

She wouldn't forget it, just as she wouldn't allow fear and intolerance to stop her from bridging the centuries-old gap between mage and mortal. She had a duty to make her country as wonderful as it could possibly be— and regardless of how her choices were received, she'd do her duty with grace and humility, just as her father had before her.

XXXII

Aurelia had spent her entire life training to be Akkinor's queen. She learned from her father, the king, and from Linden's father, the king's best man. She learned from tutors, priests, nobles, medics, servants—everyone she could, really. Edmund often told her that it wasn't enough to simply inherit a crown: one had to earn it, and the only way to be deserving of such a responsibility was to learn from the people who, one day, would depend on her.

There was one thing, however, that Crown Princess Aurelia Brentwood never had the chance to learn. One thing that nobody in Akkinor could've attempted to teach her. One thing that, whether the majority of Akkinorians approved of it or not, could've changed the state of affairs across the entire realm—but only if two or more world leaders were brave enough to learn it for themselves.

Alliances between the continents didn't exist. The sole exception was Akkinor and Quapebet, but even so, the alliance was greatly limited. The two peacefully shared a border—the Myran town of Vilgh and the Quenosi town of Azhor—and the Cerulean Sea between southern Akkinor and northern Quapebet. There was a trading agreement between them, whereas the import or export of goods between other civilizations existed on an as-needed basis. The Isalders, for example, may have traveled to Seaport to purchase Akkinorian goods, but there was no legal agreement stating that the two countries had to exchange goods.

Even so, there was no political or military alliance between Akkinor and Quapebet. Aurelia couldn't send a plea for assistance to Emperor Timman Kaplo, Sixth of His Name, while their alliance was limited to shared territory and trade. If she wanted the Quenosi Army to stand behind her in the war to come against her brother, she'd have to undergo a long, strenuous process with the emperor—a process she simply didn't have time for.

Now she had the opportunity to do something perceived by the masses as unthinkable: unite Akkinor with one or more kingdoms of Carthe. The two continents had been independent—and adversarial—of each other since the First Mortals settled on either landmass. The closest they'd ever come to such an agreement had been when her parents agreed to support the Ashfords of Omara in organizing trading deals with Caedian merchants. Even when the Cristos men were sent to Akkinor as diplomats, neither Reyna, her father, or Aurelia's grandfather had ever considered a formal alliance.

Two weeks after her arrival in Taundosa, Aurelia stood on the other side of Reyna's door, anxiously awaiting her scheduled audience with the Golden Queen. She was waiting for a few moments before the door to Reyna's study opened. She recognized the man's dress and accessories enough to identify him as a Taundosan nobleman, though she couldn't be sure of which district he governed. He bowed to her, politely kissed her knuckles, and welcomed her to the City of Gold before scurrying away.

As she watched him go, she couldn't help but notice the trickle of sweat dripping down the back of his neck. She gulped nervously, praying to the Almighty that Reyna's temperament that day wasn't nearly as sour as the lord's demeanor suggested.

Upon hearing Reyna's cue, Aurelia entered the study. She took the lord's still-warm seat on the other side of Reyna's desk as the latter finished scribbling on a piece of parchment.

"I was pleased to receive your request for an audience today." Reyna still hadn't glanced up from the letter she was crafting. "You'll be relieved to know that the Goldmen apprehended two additional assassins here in the capital—Akkinorians who arrived in southern Carthe by smuggling themselves aboard a Bozari ship departing from the Syren Isles. If you'd like to punish them yourself, I won't object. They're your people, after all."

Aurelia's eyes hardened. "They ceased to be my people the moment they accepted the assignment to murder me. They're at your mercy while they're on Taundosan soil."

"As you wish." She finished writing, folded the parchment, and sealed the letter with glittering golden wax before stamping it with the seal of the Caltheos family: a phoenix. After putting the letter aside, she folded her hands on the desk and gave Aurelia her full attention. "Now, what would you like to discuss?"

Aurelia cleared her throat. "I know Lord Cristos has informed you of my desire to ally Akkinor with Taundosa. He seems to think that you're willing to make such an agreement. I'd like to hear it from you."

"The Lord Hand is quite right. I'd very much like to see a future in which Taundosa and Akkinor are friends. I will not, however, enter such an agreement with haste simply because your reign has been threatened. I admire the measures you've taken for your country—truly, I do—but everything I know about *you* stems from what I recall about your father. If this alliance comes to pass, it will exist in perpetuity. Our names will be associated with it for centuries to come. You and I must be transparent with one another, Your Grace. I don't wish for either of us to bring shame to our great nations because we're unfamiliar with each other's character."

Aurelia opened her mouth to respond, but no sound emerged. Now more than ever, she wished an arrangement like this one had been solidified before her time. If it had, she'd have something to study— something to dictate her next move, something to guide her through this uncharted territory.

On one hand, she agreed with Reyna. They needed to establish an honest and trusting relationship before they promised their two countries to one another—like any decent marriage, really. On the other, she feared her character wouldn't impress a ruler like Reyna Caltheos.

"All right." Aurelia swallowed the lump in her throat and raised an eyebrow. "What do you wish to know?"

Reyna stood from her chair and walked around the study. "When I met your father, he told me that all leaders are motivated by one core value. He, for example, sought to inspire honor amongst his people." She stilled for a moment and raised one perfectly arched eyebrow. "What motivates *you*, Your Grace?"

Aurelia didn't have to think before she answered: "Justice. I was raised to believe that justice motivates us all."

"If that were true," she remarked, chuckling, "the realm would be a much different place." To Aurelia's surprise, Reyna sat in the seat beside hers. "The quest for power is the way of the world. Your current predicament proves that much. Why should I take your word that you seek justice rather than power? Surely, you wouldn't be here today if your power hadn't been taken from you."

Aurelia swallowed her temper before it could burst. "Oleander the Great used what little power he had to seize an entire country—not because he sought to control it, but because he sought to save it. You don't know me well, Your Majesty, but you know my brother even less. I may be the only person in Carthe who understands what he's capable of. What he desires above all else. What he despises with a burning passion. What he believes Akkinor should be." She cleared her throat when a sudden thickness hindered her ability to speak. "While he sits on the throne, there's nobody to speak for the commoners. They're alone."

"Your nobles don't fight for their own?"

She brushed off the twinge of annoyance she felt at Reyna's accusing tone. "Lord Cristos has graciously written to several Akkinorian nobles, and I'm certain their responses will highlight what horrors my brother has inflicted during his time as king. I assure you, any nobles with loyalty to me are too frightened to speak against him—particularly when he has hundreds of Isalder mercenaries prowling the country. The others would sooner be put to the sword than betray him. He feeds their indulgences, and they're more than happy to let him in exchange for their support."

"I see."

Sensing that she'd yet to convince Reyna of her worth, Aurelia attempted a new tactic. "May I tell you something in confidence, Your Majesty?" Reyna nodded as a curious glint sparkled in her eyes. "In truth, I don't care if I ever see my throne again. I'm here not because I wish to wear a crown, but because I won't rest while my people are suffering at the hands of a cruel and selfish king. So long as Akkinor has a good and just ruler on the throne, I'll be content—even if that ruler isn't me."

Reyna stared at her, face blank and eyes unblinking, until she broke out into a smile so wide that it plumped her cheeks and squinted her gaze.

"All right," she whispered. "I believe you."

Aurelia stared right back, dumbfounded. Perhaps, she thought, Reyna was searching for that confession all along—a confession proving that Aurelia's heart lay not with her throne, but with her people. Better yet, it was a confession Aurelia had needed to make to herself from the moment she fled Akkinor.

"I have a few questions of my own," Aurelia continued. Adrenaline was coursing through her veins and filling her belly with giddy fire. "You say my father inspired you. How?"

Reyna sighed. Rather than replying, she stood from her chair and approached a slender, narrow table to the left of her desk. Two golden chalices and three jugs of wine rested atop the table. As Aurelia watched her, the Golden Queen filled the chalices with blue wine and returned to the chair. Aurelia accepted the chalice with a smile and took a tiny sip of the Taundosan delicacy. She made a sour face and forced herself to swallow. Compared to the smooth, decadent tannins of the red and white wines brewed in Myra, Taundosan blue wine was sweet, tangy, and made with so much sugar that it was grainy and slightly thick. Aurelia held the chalice in her lap out of politeness, but she had no intention of consuming another drop of the syrupy drink.

"I found myself engrossed in a bit of a scandal when I met your parents," Reyna murmured after a prolonged silence. "My father and his court hoped he would sire a son, so I wasn't raised to inherit the throne until my mother passed when I was ten years old. My father loved my mother tremendously, you see, and refused to remarry even for the chance of having a son. I had only four years of preparation before I ascended the throne. I had no women on my court—only men who insisted I produce heirs as quickly as possible. Without female guidance, I didn't know exactly what that meant. I understood how a woman came to be with child, but I was unfamiliar with the societal restrictions of childbearing. I soon found myself engaged in a physical relationship with the son of one of my noblemen. As intended, I quickly fell pregnant."

Aurelia froze. She hadn't realized that she'd been running her index finger over the rim of her chalice until she abruptly stopped. Her shock, however, was no match for the shame in Reyna's eyes.

"The error of my ways was soon explained to me," Reyna continued. "I met your parents about five weeks before I gave birth. I was hardly sixteen. My advisors told me to send the child away, as no man would marry a ruler who bore a child out of wedlock. I'll never forget what your father said to me when I confided in him: 'It's more honorable to love another man's child than to subject the child to a lifetime without love.' I decided then, much to the chagrin of my court, that I wouldn't dispose of the infant. If a man were worthy of a place at my side, he'd raise my child as his own with love and honor. I would've sent my baby away if not for your father. I never would've known the incredible person she is."

Aurelia cleared her throat. "What happened after?"

"I gave birth to a daughter—Maryn, after my mother—and met my husband a season later. He visited the palace on business, and when the baby began to cry during our audience, he sent the governess away and rocked her until he left. He visited again not long after to propose marriage. We've been married for more than two decades now."

"That's very sweet. What became of your daughter?"

Reyna sighed. "I wasn't permitted to name her as my heir due to her illegitimacy. She was given every other privilege of being the daughter of the queen, though. She married a Bozari duke about two years ago—they're very happy together. I'm to be a grandmother next season."

"At your age?"

The pair laughed. "I haven't quite come to terms with it, in truth," Reyna teased. "Either way, I wouldn't be here if not for your father. He showed me the true meaning of honor. I shall never forget it. Maryn will never forget it, either." She raised a kind, playful eyebrow. "Is there anything else you wish to discuss?"

There were dozens of things Aurelia wanted to ask, but if she did, they would've sat in the study for the next fortnight. Instead, she took the opportunity to know Reyna not as a queen, but as someone she might grow to consider a friend. The things they discussed had no direct correlation to their reigns or their kingdoms or their aspirations—they simply shared stories about their families, their homes, and their pasts until the chiming of the dinner bell tore them apart. In those few hours, Aurelia learned more about her future ally through an informal exchange of stories than she would've through stuffy political audiences.

When they left to meet the others for dinner, Aurelia set her still-full chalice of blue wine on the tea table, and the fierce laughter that followed (from both she and Reyna) rattled the entire palace.

***

One day later, Aurelia returned to Reyna's study to finalize the promise of justice and comradery between the two monarchs. The queens were joined by four additional presences: Prince Vyar Caltheos, Reyna's husband, was the Master of Legal Affairs in Taundosa and therefore responsible for overseeing political agreements; Ser Barvel, General of the Goldmen, was serving as witness; Arian, as Lord Hand, was a representative of Taundosa; and Jack, as the only other Akkinorian in Taundosa, was representing their country on Linden's behalf.

Aurelia's heart had been filled with dread from the moment she woke that morning—not because she was anxious to finalize the alliance, but because she was reminded, once again, that Linden wasn't with her. He should've been standing by her side while she made history, but instead, he was likely imprisoned by Aurelia's own brother or, gods forbid, dead.

"Your Majesty." Aurelia tipped her head in greeting while she and Jack took their respective places in the study. "This is quite an exciting day for us, isn't it?"

Reyna smiled. "We're changing the world today, Your Grace. Are you ready?"

Aurelia's eyes sparkled. "More than you know."

The terms of the alliance were simple. Both queens agreed to fight for one another when called upon to do so, to host one another and their people when they were in need, and to help one another prosper through trade and commerce. While Reyna promised the full force of the Goldmen,

Aurelia promised the full force of the Royal Army. In dire situations, the monarchs would request support from their nobility (and, subsequently, the armies owned by each noble family). Each queen also promised assistance from naval fleets and protection when traveling through the other's territory.

"Has anyone anything more to add?" Vyar hurriedly scribbled the terms on two separate pieces of parchment—a contract for each party to sign. When nobody spoke, he nodded and continued scribbling. "Just a moment, please."

Aurelia met Reyna's eyes. "I must return to Akkinor as swiftly as possible. Departing Carthe from Caedia would delay my travels. It'd be most beneficial if I were to set sail from Khaba, but, as you know, the Esposi aren't fond of Akkinorians. We won't make it halfway across the Alka without their consent, and it will be difficult to acquire that permission when they hear of my situation. Have you any suggestions for me?"

Reyna smiled. "Captain Lukos of Espos owes me a life debt. I'm confident that he'll allow my fleet to make passage to Akkinor with you onboard, but it'll only be a means of repaying a debt. Should Akkinor attempt to cross the ocean again in the future, Captain Lukos won't approve. You must remember that."

"I understand. Thank you."

The Queen of Taundosa tipped her head in response. Aurelia let out a long exhale of relief as they waited for Vyar to finish crafting the documents. Crossing the Alka—the largest body of water in the realm, and the ocean separating Akkinor from Carthe—hadn't been a possibility until that day. It was controlled by the pirates of Espos, a large island southeast of Carthe, and the Esposi hadn't been friendly with Akkinor since Oleander's Rebellion. The pirates were loyal to the Cherrane family and refused to break bread with Alora's usurper. Captain Lukos, the ruler of Espos, hated the Brentwood family as much as his predecessors. An Akkinorian ship hadn't sailed through the Alka in hundreds of years, despite it being the fastest route from Akkinor to Carthe. Without Reyna's interference, the Carthinian fleets allied with Akkinor would've been wrecked within a day of departure if the Esposi knew that Akkinor's queen was traveling among them.

"It's time," Vyar announced. Aurelia straightened in her seat as he placed the two contracts on Reyna's desk. "On this day, the kingdom of Taundosa shall become allied with the country of Akkinor. The union has been solidified by Her Majesty, Reyna Maryn Caltheos, First of Her Name, Queen of Taundosa, and Her Grace, Aurelia Emmeline

Brentwood, First of Her Name, Queen of Akkinor. Should this union ever be broken by bloodshed or betrayal by their descendants, the good names of the two monarchs shall never be tarnished."

He handed a quill and an inkwell to Reyna. "Do you, Reyna Maryn Caltheos, Queen and Protector of Taundosa, swear to bear arms alongside the country of Akkinor, to assist them in their hours of need, to defend their people when called upon, and to remain loyal to them throughout your reign and the reigns of your descendants?"

Reyna signed her name on both documents. "I swear so to do." As a bead of sweat formed above her sharp, dark eyebrows, she handed the quill to Aurelia and smiled. The Queen of Akkinor was shaking so greatly that it nearly fell from her grasp.

When the same pledge was recited for Aurelia, she repeated the five words and signed her name on both documents. As she did so, she felt an invisible weight being lifted from her chest. The sight of her signature beside Reyna's made her feel more powerful than she'd ever dreamed of.

"Ser Normyn Barvel," Vyar continued, "you are here to bear witness to the signing. Should you find any objections to this union, your lack of a signature will deem the alliance invalid." The General accepted the quill, hesitated for only a moment, and signed his name on both documents. "Excellent. Now, Mister Jack Sherbourne, you've been asked to represent Akkinor on behalf of the people. Should you find any objections to this union, your lack of a signature will deem the alliance invalid."

Jack didn't waste a moment before signing, and in typical Jack fashion, he winked at Aurelia as a wicked smile usurped his lips. He handed the quill to Arian as Vyar asked the same of him on behalf of Taundosa.

Arian's dark, wonder-filled eyes were wide with eagerness. "And so," he murmured, scribbling on each document, "it is done."

For the first time since her escape from Akkinor, Aurelia felt like she could breathe again. Not only had she finally found her way home, but she'd just made a deal that would change the world. When word spread of the alliance, Akkinor and Taundosa would be officially regarded as the most powerful kingdoms in the realm.

"Lord Cristos," Reyna said, "please send ravens to our allies in Krotis and Bozar. I should think they'd like to partake in this alliance with Akkinor. We shall begin discussing a strategy as soon as every possible alliance has been solidified." She turned to Aurelia. "Each resource in the palace is at your disposal, Your Grace. As long as Lord Cristos keeps me informed, you may do as you see fit until your departure from Taundosa."

Aurelia could've sobbed in relief, but she maintained her composure. "Thank you, Your Majesty. I have no words to express my gratitude towards you. Akkinor will be forever in your debt."

"Debt is nonexistent between allies," the raven-haired queen replied. The lines around her eyes, the only sign of her middle age, deepened when she smiled. "It's an honor for the City of Gold to be allied with Akkinor. There's nothing to repay."

For many years, Akkinor had been the strongest force in the east while Taundosa was the strongest force in the west. Both nations acknowledged one another, but neither dared to overstep. Maintaining neutrality was safer than risking war or suggesting an alliance. Aurelia and Reyna were the first rulers brave enough to change that. So long as the two allies dominated each half of the world, they'd be unstoppable.

An idea popped into Aurelia's head. "Arian?" He raised an eyebrow in response. "When you've finished writing to the nobles of Carthe, would you be so kind as to help me craft another letter?"

"Certainly. Addressed to whom?"

"The Scorpion of Akkinor."

XXXIII

*F*or the eyes of the usurper, Archibald Brentwood:

  This letter comes to you from the Kingdom of Taundosa. On this day, Her Majesty Queen Reyna allied Taundosa with the great nation of Akkinor. The terms are as follows: Taundosa shall lend its swords to Akkinor in our times of need, enhance the wealth and prosperity of our country, and negotiate peace between Akkinor and our hostile neighbors. Unfortunately, the terms apply solely to the rightful Queen of Akkinor. A usurper isn't sanctioned to receive the benefits of the alliance.

  Upon my return to Akkinor, you shall face multiple Carthinian armies, two Carthinian fleets, and a coven of mages who have sworn fealty to me. I offer you the chance to surrender the throne before blood can be spilled on Akkinorian soil. Should you do so, you and your fellow conspirators will be promptly arrested and tried for your crimes against the crown. Surrender will exempt you from execution. Should you neglect to surrender the throne, I will have no choice but to respond with the full force of my defense, and your execution will be inevitable. I hope you make the right decision.

  Sincerely,

  Li.

Aurelia leaned back and nodded. "It's quite good."

Arian raised an eyebrow. "Good enough for your brother?" She shrugged. "You're giving him the opportunity to surrender. You and I both know that he'll likely ignore this offer and respond with the full force of Akkinor's military. If there's anything we can add that might diminish his anger, we'd be wise to do so."

"He'll be furious anyhow. As long as I live, he'll be angry. What he needs to know is that my forces are stronger than his—that he can't win.

Escaping execution is the only thing that might appeal to him, but it's still not enough to encourage surrender."

"He's too proud," Jack added, yawning. "That weasel will never surrender the throne. Not after what he did to take it in the first place."

"Pride has nothing to do with it," Aurelia retorted. "It's greed. The only way to reach such a gluttonous person is to threaten him with losing everything. This is the best we can do."

He frowned as he peered over Arian's shoulder at the letter. "Why didn't you sign it with your full name and your titles? I thought that was customary of royalty."

"It is." She swallowed the lump in her throat as she gazed at her nickname on the parchment. "My brother is fully aware of my titles—after all, he's claimed them as his. He needs no reminder of where I stand in our country. What he *does* need reminding of is the bond we once shared as siblings."

Originally, she *had* signed the letter using her full name and titles. She'd changed her mind upon remembering Archie's childhood nickname for her—*Li*. If the threat of execution wasn't enough to inspire his surrender, she hoped a glimpse into their past might do the trick.

Arian rolled the letter into a scroll and stamped it with the seal of Taundosa. Aurelia and Jack joined him on a walk to the observatory, the highest point in the palace, where Reyna kept the messenger ravens. The observatory was a circular-shaped balcony with gold bars around the perimeter for safety, but there were no real walls and no roof. They scaled a winding, spiral staircase to the platform, where a plethora of ravens were housed in cages. Arian opened one of the cages—labeled with a sign that read *the Palace of Akkinor*—and tied the scroll to the ravens' talons. They watched the bird disappear into the sunset as it fluttered off to the east.

"Do you suppose he'll actually read it?" Jack asked, squinting.

Aurelia clenched her jaw. "He was always a curious boy. He may not tell another soul about it, but he'll read it for himself and pretend like it never existed."

Arian exhaled. "I can't imagine how my friends raised a child like that."

"Nor can I."

"Will you ever forgive him?"

She snapped her eyes over to her uncle. "He's my brother. It's my hope that one day, I can forgive him for what he's done. I can't say the same for my people, though. If he hurt Akkinor like he hurt me, they won't be so merciful. My personal feelings won't matter when the time comes to punish him for his crimes."

"You're the queen," Jack uttered, as if she'd forgotten who she was. "You're not required to earn the approval of your people before making a decision. If you want to show him mercy, the people have no choice but to accept that."

She stared at him. "How would that make me any different from my brother?"

"Well..."

"I won't abuse my power because I have a crown and they don't. *That* is when empires start to crumble."

Her uncle glowed with pride. "You sound like your father."

Aurelia beamed.

The three of them lingered in the observatory for a few moments longer. Dinnertime had passed long before, and it was nearing bedtime in Taundosa. As she thought about crawling into her bed after such a long day, she realized the sun was still setting in the sky. It should have disappeared hours earlier, but there was still an orange glow on the horizon. Before she walked down the spiral staircase, she hesitated and stared at the skylight.

"Aurelia?" Jack furrowed his eyebrows. "Is something on your mind?"

"I was just wondering why it looks like—"

"—the sun is still awake?" Arian finished. He looked amused.

"Well, yes," she said honestly, blinking at him. "How did you know that?"

"It's a common revelation for people who see the sun set in Taundosa for the first time. Haven't you heard the saying? 'The sun never sleeps in the City of Gold.'"

Jack made a face. "That's nothing more than a reference to the kingdom's fortune. It tells you right there—*the City of Gold*. The moonbeams reflect on the gold, creating the optical illusion of sunlight. This is the only place in the world with enough gold to make that possible."

"But what if it's more than a recognition of our prosperity?" Arian had a look in his eyes that made goosebumps form on Aurelia's skin. He seemed like a little boy who still believed in tall tales and old folk stories. She could practically see his imagination running wild when he spoke. "Even the moonlight isn't strong enough to create such an illusion."

Jack furrowed his eyebrows. "No other explanation is logical."

"I don't recall anyone saying a word about it being *logical*," Arian replied. "What happened to the little boy in you, Mister Sherbourne?"

Aurelia laughed so hard that her breath caught in her throat, resulting in a horrible, primal snort that rattled her own eardrums. Her companions stared at her, shocked to hear such a sound from a queen's mouth, as she chuckled into her hand—releasing another gods-awful noise—and used the other to fan her warming face.

While Arian chuckled at his feet (mindfully avoiding Aurelia's amused gaze), she turned her attention to Jack. He was peering at her with his mouth set in a thin line as if displeased by her laughter at his expense, but when she saw the way his flushing cheeks wobbled and how the lines around his eyes deepened, she knew he was trying with everything he had to keep from laughing.

Grinning, she turned back to Arian. "What were you saying?"

He coughed to mask the one last, lingering chuckle lurking in his throat. "Where was I? Oh, yes. The sun doesn't truly disappear into the horizon line. Not in any direction. Even in the latest hours of night, there's a band of orange light on the horizon surrounding Taundosa."

Jack still wasn't convinced. "That's impossible."

"How so?"

"We saw nothing of the sort in the Ngora Valley. I haven't heard the saying apply to Bozar, either. How can it be that the sun doesn't set in Taundosa, but it sets in the kingdom's bordering lands? It's impossible. The sun doesn't stay awake for one kingdom."

"Gianla," Aurelia piped up. While Jack stared at her, Arian erupted in a grin. "The sun goddess. She's the Almighty of Taundosa, isn't she?"

"She is." Arian's eyes sparkled at her. "Clever girl."

It wasn't a difficult conclusion to come by for someone with a royal's education. At the dawn of time, the first people to claim the Taundosan lands had just fought their way through the scathing desert. The terrain south of the desert was near idyllic for settling, but the harshness of the sun made the living conditions unbearable. People were dying by the dozens of heat stroke, infected sun blisters, and dehydration. The first people in Taundosa recognized the gods but didn't worship them as strongly as other civilizations. In a desperate attempt to make Taundosa inhabitable, they built the first sacred temple in the city and dedicated it to Gianla. After eight days of prayers and sacrifices, a miracle occurred, and the sun had mercy on the people. When the monarchy was formed, the first ruler created the eight territories of Taundosa in honor of the eight days they'd spent praying to Gianla.

"We have a beautiful temple for Gianla in Agotia. The Elotheon," Arian told them as they left the observatory. "It connects to Ardiham Castle. We have access to Gianla at all times of the day."

"That sounds wonderful." Aurelia smiled. "I'd like to see Ardiham Castle before our departure from Carthe. May we go?"

His dark eyes glistened with both grief and excitement. "We shall leave at dawn."

***

"I've arranged for you to spend the remainder of your visit in Agotia," Arian announced. He, Aurelia, and Jack all winced when the carriage took them over a colossal bump in the road. Jack, being as enormous as he was, smacked his head on the roof and grunted. "Queen Reyna will be hosting a few Carthinian nobles at the palace in the meantime. It's dangerous enough for so many nobles to be in one place for an extended stay—I won't risk your life by allowing you to remain in the palace alongside them. They'll arrive in Agotia at week's end to meet with you, but they requested a private audience with Queen Reyna before then. There's nothing to fear from that meeting, though. Her Majesty has nothing unkind to tell them."

She furrowed her eyebrows. "Are they expecting Reyna to gossip about me?" When he simply pressed his lips in a thin line, she sighed. "Somehow, it's comforting to learn that nobles on all corners of the world are fond of gossip. The lords and ladies of Akkinor have always been relentless."

Three of Reyna's allies in Carthe had agreed to meet with the Queen of Akkinor. She was eternally grateful for their decision, but she was still a foreigner, and not even the support of Taundosa's queen was enough to convince the nobles of her cause. They'd require proof of Aurelia's worth directly from Reyna's lips—not from a piece of parchment declaring Taundosa's loyalty to Akkinor.

Despite the matter of her allies, Aurelia was excited for her stay at Ardiham Castle. The jittery feeling in her stomach was the same feeling she had when she'd visited Eldford Keep in Myra, the Brentwoods' family home. She'd always been excited to visit the place where the first Brentwoods settled and created a legacy that would exist for thousands of years. Now, she was anticipating her arrival at Ardiham Castle, the ancestral home of the Cristos family—her blood.

Ardiham Castle wasn't as grand as Queen Reyna's palace, but in the City of Gold, *everything* was breathtaking. Aurelia shifted in her seat to look out the window when the carriage rode through the tall, glittering golden gates of the castle grounds. The castle wasn't very tall—only two stories—but it was long, winding, and built like some sort of puzzle. Even from outside, she saw that the estate was a maze full of twists, turns, and hidden corridors. The entire castle was made of white limestone that seemed to sparkle, but it was covered in gold decals, statues, accents, and carvings. A flag bearing the sigil of the Cristos family flew from the top of the observation tower beside the Taundosan emblem.

"Oh, uncle, it's lovely!" she exclaimed as the carriage rolled to a stop. Arian and Jack laughed when she opened the carriage door herself and hopped to the ground before the driver could assist. They followed as she gazed up at the castle with goosebumps peppering her skin. When she closed her eyes, she felt the presence of her relatives who'd once stood exactly where she was: her mother, her father, her grandparents. After five-and-twenty years, she'd finally joined them.

Arian's eyes glistened with tears. "Welcome home, Aurelia."

All she could do was grin.

Arian led Aurelia and Jack to the front steps of the castle, where a female attendant was waiting for them. "This is Emely, our stewardess."

Aurelia smiled at the woman as she greeted her, but the stewardess seemed dazed. Emely was about Arian's age, perhaps a bit younger, and she gazed at Aurelia like the queen was a figment of her imagination. She was wide-eyed, slack-jawed, and perfectly silent throughout the introduction.

"As you know," Arian continued, "this is Her Grace, Queen Aurelia of Akkinor. The rightful heir of King Edmund II and the daughter of Lady Katryna." At Katryna's name, Emely inhaled sharply. "Please treat her exactly as you'd treat me. Ardiham is her home as much as it is mine. And though he doesn't have a connection to Agotia, Mister Sherbourne is as good as family now. He'll be shown the same respect and hospitality as Her Grace."

Aurelia smiled again. "Thank you for hosting us. My uncle has spoken so highly of you and of the estate—I'm eager to experience life in Agotia for myself."

Emely swallowed and curtsied. "We are pleased to have you here, Your Grace." She cleared her throat and met Arian's eyes. "She sounds like her, too."

The lord chuckled. "I know."

Aurelia didn't have to ask. She didn't know much about Katryna Cristos, but judging by the way people seemed to glow when they talked about her, Aurelia knew that being compared to her mother was a compliment unlike any other.

***

"A letter has arrived for you, Your Grace."

Archie waved a dismissive hand, neglecting to look up from his task. "Give it to the Hand."

"Lord Silio is indisposed at present, my king."

"Leave it for him, you incessant fool."

The messenger cleared his throat. "The Assembly strongly urges Your Grace to read the letter at once. It appears Your Grace has received word from the Palace of Taundosa."

"Taundosa?" Archie looked up from Sereia's tanned shoulder, lifting both his hand and an ink-laden needle from her flesh. "What on earth do those hedonistic savages want from me?" When the messenger only stared at him, Archie crawled out of bed to cross his chambers and snatched the letter from the man's trembling fingers. The messenger continued to stare as Archie ran his fingers over the golden seal. "Go on. You've done what you came for."

Flushing crimson, the messenger quickly bowed before bustling out of the room. Archie stood by the hearth to utilize the firelight as he tore the seal. A foul, sickening feeling gurgled in his belly upon recognizing the writer's hand. The signature was meaningless; he would've known his sister's hand anywhere.

He might've opted against reading the letter and simply tossed it into the hearth if it hadn't been sent from Taundosa. A handful of assassins he'd deployed to hunt for her had confirmed that she'd fled to Carthe, but until now, he hadn't known her specific location. Now he did, and a part of him wished he'd remained oblivious—but his sister had forced his hand by revealing hers. She'd found allies, and better yet, she'd found them amongst some of the wealthiest and most renowned individuals in the realm.

His hands tremored as he scanned the message. "Fuck."

"Y-Your Grace?" Sereia, still laying on her stomach, leaned up on her elbows to glance at him while covering her exposed breasts with a sheet. The half-finished tattoo on her shoulder—the letter A in the king's handwriting—dripped blood down her back. "Is...Is everything all right?"

Archie gritted his teeth, silent, and reread the letter for the third time. He barely registered the sound of rustling from behind. A moment later, she set a hand on his shoulder in an attempt to inspire comfort. Archie whirled around and struck her across the face with enough force to catapult her to the ground. She fell to her knees, whimpering, as a bright pink spot blossomed on her cheek.

"Get out." He barely recognized his own voice when he spoke through gritted teeth. Sereia stared at him, tears bubbling on her dark lashes, as her cheek began to swell. "*Get out!*"

When Archie reached for the sword on display above the fireplace—his father's prized blade—Sereia yelped, fumbled to her feet, and scampered out of his bedchamber wearing nothing but his incomplete initial on her shoulder blade.

Guilt struck him for a moment as he listened to her sobs echo through the corridors. He hoped he hadn't marred her pretty face; it wasn't in his nature to break his favorite toys. He'd taken many women to bed over the years—none of them memorable nor anything special—but he was especially fond of Sereia. When he saw her visiting her husband at the palace one day, he knew he had to have her. It wasn't as if she or her husband could deny the king his desires, so neither ever uttered a word about it. And if the crown wasn't enough for them to obey his every whim, he was making sure both Sereia and her husband knew who she belonged to. Cattlemen claimed their herds with brands, too—it was just the way of things.

As his guilt faded along with the sound of Sereia's weeping, Archie turned his attention back to the letter. In an instant, fury replaced every drop of guilt in his veins. He'd hoped his sister was dead by then—either killed by one of his assassins or lost to the savagery of Carthe—but instead, she'd somehow managed to acquire enough support to see her home to Akkinor. And, much to his chagrin, she now stood a fighting chance against him during a battle for the throne.

Before he could read it for a fourth time, he crumpled the parchment and tossed it into the flaming hearth. His eyes, clear and blue like his father's, looked amber when he glanced at himself in the reflection of a clock on the mantel. Lore claimed that Igneus, the strongest of the four Elementals, had eyes that seemed to reflect firelight even if there were no flames to be found. Mages and mortals alike had attempted to seize Igneus's power just as Archie's sister threatened to seize his. Whatever his sister and her army of heathens attempted to throw at him, he'd reciprocate tenfold. It was only in his nature, after all.

He crouched down by the hearth and watched the letter shrivel into blackened flakes. His voice was nothing short of a hiss: "I'm sorry, *Li*. I can't yield what's rightfully mine. I do hope you're enjoying yourself in Taundosa—I shall send your head to the Golden Queen after I sever it from your neck. Then you can spend the rest of eternity in the City of Gold."

When the letter was finally reduced to ash, Archie ran a hand through his hair and turned from the hearth. A cartridge of ink and a long, thick needle still rested on his bed. Remembering his task for the evening, he opened the door and shouted for the nearest guard.

A soldier appeared before him in seconds. "Yes, my liege?"

"Find the girl and bring her here. I haven't finished with her. We can't have her running about unmarked, can we? Just about any man could have her."

The soldier's cheeks reddened. "As you wish, Your Grace."

Not five minutes later, Archie and Sereia resumed their previous position on his bed while the latter, trying her utmost to keep from squirming, begged her husband—the soldier—for help.

If he heard her, he never came. He'd accepted her fate (and his own) as a plaything owned, wholly and completely, by the King of Akkinor.

XXXIV

Aurelia watched Emely in silence as the stewardess bustled around the queen's bedchamber. After Arian showed Aurelia to her new rooms in the castle, Emely arrived with clean clothing, toiletries, and fresh linens for the suite. She'd barely spoken a word to Aurelia since her arrival, and the queen noted that Emely was avoiding her gaze.

Aurelia sat on the edge of her bed. "Emely?"

"Yes, Your Grace?"

Aurelia smiled and patted the empty space to her left. Something flashed across Emely's eyes—nostalgia, perhaps?—as she sat beside the queen.

"You look at me like I'm a ghost," Aurelia said lightheartedly. A deep flush colored Emely's cheeks. "It's all right. I understand. But something else has been bothering me since our arrival this morning—I know nothing about you. You've worked for the Cristos family for many years, haven't you?"

She nodded. "Yes, Your Grace. Your grandmother hired me as a maid when I was a girl. She promoted me to stewardess not long after. I've lived and worked in Ardiham Castle for over five-and-thirty years now."

"You must've known my mother well, then."

Emely's eyes glistened. "Yes, Your Grace."

"Aurelia, please." Again, the stewardess's eyes flashed. Aurelia cocked her head to the side, confused. "Have I said something to offend?"

"No, no." Emely stared at her hands in her lap and exhaled. A small, distant smile formed on her lips. "Your mother banned the use of titles and formalities by her employees. It was especially important to her that the Cristos family staff viewed her as a friend, not as a superior. She had a glorious soul. I've never met anyone quite like her."

"You must miss her very much."

The stewardess forced another smile. "Very much, yes." She hesitated for a moment, as if she were uneasy about continuing the conversation. "Your Grace—"

"Forgive me for prying." Aurelia tucked a piece of hair behind her ear and smiled sheepishly. "I knew nothing of my mother until I arrived in Taundosa. My uncle has spoken of her, but I know it causes him great pain to share her with me. There are few people left in the world who knew her well. I'd like to get to know her before my time in Taundosa comes to an end."

"Apologies. I-I haven't had cause to speak of Katryna in many years. Now that you've arrived...You are so much like her, Your Grace. I feel as though I'm speaking to my friend again." The smile on her thin lips became genuine. "I was in the birthing suite with Katryna on the day you were born. She trusted few in this world as much as she trusted me and Estylle. We—"

"Estylle?" Aurelia couldn't keep herself from interrupting. She was baffled to hear the name spoken from the lips of someone who'd never left Carthe. "My governess's name is Estylle."

The stewardess smiled. "They're one in the same. Estylle was a young girl when she was hired as Katryna's personal attendant. She wasn't the best or most experienced maid in the castle, but Katryna refused to search for a replacement. She looked after Estylle. They became extremely close. After you were born, Estylle cherished you like her own. She nearly threw a fit when Arian told us that King Edmund and Queen Cressida were taking you to Akkinor. In Estylle's eyes, you were her last connection to her dearest friend."

Aurelia paused to process what she'd heard, and for a moment, the only thing she could think was, *of the many times Estylle spoke of my mother, how often was she referring to Katryna Cristos?*

"So my parents offered her a position as my governess and took her to Akkinor with me," Aurelia concluded. Emely nodded. "My word! I never knew Estylle had been with me since before I was born. I thought my parents hired her from an old friend in Myra." A dark, empty pit formed in her stomach. "I-I wonder what happened to her."

Fear flashed across Emely's face, but it was gone as quickly as it came. "In my experience—especially with Anysa Cristos—I've found that a child's governess is more of a parent than a child's mother and father. Maybe he would've spared her. He can be angry with you and your parents, but Estylle never wronged him. Why harm her?"

You don't know my brother, Aurelia wanted to say. But there was no point in making Emely worry about the friend she hadn't seen in over two decades. Aurelia didn't want to make herself believe in the inevitable more than she already did, either. Until she uttered it aloud, there was hope for Estylle. There was hope for everyone who'd been in the palace when Archie took the throne.

At Aurelia's silence, Emely cleared her throat. "Most of our staff has worked in the castle since His Lordship was a child. We've served the Cristos family for many years, and I'm not the only one whose life was touched by Katryna. We haven't had anyone to talk to about her in a long time. I-I'm certain the staff would be thrilled to tell you about her."

The queen's heart leapt. "I'd like that very much."

The stewardess guided Aurelia out of her bedchamber and into the hallway, where Jack was emerging from his suite. He smiled at her and offered his arm for her to take. The three of them walked through the winding, twisting hallways of Ardiham Castle to the grand staircase, which they took to the first floor. Aurelia was surprised when Emely took them through the dining hall to the kitchens, where the staff was having luncheon. Over a dozen employees rose to their feet and either bowed or curtsied to Aurelia.

"Apologies for interrupting your meal," Emely mused. "Her Grace is curious to know if you can recall a story or two about our Katryna."

A white-haired man in cook's clothing snorted. "A story or two. Hmph! I got more stories about that girl than I got about my own children. This place was never dull when she was around, that's for sure."

"Brightest girl I ever met." A middle-aged woman with amber eyes didn't look up as she peeled an orange with a paring knife. "Smart as a whip. Real funny, too. Real funny."

The eldest employee, a female baker with dark skin and gray hair, popped a berry in her mouth while gazing at the queen. Aurelia met the baker's eyes, and as the two stared at one another, a beacon of light seemed to shine between them. Finally, the old woman chuckled and wiped her hands on her apron.

"You remind me of her." She shook her head and chuckled again. "I recognize the look in your eye. Our Kitty was born with it."

Aurelia raised an eyebrow. "What look, madam?"

"The look of someone who wants to make the world a better place."

"What makes you say that?" When she sat down at the long wooden table with the staff, Jack did the same. The employees exchanged surprised looks, but their surprise quickly morphed into joy.

"She lived a privileged life," the old woman said. "She grew up in a castle in the richest place in the world. A noble girl, a mage, a daughter, a sister, a friend. She had everything anyone could ever want. But she wasn't oblivious. She wasn't selfish. She immersed herself in the lives of the common people. Wanted to help them by taking on their hardships as her own. Whenever she had the chance, she tried to make a difference." The baker gestured to Aurelia with a berry between her fingers. "You have that same look in your eyes. Maybe you'll finally be the one who makes a difference."

The queen sighed. "That's all I want. I've tried to improve things throughout my years on the throne, but it's never been enough. And now it seems my reach has expanded to the rest of the world, too. If I can change Akkinor for the better, maybe I can do the same for others—or maybe it's an impossible dream."

"You're a Cristos." The baker's chestnut eyes shimmered. "I've seen the Cristos women do the impossible. You're no exception."

"Neither was your mother." The white-haired cook took a bite of meat from a bone and smacked his lips. "I remember her fifteenth name day. Agotia was suffering through a lack of drinking water at the time. The fountains in the gardens contain freshwater for the animals. Our Kitty opened the castle gates for the people and let them take water from the fountain home in buckets. That night, it rained in Agotia for the first time in weeks."

Our Kitty, Aurelia thought. *She was one of them. She'd belonged with them.*

Her smile wavered. "You speak of her as if she were a goddess brought to the earthly realm. You loved her so deeply that you've sworn to keep the secret of my parentage safely within these great walls. I knew of only few people who would've done the same for me in Akkinor, and I know even fewer now." She sighed. "I hope the legacy I leave behind is half as profound as hers."

"Oh, you will." The old baker released a short laugh. "I'm telling you, child. It's *the look.*"

"I know it, too," Jack piped up. Surprised, Aurelia turned to him with raised eyebrows, as did the staff, equally miffed by his sudden input. "I couldn't put my finger on it until now, but I suppose that's what brought me to you. It has to be."

Aurelia's heart thumped sporadically. "What look?"

"I don't know. It just happens sometimes, randomly, when I look at you," he said with an innocuous half-smile. "Usually when you're thinking or listening to someone speaking to you. It's a bit of a thoughtful expression, I suppose, but it's more than that. It welcomes us. It's a trusting sort of thing. I look at you in those moments, and I know—without a fraction of a doubt—that you'll do your best by me. I felt it from the moment I first looked into your eyes. It's your spirit, my love. It shines from within for all to see, and it captivates us." When he and Aurelia both realized the servants were staring at them, bemused, he cleared his throat and eyed them sparingly. "I take it Her Ladyship had a similar way of affecting people?"

"Oh, yes. Very much so." Emely solemnly bowed her head. "The world was a better place when Katryna Cristos lived and breathed. Agotia has missed her terribly." She smiled at Aurelia. "The gods have answered our prayers, Your Grace. They took Kitty from us, but they've sent you in her place."

Aurelia smiled, but her chest felt tighter. She'd spent her entire life believing that her parents were the most incredible people in the world. She believed that Edmund and Cressida were one-of-a-kind, but her birth mother...Katryna Cristos seemed like the kind of person who only came around once in a millennia. How could Aurelia not have known her until now?

Aurelia met the old baker's eyes. "My uncle tells me that my mother was quite the acrobat."

"Oh, yes." She chortled and licked her berry-stained fingers. "Always climbing and hanging from things. Her body was covered in scars—just like you." Blushing, Aurelia rubbed her hands against her exposed arms, which were scathed with pale markings from years of getting herself into trouble. "Darryn Atwood used to lose her in the gardens for hours. She'd often hide in the trees like a squirrel. She liked causing trouble."

As the employees shared stories with Aurelia and Jack about the late Katryna Cristos, the Queen of Akkinor finally felt like she knew her mother. Katryna was no longer a name belonging to a ghost—a ghost who'd brought Aurelia into the world and left it moments later. Now, she was a woman who'd touched the lives of everyone she met, whose death still haunted the people closest to her after more than two decades.

After throwing her head back and laughing at the old baker's story, she opened her eyes and saw a figure across the room. She sobered as she focused on her uncle, who was silently standing in the doorway of the kitchens as he listened. His cheeks were glistening with tears, and one hand was covering his mouth as if he were trying to keep a sob from escaping his throat.

"You shall have to excuse me," Aurelia said to nobody in particular. "I believe there's someone else who's most eager to tell me about my mother."

Jack's eyes snapped to Arian. "Go on. I'll be fine here."

By the time she said her goodbyes, Arian had left the kitchens and made his way upstairs. Aurelia found him exactly where she'd expected to: standing by his lonesome in a hall of portraits dedicated to the Cristos family, gazing at his sister as her lifeless painted eyes stared back at him.

Arian was silent as Aurelia stood at his side to study the portrait. Katryna had been almost two years younger than Aurelia when she died: just barely four-and-twenty. She had a mature face, making her appear several years older, and the kind of beauty that rivaled that of the gods. Her thick, dark brown hair—falling in loose curls—cascaded over either shoulder and shone against an unseen source of light. Her eyes, bluer than the sky and framed by long, dark lashes, were so bold and bright that it was nearly impossible to focus on anything else. Her skin wasn't rich and tawny like Arian's, but deeply tanned like the dunes of the Ngora Valley.

According to the Cristos family tree she'd seen earlier in the day, Arian was the half-brother of Katryna and Anysa. His mother, a Taundosan nobleman's daughter, was killed by a cannibalistic tribe when Arian was an infant. Not long after, Dyron married Sylvina Melrayis, the daughter of a Bozari duke and a Kanish highborn woman. Other than the differences in complexion and eye color, though, Arian and Katryna shared many similar features. It wasn't difficult to understand how so many people failed to recall the truth of Arian's parentage.

The most mesmerizing thing Aurelia noticed was the golden locket that hung from Katryna's neck: the same one Aurelia had worn every day since she was old enough to understand its value.

She thought aloud: "I wonder what her voice sounded like."

Arian smiled faintly. "She was rather tranquil. The calm before the storm, as our father liked to say. She always sounded respectful, even when she was trying to be menacing, and she was firm, too. One could rarely find cause to argue or disagree with her. She sounded so sure of herself, even when she wasn't, and she had a particular talent when it came to making insults sound like praises."

"Naturally," she teased, making him chuckle again. When his laughter died down, she took the opportunity to ask the question she'd been thinking about since the moment she learned about her mother. "I was curious to know if there are crypts in the castle. Perhaps a mausoleum for the Cristos family. I-I'd like to pay my respects while I'm here."

"I expected as much. We do things a bit differently in Taundosa, my dear. There are no crypts or cemeteries. In fact, we needn't move an inch to visit Katryna's final resting place. We're already here."

Aurelia furrowed her eyebrows. "I beg your pardon?"

Amused, he took a few steps forward and reached for the right side of the thick gold frame encasing Katryna's portrait. Aurelia heard a clicking noise as Arian pulled a hidden latch in the frame. Her eyes widened when he pulled it forwards, causing the entire portrait to swing open like a door. Behind it was a square-shaped niche in the wall where a single urn rested.

"This is how Taundosan highborn bury our dead," Arian told her. "We are cremated, and our urns are kept behind our portraits. It's a bit morbid, I suppose, but in my opinion, paying our respects to the remains of our loved ones becomes more personal when we can do so while gazing upon their faces."

She and Jack had wondered why there were so many portraits in Ardiham Castle, and it all made sense now that she knew what purpose they served. Still, it was hard for her to fathom that her mother's remains had been resting on the other side of a painted canvas. It was eerie, to say the least, but comforting at the same time.

Arian smiled when he saw her staring at the urn. "Magnificent, isn't it? Every urn is designed specifically for the deceased. They're all adorned with colors and symbols that reflect their character so we may never forget who they were in life—and to inform those who never had the chance to know them as we did."

The dark blue base of Katryna's rounded urn was accompanied by gold embellishments—most notably, paintings covering nearly every inch of the smooth, curved surface. Aurelia identified most of the images and what they symbolized: the sigil of the Cristos family, red and gold with a dragon at the center; the emblems for Agotia and Taundosa; and the symbol of Taundosa's Almighty, Gianla, to recognize Katryna's religion.

"It's beautiful. I imagine she would've liked it."

"I certainly hope so." Arian closed the painting and secured the latch, then stepped back and sighed as he gazed at his sister's smiling face. "Not a day has passed when I don't question the decision I made five-and-twenty years ago. I thought I knew my sister well, but I'm not so sure anymore. I can't say for certain if she'd be angry with me for letting you go. I don't know how she'll greet me when we meet again in the afterlife."

Aurelia set a comforting hand on his arm. "The events of the last few years may have been trying, uncle, but I'm pleased with my life. I'm not an unhappy person. I love my home, my friends, and my position. I take pride in who I am and who I've become. None of it would've been possible without the decision you made."

He didn't look convinced. "I promised her I'd look after you. I promised her I'd tell you how much she loved you every day."

"She died so I could live. You never needed to tell me how much she loved me. She showed me herself."

The deep brown hue of Arian's eyes nearly disappeared beneath a thick layer of bubbling tears. He opened his mouth to respond, but no sound emerged. Aurelia, smiling at his tenderness, clutched his forearm between her hands and rested her head against his bicep as she turned her gaze to the portrait again. She'd been so distracted by Katryna's beauty that she hadn't noticed what her mother was holding until then: a bouquet of delft blue hyacinths held together by a matching ribbon tied around the stems. The stems sat daintily between Katryna's hands while the star-shaped blossoms rested against the length of her arm.

Aurelia's lips parted with a small chuckle, but before she realized what was happening, she'd begun to cry. Arian slithered his arm from between her hands to pull her into an embrace as he questioned the reason for her tears, but she waved him off and assured him that she was all right.

She wiped the tears from her cheeks and forced a smile. "Was she fond of hyacinths?"

"Very much so. They were her favorite. She liked the blue ones in particular, but she was fond of the apricot ones, too."

Another laugh-turned-sob escaped her throat, visibly concerning him, but she neglected to share the reason for her sudden outpour of emotions. It was no coincidence that Aurelia's favorite flower happened to be her late mother's favorite, too; and while she was certain the fact would've brought a smile to Arian's lips, she kept the revelation to herself. It was something she'd keep hidden away in the corners of her mind—something to exist in her memory for nobody but herself and the beautiful, extraordinary, tragic Katryna Cristos.

XXXV

O h, Jack, catch it!"

"It's only a pest." He snickered and scooped the insect out of their bathwater, and when he held up the half-drowned creature, she hugged the edge of the bathtub and howled in protest while kicking his legs. "All right. Calm yourself, woman!"

She glared at him as he squished the insect with a nearby candle holder. When she was sure the eight-eyed, six-legged creature was gone for good, she allowed herself to relax in the tub once again between his hulking legs. She felt his palms rubbing her lower legs as he attempted to make peace after teasing her. She responded to his peace offering by splashing him with lukewarm bathwater, making him flinch and rub his eyes.

He snorted into a laugh. "So much anger, all because of a harmless insect. How strange. I've never known you to be afraid of anything."

"I've always hated insects. I was terrified of the dark as a child, too. Not so much anymore. Now...You know what terrifies me as an adult. Something much greater and much harder to kill than an insect."

He grimaced. "I know. Would *you* like to know what terrifies me more than anything in the world?"

"An empty coin pouch?"

His eyes darkened. "No."

"Blue wine?"

"Close, but no."

Aurelia laughed. "Oh, I don't know. What on earth could terrify Jack Sherbourne?"

"The ocean," he admitted. The smirk disappeared from her face. Until then, she thought he'd been teasing her. "I've never been fond of it. Most Omarans live entire lifetimes without seeing the ocean. Even fewer know how to swim or sail. I've always been frightened of what lies beneath the surface. You must understand that better than most."

She did. It'd been over five years since Edmund and Cressida were lost at sea. Aurelia had loved the ocean before it swallowed her parents, but now it was one of her greatest adversaries. If not for the angry seas and storms on that dreaded night, she would've had the chance to give her parents a proper burial, and she would've had remains to visit in the crypt rather than empty tombs.

She often imagined what that fateful night had been like. Crewmates who'd survived the wreck claimed it'd happened suddenly: the ship sailed into an unforeseen storm in the middle of the night, when little could be seen other than the crescent moon cowering behind dark clouds. One moment, the ship was sailing smoothly across the Crystal Sea. The next, sailors were either jumping overboard or being thrown into the sea as enormous waves crashed atop the ship and flooded the decks. The survivors claimed that a tremendous lurch disrupted a bookcase in the Brentwoods' cabin, forcing it onto its side and blocking the door before they could flee. Soldiers and sailors alike tried in vain to open the door from the other side while Edmund and Cressida struggled to move the bookcase, but it was too heavy to budge. Their only other option was to jump into the sea via the portholes, but either way, it was unlikely they would've survived.

She wondered if they *had* attempted to flee through the porthole. Edmund was a stout and burly man at the time of his death—she couldn't imagine his large belly fitting through the porthole. He would've insisted that Cressida try to save herself, but Aurelia knew her mother, and Cressida wouldn't have left Edmund. If one had the option to die alone or in the arms of their beloved, the latter was almost always the favorable option.

She hoped that was how it'd happened. She hoped they'd taken their last breaths together, wrapped in each other's arms as seawater flooded their cabin through the portholes, so neither had to live a single moment without the other.

"I hadn't sailed until I escaped," Aurelia shared. Jack raised an eyebrow, but he didn't seem as surprised as he was interested. "That shipwreck ruined my life, Jack. I could live another hundred years without sailing the seas again, and I'd be content."

"So would I. The ocean didn't kill my family, but it's the only thing in the world that each and every civilization has yet to understand. Unconquered, unclaimed, unpredictable. It matters not the origin of the flags that fly with the sails of a ship. Akkinorian, Carthinian, Esposi...We all become equals at sea. We're all at the ocean's mercy."

The thought made her shiver. Aurelia distracted herself by leaning forward to pluck a sprig of lavender from Jack's tanned, chiseled chest. He took the opportunity to pull her onto his lap and brush his nose against hers, teasing her with a kiss that didn't come.

"Your antics have already made me late for one meeting this week, Jack. We don't have time—"

"Oh, would you hush and kiss me already?"

Grinning, she tipped her head downwards and kissed him fiercely, as if his lips were a delicacy that'd be taken from her at any moment. Their wet, naked bodies were slippery against one another, and thick chunks of hair stuck to them like glue. *Very romantic, indeed,* she thought. When Aurelia broke the kiss, she set her hand on his cheek and gazed into the beautiful eyes she adored so much. Jack grinned when he saw the way she was looking at him. He only grinned like that when he was with her, she'd noticed, as if no other soul in the realm was worthy enough to see it.

"Lily dear," he teased, "would you like to hear something wonderful?"

She traced his lips with her fingers. "Yes."

"I am furiously, incandescently, eternally in love with you."

A jittery feeling erupted in her stomach as a wide, wobbling smile washed over her lips. "I love you, too."

His entire body relaxed against hers. "Thank the gods."

"You doubted it?"

"Doesn't everyone?"

"Fair point. Would *you* like to hear something wonderful?"

"Always."

"You're the first person in the world to say that to me," she confessed. He blinked in surprise. "Other than my parents, of course. Nobody else has ever said that to me before."

He stared at her as if she'd said it only to appease him—he didn't believe her in the slightest. As he recognized the sincerity in her eyes, he softened, sighed, and held her more tightly into his warm, sopping embrace. She hadn't realized how tragic her admission sounded until his sympathetic exhale tickled her ear.

Tragic or not, it was true. Besides Jack, only her parents had ever said those three words to her. She'd never heard it from Archie, from Linden, from Cicely. She knew her friends loved her, but they'd never said it. She knew she was well-liked by many, too, but not loved. Even if others *had* said it to her, she wasn't certain she would've believed them. She was, after all, the one individual in Akkinor whom everyone sought to please. It was difficult to believe that someone beyond her family could love her without rhyme or reason.

"Thank you, Jack," she murmured into his neck.

"For what?"

"For saving me that day in the forest. I don't know if I ever said it. Not properly, anyway. So thank you."

"Don't thank me. My intentions were purely selfish."

She laughed. "I knew it."

***

Three unopened letters rested hauntingly on Arian's desk. Aurelia sat on one side of the desk, staring at the letters in silence, while Arian and Jack did the same from the other side. Neither had spoken a word since Aurelia and Jack, still damp from their shared bath, arrived at Arian's study moments earlier.

All three letters were addressed to Lord Arian Cristos, but the messages they contained were meant for Aurelia. Only a few weeks earlier—before finalizing the alliance between Akkinor and Taundosa—Aurelia and Arian had crafted a total of seven letters destined for Akkinor. The purpose of the correspondences wasn't simply to surmise which Akkinorian nobles remained loyal to Aurelia, but to understand exactly what was happening in Akkinor under Archie's rule.

Jack spoke first: "We should open them."

"How insightful of you." Aurelia peered at Arian with raised eyebrows while Jack glared at her. "Where shall we begin?"

Arian patted a letter stamped with the seal of the Normindi family. "With your uncle."

Before she was Cressida Brentwood, Aurelia's mother was Cressida Normindi, eldest daughter of Brennen Normindi, Lord of Sadia. Oleander the Great had appointed the Normindies as Sadia's rulers to replace the Spirres after the latter stood behind Alora Cherrane. Years after Edmund and Cressida were married, though, the Spirres rebelled against the Normindies and overthrew them for control of Sadia.

Andren, the eldest Normindi child, hadn't responded to Aurelia. She knew why: the Spirres intercepted every letter that left his desk, as they feared he'd rise against them and take his place as the rightful Lord of Sadia. So long as the Spirres stood by Archie, Andren couldn't risk communication with Aurelia. He'd be labeled a traitor if he wrote even a word to his niece, and Archie wouldn't blink twice if the Spirres decided to execute Andren for treason.

The letter had been written by Rien Normindi, second child of Lord Brennen and Lady Eleana, who now lived as husband to a Sadian duchess. He'd always favored Aurelia over Archie (just as he'd favored Cressida over the other Normindi siblings), but even so, he couldn't explicitly state whether he'd support Aurelia. The Spirres didn't watch him as closely as they watched Andren—Rien had no claim to the Sadian throne while his elder brother lived—but he couldn't risk stating his loyalties for fear of interception. Still, he offered other valuable information that sent a chill up her spine:

So much has changed, dear niece, in your brief absence. The coin and resources needed to repair the Folly following the infiltration was seized from the civilian funds at the Bank of Akkinor. The common people have been severely deprived of necessary goods. As such, many have turned to looting and pillaging to acquire the resources needed for their survival. In response, the king has altered the punishment for theft from imprisonment to one-hundred lashes at the whipping post. Sadia alone has buried hundreds in mass graves who perished after the lashings, as our medics are unable to acquire or afford the necessary treatments.

You must know by now that the king has purchased Isalder mercenaries to defend both the crown and his closest allies. Though I've yet to see this with my own eyes, I've heard tales of horror from noblemen across Sadia. Our men, women, and children are being beaten, raped, and killed each day. Curfews and an increased number of soldiers at the borders of each Sadian territory have made it impossible for any Sadian citizen to leave the kingdom. Even the highborn must adhere to strict rules and regulations. It's my understanding that those who've managed to escape by sea are now residing on Marooner's Chain. May the gods have mercy on them.

Jack shivered violently when Aurelia finished reading Rien's letter aloud. "If our people would rather live on the archipelago than on the mainland, then things are worse than we feared."

Marooner's Chain, the cluster of isles west of the mainland, was Akkinorian territory. The archipelago didn't share the country's prosperity or wealth. Since the old days, the treacherous islands served as home to laborers—normally prisoners or those in exile from the mainland—who worked meager jobs. Residents lived in poorly made shacks, waded through muck and grime to get from one place to another, and had grown accustomed to the dreariness that characterized the isles. Needless to say, no Akkinorian dreamt of making Marooner's Chain their home.

Aurelia cleared her throat. "Let's continue."

The second letter had also been written by one of Cressida's siblings: Selsa, the fifth of six, who was married to a Holosi duke. Like her brother,

Selsa hadn't disclosed whether or not her husband and his army would stand behind Aurelia. That was very well, she thought; the responses alone were enough to suggest that both Rien and Selsa—and their families—still believed in Aurelia and her reign. They wouldn't have risked interception (and their lives) to offer updates to their king's nemesis unless they remained loyal to her.

"My word." Her eyes, already too large for her face, strained as they bugged out of her skull. "My aunt writes that many Holosi nobles have been imprisoned by my brother since my departure. They were unconvinced by Archie's stories regarding the uprising. They voiced their suspicions, and they were tossed into the dungeons for it. If they don't agree to fight for him, he'll execute them."

Jack's face paled. "What about Lady Tarre? I can't imagine she'd allow such a thing."

Arian sighed. "She hasn't another choice."

"He's right," Aurelia murmured. "She may be the Lady of Holos, but she can't protect her nobles from Archie's decree. There's nothing she can do. Even if she could..." She shook her head, defeated. "She's been at death's door for years now. Her heir and their advisors have been ruling Holos on her behalf since before my parents died. She may not even be aware of what's happening."

"I'd imagine," Jack added, "her regents aren't happy that their nobles have been thrown into prison."

"No, they're not," Aurelia confirmed, still reading Selsa's letter. "Holos has always been the most independent kingdom. Even Omara has grown to rely on the monarchy more so than Holos. Its rulers don't approve of Archie's interference with the way they governs their people. My aunt seems to be suggesting that Holos won't stand behind my brother on the battlefield—but then again, we can't know for certain."

"Maybe we can," Arian said lowly. She looked up from the letter and raised an eyebrow. He'd been reading the last of the three letters, now with his mouth pressed in a thin line and his bushy eyebrows furrowed over his deep-set eyes. "I wrote to three Normindies, Gemma Stone, Silas Crowland, and my old friend from Laynoa. Silas Crowland responded."

Aurelia shifted excitedly in her seat. She'd been holding onto hope for Lord Crowland. Of the six Akkinorian kingdoms, the Brentwoods shared the strongest connections to Myra. More so than any other noble in the country, Lord Crowland had offered his guidance at the beginning of Aurelia's reign. He treated her not only as a new queen, but as a daughter who'd just buried both of her parents. He was empathetic, selfless, and as generous as they came. He certainly wasn't the kind of man to raise arms against someone he respected and admired.

She expected that Lord Crowland, a man she considered a friend, would promise to fight alongside her on the battlefield. Rather, he opened her eyes to something she hadn't previously considered—something she *should've* considered immediately after her departure from Akkinor.

"'...by an unexpected stroke of luck, the king permitted me to leave Myra for an audience in Holos to discuss an order of painted glass—an order I placed on behalf of the king, who requested that his lodgings at Eldford Keep be redesigned to suit his royal tastes,'" Arian read. "'Her Ladyship's closest advisors performed numerous calculations that suggest an upcoming period of poverty not only for Holos, but for the entire country. If the king doesn't answer our pleas to maintain Akkinor's wealth by the end of the current year, Holos will respond by seeking independence from the country. I don't need to continue for you to grasp how detrimental that would be for our people.'"

Aurelia's heart plummeted to her knees. "Heavens above."

"Allow me to ensure that I'm understanding this correctly." Jack's tanned skin had paled significantly by then, and the playful radiance in his eyes had been replaced by melancholy. "If Archie refuses to cease his spending for the good of the country, Holos will attempt to secede from Akkinor to become its own nation. Civil war will break out across the country—particularly if Myra and Omara follow suit."

"That's right." She hadn't realized how violently her hands were shaking until Jack reached over to still them. For the first time since arriving in Taundosa, she felt a sharp pinching sensation behind her eyes: a familiar yet distant feeling induced by both stress and caution, and a feeling that'd been almost entirely unknown to Lily Linden. It was, simply put, an experience unique to kings and queens. "Thousands will die. Kingdom will turn on kingdom, making it near to impossible for the people to receive supplies from elsewhere in the country. It'll be a bloodbath." She removed her hands from his and ran them through her hair. "On a brighter note, Lord Crowland's letter confirms that Myra and Holos haven't been swayed by my brother. We're still uncertain about Omara, but Omarans aren't warring people. They'll avoid the fight at all costs."

"If they refuse to choose a side," Arian added, "your brother may command it by executive order."

"And I will not. Only one of us will be forcing a peaceful kingdom to bear arms. Lord Ashford knows I'd never ask such a thing of him, and if I have the chance to negotiate before blood can be spilled, I'll make sure he remembers that." She cleared her throat and gestured towards the letter. "Continue, please."

Arian returned his gaze to the letter. "There isn't much left. It would appear that the schoolhouses and infirmaries you commissioned have been shut down and returned to the nobility. A Myran vineyard was demolished and turned into a menagerie for exotic animals Archie purchased from Quapebet. Civilian funds held in the Bank of Akkinor have been used not only to purchase Isalder mercenaries, but to provide them with lodgings and goods the people desperately need."

If Lord Crowland's report was accurate, then approximately half of the civilian funding had been spent since the uprising. Since taking the throne, Aurelia had used one-sixth of that funding per year, and every last bit of coin was spent on the people. Archie had spent all of it either on himself or on additional swords. The civilians and even the lower-ranking highborn hadn't received a cent of what they were owed since the uprising.

It made Aurelia's soul ache to learn what her brother had done during his time as king, but Arian was right: she was now entirely certain that, at the very least, half of her nobility wouldn't support Archie in the war to come. It was right there in front of her—they didn't approve of the things he'd done, and they wanted the country restored to what it'd been when Aurelia sat on the throne.

A part of her wanted to believe that Lord Bradley Reilly would change his mind, but as she thought about it, she realized she'd lost his support long ago. Unless she agreed to marry him, he'd stand behind Archie, and all of Laynoa along with him. Archie would've promised him something grand in exchange for his services, while the only thing Aurelia could promise him was exactly what he already had.

"Keep these in a safe place," she told her uncle. "We mustn't allow anyone beyond this room to see them. Certainly not before tomorrow's events, anyway."

Jack's mouth twitched. "When are they due to arrive?"

"Between breakfast and luncheon," Arian replied.

"I suppose it's a good sign," Aurelia offered. "They agreed to meet with me here at Ardiham Castle, but they didn't have to. Her Majesty must've been quite persuasive."

The following day, Ardiham Castle would welcome Queen Reyna, two Bozari noblemen, and one Kroti noblewoman for an audience with Aurelia. The three guests had already spent several days at the palace with Reyna to discuss potential alliances with Akkinor and what it meant for their kingdoms. Had their conversation gone poorly, the three nobles would've returned home before making Aurelia's acquaintance.

If they refused her request, she wasn't certain that her forces alone would be enough to defeat her brother. Myra, Holos, and possibly Omara would offer their swords, but Sadia and Laynoa wouldn't. The Royal Army of the Folly swore to serve only the monarch—each individual soldier would have to decide for themselves who the rightful king or queen of Akkinor was.

Even with the Goldmen, the Agotian Army, and Taundosa's navy, Aurelia and her Akkinorian allies were at a disadvantage. All three were extremely modest. Taundosa didn't have nearly as many fleets as needed to carry the two armies across the sea. Without Bozari and Kroti fleets to assist, the number of foreign allies on Aurelia's side of the battlefield would become even smaller.

Her life was in the hands of three foreign rulers with no love or loyalty for Akkinor or its queen. If she couldn't convince them to fight for her, she wouldn't live to see another Akkinorian sunrise. She couldn't let that happen.

XXXVI

Aurelia found Jack waiting for her outside of Arian's study. He was dressed in the best clothing the servants could muster for him, his wild curls combed back and his face free of stubble. He looked handsome as ever, but the way he tugged at his collar and readjusted his trousers made it clear that he wasn't fond of highborn attire. If he'd had his way, he would've marched into the study wearing the same clothing he'd donned when he and Aurelia first met.

She raised an eyebrow. "Are they nearly finished?"

"Nearly. Your uncle has been conversing with them for quite a while, though. Is that a good thing or a bad thing?"

She chewed on the inside of her cheek, but the door opened before she could reply. "Good afternoon, Your Grace. Mister Sherbourne," Arian greeted. "We're ready for you now."

When they entered the study, the three nobles immediately rose to their feet to welcome her, but Aurelia lost her voice before she could utter a word. She felt a sudden, heavy aura embracing her as soon as she stepped foot into the room—a powerful, distinctive sensation. There was no doubt in her mind that Arian wasn't the only mage among them.

The first person her eyes found was a middle-aged man whom Arian politely introduced as Jalhor Zhaaran, Lord of Orestes—the northernmost quadrant of Bozar. His shoulder-length hair, dark gray and scraggly, blended into the bushy beard that concealed most of his face. A long, jagged scar ran across his forehead between the deep lines of his aging skin. The most intriguing thing about the lord, though, was his eyes. They were a bright purple color, smooth and vibrant like violets, and so fascinating that Aurelia could hardly look away from him.

Balor Zhoqa, Lord of Kazamir—the Bozari quadrant nestled between western Taundosa and eastern Khaba—was unfortunately next in line. He ogled Aurelia like a prized mare, taking in every inch of her with hunger boiling in his brown eyes. His sepia skin was peppered with moles of various shapes and sizes, and his head was bald with a port wine birthmark in place of hair. He wore a crisp dark blue suit adorned with medals, but he didn't seem to take much pride in his appearance: his face was sallow and waxen, his fingernails were black like he hadn't bathed in weeks, his teeth were yellow, and the whites of his eyes were jaundiced. He did, however, take enormous pride in the titanic sword tucked safely in its sheath at his side. The intricate golden handle suggested it was a prized possession—likely a family sword—and Aurelia's assumptions were confirmed when he refused to remove his hand from the hilt.

It was impossible to read the thoughts of Lady Odeya Swann of Runeia, one of the five provinces of Krotis, the third and final noble. She wore heavy silver chains adorned with diamonds that covered her face and flowed down her back, chest, arms, and fingers, as if the chains were a part of her being. Her lilac dress was made up of sheer layers that left her wrinkled, sagging arms bare but covered her head and hair. Her arms and fingers were tattooed with black ink, much darker than her russet skin, in a way that seemed to snake around the chains. From what Aurelia could see beneath the chains, Lady Swann had the same sharp, feline eyes as Kaia.

Arian beamed at the nobles. "Allow me to introduce Her Majesty, Aurelia Brentwood, Queen of Akkinor, and Mister Jack Sherbourne, a native of Akkinor and traveling guide of Carthe."

She smiled at the nobles. "I'm charmed to finally make your acquaintances. Though I've heard many things about each of you, I never dreamt I'd have the pleasure of meeting you. It's a tremendous honor."

"Likewise, Your Grace," Lord Zhoqa purred. The smile playing on his lips was nothing short of suggestive. When Jack shifted his weight, the lord gave him a sidelong look. "'Traveling guide of Carthe', eh? Is that another term for 'the queen's mistress?'"

Jack's eyes flashed and narrowed to slits. "If it were, my lord, I'd be the most envied man on all sides of the world."

The air felt thick with tension as Jack—ever the veteran swordsman—casually settled his hand on the hilt of his sword. Lord Zhoqa, too, sharpened his steely azurite gaze while his fingers tightened on his prized blade. Aurelia would've been livid with them (particularly Jack, who insisted upon taking his sword everywhere) if not for an amusing reminder: neither of them would've instigated the other if they hadn't been armed.

Men, she thought. *Pitiful creatures without their sticks.*

"If you two gentlemen are quite finished, we have important arrangements to discuss." Aurelia sat in the chair beside Reyna's while Jack, arms folded over his chest, stood protectively behind her. "Forgive me for being blunt, but each of us is well aware of the reason for this audience. Have you given much thought to my proposal?"

"Queen Reyna and Lord Cristos speak highly of you," Lady Swann commented. "It's our understanding that your alliance with Taundosa has already been solidified. Taundosa is the one and only thing we have in common, Your Grace. Why should I pledge *my* people to *your* cause?"

"Akkinor was already the most powerful country in the realm before our alliance with Taundosa," Aurelia stated. "Despite what my foolish brother has inflicted on my country, Akkinor's reputation continues to exceed all others. Please don't take offense to my boasting—take my words as insurance. I'm as educated on the politics of Carthe as any highborn. Your positions in your kingdoms are as fragile as mine. Becoming my ally will dissuade any potential usurpers from threatening your titles. Nobody in Carthe would be fond of facing the full force of Akkinor's military, would they?"

Lord Zhaaran smiled a bit. "No, they wouldn't."

"How can we trust that you'll be true to your word?" Lord Zhoqa demanded. "Queen Reyna speaks of your father and his honor, but you stand before us because of your father's son. You have honor for *your* people, Your Grace. Will you have honor for *my* people if the time comes for Bozar to ask for your assistance, or will you become less like your father and more like your brother?"

Aurelia's face warmed with fury. She felt both Arian and Jack watching her cautiously from the corner of her eye. They knew as well as she did that her temper wasn't one to be trifled with. Letting her temper take the reins, however, wasn't a smart method of securing alliances. The better method—her father's method—was to use her opponent's own actions as leverage.

She recalled everything she'd learned about Bozar from the hours she'd spent researching the kingdom prior to the meeting. Of the four quadrants—Orestes, Iseppa, Tucana, and Kazamir—only Kazamir underwent a shift in power from the time of the Bozari civil war in the eight-hundredth century (when the monarchy became a feudal system) to the modern day. It'd been Lord Zhoqa's own father who overthrew the previous Lord of Kazamir—Zakur—in a bloody, four-year-long power struggle.

Zakur had four daughters and four sons. His sons were beheaded as incentive for his surrender, and their heads were posted on spikes across

Kazamir. Upon his victory, Lord Zhoqa's widower father married Lord Zakur's eldest daughter, then betrothed the remaining three to his sons. He had more sons than Lord Zakur had daughters, so one of the girls was promised to two of his sons.

Polygamy, it seemed, wasn't uncommon in Bozar.

"If I remember correctly, my lord, your father took Kazamir from the Zakur family after they'd ruled peacefully for one-thousand years," Aurelia said. Lord Zhoqa's cheeks turned pink. "The late Lord Zakur was your wife's father, was he not? Each of her brothers was murdered by your father. You may speak of my brother's lack of honor if you wish, but only if you have the humility to acknowledge the dishonors of *your* family, too."

"I beg your—"

"Enough," Lord Zhaaran snapped. The younger lord clamped his jaw shut and narrowed his eyes. Lord Zhaaran softened as he turned his purple gaze to Aurelia. "You're correct, Your Grace. Orestes will be untouchable with Akkinor at our side. It's an irrefutable offer, I think, and one that shall benefit us in more ways than one. So long as Akkinor responds to our call in times of need, we shall do the same. My army is yours in the fight to come—and in the fights that may happen in the future. Can you say the same for me?"

She didn't bat an eye. "In perpetuity, my lord."

Lady Swann tapped her pointer finger against the wooden armrest of her chair. Her chains clinked against the chair as she did so, causing all focus to turn to her. She eyed Aurelia silently and diligently, and the young queen mirrored her gaze. The two stared at one another until Lady Swann broke eye contact, frowning beneath her mask of chains and diamonds.

"In perpetuity," she repeated. "That's a lofty promise to make. I do believe you're true to your word, Your Grace. However, I remain unconvinced of the benefits of such an alliance. It seems to me that I have more to lose by standing beside you than I have to gain."

Aurelia's heart thumped wildly. "My lady—"

"If you'll excuse me," Lady Swann continued, "I haven't had cause to visit Agotia in my lifetime. I'd like to tour the castle before my carriage departs."

With the rattling of chains and the screeching of her chair, Lady Swann was gone, and all hopes of an alliance with Runeia fizzled away.

Aurelia stared at the door, mouth agape, as her fingers curled into fists. She forced herself to blink a few times when her eyes burned. She'd accepted that it wouldn't be easy to sway the Carthinian nobles into supporting her, but she'd prepared for more negotiating before they approved or denied her. Her confidence—previously a fiery sphere igniting her insides with determination—was now nothing but a miniscule, dwindling spark desperately searching for something to cling to.

"Aurelia—" Jack started.

"The old woman has more wit than the rest of us combined," Lord Zhoqa interrupted. He took a pipe from the inside pocket of his coat and lit it with the flame of a candle on Reyna's desk. He leaned back in his chair as he exhaled a puff of smoke, seemingly unaware of (or careless to) the way the earthy-smelling fog encircled those around him. "I stand behind Her Ladyship. Apologies, Your Grace."

Aurelia hardly heard him. She was still staring at the door as if waiting for Lady Swann to return with a change of heart. The others—even Jack—were bickering over Lord Zhoqa's hasty decision, but Aurelia couldn't bring herself to participate. She wondered where she'd gone wrong during her argument, and what she might've said to sway Lady Swann rather than push her away.

She'd entered the meeting with every ounce of faith in Lady Swann. She thought the old woman would feel a sense of kinship towards her fellow female ruler. The three women in the study were the only females currently holding power across the realm—Aurelia assumed that would've meant something to Lady Swann. Apparently, it didn't.

The room silenced when Aurelia stood from her chair. When Arian inquired after what she was doing, she replied, "Securing an alliance." Then, without another word, she excused herself from the study and scoured the halls for the Lady of Runeia.

Emely spotted Aurelia and directed her towards the Hall of the Divine: a long, seemingly empty room in the western corridor of the castle containing nothing but paintings of magic, the gods, and the Elementals. Aurelia and Jack had been given a tour of the room by Arian not a day prior. Other than her parents, they were the only Akkinorians in history ever permitted to visit the room.

Aurelia found Lady Swann standing by her lonesome in the hall. Without saying a word, Aurelia joined the noblewoman and silently observed the painting hanging before them. It depicted Pherena, goddess of virtues and Almighty of Krotis, tipping water from a large seashell into the mouths of slaves. Scribbled writing on the bottom attributed it to none other than Katryna Cristos.

"It's a beautiful piece," Aurelia remarked. "She was quite talented."

Lady Swann didn't glance away from the artwork. "Are you proficient at painting or drawing, Your Grace?"

"Not at all. I haven't an artistic bone in my body, I'm afraid."

"Pity. I would've expected you to inherit your mother's talent."

Aurelia stilled as her blood turned to ice. "I beg your pardon?"

"Do you take me for a fool?" Now Lady Swann was looking at her, and with the many chains concealing her face, Aurelia could see nothing but the sharpness of the noblewoman's gaze. "I can smell your Carthinian blood. Your *Cristos* blood. The Lord Hand isn't the only person in this castle with magic—every reigning noble of Krotis is a mage. Had you properly researched my people and my culture prior to our meeting, you would've known that."

Aurelia scowled. She *had* researched beforehand. She'd spent hours in the castle library reading everything she could about Krotis, Runeia, and the Swann family (and about her potential Bozari allies, too). But that meant nothing unless she could prove her diligence.

"My lady—"

"The promises you've made today are worthless—nothing more than a means to reclaim your throne," she continued. "If you weren't so desperate, you wouldn't be concerned with Krotis. We mean nothing to you or your people. Why should I form an alliance with someone who desires my resources only in times of desperation?"

Aurelia's temper flared. She wouldn't snap, not yet, but she worried for how much longer she could keep her wrath at bay.

"If all of this goes to hell, my brother won't stop simply because I'm no longer a threat to him. He'll set his sights elsewhere—on Krotis, perhaps—and make it his goal to seize territories on other continents. He wants to show the world what he's capable of. I'd rather see Akkinor allied with Krotis than infiltrating your kingdom and corrupting your culture. That's exactly what will happen if I'm unable to stop him."

"Bah." Lady Swann waved her hand. "The Kroti are stronger than you think. An Akkinorian boy-king stands no chance against us."

Aurelia didn't reply. Her mind was swimming with possible retaliations, none of which would've convinced the noblewoman to change her mind. She realized then that it wasn't enough to use Archie's immaturity and greed as incentive for gaining support. She had to *earn* the support she desired, and such a task wouldn't be a simple one.

"Perhaps I *am* desperate," she admitted, "but not for the reasons you think. I'm not desperate to wear a crown or to have my every desire presented to me on a silver platter. I'm not desperate to have millions depending on me or to claim responsibility for things I had no part in. I'm desperate because I know that every moment I spend here, my people are suffering. You're correct—I wouldn't have come to you for assistance if all was well in Akkinor. All is not well, my lady. My people are in trouble, and I can't save them from my brother's greed without your help."

Lady Swann's eyes narrowed. "If you care so greatly for the welfare of your people, why did you flee?"

She sighed. She'd been waiting for that question. "If I'd stayed, I'd be dead. Nobody in Akkinor has dared to interfere with my brother's rule thus far. It's safe to say that, if I were dead, the same would be true. Who would rise against him if I were gone? Who would protect my people from his cruelty?"

"Akkinor isn't renowned for its bravery."

That made her smile. "No, it's not. Akkinor is famed for its honor, and I won't rest while a dishonorable man damns the lives of innocents. My people deserve better than that. Everyone does."

The noblewoman was quiet for a moment. "I have an inquiry for you, Your Grace. Did you honestly believe that your reign wouldn't be contested while a legitimate male heir lived and breathed?"

Aurelia's cheeks warmed with embarrassment. "Of course I didn't. I'm not that naïve. But I never imagined it'd be Archie who'd take up arms against me. I was too trusting, you see. I wanted to believe that my brother loved me and wouldn't take what was mine—by his own accord or by the urgings of others. I suppose it was silly of me." While Lady Swann snorted, agreeing with her, Aurelia bit her lower lip and recalled what she'd researched about her companion. "Your fears would've been exactly the opposite of mine. You didn't wish to rule Runeia, did you? It fell onto your lap after a string of tragedies."

Lady Swann stared at her, mouth agape, before shaking her head and chuckling. "You surprise me, Your Grace."

"I'd hoped to."

Her chuckle morphed into full-fledged laughter, but it died down as the mood grew somber. "You're quite right. My father was Lord of Runeia. I had two brothers—one elder and one younger. The little one caught scarlet fever and died when he was all but four. Our mother jumped from the nursery window when *ze pelzhar* pronounced him dead." Aurelia sighed with pity. The Old Carthinian words translated to *the healer*. "Father died about a year later when the fever came back for him. My elder brother took his place. He and his wife produced an overabundance of children— fourteen, to be exact. He had four boys, and each of them perished before adulthood. It was his wish that Runeia be left in my hands after he died. His daughters, may the Almighty bless them, don't know the difference between red and yellow. He didn't trust them to rule."

"That's...That's..."

"Quite the spectacle, eh?"

"I'll say." Aurelia offered her a small, hopeful smile. "At least your brother maintained faith in you. He must've inflicted quite a bit of chaos in Krotis when he altered the line of succession."

"He did. My counterparts calmed when they convinced themselves that the men of our family must've been cursed. The curse didn't seem to apply to me, though. I have five sons, all of whom have reached adulthood, and the fever hasn't yet returned to claim them. I pray it never does." Lady Swann exhaled and gazed at the painting again. Talk of prayers, curses, and unorthodox reigns seemed to remind her of the reason for their conversation. "The Almighty Pherena commands me to be charitable, to lend my resources to your cause. Your heart is true, Your Grace. I admire that. I will not, however, risk everything I have for a one-sided alliance. Krotis is a stable kingdom—each of our districts is at peace with each other and with the continent. I've no need for a military alliance with Akkinor when only one of us is desperate for it. The Swann family has lost enough as it is."

"I can offer more. We have ample resources available for export to Carthe. Akkinorian bronze, Myran wine—"

"All of which sound lovely," she mused, chuckling, "but I have something else in mind."

"Oh?"

When the noblewoman extended her arm, Aurelia took it and allowed Lady Swann to guide her out of the room. They were navigating the halls of the castle now, out in the open for all to see and hear them: a purposeful decision on Lady Swann's part, as Aurelia would have to be mindful of how she reacted to whatever was suggested.

"I have seven children, Your Grace," she shared, "the youngest of whom has just reached his nineteenth year. He understands he must marry to receive his inheritance, but no woman wants to marry a man who can't stay put. My son has spent the last three years traveling the world by land and sea. He spent two seasons in Akkinor masquerading as a Caedian sailor, that foolish boy, and fell madly in love with your country. He wishes to explore Akkinor further. That brings me to my proposal: find an Akkinorian wife for my son, and my sword is yours."

Aurelia nearly stumbled over her skirts. "That's all?"

"That's all. That way, Krotis will be more than just a solution to Akkinor's current woes. Your country won't forget us when our soldiers aren't fighting your wars."

Aurelia gnawed on her lower lip, contemplating, as the pair grew closer to Arian's study. Lady Swann was clever, she'd give her that: now, she had only moments to agree or disagree before they returned to the others with a verdict.

She thought back to her conversation with Lord Crowland prior to the uprising. Both agreed that it'd be easier for Lord Crowland's eldest daughter to marry a man whose status was equal to hers—in other words, a nobleman from another civilization. Cross-cultural marriages were frowned upon but not forbidden across the world. They were common between the kingdoms of Carthe, but certainly not between continents.

Dahlia Crowland was fearful of marrying below her status because she knew that, like noblewomen of the past, her husband would undermine her as Lady of Myra—the people would always prefer a man as the face of the kingdom. If she married a Kroti nobleman, though, everything would be different. A native Carthinian would never be favored to rule over a native Akkinorian. He'd have all the luxuries of Lord Consort, but he'd never have the chance to pull strings while Dahlia and her rule were belittled.

Of course, there were other noble girls in Akkinor who would've made excellent wives for Lady Swann's son, too. Dahlia Crowland was a wonderful choice, but she wasn't the only choice.

The hardest part would be convincing the Akkinorian people to accept a Carthinian as spouse to a noble. Then again, if Aurelia succeeded in securing her Carthinian alliances, her people would have no choice but to accept the newfound relationship between the two continents.

It was a risk she'd have to take.

***

"How pleased I am that you've changed your mind," Arian said to Lady Swann. "Pray tell—what are the terms?"

Lady Swann was calm and collected. "Her Grace has agreed to marry an Akkinorian noblewoman to my son."

"Really?" Jack's voice cut through the air like a knife. The tips of his ears reddened when all eyes turned to him. "Forgive my outburst. I hadn't expected..."

"There have been many firsts in recent days," Reyna commented, smiling a bit. "I suppose something like this was bound to happen sooner or later."

"Indeed." Lady Swann snapped her gaze over to Aurelia. "I understand the poor relationship between Akkinor and Espos. The pirates will sink our ships if they spot Akkinor's flag among our sails. I'd prefer that my men and ships arrive in Akkinor in one piece. To ensure this, I will personally discuss your ability to cross the Alkamura with Captain Lukos."

Aurelia's heart pounded excitedly. "Thank you, my lady."

If Lady Swann knew that Reyna had already promised to speak with Captain Lukos, it didn't seem to matter to her. The word of not one, but *two* respected world leaders would make it very difficult for Lukos to break the promise he'd made to Reyna—Aurelia understood that much. A pirate's word couldn't always be trusted, but only a fool would dishonor two of the realm's most powerful people by making false promises. Aurelia knew Lukos in reputation only, and she didn't take him for a fool.

All eyes turned to Lord Zhoqa, who still hadn't decided since hearing Lady Swann's change of heart. Aurelia knew he was one of the many Carthinians who despised Akkinor and its people. His participation in the meeting was a mere courtesy out of respect for Reyna. Even so, as much as he wanted to deny Aurelia, he knew her offer would keep him safe and rich for the rest of his life. Only his pride stood in the way now.

He glowered at her, knowing he'd been defeated. "My sword is yours, Your Grace."

She smiled. "Thank you."

Arian summoned Prince Vyar for the official signing of the written alliances. The lords of Bozar agreed to a basic military alliance with Akkinor: both would offer their armies to one another in their times of need. Lady Swann, on the other hand, had agreed to both military and economic alliances in addition to a marital agreement for her son. As soon as the terms were written on parchment and signed by each of them, the agreements were finalized. Now, the alliances could only be broken by treason.

"It's done," Vyar announced as the ink dried. Aurelia couldn't help herself when she expelled a sigh of relief. "Congratulations. History has been made today."

Aurelia beamed at her allies. "I'm eternally grateful for your allegiance. There will always be a place at my hearth for you, should you ever require a safe haven outside of Carthe."

"Likewise, Your Grace," Lady Swann said with a smile. "Our emissaries will arrive here at the end of the week to discuss our next moves regarding the battle with your brother. On your word, our armies will march to Khaba for departure."

"My fleets are yours for the taking," Lord Zhaaran added. "I will discuss safe passage with the pirate lord, too, just to be safe."

She tipped her head. "Thank you, my lords. My lady."

Queen Reyna offered to personally escort the nobles to their carriages. Vyar bustled after them with each of their contracts in hand. When everyone had gone, only Aurelia, Jack, and Arian remained in the latter's study.

"So, Your Grace," Arian chirped, "how does it feel to be the most powerful person in history?"

She blushed. "My uncle and his imagination..."

"I'm not imagining a thing. Not in this particular moment, anyway," he teased. She chuckled at him. "My previous statement was authentic, my dear, and just as impartial. I praise you not out of familial obligation, but out of recognition. There's never before been a foreign monarch who's succeeded in legalizing an alliance with one Carthinian kingdom, never-mind three! Even your father was unable to formalize such an agreement."

"I can't understand why," she admitted. "Why me? Why now?"

"You've given them reason to believe in you," Jack said with a warm smile. "In the past, leaders have sought alliances to increase their power. They've always wanted to be the richest with the largest territories and the strongest armies. Your brother is one of those rulers, and you're not. You seek to give your people the care and concern they deserve—and to do the same for the people of Carthe, if necessary. The nobles are more inclined to lend their swords to someone who inspires them rather than someone who intimidates them."

Though his words were meant to be uplifting, she couldn't help but shiver with uneasiness. Her subjects—mainly the nobility—knew exactly what kind of ruler she was, and yet, they still weren't inspired. Those who assisted Archie in plotting the uprising knew exactly what kind of ruler he would be, too: a person who used his power, privilege, and fortune to manipulate and dominate those beneath him for his own benefit. They knew his character as they knew hers, and still, they'd chosen to risk everything to give him a crown. It was harrowing to think that the people she trusted to govern her kingdoms (and, subsequently, to be responsible for her subjects' welfare) had chosen intimidation and greed over inspiration and prosperity.

Seeking to change the subject, Aurelia met Arian's eyes. "When can we set sail for Akkinor?"

"Within the next two weeks. Our allies will send diplomats and troops as soon as they've returned home. Once everyone arrives, it should take no more than a day to strategize before we march for Khaba." He opened the door for them and smiled. "We shall discuss this further tomorrow. A carriage awaits me."

"You're not staying in Agotia?" Jack inquired.

"Not today. Her Majesty has requested that I return to the palace with her to discuss the terms of our agreement with Akkinor. There are certain military secrets that can only be discussed between a Hand and his queen." When he winked, Aurelia and Jack had to stifle their laughter. "I'll send word when I'm due to return. Emely will be present to assist you with anything you may require."

Aurelia smiled. "Thank you, uncle."

"You're most welcome, my dear."

When the three of them exited the study, Arian escorted them to the foyer and said goodbye. The couple watched him disappear into the queen's carriage before the driver urged the horses forward. In the distance, Aurelia saw three carriages being pulled in different directions: two east and one west. Her allies had gone after only moments of conversing, and soon they'd send troops in their place. Nobles, she'd noticed, were the only creatures in the world capable of multiplying faster than rabbits.

Aurelia and Jack made themselves busy by promenading across the grounds of Ardiham Castle. After a few moments of walking in contemplative silence, Aurelia looked up at Jack. His eyebrows were furrowed, creating a harsh line between them, and his lips were turned downwards in a scowl. It was a funny expression, but it was clear that something was troubling him, too. When Aurelia reached over to take his hand, he snapped out of his daze and smiled at her.

"Are you okay?" she asked.

"Better now. That Lord Zhoqa..." He shook his head. "I could've killed him with that big ugly sword of his, right then and there. He would've deserved it, too. He's a wretched excuse for a man."

"Is this because he asked if you were my mistress?"

"It's because he was more interested in your breasts than your words."

"Men want what they can't have." She shrugged. "It's a universal cycle that claims responsibility for many of the world's tragedies. I'm here because of that. Lord Zhoqa may have denied an alliance with Akkinor because of that. You mustn't let it bother you, Jack. Instead, you must learn to be clever—much like you were today. A smart, quick response tends to have a much better effect than swinging a sword."

"Ever the voice of reason, my love. You were quite impressive today, too. Who taught you how to negotiate like that?"

"My father. Negotiation is a monarch's greatest weapon, especially when collaborating with people who aren't our own. I was lucky to have Reyna and Arian vouching for me. The nobles may not have given me a chance if Reyna hadn't entertained them."

"Maybe. Why do you suppose Lord Zhaaran was so quick to accept your offer?"

"I don't know." She raised her eyebrows at him as a sudden thought popped into her head. "His eyes were interesting, weren't they? I've never met anyone with purple eyes. Is that a common trait among the Bozari?"

Jack looked amused. "You haven't heard the stories?"

"What stories?"

"About the *lak'kari*, of course!"

She rolled her eyes. "*Lak'kari* are Carthinian folklore, Jack. Stories invented to frighten children and inflict morals upon those who have none." When she saw the look on his face, all traces of humor disappeared from her being. "Are you perfectly serious?"

Of course he is, she thought. If anyone had reason to believe in silly folk stories, it was Jack. The man she loved may not have been one to accept stories of religious salvation and miraculous blessings from the gods, but he was certainly a believer in magic. His time in Carthe had exposed him to magic of all kinds—including mages with more stories to tell than any average mortal in Akkinor.

"Very," he replied. "When the forest was uninhabited, it was overwhelmed with purple flowers that came to be known as *violets*. The first people to find the land were mages who discovered a multitude of purposes for the violet flower. Such extreme exposure caused their eyes to absorb the purple pigmentation. They harvested every violet in the forest until nothing was left—not even seeds to regrow the flowers from scratch. The coven was then unable to perform certain ceremonies, use certain healing remedies, or even eat certain foods without the missing ingredient. It became nearly impossible to live without. They'd used up the only valuable resource of the terrain, so they returned to a nomadic lifestyle and abandoned the forest altogether. The moral of the story is that—"

"—greed has consequences," Aurelia finished.

"Precisely."

"*Lak'kari* is the Old Carthinian word for *demon*. Everyone knows that. Did the ancient people believe the settlers of the Violet Forest to be demons because of the color of their eyes, or because of their selfishness?"

"A bit of both. Only the direct bloodlines of the first settlers have purple eyes. Those who know the story are able to identify them, but those who don't are led to believe that these people aren't human. It's something of an eternal punishment for the selfishness of the first settlers. Not only is Lord Zhaaran a direct descendant of the *lak'kari*, but he's also a mage. Everyone who sees him knows exactly who he is and what he can do."

Aurelia recalled the way Lord Zhoqa had obeyed his fellow lord. "That makes him quite powerful here in Carthe, doesn't it?"

"Remember what I said earlier. Most people would rather *willingly* follow someone who inspires them rather than someone who intimidates them. Lord Zhaaran is an intimidator, not an inspirer. That's why his family has had influence in Bozar for over a thousand years. That's why Captain Lukos will allow Zhaaran ships to cross the Alka into Akkinor—because nobody, not even that foul Lukos, will deny a person who's descended from the first sinners of mankind."

She couldn't imagine how the kind old man she'd met only moments before had come from such a legacy. She hadn't thought much of his purple gaze—only that it was interesting. She felt foolish after realizing that everyone else in the room had been well aware of Lord Zhaaran's ancestry. But then again, Aurelia knew better than anyone that blood was not the only marker of a person's character.

"Hmm," she muttered. "I must've slept through my lessons when we learned about the Zhaaran family."

"They don't often teach that story in Akkinor." Jack yawned as she furrowed her eyebrows. "Our homeland has its own stories, Aurelia, as do our people. If you want to learn the stories of Carthe, you have to hear them from the people whose ancestors experienced it for themselves." His lips curled into a smile when he saw the dissatisfied look on her face. "Don't fret, lovely. One day, people will be walking across these very lands, telling stories about you."

"What will they say?"

"There was nobody like you before you came, and there was never anybody like you after you were gone."

XXXVII

"Aurelia?"

The queen didn't so much as twitch at the sound of her name. She hadn't spoken or even moved an inch since Emely brought her to Arian's personal parlor hidden deep within Ardiham Castle—a private room reserved solely for the Lord of Agotia and his closest confidants. Arian had given Emely permission to share the parlor with Aurelia, and she hadn't understood why until she saw what it contained.

In Taundosa, it was illegal to own or display paintings, artifacts, sculptures, and the like from non-Carthinian cultures. Hanging on the wall in the parlor, however, was a portrait of the Brentwood family that'd been painted on Aurelia's eighteenth name day. An identical portrait was on display in the Palace of Akkinor, so Aurelia assumed her father had commissioned a duplicate for his dearest friend. It was the only way for Arian to watch his friends and his niece grow from across the sea—even if ownership of such a thing put him at risk of a scolding from Reyna.

Jack stood beside her and observed as she stared at the painting. "What are you thinking?" he asked, breaking the silence.

"That my parents are turning in their graves at the thought of what's to come."

Jack followed her gaze and studied the portrait along with her. Aurelia herself hadn't changed much since her teenage years. Her reddish-blonde curls, vibrant blue eyes, and defined features were the same as they'd always been. Her brother, on the other hand, had changed dramatically. He'd been fifteen when the painting was commissioned, so he was much scrawnier and smaller then. His smile was adventurous, his face was hairless, and the boyish glint in his eyes was as active as ever. The only thing that hadn't changed was the wild mop of blonde hair on his head. Nobody had ever been able to tame it—or him.

"Aurelia..." Jack didn't seem to know what to say. "They understood the laws as well as we do. Nobody—not even a person of royal blood—is above or beyond the law."

"I know that," she snapped. "Robert Cherrane didn't go to war against his brother, Jack. Neither did Alora, or Oleander, or any Akkinorian ruler who came before me. No monarch's sibling was ever foolish enough to incite a war like that, either."

Once more, Jack was silent. He hadn't seen the worst of her temper yet—she prayed he never did—but by that point, he'd recognized how easy it was to anger her. Nowadays, it seemed, her body was composed of so much rage that she no longer had to fear her temper exploding. She was angry constantly, even if she didn't realize it, and despite how desperately she fought to control it, she was beginning to wonder if the gods were pitted against her.

In the three days that followed her alliances with the nobles of Carthe, Aurelia had come to a painful realization. It didn't seem likely, given the circumstances, that Archie would accept her terms of surrender to save his own life. One sibling couldn't live while the other survived—that's the deal he forced them into. One way or another, reclaiming her throne meant signing her brother's death warrant.

If she'd had it her way, she would imprison him for life, regardless of how he responded to her letter, but even the queen didn't have that option. The law stated that a traitor of royal, noble, or lowborn blood couldn't stand on Akkinorian soil or breathe Akkinorian air. Some monarchs chose to exile traitors rather than execute them, but in Archie's case, that much was impossible. Aurelia would be perceived as a weak and spineless ruler for allowing her brother to live after he usurped her throne.

"Would you care to hear what I think?" Jack inquired. She glanced over at him and sighed. "I think your parents understand that you must do what's necessary for yourself and for your country. Archie is a plague on Akkinor, and you are its cure."

Her eyes welled with tears. "They must've suspected something. They must've anticipated that Archie would do something like this one day. I doubt they predicted a fight of this caliber, but either way—"

"—he's their son. Maybe they knew of his jealousy, but they certainly didn't expect him to do something like this. If they had, we wouldn't be here today."

Another burst of anger bubbled up in her stomach as her tears grew hot. "I wish they had. I wish they'd taken the time to know him for who he truly is." Her hands were balled into fists, her heart pounding with rage—and yet, she didn't know who exactly had frustrated her so deeply. "Had they done so, I wouldn't be forced to return home knowing that my success means sending my brother to the gallows."

He set a gentle hand on her arm to calm her. "It's not a simple task to rule a nation. You know that better than anyone, my love. I can't imagine how awful you must feel, but you're doing the right thing for you, for Akkinor, and for our people. I know nothing I say will make you feel better, though. Not for a long time."

A sharp pang pierced her heart. "He was never a good sibling, son, friend, or prince, but he *is* my brother. My baby brother. The earliest memory I have is holding him in my arms for the first time. I used to think that I was made to look after him. I was a sister before I was a queen, but he never wanted nor needed me, and I refused to accept that. Now...Now his remains will lay in the crypt, head severed from his body, because I must give an order."

"He chose his fate, Aurelia."

"*I* chose his fate." A long, melancholy sigh escaped her. "And he chose mine."

***

Seldom did Aurelia recognize Arian's flamboyant presence while in his company. The largeness of his being was, however, felt almost painfully in his absence. One didn't truly realize how fortunate one was to stand in his presence until he was gone.

She'd never met a person like him in her lifetime, and she was certain she never would again. He, like his late sister (so she'd been told) was one of a rare few. His individuality was derived from a multitude of characteristics: the mystical light behind his eyes; the way his imagination offered a sense of childlike curiosity and naivety, even for a man of his age and experience; and how regardless of the turmoil unfolding around him, Arian never ceased to bring joy to everyone whose life touched his.

Only a few hours after Aurelia and Jack conversed in Arian's private parlor, the Lord of Agotia returned to Ardiham Castle. Jack, sensing that Aurelia needed a bit of cheering up, requested Arian's immediate return to the castle. Aurelia wanted to be upset with him for pulling Arian away from his duties with Reyna for something so silly, but the moment she saw her uncle's playful gaze, she was infinitely grateful for Jack and his ability to predict her needs.

When Arian returned after dinnertime, the trio made themselves comfortable in the same parlor from earlier in the day. Aurelia was hesitant to return at first—she didn't wish to see Archie's face staring at her again—but it wasn't nearly as painful as it'd been before. Somehow, seeing her parents' faces in the same room as Arian brought her comfort. It was as if they were meant to exist in the world as a trio, like puzzle pieces that'd never fit quite right so long as they were apart.

Arian wouldn't admit it aloud for fear of disrespecting his queen, but he seemed glad to be home. He was far more tranquil at Ardiham Castle than he was at the palace: he spoke with a gaudier octave, relaxed when he sat rather than perching with near-pristine posture, and allowed himself numerous rounds of drinks rather than stopping himself at one. The castle was, after all, where he'd spent most of his life. It made perfect sense that he was more at ease within the winding, puzzle-like walls of Ardiham Castle than he was anywhere else.

The only place she imagined he'd be equally as comfortable (if not more) was the same place that brought *her* the most serenity, too: the Palace of Akkinor. Even after everything she'd learned, it was still baffling that Arian—as Taundosan as they came—had been raised in her home. They'd been tutored in the same classroom. They'd sat at the same dining table for every meal. They'd walked the same halls, tripped over the same uneven tiles, stolen sweets from the same pantry. Their childhoods had mirrored each other's in more ways than one, yet there were only a handful of Akkinorians alive who had any recollection of Arian Cristos.

The following evening would be their last in Taundosa. Upon his return to Ardiham, Arian proclaimed that they'd spend the night (the "eve eve" of their voyage, in his own words) enjoying the peace of each other's company rather than plotting for the future. There'd be time enough for strategizing in the morning, he'd insisted, and Aurelia was far too exhausted—mentally more than physically—to argue.

She was resting on a plush scarlet couch beside Jack, her legs folded to the side and her arms snaked around his, while laying her head on his shoulder and burying her bare toes between the cushions. Jack sat with his feet firmly planted on the ground and one arm draped over the couch beside him. His other arm fell over Aurelia's back as he balanced a chalice of Kanish wine on her hip. Arian was perched in a matching armchair to her immediate right, feet resting on a tiny ottoman, with his third glass of wine in one hand and a smoking pipe in the other. When the glass tipped in his grasp, threatening to stain the pretty cream-colored rug with pink liquid, Arian responded in time with his powers to carefully return the wine to the chalice. It was a near-instinctive response, and one he'd conjured before the liquid was halfway to the floor.

Jack took the opportunity to ask, "Was the late king fond of magic, my lord?"

"Ed? Most certainly." Arian tucked a gray curl behind his ear as he sipped from his chalice. "Our governess, Charity, used to say we were like *Vilifsir vi Sielashi.*"

While Aurelia burst out laughing (barely avoiding a snort), Jack frowned. "What on earth is that gibberish?"

"It's Quenosi for *The Emperor's Marmoset*," Aurelia explained. "It's an old children's story. Haven't you heard of it?" He shook his head, still frowning, as both Aurelia and Arian chuckled at him. "Quapebet is crawling with exotic animals. It's said that a handful of emperors turned the palace into a menagerie—they thought the animals were sacred and wished to have the creatures treated like royalty. Emperor Timman III supposedly inspired the story. He was infamous for taking his pet monkey along on his every endeavor. The monkey would perform tricks for the emperor and his court."

Jack raised an eyebrow at Arian. "And your governess utilized this phrase because...?"

"Why, because of the many magical tricks Ed demanded I perform for him!" Arian exclaimed. Aurelia and Jack laughed at the amused, exasperated look on his face. "Only our governess—and Ed's parents, obviously—knew about my magic, so dear Charity would sit in the audience with Ed while he ordered me about like a magical jester." He tried to look disappointed by his closest friend's antics, but he couldn't manage it; in fact, the shimmer in his eyes was bittersweet. "I miss those days. We had quite a bit of fun, the two of us."

"I imagine you must've gotten yourselves into trouble, too," Jack commented.

"But of course! Ed would've died an adolescent and a virgin if not for me."

Aurelia choked on a gulp of wine from Jack's chalice. "Good heavens."

Jack was cackling. "Oh, do tell!"

Grinning from ear to ear, Arian abandoned both his pipe and his chalice before springing up from his seat. "This story requires a bit of a show, I'm afraid." The couple laughed as they straightened to appear more like a proper audience. "The year was 1940 Post Creation. Two young men, just shy of fourteen years, were forbidden from joining their fathers for a hunt by one *particularly* overbearing mama."

Aurelia covered her mouth with her hand to muffle her laughter. She didn't remember much about her grandmother, but she knew Charlotte Brentwood had been quite the victim to her nerves.

Arian, reenacting the incident as if he were a theater actor performing a monologue, pranced about the parlor with waving arms and twirling feet while offering impersonations of those he once knew. It was almost difficult to remember that the man standing before her—the man who, after three glasses of wine, was impersonating the late Queen Charlotte with a linen napkin on his head to mimic her infamous locks—was also one of the most powerful people she'd ever encounter in her lifetime.

With an exceptional degree of devotion, Arian finished the tale of the day he and Edmund nearly lost their lives. The two boys decided to sneak out of the palace to hunt a stag while their fathers headed a separate hunting party in the forest between Seaport and the Folly. The boys soon found themselves lost in the forest and unable to find their way back to the Templar's Road. When they realized they were being chased—not by the stag, but by starving, feral hounds—they ran in hopes of finding civilization. Instead, the pair of them stumbled over the edge of a cliff they hadn't seen coming.

Aurelia knew the cliff in question. The northern border of the Folly was primarily composed of woodlands and sat high above sea level. The thickness of the foliage and the slant of the cliffs made it nearly impossible to see the ocean ahead. If one didn't know about the cliffs beforehand, one wouldn't know about them until they almost fell over the edge and plummeted several hundred feet onto the jagged rocks below.

At this point in the story, Aurelia and Jack ceased being amused by Arian's flamboyancy. Both were genuinely curious to hear how Arian and Edmund had survived the incident. Perhaps they'd narrowly avoided being impaled or crushed by the rocks, but the seas were especially rough at the bottom of the cliffs. If the current didn't sweep them out to sea, the violent waves would've thrown their bodies against the rocks and drowned them.

"For a fraction of a second as we fell," Arian continued, "I felt a strange, distant pull in my chest. Magic. I held out my hands—just like this—and the water below rose like a cyclone. It caught us gently, like a blanket, and carried us to land again. We sat there on the grass, sopping and traumatized, while the hounds ran off in fear of the water. Our fathers found us accidentally while searching for the stag. A servant delivered us back to the palace, and your darling grandmother gave the both of us a firm slap across the cheek."

"My word." Aurelia stared at him, dazed and intrigued by his storytelling, as she struggled to imagine her father being carried to the top of a cliff by a magical, watery tentacle. "Staring down at the rocks...You must've seen the exact moment of your death."

"We did. It would've been a horrible way to die—I suppose that's what my power was trying to tell me." Exhausted from his demonstration, Arian sunk into the armchair again and coated his parched throat with wine. "You experienced your fair share of near-death experiences, too, so I've heard."

Aurelia flushed crimson. "Once or twice."

"Oh, now you *must* tell us," Jack teased, pinching her sides. She slapped his arms to stop him when his fingers jabbing at her ribs made her jump. "You speak of your troublemaking ways, but I've yet to hear proof of it!"

"Get off me, you rotten fool." She pushed him away, making him cackle, and toyed with the ends of her braid while her lingering blush made her face hot. "I suppose I can tell you about the day Linden nearly got me killed. That story always made my father laugh."

Arian guffawed. "Now I'm intrigued."

Grinning, Aurelia told the tale in exquisite detail, though she refused to perform it as Arian had, as her best efforts wouldn't have come close to the marvelous show he'd put on for them.

It'd been the first night of the Changling (marking the end of spring and the beginning of summer) when she was ten. Her parents forbade her and fourteen-year-old Linden from partaking in the festivities after dark. Disobedient as ever, the pair snuck into the gardens—relying heavily on Linden's spiderlike movements—and decided they'd scale the wall so they could watch the celebration without leaving the grounds. It was an easy task for Linden, a strong teenager by that time, and for Aurelia, who'd gotten more than enough practice after years of climbing trees.

They'd reached the top of the wall and sat there, legs dangling over the edge, as they watched the festivities from afar. They'd brought sweets with them, so they snacked on raspberry tarts and chocolate truffles while listening to playful jigs in the distance. They watched the civilians, no larger than ants, roaming the streets of the Folly while drinking wine, munching on treats, and tossing coins at the jesters. Jousters left their tents in search of the women who'd thrown favors at them during the day's tournaments. Actors, singers, and acrobats welcomed visitors to their tents for short encores of their previous performances, and the children who'd been allowed out after dark lined up outside the tents for autographs and mementos.

Aurelia and Linden were sitting atop the wall for over an hour before they realized something: it'd be exceptionally harder to get down than it was to climb up. Linden attempted it first and managed to use a thick, winding bit of ivy as rope to assist his descension. He guided Aurelia from beginning to end when it was her turn to do the same. Unfortunately, his method didn't work for the then-Crown Princess, as the length of ivy snapped from the top when she was halfway down the wall.

She'd landed hard on the ground, the breath stripped from her lungs, with her wrist bent awkwardly beneath her. Linden rushed to her aid immediately and helped her steady her breathing before carrying her into the palace for a visit to the infirmary. As he lifted her, the friends turned their gazes to something on the ground a few inches from where Aurelia had landed: a cluster of thick, prickly blackberry bushes blooming with fleshy fruit and sharp, jagged thorns. If she'd fallen onto the bushes, it may not have killed her, but the thorns would've maimed her for life.

"My parents and Robert had been in the city watching the last concert of the evening," Aurelia finished. "A messenger fetched them while I was being treated. By the time they arrived, my wrist—broken in two places—was wrapped in bandages, and the medic was treating the flurry of cuts I'd earned on the climb. My dress was torn to shreds. They demanded an explanation from Linden, but it wasn't his fault. I would've gone with or without him. He wasn't punished, but Mother withheld dessert from *me* for the next fortnight."

"What a rascal you were, Aurelia Brentwood," Jack teased. "I'd have been at my wit's end if I were your parents. What if you'd fallen over the other side of the wall? The exterior perimeter of the grounds is marked by stakes, isn't it? It's a precautionary measure to prevent intruders from climbing the walls."

"That's right. Linden warned me about the stakes while we were fleeing the nursery, but I wouldn't have it. I was a bit intrepid as a girl, I'm afraid."

Arian chuckled. "My poor friends!"

"We had a good laugh about it after," Aurelia insisted. "My legs are perpetually scarred from it. Father said it served me right."

Jack snorted. "I'll say."

She whacked him in the chest with the back of her hand. "Don't be so impish about it."

He blinked at her. "Sometimes you really do sound like a common tavern wench, you know." She laughed so hard her chest ached, though she couldn't help but respond to him with another whack to the chest. "I'm serious. That vocabulary of yours certainly makes it easy for you to masquerade as a commoner."

She watched him, bemused. "Everything Lily Linden told you about my life is true. I spent half of my life in the palace as the future queen, but I spent the other half engrossed with the civilians. Remember the story I told you about churning butter with the old blind woman in the village? I might've adopted a few foul words that day. She was a spitfire."

He stared, lips parting, as Arian laughed into his hand beside them. Aurelia laughed, too, when she saw the crazed look in Jack's eyes. She'd said it to him a dozen times since he learned the truth about her, but only now was it finally hitting him that Lily Linden and Aurelia Brentwood were one in the same. She was determined, clever, vulgar at times, but very passionate, too—the same girl she'd always been.

XXXIII

Aurelia heard the door creak open behind her, but she made no move to acknowledge her guest. She simply stared through the gap in the golden bars encasing the balcony as the district of Agotia quieted for the night. The walls encircling Ardiham Castle were tall, but because the estate had been built atop one of the few hills in Taundosa, she had a near-perfect view of the sleeping villages below. Her legs dangled over the edge of the balcony, shins nestled between golden bars, as her slender fingers curled around the cool metal. She glanced briefly to her side when Jack sat beside her, legs folded like a pretzel, and set a comforting hand on the back of her neck.

"It's getting late," he murmured. "You should come to bed soon. We have a long day ahead of us tomorrow."

"Soon."

He hesitated for a moment. "Is something on your mind?" She exhaled and stared down at her lap. "I know how saddened you are to say goodbye, but you may return in the future. Ardiham Castle is as much your home as Akkinor. The gates will never be closed to you."

"I know. Leaving Agotia in the morning won't be easy, but it's never been my intention to stay—that much hasn't changed."

He paused again. "What is it, then? What's troubling you?"

Aurelia took a long, deep breath. "I realized something after we left Arian tonight. If I wanted to, I *could* stay here. Archie may not be the ideal ruler for Akkinor, but he *does* have a claim to the throne. His claim is as good as mine here in Agotia. If I wanted to, I could stay here and become Lady of Agotia when my uncle dies. That's what I was meant to do before my mother and father arrived in Taundosa all those years ago. I could stay here, in my ancestral home, safe and sound with a district to look after rather than an entire country. It'd be much easier, wouldn't it?"

"I suppose. But would it be the right thing to do?"

She smiled faintly. "No."

"No." He set his hand on her thigh and followed her gaze. "You were raised in Akkinor for a reason. Maybe it *would* be easier to let Archie have the throne and live out the rest of your days as a Cristos, but that's never what you were meant to do. You were meant to rule."

She released a long, painful exhale and reached for something under her leg. He furrowed his eyebrows when she produced a scroll with a broken seal. As she handed it to him, his eyes studied the seal: the sigil of the Kaplo family of Quapebet.

"What's this?"

"A letter from Emperor Timman VI," she replied. "My father reigned for thirty years without a single correspondence from the Quenosi emperor. In my five years, he's written to me twice. Neither letter carried good news." When she saw that he was looking at her rather than reading the message, she sniffed and nodded her head. "Go on, then. Read it."

He gave her one last look before tipping his head downwards. "'For the eyes of Her Grace, Queen Aurelia of Akkinor. On this date, I received a proposition from the usurper Archibald Brentwood, who initiated a call-to-arms in accordance with the limited alliance between the great nations of Quapebet and Akkinor. As stated in the treaty signed by our predecessors, Quapebet is only obliged to respond to Akkinor's *rightful* leader. It's my understanding that Her Majesty the Queen has found refuge in the City of Gold. Until your return to Akkinor, the alliance between our two nations has been frozen. Quapebet and Akkinor are now in a state of neutrality. I humbly request an audience upon your return to Akkinor to discuss the reason for your abandonment of your responsibilities to our country. Sincerely, Timman VI Kaplo, Emperor of Quapebet.'"

Aurelia grimaced. She'd all but memorized the contents of the letter since the raven from Quapebet arrived an hour earlier. Akkinor had been allied with their neighbors to the south since the days of old, as the two countries were the only civilizations to share a portion of their conjoined continents. Trade between the two was more efficient and profitable than it was between other nations, so the alliance was one of economic benefit. Since the treaty was forged, the rulers of either country had kept a safe distance from one another, conversing only when absolutely necessary. It was a weak alliance that could've snapped at any moment—and it had.

Aurelia was still alive, and as long as that remained true, she was the rightful Queen of Akkinor. Quapebet respected the chain of command more than anything else. Archie made a mistake by telling the emperor that she was still alive—and better yet, where to find her. Until Quapebet heard news of her death, they'd never support Archie or the whole of Akkinor. Even so, Archie had slandered her name to Akkinor's nearest and oldest ally. Winning the battle against her brother would be only the first step in convincing the emperor to resume the alliance.

There was another letter that arrived for Aurelia that night, but she couldn't summon the strength to tell Jack about it yet. It'd come directly from the desk of Archibald Brentwood, First of His Name, King of Akkinor. Archie had received Aurelia's letter, and more than that, he'd read it himself. He'd refused to surrender, as expected, and for a boy with such malice in his heart, he'd been surprisingly polite.

She could still see the words—slightly smudged because of his left-handedness and the amount of pressure he'd put on the quill—flashing through her mind: *You committed treason when you fled the country rather than staying behind to fight for our people. Nobody will stand behind a traitor who ran in the face of danger, only to return with even greater dangers at their side. Your place is among the savages you sought out instead of the people you abandoned. Akkinor will be just fine in the hands of its rightful king. If you disagree, you shall come around when we meet on the battlefield.*

There was more, of course, but it wasn't anything of great importance—nor anything she wished to think about in further detail.

She knew her brother so well that she could imagine the moment he'd crafted the letter. He'd be sitting at her desk while crafting a message that needed just one draft. He never stopped to think about anything: he'd write exactly what came to his mind without going back to read it over again. Even in the privacy of his study with no subordinates to observe him, Archie would've worn their father's golden crown on his head, all because he valued the appearance of power more than what it truly represented.

"That's good, isn't it?" Jack asked. "When we reach Akkinor, the only army we'll be facing is your own. The only potential ally for Archie to turn to is Quapebet, but they've declared a state of neutrality until the rivalry has been dealt with. Your forces may not outnumber his, but you certainly have more *support* than he does."

She sighed. "Akkinor has just lost trade relations with our closest ally. Are you aware of how greatly we depend on Quapebet for our goods? The majority of our spices, limestone, and cotton come from there. Losing even a week's worth of goods will be disastrous for our economy. It'll take years to recover from that damage, Jack. *Years.*"

"Your brother—"

"—is a fool. He took a risk and it failed. The emperor would've kept his distance from Akkinor as he and his predecessors have done for centuries, but Archie forced them to respond. My people will suffer for that, and I'll have an even larger mess to clean when I return."

Jack paused for a moment. "You still have something that Archie never will, Aurelia."

"What's that?"

"People who believe in you," he said with a smile. "Akkinorians are honorable people—they wouldn't follow Archie if they knew he was responsible for the uprising. Everyone in Akkinor is following him because only he has a claim to the throne in your absence. They don't know what really happened to you, do they? You'll return home to show our people what you've done. You'll prove to them that you've never stopped fighting for them. They'll flock to you, just as the people here have. Not only will you have the support of Akkinor, but you'll have the support of three powerful kingdoms to help you repair the damage from Archie's reign. Quapebet will return to you when they realize their mistake."

She closed her eyes. "I'll be facing so much hysteria in the weeks to come, but somehow, despite how easy it'd be to live out the rest of my days in this kingdom...somehow, the hysteria calls to me, Jack."

"Because you love your country and your people. That's the difference between you and your weasel of a brother—if he had the opportunity to run and hide, he'd take it. You wouldn't. You ran, but you never had any intention of hiding. That's what matters."

As she stared out at the sleeping district, her eyes began to burn. She didn't realize she was crying until Jack reached forwards and brushed a tear from her cheek. She sniffled and wiped her eyes, removing any trace of emotion from her face, before turning to Jack and forcing a smile. She didn't want to look as disheartened as she was going to sound.

"I'm scared, Jack."

His eyebrows furrowed, almost as if he were startled, but his expression quickly smoothened. "Scared of what, Lily dear?" She rolled her eyes and chuckled a bit, but her eyes still stung. "There's nothing to be frightened of. One way or another, the sun will shine as brightly for you in Akkinor as it does here in Taundosa. I promise." He leaned towards her and pressed a tender kiss to her cheek. "I'll be waiting for you inside."

He pulled himself to his feet and disappeared into her suite, closing the balcony doors behind him and leaving her to muddle by her lonesome.

In the morning, a carriage would take them through Taundosa, Bozar, and Khaba. Everyone hoped they'd make it to the coast of Khaba within a day or two, but that was if—and only if—they neglected to stop for more than a few minutes at a time. Then, as long as the seas were kind, they'd arrive on the shores of Akkinor after a few weeks of sailing.

Aurelia knew what she was facing in Akkinor. She'd always known—it was *her* country and *her* people, after all. If she knew her brother, he'd be initiating a call-to-arms for every kingdom in Akkinor. That meant she'd be facing six armies, trained assassins, and whichever foreign mercenaries he'd hired to fight for him. The monarch's Royal Army already outnumbered every other army in the world, and with the lords and ladies of Akkinor being forced to supply their own troops, Aurelia would be vastly outnumbered, even with her Carthinian allies.

Jack believed that all nobles of Akkinor were unaware of the details surrounding Archie's ascent to the throne. Aurelia knew better, but she couldn't tell him that. She didn't want to see the hope fade from his eyes. Her advisors, nobles, and soldiers were all led to believe that their queen fled the country during an enemy attack, leaving Archie to become their hero while she drank blue wine and ate sugared nuts across the sea. They'd fight for Archie until she showed them how their new king had lied to gain their favor. Her only hope was to rely on people like Lord Crowland, whose disapproval in Archie outweighed whatever they'd been told about their queen's disappearance.

Even so, there would be those who defended her brother in perpetuity, no matter the circumstances of his ascent to the throne. Archie was the sole male heir of King Edmund II, and in their eyes, he was Edmund's *only* heir. Even if a handful of highborn decided to join Aurelia's side after learning the truth, there would always be those who'd rather die fighting for a king than live bowing to a queen.

***

Aurelia bit the insides of her cheeks and watched as a large carriage slowed to a stop in front of the Palace of Taundosa. The natives watched from their homes or their spots on the streets, wide eyes full of intrigue and awe, as they had been since Aurelia's carriage arrived from Ardiham Castle an hour prior. Inside the carriage sat an emissary from Runeia, and behind it were ten troops sent by Lady Swann. When they marched eastwards, they'd be joined by troops from the Zhoqa and Zhaaran families of Bozar.

"It's time." Jack set a hand on the small of her back as the last of the Taundosan soldiers fell into place beside their Kroti allies. "We should exchange parting words with Her Majesty. Your uncle is hosting the emissary in the meantime. He hopes to leave Taundosa by the end of the hour."

"Join him, won't you?"

He furrowed his eyebrows. "My love—"

"I wish to speak with Her Majesty in private. Queen to queen." His eyes flashed with understanding, and he responded by pressing a gentle kiss to her cheek. "I shall meet you in the foyer."

Jack nodded. Without another word, he disappeared from the balcony and left her to herself. She clenched her jaw when she saw the diplomat emerge from his carriage. Below her, she spotted her uncle walking down the grand steps of the palace while Goldmen opened the massive gates for him. Without Linden, Arian had assumed the duties of Aurelia's Lord Hand; thankfully, Reyna had allowed him to do so as a favor to Aurelia.

Aurelia knew her time was running out, so she left the balcony and reentered the palace in search of Reyna. As she walked the glittering golden halls and murmured greetings to the palace staff, she wondered if she'd ever return. She hoped she would. One visit to the City of Gold wasn't enough, not for anyone. Saying goodbye to the place that'd offered her refuge wouldn't be easy, but the new alliance between Akkinor and Taundosa made the prospect of returning that much more plausible.

When Aurelia arrived at Reyna's study, the soldiers positioned outside of the door knocked and waited for confirmation from their queen. Upon receiving it, they opened the door for Aurelia and closed it as soon as she was on the other side. The two monarchs, one on either side of Reyna's desk, curtsied politely to one another before sitting.

Beside Reyna's chair was a small bassinet adorned with a golden mobile. A tiny babe—a girl, judging by her frilly white dress—snored softly with one hand firmly grasping a chunk of black hair.

Aurelia peered down at the infant and smiled. "What a sweet little thing. Your youngest?"

Reyna nodded, beaming. "The Princess Eida. I have three others, too. All boys." She tore her eyes away from her daughter and reached for a pitcher. "May I interest you in a cup of wine?" When she saw the way Aurelia instinctively wrinkled her nose, the Taundosan queen laughed. "I suppose I should've expected that. Blue wine isn't as popular elsewhere as it is in Taundosa."

"Too sweet for my taste." Aurelia paused for a moment. "Thank you for allowing Jack and I to stay in Taundosa. It's been an honor making your acquaintance, just as it's been an honor to become your ally."

Reyna glowed with pride. "Likewise. I've thought highly of Akkinor since I was a young girl—the honor is all mine. I sincerely hope that our descendants don't break the treaty of peace and respect we've fashioned." She took a sip of blue wine, swallowed, and raised an arched eyebrow. "Have you everything you'll need for the journey?"

"Ample amounts of everything, thank you. His Lordship has seen to our needs in all aspects. You're lucky to have him as your Hand."

"I am. You're just as lucky to have him as your family."

"Indeed." Aurelia smiled at the secretive shimmer in Reyna's eyes, then shifted in her seat and cleared her throat. She'd come for something other than gratitude and flattery, and judging by the way Reyna watched her, it was clear the Golden Queen was aware of it. "May I ask you something, Your Majesty?"

"Please."

"Why did you speak for me?" she inquired. Reyna furrowed her eyebrows at the question. "Forgive me for being plain, but it seems odd that all three nobles agreed to an audience with me after one conversation with you. Did you vouch for me out of respect for my family, or because you truly have faith in my success?"

Reyna sighed. "I'll always have a great admiration for your father. I also have a deep loyalty to Arian Cristos. But I won't advise my fellow rulers to send their men to war for a foreign monarch because of admiration or loyalty. I admire many people, Your Grace. I'm more loyal to others than I am to Lord Cristos. I may have offered my own services to you because of those things, but I wouldn't have risked so many lives and such crucial alliances because of them." She tipped her head to the side as if analyzing Aurelia, then smiled and straightened again. "I was a young queen once, too. I dreamt of changing the world. When I look at you, I see myself, long ago when your mother was older than me."

"You knew her?"

"A bit, yes. She was lovely." Reyna's fluorescent eyes shimmered with emotion. "You remind me of her, though you're a bit more poised than she was. She was a rather playful girl." Both chuckled. "Katryna could've conquered the world, had she been given the opportunity. Everyone in Taundosa believed that. I liked to believe that about myself, too. You *have* the opportunity, Your Grace. The world deserves the chance to see what you inspire."

"Thank you, Your Majesty."

Reyna beamed. "You are the product of many remarkable people, yet I see so much independence within you. I hope that makes you the kind of ruler whom I believe you to be. My prayers will be with you on the battlefield." She held up her half-full chalice of wine, the vibrant color of the anemone flower, and declared, "Forward, good man—"

"—ever forward." Aurelia smiled. Those were parting words, as both were aware, so she stood from her chair and turned towards the door. As she took a few steps forwards, something compelled her to stop and look back at Reyna. "What kind of ruler do you believe me to be?"

The Queen of Taundosa mirrored Aurelia's smile. "The kind who sees war for what it really is."

Aurelia instinctively wrapped her fingers around her locket. Reyna's sharp, hawk-like gaze followed Aurelia's movement. In that moment, Aurelia knew that Reyna had been keeping Cristos family secrets for a *very* long time.

XXXIX

What's going on?" Arian's voice pierced Aurelia's eardrums as he hollered to the driver through a small opening in the carriage. They hadn't been riding through Bozari territory for long before the entire coach was brought to a halt. They couldn't see what was happening around them, as the carriage was surrounded by Goldmen who were so numerous that they resembled a chain of shields and armor rather than soldiers.

"Nothing to worry about, m'lord," the driver replied. "The peasants are flooding the streets. Just trying to catch a glimpse of Her Grace, I'd assume. We'll keep moving when they lose interest."

Jack snorted. "We'll be here until the end of the week, then."

Aurelia tried to look through the window, but the soldiers were still blocking her view. Of course, they'd expected some type of interference from the Bozari people. Only two of the kingdom's four reigning nobles had been allied with Taundosa, so therefore only two had been willing to form an alliance with Akkinor. The other nobles wanted nothing to do with a foreign ruler. Prior to their departure from Taundosa, Lord Zhaaran's emissary had warned them of the possible greetings they'd receive from the Bozari. While some were intrigued and excited by the idea of being allied with Akkinor's queen, others were afraid the alliance would cause civil unrest in Bozar.

"The Bozari troops have already joined us," Arian uttered, annoyed. "If their people hinder our travels, the soldiers will intervene."

Aurelia frowned. "With force?"

"If necessary, yes."

"Oh, uncle, they mustn't." At his puzzled expression, she exhaled. "If the people want to see me, so be it. If they want to yell profanities and curse my name and throw things at me, so be it. They're already uneasy enough as it is. I'd rather not cause such unnecessary violence because a few villagers are blocking the road. That isn't a very wise way to start an alliance with the Bozari."

He smiled. "No, it's not. You're noble to think this way, Aurelia, but it isn't safe for you to leave the carriage. Southern Carthinians are different from the northern Carthinians you met on your journey to Taundosa."

"How so?"

"The other side of the Ngora Valley is intended for travelers and tradesmen," Jack told her. "Caedia, the forest, the desert—those territories are hardly inhabited by anyone other than the tribes and innkeepers. Nobody actually *lives* in northern Carthe other than in Kanibar and Dofell. It's for foreigners and businesspeople to do their bidding before going on their way. This side of the valley is different. Most natives have never left their villages and kingdoms, and even fewer have left Carthe at all. The people surrounding us haven't been exposed to many foreigners in their lifetimes. That can be dangerous."

"What can they do with so many soldiers surrounding me?"

Jack and Arian exchanged looks. Neither had a genuine answer for her. The Bozari natives might've verbally attacked her, but there were far too many people protecting her for any harm to come to her.

"Wait," Jack said as she reached for the carriage door. She sighed exasperatedly and raised an eyebrow at him. "What if your brother has assassins posted in Bozar? They'd rather die trying than not try at all. Is that a risk you're willing to take?"

She gave him a look. "You worry too much." He scoffed at her, offended. Arian laughed. "I'll be fine. We'll all emerge from this experience better than we were before, not worse. If you two gentlemen would rather wait for me here, you may do as you wish."

Without another word, she pushed the door open and peeked her head outside. Jack and Arian were both rustling behind her, so she knew they'd be following rather than hiding out in the carriage. It was still nearly impossible to see their surroundings from her stance, as the Goldmen towered over her with their arms locked and their collective legs looking like bars of a prison cell. The only way for an outsider to penetrate their barrier would be to attempt crawling between the soldiers' legs, and even then, only a child was petite enough to manage that. If Aurelia wanted to see the people—and for *them* to see *her*—she needed to open the barrier.

What she *could* see, though, captivated her. Taundosa's terrain was similar to the desert, but Bozar was different. The cerulean sky above their heads was cloudless, and the air wasn't nearly as dry and hot as it was in the west. The cobblestones beneath Aurelia's feet were imbedded with patches of dirt and grass, not sand, and a cool breeze caused the palm trees to rustle and sway. It must've been a beautiful place to live—especially with a view of all four noble castles atop their hills in the distance.

Aurelia approached one of the Goldmen. "Excuse me." Upon realizing who was speaking to him, the soldier removed his helmet and took a knee as a demonstration of respect. "You wear the crimson sash of a knight on your armor, Ser—?"

"Xantos, Your Grace."

"Ser Xantos. Forgive me if I'm mistaken, but I'm assuming you're in charge of these men. I'd like to see a bit more of the kingdom while we pass through. If I wasn't wrong to assume, please command half of your men to fall into line alongside the troops from Krotis and Bozar. The other half will remain where they are."

The soldier nodded. "At once, Your Grace."

As she stepped back to stand with Jack and Arian, the knight barked new orders to the Goldmen and returned to his position among them. As Aurelia requested, half of the Goldmen stepped out of line. They marched backwards until they were positioned behind the carriages and wagons alongside the other three noble armies. Only half of the Goldmen remained in their former positions. Now, Aurelia could see the entire village, and the entire village could see her.

Jack settled his hand on the hilt of his sword. "I don't like this."

"Be quiet."

Neither Jack nor Arian made a move as Aurelia walked along the perimeter of the soldiers' protective circle. She walked the circle entirely, studying the village and its people without saying a word. She could hear them muttering and whispering to one another in their native tongue while they observed her. Surprisingly, though, none of them booed or threw things or cursed at her. None of them so much as *twitched*.

Then, entirely by accident, she locked eyes with someone who towered over everyone else: a young boy watching her from his spot on his father's shoulders. Her eyes lingered on the boy rather than passing him by. It was the tears in his clothing, the lack of shoes on his feet, and the sunken appearance of his face that caught her attention. When the boy realized she was staring at him, he smiled and waved like she was an old friend.

Startled but moved, Aurelia returned his smile. Instead of walking in silent observance, she slipped through the gap created by the soldiers. Jack hissed something at her from behind, but she ignored him and kept moving. The Goldmen stood on either side of her, following her through the protective circle and onto the crowded streets. The boy's father, upon realizing the queen was walking towards him, put his son on the ground and squared his shoulders. A bead of sweat trickled down the side of his face.

"Good-Good day, Your Grace," he stammered.

"Hello." She crouched down in front of the boy and smiled again. "Thank you for inviting me into your village. I'm extremely grateful to you and your neighbors for allowing me to travel upon your roads."

The boy sighed. "I have not much to give, Majesty." He set something on her palm and smiled. "For your troubles."

They expect me to collect from them, she realized. She wondered how many nobles in Bozar earned their riches by collecting coin and valuables from the commoners. She was starting to believe that the natives weren't uneasy because she was a foreign intruder, but because they were uneasy to see *any* highborn person taking a tour of their village. To the Bozari, a highborn presence in the villages must've meant that some sort of compensation was due—that families were sacrificing a day's worth of food to fund the nobility's lavish lifestyle.

When she looked down at her hand, it took everything she had to keep from bursting into tears. A tiny wooden soldier sat on her palm and left chips of blue and red paint sticking to her skin. It was missing an arm, and one leg was bent at an awkward angle. Even the soldier's face had been rubbed away with only an eye and the lips left behind—faded images of what was once an exquisitely crafted toy. It was clear that the soldier had been loved deeply, but there it was, in her hand rather than the boy's.

"How lovely," she mused. "Thank you. But won't you be missing him?"

"Yes, Majesty, but Pa says you need soldiers." He gestured to the toy. "He is strong. He protects me. You, too."

"I'll take excellent care of him. What's your name?"

"Oslo."

"Well, Oslo, it would be incredibly rude of me to accept this great treasure without offering something in return. Is there anything I can do for you? Or for your Pa, perhaps?"

His father bent down to whisper something in his ear. Oslo nodded and told her, "Ma liked pretty glass. Pa wants to make her the window."

Aurelia eyed his father for clarification. The young man, no older than Aurelia herself, cleared his throat. "My wife died two weeks ago. She was fond of painted glass. Overly fond, really. It's impossible to find on this side of Carthe. I-It was her last wish for me to build a painted glass window in her memory. W-We couldn't afford a real tombstone."

A sharp pang pierced her heart. "That can be arranged. I will personally commission an order of Holosi painted glass upon my return. Your wife will have her window, sir—as will each of your neighbors. Now you may see your wife's memory in every window in the village."

"Thank you, Your Grace." The man's eyes welled with tears. "I hope the seas are kind to you."

"Thank you, sir." She hesitated when she saw the bronze coins nestled in the man's fist. "Why are you and your neighbors prepared to compensate me? One would assume that I'd be expected to compensate *you* for traveling through your territory."

The man's piercing blue eyes seemed to dull. "It's the law, Your Grace. When an individual of highborn blood arrives, we must offer what little we have as a token of our gratitude for your leadership."

Aurelia failed to suppress her scowl. "That's not how things are done in my country. Quite the opposite, in fact."

As she pondered—well aware of the many gazes observing her every move—she recalled the last wonderful day she'd spent in Mistcairn playing knucklebones with a group of starving children. Before she realized what she was doing, she removed her earrings (a gift from Reyna, gold-plated and encrusted with sapphires), set them on the man's palm, and curled his calloused fingers over the jewelry as he watched her with his jaw unhinged.

"I can see in your eyes that you are an honorable man," she told him. "You'll do what's right not only for you and your son, but for your community. Do with these what you will, but only if you can give me your word that you will proceed in the best interests of all."

He stared at the earrings, glanced up at Aurelia, and turned his gaze to the jewelry once more. Tears leaked from the corners of his eyes and splashed on the sapphires, giving the illusion of deep ocean water as the droplets reflected the sunlight. He opened his mouth to reply, but no sound emerged. Aurelia merely smiled, squeezed his arm in response to his nonverbal thank-you, and tousled Oslo's hair in farewell.

Before turning away, Aurelia spotted the man gesturing with his hands from the corner of her eye. He was speaking the language of the mutes—a language solely dependent on signals and gestures commonly used in Bozar, as the Bozari were known to remove a person's tongue as punishment for petty crimes. The punishment had become so common that the average Bozari, mute or not, was proficient in the language.

When Oslo's father signaled to their neighbors, those nearest to him mimicked his message for the observers in the distance, and the very foundation of the Bozari's reluctance fractured before Aurelia's eyes. The commoners crowding the caravan of wagons and carriages stepped away to allow passage across the road. Some, inspired by Oslo's sacrifice, fumbled through torn pockets and droopy linen bags for whatever treasures they could spare. When they began approaching Aurelia with their cupped hands outstretched in her direction, she commanded the Goldmen—weapons raised in preparation to defend her—to stand down.

"*Sasoma! Sasoma!*"

A trio of men each holding a young girl—no older than eight at most, and all wearing identical white frocks—pushed their way through the crowd until they were directly in front of Aurelia. She easily translated the Old Carthinian word *sasoma* to *majesty*. Just as easily, she recognized the glint in the men's eyes as nothing short of desperation.

The trio attempted speaking to her over the roaring of the crowd, and while she was nearly fluent in Old Carthinian, she failed to understand their unique dialect. Oslo's father, sensing this—and likely feeling the need to repay her somehow—translated:

"They've come to ask for your help," he told her. "Their daughters— among others—have been selected by Lord Zhoqa as brides for his knights. The oldest of them is all but nine. These men humbly ask you to intervene before their girls are taken away next season."

Aurelia's back stiffened. Children and even infants were often promised to future spouses by their parents on all corners of the world, but rarely were they forced to wed before their coming of age. Child brides didn't exist in Akkinor, so Aurelia had always assumed they didn't exist in Carthe, either. Not only had she been wrong about that, but she was now realizing they existed in Bozar, of all places—particularly here in Kazamir, one of the two Bozari districts Aurelia had promised to defend and protect. She wasn't certain she could turn a blind eye to her new ally's atrocity, even if it threatened to weaken their alliance.

The eldest of the fathers stood closest to her. His daughter, five or six years of age, clearly didn't understand what her future held.

Smiling, Aurelia tucked a lock of the girl's hair behind her ear. "I will write to His Lordship when I reach my lodgings this evening," she murmured. Oslo's father translated on the trio's behalf. "Our alliance as it currently stands is strictly military, but that's subject to change. I'll offer him a free shipment of Akkinorian bronze every season if he agrees to free the children and disband the practice indefinitely."

One of the men muttered something, to which Oslo's father turned to her and said, "And if he refuses?"

A lump formed in her throat as she spotted blue ink staining each of the girls' fingers. She recalled the practice of *feyh czarareth*—meaning *one who is owned* in the common tongue—from her studies. When a Bozari woman was betrothed, a combination of herbs and dyes was slathered over her fingertips to semi-permanently stain her skin, identifying her as a bride until the day of her wedding.

"If he refuses," Aurelia said carefully, "I will ask him what he desires in exchange for abandoning this practice, and I will give it to him. You have my word."

The relief on the fathers' faces was almost enough for her to ignore the uncertainty bubbling up in her gut. Such a promise would've been easy to keep before the uprising, but now, she didn't know what her country was capable of giving away for free—if anything at all. And if she failed to defeat her brother, it wouldn't matter what she was able to offer Lord Zhoqa. She'd be dead, and any hope she'd given the Bozari to see their children protected would fizzle away like it'd never been there at all.

She wasn't just fighting for the people of Akkinor anymore. She was fighting for the people of Kazamir, Orestes, Runeia, and Taundosa, too. Perhaps it was foolish of her to make such momentous (and easily broken) promises to people who weren't her own—or perhaps it was exactly what she was meant to do.

The fathers, still holding their daughters in their arms, fell to their knees and thanked her through their sobs. Those nearby who'd overheard the exchange used gestures, once again, to spread word of Aurelia's promise to the others in the village. Like the fathers, the other commoners fell to their knees as if in prayer. Some kissed her shoes and reached out to touch her hair. Others simply flattened themselves to the ground, still holding out gifts and treasures for her to accept, while speaking to her through tears in an unfamiliar tongue.

Overwhelmed yet empowered, Aurelia tried her utmost to politely decline the gifts without offending them. Many shook their heads at her refusal and dropped the items at her feet: old trinkets like brooches and pipes, notarized pages from holy books, and lengths of ribbon and other textiles. When it became clear to them that she wouldn't take the gifts, they abandoned their efforts and grasped the hem of her skirt, yelling over one another while speaking the same distinctive dialect. As she attempted to make sense of their language, she realized many of them—if not all— were repeating the same phrase.

She looked up at Oslo's father. "What are they saying?"

The man smiled. "*Feyh hishil ru zatyb.* 'One Forged in Gold.'"

When the First Mortals rose against one another (as they often did), the gods delivered individuals of great promise to the earthly realm in hopes of restoring the fundamental pillars of humanity. The bringers of peace, unaware of their destinies, bore the golden blood of the gods in their veins. Upon restoring harmony and unity to the realm, the Ones Forged in Gold would weep golden tears as the gods had before them, and humankind would awaken to greet a new age of salvation.

Aurelia knew the passage well. Numerous variations of the Creation Story existed across the realm, and each spoke of divinely chosen individuals said to be the bringers of peace during times of tragedy and turmoil. The golden blood of the gods created humanity, and only the golden blood of the gods could save it.

"I'm not—" she started, unaware of what she'd say next.

"What you are and what you are not don't matter to them. To us." The father's smile widened to reveal two missing teeth on the bottom row. "We have been treated like hounds and slaves for our entire lives. No ruler before you has ever treated us any differently. We won't forget that."

Aurelia's heart pounded so violently that she could no longer hear the commoners' speech over the roaring of blood in her ears. She stood still and mute while the people bowed at her feet and wept onto her shoes. She may have remained there for some time, had Jack not approached from behind and set a hand on her shoulder to signal their departure. It didn't feel right to walk away when she saw the way they were looking at her. A simple act of kindness had given them hope again—in what, she didn't know, but the recognition of what she'd done entranced her anyhow.

She said goodbye to Oslo and his father, waved to the civilians as they cried out for the One Forged in Gold, and followed Jack to the carriage. The sea of commoners parted for them as they walked, and each individual—the young, the elderly, the crippled, the strong—took to their knees when she passed them. Even when she and Jack were inside the carriage with Arian, the Bozari commoners remained on their knees on either side of the road, shouting blessings and thanking the Almighty for the day's good fortune.

Nobody uttered a word until the carriage jolted forwards. "That was..." Jack trailed off, eyes wide with astonishment and a touch of alarm, as Aurelia struggled to stabilize her breathing. She hadn't realized she'd been holding her breath until the thousands of pairs of eyes watching her reduced to two. "I've visited Bozar over a dozen times, and never before have I seen something like that."

"Nor have I," Arian agreed. "The Bozari commoners have never been anything but frightened and distrustful of the highborn. Not since the kingdom was a monarchy, I'd imagine. That was most impressive, my dear. Most impressive indeed."

Aurelia tried to smile but was unsuccessful. "It was an interesting encounter, but they didn't seem to understand that I hadn't come to collect from them. They were rather insistent that I accept their goods, but I couldn't. They have so little as it is."

"Don't you see?" Arian's dark eyes twinkled with wonder. "They were prepared to give you their coin because it's expected of them. They sacrificed whatever *treasures* they had on their beings not because it was expected, but because you did the same for them. They mimicked your actions for a reason: 'The Ones Forged in Gold would lead with altruism and compassion, and the First Mortals would mirror their behavior until humanity was restored to its former glory.'"

Her lips parted. "You don't mean to say you agree with them, do you?"

"Why shouldn't I? Even if it's untrue, there's no harm in faith. What you did today has given the Bozari reason to hope for a brighter future. It's the only hope they've ever known."

Aurelia gnawed on her lower lip, still in disbelief, and met Jack's gaze. "You've never been one to believe in religious tales. What do *you* think?"

He hesitated for a moment. "Those Forged in Gold haven't been proven as truth or legend because they've never been named. Many believe Oleander the Great was one of them, among others, but nothing has ever been proven. That, however, doesn't mean they don't exist. The gods wouldn't have written them into the Creation Story if they didn't exist."

"But—"

"The odds of you—or anyone else—being Forged in Gold are slim," Arian intervened. "That doesn't matter, though. What matters is what the people believe."

Aurelia winced. "This particular village may believe, but the rest of the world doesn't. Akkinor most certainly doesn't, and its people are the ones I must inspire."

"Word spreads as quickly as lightning strikes. What you did today may not mean anything to the majority, but it *will* mean something to those desperately clinging to their last sliver of hope. Given what we know about your brother's reign thus far, the Akkinorians have become the most hopeless of us all. They'll see you as you are when we return to Akkinorian shores, just as the Bozari have."

Her cheeks burned crimson. "I didn't intend for this. I only wished to lessen their pain as much as I was able to."

"That's enough," Arian pressed. "Had you done so merely because you wished to earn their favor, they may not have responded as they did. 'Hope stems not from the actions of one seeking power and glory, but from the actions of one whose soul has been promised to the betterment of all.'"

"A wise saying," Jack commented. "To whom must we thank for it? Yourself? Lord Dyron?"

Aurelia smiled. "My father."

Jack's gaze—both innocent and wicked at the same time—mirrored his smile. "Which one?"

"Edmund, you big idiot," she teased, jabbing her pointer finger into his chest. The trio laughed. "He used to say that bestowing gifts without expecting anything in return was the best way for highborn to prosper. Almighty Buen favors those who use their prosperity to help others without the desire for compensation. He rewards us for generosity rather than selfishness. My father also used to say that there's a fine line between generosity and—"

"—foolishness," Jack finished. Aurelia blinked at him, surprised, while Arian raised his eyebrows. Jack merely shrugged. "That saying originated in Omara, actually."

Across from them, Arian's eyes shifted to meet Aurelia's gaze. She knew they were thinking the same thing: Edmund had learned those words from Alistair and Isobel Ashford, former Lord and Lady of Omara. Not only were the Ashfords and the Brentwoods connected in government, but they were connected as friends, too. It'd been Alistair and Isobel who persuaded Edmund and Cressida to open trade relations in Caedia. It'd also been Alistair and Isobel who escaped on a lifeboat while Edmund and Cressida sunk to the bottom of the ocean.

The Quenosi Emperor sent a letter to Aurelia a few weeks after her coronation when Lord and Lady Ashford washed up on the shores of Quapebet. It was considered an act of treason to abandon the monarch in their time of need, and the betrayal was made even worse because of the kinship between Ashford and Brentwood. The country wanted to see Alistair and Isobel hanged for leaving Edmund and Cressida to die. Aurelia, wanting to keep civil relations with Omara, decided to exile the former nobles to Quapebet rather than execute them. She hadn't heard from them since.

Even after exiling his parents, Lord Bryan Ashford wasn't cold towards Aurelia. He was as Omaran as they came: there were no grudges to be held and no vengeance to seek. Bryan understood what his parents had done and accepted their punishment. Neither he nor Aurelia thought it wise to mention Alistair and Isobel after that. Aurelia respected his grief enough, too, to neglect mentioning her parents' names in his presence.

It suddenly occurred to her that Arian must've been acquainted with Alistair and Isobel. After all, he was Edmund's best friend, and he would've been Hand of the King, had life not intervened. Aurelia had only known the Ashfords as businesspeople, but Arian had likely known them as friends, too.

The caravan stopped on the southern border of Iseppa, the easternmost quadrant of Bozar, to feed the horses before proceeding into Kazamir. The brief stop gave Jack the chance to rush into the woods to answer nature's call. While he was gone, Aurelia took the opportunity to turn to Arian about the Ashfords. Even if the former nobles meant little to Jack, it was never kind to speak of such things in the presence of an Omaran. They were normally compassionate and honorable people, and dredging up such a scandal would only cause unnecessary tension.

"Uncle," Aurelia said, "do you remember the Ashfords?"

"That man of yours got you thinking, did he?" When she shrugged, he responded by exhaling and pulling at his beard. "I wish I could tell you that I haven't thought of them in years. In truth, I think about them often. Alistair wasn't a prominent presence in the government until after your parents were married. That's when he suggested that Omara be the first to open trade relations in Carthe, which required a great deal of work with your father. My time in Akkinor was over by then. I met Alistair and Isobel briefly at the wedding, but I never knew them as Ed and Cressy did. Not until all four of them came to visit me in Taundosa before you were born."

"Did you care for them?"

The corner of his mouth twitched. "I could've. We were never given the chance to become friends. To me, they were your father's subordinates. To them, I was Edmund's childhood friend. We never thought much of each other, but we could've. Nobody was responsible for the lack of care between us."

"I exiled them." She felt her eyes burning, but she refused to shed a tear. "Everyone—Linden, Archie, my advisors, the nobles, the commoners— told me to behead them and leave their corpses to the scavengers. B-But I remembered hearing the way my father would laugh when he and Alistair were together. My father never laughed like that with anyone else. Except you, I imagine." That made him smile. "I remembered how my mother would join Isobel for tea every fourth day. She left home at the same time every week, then returned hours later, drunker than a sailor. I quickly learned that *tea* was a synonym for *rum*."

Arian laughed. "Your mother could certainly hold her liquor."

"Yes, she could." Aurelia sighed. "I knew my parents wouldn't have wanted me to punish their friends like that. Regardless of the circumstances, my parents would've advised me to seek another route. And I did. Some called me foolish and naïve, but others called me wise for salvaging peace with Omara. I didn't spare their lives simply for Omara, uncle. I spared their lives because they were friends."

His eyes darted between hers. "For the first year after the accident, I imagined every way I'd punish them for abandoning your parents. They claimed Ed and Cressy were trapped and unable to be saved. Maybe I'm a fool, but I would've let myself sink to the bottom of the ocean before I abandoned my friends. Leaving them to die..." As he shook his head, his face crumpled with emotion. He smoothed it out and inhaled sharply. "I wouldn't have the strength to live with myself if I survived while my friends drowned. Even now, I struggle to forgive Alistair and Isobel for not trying as hard as they should've. But sparing them was the right thing to do, my dear—for your parents, for Omara, and for Akkinor."

She forced a smile. "Would you have done the same thing?"

"I would've swung the executioner's sword myself, but you're better than I am. You're smarter, kinder. Just like my sister."

Her heart ached. "You've experienced so much loss in your lifetime. How have you carried on? How do you wake each morning without feeling like the world has failed you?"

"Because the world hasn't failed me. Not yet. I thought I was the last of the Cristos family, Aurelia. Then you came along. I thought I'd said goodbye to my two best friends. Then you arrived in Taundosa. The people who loved me—the people who are no longer with us—left me with a reason to wake each morning. When I look at you, I feel like I'm looking at my sister again." His eyes sparkled with tears. "Your voice sounds like hers, too, but your speech is Edmund's. You speak like you're reading from his letters. There's a grace about you that can only exist within Cressida's daughter. Every movement is a mirror of hers. How can I claim that the world has failed me when the gods have blessed me with a second chance at family?"

"I hadn't seen it that way." She wiggled her eyebrows. "Have you decided to consider Mister Sherbourne as your family, too?"

He grunted. "Your father's ghost will blacken my eye if I say yes."

"Oh, most certainly."

XL

I hope everything is suitable for you, Your Grace." Emissary Zhaama, sent on behalf of Lord Zhaaran, stood in the doorway of Aurelia's bedchamber with his hands clasped behind his back. "This estate belongs to the Zhoqa family. You won't be disturbed by the common people throughout your stay. Our men are posted at all entrances and exits to ensure your safety. Should you need anything at all, please don't hesitate to call on the household staff."

Aurelia tipped her head in gratitude. "Thank you. When will we depart for Khaba?"

"After breakfast, Your Grace."

"Splendid. Thank you."

The emissary bowed to her and excused himself from the bedchamber. Now that he was gone, she allowed herself to relax and plopped down on the bed to soothe her aching back. She'd nearly forgotten how ailing it was to travel by carriage for hours on end. Fortunately, Arian had anticipated this and organized a night's stay in Kazamir, the southwestern district of Bozar, at one of Lord Zhoqa's family estates. Come dawn, Aurelia and her caravan of allies would cross the remainder of Kazamir into Khaba to meet their fleets on the southern coast of Carthe.

As she waited for Jack (who was confined to the washroom, as motion sickness from the carriage caused his luncheon to make a reappearance), there was a knock at her door. Two footmen greeted her with the only effects she and Jack had taken from Taundosa: two chests, one for each of them, containing the clothing and other items gifted to them by Reyna during their stay in the City of Gold.

Because it was customary in Bozar for highborn to dine in their bedchambers, Aurelia didn't hesitate to change into her night clothes as she awaited the arrival of her dinner. While fishing through her chest for a nightdress, she spotted something she hadn't noticed when her Taundosan maids were packing her things: a small, drawstring linen bag woven with strands of sparkling golden thread. A folded slip of parchment was attached to the drawstrings by a golden wax seal stamped with the image of a phoenix—the sigil of the Caltheos family.

Aurelia unfolded the parchment and read its message: *I pray you won't need this on your future endeavors. If the time comes, however, let this be a reminder of what we've accomplished together. The sun shall never set on an ally of the City of Gold. With luck, Reyna.*

Smiling, she opened the linen pouch and poured the contents onto her palm. A smooth, round stone no larger than a cherry plopped onto her hand. She recognized the onyx-and-azure stripes instantly from a description in a book she'd read at the Palace of Taundosa. It was *elvemar*— a stone born from the egg of a Bozari python, a magical species native to southern Carthe, that bore the power to heal any injury when placed within the victim's mouth. Back in Taundosa, Arian had told her that elvemar was nearly impossible to find outside of Carthe.

Aurelia returned the stone to the pouch and nestled it deep within her chest for safekeeping. As she continued weeding through her things for a nightdress, she saw one of Jack's possessions—a golden medallion gifted to him by Arian as a thank-you for protecting Aurelia on her journey. Tsking him for being so careless with his things, she opened his chest to put the medallion in its rightful place. Before she could set it down, though, she spotted something curious: a palm-sized Akkinorian bronze lapel pin that'd likely spilled out of Jack's knapsack while the chest was in transit. She hadn't seen Jack touch the knapsack since they were safely within the Palace of Taundosa, nor had she ever thumbed through its contents.

She would've thought little of it if it were any ordinary pin, but it wasn't. She recognized it instantly: she'd placed an identical pin on Bryan Ashford's suit coat at the ceremony proclaiming him as Lord of Omara. The figurine attached to the pin was a horse with emeralds for eyes— emeralds for the color associated with the Ashford family, and a horse for the family's sigil. Each member of a noble family was required to wear their pin when attending ceremonies or conducting business, and the odds of a commoner coming across one were slim to nothing.

Aurelia tried to convince herself that, given Jack's time and history in Carthe, he'd simply found, stolen, or purchased it at an illegal market. But every scenario she conjured was vastly unlikely. Akkinorian bronze was a coveted good on the western continent, and a man like Jack—a man who'd bartered everything but his horse to afford his nomadic lifestyle—wouldn't have hesitated to sell the pin to the highest bidder. Any Carthinian would've offered anything Jack desired for the chance to melt the pin and use the bronze for something more practical. It didn't add up.

She'd suspected from the day they met that there were things Jack was keeping from her. She—having secrets of her own—hadn't pushed him to tell her. She'd respected his privacy and his need for secrecy, just as he'd done for her, and chosen to believe that he was who he'd claimed to be: an Omaran soldier who'd fled Akkinor nearly six years earlier for a life of adventure in Carthe. She realized now that his tales were lies, and she was ashamed of herself for failing to notice until a silly lapel pin revealed the truth.

As she continued to dwell on it, she recalled more than one suspicious incident she'd brushed off since their first meeting. The more she thought, the more she was convinced she knew exactly who Jack Sherbourne really was.

I may have left Akkinor eventually, but the target on my back was particularly convincing at the time.

I left Akkinor for a reason. I swore I'd never return.

I'm certainly no lord, Aurelia. I couldn't say.

As dark spots clouded her vision, the door to the washroom opened, and a gray-faced Jack emerged with a groan. He smiled when he saw her perched on the bed across from him, but upon recognizing the fury and betrayal in her eyes, his smile faded, and his complexion grew even paler.

"Aurelia? Is everything all right?"

She tossed the pin onto the floor by his feet and winced when it clattered against the wood. His eyes enlarged as he realized what the object was. When he finally looked up at her again, every ounce of blood had drained from his face.

The Queen of Akkinor didn't bat an eye. "Have a seat, Mister Ashford."

***

The tension radiating between Aurelia and Jack was suffocating as he stared at her from across their bedchamber, still and silent, appearing sicklier than he had prior to expelling the contents of his stomach. More emotions than Aurelia could count passed over his face: guilt, relief, fear, dismay—the list was eternal.

"Aurelia," he whispered, "I don't under—"

"You understand perfectly." A cruel, humorless laugh gurgled in her throat. "I must admit, I didn't anticipate this. I should've, but I didn't. Did you enjoy playing me for a fool? Was it entertaining for you, wondering if I'd ever put the pieces together?"

"Of course not!" His oceanic eyes bugged out of his skull as he rushed towards her. He knelt on the floor in front of her and attempted to take her hands, but she wrenched them from his grip. "Aurelia—"

She stood abruptly, nearly trampling him, and trudged off as if to storm out of the room. She closed her eyes as she faced the door and took one deep, calming breath. She knew what might happen if she let her temper get the best of her, and this wasn't a conversation she wanted to lose to a blind rage.

"About six years ago," she said quietly, "the palace received word of an attack on the Templar's Road in Omara. Religious radicals overwhelmed a caravan of travelers including five soldiers, two emissaries, and the heir to Lordship of Omara. Save one lone soldier burdened with telling their tale, the entire caravan was slaughtered and sacrificed. The country mourned the loss of Arthur Ashford, and his brother became Lord of Omara one year later after their parents' exile." Blinking through hot, angry tears, she turned to face him again. "You're Arthur Ashford, aren't you?"

Guilt was etched into every crevice of his face. "Yes."

Aurelia's eyes fell shut again. Never before had she felt like such a fool. She'd often prided herself for her cleverness, and yet, she'd allowed her feelings for Jack to fog her judgement. The signs were all around her: an Omaran citizen who'd left the shores of Akkinor over five years prior; a commoner who somehow recognized the ballads of the highborn children; a man who held himself with the poise and dignity of a noble, but who claimed to be nothing more than a soldier; and a person who never spoke of his family, but who had a debilitating fear of the ocean.

He wasn't Jack Sherbourne, former citizen of Omara and traveler of Carthe. He was the presumed dead Arthur Ashford, former heir to Lordship of Omara, and eldest son of the disgraced Lord Alistair and Lady Isobel Ashford.

Their lives had been connected long before their first encounter in the Violet Forest. Their parents had been friends for decades. Edmund and Cressida had taken many trips to Carthe with Alistair and Isobel, and the two couples were constantly visiting one another at their homes. Aurelia's parents had seen quite a bit of Arthur when they visited Omara. She assumed that all four of the Ashford children had visited the palace during her lifetime, too. She and Jack had probably crossed paths more times than they realized when they were children who didn't know any better.

"I don't wish to look at you," she murmured. She heard him sigh. "I would, however, be most inclined to hear whatever explanation you've prepared."

Jack cleared his throat. "The story as you've heard it is true, for the most part. We were attacked on our way to Sadia. When the radicals were preparing us like pigs for slaughter..." He trailed off, cleared his throat again, and took a deep breath. "There was an adolescent among them. No older than fourteen. I could see in his eyes that he disapproved of his peoples' behaviors. I managed to speak with him when the others were distracted, and we made a deal: if he cut me loose and set me free, I'd help him escape. He agreed."

Aurelia, now with her eyes open, began to pace. "And then?"

"We slipped away and ran until we came across a farm. Stole the horses in the stable and rode to Seaport. I was planning to see him aboard a ship to Carthe before I sought salvation at the palace. He reminded me of something I'd forgotten—religious radicals don't abide by our customs or laws. His people knew who I was, and as such, they wouldn't stop until they reclaimed their intended noble sacrifice." He stifled a bitter laugh. "Your father would've been unable to punish them anyway. That's the law. So instead of risking my life and the lives of my loved ones, I joined him and traveled to Carthe. I intended on staying only for a few weeks. Then I heard about my parents, and I knew I had to stay. My brother was more suited for lordship than I—he always had been."

She tried to think of a counterargument, to no avail. Oleander the Great had passed a royal decree following the rebellion that banned religious persecution in Akkinor. Those who didn't worship Buen as their Almighty—and whose religious practices weren't customary or traditional—were free to worship whomever they pleased, however they pleased. Even the monarch couldn't punish them for actions committed in the name of religious freedom. It was one of many ancient (and toilsome) laws established by Oleander the Great, who promised the radicals eternal religious freedom in exchange for their support in the battle against Queen Alora.

If Jack had gone to Edmund for help, Aurelia's father would've had his hands tied. He couldn't punish the radicals for attempting to kill a nobleman's son, as some of their rituals demanded a highborn sacrifice. Even with ample protection detail, Jack would've risked his life every day he traveled beyond the walls of Witton Castle.

Still, Aurelia couldn't overcome her feelings of betrayal. "You lied to me, Jack. You've lied to me about who you are from the moment we met."

"You lied to me, too."

"This is different," she seethed. Now she was gazing at him again, and the sheer ferocity of her glare made him appear to shrink in size. "I was a queen with a bounty on my head. You are supposed to be dead. Even so, you should've told me the truth the moment you learned the truth about me. You shouldn't have been so furious with me after you learned the truth, either. It wasn't right."

"I'm sorry, my love. I didn't intend to cause you any distress. I was merely...I was merely concerned with placing you in an unfavorable position. You said it yourself—I'm supposed to be dead. Even if I wasn't Lord of Omara when I fled, I was still my father's heir. The people may wish to try me as a traitor for abandoning Omara. I didn't want to add that to your extensive list of responsibilities. Not yet."

She softened, but not by much. He was right about that, too. "I'm the queen, Jack. So long as you stand by my side, you needn't worry for how our people respond." She shook her head and scoffed. "Arthur Ashford, alive and well, having spent the last five years in Carthe. I never imagined..." She sighed and returned to her seat at the foot of the bed. Jack was still crouched on the floor where she'd left him. "Why didn't you write to your family? To let them know you were all right?"

"Because they would've done everything in their power to bring me home," he said. She frowned, puzzled. "I was frightened, in truth. Frightened of the radicals and of the reign of terror they might've set upon my family if they knew where I was. That, and, well...It was a gut feeling, really. As if I was meant to stay on this continent. As if I'd have a greater purpose here." He offered her a small smile as he brushed hair from her face and cupped her cheek. "You were that purpose. You are my purpose."

She allowed herself a smile, too. "We were fated for one another, weren't we?"

Jack grinned. "We met as children, you know. You were far too young to remember, but I certainly do. Our mothers put us in a room with Bryan and our governess while they had tea. I got us into trouble."

"I don't remember that. I don't remember ever meeting you, come to think of it. You were never present at Witton when I visited. You never came to any events at the palace or elsewhere, either. Why is that?"

He grimaced and retracted his hands. "I didn't get along splendidly with my father. We tended to disagree over our different perspectives on life. He'd bring Bryan with him on trips to the other kingdoms instead of myself. My brother was willing to endure balls and parties and such, and my father was always willing to take him. He'd send me away on business trips rather than take me along. While my brother danced at your name day parties, I sat in musty offices and completed the cumbersome tasks my father asked me to finish on his behalf."

Aurelia scowled. That didn't sound like the man she loved. Jack hadn't been fond of enduring the boring business meetings Aurelia had asked him to attend in Taundosa. He was a fighter and a survivor, not a businessman. He loved the thrill of an impulsive adventure, the liberating feeling of galloping through the trees with Sterling, and the independence of doing whatever his heart told him to do. He was a free spirit, her Jack. Perhaps *that* was why his father had restrained him.

Jack had spent the majority of his life in a cage with clipped wings, and he'd freed himself all on his own. She couldn't remain angry with him for that.

"I didn't know," she whispered. "I'm sorry."

He waved her off. "It's all right. I decided to let my soul guide me all those years ago, Aurelia. I knew what would happen if I ever returned to Akkinor, and I've prepared to face those consequences as the country sees fit. My biggest and only regret, though, is hurting you while I attempted to protect my own fate. I should've been honest with you."

"Yes, you should've." She smiled and brushed a curl from his forehead. "You must really love me to come back and risk your life." As the realization settled in, the smile faded from her lips, and tears bubbled on her eyelashes as her chin began to tremble. "You must really love me."

***

Bryan Ashford glanced down at his hands when he felt a sudden stinging sensation along the pads of his fingers. An inaudible curse escaped his lips upon spotting tiny pinpricks of blood blossoming over his fingertips. Dark crimson droplets had already stained the armrest of his chair: a wooden structure whose seat was far too low to the ground, and whose backrest extended several feet above Bryan's head. It wasn't the bronze, emerald-encrusted throne he'd grown accustomed to utilizing when he visited the Palace of Akkinor, but a dusty, termite-eaten seat likely taken from storage.

The former queen had commissioned exquisite thrones for each of her nobles to use during their visits to the palace. Though the magnificent seats were removed from the throne room when the nobles weren't in attendance, they always returned in time for Akkinor's five leaders to arrive. The thrones hadn't been seen since the queen's brother took her place as monarch, as the new king didn't wish to present himself as equal to his subordinates by providing them with thrones that rivaled his.

Three wooden chairs sat on either side of the king's enormous, gold-plated throne, but only one—reserved for the Lord Hand—was empty. Lord Crowland of Myra sat directly to Bryan's right, and Lady Tarre of Holos to *his* right. Lady Spirre of Sadia sat across from Bryan, with Lord Reilly of Laynoa seated between the noblewoman and the Lord Hand. Of the five faces present in the throne room, each of them knew the reason they'd been summoned to the palace that day. Only two—Lady Spirre and Lord Reilly—were entirely at ease, as they conversed and chuckled with one another. The remaining three hadn't uttered a word since they arrived.

Lady Spirre was in oddly high spirits for someone who'd just received a scolding from the king. Having deduced her plans to marry him to her niece (seven years' his junior at fifteen), the king had supposedly reprimanded her loud enough for the entire palace to overhear the exchange. Servants and soldiers tended to gossip, so it wasn't long before the rest of the country heard about what'd happened. Not long after, the king sent copies of the same letter to every noble in Akkinor, demanding they cease their efforts to marry him to the eligible young women in their families. He, like most unmarried young men, didn't seem interested in taking a wife until he exerted his energy on as many maidens as he desired.

At the least, he seemed unwilling to take a bride while knowing he'd dishonor her by warming his bed with mistresses. It was perhaps the last thread of honor he maintained that connected him to his late father. Without it, only his looks and his name offered him any relation to Edmund Brentwood.

Just then, the doors opened, and the king strode into the throne room with the Lord Hand trailing several paces behind him. Upon his arrival, his guests rose from their seats to bow or curtsy in greeting. Nobody returned to their seats until the king was comfortably perched on his throne. Even then, the audience was delayed by several seconds as Lord Crowland struggled to assist Lady Tarre in lowering her brittle, aging body onto the much-too-low chair she'd been provided with.

The old woman hadn't had the strength to climb out of bed in years, but the king—insisting upon a meeting with all five reigning nobles, not their representatives or advisors—refused to exempt her from the audience. Since her arrival that morning, she'd done nothing but fall asleep in her chair and ask Lord Crowland what she was doing at the palace. Her son, the acting Lord of Holos, was probably ripping his own hair out as he imagined what his poor, senile mother was saying or doing in the king's presence.

King Archie adjusted his lopsided crown. "Thank you for arriving so swiftly. We must discuss a matter of great importance—a matter which requires extreme haste and dedication. It's come to my attention that my sister has somehow managed to woo the Queen of Taundosa and her allies from Bozar and Krotis. She threatens us with a massacre if we fail to abide by her terms. With that being said, each of us in this room must prepare our men for war."

Bryan stiffened. After a moment of deafening silence, Lord Reilly was the first to speak: "When can we expect her?"

"Uncertain. I have scouts posted on every ship currently sailing the Crystal Sea. They'll send a raven as soon as she's spotted."

"All due respect, my king," Lord Crowland intervened, "but that won't do us much good if she takes the Alka. The Esposi may not be fond of us Akkinorians, but if she's sailing aboard Carthinian ships—"

"A fleet of Carthinian warships destined for Akkinor would certainly catch the pirates' attention." Tyren Silio, Hand of the King, eyed the nobleman with caution and disdain. "She wouldn't make it halfway across the Alka. We needn't worry about that."

"Either way, we shall have more than enough time to prepare our troops and deliver them here to the Folly," the king continued. "I'd suggest deploying your troops to the Folly immediately for training and preparations. So long as they're already here, we needn't worry about being unprepared for yet another ambush."

Lord Crowland raised an eyebrow. "And what of the commoners?"

King Archie blinked at him. "What about them?"

"Where shall we evacuate them to prior to the battle?"

"We won't be evacuating anyone."

Another round of silence pierced the throne room. Even Lord Reilly and Lady Spirre, the king's closest allies among the highborn, had shock and concern etched onto their faces. They may not have had any real love for the commonfolk, but at the very least, their honor prevailed enough for them to remember wartime protocol.

"We need them." The king's sharp, somewhat adolescent voice rang out again when he realized his mistake. "Half of them are able-bodied young men who scorn my sister's name for abandoning them during their time of greatest need. They won't hesitate to join the fight against her— soldiers or not. The other half will protect us from her allies' savagery. Her troops will have no choice but to lay siege to everything in their wake before they reach us on the battlefield."

Bryan's clear blue eyes widened. "But, Your Grace—"

"I won't hear another word of it. It's decided." The king narrowed his eyes as a pesky lock of thick blond hair fell over his forehead. "Have you something else to say, my lord?"

Bryan shifted in his seat, uneasy. "As you know, Your Grace, Omarans aren't warring people. We haven't had cause to deploy our troops in—well, ever. My men aren't trained for war, but for guardianship. It's written into the Accords that Omara may not raise arms against others unless the matter threatens the survival of our kingdom."

"I *am* the Accords," the king snapped. "I *am* the law. I don't care about what your ancestors believed was right. I don't care that your men are incompetent. We need every sword we can get if we're to defeat my sister. One way or another, four armies of lawless heathens will invade our country and tear it apart in my sister's name. Omara won't be exempt from their conquest simply because you claim to be a peaceful kingdom. If you disagree, please speak now—there are more than enough highborn willing to claim Omara as their own if you prove to be incapable."

Bryan's cheeks warmed. "Yes, Your Grace. I understand."

"I should hope so. Your sisters are far too young and far too beautiful to find themselves in early graves because of your disobedience."

Bryan's blood turned to ice in his veins. The king maintained eye contact for just a moment longer before he addressed Lord Reilly regarding the latter's plans for the former queen. Bryan hardly heard a word of it. The king had only mentioned Bryan's two younger sisters, but everyone in the room knew the threat extended to the entirety of the Ashford family: including Bryan's wife and their three young children. If Bryan failed to support the king in the latter's war against his sister, he wouldn't just lose his own head—he'd be signing the death warrants of everyone he loved, too.

There'd been plenty of moments in the past five years when Bryan missed his late elder brother, Arthur—known to those closest to him as *Jack*, his middle name. There hadn't been nearly as many moments when Bryan wished his brother had survived long enough to become lord in his place. This was one of those moments. Jack certainly hadn't been built for lordship (nor trained for it—their father's doing), but he'd been born to lead. He was cleverer than Bryan; clever enough that he could've moved mountains if it meant protecting his family and his subjects. Had it been Jack sitting in the Lord of Omara's chair that day, he would've found a way to preserve Omara's values without damning those he loved.

Bryan sighed. He wondered what might've happened if that cleverness had been enough for Jack to survive what'd been done to him all those years ago. If only that cleverness, compassion, and courage had been granted to their father's second son, too. If it had, Bryan would've found his voice rather than keeping mum while a boy in a crown threatened everything he held dear.

"I shall see each of you on the battlefield." The king rose from his throne, prompting the others to follow suit. His eyes seemed to land on all five faces for longer than necessary as his gaze traveled the room. The look of his eyes mirrored his father's almost exactly, but the way they shined with such malice, selfishness, and hunger for power would've made Edmund turn in his grave. Before he left, he offered the nobles one final piece of advice—or a warning, depending on one's preference: "Don't forget who rescued you all those weeks ago, and don't forget who put you in a position to be rescued."

XLI

H ere we are." Arian peered through the carriage window and grinned before sinking back against his seat. His eyes found Jack. "Have you spent much time in Khaba, Arthur?"

Jack grunted as Aurelia and her uncle cackled. "I have, and please, refrain from using that awful name." Aurelia snorted and attempted to mask it with a cough. "Of all the *A* names common to Akkinor, I shall never understand why my parents chose *Arthur*."

Aurelia cracked a smile. "It doesn't suit you very well, does it?"

"Hence the reason I've only used my given name professionally. Nearly everyone has called me Jack since I was a babe."

"I remember hearing Cressy speak fondly of a Jack," Arian recalled. "I hadn't quite put it together."

Each Akkinorian kingdom had its own naming traditions, but no kingdom admired those traditions as greatly as Omara. The children in each family were named in alphabetical order: the Ashfords, for example, were Arthur, Bryan, Cecelia, and Daniella. Middle names were adopted from relatives or close family friends. According to Jack, he received his namesake from a friend of his father's, Jack Halloway. As Aurelia had only ever heard of Arthur Ashford professionally, she'd never known that he preferred to be called *Jack*.

Arian wasn't shocked by Jack's true identity. In fact, he wasn't nearly as surprised as he should've been. Though he'd never admit it, Aurelia had a sinking feeling that Arian had known the truth all along. After all, a mage with Arian's skill could deduce more about a perfect stranger than the latter's closest friends could.

After departing Kazamir early that morning, Aurelia and her allies had finally arrived in the port province of Khaba. She'd imagined it would be a mirror image of its twin, Caedia, on the other side of the continent: crowded docks and shipyards, drunken sailors stumbling across the roads, horses and mules pulling wagons of trading goods.

Khaba wasn't like Caedia, and that had become clear as soon as the carriage crossed the border from Bozar. The first thing she noticed was the houses (hovels, really) lining either side of the cobblestone road. The breeze from the ocean was chilly, so it wasn't surprising to see smoke billowing from the chimneys. Children were playing games outside of their homes, women were tending to laundry on the clothing lines, and men were fixing leaky roofs or corralling livestock. Most of them paid little to no attention to the carriages and troops traveling by, as if an army passing through their little town was commonplace.

"How odd," Aurelia remarked. "People live here?"

Jack nodded. "With so few travelers entering Carthe through the south, Khaba has become much more bearable than Caedia. Caedia...It's always busy. Never exactly quiet. It's dangerous, too. Nobody wants to live in a place that exists solely for outsiders."

"So many years of courting travelers has made Caedia uninhabitable," Arian added. "Khaba is secluded. Quiet. Most foreign travelers never make it this far into the continent. The families who live in Khaba have lived here for hundreds of years. Nobody bothers them, so why leave?"

Aurelia peered through the window of the carriage in silence as they quietly moved towards the docks. The civilians continued to pay her no attention, and the troops didn't seem to frighten them in the slightest. The people of Khaba may have been ignored by the rest of the world, but the terrain had certainly been made useful over the years. Highborn fleets floated off the coast at all times, so it wasn't uncommon for the Khabish to see so many people crossing their territory. Aurelia simply couldn't understand why they were so unbothered by the constant interruptions.

When the carriage was brought to a halt, the driver turned to them. "It will be a few moments before the rowboats arrive. You're welcome to wait here before I return to Taundosa."

"Thank you, good man." Arian reached into the breast pocket of his suit and produced a heavy pouch of coin. The driver appeared pleased when he felt the weight of the coin on his palm. Arian turned back to Aurelia with raised eyebrows. "Shall we stretch our legs?"

"Please."

Jack hopped out of the carriage and held the door open with one hand while offering the other to Aurelia. She smiled and accepted his assistance as she stepped onto the ground. It wasn't desert sand like Taundosa or rainforest soil like Bozar, but beach sand and rocks, hard and sharp beneath her shoes, that made a crunching noise with every muscle she moved. The sweet, salty smell of sea air wafted through her nostrils as the breeze lifted her curls from her shoulders.

"Excuse me for a moment." Arian gestured over his shoulder, where the Carthinian emissaries were waiting for a word. "I must settle a few arrangements with our allies before the rowboats arrive."

Aurelia nodded. "Of course."

She minded him as he approached the emissaries with a grin and outstretched arms. A smile formed on her lips at the sound of his hearty, lively voice echoing throughout the streets. She'd miss the sound terribly when he returned to Taundosa, but she wouldn't forget it—nobody who met Arian Cristos could forget the sound of his voice.

Jack cleared his throat. "Aurelia?"

She tore her eyes away from her uncle. "Yes?"

"Those don't look like our boats."

She followed his gaze to the water. In a split second, she spotted over a dozen rowboats making their way towards the docks. The boats were filled to capacity, and not one sailor aboard wore the colors or sigils of Aurelia's Carthinian allies. In the distance among the many Carthinian fleets, a handful of ships had laid anchor at sea, all bearing the same scarlet-red sails that reminded Aurelia of the flocks of cardinals that often flew by her bedchamber window in Akkinor.

As a pit settled in her stomach, a wall of gold formed a circle around she and Jack. The Goldmen were firmly positioned between Aurelia and their uninvited guests, making it impossible for her to see anything further.

"What's going on?" Jack demanded. "Where are our boats?"

"Still at sea." One of the soldiers turned around fully to face Aurelia. His shoulders were still pressed against those of his comrades. Even with his new stance, there were no gaps in the barrier. "It appears we've been joined by Captain Lukos of Espos, Your Grace."

Aurelia's heart hammered. "Captain Lukos?"

"Yes, Your Grace."

"Are you certain?"

"Yes, Your Grace."

She looked to Jack for assistance, but he only stared at her. The man she loved had traveled every inch of Carthe in the near-six years since he left Akkinor, but unfortunately, Espos wasn't Carthinian territory. He'd never stepped foot on the island. Arian and the emissaries may have had better luck, but they were indisposed, and Aurelia was running out of time before Captain Lukos attempted to break her protective circle.

"Step aside please, gentlemen," she commanded before she could stop herself. None of the Goldmen moved an inch. She furrowed her eyebrows and tried again, louder: "Move aside. I'd like a word with Captain Lukos."

"Aurelia—" Jack started.

When she shot him a nasty look, he clamped his jaw shut and silenced. The Goldmen hesitantly moved aside for her, creating an opening that made a path directly to the docks. She took a few steps forwards, trying her utmost not to tremble, as the rowboats arrived on the rocky shoreline.

It wasn't hard to identify Captain Lukos among the pirates. When he stood, he was taller and heavier than the others, and his men cowered away from him on instinct. He was older than Arian with long, sandy hair that'd begun to gray at the roots. His beard was already gray, though the left side of his face was hairless from a monstrous burn across his cheek. One of his hazel eyes was missing, leaving nothing but an empty socket and a jagged silver scar across his skin. He was deeply tanned from the sun and unfathomably filthy, too. His clothing was torn, dirtied, and stained, but the captain's hat on his head and the sash across his midriff were pristine. He moved with a limp, as if one of his dusty black boots fit better than the other, and didn't dare lift his hand from the hilt of his sword.

The Esposi were an interesting people. Long ago when the first settlers inhabited the island, they traveled there from Akkinor or Carthe. Some had noticeably light or very dark skin like Akkinorians while others had the characteristic brown skin of most Carthinians. As the early humans continued to migrate over the centuries, people from Quapebet, Glacier Bay, and the islands also decided to settle on Espos. No monarch or noble family was ever appointed, as most settlers were sea-faring people who spent the majority of their time sailing the world. As the decades passed, Espos became something of a place for outlaws from around the realm to settle, so no two people quite looked the same.

Espos functioned on a unique form of hierarchy. There were no highborn individuals governing the island nor any soldiers present to enforce laws. The island itself was almost as independent as the Violet Forest or the Ngora Valley. Things were different aboard the ships, though. Every captain of every ship was viewed as a king by his crew. When a captain retired (which normally only happened when one perished), their potential successors—their first mate, the quartermaster, or any other crew member who believed they had a claim to the ship— battled each other for the title until only one remained.

Every captain, pirate, and civilian responded to the Captain of Espos. Though he wasn't responsible for most aspects of leadership (like establishing or enforcing laws and providing his people with survival necessities), his word was law. He told every ship where to sail and what to do. He claimed a portion of every bounty they discovered or stole. The Esposi didn't seem to mind being ruled by such a bully, though. It was the way their culture functioned, after all, and the way it had for generations.

There'd been so many captains of Espos over the centuries that the exact number was immeasurable. It could've been hundreds or even thousands. It hadn't always been that way, but history didn't matter to the Esposi anymore. The names and legacies of former captains had been long forgotten or ignored, all to give the current captain as much authority as possible. After all, if the people didn't compare him to his predecessors, they couldn't hold him to any ancient promises or practices—he could do whatever he pleased, and the people would have no choice but to obey.

"Buen give me strength." Jack's voice from behind interrupted Aurelia's thoughts. "He's even worse than I imagined."

"Mind your tongue."

He ignored her. "I really think we should wait for Lord Cris—"

"Captain Lukos." Aurelia took a few steps forwards, still flanked by Goldmen, as Lukos climbed a rocky hill to meet her on the flat road overlooking the docks. They stood a safe distance apart from one another, and the other pirates watched the interaction as they guarded the docks behind their captain. "We weren't expecting you."

He didn't seem fazed by her. "I wanted to see ye off for me-self." It took everything she had to avoid wincing at the sound of his voice: raspy and rough like stone against stone. "Had to make an impression before I decide what to do wit ye."

"I beg your pardon?"

The captain shifted his weight between his feet and spit a wad of chewing tobacco onto the sand. "I canna help but wonder, Y'Grace, if ye paid three highborn to butter me up so I don't blow ye wee fleet to bits." Instinctively, Aurelia leaned backwards and made a face, offended by his insinuation. His eyes flashed, and after a moment, it seemed like the old man had tempered. "Ye pay 'em or not?"

She narrowed her eyes. "No."

"So three highborn spoke for ye on they own?"

"It would appear so."

He almost looked impressed. "Ye got three highborn to speak on yer behalf. One by one, they came. Never seen somethin' like that before. Never cared to hear about Akkinor's girl-queen before, either." When she

379

scowled, he grinned and revealed a mouth full of blackened, rotting teeth. "Ye got fire for such a wee thing. No wonder they came."

She held her head high. "You know what I want. You and I don't have to be friends, Captain. In fact, I don't want us to be friends. The only thing I want—the only thing I want *presently*—is to return home as quickly as possible. My brother threatens you just as he threatens the people of Akkinor. Surely Espos is one of many problems my brother aims to solve with his newfound power—I'd be surprised if it weren't. If things are to be returned to the way they were *before* the uprising against me, my feet must touch Akkinor's soil before the damage is irreversible. That requires me to sail across the Alkamura." He blinked in surprise. That made her smile. "That's right. I may be a queen, but I have enough humility to admit a wrongdoing. You have my respect, Captain Lukos. I hope I've earned yours."

Now he *was* impressed. "Ye may cross. When his head is in the ground, we will meet again to discuss this *humility* ye speak of."

She extended her hand. "For clear skies—"

"—and steady seas." He reached out and clasped her forearm as she did the same to him. They held the grasp for a moment before releasing one another. "Been a pleasure, Y'Grace."

"Likewise, Captain."

He held her gaze for a long moment, then turned to face his crew and made a motion with his arm. One by one, the pirates turned back to the docks and boarded the rowboats. Aurelia's heart pounded as Lukos stepped onto one of the boats and met her gaze. He no longer seemed threatening or callous; in fact, he almost appeared calm. He held her gaze until the boats were untied from the docks. When they began paddling out to sea again, he turned to face the horizon with his back to the Queen of Akkinor.

"Good heavens." Beads of sweat dribbled down Jack's face. "No man has ever frightened me before today. I certainly wasn't expecting him to see us off. Form a blockade around our fleets, yes, but not see us off."

"You heard him. Three Carthinian highborn personally asked him to allow me safe passage across the ocean. The Queen of Taundosa, Lady Swann of Krotis, Lord Zhaaran of Bozar...That doesn't happen every day, does it?"

He smiled at her. "No, it doesn't."

"He needed to meet me for himself. He needed to know if I'm worth the effort."

"You seem to have convinced him." They both stared at the ocean as the Esposi rowboats shrunk into the distance. "How did you do that? No Akkinorian ruler in hundreds of years has managed a civil conversation with a Captain of Espos. Those who've dared to meet with one have almost always returned home with some sort of injury. Not a day passes when I'm not impressed with you, my love, but today you've baffled me."

She shrugged. "It was simple. *Alkamura.*"

"Is that pirate-speak or something?"

She gave him a look. "The Alkamura is the full and accurate name for the ocean. The Almighty of Espos is Alkamura, Jack. The sea goddess. When Oleander won the war, the Esposi were loyal to the Cherrane family. Oleander offered to spare them from punishment for supporting the Cherranes if they accepted his terms of surrender. The Esposi accepted his terms at first, then violated them by laying siege to every Akkinorian ship that crossed the ocean. In retaliation, Oleander declared that the ocean would become known as the *Alka*, not the Alkamura. It's been an ongoing war between our two peoples ever since."

"So you earned Lukos's respect by using the proper name of the ocean, inspired by his culture's Almighty, which every king before you has refused to do." Jack smiled. "Brilliant. What a shame—so much conflict over a matter of terrible hubris."

"Indeed. For Akkinor, it's a matter of establishing consequences for a lack of honor. For Espos, it's a matter of respecting another man's culture. Where does one draw the line between honor and respect, Jack? Whose pride can bear to concede first?"

His eyes sparkled as he gazed at her. "Honor, apparently."

"Yes. Honor." She smiled a bit. "The Esposi have been punished for their ancestors' actions long enough, and in a way, so have we Akkinorians. Our country could've been leagues ahead of where we are now if we'd been able to trade with Carthe these last few centuries. The diplomats accompanying us home can tell our people about how Carthe wishes to trade with Akkinor, and the only way to do that is through use of the Alkamura. Nobody will protest when they realize how desperately we need trading partners in Carthe. They won't see it as a matter of pride anymore—they'll see it as a matter of survival."

When she saw the way his eyes shined for her, she knew she'd done the right thing. She hadn't expected Captain Lukos to seek her out, so she hadn't known what she'd say until the words spewed from her lips, but she had no regrets about the things she said to him. Her impulsive words were exactly what she needed to help her country out of the hole her brother had dug.

"What now?" Jack asked, brushing a lock of hair from her face. "How shall we proceed, Your Grace?"

"With caution. Captain Lukos may have given us permission to cross the ocean, but a pirate's word can't always be trusted. We must be vigilant on this journey." A smile passed over her face when she spotted dozens of rowboats peppering the ocean. It wouldn't be long before they were setting sail for Akkinor. "Let's find my uncle. It's almost time for us to say goodbye to Carthe."

They stopped at the docks to say goodbye to Scotch and Sterling, who'd be taken aboard another ship with the rest of the cavalry's horses. The pair offered their horses two fleshy red apples each as a parting gift before their journey began.

"It's time to go home, Scotch," she murmured, brushing his chestnut mane. "Another adventure awaits us."

"So it would seem." Jack outstretched his hand and smiled at her. "Are you ready, my love?"

She glanced to her right at the glittering ocean and took a long, deep breath. She didn't know when her feet would touch Carthinian soil again, but she hoped it'd be soon. She wasn't ready to say a permanent goodbye to the place she had grown so fond of: the place of her birth, of her ancestral home, and of the mother she never knew. Somehow, though, she knew she'd return. Carthe was her home as much as Akkinor.

She threaded her fingers through his and squeezed. "Ready."

XLII

Aurelia wrapped her arms around herself and shivered when a gust of chilly air blew her hair from her shoulders. The salty spray had her blinking and shielding her eyes, while the rotten, somewhat sour smell of marine life and sailors' stench made her wrinkle her nose.

She jumped in surprise when a thick, muscular arm snaked around her waist. At her side, Jack chuckled and tightened his arm around her. He must've felt how chilly she was, as he was soon taking off his coat and draping it over her shoulders. She smiled fondly and tucked herself into his side, relishing the heat from his body against hers. He kissed the top of her head and held her closer while releasing a long, contented exhale.

They'd been at sea for seven days since departing Khaba. So far, Captain Lukos had been true to his word, as their fleets had been sailing the Alkamura without problem. Esposi ships were sailing nearby, lurking as always, but they paid no attention to Aurelia's fleets.

In just a few days, they'd reach the western coast of Akkinor, where Archie's forces would be waiting for them. As they inched closer, Aurelia was haunted by memories of her escape and of the very reason for it, as told by Archie to the Akkinorian people—a reason which, depending on Archie's persuasiveness, might've left Aurelia without a single ally amongst her own people.

Jack was studying her. "I can see the anxiety in your eyes. You've nothing to fear, my love. Your people are following Archie blindly. The only word they've had cause to trust is his. When they see you and everything you've done...Their swords will fall at your feet."

"I hope so."

His chest rumbled as he laughed. "Look around. No monarch in history has succeeded in accomplishing what you have. Not even Oleander."

The thought sent shivers up and down her spine. She did as she was told and surveyed her surroundings, soaking in every last detail. The fleets surrounding her ship could be seen for miles, all carrying soldiers, horses, and weapons leant to her by some of Carthe's most powerful rulers. The rulers themselves may not have been fighting at her side, but they'd each sent a powerful diplomat in their place. Arian, too, had enlisted the assistance of a coven of mages who were loyal to him; more importantly, loyal to the entire Cristos bloodline. And, of course, there was Jack, who was something of a super-soldier himself—according to him, anyway.

"They think I abandoned them," she reminded him. "My people think I escaped the country and left them in the hands of barbarian usurpers. In a way, I did. I wasn't aware of Archie's betrayal until well after I met you."

"You had no choice. The monarch must think of their survival first if they hope to aid their people."

She shook her head. "Will they believe me if I tarnish the name of the king who came to their rescue while their queen fled?"

"Of course they will. They've seen what you've done for Akkinor in five years, Aurelia. Archie has brought them nothing but pain and suffering in less than a year. Nobody is unaware of that."

That made her wince. She was mortified of what she'd find upon returning to Akkinor. Archie was a greedy man—still a boy, really—who relished the privileges of being king. His army of mercenaries had created a massive dent in Akkinor's bank, and he would've required even more compensation to keep his allies quiet about the things he'd done. The wealth and prosperity that generations of Brentwoods had worked to build was threatened, and Aurelia was terrified of how long it would take to reverse the damage.

Before she could respond, Arian manifested at her side. "Good morning, my dear. We've started discussing our strategy for our arrival in Akkinor. Your presence is needed before we can proceed."

She nodded. "Of course."

She and Jack followed Arian below deck, where a handful of strategists were gathered around a large table in the captain's study. The three noble diplomats, in addition to the generals of each army (save Normyn Barvel, who'd sent someone in his place while he remained in Taundosa as Reyna's temporary Hand), were staring down at a map of Akkinor spread over the table. Small figurines symbolizing each army were positioned on the map, though the men were rearranging the pieces and arguing over the placements. When they saw Arian walk into the room with Aurelia at his side, each of them straightened and bowed to her.

"Your Grace." Ser Xantos, a Goldman, tipped his head in greeting. "We've begun preparations for our arrival in Akkinor. Unfortunately, we aren't familiar with the terrain or the troops. Your input is most valuable."

She approached the table and wrapped her fingers around the mahogany edges. Nobody uttered a word as she examined the map and the figurines from left to right and back again. Each figurine represented one troop, and based on the presences on the table, Aurelia's forces were still outnumbered by her brother's.

"My brother will be expecting us in the capital." She grabbed a handful of figurines representing Archie's troops and repositioned them from Seaport to the Folly. "I doubt we'll find anyone waiting for us when we dock in Seaport. It's far too small and clustered for so many men. The Folly's terrain is better suited for a fight."

Jack was frowning. "The Folly has the largest civilian population on the western half of the country. The most damage will be inflicted in the capital, so we can expect a high number of both civilian and military casualties. Your brother doesn't strike me as the type of commander to evacuate civilians."

She flinched. "The civilian casualties will be the least of his concerns. That's why we'll make them a concern of ours."

The men exchanged looks. "How do you propose we do that?" asked the emissary from Krotis. "All due respect, Your Grace, but it'd be a tremendous waste of our resources if we focus on evacuating the city. We don't have enough men to face the entirety of your brother's forces if half of our troops are elsewhere."

"We're fighting this battle for the people, my lord. I won't reclaim my throne while hundreds of wagons carry innocent bodies to the trenches," she said. "Archie wants to fight in the place where the most casualties will be inflicted. He wants the people to associate me with that damage. If he wins, I'm to blame for everything. If he loses, there will be nothing left of the Folly for me to govern. That's his strategy—to force me into impossible situations." She blew a curl from her eyes and rearranged the figurines again. "The Kroti will travel through the forest and engage evacuation protocol of the civilians in the Folly. They'll be escorted to Seaport, where they should be safe for the duration of the battle. The other troops will take the Templar's Road to Oleander's Valley and the palace."

"They're already expecting us," Arian added. "A surprise attack is pointless. As soon as they spot our fleets at sea, they won't be focused on the civilians."

She nodded. "Precisely."

"The Goldmen are the strongest. We'll be on the frontlines," Ser Xantos proclaimed. "Lord Cristos is overseeing the mages. They'll be positioned around the perimeter to keep the battle contained. Our goal is to limit the fighting to the valley and the front gates of the palace. If we make it to the palace, we can infiltrate it and take it back from your brother's forces. He'll most certainly have men surrounding the grounds, so it won't be an easy task."

"Leave the palace to me." Aurelia wrapped her fingers around her locket. The men furrowed their eyebrows and exchanged looks with one another, but she ignored them. "My primary concern is keeping Archie's forces from seeking shelter. The palace is the safest place in the Folly for both sides, and if his men manage to make it inside, our only chance of victory means destroying the entire estate. How many men do we require to stand guard outside the gates?"

The knight shrugged. "Two hundred at most."

"I'll lead them," Jack offered. Aurelia frowned at him. "Fighting our way through Archie's forces won't be easy, but we can do it. I might suggest presenting a united front—soldiers from all armies, standing arm-in-arm to protect the center of their ally's kingdom."

She smiled at him. "Clever."

Ser Zhaama cleared his throat. "We'll have archers positioned on high ground and on cavalry. The rest of our men will be on foot. The troops have strict orders to wait for your signal, Your Grace. How would you like to proceed upon meeting your brother's forces on the battlefield?"

"Well..." She gazed down at the map and sighed. "Negotiation is my first strategy. Most of Archie's allies are under the impression that I abandoned them. They're fighting for him because they believe me to be the enemy and my brother to be their hero. It's my hope that the nobility will hear me and see Archie for what he is. If there's any chance of them surrendering before blood can be shed, I'll take it."

"The nobles may decide to fight for you, but the mercenaries and assassins he hired fight for coin," Arian reminded her. "They won't betray your brother so easily. We may not find ourselves fighting your kin, but we'll certainly find ourselves fighting."

"I'm not frightened by a few mercenaries." She looked around at the men and raised an eyebrow. "Are you?"

No reply. Instead, they stared at her with a glint in their eyes that felt oddly and obscurely familiar. It was the way Linden and Cicely would look at her when they were proud of her. The look that told her she was doing the right thing—that she was the queen Akkinor deserved.

Aurelia's time in Carthe had changed her, she knew that, but despite the person she'd become, the best parts of her remained. Upon realizing that, the fear and anxiety that'd been bubbling in her stomach since departing Carthe began to fizzle away. In its place, adrenaline coursed through her veins.

***

Jack let out a strident, guttural moan as he tucked his head between his knees. Aurelia sat on the bed beside him and rubbed his back comfortingly, but the rough swaying of the ship was irking her, too. Both jumped when the rocking disturbed knick-knacks from a nearby table and sent them rolling across the floor.

Carthinian highborn rarely traveled by sea, which meant that none of their ships were built with living quarters suitable for them. The ship's captain had been kind enough to sacrifice his quarters for Aurelia and Jack. While she was eternally grateful for that (she had no intention of sleeping on a hammock surrounded by drunken sailors), she wished the captain hadn't been such a collector. Bookshelves and antique cabinets clung to the walls, all filled to the brim with miscellaneous prizes, collectables, and mementos, but nothing was spared from the raging seas when the ship rocked from side to side. The sound of the captain's precious collection falling to the floor only made the experience worse.

Jack lifted his head from his knees, his face a sickly shade of gray, and peered at her through the dim candlelight. "We haven't stopped rocking in hours. When will it end?"

"We've sailed through the heart of it. It won't be long now."

"How are you so calm? After what happened to our parents..."

She sighed. "As a queen, there are things I simply can't avoid. I thought I could avoid the sea, but it's impossible. It terrifies me to no end, Jack, but I can't let fear of the past stop me from returning to Akkinor."

He shivered. "Do you suppose it's a sign? We have a day left on our voyage, and here we are, stuck in the eye of a storm. Is this some sort of warning?"

"I refuse to believe that." She frowned when she saw the uneasy glint in his blue eyes. That night, they were as dark and chaotic as the seas. "Are you nervous, Jack?"

"Aren't you?"

"No. Not anymore." She set her hands in her lap and looked down as she fiddled with her fingers. "I've been waiting for this since the day I fled, despite how terribly it could end. I see no point in thinking about that terrible ending. I'd much rather think about the best possible outcome."

"What's that?"

She smiled. "We win this fight without turning the Folly into a graveyard. My brother is dealt with as seen fit. My alliances remain strong. We reverse the damage Archie caused and bring Akkinor back to its rightful state. I will continue to rule until the day I die, when our child takes the throne and carries on the Brentwood name."

That made him beam. "Do I have to take on the Brentwood name, too?"

"Most definitely."

He guffawed and reached for her, tickling her sides and sending tingles throughout her body. She almost forgot about the rocking of the ship as they tossed and turned on the bed. It wasn't long before their playful game ended up with both of them rolling off the bed and hitting the floor with a thud. They were laughing and gasping for air as Aurelia lay on top of him, staining his white shirt with tears of joy.

Suddenly, with one jerky movement, he sat up on the floor (still with Aurelia on his lap) and stared into her eyes with a look that made her shiver. A light had formed behind his eyes that wasn't there before: a light that made her both giddy with excitement and somewhat terrified of what would spout from his lips next.

While Aurelia demanded to know what he was doing, Jack sprung up from the floor and knelt beside his chest of belongings. Aurelia remained on the floor, amused yet puzzled, as Jack collected something from his chest before turning his attention to Aurelia's. She laughed at his odd behavior until he turned around to face her while holding two items for her to see. Every ounce of amusement faded from her being upon recognizing the twin bands crafted from twine.

"Jack—?"

He crouched beside her and held the smaller of the two bands between his fingers. "Weeks ago, I placed this on your finger for one reason: survival. It was perhaps the only way for us to reach our destination without fuss. I didn't ask your permission then, nor did I care at all for what this represents. I realized rather quickly after our experience in Dofell that you deserve more than that. No man on either side of the world is worthy enough to place a band on your marital finger unless you've chosen them, too. It's been my intention to marry you from the moment I decided to follow you home to Akkinor. I don't wish to wait until after the battle to make my intentions clear. If either of us happens to die on the battlefield, we'll die knowing we belonged to someone—that we chose someone, and that someone chose us in return."

Her eyes stung with emotion. "Was that meant to be romantic?"

"In a way." That infamous, wicked smile appeared on his lips for a moment before it was replaced by tender sincerity. "I don't know what will happen tomorrow or in the days that follow, but I *do* know that I've chosen you every second of every day from the moment we met. I'm asking your permission now to place this band on your finger—to promise myself to you wholly and eternally, and to promise that I shall never again forget what it represents. You are my love and my life, today and every day. I'd be a fool to waste what could be our last night together by failing to ask for your hand." Smiling through glassy eyes, Jack gently took her hand in his and held up the twine band. "Will you do me the honor, or shall I throw myself overboard instead?"

Laughing and sobbing in unison, Aurelia took his face in her hands and pressed a wet, sloppy kiss to his lips. She was blubbering so fiercely that she didn't realize if her affirmative response had been coherent. Fortunately, Jack seemed to excel in translating her garbled speech, as he grinned from ear to ear and slipped the twine loop onto her finger.

He leaned in to embrace her, but she held out a hand to stop him. While he frowned in confusion, she took the larger of the two bands and slipped it onto his finger, too. He raised a curious, amused eyebrow in response.

She offered him a weak smile. "It's a silly tradition for the man to wear his ring only after the marriage ceremony. My ring alerts the masses that you've chosen me. Yours tells the world that I've chosen you, too."

The smile on Jack's lips was so genuine that Aurelia felt as if hers was inconsequential in comparison. His bright, swirling oceanic eyes brightened with adoration as he swept her into his arms and sealed the gap between them with a kiss that could've tilted the world. She smiled at the salty taste of his lips—mainly because she wasn't sure if the tears melting into her mouth were his or hers.

Aurelia, suffocated by both memories and dreams for the future, internally thanked the gods not only for leading her to Jack, but for creating him as he was. She'd spent her entire life wondering if it were possible to marry for love as a woman of her status. Suitor after suitor had lined up on her doorstep since she was a girl, all hoping for the chance to marry Akkinor's future queen. She'd never even *liked* any of them, let alone felt the capacity to love them. Even in all her years of secretly romancing the men she could never have, she'd never felt a real connection until she met Jack. The Queen of Akkinor had waited far too long for the chance to marry for love, and here it was, staring at her like she was the most divine creature in all the world.

This wasn't a man wishing to marry the queen to seize her power for himself. This wasn't a man who looked into her eyes and saw the prospect of unbridled authority. This wasn't a man who praised her and showered her with half-hearted, misplaced outpourings of affection simply to earn her favor. This was a man who loved her as deeply as she loved him—a man who, noble blood or not, sought nothing more than an eternity at her side. If that were untrue, he may have waited until she emerged victorious on the battlefield to request her hand.

This was the man she'd been waiting for: a man with Akkinorian blood pumping through his heart, and the spirit of Carthe igniting his soul.

XLIII

urelia stared at her palm against Jack's as their matching twine bands brushed together. She could feel the heavy pounding of his heart against her back and his anxious breaths against her ear. She wanted to feel safe in her spot in his arms, but the familiar stench of Seaport made it impossible for her to feel anything other than uneasiness. Neither of them spoke a word until someone knocked on their door. Sighing, they stood from the bed and opened it, revealing Arian on the other side.

The look on his face was grave. "It's time, Your Grace."

She swallowed. "We'll meet you shortly."

She closed the door and turned to face Jack, whose attempt at a comforting smile failed miserably. They had a silent conversation with their eyes as they exchanged the words that'd been lodged in their throats for hours as their ship approached the coast of Akkinor. They wrapped themselves in each other's arms until their time was up, then helped one another suit up in the metal armor that'd haunted them in the corner of their room for weeks.

After dressing, Aurelia caught sight of something resting atop the clothing in her chest: a small linen bag woven with golden thread. Remembering the gift from Reyna, she slipped the elvemar stone into the pocket of her trousers, hoping she wouldn't have to use it, and smiled when it clinked against the tiny, weathered soldier gifted to her by Oslo.

While Aurelia strapped her sword and sheath to her waist, Jack held something out for her. She blinked in confusion when she saw her bow and sheath of arrows—*Kaia's* bow and sheath of arrows. She hadn't seen them since the attack by the maid in Taundosa. Until now, she hadn't needed them.

"You're better with a bow," he said.

She smiled and accepted the weapons. She felt strange with a sword strapped to her waist and a bow slung over her shoulders—not as Lily Linden, but as Aurelia Brentwood. She'd trained for something like this, as every monarch before her had done, but she hadn't seen war in her lifetime. She'd never marched onto a battlefield and prepared herself to spill blood. The feeling didn't sit well with her, but she knew there was only one way to achieve the outcome she desired.

Hand-in-hand, the couple joined their allies above deck where the crew was preparing the rowboats. She shuddered at what little she could already see of Seaport: warning lanterns had already been lit by Archie's scouts. It wouldn't be long before the entire kingdom was made aware of her return.

Jack set a hand on her back. "Are you all right?"

"Fine." When she saw the look on his face, she cleared her throat and tried again. "I'm fine. It's just...The last time I was here, I was running for my life."

"You'll never have to do so again. Not as long as I live and breathe."

She smiled, but it was so forced that Jack winced at the sight of it.

They were soon approached by Arian, who told them that the Kroti troops had already arrived at shore and were making their way through the woods in preparation for the evacuation. The moment she'd been waiting for had finally arrived, and the anticipation was cutting her apart like a knife.

She and Jack boarded a rowboat with Arian and sailed to shore. Her hands shook in her lap and her heart pounded so loudly that it drowned out the sound of the crashing waves. As the village grew closer, she realized that not one soul roamed the streets. The shutters on the windows of every home were closed, the doors bolted shut, and even the chimneys expelled no smoke from the fireplaces. As far as the people must've known, they were being attacked by Carthinian troops—they were completely unaware that the troops were being headed by their queen.

When the boat finally arrived at shore, Jack stepped out first and offered her a hand. She inhaled sharply as her boots sunk into the dark, wet sand of the Seaport beach. A nippy breeze lifted her curls from her shoulders and made her shiver. She forced herself to keep moving forwards, to follow the traffic of soldiers making their way to dry land, until her feet hit the grass and cobblestones of the streets. She took a long, deep breath of the Akkinorian air she'd missed so dearly, but somehow, her homecoming wasn't as relieving as she'd imagined it.

Soon enough, the entirety of their forces arrived on land. Aurelia and Jack mounted Scotch and Sterling, respectively, as Arian and the other commanders followed suit. Aurelia instinctively wrapped her fingers around her locket as she peered over her shoulder at the soldiers. The banners of Akkinor, Taundosa, Krotis, and Bozar flew high in the wind. The sun reflected off the glittering gold armor of the Goldmen (who were frightening enough as it was), and blinded anyone who dared to look in their direction.

Arian raised an eyebrow. "On your word, Your Grace."

Aurelia's heart hammered. "Forward, good man, ever forward."

With one wave of her uncle's hand, the soldiers began to march, and the horses reared forwards. Aurelia's body tingled with both terror and anticipation as Scotch's hooves kicked dirt into the air. They moved forwards to follow the Templar's Road—the path that'd take them directly to the Folly—while all thoughts of turning back disappeared.

Soon enough, the palace was visible through the foliage. The Kroti soldiers were hiding in the forest (all wearing purple-and-gold strips of cloth around their biceps to signal their allegiance to Akkinor, as to not alarm the civilians), waiting for the signal to infiltrate the villages, as the others followed their commanders towards the gates of the Folly. Aurelia's breath caught in her throat when they arrived and saw that the gates were already open. Archie was inviting them inside for the entire Folly to see. The troops halted before entering, waiting for Aurelia's final signal. She hesitated for a moment, staring at the place she called home, before urging Scotch forwards once more.

Finally, Archie's troops came into view. All six Akkinorian armies were waiting at the bottom of a mountainous grassy hill. It was the same battlefield—Folly Hill—where Oleander Brentwood defeated the Cherrane family and won the rebellion.

The world seemed to move slowly, very slowly, as the two armies settled across from one another on either side of the battlefield. Aurelia couldn't see her brother, but she *did* see the lords and ladies of Akkinor heading their respective armies. The banners of Myra, Omara, Holos, Laynoa, and Sadia flapped in the breeze as a horn blew to signal the arrival of Aurelia's troops. She counted her breaths and waited as the sea of soldiers parted to make way for her brother.

The sight of Archie's face made her stomach churn. The Scorpion of Akkinor looked the same as when she saw him last: short blonde hair, bright blue eyes, and a reddish beard far too unkempt for a royal. He wore Akkinorian bronze armor and held their father's prized sword at his side. Each of their father's medals—symbolic of his many accomplishments—adorned Archie's armor as if they'd been welded to the metal.

So it's come to this, Aurelia thought. *Insulting our father's memory by claiming his achievements as your own. A spineless act, brother, even for you.*

"The traitor returns!" he bellowed. "You've lost the element of surprise, sweet sister, just as you'll lose many things today—including your life."

She cocked her head to the side. "My poor, foolish brother. How blindsided you've become! I've lost nothing, nor will I lose anything today. My reign was merely interrupted by the uprising you orchestrated. As you can see, I've come to free Akkinor of its usurper, and I've come *very* well prepared."

He raised an eyebrow, feigning confusion. "Usurper? You're mistaken. Almost three seasons ago, our great country was attacked. You, Queen and Protector of Akkinor—you abandoned your people when we needed you most. As next in line to the throne given your *reluctance* to marry and produce heirs, I assumed the role you discarded. I protected our people in Akkinor's time of need while you fled to protect your own life. From where I stand, you are no queen. You're a traitor who deserves to be hanged for treason. A traitor who abandoned her people in exchange for the likes of foreign barbarians. Give yourself up, sister. Save the many people who could lose their lives today because of you. Do one last justice to the country you turned your back on."

"Is that what you've told them? That I abandoned my country in the midst of an attack?" she demanded. "You're a liar and a cheat, dear brother, and nobody wants that type of king sitting on the throne. I'm no traitor, and you are no king." She glanced around at the lords and ladies on his side. "Seasons ago, somebody from inside the palace walls hired mercenaries and assassins to infiltrate the capital and murder me, and to destroy everyone who remained loyal to me. I fled not only to save my own life, but to acquire the manpower and resources needed to rescue Akkinor from its usurpers. Today, I come to you with four Carthinian armies who are loyal to me. I've successfully allied Akkinor with the great leaders of Taundosa, Bozar, and Krotis; not merely to reclaim what's mine, but to utilize my allies' strengths in restoring Akkinor to its former glory."

Lord Crowland of Myra met her eyes. "Your Grace—"

"Say another word and you'll meet your death," Archie threatened. "This woman betrayed you and left you at the mercy of savage intruders! There are no limitations to what she'd say to sway you into thinking otherwise."

Lord Crowland ignored him and kept his eyes trained on Aurelia. "You shocked the country when you fled all those weeks ago. Your betrayal was seen as treason of the highest degree, but deep down, I knew the queen I became so fond of would never betray the country she loves so dearly. I've struggled to understand that betrayal in your absence, just as I've struggled to understand how mercenaries were able to infiltrate the capital at all."

"I, too, am struggling to understand why you betrayed our country only to return with allies at your side." Kallan Tarre, Regent Lord of Holos, had the barest hint of a smile on his lips when he turned to her. "Have you returned to fight us, Your Grace, or to fight *for* us?"

Aurelia didn't so much as blink. "I've spent the last three seasons fighting for Akkinor from across the sea. I'm prepared to continue that fight today. You, my lords and ladies, have witnessed the downfall of our great country better than I in the time that's passed since the uprising. I urge you now to ask yourselves—would your so-called king fight for you as I have, or would he leave you to fight and die for the war he inflicted?"

"Listen to yourself!" Tyren Silio, a banker with whom Aurelia had once done business, hollered at her while Linden's lapel pin—identifying him as Lord Hand—gleamed against his chest. "Where were you in the aftermath of the invasion? Sailing to Carthe to lay with man-eating barbarians, that's where. Say what you will, but the country knows who stayed behind to protect them while their leader fled like a child."

As Archie's supporters cheered, Aurelia raised an amused eyebrow. "All monarchs have an escape plan in the event of a crisis. My father, your beloved former king, was diligent in preparing me for that. Me, his heir—*not* his only son. If my father wished for his son to rule in my stead, why would he ensure my safety and not my brother's?" She tossed a glance at Archie, whose entire face had turned crimson with anger and humiliation. "Instead of returning to the palace when the siege came to an end, I left to find support—to find people willing to defend Akkinor as I would. I believe I was right to do so, seeing as though the men who nearly destroyed the Folly are some of the very same men standing behind my brother today. Do you not find it odd that my brother hired Isalder mercenaries into his service after letting them lay waste to the entire Folly?"

Kallan Tarre's eyes ever-so-slightly snapped to the man standing directly beside him. Aurelia recognized him instantly as Carlton Moor, Duke of Gendrie in Holos—and husband to Aurelia's aunt Selsa. In that moment, Aurelia knew for certain that Arian's brief correspondence with Selsa Moor hadn't been as clandestine as they thought. The Tarres had known from the moment Selsa received the letter from Taundosa that Holos would be fighting beside its rightful queen.

In the blink of an eye, both Kallan and Lord Crowland urged their horses forwards to join the Carthinian armies. Their soldiers retreated and followed suit, cheering, and raised their swords in the air. Pride gurgled in Aurelia's stomach, but she knew it wasn't enough. Unless she could convince all of them, it'd be impossible to stop blood from being spilled in the Folly.

It wasn't long before their change of heart inspired others. Lord Ashford of Omara didn't hesitate to lead his men to Aurelia's side, and neither did three of her advisors: Lords Gideon, Baylor, and Rudal. Two Sadian armies, led by Andren and Rien Normindi, crossed the battlefield next. A Laynoan duke and husband of Edmund's sister, Odessa, urged his men to follow suit—as did Duke Lucan Stone, Linden's brother-in-law, and his soldiers. Every other Laynoan and Sadian, though, stood firmly behind Archie. Dozens of Royal Army soldiers and their leaders switched to Aurelia's side, too, giving the siblings an equal number of Follian supporters.

"Traitors!" Archie's hands trembled on his horse's reins. "You will hang for your betrayal and your treason against your king! Do you wish to fight for the woman who abandoned you? The woman who left you in the hands of intruders until I took her place? I *saved* you!"

"You saved us from nothing," Kallan retorted. "Her Grace speaks the truth. No army of intruders could infiltrate the Folly without safe passage from someone inside the palace. Royals are the first to be evacuated from a dangerous scene, should they ever be compromised, and yet, you stayed in the Folly. You failed to escape and declared yourself king without so much as a scratch on your body."

"The supposed intruders ceased their reign of terror as soon as Her Grace fled the country," Lord Crowland added. "And the Royal Army magically doubled in size. How can you explain that?"

Archie tried to maintain his composure, but he looked and sounded more like a child than he ever had before. "I-I paid them to join the army! I used the crown's money to protect my people as a good ruler should!"

Lord Ashford's eyes blazed with a wrath Aurelia hadn't expected from him. "You forced us to participate in this battle to defend against a traitor. We're a peaceful kingdom, and you forced our hand. Only a tyrant would do such a thing. A tyrant who craves power above anything else, and a tyrant who can't afford to lose. You have betrayed your country. You have put us at risk today. While you sat on your throne taking money from our people to pay intruders and assassins to do your bidding, our queen has made history and protected Akkinor from across the sea. I vowed to never wield a sword unless forced to do so, but today, I shall wield it with pride for my queen."

The Omaran soldiers lifted their weapons into the air and cheered. Archie's remaining soldiers immediately filled the gaps in their ranks, still not reacting or striking without a command from their leader. Aurelia saw her brother's face pale when he realized how many troops he'd lost before the fighting had even begun; then his fear turned into greed, as it always had, and a ruthless smirk spread over his lips.

"Your blood will stain the earth today!" he yelled. "Your betrayal will be noted if you survive. Omara, Holos, and Myra will exist only in memory. You've chosen to follow a traitor—for that, you will die."

"And you will burn," Aurelia promised. A memory from Taundosa struck her as she stared into Archie's hungry eyes. "The price of death has surpassed the price of life, brother. You're sacrificing innocent lives by refusing to lay down your sword."

"You have fire in your words, not in your heart. But if you wish to play with fire, so be it. When the world hears of what happens here today, you will be the villain of their stories. The Queen of Ashes."

His men cheered and whooped for their king, but Aurelia wasn't so frightened by his words. In fact, she had a few words of her own—just not intended for her brother.

While he riled his soldiers and prepared them for battle, she unscrewed the caps on either end of her tube-shaped golden locket. As the caps fell onto the grass, lost forever, she murmured the words her parents had embedded in her head since she was old enough to speak them. When she finished, smoke spewed from either end of the locket, creating a haze that enveloped Aurelia completely. She could hear Archie mocking her, demanding to know what tricks she was playing, as those around her shuffled and muttered to themselves. The billow of smoke rose into the air and disappeared into the clouds like it was never there at all. She kept her gaze focused on her brother, who was staring at her with amusement shimmering in his malicious eyes.

"If that was an attempt at an escape, I'm afraid you've failed miserably," he sneered. "There's no escaping this, sister! Your blood is mine to spill."

She merely stared at him, waiting for him to grow weary of his threats. Finally, when his eyes flashed, she knew the time was near. When he opened his mouth to speak, an earth-shattering shriek echoed throughout the Folly. Everyone shifted and yelled and searched for the source, but it was nowhere to be found. Then an enormous shadow concealed the sun, coating the battlefield in a blanket of darkness that seemed to eliminate all light from the world, and Aurelia's final hand was played.

To her right, Jack was trying to speak to her, nervously stammering about what she had done.

To her left, Arian was laughing.

When the sun shone again, a screech echoed across the battlefield as a powerful gust of wind rattled the trees. In the blink of an eye, an enormous dragon sailed above their heads in a flash of steel-blue scales and golden eyes. He circled the clouds, causing the soldiers to scream and some of them to run for cover, as his shrieks grew shriller. Aurelia sat in silence, watching the terror on her brother's face unfold as he witnessed something that'd only existed in tales of old.

Calmly, Aurelia dismounted Scotch and began to walk. Jack and the others were calling after her, demanding that she return to their ranks, but she ignored them. She was well aware of Archie's archers aiming at her, ready to take the shot at his command, but she wasn't frightened by them. In fact, they seemed more frightened by *her*. Their terror was enhanced when the dragon, named *Halvor* for the minor god of protection, slowed his pace and landed on the ground behind her. He stood with his wings on either side of her, protecting her from any threat that may have approached, and released another ear-piercing shriek that sent a gust of wind towards Archie's troops.

She smiled. "As you can see, I have more than enough fire in my heart to spare!"

"I-Impossible!" The fear in Archie's eyes was almost enough to make Aurelia feel guilty; *almost*. He looked around at his men, who cowered behind their swords and shields, and pointed towards Halvor. "Do you see what she's done? The traitor has brought a beast to Akkinorian shores!"

Aurelia narrowed her eyes. "Your men are afraid. Your words mean nothing to them. Do you see now what your actions may result in? I'm more than capable of burning you and your men to the ground. Akkinor will be mine again with a snap of my fingers—but that's the difference between you and I, Archie. If this power were in your hands, the entire country would be reduced to nothing but ash for the chance to keep your crown. I refuse to destroy my home as you have. This is your chance to surrender—I'd suggest you take it."

She recognized the look in his eyes. It was the same look he wore when they were children, when he was struggling to decide if he'd throw a tantrum to get his way. It was exactly the look she was hoping to see when she unleashed Halvor into the world. Archie, along with every soul on the battlefield, had now witnessed the true power she held. They'd all seen what the rightful Queen of Akkinor was capable of. It was Aurelia's secret weapon, and more importantly, it was the only hand she could play that yielded any hope of preventing Archie from inciting the battle.

"You threaten us with a massacre," he accused. "Is this how you plan to reignite your rule? I overestimated your intelligence, then. What kind of ruler does that make you, sweet sister? The kind who incinerates her people for a title and a crown?"

She scowled. "The kind who sees war for what it really is."

"Which is?"

"Sorrow," she replied. "I won't ask you again, brother. Surrender now or face the consequences. Nobody needs to die today. There's more honor in surrender than there is in war."

His eyes flashed. They'd both heard those words from Edmund's lips more times than they could count. Still, Edmund's spirit wasn't enough to wipe the merciless expression from Archie's face. When Aurelia saw the malice in his eyes, she knew her last attempt to dissuade him had failed.

"Bring the prisoner forth!" Archie commanded.

The sea of men behind her brother parted to make way for the person he'd summoned. Aurelia's chest heaved as she watched two soldiers drag a man forwards and drop him at Archie's feet. When the prisoner lifted his head, Aurelia had to cover her mouth to keep a strangled cry from escaping her throat.

Linden, her dearest friend, had never looked so terrible in the five-and-twenty years Aurelia had known him. He wore nothing but filthy rags to cover his modesty, and his dark skin was peppered with more wounds than she could count. Every inch of him was covered in deep gashes, bruises, burns, and ligature marks. His dark hair, once short-cropped, had grown long and untamed. He was no longer the strong soldier Aurelia remembered, but skinny and so gaunt that she could see each of his ribs. His eye sockets were hollow, his cheekbones sunken. Even from afar, she could see the lack of luster in his dark eyes. He was shackled around the ankles and wrists, with Archie holding the other end of the chains as if Linden were an untrained hound.

"You offered me a choice. Now I'll offer the same to you," Archie told her. "I know you, sister. Even when you begin to lose this fight—and you will—you won't unleash that beast on your people. It's not a threat to me, and neither are you. This is your final chance to surrender yourself to avoid bloodshed. If you refuse, I'll start with him."

When he yanked the chain, Linden gasped and fell to the side. Aurelia's heart broke for her friend, who could barely lift his head to look at her. When he mustered the strength to meet her eyes, the look he gave her made her chest tighten in a way that scared her half to death.

Lucan Stone spoke before Aurelia had the chance. "You will do no such thing!" When he surged forwards by several feet, his men followed. Only when Aurelia held up a hand did they cease to move. "You removed the Lord Hand from power immediately after the uprising. The law states that an individual removed from the monarch's court must be extradited to their place of birth. Ser Elliot is a native of Lockshaven and brother to my wife—as such, he is my charge. Honor and law demand that you release him into my custody."

Aurelia tore her eyes away from Linden to observe the remaining Laynoan soldiers standing behind Lord Reilly. Many were exchanging perplexed looks with one another. The duke played a clever hand: he knew as well as anyone that an Akkinorian's honor was more valuable than their ability to swing a sword. If Archie knowingly broke a law of honor, the Laynoan soldiers—in spite of their loyalty to their lord and their king— might've been swayed to fight for the other side.

Archie, as predicted, was unfazed. "Every man, woman, and child of Akkinorian blood is my charge. The former Lord Hand has been a prisoner of the crown because of his refusal to cooperate following the uprising. I won't allow him to walk free." His icy eyes landed on Aurelia. "Unless, of course, the traitor agrees to my terms."

"I won't surrender myself to a usurper," she said hoarsely. "You stole my crown, brother. I didn't come all this way to place it on your head myself."

His bright eyes were vicious, but they shone with knowing and disbelief, too. He knew as well as she did that bartering Linden's life was perhaps the only persuasion tactic she would've considered. In truth, the one thing stopping her from considering a deal with Archie was his dishonor: if she agreed to surrender to save Linden's life, Archie would've killed him anyhow. He'd never been the type to keep his word.

He dismounted his horse and stood behind Linden, then produced a dagger from his sheath. Aurelia gasped as he grabbed Linden by the hair and yanked his head back, holding the blade close to her friend's throat. Behind her, Halvor let out an angry snort that sent a gust of warm air blowing through her hair, and Duke Stone hollered a string of profanities that rattled Aurelia's eardrums. Her hands balled into fists at her sides when she saw a drop of blood rolling down Linden's throat.

"Choose wisely, Aurelia," Archie advised. "This is your last chance."

For the first time since meeting her brother again, she felt hopeless. In that moment, the Queen of Akkinor was a little girl wishing she could turn to her best friend for comfort. She could've sworn she was six years old again, having just fallen from a tree and scraped her knees on the ground. Linden was at her side in a moment, tending to her injuries and telling jokes to distract her from the pain. Then she blinked, and the reality of her world came crashing down like a tidal wave. She did the only thing she knew how to do: she looked at Linden with a pleading look in her eyes, as if his words were the only ones that mattered—because they were.

Linden nodded to her as tears rolled down his cheeks. "One life isn't worth losing your country." He winced as Archie pressed the blade deeper into his throat. It took everything in Aurelia's power not to run to them, to crash into his arms and hold him for dear life. "You're the light that shines on Akkinor, Aurelia. You're our kingdom's most precious gift. And...And above all, you're the greatest friend I've ever known. I love you very much." He closed his eyes as the sun reflected off the tears on his cheeks. "Long live the queen."

With one swift motion, Linden's throat was cut, and Aurelia's dear friend fell to the ground in a pool of his own blood.

She stood in silence, lips parted in shock, as hot tears poured from her eyes. She wasn't focused on her brother as he cleaned his blade and mounted his horse again. She was only focused on Linden, whose lifeless body would soon be trampled beneath pounding hooves and marching boots.

"Coward!" Duke Stone's voice echoed throughout the field. "Look at the man you call king, Laynoans! Don't give your lives for a man without honor!"

Aurelia didn't see or hear what happened next. She didn't know how many (if any) Laynoan soldiers abandoned Archie to fight for her. She was numb, trapped in a limbo deep within her own mind, unable to return to the mortal world after witnessing such horror. She'd spent the last three seasons wondering if Linden was still alive: if he'd been slain during the uprising, mere moments after sending her off to Seaport, or if he'd succumbed to his injuries after weeks of being tortured for information. Relief bubbled up in her chest when she first saw him—battered and broken, but alive—and now that relief had transformed into something resembling whiplash as she watched his blood mix with dirt to form a puddle of crimson mud.

He'd survived all this time, only for Archie to use him as a pawn for commencing bloodshed. There was no greater dishonor for an Akkinorian knight than to initiate a conflict rather than to disarm it, and now that Archie had sullied Linden's oath, Aurelia had something beyond her crown to fight for: not vengeance, but justice.

Feeling like her body wasn't her own, Aurelia turned to face Halvor. His reptilian eyes stared deeply into her soul as his growling echoed the pain she felt inside. Halvor, like the woman he'd been destined to protect, was prepared to avenge the friend they'd lost.

"Fly," she whispered.

XLIV

As Aurelia brushed by the dragon to return to Scotch, Halvor broke out into a run towards Archie's troops. The soldiers immediately began yelling and shooting arrows at him, but Halvor's thick, armored skin easily deflected every shot. When he gained enough momentum, he lifted into the sky before he could trample Archie's troops. Aurelia wiped the tears from her cheeks and climbed onto Scotch's back as she watched Halvor coast towards the palace. Everyone on the battlefield watched, too, as the enormous creature landed on the tallest tower and released a bellowing screech.

"Aurelia," Jack said hurriedly, "I-I don't—"

"Halvor will protect the palace. Archie's forces have nowhere to go," she assured him. "Halvor will remain there unless called upon by me."

"H-How...?"

"Halvor is bonded to the women of the Cristos family," Arian explained. Other than her parents, Linden, and Aurelia herself, Arian was the only person who'd known about Halvor before that day. "A soul connection, to put it simply. They're of one mind."

She shifted in her saddle and shot daggers at Archie with her eyes. Her brother was waiting for something, and it was becoming clearer by the minute. She could see the greedy glimmer in his eyes even from across the battlefield. Her heart thumped wildly—she recognized that look all too well.

"U-Uncle," she stammered, "we need the shields. *Now.*"

Arian didn't stop to question her. He held his hand out with his palm facing the sky, and a bright burst of white light quickly shot into the clouds—a signal. A moment later, a glittering veil cascaded around Aurelia's troops. At the exact same time, Archie's Isalder mercenaries emerged from the deciduous trees with weapons in hand. When they came in contact with the magical shields erected by Arian's coven, the flesh and bone melted from their bodies and turned into a sickly pool of gunk on the grass.

When Aurelia raised her hand, battle cries spewed from her allies' lips as they blew by in flashes of white and gold. Archie's men responded in time to meet the Goldmen halfway across the battlefield. The Bozari troops weren't far behind, while the remaining Taundosan troops stayed back to defend against the mercenaries who'd survived the shield. When Arian sent another burst of light into the air, he signaled the mages to surround the perimeter of the battlefield to keep the fighting contained.

"I will join my brethren," Arian called over the clanging of swords and blood-curdled screams. Before he left, he set a hand on Aurelia's sheath and closed his eyes. His hand glowed for a moment before the warm golden light faded. "There. Now you shall never run out of arrows."

She smiled. Having a mage at her side really *did* make all the difference. "Thank you."

He squeezed her shoulder for encouragement. "Good luck."

Next to her, Jack grasped her wrist. "That dragon of yours may be capable of defending the palace from the outside, but we're uncertain of what awaits us inside." She wished she could see his expression, but his entire face was concealed by his helmet. "You know what I must do. I'll see you on the other side."

"Likewise." She smiled painfully. "Good luck."

Jack winked at her before he and Sterling galloped off into the chaos. Aurelia took a long, deep breath and murmured a quiet prayer. This was the moment she'd been waiting for since she was smuggled onto a ship destined for Carthe, and yet, no amount of adrenaline could stop her from wondering if she was strong enough to survive it.

Still surrounded by Goldmen, Aurelia took her bow from her shoulder and nocked an arrow. She was still trapped in the cluster of mercenaries, which gave her the chance to shoot the foot soldiers from her position on Scotch's back. Her heart hammered when more mercenaries emerged from the trees, wrestling with the Bozari archers who'd been hiding in the forest. It wasn't long before the Goldmen surrounding her were occupied. She realized then, as the fighting inched closer and closer, that relying on a long-distance weapon like a bow wouldn't do her much good. With a deep breath, she slung the bow over her shoulder again and drew her sword. She prayed to Buen—and to Kaia—that for once, she'd be better with a sword than a bow.

A Laynoan soldier on horseback charged her, sword catching the light from every angle, but the poor man underestimated the woman he once called queen. While she deflected his blow, he took too long to recover, giving her the opportunity to stab him in a weak spot in his armor. She removed her sword in time to deflect another attack from a Sadian. She knocked the soldier from his horse and urged Scotch deeper into the heart of the fighting, where she was hoping to find her brother.

As they galloped through what already resembled a graveyard, Scotch released an ear-piercing shriek of pain and threw Aurelia from his back. She fell onto the ground with a thud and rolled until she was forced to a stop by colliding with a headless corpse. She rotated from her back to her stomach and pushed herself onto her knees, desperately searching the chaos for her horse. When she found him lying in the dirt with a terrible wound in his gut, whatever remained of her heart began to break.

"Scotch." She fumbled to her feet and tried to run to him but was intercepted by a mercenary with a spear. When he charged her, she rolled out of the way and managed to cut the backs of his knees. He hollered and collapsed but didn't yield. She narrowly deflected the spearpoint and drove the tip of her blade through his foot. As he fell to his knees, she slit his throat and let him fall face-first onto the dirt.

As she turned to face the next threat, a hot substance sprayed the left side of her face. She lifted her fingers to her cheek and realized it was blood. In a state of adrenaline and chaos, she had to remind herself that the blood wasn't hers.

When she glanced in the direction of the blood spray, she saw the body of Alwen Gideon, one of her advisors. He'd discarded the ivory cape he'd worn to express his allegiance to Archie, thus signifying his new allegiance to Aurelia. His severed head rolled across the grass until it lost momentum by crashing into a boulder. A sickening crack rattled her eardrums when the stone fractured his skull.

He wasn't the first friend to die that day, and he wouldn't be the last. Aurelia knew that much for certain. What she didn't know was whether she'd be facing more friends or enemies when she won the battle. But as she watched her friends and allies drop like flies around her, *when* started to feel more like *if*.

***

Every life you claim is another medal you've earned. When a respectable gentleman wishes to conduct business with another, who do you suppose he'll choose—the man whose victories gleam on his chest, or the man whose only adornment is a rose on his lapel?

With each swing of his sword, Tyren Silio heard his father's grating voice echoing in his head. Duke Landen Silio was likely fighting at the center of the battle, slaying every barbaric Carthinian and traitorous Akkinorian who crossed his path. He'd probably forgotten that his two sons were on the battlefield with him—and yet, Tyren kept his eyes peeled for the duke, wanting his father to watch him earn his achievements.

Tyren had been named Hand of the King by his old friend, but even *that* hadn't been enough to impress his father. Landen had taken Tyren's honorary lapel pin from his suit coat and thrown it across the room when he first saw it. *A mere banker like you has done nothing to earn your place at the king's side*, the duke had said. *Medals and honors mean nothing when they're handed to you on a whim.*

Perhaps Tyren *hadn't* done anything worthy of becoming Hand of the King—other than befriending the right person at the right time—but he would. Today.

While inching closer to the palace, Tyren stabbed a female mage in the gut before she could kill a Sadian soldier. Another mage nearby shouted her name—Lyra—and set his vengeful eyes on Tyren. Before Tyren could respond, the tip of a blade emerged from the mage's throat, and he fell to the ground in a heap. Tyren's elder brother, Landen II, gave the former an unimpressed look before darting away.

Grinding his teeth, Tyren scoured his surroundings for a formidable opponent—one he'd be able to best after a bit of a fight, and one whom his father and brother would praise him for killing. Queen Aurelia was the most obvious choice, but Archie had ordered his men to leave his sister for him. One of the traitorous Akkinorian leaders—Silas Crowland, perhaps—felt like the next best option.

Upon spotting the middle-aged Carthinian man who'd stood beside Queen Aurelia until the battle began, Tyren knew he found his opponent. The man was clearly an important individual in Carthe, and Tyren had a feeling that Queen Aurelia would be severely weakened if this man were dead—making him one of the worthiest opponents on the battlefield.

When the short, gray-haired man turned his back, Tyren broke out into a sprint with his sword raised and a battle cry rising up in his throat. He didn't realize how close he'd gotten to the palace—nor to the queen's dragon—until the massive, blue-scaled beast flickered its gaze to Tyren.

As Tyren slowed and stumbled, the man seemed to recognize the dragon's behavior—the hunger in its eyes, the curling of its lips, and the way it lowered its head to the ground like a cat prowling for a mouse—and turned to face his attacker. Tyren was only a few yards away from him now, and while the dragon was frightening, Queen Aurelia had said herself that she wouldn't let it destroy her home. Tyren didn't think she had the stomach for it, either. A dragon that was nothing more than a pawn for a foolish woman's mind games didn't scare him—and at the very least, his opponent didn't seem worried, so why should he?

As he met eyes with his target, Tyren shouted and ran forward again, raising his sword in preparation to strike. The man only stared at him, calm and motionless, without so much as a dagger in hand.

Then a blinding orange glow rose up from behind the man, just above his head, and the last thing Tyren saw before being set ablaze was the man's face as his lips curled into a smile.

***

Aurelia gazed around, overwhelmed, as she tried to identify which soldiers were fighting for her and which were fighting for Archie. Some soldiers of the Royal Army had switched sides in the middle of the chaos, but the Laynoans and the Sadians were as loyal to Archie as ever. Only a handful of Laynoans, it seemed, had been swayed by Duke Stone's reminder of what it was to be Akkinorian.

Upon seeing Bryan Ashford struggling with an assailant, Aurelia exchanged her sword for her bow and sent an arrow sailing through the attacker's throat. The mercenary fell to the ground in a lifeless heap as the young lord met her gaze and struggled to catch his breath.

She inhaled sharply when their eyes met. She'd been acquainted with him many times before, but now that she knew of his connection to the man she loved, she saw him in an entirely different light. He was almost identical to Jack, his elder brother, with the primary differences between them being Bryan's long, curly brown hair and crystalline-blue eyes. Though he didn't have the ocean in his eyes as his brother did, the kindness and valor radiating from him proved that he and Jack were more alike than either of them realized.

A part of her wanted to tell him that his brother was alive—not only alive, but fighting on the very same battlefield.

Now, however, wasn't the time for sentiment.

"Thank you." He took note of the blood on her face and frowned. "Are you hurt, Your Grace?"

"No, I'm all right. Thank you for your help today, my lord. I never—"

"I know. That's why I'm here—because you never would've asked." His eyes landed on something behind her. He grabbed his dagger from its sheath and threw it before she could blink. When she looked over her shoulder, she saw a female assassin wielding a spear standing there. She fell backwards, choking on her own blood, with the dagger piercing her throat. Aurelia turned back to him and raised her eyebrows, and he only shrugged in response. "We don't like to fight, my queen. That doesn't mean we don't know how."

"Understood. My lord—how are there so many of them? I wasn't under the impression that my brother's mercenary army was so large."

Lord Ashford plucked a spear from the gut of a nearby corpse. "He's been embezzling funds from the people. He probably purchased more mercenaries after you escaped, and again when he heard of your plans to return. I hear he even turned to Isalder rogues on the Syren Isles and the pirate ports—a very costly thing."

She sheathed her sword and took her bow from her shoulder. She pulled an arrow from her sheath and nocked it, then aimed towards one of Archie's soldiers as the man threatened a Taundosan mage. The mage was distracted by pulling tree roots out of the ground and strangling enemy soldiers in her vicinity. Before the soldier could impale her, Aurelia sent the arrow flying through his neck.

"Be safe out there," she advised, reaching for her sword again. "I hope to see you again when this bloodshed comes to an end."

"Likewise, my queen."

As she dashed away, she felt a pressure in her ears. In the distance, it sounded like someone was calling her name. She looked around for the source and eventually found her uncle a few yards away. He was cut and bruised, but otherwise unharmed. He gestured with his hands and turned to face the palace. She followed his gaze and clenched her jaw when she realized what he was trying to tell her. Despite Halvor and Jack's troops protecting the palace gates, Archie was urging his men to retreat.

She knew why Arian was concerned. Jack didn't have enough men to prevent the entirety of Archie's forces from retreating into the palace. Halvor wouldn't respond unless ordered to do so by Aurelia. One way or another, the fight was being brought to the front doors of the palace. How her forces responded, though, was entirely up to her.

With a deep breath, she wrapped her hand around her locket and closed her eyes. She was murmuring Halvor's name when something hard and strong hit her in the back, sending her face-first onto the dirt and knocking the air from her lungs. Her sword fell from her hands as she struggled to climb to her knees. When she was standing with her sword in hand again, wheezing and gasping for air, she came face-to-face with her assailant: Lord Bradley Reilly.

***

The last thing the King of Akkinor saw before turning his back on the battlefield was his Hand being engulfed in flames and running in circles, guttural screams tearing through his body. While he was flailing about like a headless chicken, the dragon plucked Tyren off the ground and swallowed him whole, later belching triumphantly as a combination of flames, smoke, and charred body parts spewed from its massive jaws.

Archie turned away, desperately trying to control his trembles of fear, as two of his most loyal soldiers urged him to keep moving. Prior to his sister's return, these men were tasked with guiding the king to a safe place where he could wait out the battle until his forces overpowered hers. They'd managed to pull Archie from the field of combat before he was caught in the thick of the battle, so now the only task that remained was making sure he reached his safe haven.

As Archie and the soldiers rode east—careful not to draw attention to themselves by running like shameless deserters (which, of course, they were not)—he spotted a large, grassy hill in the near distance. On the other side of the hill was the River Gilsad, and upon crossing the bridge, they'd be leaving the Folly behind for Omara. There were plenty of places along the Omaran border for Archie to take shelter until the battle ended, and nobody—least of all the peace-loving Omarans—would dare to say or do anything if they happened to come across their king.

Hollering voices from behind compelled Archie to look over his shoulder. A group of five Carthinian soldiers were chasing after him and his protectors—on foot. Archie jerked his horse's reins to gain distance, only to be thrown onto the ground when an arrow pierced the steed through the neck. He barely registered the sound of his men yelling and the sight of them dismounting their horses to rush to his aid. He didn't have a breath left in his lungs, and his vision was corrupted by dark splotches, but somehow, he was able to steady himself when the soldiers hoisted him to his feet.

The Carthinians (Bozari, judging by their fiercely blue eyes) were apparently much faster than the average Akkinorian soldier, as they were surrounding the three men before Archie's ears had ceased to ring from his fall. He drew his sword—the first time in his life he'd ever done so in a matter of life and death—while his soldiers stood on either side of him, protecting him as well as they could.

As the Bozari closed in, one hissed something in their native tongue that neither Archie nor his soldiers understood. One of them lunged forward, and the Akkinorian to Archie's right leapt to meet him. Another struck at the second Akkinorian soldier, and the remaining three merely circled Archie like a trio of panthers preying on a rabbit.

Archie's stomach churned as he observed the fighting. His men were strong but slow, and every time they lifted an arm or put a foot forward, it looked like they were using every ounce of vigor in their bodies to move. The Bozari, on the other hand, resembled dancers more so than fighters: they moved swiftly and gracefully, were light on their feet, and didn't break a sweat. Even before the first Akkinorian fell, Archie knew he wouldn't be making it to Omara that day. The Bozari were wolves, and Archie and his men were sheep.

When both Akkinorians fell to the ground, the Bozari turned their full attention to Archie. Two of them spoke to him, but he still didn't understand a word of their barbaric gibberish. He could see the bloodlust in their eyes, so he did the only thing he could think of: turned and ran for the hills.

He heard them chuckling behind him, but he paid them no heed. Five Carthinian savages had no business killing the King of Akkinor. His sister would've given her men the same order Archie gave his own: to leave her rival for her to deal with. Maybe they'd put him in shackles and deliver him to his sister, but they wouldn't harm him—they had no right to.

Then a white-hot pain in his gut knocked him to the ground as he attempted to climb a hill. He tumbled down the sloped side, rolling and screaming, until he lost momentum by colliding with something sturdy: a pair of boots. He looked up at the Bozari soldier's face as black spots clouded his vision again, but he couldn't summon words—because of fear or pain, he didn't know. The soldier was the only one of the five armed with a bow and arrows, and his lips curled into a satisfied sneer when Archie brought a shaking hand to the burning sensation on his abdomen. Archie tried to remove the arrow from the unprotected chunk of flesh between pieces of his armor, but it only snapped in half.

Archie tried rolling to reach for the sword he'd dropped during his escape, but the soldier stepped on his hand, making the king howl in agony once again. The soldier crouched down beside him and ran the tip of a dagger along Archie's cheek. He said something that Archie didn't understand, then tried again in the common tongue:

"Surrender."

Despite his injury and fear, Archie was a king, and he had no intention of giving up. Instead, he spat in the soldier's face. The soldier laughed at Archie, neglected to wipe the saliva from his face, and severed Archie's left index finger in the time it took the king to blink.

Archie screamed and thrashed as he watched blood spray from whatever was left of the digit. Two other soldiers held him down by the knees and shoulders while the first—still with Archie's saliva dripping from his face—took another finger, and then another. Archie would've passed out from the pain, had the shock of everything failed to numb him, but he was forced to remain conscious as the soldier seemed to be collecting trophies for him and his comrades. Before he could take the fourth and fifth fingers for his friends, one of them stopped him by uttering something Archie couldn't understand.

The soldier with the dagger stepped away and kicked Archie in the gut, angering the arrow wound. "My friend saves your life," he told the king. "We must not take what belongs to the queen."

As the Bozari turned away, preparing to leave Archie and rejoin the fight, Archie used his last bit of strength to prop himself on his side and grab the soldier's ankle. He opened his mouth, preparing to clamp his teeth down on the soldier's flesh, but he was too slow. The soldier responded by kicking Archie in the face, and the blinding pain of feeling his jaw break almost knocked him out. He wanted to scream, but he couldn't—his jaw wouldn't open.

The soldier straddled Archie, forcing the arrow deeper into the king's gut, and traced Archie's cheek with the tip of his dagger once more. Archie's screams lodged in his throat as he felt the dagger tear his face open from the top of his cheekbone to the corner of his mouth. The wound was so deep that he could feel blood filling the hollows of his mouth, and as he writhed beneath the soldier's weight, the pain of every other injury he'd sustained increased tenfold.

"A king should know better than to strike the man who spared his life," the soldier seethed. A grin formed on his lips. "But you're no true king, are you?"

He stood, but before he and his fellow soldiers walked away, he turned Archie's head and planted his boot on Archie's uninjured cheek, shoving the open wound into the dirt. Archie blacked out from the pain for just a few moments, but not before the soldiers—now seemingly uninterested in their trophies—tossed his severed fingers onto his chest.

When he woke, still blinded by pain and unable to speak, one last, strategic thought popped into his head. The soldiers would tell his sister exactly where to find him if her forces managed to defeat his, and he wouldn't survive very long after he was captured. If he managed to hide, perhaps he could recover his strength enough to flee before she found him.

Mustering every bit of strength he could, Archie crawled toward the battlefield and kept his eyes trained on the only destination he could find: a pile of bloodied, battered corpses with Archie's coin in their pockets.

Just a bunch of scarecrows, really.

XLV

I suppose I should be more surprised than I am," Aurelia managed, ignoring the throbbing pain in her back. "Did I truly offend you so fiercely?"

"Five years." Lord Reilly pointed his blade at her chest. "For five years, I tried to make you my wife. I could've been the second-most powerful man in Akkinor. You never even considered my proposal, did you?"

"No, I didn't. I'm certainly glad for that now—you're as vile as my brother. There's nothing that motivates men like you other than power."

"Power motivates us all."

She shook her head. "No, it doesn't."

"Yet here you are, the most powerful woman in the world, making sure everybody knows it," he replied. The tip of his blade trembled against her breastplate as clumps of sweaty, chestnut hair fell over his wide eyes. "I pitied you once, you know. Rejecting suitor after suitor made you undesirable—the opportunity to claw at your power was the only reason any of us continued our efforts to court you. But you don't deserve my pity. You're as bad as the rest of us. A selfish, greedy woman who's too vain to share her power—even for the chance of having a husband."

"That's where you're wrong." She held up her hand to show him the twine ring Jack had tied around her finger the night before. "I *have* shared my power, Lord Reilly. Just not with you."

His eyes blazed. "You wicked little—"

"Careful." Relief flooded through Aurelia's veins when she recognized Jack's voice. Jack managed to wrap his arm around Lord Reilly's neck before the latter could react, then pinned the lord's arm so tightly that he was forced to drop his sword. "No title, no money, no power—and yet, I'm set to marry the queen, and *you* will be first in line to meet the hangman on execution day. Funny how that works, isn't it?"

"Let this be a lesson," Aurelia stated as Lord Reilly's chestnut eyes rolled back into his skull. He was losing consciousness from the force of Jack's arm against his throat. "Men who crave power will always fall to formidable women."

When Lord Reilly fell unconscious, Jack released him and let him plop to the ground. He stepped over the lord's limp body and took Aurelia's face in his hands, checking to ensure that the blood on her face wasn't her own—exactly what his brother had done moments earlier. She studied him as much as he studied her. When they were both certain that neither had been gravely injured, they released each other and exchanged tired smiles.

"You're supposed to be guarding the gates," she recalled. "Has something happened?"

He grimaced. "There are more of them than we prepared for. That creature of yours is frightening, but he hasn't dissuaded the retreaters." When she didn't answer, he stared at her and scrubbed a hand down his face. "I think—"

"I know."

She glanced up at the palace as Halvor turned his massive head in her direction. They met eyes, and for a moment, it seemed like the two were having a conversation. Then he lifted off from the tower, shrieking, and landed on the ground in front of the walls dividing the palace grounds from the battlefield. He released another screech at the men who tried to pass him—even going as far as to tear one of them in half with his teeth.

"When all of this is over," Jack said, "I'd like to hear about how you were able to keep a dragon in a necklace."

Aurelia laughed. "You will. For now, I must reach him before Archie's forces overwhelm him. He'll respond instinctively if he feels threatened, and I meant what I said about being better than my brother. I'd rather not turn the Folly into a graveyard."

He rolled out his shoulder and adjusted his grip on his sword. "Let's go." When she started to protest, he shook his head at her. "I'm right by your side, Lily dear. You'll be wasting precious energy if you attempt to fight me on that."

She smiled. "Okay."

As much as she hated the idea of Jack following her through the bloodshed, it was pointless to argue with him. Now that they'd reunited, nothing short of death would separate them again—not even the mass hysteria and chaos unfolding across the path they needed to take to reach Halvor. The fighting was the thickest there, as Archie's forces were attempting to retreat into the palace while Aurelia's forces tried to stop them. Getting to Halvor wouldn't be easy, not from their position, but Aurelia's most loyal protector had become their last hope.

The surrounding village was already engulfed in flames, but not by Aurelia's command. Archie's mercenaries had torched the homes and shops to inflict maximum damage upon the Folly. Luckily, Aurelia couldn't see or hear any civilians being dragged from their homes or murdered in their beds. The troops from Krotis had successfully evacuated the city and relocated the civilians to Seaport. As long as Archie's forces were contained in the Folly, the people would be safe.

None of that mattered if the enemy took the palace, which would've left Aurelia with one option: destroying her home and everything inside. Anyone left inside the palace as collateral damage—servants and their families, friends, and the like—would be lost forever.

As they trekked to the palace, an arrow whizzed through the air and nicked Aurelia's upper arm. Startled, she cried out and dropped her sword to the ground. While she turned to collect her weapon, Jack engaged in a battle with a man twice his size. Luckily, Jack was the better swordsman, and the assailant was choking on his own blood in a matter of seconds. Jack turned to inspect Aurelia's arm, and upon seeing that it was fairly minor, turned his attention to a dark stain on his shirt.

Aurelia's eyes widened. Jack touched his palm to his side and inspected his hand, which was now stained with a thick coat of blood. He grimaced, but the adrenaline of the fight seemed to give him strength. He gave her a nod, a smile, and a quick look of encouragement before leading her further into the heart of the fighting.

Her arm was getting weaker and weaker with each movement, and she could see that Jack was beginning to slow down, too. Halvor was still a distance away from them and was growing more overwhelmed by the second. The bond between dragon and mistress would keep him at bay for a little while, but skin-to-skin contact was crucial during times like this: without a physical connection to strengthen the bond between souls, Halvor would respond instinctively to the threats surrounding him. If Aurelia was unable to take control, every soldier in Halvor's proximity would be at the mercy of a beast who stood taller than the palace. Dragons were intelligent creatures—arguably even more intelligent than humans—but on that day, it was nearly impossible to tell allies apart from enemies.

Aurelia threw her sword when she spotted an archer setting her sights on Jack. The woman was impaled with the sword before she could release the arrow, and Aurelia was able to recover her weapon in time to defend herself from another attacker. The Isalder was much stronger and more skilled than herself, but bearing arms against the queen seemed to panic him. His arms trembled as their blades met, and she was able to shove him backwards before his sword kissed her throat. Jack approached him from behind, sweating and panting from defending against another assailant, and cut his throat with one quick movement.

Her heart hammered when she saw the spreading of blood on his shirt. "Oh, Jack—"

"We have to keep moving." His face was ashen, but his eyes were as alive as ever. "Keep your head high, Aurelia. Keep—"

She whipped around at the sound of heavy footsteps and blocked a soldier's sword with her own. As they struggled against one another, she reached into her sheath with her wounded arm and gritted her teeth through the pain. She attempted to stab the man with an arrow, but he managed to lower his sword and cut her thigh before she had the chance. When her legs gave out, she let out a yelp of pain, prompting Jack to stab the man and whirl around in time to defend himself against yet another attacker. While he and the soldier battled, Aurelia regained her footing and shoved the arrow into his attacker's throat.

She reached for Jack's hand and squeezed. "You are my love and my life, today and every day."

He forced himself to smile, revealing blood-stained teeth, and wiped at his split lip. "And you are mine. Today and every day."

She smiled, eyes growing bleary with exhaustion, as the pair pushed forwards once more. They'd almost reached Halvor by then, but the crowd of soldiers surrounding him was nearly impenetrable. Despite the chaos around her, she took a long, deep breath and focused on Halvor's reptilian eyes. Her old friend felt the strengthened connection between them and turned in her direction. When they met eyes, blue against gold, he released an ear-piercing shriek that rattled the world from east to west.

His enormous, spiked tail whipped from side to side, knocking soldiers from their feet and sending them flying into the air. In the blink of an eye, his massive mouth dipped downwards and tore three men in half. Some soldiers ran in fear as Aurelia had hoped, but others were still more afraid of Archie's wrath than of being torn to pieces by a dragon. As she watched Halvor clear a path, Jack took her elbow and squeezed. He'd found her an opening, but now, it was time for the queen to continue on alone.

She bounced on her feet for a moment before breaking out into a sprint. With Jack protecting her from behind and Halvor from the front, her primary focus was to run. She jumped over bodies like hurdles, dodged whizzing arrows and flying daggers, and slid across the blood-stained dirt so aggressively that her trousers tore at the knees. She was running again before she knew what was happening, but soon enough, she regretted not crawling to Halvor on her hands and knees.

She'd been running like war wasn't raging around her, and she'd let her guard down. She was close enough to Halvor that she could feel the heat of his breath when something sharp sliced her face—so impactful that her head whipped backwards, weighing her body down and resulting in the back of her head slamming against the ground.

Her vision faded to black, the sounds of battle reduced to silence, and one lone, strangled gasp escaped her throat before the world around her disappeared completely.

***

He'd lost her.

He'd turned his back for a split second, and he'd lost her.

Jack scoured his surroundings, but he couldn't find her anywhere. It was like she'd disappeared into thin air. Maybe he'd simply lost her in the chaos, or maybe...maybe she'd gotten captured and dragged away—or worse, killed and left to be buried beneath corpses as they fell, only to be trampled on and disfigured beyond recognition. Every possible scenario ran through his head, and it wouldn't stop until he found her again.

He kept worrying and searching as he fought, to no avail. His concern for Aurelia disappeared for just a moment when an enormous Isalder mercenary charged him with a club in hand. Jack deflected the blow and tried to kick the man in the gut, but his foot bounced off the man's bulging belly like the Isalder was made of rubber. Fortunately, large men tended to be rather slow, and Jack had adopted some speed after his many races with Aurelia. He rolled across the ground, and in the time it took for the Isalder to turn, Jack was able to stab the man in the back, severing his spine in two.

He'd somehow lost his helmet not long after the fighting began, and he wished he hadn't when an arrow missed his head by inches. The rest of his armor hadn't done much to protect him, though. He'd been able to ignore the wound in his abdomen for the most part, but now that the adrenaline was wearing off, the pain was getting worse and worse by the minute.

As he turned toward the palace, still searching for Aurelia and covering his bleeding wound with his hand, he saw an Akkinorian soldier straining against an Isalder mercenary. Jack lifted his sword again, intending to assist his fellow Akkinorian, but he didn't need to. The soldier stabbed the mercenary through the eye with a dagger, and when the body fell to the ground, the victor reclaimed his dagger and turned.

The world seemed to still for a moment when Jack met the soldier's gaze. He wasn't a soldier at all—he was a nobleman, the very same nobleman who'd taken Jack's place as Lord of Omara.

As Bryan's eyes bugged out of his head, he opened his mouth to speak before closing it again. When he tried once more, no sound emerged, but Jack recognized the word playing on his brother's lips: *Jack*.

Jack took a step forward, intending to show Bryan that he was real and not a ghost, but he didn't get the chance. From the corner of his eye, he saw a figure rise from the ground several yards from him—a figure with a head of dirty, blood-stained hair, but hair Jack would recognize anywhere: long, golden locks woven with strands of copper and auburn. He knew it was her the moment he saw her hair, which meant that anyone else searching for her—friend or enemy—would recognize her, too.

Jack looked at his brother once more, murmured an apology Bryan couldn't hear, and ran for the woman he loved before somebody else got to her first.

***

Aurelia gasped as her eyes shot open, and for a moment, she forgot where she was. Her vision was blurry and hazy, and the only thing she could see was the smoky, darkening sky above. The sounds of war were muffled at first, but as the seconds passed, they became so earsplitting that her head—already aching and throbbing from her fall—felt like it was close to imploding.

Slowly and cautiously, she pushed herself to her knees, feeling as though time had halted. She brought a hand to her cheek and winced at the stinging sensation that followed. She barely registered the bloody arrow resting beside her and the interaction in front of her, in which Alryn (the fire mage from Taundosa) was incinerating a Sadian soldier with his flames.

With her bloodstained hands resting on her knees, she closed her eyes and counted her breaths, slowly mustering the strength to rise again. The noises surrounding her were still muffled as if the battle was raging beneath the tides. Amidst the distant sounds of chaos, though, a voice echoed in her head and drowned out everything from Halvor's shrieks to the blood-curdling screams of dying men—a voice Aurelia recognized better than her own: Edmund's.

"If you ever find yourself at war," he'd once told her, "remember this, and remember it well: it doesn't matter how many lives you claim, how much land you seize, or how formidable you are in combat. What matters is how many friends you save—and foes, if they're worthy. Whether you win or lose, the friends you saw to the end will make sure history remembers you for the good you did, not the tragedy you participated in."

"But what if I *do* lose?" Even at twelve years old, Aurelia had known that the opposite of victory was death.

Edmund had only smiled. "Fret not, little one. If you lose, you'll still have won something by fighting for what the realm needs, not what you desire. You see, the way history remembers us is almost entirely dependent on motivation. Victors come and go, and history struggles to recall each of their names. It'd be like documenting every tree that loses its leaves and gains them back again: an impossible task, even for the most diligent of scholars. That's why you must always fight for those who, like you, have the most to lose: when all is said and done, the people you showed grace and mercy to will be the ones responsible for deciding how the realm remembers you."

An ear-piercing shriek snapped Aurelia's gaze to the side, where the orange glow of sunset beamed behind Halvor's body and cast a massive shadow over the battlefield. The memory of her father retreated to the farthest corners of her mind, the scene unfolding around her returned, and she remembered what she was meant to do. Halvor hadn't moved from his previous position, though she could see in his eyes that he was growing restless. If she failed to reach him before he defended himself against the troops closing in on him, she'd lose her chance at becoming the leader her father taught her to be—after all, a victory won by massacre was no true victory.

She ran for the dragon again as if every blade, every arrow, and every spear aimed in her direction would bounce off her flesh like her entire being was crafted from Akkinorian bronze. Just as Halvor released another bellowing screech, she found herself tripping to the ground, now eye-level with his talons. She scrambled to her feet and sheathed her sword, then hurriedly clambered on his back while he deflected the arrows being aimed at his mistress. From her position on Halvor's back, she searched the crowd for Jack and met his eyes. Jack knew what she meant by her quick glance and immediately commanded their troops to run. As her allies began evacuating, Archie's soldiers took the opportunity to press forward, still intent on following their king's order to retreat into the palace.

Aurelia took a long, deep breath and tapped Halvor's scales once, twice, three times. On her signal, he turned his head to the left and released a powerful stream of fire that ravaged every man and woman in his path. As he craned his head from left to right, igniting everything in his wake,

Aurelia winced at the heatwaves burning her skin. Smoke billowed into the air and transformed the sky from a serene blue to a sickly gray.

As the smell of burning flesh filled her nostrils, Aurelia urged Halvor forwards. He stomped over the charred bodies and burning soldiers, roaring as he charged towards the battlefield, and let out another stream of fire when Archie's soldiers attempted to stop him with spears and arrows. On Aurelia's command, Halvor slowed to a stop and lowered his head to make her visible to the survivors on the battlefield.

"Today, friends and family have raised their swords against one another to fight a battle for greed. You've taken orders from a usurper and a traitor for reasons even *you* don't understand. And the rest of you, wherever you may hail from, have raised your swords to a queen in exchange for blood money. Enough lives have been lost today. You've seen what my allies can do. You've seen what I'm capable of. I won't burn my city to the ground, as my brother would. I won't burn my people to the ground as my brother would. I can, but I won't. Nobody else needs to die today. If you lay down your weapons, no harm will come to you. You have my word."

Nobody moved or spoke. Across the battlefield, she saw friends and enemies staring at her with both fear and wonder in their eyes. Before Archie's troops could respond, one figure surged forwards and released a battle cry as she charged Halvor with a spear in hand. Aurelia recognized Lady Daena Spirre of Sadia, wife of Terren Spirre, whose throat she'd cut on the battlefield several hours earlier. Their two sons, both under the age of sixteen, had also died on the battlefield after being forced to fight by a Sadian tradition, which demanded that all noble boys over the age of thirteen bear arms during wartime. Before she could avenge her husband and her sons, Lady Spirre was swallowed whole by Halvor, and the last of the Spirres was gone.

Aurelia winced, but she knew Lady Spirre was an example. She couldn't be touched so long as Halvor lived and breathed, and nobody in the world had the power to defeat a creature of his strength. The battle was already over; it was only a matter of waiting for Archie's troops to realize it, too.

And so they did. After a few moments, Archie's soldiers lowered and dropped their weapons. Sheaths were emptied, swords clattered to the dirt, and bowstrings snapped upon contact with the ground. When they were disarmed, they collapsed to their knees in surrender with their hands behind their heads.

Even when her allies began to cheer, the only sound Aurelia could hear was the pounding of her own heart—and Halvor's—in her ears.

XLVI

The sun had set and risen again by the time Aurelia's ears ceased to ring. Even then, her body felt weightless, as if she were floating through the clouds in the world beyond. Paired with the ash blowing in the wind like snow, the orange glow of the sunrise made it appear as though the kingdom was still ablaze. Aurelia wondered if it would ever look as it did before.

After the battle ended at dusk, Aurelia hadn't been given the chance to rejoice or rest. There was much to be done: finding her allies in the smoldering remains of combat, locating and apprehending her surviving enemies, bringing the Follian civilians home from Seaport, and the like. Even with the many voices of leadership helping her pick up the pieces, nobody seemed willing to do anything without Aurelia's command. She hadn't realized how long the process took until the sun rose to welcome a new day.

Aurelia was vaguely aware of a presence at her side, but it took her longer than usual to sense her uncle's unique energy. When she looked at him, the rising sun cast beautiful rays of golden light on his face, and she saw flecks of gold in his eyes that she could've sworn hadn't been there before. He said something, but the ringing in her ears drowned out the sound of his voice. As the ringing slowly faded, he realized she hadn't heard him and gave a slight chuckle.

"I asked if you've been examined by a medic, Your Grace," he repeated. She exhaled. "I shall take that response as a no. I must encourage you to accompany me into the palace. You'll do well to have yourself healed before you stress yourself further."

"All right." She turned from the battlefield and towards the palace, taking Arian's arm and allowing him to escort her through the gates. As they walked, she watched her boots create prints in the ashes coating the ground. "I haven't been home in almost a year," she shared as she looked up at the palace.

"Are you nervous?"

"A bit." She shivered at the sound of her feet against the familiar marble steps leading to the front doors. From what she could see of the foyer, it looked exactly as she remembered it. She brought Arian to a halt and sucked in a deep breath. "When were you here last?"

"I visited briefly about twenty years ago. You were five at the time, your brother two. I came for your grandmother's memorial and was gone two days later. We met momentarily, you and I, but the circumstances of my visit kept us apart for most of it. You were in quite the rush when we met. Your exact words were, 'It's a pleasure, but I really must be going.'"

Aurelia chortled. "You never told me that."

"Yes, well..." He sighed. "Some memories are better left for opportune moments such as this." He patted her hand on his arm and offered her an encouraging smile. "Welcome home, Aurelia."

She released a long, shaky exhale and released him. When she took her first steps into the foyer, she felt something wash over her that she couldn't quite identify. Nostalgia, perhaps? Anxiety? Terror? A mix of all three, she decided. Even with the many emotions paralyzing her, she forced herself to move forward. The moment she'd waited for was finally here: she was home.

All evidence of the uprising had been scrubbed away: the wallpaper had been replaced, the marble floors were squeaky clean, and the blood spatters had been cleaned from the artifacts, lighting fixtures, and furniture. The one difference was the enormous portrait of the monarch hanging in the foyer. Aurelia's portrait had been taken down and probably destroyed, only to be replaced by a painting of her brother.

"Remove that wretched portrait at once," Arian instructed a soldier. Aurelia thanked him with a faint smile, but she couldn't bring herself to look away from it until the soldier hauled it away. Her uncle set a comforting hand on her shoulder. "Let's go."

Silent, she followed him through the corridors to the ballroom, where a makeshift infirmary had been organized in the massive space. She wrinkled her nose immediately at the state of the soldiers being tended to by medics and mages. Most were covered in blood, soot, and dirt. Men howled in pain and shrieked at the sight of missing limbs. Medics covered corpses with sheets and left the bodies for the uninjured soldiers to load into wagons.

Aurelia frowned. "These people need the medics more than I do. I'm perfectly fine. I can wait—"

"You'll do no such thing," came a voice from behind. She smiled tiredly when Jack set a hand on the small of her back and kissed her cheek. He seemed exhausted and weakened, but luckily, he'd already been treated for his injuries. "Your wounds are minor. It'll take only a moment."

She sighed. "All right."

"I must discuss our next moves with our allies," Arian informed them. "Find me after you've been examined. There's another matter that requires our attention."

The queen wrinkled her nose. She knew exactly what he was referring to—her brother. Nobody had seen him since the battle began. Aurelia's soldiers were now searching every evacuated home in the Folly, believing he'd hidden himself away to avoid the fighting, but everyone was well aware of a terrifying possibility: Archie might've fled.

Jack escorted her to an empty cot in the middle of the ballroom, where a medic immediately approached her for an examination. Her wounds were minor and shallow, so all she required was a bit of healing salve and bandages. A mage approached her and offered to heal her injuries indefinitely—including erasing the scars from her skin—but upon seeing the soldiers' wounds, she declined. There were only a few mages present who were adept at healing, and their energy was too precious to be wasted on Aurelia's minor injuries.

She hesitated briefly when the medic offered her a handheld mirror, believing Aurelia would change her mind upon seeing her face. She inhaled sharply at the sight of a long, jagged scar over her right cheek—the scar she'd earned at the end of the battle when an arrow knocked her to the ground. The medic had treated the wound with salve, so it'd leave a thick white scar behind when it healed. The marking wasn't one that could be easily concealed by cosmetics and the like, either. A part of her wanted to be rid of it to preserve her beauty, but the more dominant part of her knew the mark was one she was meant to bear.

"Aurelia?" Jack stared at her with raised eyebrows. Again, she'd been too lost in her head to realize someone was speaking to her. He brushed hair from her face and smiled. "You should get some rest, my love."

She shook her head. "There's much to be done. Halvor—"

"—is fine. He's perfectly capable of looking after himself." The silly grin she loved so much reappeared on his lips. "I believe you owe me a story. How did you manage to house a dragon in a locket?"

She smiled as she clutched her now-empty locket. "Arian told me everything in Taundosa. He can provide you with the more precise explanation of how it came to be. This necklace—and Halvor—has been passed down to the women of the Cristos family for generations. My parents told me about Halvor when I was old enough to understand why he had to be kept secret, but they didn't disclose how he came to be mine. During the persecution, Halvor's mistress cast a spell on her locket so it would contain him: not quite a prison, but a magical place between worlds where he could exist until he was freed again. Another spell protects the locket from releasing him when opened. That's why I needed the sorcerer in the dungeon. Linden took the necklace to him during the uprising and had him break the spell, which allowed me to free Halvor on my own."

"How long has he been in the locket?"

"Several centuries, I'd imagine. Give or take."

"And he's tame?"

She gave him a look. "No wild animal can be tamed completely, Jack. Dragons weren't meant to be humanity's slaves. Not like the little domesticated ones alive today. I spent many days and nights studying dragons when I first learned about Halvor. They're the kind of creature that chooses their own master or mistress. When they've chosen a person to protect and serve, they become incapable of harming or disobeying that person and their entire bloodline. Halvor chose one of my ancestors a long time ago. He's proven today that he's still as loyal to the Cristos family as he was all those centuries ago."

"Incredible. Do you suppose there are others out there? Dragons of old, being hidden away by the descendants of their masters and mistresses?"

A deep sigh escaped her. "I hope so."

***

"Any sign of him?"

Arian grimaced. "No."

Aurelia sighed and averted her gaze. It'd been hours since the end of the battle, and still, not a soul had seen Archie. With each second that passed, Aurelia was beginning to wonder if her fears were warranted—if Archie had, indeed, fled the Folly for Seaport and sailed off to salvation elsewhere in the world.

She was exhausted, hungry, filthy, and desperately craving nothing more than a night's sleep in her own bed, but she couldn't rest until Archie was found. She needed proof of his departure from Akkinor so she could order her men to search for him. If he hadn't fled the country, then she needed to find him before he did something even more foolish than usurping his queen.

Standing to the left of Aurelia as she sat on her throne, Jack turned to her. "Lily, dear," he said cheekily, "there's no better place to hide than directly under our noses, is there?"

Her lips parted. "You think he's here? On the grounds?"

"He must be. He knows every crack and crevice of the palace. I've been thinking about it, and I don't suppose he's clever enough to have planned an escape from the country. He doesn't have enough foresight for that. In his mind, he didn't need an escape because he'd be victorious on the battlefield."

Aurelia's grin matched Jack's. She hadn't thought of that, but he was certainly right: Archie never expected to lose. An unplanned escape from the Folly wouldn't have worked in his favor, what with the massive number of Carthinian soldiers in the kingdom, and he wouldn't have orchestrated an escape before the battle if he had no intention of losing. That alone was enough to give her an idea of where he might've gone.

"If you'll excuse me," she muttered, rising from her throne, "I'm off to have a word with my brother."

Both Jack and Arian insisted upon accompanying her, but she refused. This was something she needed to do alone. She didn't want to face her brother for the first time after the battle with allies flanking either side of her. She wanted him to see her alone, without a dragon or a Goldman or an Akkinorian swordsman by her side.

As she roamed the halls, ignoring the many faces surrounding her, she was unable to fully appreciate the wonder of what she'd done. For the first time in history, Akkinorian and Carthinian soldiers fought side-by-side on the battlefield. Now, they were celebrating their victory with shared pints of ale, tending to each other's wounds, and exchanging stories from their respective homelands. The animosity between the two continents seemed to have evaporated.

But Aurelia wasn't concerned with all of that now. She was too distracted by thoughts of her childhood, by the memories clinging to the walls like sconces. All members of the royal family were trained in combat, and as such, she and Archie had undergone numerous training sessions together. She remembered one particular instance when she and her instructors couldn't find ten-year-old Archie in the training hall. After hours of searching the property, it'd been Aurelia who'd found him. Not wanting to train that day, her brother had concealed himself beneath heaps of scarecrows—lined up against a wall in the gardener's shed like firewood—so well that she'd only found him after hearing him sneeze.

When reprimanded by their father, Archie had replied, "Why should I fight when I can hide until it's over?"

Aurelia would never forget their father's response: "A leader who hides from conflict while his men give their lives in his name is deplorable, shameful. If you hide while others win a war on your behalf, you *must* have enough humility to admit that the victory isn't yours to claim. You can't claim what you didn't earn."

Aurelia made her way to the exterior of the palace and instructed two Goldmen to escort her to the battlefield. As expected, soldiers were loading bodies into wagons to be transported elsewhere. What with there being so many corpses strewn about, she wasn't surprised to find that a large number of them had been piled atop one another.

She knew where each of the bodies would be taken. Akkinorian soldiers would be returned to their native kingdoms and buried in family crypts or cemeteries. Carthinian soldiers, as customary on the western continent, would be placed on funeral pyres, floated out to sea, and set ablaze by flaming arrows. Archie's mercenaries, on the other hand, would be taken to the barren northern mountains of Sadia, where the corpses would be buried in mass graves.

Nobody who'd fought for Archie knew what to do with the dead. He hadn't given any thought to funeral rites before he sent his men to combat. There he was, forcing thousands upon thousands of people to wage his war, all without having any intention of honoring them if and when they died for him.

Aurelia studied the heaps of bodies while soldiers hefted the remains for transportation. Several yards to her left sat a hulking pile of Isalder corpses. *Scarecrows*, she thought. Every last one of them, as she'd seen with her own eyes, perished instantly when a powerful mage's shockwave stopped their hearts. They'd collapsed atop one another near the center of the battlefield. Her eyes locked on one corpse in particular: a thin man wearing Isalder furs, laying face-down on the ground, with his head of golden blond hair stained with blood and dirt.

"Awfully dark for Isalder hair, isn't it?" she said to nobody in particular.

One soldier coughed. "Your Grace?"

"Move them."

Obeying their queen, the soldiers lifted the bodies from the heap and laid them side-by-side on the grass. She held out a hand to stop them when the body in question twitched ever-so-slightly. With a pounding heart, she fell to her knees and rolled the body over. A gasp escaped her lips when she set her gaze on her brother's face.

The soldiers barked orders at one another, hollering that the usurper had been found, but Aurelia motioned for them to cease upon feeling the shallowness of Archie's breathing. A monstrous gash on his right cheek was so deep that she could see his teeth under layers of blood and torn flesh. A broken arrow protruded from his gut, and when she glimpsed at his hands, she counted only seven fingers.

A Goldman cleared his throat. "Is he...?"

"No. Not yet." Aurelia couldn't look away from him, despite the horrors of his appearance, as she tried desperately to convince herself that she wasn't to blame for her brother's suffering; only he was. She opened her mouth to ask the soldiers to fetch a medic, but before she could speak, she felt a heavy weight along her thigh. Her lips parted when she reached into her pocket to produce the elvemar stone. "Thank you, Reyna," she whispered.

Grimacing, she forced Archie's jaw open and tucked the stone into the left side of his mouth. Her heart hammered as she waited for the stone to take effect. She didn't wish for her brother to suffer before death, nor did she wish for him to escape a trial for his crimes. And though he'd wounded her more deeply than any other had before, she didn't want to see her little brother die.

She inhaled sharply when the wound on his cheek began to heal. She could hardly believe her eyes as his flesh seeped together like liquid, rebuilding the missing part of his cheek. At the same time, the remaining piece of the arrow expelled itself from his gut, sealing the wound. His fingers didn't return, but the bloody stumps where his digits had been closed like they'd been sewn together.

When his eyes snapped open and a strangled gasp escaped his lips, Aurelia commanded the soldiers to leave them. She took a few steps backwards—still frightened of him, even in his current state—and watched with wide eyes as he brought himself to a sitting position.

"You've been most fortunate to live to see another day," she said hoarsely. He blinked, still dazed, before his cold gaze met hers. "Tell me, brother—did you even attempt to fight before you ran and cowered beneath the corpses of your mercenaries?"

Archie ignored her inquiry. "It's over, then?"

"It's been over for hours now."

He didn't move an inch. "Come to escort me to the dungeon yourself, have you?"

"Not quite. Soldiers are over there—they'll come for you after we've spoken."

His head bobbed as if he wanted to nod, and he stiffened when his eyes flickered up to her left hand. "Which Carthinian heathen did you trick into accepting your hand? That's how you secured your silly little allies, isn't it? You refused to marry your own kin for years, but the moment an opportunity for power presented itself—"

"Careful, brother," she warned. The cool edge in her voice must've been chillier than intended, as he recoiled just enough for her to notice. "I secured my alliances because of the quality of my character. I wouldn't expect you to understand that. Carthinians aren't heathens, for one, and for another, my betrothed isn't from the west. It's Arthur Ashford. He's more Akkinorian than you are, for gods' sakes."

The corner of his mouth twitched. "Arthur Ashford is dead."

"He was *presumed* dead. He's very much alive. I'd fetch him for you, but I don't suppose he'll be as patient with you as I am."

"Hmm." He paused for a moment. "It's a shame it took you so long to find him. Perhaps none of this would've happened if you'd met him sooner."

"What's that supposed to mean?"

"Oh, come *on*," he snapped. A scowl corrupted her lips as his childlike intrigue was, once again, replaced by resentment and bitterness. "You can't be that daft. If you and your deserter plaything had met and fallen madly in love a few years ago, you'd have an heir or two by now. Nobody would've placed a crown on my head if you had a child to take the throne in your stead." A cunning twinkle illuminated his eyes—a look so weathered and calculating that for a moment, Aurelia didn't recognize her own brother. "Why do you suppose I fought the idea of marriage so fiercely?"

Her lips parted as he sneered at her. She felt silly—not simply because her brother had played her like a fiddle, but because she hadn't held him in high enough regard to even *suspect* he'd be such a clever strategist.

She hadn't hidden the fact that she was waiting for Archie to marry before she considered her own marriage. Her list of concerns would grow by the dozen when she was married, and she didn't want Archie's future included in that list. So long as he remained unmarried, so would she—but that'd left her without a true heir, too. By sidestepping every proposal Aurelia brought to him, he assured his place in the line of succession. He'd been playing her for *years*.

She wanted to holler at him, to say every ugly thing that'd been brewing in her brain from the moment she learned of his involvement in the uprising, but she couldn't do it. This may very well have been the last conversation she'd ever have with her brother; if there was any time to be honest with him when nobody was around to hear, it was now.

Anxious, she rubbed her palms on her thighs and swallowed the lump in her throat. "I must've been a dreadful sister to you, Archie, for you to do the things you've done. I'm sorry."

His face contorted with disgust. *"You're* apologizing to *me?"* When she stared at him, her silence seemed to peeve him even more. "Is this some sort of trick? Are you playing me for a fool, or are you simply proving that you're just as idiotic as I've always thought you to be?"

Her blood boiled, that infamous temper of hers threatening to strike, but she refused to snap. Instead, she laughed. "I must say, it's comforting to know that some things never change."

He raised an eyebrow. "Pray tell."

"You're still the same boy, Archie. Even now. Even after everything." He stared at her blankly, not understanding. "You've never been someone who is happy—or even *content*—with what's already yours. You were once among the most blessed people in the realm, but you were too blinded by greed and resentment to appreciate it."

His eyes narrowed. "And what's that? What did I have before the throne, sister? You? A title? A noble girl from Myra waiting for me?"

"Well, yes," Aurelia said, blinking at him. "Before this mess, you had everything a person could hope for. You were loved, wholly and completely, by wonderful people. You lived in a palace, brimming with the comforts that most people can only dream of. You were set to inherit one of the largest castles and one of the most formidable dukedoms in the country. None of it was ever enough for you. It grieves me to know that you were too displeased with your own good fortune to consider the misfortunes of our people."

"Love is supposed to be unconditional, isn't it?" he demanded. She observed him, perplexed. He shook his head and scoffed. "I was never as loved as you like to pretend. I was never *unsatisfied* with being as lucky as you say. I was simply aware of the inevitable truth of my life—that somebody will always be loved more than me because I wasn't born to wear a crown."

Her heart ached. "That isn't true. You're my brother, despite—"

"Despite what I've done to you?" With his unkempt blonde hair and grimy, blood-stained skin, he looked more like a prisoner than he did a prince. "I'm to be executed, Aurelia! I broke eleven of the Accords and sent assassins to murder you! You've sentenced me to death, but you claim you still love me? Have you any sense at all?"

She narrowed her eyes. "If you knew what it means—what it *feels like*— to love someone, you'd understand." She kicked a rock by her foot and chuckled humorlessly. "You were always meant to end up where you are today, brother, and maybe I've always known. But I've always loved you anyway." No reply. She sighed. "There's another question I'd like to ask, and please, do me the kindness of telling the truth. Was this *all* your doing? Did you plot everything yourself, or did others compel you to rise against me? Did you start planning for this the moment Mother and Father were gone?"

"That's more than one question." Angry red splotches spread over his cheeks at her mention of their parents. "But no, it wasn't entirely my doing, and I didn't plot to murder you while we mourned over empty tombs. It was three years ago when Daena Spirre planted the idea in my head. She came to me just after you refused her proposal to betroth you to her son."

Aurelia grimaced. "He was twelve. I was two-and-twenty."

"A far-fetched idea, even for me." He swallowed like vomit had filled his mouth, then clenched his fists to conceal the stumps. "She thought you were failing the country by refusing to marry and further the line of succession. She said that men are always more dutiful than women, and Akkinor would do well to have a strong man on the throne, just as we've had for centuries. She tried convincing me to marry her niece, too, but I wasn't thinking about that."

"What were you thinking about?"

"How every king before Father disposed of their firstborn daughters to ensure they'd have a male heir—even Oleander the Great. He had three daughters before his wife gave him a son, and he sent them all away. Father had every opportunity to do the same with you after I was born, and he refused. Steadfastly, might I add. He made me the laughingstock of the realm by choosing you over me. Daena reminded me of what I always knew: everyone thought something was wrong with me, because why else would Father choose a *girl* to rule when he was blessed with a son?"

Aurelia scowled. "He chose to respect the line of succession because it's the law. He did the honorable thing instead of what society deemed suitable. That was always his way, Archie, and you know it. His choice wasn't a reflection of you or how he felt about you." He hung his head, refusing to reply. She exhaled and tiredly pinched the bridge of her nose. "Before I summon the soldiers to apprehend you, there's something else for us to discuss. You have the same right as any prisoner on death row to—"

"—write one final letter to a loved one?" he finished. "Who's left for me to write to? Everyone's gone. My only remaining relative is condemning me to death. What would you have me do?"

"I've done my part. You have the right to craft one final letter before your execution. You may do as you please with that."

Again, she was met with nothing but silence. She sighed irritably and called for the soldiers as she prepared to return to the palace. As two Akkinorian knights and two Goldmen joined them, armed with swords and shackles, she heard a quiet mumble escape Archie's lips. He still hadn't risen from the ground, and if she knew him at all, she was certain that he'd remain seated until the soldiers were forced to carry him away.

"Do you have something to say?" she asked.

She paused for a moment when she saw how frail and small he'd become. She was reminded of the six-year-old boy who'd come to her for solace after accidentally killing a toad he'd been playing with. The young prince hadn't understood the tragic effect of keeping a living creature in a wooden chest with no air. He'd had the same look on his face as he did now—only this time, he wasn't being introduced to the god of death, but rather preparing to meet him. It seemed he finally understood the severity of what he'd done and what it meant for him.

"Come here, Li." She hesitated, not wanting to give in, but the childlike tone in his voice—and his use of her nickname—compelled her to approach him again. "I-I have a request."

"What is it?"

He paused for a moment. "I-I don't want to write a letter. I'd like something else." She stared at him expectantly as he smacked his dry, bloodied lips together. "One final song. That's it."

She didn't have to ask. "All right."

His eyelids fluttered shut, relieved. With a heavy, pounding heart, Aurelia turned away from her brother and allowed the soldiers to escort him to the dungeon. She waited for them to cross the battlefield before motioning for the Goldmen to accompany her back to the palace. As she walked with the two Goldmen trailing behind her, it took everything she had to keep from crying, despite knowing her brother wasn't deserving of her tears.

She should have anticipated his request. Archie's pride and joy for the entirety of his two-and-twenty years was the pianoforte. He'd learned to play by the time he was four years old. It was his favorite thing in the world, even when it seemed like nothing could bring him joy.

She knew to expect some backlash from the nobles and her advisors, as they wouldn't be happy with her fulfillment of Archie's request, but it was a risk she'd have to take. After all, the song would be her last gift to her baby brother before she sanctioned his beheading.

XLVII

urelia leaned her back against the golden bars of the balcony and watched the interaction before her. At the opposite end of the hallway, Arian and Estylle laughed and wept in each other's arms. They hadn't seen one another for twenty years. Aurelia was more than relieved when she saw her governess roaming the halls after the battle, but Arian had nearly lost his footing when he spotted his old friend.

Unfortunately, Estylle was the only familiar face Aurelia had seen since the battle, as most had been killed during the uprising. Cicely had been shot with an arrow after attempting to shield a maid's young son with her own body. Buck was killed in the fires set in the Folly while trying to help the people escape on horseback. Even elderly Madame Bettley, the stewardess, had perished along with her entire family after her home was set ablaze while they slept.

Three members of her Assembly—Calder Byrd, Leith Rowe, and Zinnia Summerhill—died at Archie's hand. The former two were killed within weeks of Aurelia's departure from Akkinor when they were caught attempting to flee the Folly for their native Holos. They'd apparently hoped to inform the Tarres of their suspicions regarding Archie's ascent to the throne. Perceiving their intentions, Archie had them captured and beheaded before they could leave the Folly.

Aurelia had been more surprised to learn of Zinnia's death, as the late advisor often warmed Archie's bed prior to the uprising. According to a surviving advisor, Zinnia boldly questioned Archie regarding his ascent not a week after the uprising while the two were in bed together. Archie killed her with his hunting knife while she lay naked beside him, and the servants spent the next three days scrubbing her blood from his chambers.

Braddock Wallace and Stephen Median, native Sadians, had supported Archie due to both preference and respect for Lady Spirre. They both died in battle: Wallace was killed by a Goldman's sword through the heart, and Median met his end when he was swallowed by Halvor. The last dead advisor, Alwen Gideon, was beheaded on the battlefield after solidifying his allegiance to Aurelia.

The only members of the Assembly to survive were Henry Rudal and Frederick Baylor. The two Follian-born advisors were fiercely loyal to Aurelia, but they'd managed to survive by pretending otherwise. Even their fellow advisors hadn't questioned their loyalties when they declared their support for Archie. When the battle began, though, the lords didn't hesitate to join Aurelia's troops. She would've been terrified of their effortless deceit if she hadn't been so amazed by it.

Even after learning about how many lives had been lost during her time in Carthe, she couldn't bring herself to weep for them. She wanted to mourn them, to grieve them properly, but the shock of the battle hadn't worn off yet. For all she knew, it never would.

Wanting to give Arian and Estylle a few moments of privacy, she turned to face the courtyard. It'd been untouched by Archie and untouched by the battle, so it was the one place in the Folly that was as pure as it'd been on the day she left. The courtyard had been her mother's favorite project, and after visiting the gardens of Taundosa, Aurelia realized that Cressida had gathered most of her inspiration from her visits to Carthe. Even from across the sea, she was happy to see that reminders of Taundosa were all around her.

Her uncle appeared at her side a few moments later. "Estylle is perfectly fine, all things considered. Your brother didn't touch a hair on her head."

"He would've, had he known the truth."

"Thank heavens he did not."

The pair stood in silence and watched Halvor circle the palace overhead. The dragon had been keeping himself busy by monitoring the property, and the people who came and went were doing their best to avoid him. The locket still hung from Aurelia's neck, but she'd lost the caps on the battlefield. It was never her intention to reimprison her great protector after revealing him on the battlefield. Halvor had been hidden from the world for far too long—he deserved better, and the world deserved to experience the majesty he brought to the realm.

"There's a reason why Brentwoods stopped training falcons," Arian said as they watched Halvor. "Do you know what it is?"

"I'm afraid not."

He smiled as the clever twinkle in his eyes shined brighter. "They started training dragons instead."

Her eyebrows furrowed. "I beg your pardon?"

"Didn't your father ever tell you?" Her silence was response enough. "The Brentwoods trained falcons until the day you were brought home to Akkinor. When we were young, your father had a falcon called Hzarl. He and your grandfather used them as messengers, fighters, protectors. When your father learned about Halvor, he thought it was time for a change. He ceased the use of falcons in favor of something greater. He knew you were the start of a new era for this country, Aurelia. We all did."

Her eyes welled with tears. "I remember the first time I met Halvor. It was my sixteenth name day. My parents took me to a secluded field on the outskirts of Myra and released him. My mother told me not to be afraid, but I wasn't. I knew he wouldn't harm me. I-I knew he was meant for me." A sudden thought struck her. "May I ask you something?"

"Always, my dear."

"Did you ever resent my mother because of Halvor?"

"No." His reply required no thought. "I was raised to understand that Halvor would never be mine. If my parents had a daughter, Halvor would be hers. If not, he'd be inherited by the next Cristos daughter—mine, perhaps, if I ever married. I suppose it's something the men of our family have understood from the beginning. The laws of succession are somewhat set in stone when it comes to magic." He squinted to get a better look at Halvor as the dragon soared above the clouds. "Perhaps I was spiteful as a boy, but when Katryna was born...It was difficult to be envious after witnessing their bond. I've always known that he would never have a connection like that with me or any other man in my family."

"Did she release him often?"

"A dozen times, I'd say. Maybe more."

"What?" She gawked at him, lips parted in shock, as he chuckled. "Why, that's outrageous! I'd only released him twice until the battle. The risk of him being seen was too great."

"You met the staff at Ardiham Castle. They're rather loyal to the Cristos family, don't you think?"

A smirk formed on her lips. It made perfect sense: if those employed by the Cristos family were loyal enough to keep the truth of Aurelia's birth a secret, then surely they would keep mum about their mistresses being in possession of a dragon. The gardens at Ardiham Castle weren't grand or majestic like the gardens at the palace, but they were certainly large enough—and with walls high enough—for Halvor to be released without being spotted by pesky civilians.

"I imagine he wasn't able to fly at Ardiham," Aurelia commented. He grimaced in response. "Where did she take him when she wished to fly?"

"The desert, mostly." A gurgling laugh escaped his throat. "There must be dozens of mad people in the realm claiming to have seen a dragon in the Ngora Valley!"

"Those poor souls," she teased, mimicking his laughter. "I'm certainly glad his prison was never permanent. It would've been a shame if he were unable to meet each new mistress in the flesh. Now that he's free, though, he shall never see the inside of another prison again."

Arian was smiling. "I'm proud of you, Aurelia."

"Thank you." She sighed and turned away from the courtyard as a subsequent thought popped into her head. "Have you any news on the sorcerer in the dungeons?"

"Murdered after the uprising. Archie tortured him for information, but the poor man didn't know a thing."

She'd worried about the sorcerer since she fled Akkinor, so she was almost relieved to hear of his execution. Archie knew Aurelia kept that man in the dungeon for a reason, and the latter only knew that there was a protection spell on Aurelia's locket. He had no knowledge of what the locket contained.

Before Aurelia could retire to her bedchamber for some much-needed rest, she had one last item on her agenda for the day. Arian escorted her to a private room within the palace's infirmary wing, where Jack was waiting for them.

Her uncle raised an eyebrow as he set his hand on the doorknob. "Are you sure?"

Aurelia nodded. "I'm sure."

He hesitated, still troubled about fulfilling her request, before sighing and opening the door. Inside the empty room was a single stone table, and atop that table was the corpse of the former Lord Hand. Aurelia's heart plummeted to her knees at the sight of Linden's mangled, deformed face. Lord Crowland had discovered the trampled body on the battlefield, and he thought it was only right to give Linden a proper burial beside his father in the palace crypt. Aurelia couldn't have agreed more, but burying her best friend wouldn't have felt right until she said her final goodbyes.

According to Estylle, Archie's supporters had apprehended Linden while he was preventing them from following Aurelia to Seaport. Charged with aiding Aurelia's escape and desertion of her people, Linden was confined to the dungeon. He was tortured for information, but he hadn't disclosed a single detail. When Archie realized that Linden would never betray her, he chose to keep Linden locked up as a bargaining chip for the day Aurelia returned.

If Estylle's source was correct, then Cicely, too, had been confined to the dungeon when Archie's men found her—barely clinging to life—after the siege came to an end. When she died of her injuries just a few weeks later, she'd been in the cell directly beside Linden's, and he'd been forced to sleep beside the corpse of the woman he loved for days until she was finally taken away. Nobody knew where her remains had been buried, either. Archie made sure nobody ever would.

She could feel the tears leaking down her cheeks, but she couldn't move a muscle to wipe them away. She could only stare at Linden, trying to make sense of what remained of him, as his charming voice echoed in her head. She lifted a shaking hand to his and clasped, but her pain intensified when she realized he'd never hold her back again.

"Leave us," she whispered.

"Darling—" Jack began.

One sharp look was enough to silence him. He and Arian excused themselves from the room and closed the door behind them. She sniffled through tears and tightly grasped Linden's arm with both hands, wincing at the feel of his cold skin and deteriorated muscles.

"Oh, Linden. I'm so sorry, my friend. Only the gods know what you endured at my brother's hand. I-If you'd been with me..." She choked on her words and took a moment to catch her breath. "I miss you, Linden. I shall never forget you nor the love I have for you. I promise."

She could hear his voice in her head, see his bright smile, feel his warmth as he walked her through the gardens. She remembered gazing down at him, both laughing, when he'd find her hiding in the branches of a tree. She could even remember being eight years old, having stayed up through the night with haunting dreams, and leaving her bedchamber in the morning to find him sleeping outside of her door. He'd protected her from the moment she was brought home to the palace, and now he was gone.

The door opened and closed again. She didn't have to look to know it was Jack. He stood by her side in silence, giving her a moment to collect herself, before setting a hand on her back to comfort her.

"Would you like to know something, Jack?"

"Of course."

"I never lied to him. Not once." Aurelia sniffled. "I've lied to everyone else in my life, but never to Linden. It was never safe nor proper to tell the truth to anyone else. I couldn't confide in my parents about certain things because they were, well, my parents. Archie never cared. Cicely, though I loved her dearly, was never skilled at keeping things to herself. The maids gossiped with the kitchen staff, the kitchen staff gossiped with the stable hands, the stable hands gossiped with the guards. There was never anyone to confide in. Nobody but Linden. Even in Carthe...I lied to you, to Kaia. I had no choice."

"What made him so different?"

She smiled faintly. "He'd sit by my crib every day when I was a babe. He knew it was his duty to protect me, even as a young boy. When I told him something in confidence, he kept it to himself. He never saw reason to betray my trust. He listened, gave advice when need be, and never told a soul without my permission. I was never worried about him telling anyone or betraying me. He was the only person in the world whom I could say that about. Things changed when I came to Carthe, but Linden never did. He was loyal until the end."

She thought about the things her brother had tortured Linden for. As the Lord Hand, he knew the country's secrets *and* he knew Aurelia's. He knew about her weaknesses, Halvor, the escape plan, the sorcerer in the dungeon. If anyone wanted to ruin her beyond repair, Linden was the person they'd turn to—but he never said a word, and if he had, Aurelia may not have won the battle.

"You heard him," Jack offered. "He loved you very much. Everything he endured, everything he sacrificed...He did it out of love and loyalty. That's the most precious gift anyone could ask for."

She wiped her eyes and hovered her hand over Linden's face. She couldn't bring herself to touch him. "Goodbye, Linden. Rest in light."

They started for the door, but she couldn't muster the strength to leave the room when they reached the exit. She peered over her shoulder at the table and held her breath to keep from crying. Her soul was aching, but she knew that one day, she and her closest companion would meet again. That reminder was the only force strong enough to propel her forwards.

"You never told me about what happened with Archie," Jack said as they left the room. "Was he a bear?"

"Of course he was. I...I didn't tell him about the elvemar. I don't think he knows that he would've died of his injuries, had I not found him when I did. He'll never know I saved his life."

"Why did you?"

She sighed. "Because he deserves to stand trial for his actions...and because I couldn't bring myself to let him die."

"Why not tell him, then?"

"Does it matter? He's going to lose his head eventually, and only I can stop that from happening. I can, but I won't. He knows that. It doesn't matter that I saved his life when I'm condemning him to die anyway." She took a long, deep breath and ran a hand through her curls. "He declined his right to a letter and asked to play one final song on the pianoforte. I accepted."

Jack was silent for a moment. "That's generous of you."

"I suppose." She shook her head and bit the insides of her cheeks. "When I saw him there...He looked like a boy again, Jack. I-I couldn't leave him without giving him something. One last gift."

"He deserves no gifts from you, Aurelia. That's what makes you better than he is."

She forced a smile, but it soon faded. "I thought I'd feel better after we won. I thought I'd be thrilled to have my throne back, but I'm not. All I can think about is how many lives were lost. How many lives *will* be lost."

"That's what war is, my love: sorrow, exactly as you said. Nobody emerges from the battlefield without leaving a piece of themselves behind." When she remained silent, he brushed his fingers over her arm and gazed into her eyes. "Despite everything, you should be proud of yourself. You were an incredible leader on that battlefield. We wouldn't have succeeded without your knowledge of Archie's movements."

She sniffled. "That's why he was doomed to lose—I knew exactly what he'd do. When you love someone, you come to know everything about them. That's how I know my brother never loved me, Jack. He never knew me at all."

***

Aurelia had always been jealous of the way Archie's hands could understand a pianoforte. He had long, slender fingers—*perfect for picking pockets*, as their father liked to joke—that seemed to glide across the keys like his own kind of magic. His hands never looked natural when he was holding a sword, shooting an arrow, or even grasping a horse's reins. Nothing seemed as inherent as his hands on a pianoforte's keys. Even now—with just seven fingers and three short, fleshy nubs—he played with the same grace he always had. The music may not have sounded quite right, but he didn't allow his loss to stop him. After all, it was the last song he'd ever play.

Archie wasn't fond of much in the world, but he *was* fond of music. The pianoforte was the only thing that'd ever brought him joy. It was the only present from Aurelia he'd ever truly cherished.

She remembered how angry he was when she broke his favorite pianoforte—their mother's since childhood, which she'd taken with her when she moved from Arrenwood to the palace after her wedding to Edmund. Aurelia had snuck out a ground-level window to hide from her tutor in the garden, and she'd forgotten to close it after making her escape. A hurricane struck the Folly not long after, and everyone was so concerned with finding Aurelia (who'd taken shelter in the greenhouse) that they hadn't bothered to make sure the windows were closed. Ferocious winds and heavy rainfall flooded the room with water, twigs, and debris from across the property. Archie's pianoforte—which sat directly beside the window, as he liked to play beneath the sunlight—had gotten water-logged beyond repair, all because of one open window.

It was a child's accident, of course, but he'd never looked at her with such hatred until that day. He didn't speak to her for weeks after it was broken. Luckily, the joy returned to his eyes when she gifted him with a mahogany pianoforte that seemed made for the prince's hands. It was the one time Archie had ever said *thank you* to his sister and meant it.

Aurelia watched in silence as the music echoed throughout the room. Soldiers stood at the entrance while waiting to escort Archie back to the dungeons. She'd permitted Arian, Jack, and Estylle to witness Archie's final song along with her. They hadn't uttered a word since the moment Archie was brought to the room in chains, and he hadn't acknowledged any of them.

She'd expected the chains around her brother's wrists and ankles to disturb his playing, but they didn't. It almost seemed as though he'd learned to play with shackles constraining his limbs—as though he'd always been a prisoner. He was still wearing the clothing he'd worn to battle, though every inch of him was covered in grime and dirt. With his back turned, he looked like a stranger. Maybe he was.

Aurelia recognized the song as soon as he began to play. Their mother had often played it for them when they were children: it was a sort of lullaby in Akkinor, meant to be sung rather than played, but Cressida had shared Archie's love of the pianoforte. Aurelia didn't know whether to be distressed or provoked by his choice of song. They both knew what Cressida's song meant to them, and it didn't surprise her that he chose to end his time on earth by honoring their mother. Unfortunately for Aurelia, the only thing she could think about was how their mother would feel if she were alive to see one child executing the other.

When the song came to an end, Archie set his hands in his lap and stared at the keys as if the pianoforte would save him from what was to come. Aurelia hadn't realized the soldiers were waiting for her signal until Jack touched her elbow. She nodded once to the soldiers, fighting through stinging eyes, and watched silently as they collected Archie from the pianoforte. He stood with a sigh and let the soldiers take him by the arms, seemingly unfazed by his chains dragging across the floor.

As they passed Aurelia to exit through the doors behind her, she impulsively asked them to halt. Every soul in the room seemed confused by her request—everyone except for Archie. Somehow, her brother had anticipated that she wouldn't let him leave without exchanging parting words. She held her breath and approached him cautiously, not bothering to excuse the soldiers before she spoke:

"That was lovely."

Her brother clenched his jaw. "Mother's song."

"I remember."

The circles under his eyes were darker that day, and his voice sounded different when he croaked, "Why did you agree to it?"

She frowned. "I swore an oath to show mercy to my people. That includes you."

He appeared neither satisfied nor dissatisfied with her response. With one nod of her head, the soldiers urged Archie forwards and led him out of the room. She watched him go, knowing that the next time they saw one another, it'd be execution day. It was her brother's last night on earth, and he'd spend it alone in a prison cell until morning.

Estylle wiped her tear-stained cheeks. "That was very kind of you, Aurelia." Her eyes found Arian as a smile formed on her thin lips. "Katryna would've done the same."

"Most definitely." Arian cocked his head to the side as he studied Aurelia. Jack, too, didn't seem to know what she was thinking or feeling. Aurelia didn't know, either. "Are you all right, my dear?"

The queen shrugged. "I bought him that pianoforte, you know. I'd broken our mother's when I was a child. He was so angry with me—I thought he'd never speak to me again. My father helped me design a new pianoforte as a name day gift for Archie. T-That was the only time he'd ever thanked me for anything."

Jack set a hand on her shoulder and squeezed. "You were so good to him. It isn't fair that your kindness wasn't reciprocated. You've done all you can for him now—the rest is in the gods' hands."

She didn't reply. Earlier that day, the remaining members of her Assembly joined she and Arian for several criminal trials. Each of the high-ranking officers who'd refused to surrender to Aurelia had been condemned to hang, as required by law. Archie and his fellow highborn, like Lord Bradley Reilly, had broken their oaths to the crown and were deemed traitors. While Archie was beheaded as customary for a traitorous royal, the nobles would be hanged, and their corpses would be buried at

Seaport rather than within their family crypts. Their earthly punishments had been fulfilled, and as Jack said, the rest was up to the gods.

Despite the pain she felt at confirming her baby brother's execution, there was no escaping it. The only other option was to imprison him for life, and the people wouldn't have been pleased with that verdict. Archie had caused too much pain and suffering to emerge unscathed. His actions towards Aurelia, too, had been more than reason enough for such a punishment. Orchestrating an uprising, hiring and deploying assassins, murdering her two best friends in cold blood, and wreaking havoc upon her home was enough for her to know that his punishment was appropriate if not perfectly warranted.

XLVIII

Aurelia gently touched her fingertips to the bark of her favorite tree as she traced a curve between the trunk and a thick branch. She'd hidden things in that crevice since she was five years old. When she was a child, she'd hide tarts and cakes wrapped in cloth napkins. As she grew older, it was an assortment of things: books, diaries, love letters. It was the only place on the grounds that was untouched by everyone else—the one place that existed just for her.

Linden, naturally, discovered her hiding spot when she'd fallen asleep while eating cookies in the branches. She'd sworn him to secrecy, and for sixteen years, he hadn't told a soul about her favorite spot. It was his job to keep her feet firmly on the ground, but first and foremost, he was her friend. He'd keep an eye out while she hid, and sometimes he'd join her in the branches for games and snacks. They'd go missing for hours at a time, then return to the palace with fruit juice staining their lips and leaves caught in their hair.

Tears welled in her eyes and a faint smile formed on her lips when her fingers found engravings in the bark. She and Linden had used his knife to make tallies one day when they were swinging through the branches. They'd wanted to keep track of how many hours passed before an adult found them. A total of five hours passed before Cressida discovered them in the branches. Her mother had merely laughed at the friends and offered them a tray of juice and cookies.

Now, Linden and her mother were both gone, and all that remained of her adventures in the tree were tally marks engraved in the bark.

When she heard her name being called, she sighed and dropped her hand from the tree. She swung one of her legs over to the other side of the branch she was sitting on before expertly dismounting to the ground. As she brushed herself off, she saw Jack approaching her from the rear of the palace. Several guards were watching her from afar, so it wouldn't have taken him long to find her. Now that her reign had already been threatened once, there wasn't an inch of the palace grounds that she could keep secret—not even the tree she loved so dearly.

"There you are." Jack forced a smile. "I've been searching everywhere for you. It's time—"

"I know."

She didn't want him to finish his sentence. He seemed to understand when he pressed his lips together and offered his arm. She took it gingerly, but with each step she took towards the palace, she felt like her body was being weighed down by bricks.

He glanced at her while they strolled. "You don't have to go, you know."

"Yes, I do. Every monarch before me had to endure days like today. I'm not the first to condemn a loved one, either. My situation is no exception." He was still tense, and his silence was enough for her to know that he felt otherwise. "A criminal is a criminal, even if he happens to be my brother."

For a moment, Jack was silent. "It's okay to close your eyes from time to time."

Aurelia clenched her jaw, disagreeing. She knew that most eyes would be watching her that day, especially when the hangman pulled the lever, or the executioner swung his sword. Everyone in attendance would be curious to see how their queen responded to her brother's public execution. As much as she wanted to look away, it was a liberty she couldn't take. Weakness was the last thing she intended to express in front of her people. It was the last thing she wanted to express in front of her brother, too. No matter how difficult it'd be to endure, it was her responsibility, and Archie had earned his place on death row.

Jack escorted her to her bedchamber, where an army of maids began preparing her for the day's event. She stared at herself in the mirror of her vanity while the maids worked on her face and hair. They brought life to her cheeks with a pink rouge and covered the chapped skin of her lips with a pleasant rosy lipstick. Her long eyelashes were coated with a thin layer of dark tint, drawing further attention to the lovely blue eyes that'd been gifted to her by Katryna Cristos. She winced when the maids pulled at strands of her curly hair to pin it up in a low bun, leaving several wisps to frame her face. Her stomach turned when the tiara was placed on her head—she hadn't worn or seen it since the day she escaped Akkinor.

When the maids finished with her, she stood from her vanity and approached the long mirror hidden away in her wardrobe. She swallowed at the sight of herself, suddenly feeling like she was staring at a stranger.

For many weeks, she had. Lily Linden used to look at herself in the filthy, cracked mirrors of Carthinian inns and see a lost girl who yearned for her homelands. Even when her identity was revealed in Taundosa, she struggled to feel like herself again. She'd hoped that returning to Akkinor would solve all of her problems, but now...Now, she looked exactly like the woman she remembered. Somehow, the sight gave her less comfort than she'd imagined.

Arian was waiting outside of her chambers to escort her downstairs. He wore traditional Taundosan attire, his tunic adorned with medals and recognitions of his achievements, but the ever-present glint in his eyes had disappeared. He looked as troubled as she felt. Nevertheless, he offered her his arm and escorted her down the stairs in silence. Neither felt it appropriate to make conversation when they knew where they were headed. In fact, every soul in the palace seemed quiet that day. Despite what the damned had done to them, it was never a day of celebration when the executioner was summoned by the palace.

Jack was waiting for them in the foyer. In his navy suit gilded with golden emblems and medals, Aurelia finally saw him as Arthur Ashford rather than Jack Sherbourne. He'd always been a man of great poise, power, and pride, but now, he really looked like the man he'd been raised to be. Aurelia wasn't sure how to feel about it, but she was comforted to see the dumbfounded look in Jack's eyes when he caught a glimpse of *her*. They were finally seeing one another as they truly were after almost three full seasons of masquerading.

The three left the palace for the carriage that would deliver them to Oleander's Valley. The field below Folly Hill, while also serving as a battlefield, had been home to the gallows since Oleander the Great won the war all those centuries ago. It was the only place in close proximity to the palace vast enough to execute the many traitors and conspirators who'd fought for the Cherranes. Aurelia had only traveled to the valley a few times in her life, and each time when she returned, she felt like a piece of her soul had perished along with the condemned.

She was aware of Arian's eyes on her while the carriage took them to the valley. Jack hadn't mustered the courage to look at her, let alone speak to her, but Arian was like a father to her; it was one of his many responsibilities in life to worry.

"It'll be over sooner than you think," he assured her, wincing at the jolting of the carriage. "You're doing a brave thing today, my dear."

"I don't feel very brave."

Jack squeezed her hand. "The greatest among us never do."

Her eyes found the window of the carriage closest to her, and she couldn't help but stare as they passed through the Folly. The damage from the battle was still being cleaned up and repaired, so the villages were nothing like she remembered. In fact, it looked exactly as it had when she escaped Akkinor. The one difference was the lack of flames and bodies ravaging the land.

Somehow, seeing the wreckage brought her comfort, as she knew she was doing the right thing for her people. The men on death row had brought unimaginable pain and suffering upon her people, and it was only right that she follow through on her promise to punish them accordingly. It was just as she'd said to Jack: every king before her had endured days like today, and she wouldn't be the first of Akkinor's monarchs to break that tradition.

Oleander's Valley had a sinister way of making even the strongest of people feel like ants under a boot. The weight of the death that'd occurred there was suffocating. Ash from the battle still lingered, so there was a sickly coat of gray covering the entire area. The nooses had already been tied to the gallows on the scaffolding and now teetered eerily with the breeze. A lump formed in Aurelia's throat when she saw the executioner sharpening his sword beside the chopping block, where her brother's head would soon be severed from his body. The chopping block itself was stained with different shades of brown and red, as it was impossible to scrub the blood of the dead from the wood after the first drop was spilled.

To the left of the scaffolds, the soldiers had organized a viewing area. Each highborn who'd come to witness the executions was given a proper seat, while the commoners were allowed to watch on their feet from a field. Aurelia, Jack, and Arian took a few moments to prepare themselves before exiting the carriage. In that time, six additional carriages arrived carrying highborn from across Akkinor. It wasn't long before the commoners flooded into the empty space in front of the scaffolds. Now, the only people they were waiting for were those sentenced to die.

Arian wordlessly signaled for the driver to open the carriage door. As soon as Aurelia's feet touched the ground, the gravity of the situation smacked her in the face. She clenched her jaw and balled her fists to keep her hands from trembling. She was so disoriented that she hadn't noticed when the spectators bowed or curtsied to her. She simply took Jack's arm, held her breath, and followed him to their seats in the front row of the seating area. Arian sat on her other side, armed with paperwork and a pen to keep record of the executions. She glanced down at the parchment, and upon seeing Archie's name listed as one of the damned, turned away and swallowed the bile that'd risen up in her throat.

Soon, Oleander's Valley was flooded with spectators. Nobles filled every chair, including diplomats from Carthe and Quapebet. Aurelia easily spotted the surviving members of her Assembly, the lords and ladies of her kingdoms, and the dozens of other highborn families from across Akkinor. Almost every highborn in the country had come to witness the executions. As far as she was aware, the only highborn not in attendance were those who'd fallen on the battlefield.

Finally, two thumping, armored carriages rolled into the valley. Pinpricks seemed to prod at every inch of her body as they slowed to a stop behind the gallows. Soldiers armed to the teeth unlocked the back door and urged the prisoners onto the ground. Aurelia held her breath when she saw her brother's mop of blonde hair among them. He kept his head low, knowing it wouldn't be long before the spectators began shouting and throwing things at him.

Despite his arrogance, he was bested, and he'd finally accepted it.

In a single-file line, the shackled prisoners were led up the stairs of the scaffolds and positioned in front of their respective nooses. Only Archie was exempt, as a royal's punishment for treason differed greatly from a nobleman's punishment. He stood in front of the chopping block, head still tilted downwards, and stared at the blood-stained wood with wide eyes. Aurelia forced herself to focus on the other prisoners to avoid acknowledging his terror. The prisoners stood as still as statues while the executioner fashioned the nooses around their necks. The people had already begun yelling, booing, and tossing whatever useless possessions they owned. It wouldn't be long before their boos turned into cheers.

Arian, serving as temporary Hand of the Queen, rose from his seat and approached the gallows. Every soul in the valley quieted when he took his first steps. He cleared his throat and unraveled one of the scrolls he'd tucked into the inside pocket of his tunic.

"The men before you are standing accused of high treason, conspiracy, and embezzlement," Arian announced. "These crimes were committed against Her Majesty the Queen, the great nation of Akkinor, and the many thousands of citizens whom these men were sworn to protect and serve. As punishment for their crimes, the damned are hereby sentenced to death by hanging." He turned to face the condemned, who could barely lift their heads to meet his eyes. "You've been found guilty of treason of the highest degree. However, as stated in the Akkinorian Accords, you are permitted final words. Have you anything to say?"

To Aurelia's surprise, the prisoners spoke. One by one, they offered their sincerest apologies to the people, the country, and their queen. Even

Bradley Reilly offered words, but he seemed less than apologetic when addressing Aurelia herself. That much hadn't shocked her.

"May the Almighty Buen forgive you for your sins, and may the god of death serve you in the afterlife as you served those on earth," Arian finished. "In the name of our savior Oleander Brentwood, by order of Her Majesty the Queen, you will now answer for your crimes against the crown."

With those final words, the executioner pulled the hangman's lever. Aurelia forced herself to keep from wincing when the floors beneath the prisoners' feet gave way, causing each of them to fall and dangle several feet above the ground. The gods granted some of them with the privilege of a quick death: their necks snapped as soon as their bodies fell. The others, including Bradley Reilly, were condemned to suffer by suffocation until the nooses around their necks strangled them to death. It was less than a minute before the sounds of gasping, guttural groaning, and thrashing limbs finally came to an end. By the time the soldiers mounted the scaffolds and began cutting the bodies down, no man looked as he had before. Each of them had turned blue in the face with bloodshot eyes that bugged out of their skulls. It wasn't a pleasant sight, but neither had been the bloodshed the dead men inflicted.

While the soldiers loaded the bodies into wagons, Arian unraveled a second scroll. The executioner approached Archie and forced the former prince to his knees. Aurelia's heart pounded violently at the sound of his chains against the floor. Her brother knelt in front of the chopping block, wide eyes trained on the wood, as the executioner drew his sword and waited for Arian's cue.

"Archibald Edmund Brentwood, former Prince of Akkinor, kneels before you as a traitor to the great nation of Akkinor," Arian declared. "He is charged with high treason, conspiracy, and embezzlement. These crimes were committed against Her Majesty the Queen, the nation of Akkinor, and the many thousands of citizens whom he was sworn to protect and serve. As punishment for these crimes, Archibald Brentwood is hereby sentenced to death by beheading." Aurelia saw the pain in her uncle's eyes as he turned to face Archie. "You've been found guilty of treason of the highest degree. However, as stated in the Akkinorian Accords, you are permitted final words. Have you anything to say?"

Archie's head lifted ever so slightly. "Long live the queen."

Aurelia's hands trembled in her lap. She was well aware of the many eyes on her, but she maintained her composure and didn't look away from her brother. She watched in silence as the executioner positioned Archie's head on the block. Archie was now facing his sister, but he spared both of them the pain of one final glance by keeping his eyes sealed shut. For a moment, he looked like a boy again, and Aurelia had to resist all urges to run to him.

"May the Almighty Buen forgive you for your sins, and may the god of death serve you in the afterlife as you served those on earth," Arian finished. "In the name of our savior Oleander Brentwood, by order of Her Majesty the Queen, you will now answer for your crimes against the crown."

In the blink of an eye, the executioner swung his sword, and Archie's head was severed from his body. As hard as she tried to fight it, Aurelia jumped in her seat. Her entire body shook, and her eyes widened to the size of saucers as she watched his head roll across the floor. His limp body fell to the side, blood oozing from his neck, as the spectators began to cheer.

Aurelia lost track of time as she stared at her brother's corpse. She could hear Jack saying something to her, but his voice was muffled and quiet like he was speaking to her while both were underwater. By the time she could move again, the commoners had been ushered out of the valley, and the highborn had returned to their carriages. The only people who remained were herself, Jack, and Arian as they watched the soldiers load the bodies— and body parts—into wagons.

"My love—" Jack started.

Aurelia held up a hand to silence him. She stood from her seat, prompting Jack and Arian to do the same, and wordlessly approached the scaffolds. From the corner of her eye, she saw Jack and Arian retreating to the carriage while several of her soldiers stayed behind to guard her. She paid them no attention as she stood face-to-face with the chopping block. For a moment, the only sound she could hear was the *tick-ticking* of blood droplets as they fell from the block to the floor.

Then, as if he could feel her pain and anguish, Halvor flew overhead and released an ear-piercing shriek that shook the trees. He landed on the ground behind her and took a few steps forward. When she could feel his hot breath behind her, she closed her eyes and allowed silent tears to flow down her cheeks.

Arian had ordered the soldiers to leave her by then, and every person on the valley began departing for the palace once more. Only she and Halvor remained. She collapsed on the grass when her legs weakened, hugging herself as best she could, and stared at the spot where her brother had previously knelt. Halvor extended his wings to encircle her, protecting and comforting her at the same time. He lowered his head to the ground, releasing a guttural moan, as the two endured a silent goodbye.

XLIX

T hey seem rather besotted with one another."

Aurelia smiled as Jack circled his arms around her waist. "They do, don't they? I daresay it was a match made in the heavens!"

He chuckled. "That Lady Swann is a clever old thing, isn't she?"

Aurelia's smile grew wider as Dahlia Crowland's laughter echoed throughout the gardens. The heir to Myra was waltzing across the grass on the arm of Erastus Swann, youngest son of Lady Odeya Swann of Runeia. The Kroti nobleman had arrived on Akkinorian soil at dawn that morning to meet Dahlia, the first of many potential wives on the list Aurelia had prepared for him. Upon introducing them, she knew immediately that there was no need for him to meet the other women; the two were perfect for one another.

She'd worried for how her people would react when word spread of a Kroti nobleman's arrival in Akkinor—not because of his general presence, but because of his purpose. He'd be granted partial Akkinorian citizenship upon marrying a native, thus becoming the first Carthinian (and non-Akkinorian) to do so.

With the war still fresh in their minds, the people hadn't given much thought to it. Perhaps they would in the future, but for now, Erastus Swann's arrival brought more good than bad. And the ship from Krotis hadn't just brought one man—it'd brought the first shipment of goods as outlined in the alliance agreement between Krotis and Akkinor. The latter was fearfully low on supplies and resources from Archie's ridiculous spending habits. Lady Swann, clever as she was, predicted this. She'd sent her son to Akkinor with supplies to be distributed across the country: specialty foods, textiles, spices, and medicines that weren't quite familiar to Akkinor, but close enough to bring solace to the people.

The cultures of the world had begun to blend, and Akkinor was too desperate for assistance to fight it. Aurelia knew in her heart that the time for disapproval would never come. Her people would grow to see elements of Carthinian culture not as war reparations, but as goods they couldn't live without. The people, like their queen, would grow to see Akkinor's newfound relationship with Carthe as nothing but a blessing.

Even with all the good coming from her Carthinian alliances, Aurelia couldn't help but wonder what Akkinor would look like if Archie hadn't attempted to steal her crown, setting all of this in motion. Maybe it would've been her brother gallivanting across the gardens with Dahlia Crowland instead of Erastus Swann. Maybe Akkinor and Carthe would remain eternally indifferent to one another, too, if Aurelia hadn't been forced to make friends from strangers. And maybe, just maybe, Aurelia never would've met Arian Cristos or learned the truth of her parentage.

Speak of the devil.

"There you are," Arian remarked, joining the couple on the balcony. "Spying on our guests, are we?"

"Only a bit," Aurelia teased. Her playful demeanor shifted when she realized why her uncle had come to find her. "It's time, isn't it?"

He exhaled. "I'm afraid so."

Aurelia wordlessly accepted Arian's arm while Jack trailed beside her. They left the balcony, cut through winding hallways and bustling corridors, and made their way to the foyer. A pit formed in Aurelia's stomach when she spotted servants carrying Arian's trunks and chests to the bailey, where a carriage was waiting to deliver him to Seaport. Arian's time in Akkinor had come to an end, and the day Aurelia had been dreading had finally arrived.

While servants packed the carriage, Arian said his goodbyes to the many souls who'd come to see him off. A sharp pang pierced Aurelia's heart when she watched him envelope Estylle in his arms first. But that pain was quickly replaced by relief when she remembered how significantly things had changed. Now that Aurelia had secured her place in Akkinor, there was nothing stopping Arian from returning whenever he pleased. The time for secrecy and distance had come to an end, and their broken family could become whole once again.

After leaving Estylle, Arian said goodbye to the many others whose lives he'd touched during both his current visit and his original stay in Akkinor. He'd already said farewell to those who'd perished before his return, too. Aurelia found him in the palace crypt early that morning: he'd been sitting on a quilt beside the tombs belonging to Cressida, Edmund, and Edmund's parents. She hadn't announced her presence for fear of disrupting him, but she'd lingered long enough to hear bits and pieces of the one-sided conversation he had with his departed friends.

Arian shook hands with Jack, clapped him on the back, and murmured something in his ear that Aurelia couldn't hear. After Jack nodded and smiled in response, Arian turned his grief-stricken gaze to Aurelia.

"Oh, uncle, must you leave so soon?" She clutched Arian's hands as if her grip would convince him to stay. "I-I know Reyna mustn't be parted from her Lord Hand for so long, but I can't imagine saying goodbye after so many years without you."

"Aurelia..." A wave of anguish passed over his face, but it was gone as soon as it came. "I'll always be your family, even from across the sea. That much has been true since the day your parents brought you home. I've cared for you from foreign lands for five-and-twenty years, and I will continue to do so until the day I die. When you need me, I'll be here in the blink of an eye. If not, you know by now that the gates of Taundosa are forever open to a Lady of Gold."

Her eyes stung with tears. "I love you very much, uncle."

"And I you, my dear." Arian released her hands and pulled the queen into an embrace. Aurelia hugged him tightly, squeezing her eyes shut as she rested her chin on his shoulder. She inhaled the familiar scent of Taundosa—charred nutmeg and citrus, the aromas associated with magic—that lingered on his clothing. When they separated, he took her hands again and smiled. "I have a parting gift for you."

She furrowed her eyebrows. Before she could continue, a carriage rode through the palace gates and slowed to a stop behind the one that would soon take Arian to Seaport. When the driver opened the door, three strangers emerged from the carriage: a young man and two children, a boy and a girl. She recognized them immediately as Carthinians. They all had light brown skin, dark hair, and eyes either as brown as chestnut or as green as jade. Their features were sharp and distinct, with feline eyes that seemed to be on high alert. The clothing on their bodies was traditional Carthinian, though neutral and plain like the dress of the commoners.

"Good day," Arian greeted, approaching them. The man held the children close to his sides, still uneasy, as Arian extended his hand for him to shake. "Mister Bolas, I presume?"

While the man nodded, Aurelia's ears perked up. "Bolas?" she repeated. She followed her uncle to approach the strangers. The man nodded and bowed to her. "Have you any relation to Miss Kaia Bolas of Kanibar?"

The man's eyes widened. "Kaia is my younger sister." He seemed surprised to hear his sister's name from Aurelia's mouth. "Ansyl Bolas, Your Grace. And my other siblings, Thea and Mycah."

Aurelia studied each of them, still awestruck, as the puzzle pieces began to fit into place. She could see similarities between the siblings and her old friend. Mycah, a young boy of no more than ten, had his sister's mischievous jade eyes. Thea, who Aurelia estimated to be about eight or so, was the spitting image of Kaia, aside from her golden-brown eyes. Ansyl resembled Kaia the least, but Aurelia knew by looking at him that they shared the same smile.

Arian turned to face his niece. "I sent a raven to Duke Glenas in Kanibar. He kindly agreed to forward a message to the Bolas family. Mister Bolas had become unemployed following his sister's disappearance, but he'd previously trained with the Kanish army under General Greykas. He has ample military and political experience. You're in desperate need of a new Hand, Your Grace. As temporary replacement for Ser Elliot, I took it upon myself to find someone permanent to fill the role."

The queen was speechless. She still couldn't take her eyes from the siblings, who reminded her so much of her friend that she wanted nothing more than to curl up and cry.

She was suddenly aware that the siblings didn't know what'd happened to Kaia when she disappeared all those weeks ago. They knew nothing of Kaia's time with the Queen of Akkinor, nor why Lord Arian Cristos of Taundosa would summon them to a country across the sea.

Upon realizing that they were waiting for her to speak, she cleared her throat. "It's a pleasure to have you here. My uncle was very clever and even more considerate to invite you to Akkinor. Your sister was a dear friend of mine during my time in Carthe. I cared for her deeply."

Ansyl shifted, dark eyes widening. "Do you...Do you know what happened to her?"

"Yes." A sharp pang pierced Aurelia's heart. She could hardly bring herself to say it aloud. "Your sister was killed while we were crossing the Violet Forest. S-She was struck by an arrow laced with phoenix blood. I was unable to save her. For that, I offer my deepest condolences. She was a spectacular woman and an even better friend."

As the children curled into his chest and cried, Ansyl held his head high and nodded through his tears. He attempted to say something to her, but his grief overpowered his ability to speak. His face crumpled and reddened, and in seconds, he was kneeling beside his siblings and sobbing. Aurelia, too, had silent tears leaking from her eyes.

"I'd be honored to offer you permanent residence in the palace," she affirmed. The siblings looked up at her through their tears, stunned and silent. "I'd give anything to have Kaia here with me, too. She would've been named Hand of the Queen in a heartbeat if she were here. I can sense her within you, Mister Bolas, and I know you'll be as excellent in this position as your sister would've been. The choice is yours. If you wish to return to Kanibar, you may. If you'd like to stay, Akkinor is your home."

Ansyl was speechless. "But my siblings—"

"They're welcome to stay. There are plenty of rooms in the palace, Mister Bolas, and an ample number of people to watch over them in your absence. They'll have access to the greatest tutors, physicians, and caretakers Akkinor has to offer."

He glanced between her eyes, searching for a hidden agenda that didn't exist. He seemed to feel Kaia within Aurelia, just as Aurelia felt Kaia within him. The Kanish girl had left a permanent mark on the queen's soul, and Ansyl could sense it as much as Aurelia could feel it. Kaia had told Aurelia about the difficulties of Kanish life—the family would be better off in Akkinor than in their place of birth. Akkinor was a fresh start for a family who'd lost the glue that held them together. If Kaia were still alive, both Aurelia and Ansyl knew she would've urged them to stay.

"We'd be honored to accept your invitation, Your Grace." Ansyl forced a smile and squeezed her hand in gratitude. "Thank you. Thank you very much."

"It's my pleasure. Kaia wasn't only a friend, but someone whom I grew to consider family. Water, in this case, is as thick as blood, Mister Bolas." She squeezed his hand and smiled. "Welcome home."

When the family collected themselves, Arian summoned a servant to escort them into the palace. Aurelia's heart ached with the weight of Kaia's loss, but she knew her dear friend wasn't gone forever. Now that the Bolas siblings had arrived in Akkinor, she and Kaia were connected for eternity.

"Thank you, uncle," she said, embracing him again. "You have no idea how much this means to me."

"Everything is as it should be," he murmured. "You'll find that Mister Bolas is more than qualified. In a way, his presence is similar to mine when I stood by your father's side. A foreign Hand isn't always accepted in this country at first, but he'll prove himself to the people when they witness what he has to offer. I know he's no replacement for Linden, and the loyalty of your late friend can never be matched by anyone on this earth, but you and Mister Bolas are connected by someone whom you both loved. As long as that love prevails, he'll be faithful to you."

She smiled through her tears. "You do so much for others without expecting anything in return. I wouldn't be standing here without you, uncle. I owe everything to you. I fear I'm incapable of expressing how grateful I am for the many years of life you've given me."

He took her face in his hands and brushed her tears away. "Our family is gone, Aurelia. Yours, mine, ours. Everyone we loved has been taken from us, but when I look at you, I see a piece of everyone we've lost. My parents, my sisters, my friends. I hope you can say the same about me."

"I can. Always."

"That's the only gratitude I require. I shall miss you very much. Write to me, won't you?"

"Every day. I promise."

His eyes welled with tears, but he straightened up and inhaled sharply before they could spill. "Forward, good man—"

"Ever forward." Aurelia smiled. "Until we meet again."

L

Two ravens arrived this morning, Your Grace."

Ansyl took the scrolls from the servant's platter and examined the seals. "A letter from Emperor Kaplo, and a letter from Lord Zhoqa," he announced. As the servant bowed and left the throne room, Ansyl carefully studied the scrolls, searching for any sign of tampering or poison. "They seem to be acceptable for your hands, Your Grace."

"Thank you." Aurelia accepted the scrolls with a smile. Ansyl and Jack watched in silence as she broke the seal on the first letter. Her eyes scanned the correspondence as she read the brief message from Emperor Kaplo. She couldn't help but grin by the time she finished. "It seems the emperor received my last message. He congratulated me on my return to the throne and complimented my methods of returning to Akkinor. He's agreed to reinstate the terms of our alliance now that I've returned."

Jack lit up. "That's wonderful!"

"Indeed." She gave the letter back to Ansyl and broke the seal of the scroll from Lord Zhoqa of Kazamir. The message was longer than the first, so it took her a few moments to read it. Again, she smiled. "Lord Zhoqa sends his gratitude for the shipment of Holosi painted glass that was delivered to Bozar. He's agreed to my proposition: a shipment of Akkinorian bronze will be delivered to Kazamir once each season, and in exchange, he'll disband the practice of child brides."

Aurelia made two promises when she traveled through Bozar: the first was to deliver painted glass windows to a motherless boy and his father, and the second was to free the dozens (if not hundreds) of young girls who'd been promised as wives to Lord Zhoqa's knights. One of her first orders of business after reclaiming the throne was keeping those promises. She'd sent painted glass not only to Oslo and his father, but to every home in the village—and to all four of Bozar's lords, despite being allied with only two of them. She'd expected Lord Zhoqa to demand more than bronze in exchange for abolishing the practice of marrying off young girls to the highest bidder, but he'd been more than pleased with her offer. After all, Kazamir would soon become the only Carthinian territory to possess enough ore to put Akkinorian bronze swords in the hands of every soldier. Not even someone as unseemly as Lord Zhoqa was foolish enough to decline arming his men with nearly indestructible weaponry.

Aurelia had strengthened her relationships with the nobles of Akkinor, too, in the time that had passed since the battle. Her maternal uncle, Andren Normindi, claimed his ancestral seat at Arrenwood in Sadia as the kingdom's rightful lord. What remained of the Reilly family had either been arrested or banished from Akkinor following Bradley's execution. Instead, Gemma Stone, younger sister of Ser Linden Elliot, was now serving as Lady of Laynoa.

The Assembly had collectively agreed that Jack's fate rested in his brother's hands. If Bryan wanted to see Jack punished for deserting Omara, a trial would be held. Fortunately, Bryan had no intention of treating Jack like a criminal. He knew that he was meant to be Lord of Omara, just as he knew that Jack's place was at Aurelia's side.

Following their support on the battlefield, Aurelia grew closer to the nobles of Myra and Omara, but still—even with Jack as her soon-to-be husband—she felt that her relationship with Omara was strained. In an effort to repair the bond between Brentwood and Ashford, Aurelia sent word to an emissary of Quapebet to politely request that his men locate Alistair and Isobel in exile. When the former Lord and Lady of Omara were found and returned to Akkinor, they'd be granted a retrial by Aurelia and the Assembly. The queen sincerely hoped that her advisors would allow the Ashfords to return home; they'd been punished long enough for something they couldn't control.

As the political corner of Aurelia's mind worked tirelessly to catch up with the aftermath of her success, she remembered something that both excited and terrified her. She'd been so distracted that she'd nearly forgotten the agreement she made on the shores of Khaba.

When his head is in the ground, we will meet again to discuss this humility *ye speak of.*

"Ansyl," she said, "please respond to Lord Zhoqa and Emperor Kaplo on my behalf. There's another matter that needs my immediate attention."

"At once, Your Grace."

While he excused himself, Aurelia stood from her throne and took Jack's arm. "What are you up to, Lily dear?" he teased as they left the throne room. "What could be so urgent?"

"Piracy."

He looked puzzled. "Piracy?"

She nodded, though it was clear that he still didn't understand what she meant. When they arrived at her study, she sat at her desk and produced a piece of parchment, an inkwell, and quill. Jack looked over her shoulder as she began crafting a proposal addressed to Captain Lukos of Espos.

He made a noise deep in his throat. "What are you—"

"Shh."

The words seemed to appear on the parchment before she knew what she was writing. That's exactly what she'd hoped for, as she knew that the pirate captain was a man who valued sincerity above all else. He wasn't a person to be coerced by fancy speech and highborn propriety. He cared not for the king or queen of a nation, but for the leader of its people. By expressing herself as such, Aurelia was making them equals.

"None of our ravens fly to Espos, you know," Jack reminded her. "No person or animal has been trained to find the island in centuries. How are you expecting to deliver this message to the captain?"

"By hand."

"By *hand*? Good gods, woman! Are you *mad*?"

Aurelia gave him a sharp look, silencing him, and continued writing. When she signed her name at the bottom of the parchment, Jack realized what she was doing. She wasn't fashioning a letter to be delivered by a raven or a messenger. She was creating a document to orchestrate a peace treaty between the country of Akkinor and the nation of Espos. If Captain Lukos were to consider it in the slightest, he'd only do so after Aurelia had delivered the parchment personally.

Later that night when all of Akkinor said their nightly prayers, Aurelia left the palace gates with nothing but a cloak and a scroll. Jack followed her to the field beyond the gates, kissed her goodbye, and watched as she climbed on Halvor's back. When the dragon lifted off into the air, Aurelia gazed down at Jack until he was no larger than an ant. They were flying above the clouds now, and before she knew it, Aurelia could see nothing but dark skies and stars surrounding her.

An Akkinorian hadn't stepped foot on the island of Espos in a thousand years, but when the sun rose into the sky at dawn, Halvor's talons dipped into the salty turquoise sea of the Alkamura, and the Queen of Akkinor changed the world once again.

***

Lukos watched his exhaled smoke melt into the cloudy haze lingering in the sky. A storm was approaching from the east, and judging by the severity of the winds and the aggression of the cresting waves, it'd be a treacherous one. But the Captain of Espos had no fear of storms nor the wrath of the Lady Alkamura: while aboard the *Lost Stinger*—a beached ship that'd washed up on inland Espos after a tsunami many centuries prior— there was nothing for anyone to fear but the captain himself.

He inhaled what remained in his pipe before snapping his fingers at a nearby swabbie. The indenture hurriedly sprinkled an earthy-smelling powder into the captain's pipe before lighting it with a match. The leggy, half-naked harlots lounging nearby—twins, as preferred by the captain— crawled to Lukos's side when he clicked his tongue. One resumed her earlier position by massaging his inverted toes, and the other (prettier than her sister) expelled soft breaths of air against his ear while he shuddered in delight.

Lukos frowned and curled his fingers around the pretty one's wrist when she stilled beside him. "I dinna tell ye to stop."

"Begging forgiveness, milord, but w-what *is* that?"

He followed her terrified gaze to the dark thunderclouds above. Upon spotting what'd caught her eye, he straightened up in his chair and squinted to get a better look. There was a vast shadow behind the clouds— a shadow that wasn't intimidating by the signs of an impending storm and appeared to be inching closer to the *Lost Stinger*.

The pirates who called the ship home alongside their captain hollered at one another and appeared on the deck in a matter of seconds. Lukos was on his feet by then, as were the harlots and the indentures, while his crew armed themselves with whatever weapons were within reach. They turned to their captain for orders, but Lukos—a man who'd seen everything the realm had to offer in his nine-and-fifty years—was miffed. He wondered if the Lady Alkamura herself had come to reward or punish him for his leadership on Espos, but then a bellowing shriek rattled the island, and the pirate captain set his eyes on the only thing in the realm to ever fill his belly with terror.

Even the frightened screams of his crew weren't enough to drown out the sound of the dragon's roars as it broke through the clouds, diving directly towards the *Lost Stinger*. Pirates and harlots alike flattened themselves to the deck when the dragon swooped downwards, just barely grazing the exterior of the ship with the tip of its wing. As the dragon soared into the sky again, Lukos spotted a flash of golden, reddish hair from the beast's back. He'd only ever seen one person with hair like the rising sun, and he was certain that she was the very same person riding the dragon like a stallion.

Before he knew it, Lukos was howling with laughter. Never before had he witnessed something so perfectly mad; it was the greatest delight he'd ever seen.

As the dragon landed a safe distance from the ship, pirates surrounded the captain with their weapons raised, all awaiting his next command. He simply watched, fingers curled around the rotted railing, as the woman climbed from the dragon's back and began walking towards the ship. The beast shrieked from behind her, and the twin harlots simultaneously fainted onto the deck upon seeing the glowing ball of fire nestled in the dragon's throat.

"Milord?" Beside Lukos, a pirate's sword shook like a leaf in his grip. "What are yer orders?"

The captain grinned. "Stand down. We have a guest."

The dragon bellowed once again, and the breeze from his exhale lifted the queen's hair from her shoulders as she trudged towards the ship. Sparks from the dragon's breath seemed to cascade over her like rain droplets. The sight made Lukos laugh again until his tainted lungs strained for air.

The storm never arrived. Others may not have understood it, but Lukos certainly did: it wasn't a storm he'd sensed approaching, but the arrival of an individual whose very essence was tethered to the making and breaking of tempests.

***

When the queen entered the throne room, each member of the Assembly rose from their seats. The nobles, accompanied by Lord Hand Ansyl Bolas, bowed or curtsied while she made her way to her throne. Nobody dared to sit until the monarch did so first. When she was comfortable on her throne, her advisors took their seats and waited for her to begin.

Aurelia was glad to see the number of advisors in the throne room— eight rather than two. It'd been an arduous task to replace her former advisors, but she was pleased with her choices. Every last one of them had expressed one or more acts of loyalty to her since she returned to Akkinor; she knew with absolute certainty that she'd never grow to doubt or distrust those sworn to guide her throughout her reign.

Henry Rudal and Frederick Baylor were joined by another native Follian: Megara Witton, one of Aurelia's distant cousins on her father's side. Along with Lady Witton, three additional women had been appointed as the queen's advisors to establish balance between the sexes: Marilla Page of Holos, Emilia Litten of Sadia, and Ophira Paul of Laynoa (the latter of whom was Linden's maternal aunt). Sylvan Halloway of Myra, a nobleman normally tasked with overseeing matters in Eldford on Aurelia's behalf, had also been appointed as an advisor.

The eighth and final member of the Assembly was a bit different from the others. She'd been introduced to Daniel Chilton, a native Omaran, a week prior by Erastus Swann. The latter had befriended Chilton (a young soldier whose uncle was an Omaran earl) during a visit to Akkinor. When Erastus overheard Aurelia's desire to hire a mage into her personal service, he recommended Chilton. She'd been presented with a wonderful idea: rather than utilizing Chilton as a second, magically enhanced Lord Hand, she'd offer him a seat on the Assembly. If she wanted to properly reintroduce magic to Akkinor, she'd need a mage amongst her advisors.

"Thank you for joining me today," Aurelia said cordially. "I understand that each of you has been more than busy as of late. My brother's brief reign caused more damage than we realized. I thank you for your care and dedication to your duties." The nobles tipped their heads in response. She cleared her throat and continued, "As you know, during my time in Carthe, I made the bold and necessary decision to ally Akkinor with several nobles of the continent. Whilst the arrangement between the lords of Bozar are strictly military for now—excluding our bronze and glass shipments to Kazamir—we've promised trade relations with Queen Reyna of Taundosa and Lady Swann of Krotis. I expect further trade relations to emerge with Lord Zhaaran of Orestes, too."

Ansyl nodded to her. "Emissaries from Orestes have already sent ravens with proposals for these trade relations. They're waiting for our approval before the arrangements can be confirmed."

"Excellent! We'll examine the documents at our earliest convenience. However, I believe now is the time for us to discuss our *other* plans for the west." She raised her eyebrows at her advisors. "Anyone?"

Lady Page cleared her throat. "What plans for the west, Your Grace?"

"I'm referring to the Alka," Aurelia said directly. Nobody spoke—they were too busy gawking at her. "I understand that we forbid travel of any kind through the Alkamura, but I believe it'd be worthwhile to reconsider."

"A lovely thought, Your Grace," Lord Baylor mumbled, "but it's rather...unimportant. Your brother inflicted quite a bit of damage on the people." He looked around at the advisors and swallowed nervously. "That was once the incredible thing about Akkinor—so few were impoverished. So few were indebted. It was wonderful before, but when the money ran out...It didn't pick us off one by one. The poor didn't fall first with the rest of us not far behind. Everyone came crashing down together. Peasants, highborn families, nobles. We need this problem solved, Your Grace. Quite quickly."

She smiled. "The Alkamura offers faster trading routes between Akkinor and Carthe. Few people from the southern half of Carthe have traded with our country precisely because of our situation with Espos. I had the pleasure of meeting a few of them. I spoke with nobles who offered an exchange of goods that would greatly benefit this country. Gold, livestock, grain, horses—anything we desire." Their eyes widened as they exchanged interested looks. "Use of the Alkamura will make us rich. It won't take long for the country to recover from what my brother inflicted."

Lord Rudal shook his head. "It's impossible. Despite your being granted safe passage across the Alka to return to Akkinor, we maintain hostile relations with the Esposi. Our ships will be attacked, and our sailors murdered before we can trade an ounce of grain with the Carthinians."

"I've negotiated a peace treaty with Captain Lukos of Espos," she announced. Her advisors' awe and disbelief almost made her chuckle. "I departed Akkinor at nightfall yesterday and personally discussed these relations with Captain Lukos. As many of you may know, my safe passage from Khaba to Seaport was orchestrated by the simplest of actions. As of now, we shall proceed by referencing the ocean as the Alkamura, not the Alka."

"Your Grace—"

"It's done," she declared. "I understand that this is a matter of great pride for our people. The damage my brother inflicted will take years to correct if we don't proceed with cleverness and humility. I've secured safe passage across the Alkamura for every ship with Akkinorian sails. The Esposi agreed to share their territory with our fleets. We'll be free to dock on the southern coast of Carthe and conduct business as we see fit. I apologize for organizing this treaty without consulting you first, but I believed it to be a matter of extreme importance that couldn't be negotiated."

Silence echoed throughout the throne room for so long that Aurelia's ears began to ring. She examined the expressions of each and every member of her Assembly as they processed her words. She knew her actions would lead to hesitation, and her advisors weren't the only people in the country who'd express displeasure at her decision. But peace with Espos would allow Akkinor to thrive as it never had before, and it was a gamble the country had no choice but to make.

"I agree with Her Grace," Lady Witton proclaimed, breaking the silence. "Use of the Alkamura is essential for restoring Akkinor to its former glory."

"It's by the grace of the Almighty that our people shall sail the Alkamura once more," Lady Paul agreed. "If a full-grown dragon can fly over Akkinor for the first time in a thousand years, then surely we can sail the ocean as our ancestors did before us."

Aurelia smiled. "Do I have your approval?" One by one, each member of the Assembly offered her a slight nod. "Wonderful! Now, before we proceed with arrangements for the Alkamura, I'd like to earn your favor on one other matter that is dear to my heart. Tell me—how long has it been since the persecution?"

Lord Rudal thought for a moment. "Well over a thousand years, Your Grace."

"As such, I feel strongly that we've evolved beyond the petty squabbles that incited the horrors we're all familiar with. Every man and woman who fought beside us on the battlefield witnessed the loyalty, integrity, and sheer power of the Carthinian mages. If we wish to rebuild our country into the realm's most powerful nation, we can't continue to force our mages into hiding because of something that occurred over a thousand years ago. The citizens of Akkinor have turned on one another enough as it is. We must unify our people—*all* of our people."

Chilton raised an eyebrow and smiled. "Where shall we begin, Your Grace?"

She hesitated. Glancing around at each of her advisors, she studied the expressions on their faces and the glints in their eyes. She was suddenly taken back to the night of the uprising, when she shared her last meal with her dear friends. She'd made an executive decision then about the Spirre family's overspending, and her choice had caused her friends to look at her with more pride than she thought she deserved.

Now, her advisors were looking at her with the same admiration she'd cherished from her friends. Once more, she reminded herself that as long as her people looked at her like that, she was exactly the queen Akkinor deserved.

Archie had warned her that her actions on the battlefield would cause the world to know her as nothing more than the Queen of Ashes: a traitor to the greatest country in the world, whose rise to power would turn Akkinor into a graveyard of bone and ash. But she wasn't the person he thought her to be, nor the person she was before he'd taken everything from her.

Later that night, she knelt in front of a window in her bedchamber and gazed up at the heavens as she had hundreds of times before. She murmured prayers for everyone who'd made sacrifices to see her on the throne again, and she uttered one for Archie, too—not because he deserved her prayers, but because of what his terrible deeds allowed her to achieve. She didn't realize she was crying while speaking to the midnight stars until she felt a cool wetness on her face. She brought her fingers to her cheek to brush them away, and upon glancing at her hand, she nearly lost her balance and fell to the side.

Upon restoring harmony and unity to the realm, the Ones Forged in Gold would weep golden tears as the gods had before them, and humankind would awaken to greet a new age of salvation.

THE GOLDEN ONE TRILOGY IS NOW COMPLETE! GET ALL THREE BOOKS ON AMAZON!

Keep reading for a sneak peek of Book 2, Forged in Ashes!

1989 Post Creation

Arian Cristos, Lord Hand of Taundosa, didn't care for the north. Of course, one's definition of *the north* depended greatly on one's place of birth. The Isalders of Glacier Bay, for example—the northernmost continent—referenced the barren, jagged Ealair Mountains inhabited by ruthless clansmen and ravenous beasts. The people of Quapebet might've referenced either the empire's agricultural districts or its many swampy wetlands. In Carthe, Arian's native continent, *the north* referred to everything above the Ngora Valley desert.

Of the four northern territories, Arian had his reasons for frowning upon each of them. Caedia, a port province and the northernmost Carthinian territory, was a place of pure chaos. Travelers from across the realm fought tooth-and-nail to barter whatever they could with whomever they could, and when that didn't work, they did what was necessary to return home with coin jingling in their pockets. Courtesans flanked the streets at all times of the day, hoping to catch the eye of a handsome sailor or traveling merchant before they returned home. Thieves and rapists lurked in the shadows, concealed by alleyways and darkened street corners, awaiting unsuspecting victims.

The Violet Forest spanned across the majority of northern Carthe, and while its unique beauties were abundant, it wasn't like the realm's other woodlands. Native tribes prowled the land in search of travelers to steal from, rape, and sometimes eat, depending on their customs. Woodland creatures, far too familiar with being hunted, seldom left the safety of their tree or cave dwellings, forcing humans to survive on little other than berries and nuts. Criminals and predators of all kinds used the forest as their hunting ground: after all, nothing was illegal in the Violet Forest, and nobody—not even royalty or nobility—could escape those who'd become one with the land.

The kingdom of Kanibar was perhaps the nicest and most similar to the southern territories. Arian had only visited thrice in his lifetime, and with each trip, he came to the same conclusion: Kanibar resembled the eastern country of Akkinor more than it did Carthe. Its ancient history and cultural identity had been lost to time, now existing only in texts and art, just to be replaced over several decades by what the Kanish believed a stable society to be. Arian often wondered if the Kanish were aware of how closely their homelands reflected the kingdoms of Akkinor—a place most Carthinians chose to despise, even if they were unaware of the reason for their animosity.

The last of the four northern territories was the worst of them. Dofell had been the center of the world during the old days: it was the first established Carthinian civilization, the original division between the north and the south, and the magical capital of the continent. It was said that, long ago, a portal between the mortal world and the heavens existed in Dofell—a portal capable of bringing magic and divinity to the realm on the gods' behalf.

The Great City (a nickname for Dofell, as the words 'city' and 'kingdom' were used interchangeably during the old days) had fallen almost two hundred years before Arian's birth. The reasons for its downfall were as numerous as they were unmendable. Whatever magic still lingered in Carthe certainly hadn't stayed in a place marked by such dreariness. Enormous, ghastly stone walls encased the entire kingdom, breaking all ties to its neighbors and isolating it from the world.

The Lord Hand of Taundosa didn't normally travel beyond the south, but when his queen gave a command, Arian obeyed. She'd sent him to collect a package from one of her contacts in Caedia—him, not a troop of soldiers or a handful of trusted knights. Queen Reyna Caltheos hadn't told him what it was or why she needed it so desperately, but she trusted no other like she trusted her Lord Hand, so only he could make the exchange.

Traveling across the barren Ngora Valley was an arduous task for the average person, but it hadn't been too difficult for Arian. He was a mage, for one: seldom was there a problem magic couldn't solve, especially for a practitioner of his skill. For another, he'd spent most of his life familiarizing himself with his homeland and its many dangers. The continent didn't favor natives over foreigners, but one's odds of surviving were much greater when one was raised within the chaos.

Now, after a surprisingly quick and easy trip across the desert, Arian had finally arrived at the gates of Dofell. Other than a camel, he was alone, with nothing but a satchel slung over his shoulder and a gold-plated dagger strapped to his waist. About a dozen groups of people, all accompanied by Dofelli traveling guides wearing blue-and-yellow face coverings, loitered by the gates as they awaited their cue to cross the threshold into the desert.

Perhaps half of them would make it to the gates of Taundosa. The other half would die on the journey. Some would succumb to dehydration and starvation. Others would be too weakened by the boiling sun and torrid desert heat to muster the strength to press forward. The especially unlucky travelers would find themselves slaughtered by desert tribes and left for the vultures.

After trading his camel for a horse, Arian took the steed's reins and guided him towards the opposite side of the kingdom, where an identical set of gates led directly into the Violet Forest. He thought he knew exactly what to expect while passing through the kingdom: shoeless children dressed in rags, begging on the streetcorners for food; gaunt-faced adults, practically skeletons, trying to make a living while desperately fighting the urge to fall asleep—or die—where they stood; and feral hounds, limping and balding because of malnutrition, digging through piles of waste in search of scraps.

Other than the hounds, Arian didn't spot anything else that normally welcomed him when he visited the kingdom. In fact, what he found was unlike anything he'd thought to expect in Dofell.

Upon passing the heart of the kingdom—the tiny, half-dead villages surrounding the Phyre family's extravagant palace—he saw hundreds, if not thousands, of people flooding the streets. Most were Dofelli, of course, but he recognized people from other Carthinian cultures, too. The steely, azurite-blue gazes of Bozari natives were impossible to misidentify, as were the broad noses and feline eyes of Kanish natives.

The Phyre family soldiers (normally stationed *within* the palace walls, not beyond them) stood in a perimeter around the palace, their shields connected like a wall of iron and their spears pointed at the crowd to keep the shouting civilians at bay. A dark cloud rolled away, allowing the sun's rays to highlight the sweat on the soldiers' brows. The civilians were armed only with stones, and so long as they neglected to use the rocks as weapons, the soldiers would leave them be.

Knowing he had a job to complete for his queen, Arian didn't linger. He pushed through the crowd, careful not to draw attention to himself by upsetting the commoners, and tried to make sense of what the people were hollering. Their garbled voices blended together, their demands fading into oblivion, as the shouts intermingled with sobs from those who recognized that their cause was a lost one.

The angry crowd hadn't been enough to stop him, but one sight *did* bring him to a halt: an adolescent girl, caked in grime from head to toe, peering into a hole in the trunk of a dead tree. Her hair was matted to her neck and back with filth, masking its true color, and when Arian turned to catch a glimpse of her face, he saw that her onyx eyes were jaundiced, her teeth were rotted, and she hadn't any fingernails.

"Pardon me." Arian approached her, keeping his steed close to his side, and cleared his throat when she didn't seem to hear him over the roaring crowd. "Pardon me, miss. Whatever are you doing?"

The girl, like so many others in Dofell, had clearly been affected by starvation-induced madness. She was muttering to herself, eyes darting in every direction, and twitching uncontrollably—either because of the bugs crawling along her scalp or the hungry voices echoing in her head. Arian couldn't be sure.

"*Alb narez lave fazeeb.*" Her hushed tone grew louder and shriller when she repeated herself. "*Alb narez lave fazeeb! Alb narez lave fazeeb!*"

Arian translated the Dofelli tongue with ease: *He has come back.*

"Who's come back, dear one?" He extended a hand, intending to set it comfortingly on her shoulder, but retracted it when he saw the louse crawling in her hair.

She grinned and pointed to the hole. "*Xib lizqe!*"

"The sprite." A frown formed on his lips. He wasn't sure he'd understood her correctly. "What sprite?"

The girl laughed so hard that her chest caved inwards and her lungs strained against her ribs, with so much childlike wonder that it breathed life back into Dofell's sordid ambience.

When her laughter didn't fade, Arian took a few steps backwards and clicked his tongue for the steed to follow. A strange feeling had washed over him, like he'd stumbled upon something he wasn't meant to see. The poor girl was ill—mentally as well as physically—and it didn't feel right to wait around for a moment of lucidity that probably wouldn't come.

As he walked off, Arian tossed one final glance over his shoulder. The girl appeared to be playing: she crouched down below the hole in the tree, and after a few seconds, she popped up as if to scare a rodent hiding in the trunk. Had Arian blinked, he would've missed the rodent in question: a tiny figure bathed in shades of leafy greens and browns, with two arms and two legs in human form, giggling as loudly as the girl herself. When the girl looked back, sensing Arian's eyes on her, the figure disappeared into the darkness of the tree, and the girl pleaded for the creature to play with her again.

A shiver traced Arian's spine from the nape of his neck to his tailbone. He mounted his horse and galloped to the other side of the kingdom, where a handful of guards were stationed at the gates. After dismounting, he approached one of the soldiers and removed a small golden token from his pocket: a token stamped with the sigil of the Cristos family on one side, and Taundosa's emblem on the other.

The guard stared at him impatiently. "May I help you?"

"I am Lord Arian Cristos of Taundosa, Hand of the Queen to Reyna Caltheos." Arian tossed the token at the soldier, who caught it swiftly and examined both sides before returning it. "I have business in Caedia, but I must ask you to send word to Queen Reyna on my behalf as quickly as possible. You'd do well to deliver my message to your king, too."

The soldier raised a bushy black eyebrow. "I'd be most obliged, my lord. What's the message?"

Arian's dark eyes flickered over to the wrought-iron gates. The Violet Forest was visible on the other side—as were the tattered remains of Kanish flags and the still-burning remnants of campfires, just barely concealed by thick foliage. A hot, uneasy lump settled in his gut. These weren't signs of a struggle or an attack, but of scouts. Spies.

"You have a sprite infestation," Arian told the soldier. "Magical creatures are all but extinct here in Dofell, as you know, but sprites are rather common in Kanibar. They're tricky little things—some say they're the only spies in the realm who can never be captured. There's a bit of uproar happening in the heart of the kingdom, too, as I'm sure you're aware. I noticed a somewhat equal number of Dofelli and Kanish commoners making demands of your fellow soldiers. Both of these things, paired with the presence of scouts just up ahead, suggest Kanibar has set its sights on Dofell." He paused and chewed on his lower lip. "Might as well ask Queen Reyna to relay the message to Aurelia of Akkinor, too. I have a feeling we shall need her."

The soldier's tanned, yellow-toned skin turned gray. "My-My lord?"

"The people seem to know something you don't, sir. I suspect your king remains unaware of it, too. The trees in Dofell have begun to speak again—that can mean nothing if not invasion. Proceed with caution, good man, and send word as soon as you can."

The soldier barely let Arian finish before he turned on his heel and darted for the heart of the kingdom. When the other soldiers at the gates turned to Arian with panic glistening in their eyes, he forced the most reassuring smile he could muster and politely requested that they open the gates for him.

Still feeling their eyes on the back of his head, Arian mounted the steed once more and set out to complete his quest. As he stared ahead at the grassy hills and blooming wildflowers, he sensed something watching him and jerked his head to the left. There, a palm-sized figure with human limbs hissed at him while perched on a wire-thin tree branch.

He sighed and turned his gaze to the forest again. "Go home, sprite. Tell your master that I know, and soon enough, the others will, too."

Arian didn't know if the creature obeyed him or not, but that didn't matter. There were undoubtedly dozens of its kind lurking throughout Dofell, gathering intel and collecting the kingdom's secrets, at their master's behest: Willem Trevas, King of Kanibar.

Acknowledgements

For me, writing is the easy part. The most challenging part of this journey, I think, is building up the courage to share my stories with the world. Luckily for me, I have an army of supporters at my side.

Thank you first and foremost to my late grandfather, Kenneth Negrotti. The stories you told me as a little girl inspired me to create my own, and I wrote my first just a few months after you passed. I was eleven. I never would've found my source of empowerment or my life's passion without you.

Thank you to my many beta readers for your incredible feedback and support. It's an unbelievable honor to share my work with likeminded people, but even more so when those people are helpful, considerate, honest, and as passionate about my work as I am.

Thank you Aubrey for the incredible interior illustrations, and thank you Katarina for the beautiful cover art! I'm blown away by your talent and your dedication to bringing my vision to life.

To my fellow fantasy authors, thank you for welcoming me into one of the most supportive communities I've ever experienced. The outpour of encouragement and advice I've received from some of you has been overwhelming!

To my teachers: every last one of you impacted my life somehow, and without you, I wouldn't be here. I've always been grateful to you for being unfathomably incredible teachers, but I'll never be able to thank you enough for your life lessons and the many times I visited your classrooms for guidance.

To my grandparents: You're four of the humblest people I know, and I wish the world knew you as I did so you can receive the praise and admiration you deserve. You taught me the meaning of hard work and dedication. I'd like to thank my grandmothers especially: you were both working mothers for many years during a time when being a woman in the workforce was extremely difficult. I'll never be able to thank you enough for the many sacrifices you made for your families.

To my aunts, uncles, and cousins: there are more of you than I can keep track of sometimes, but the love, support, and encouragement I've received from each of you hasn't gone unnoticed. Thank you for everything.

Thank you Nina Ritter, my best friend. You're the first person to ever lay eyes on my manuscript! Because of you, *Forged in Gold* will finally be shared with the world. Because of you, this isn't a stand-alone story, but the first of a universe you helped create from the ground up. Thank you for the many days and nights we spent plotting, drafting, and vision boarding; for the long hours you spent reading, rereading, and editing; and, most of all, for the encouragement I needed to make this story a reality. Who knows—if we hadn't been roommates freshman year of college, *Forged in Gold* might still be collecting dust on my computer!

Thank you to my best friends since childhood: Gabrielle, Chloe, Brianna, Chasati, Maria, Kaley, Tess, Amanda, Kylie, Alivia, Bianca, Taylor, and Hannah. I'll never be able to thank you all enough for your constant support and encouragement. Growing up beside you, being treated like part of your families, and sharing some of the best moments of my life with you means more to me than you'll ever know. I don't think I'd have the confidence to do this without you.

Thank you to my partners in all things nerdy, Dan and Katie. The three of us hold the fantasy genre so close to our hearts, so when I made the decision to go through with publishing, I knew I had to work extra hard to create something not only that I'm proud of, but that you'll be able to lose yourselves in, too.

Thank you to my found family at Endicott College not only for your support and friendship, but for reminding me to always find fun and adventure in life. I forget that sometimes!

Thank you to my nieces, Zuri and Emerson, and my nephew, Amari, for inspiring me to tell a story about creating a better future for the next generation. I hope our world changes for the better by the time you take your places in it.

Thank you Tasha for being my family and my best friend since birth, and thank you especially for keeping my head above water when I need it most. I couldn't do life without you, and I'd never want to.

Thank you to my baby sister and my pillar of strength, Chrissy. You inspire me every day with your perseverance. Normally the younger sibling looks up to the elder, but in our case, it's reversed! I'm so proud of the person you are and the person I've become by being your sister.

Thank you to my father, Gary, for so many things that I could be writing this for the next year. Thank you for believing in me, supporting my dreams, and holding my hand through everything. Thank you for doing the absolute most for anyone and everyone without expecting a thing in return. Thank you for working as hard as you do to give us the most incredible life and to ensure that our opportunities are endless. Thank you for your many words of wisdom, for your unconditional love, and for raising me, loving me, and inspiring me.

Finally, thank you to my late mother, Terrie. Fourteen years with you was nowhere near enough. You were the one person who knew about my writing when I was young, and you always kept my secret—even though I didn't let you read anything! Your life, death, and legacy inspired this story in more ways than I can express. Cressida and Katryna are the best parts of you; the parts I wish I were more like. I've never known anyone like you. You, like Aurelia, were the kind of person who only comes around once in a lifetime—sent from heaven to make the world a better place. Thank you for teaching me the true meaning of love and family; reminding me to never let my sex interfere with earning my place in the world; and leaving me with a lifetime of memories, lessons, and advice to guide me. Everything I am and everything I will be is because of you. Thank you.

Last but not least, thank you to the readers who took a chance on a random fantasy story and made me remember why I chose to become an author. Thank you to the novelists who made me fall in love with the idea of losing myself in strange and exciting worlds. Thank you to the rest of my family, friends, coworkers, and associates who unknowingly prepared me for this adventure.

About the Author

Noelle is a pseudonym for a writer, beta reader, and editor from Boston who found her passion for writing early on and pursued it wholeheartedly. Although she is a young writer, she has been honing her craft for more than a decade, having written her first story in middle school!

While Noelle enjoys genres like romance, historical fiction, and science fiction, fantasy has always been her favorite. She fell in love with the genre at an early age after reading C.S. Lewis's *Narnia* series and William Goldman's *The Princess Bride*. Since then, her love of fantasy has only grown!

Much of Noelle's early career reflects her lifelong love of children, having worked as a nanny, infant/toddler daycare teacher, and substitute elementary teacher. However, since graduating with her BA in English Literature, she has immersed herself in the exciting realm of freelancing. When away from her writing desk, Noelle can often be found curled up with a novel or avidly working on expanding the world of her creation.

Noelle currently resides with her father, younger sister, and her feisty kitty, Nugget. *Forged in Gold* is her debut fantasy novel and marks the first of an exciting, heart-stopping series. She writes in honor of her beloved mother, who passed away from cancer in 2015.

Glossary

AGOTIA (Ah-goh-sha): Taundosan district bordering the Ngora Valley; governed by the Cristos family.

    Ardiham Castle: Ancestral home of the Cristos family.

    The Elotheon: Holy temple for Gianla.

AKKINOR (Ack-inn-or): The largest populated continent of the east; the most powerful country in the realm; ruled by the Brentwood family; composed of six kingdoms:

    Holos (Holl-os): Region in southeast Akkinor; ruled by the Tarre family.

    Laynoa (Lay-noh-ah): Region in northeast Akkinor; ruled by the Reilly family.

    Myra (Meer-ah): Region in southwest Akkinor; ruled by the Crowland family; borders Quapebet.

    Omara (Oh-mar-ah): Centermost Akkinorian territory; ruled by the Ashford family; the last kingdom seized by the Akkinorian monarchy.

    Sadia (Sah-dee-uh): Mountainous northern region of Akkinor; formerly ruled by the Normindi family; presently ruled by the Spirre family.

    Seaport: Small coastal town on the west coast of Akkinor; borders the Folly; ungoverned; the only international port in Akkinor.

    The Folly: Capital of Akkinor; home to the palace and the royal family.

        Kilwick: The largest of several cities in the Folly.

        Mistcairn: One of several villages in the Folly.

ALDA PORT: Akkinorian assassin.

ALISTAIR ASHFORD: Former Lord of Omara; father of Arthur, Bryan, Cecelia, and Daniella; husband of Isobel; exiled to Quapebet.

ALKAMURA OCEAN: Also known as the Alka; massive ocean that lies between Carthe and Akkinor; corrupted by the Esposi following Oleander's Rebellion; forbidden territory for Akkinorians.

ALKAMURA: Goddess of the seas; Almighty of Espos.

ALMIGHTY: The primary deity worshipped by individual cultures/civilizations.

ALORA CHERRANE: The last ruler of the Cherrane Dynasty in Akkinor; the last female monarch until Aurelia Brentwood.

ANSYL BOLAS: Native of Kanibar; brother of Kaia, Mycah, and Thea; former Kanish soldier.

ARCHIBALD BRENTWOOD: Prince of Akkinor; son of King Edmund II and Queen Cressida; younger brother and usurper of Queen Aurelia.

ARIAN CRISTOS: Lord of Agotia; Lord Hand to Queen Reyna.

ARTHUR ASHFORD: Former heir to Lordship of Omara; true name of Jack Sherbourne.

AURELIA BRENTWOOD: Queen of Akkinor; adopted daughter of King Edmund II and Queen Cressida Brentwood; elder sister of Prince Archie.

BALOR ZHOQA II (Bay-lor Zoh-kah): Lord of Kazamir, Bozar; ally of Queen Aurelia.

BEVERLY TARRE: Lady of Holos.

BOBOLON TRIBE: Nomadic Carthinian natives who frequent the Violet Forest; cannibals.

BRADLEY REILLY: Lord of Laynoa.

BRYAN ASHFORD: Lord of Omara; younger brother of Arthur Ashford.

BUEN (Bu-wen): God of prosperity; Almighty of Akkinor.

CARTHE: The largest populated continent in the west; a safe haven for mages and magical creatures; home to numerous civilizations:

> *Bozar* (Boh-zar): Kingdom east of the Ngora Valley; borders Taundosa and Khaba; ruled by four noble families: Zhaaran of Orestes, Zhoqa of Kazamir, Zoma of Iseppa, and Xada of Tucana.
>
> *Caedia* (Cay-dee-ah): Northernmost territory of Carthe; ungoverned port province frequented by travelers and merchants; borders the Violet Forest.
>
> *Dofell* (Doh-fell): Kingdom north of Taundosa and the Ngora Valley, south of the Violet Forest, and east of Kanibar; ruled by the Phyre family; formerly known as *the Great City*; the most impoverished kingdom in Carthe.
>
> *Kanibar* (Can-nih-bar): Kingdom north of the Ngora Valley; borders Dofell, Taundosa, and the Violet Forest; ruled by the Trevas family.
>
> *Khaba* (Cah-bah): Southernmost territory of Carthe; ungoverned port province; borders Bozar.

Krotis (Kroh-tis): Kingdom south of the Ngora Valley; borders Taundosa; governed by five noble families: Selle of Bruila, Keer of Mekya, Quagg of Osanad, Swann of Runeia, and Reesa of Vrurith.

Ngora Valley (Nih-gor-ah Valley): Vast desert that separates northern and southern Carthe; only accessible through Dofell and Taundosa.

Taundosa (Tawn-doh-sah): Kingdom east of the Ngora Valley and south of Dofell; the wealthiest Carthinian kingdom; ruled by the Caltheos family; known as *the City of Gold*.

> *Eight Kingdoms of Taundosa:* Agotia, Brorane, Cidour, Emerdes, Morvis, Thania, Trostall, and Vortea.

Violet Forest: Massive deciduous forest that lies between Caedia and the Carthinian kingdoms; home of nomadic native tribes; mostly frequented by travelers.

CERULEAN SEA: Body of water between Holos and Quapebet.

CHANGLING: A five-day celebration held in the Folly at the beginning/end of each season; attended by all highborn Akkinorians and citizens of the Folly; includes performances by jousters, theater actors, bards, jesters, etc.

CICELY POOLE: Close friend and lady-in-waiting to Queen Aurelia.

CRESSIDA BRENTWOOD (deceased): Former Queen Consort of Akkinor; wife of King Edmund II; mother of Queen Aurelia and Prince Archie; daughter of Lord Brennen and Lady Eleana Normindi.

CRYSTAL SEA: Body of water located between northwestern Akkinor and northeastern Carthe.

CULLEN FALWELL: Sadian-born assassin.

DAENA SPIRRE: Lady of Sadia.

DHYLO (Die-loh): God of knowledge; Almighty of Bozar.

EDEA (Ee-dee-ah): Goddess of the moon.

EDMUND BRENTWOOD II (deceased): Former King of Akkinor; husband of Queen Cressida; father of Queen Aurelia and Prince Archie; son of King Edmund II and Queen Charlotte.

ELVEMAR (El-veh-mar): A magical stone with the ability to heal any physical injury when placed in the victim's mouth; can only be found within the eggs of the Bozari python.

ERIC HAZE: Biological father of Aurelia Brentwood; native of Holos; former Cristos family soldier.

ESPOS: Island south of Carthe inhabited mainly by pirates.

GEMMA STONE: Wife of Duke Lucan Stone; Duchess of Lockshaven, Laynoa; sister of Linden Elliot.

GIANLA (Gee-ahn-lah): Goddess of the sun; Almighty of Taundosa.

GLACIER BAY: Northernmost continent; home of the Isalders; ruled by the Styrmodr family.

GLACIER SEA: Northernmost body of water; Isalder territory.

GOLDMEN: An esteemed organization of soldiers loyal to the Taundosan monarchy.

HALVOR: (Hal-vohr): (1) God of protection; (2) Dragon of old loyal to Aurelia Brentwood and the Cristos family.

HZARL (His-arl): God of the hunt; Almighty of Glacier Bay.

IMMOR (Ee-mor): God of war.

INESIS (In-ness-iss): God of life and death; Almighty of Quapebet.

ISOBEL ASHFORD: Former Lady of Omara; mother of Arthur, Bryan, Cecelia, and Daniella; wife of Alistair; exiled to Quapebet.

JACK SHERBOURNE: Akkinorian-born traveler of Carthe; alias of Arthur Ashford.

JALHOR ZHAARAN (Jall-or Zar-ran): Lord of Orestes in Bozar; *lak'kari* descendent and mage; ally of Queen Aurelia.

KAIA BOLAS: Native Kanish merchant.

KATRYNA CRISTOS (deceased): Biological mother of Aurelia Brentwood; sister of Arian Cristos; native of Taundosa.

LAK'KARI (Lah-car-ee): (1) Old Carthinian word for *demon*; (2) Carthinian folklore proven true; refers to the first settlers of the Violet Forest who were cursed for their greed; known as humanity's first sinners.

LAURENIA FALWELL: Follian-born assassin.

LILY LINDEN: Carthinian alias of Aurelia Brentwood.

LINDEN ELLIOT: Hand of the Queen and best friend of Aurelia Brentwood.

LUKOS: Pirate captain of Espos.

MAGES: Humans with the ability to conjure magic from the gods.

MAGICAL PERSECUTION: The annihilation of mages and magical creatures during the old days that saw the extinction of numerous races and forced surviving mages into hiding.

MAROONER'S CHAIN: Archipelago off the western coast of Akkinor; mainly uninhabitable; serves as labor towns for low-ranking Akkinorians and criminals.

MYENAR (My-enn-arr): God of judgement; Almighty of Dofell.

ODEYA SWANN: Lady of Runeia in Krotis; ally of Queen Aurelia.

OLEANDER BRENTWOOD: Usurper of Alora Cherrane during the old days; the first Brentwood king of Akkinor.

OREN LOWSTONE: Akkinorian assassin.

PHERENA (Ferr-ee-nah): Goddess of virtues; Almighty of Krotis.

QUAPEBET (Kwah-peh-bet): Continent south of Akkinor; ruled by the Kaplo family; shares the Cerulean Sea with Akkinor; connected to Myra by the neutral city of Vilgh-Azhor.

REYNA CALTHEOS: Queen of Taundosa.

ROBERT CHERRANE: The first King of Akkinor.

ROBERT ELLIOT: Lord Hand to Edmund I; father of Linden Elliot and Gemma Stone.

SILAS CROWLAND: Lord of Myra.

SYREN ISLES: Archipelago south of Glacier Bay; independent territory.

THE ASSEMBLY: An esteemed group of Akkinorian nobles serving as advisors to the monarch.

THE ELEMENTALS: The first four mages to walk among mankind, created directly by the hands of the gods to introduce magic to humanity:

> *Ceruleus* (Cerr-oo-lee-us): Elemental of air
>
> *Glacia* (Glah-see-uh): Elemental of water
>
> *Igneus* (Igg-nee-us): Elemental of fire
>
> *Terra* (Ter-rah): Elemental of earth

THE ONES FORGED IN GOLD: Humans said to be chosen by the gods to restore peace and harmony to the realm during times of peril; known to weep golden tears.

THE TWELVE: The global religion worshipped by all cultures of the realm; follows the twelve deities responsible for the Creation: Alkamura, Buen, Dhylo, Edea, Gianla, Hzarl, Immor, Inesis, Myenar, Pherena, Vyena, Xienia.

TIMMAN KAPLO VI: Emperor of Quapebet.

TYREN SILIO: Hand of the King to Archie Brentwood.

VILGH-AZHOR (Vilg-Ah-zor): A neutral trading zone on the border of southern Akkinor and northern Quapebet; named for the Myran town of Vilgh and the Quenosi town of Azhor.

VYENA (Vee-enn-ah): Goddess of blessings; Almighty of Kanibar.

XIENIA (Zee-nee-ah): Goddess of love and beauty.